quality brought him to the attention of Joshua Shaw, the son of people who had been ironmasters since the Revolution; and thus began, between the two young men of widely different backgrounds, a friendship which was to last for many years. Through Josh and his family's mills Alan was able to take the first step toward his dream. At this time too Alan fell desperately in love with and married the half-Indian girl, Minna Svenson, who possessed a vibrant beauty that made every man who saw her want her. The love between Alan and his wife was passionate and true; and it endured through the long years of Alan's struggle, his financial success at the cost of friendship and respect, and his final vindication during the dark days of the depression.

It is impossible to indicate in a few words the scope and power of Alan Kennard's story and the many scenes which make it up. There are labor troubles and bloody strikes, idyllic moments of peace and pleasure, the treacherous storms and fogs of the Great Lakes, memories of the heartbreaking beauty of Ireland. The characterizations are extremely vivid: Alan, a sympathetic and very human person despite his ruthless drive; his sons, Mark and Stacey, who in one crisis turned against their father; the strange, twisted Shaw family corroded by its own poison—all these have parts in a memorable novel which pulses with the breath of life.

The Beckoning Waters

Novels

HORIZON
SIREN SONG
HEART'S DESIRE
PACIFIC
DEEP SIX
FROM THE SEA AND THE JUNGLE
THE BECKONING WATERS

Non Fiction

THE UNCONQUERED
THERE GO THE SHIPS
LIFELINE

Juveniles

GREAT VENTURE

THE
BECKONING WATERS

—

ROBERT CARSE

CHARLES SCRIBNER'S SONS
New York   1953

This is for Elsa and Jim

The Beckoning Waters

Book One

1876

CHAPTER ONE

The ship was quiet now in the night, and the city. Alan Kennard sat on deck with the light from the 'midships cuddy at his back and once more tried to read the two letters. But the meaning of them became confused, because, he thought, each in its own way meant so much to him. And his reading wasn't the best. Maybe he had mistaken what they said, and after all his mother wasn't dead, nor Phelim Carmody in that town inland that was called Buffalo.

He folded the letters, put them back in his shirt pocket. He stood and walked the deck, feeling the slow, soft lift of the tide under the ship, hearing the murmurous slackening of her dock hawsers. She made him uneasy tonight, although out to sea he had greatly loved her. He looked aloft at the slender reach, the grace of the topmasts, then the royal and lower yards where they canted in a faint arc across the star-pale sky. She's fine. The trouble is with you, man. Never have you liked a ship in port. He was surprised by the idea, and turned as if he could find understanding of it in the city.

Mist had come along the Upper Bay. Staten Island was a gray blur through a thinner gray. Castle William lay dark and stern and low, and Castle Garden had a vague, shimmering glimmer, like the sea flowers seen beneath the surface on some tropical reef. The Jersey shore was a dull strip of brass. Over on Brooklyn Heights, the windows of the big homes shone bright, clear above the mist. But to the North, past South Street, the buildings of Manhattan gleamed. A strong place, and you're afraid of it. You're afraid of any city, and only on the sea do you think you're safe.

He leaned against the side bulwark, the wood moist and chill with the mist. Hansom cabs, carts and wagons and drays racketed over the South Street cobbles in the greenish cast of the gaslights. For the fish market, he told himself. All night long they work. While you stand here with the knowledge in your head that you're free.

Your mother's dead and you no longer have to concern yourself with her keep. That's what the letter from Ireland said. The other, from your old shipmate, Phelim, told you that there's work for you

3

inland here in America any time you want to go and join him. Say it to yourself again. You're free. The death of your mother made you so, and Phelim's letter gives you the chance to get out of a brute big ship like this. Och, what manner of man are you, staying here? Time enough that you understood. Haul ashore.

The fo'c'sle door was open a few feet from him and he could smell the place. It was a familiar smell, yet rank and foul. The blankets had been left in the bunks, and they were damp, dirty, as were the straw pallets. Over the deck was scattered the wornout gear of the sailors who had left her calling her a workhouse son of a bitch and a man-killing bastard. So she was. Down in the Le Maire Strait, when she rounded up on Cape Horn for her run East, the mate had sent the young Danish lad to the main topsail yard when nobody but the best of sailors should have gone. The lad was sick from the lack of hot food; he was part-frozen and he was scared. His hands were raw from weeks of fisting the ice-hard canvas and his body covered with sea water sores. When he fell, maybe, he was glad. You can't forget him, and you shouldn't.

Kennard started aft to the cuddy. Still, he went slowly. He hadn't conquered his dislike, his fear of the city. A city was to him a source of great trouble far beyond his comprehension. It gave a ship her cargoes, so you called there for them, and to get your orders. The agents, those mysterious, smooth-faced people, came from the city, and the doctors, the police. That was about all you knew except that the master went there for his orders, sometimes the mate. They could talk the city language, navigate around.

But a city wasn't for a sailor. Hell, no. You were like a wee bit of a stupid lad once you got a few squares past the waterfront. Even that was too much for you. Along the front, in the traps which all looked the same and where the women all looked the same, you soon were lost. The booze and the harpies did for you and you had no chance against them. Try to buy a knife ashore, or a pair of dungarees or boots. You were beat before you started. They knew you for a sailor; they stuck you with their worst and cheapest gear for the highest prices. One thing for you to do—get back aboard and stay aboard and wait for the ship to head for sea. You were cheated there, too, but in the wind, the sun, the work, and with the days between you and the shore, you could forget.

He stood by the cuddy, his bucket in his hand. He was slightly trembling. A fine sweat was on the backs of his hands. He was telling himself that he must get over the fear of the shore. Phelim had done it, and many times he had wanted to try. America was the place, too. He could remember when he had first touched this coast. Maine, yes, and a city by the name of Portland. Then Boston, Boston, Massachusetts. He'd made it up into the middle of the city in Boston on a Sunday and the streets were a good deal like at home, some of the houses, too, but not the people. They'd stared at him, and their eyes were quiet and incurious. After Boston, a couple of other coastal ports in New England, and New York, Philadelphia, up that goddamn' river, then Baltimore. On a big, wide bay. And all the time you were thinking. Can you do it, Alan? Can you make the break, man, and get away as Phelim did? Your mother, though. You have to keep sailing in these deep water ships, make the only living you know how so that she won't starve.

She's dead. Say it clear out. Your mother's gone and in the ground months ago. That's the meaning of the letter from the schoolmaster in Daigvera. He wrote you special to let you know. And Phelim's waiting for you in Buffalo. Now or never, Alan. Get along and stop playing the fool.

The mate heard him as he filled the bucket at the fresh water butt aft, and he was able to see the mate through the cabin skylight. The mate sat on the settee holding a newspaper. But the mate paid no attention to the paper. Instead, he listened to him here on deck. They were alone on board together while they tended ship. In a few minutes the mate would be up to find out what he did with fresh water. That was Gaskill's style. He was slow to start after you. But to hell and away with Gaskill. You're bound for Buffalo.

He sang straight through "The Swallow Tail Coat" while he bathed. He had a small chunk of soap the cook had rendered out to sea and he used it over every portion of his body. He looked down at his wiry, compact body, his torso brown from the tropic sun and winds, his scarred legs and broad, calloused feet. Pride in his strength came to him, and a sensuous exhilaration from being freshly clean. He took and honed his razor, began to shave. Then, while he fastened his money belt and pulled on his best jersey and the shabby blue serge suit and the high, clumsy shoes, he counted the years.

This now, it was 1876. For six, close onto seven years, he had been sailing the deep water ships. Before them were the coasters and the fishers. You've been at sea all told, all counted for eleven years, and out to China last voyage you had your twenty-second birthday. Bosun for sure in a full rigged ship when many an older man might have the job. Able to sign your name and make the figures of the arithmetic. It was when you were ten that your father was lost off the Skerries in that blow. A small man, and quiet. You can't remember much of him except the way he used to sharpen his knife on the sole of his boot. You've done well enough. If you'd stayed in County Antrim, you'd be fishing for the herring yet, or cutting turf on another's land. A bog jumper at best, with a gypsy mother at home to keep any decent girl in the village from marrying you.

Your mother, though, Alan. You needn't think of her so. A strange woman, a sad one. Fey, gone in the head a bit from the day they came to tell her that her man was lost on the sea. You won't forget, you can't, how she'd sing in the night. Sitting by the fire. Not even knowing that you were there. And the light of the peats full on her eyes and her strange, tight face. She knew the old songs and the playing of the harp and the pipes, although that last's not the thing for a woman. She was Ireland, and she was the mother to you, and you're a poor sort if you feel glad that she's dead, no matter how many's the years she kept you hard to your work.

An exquisite kind of pain held him as he remembered his mother singing and then the sights and sounds of the glen where they had lived. He listened in memory to the wind in the whins, through the hawthorn hedge and the yew tree. He heard the crying of the plover on the river, and the fierce, thin call of an eagle. There was the rush, the crash and roar of the breakers on the great stones of the Giant's Causeway below. Wind slammed whooping in the chimney to send the sparks in cascades out upon the dimness of the room. His mother cried forth from her corner, but he failed to get the words. It wasn't even the Gaelic she spoke; it was the Romany of her own people, and as he listened, the sparks whirling about him, he was contained by a deep wonder rather than fear.

"Get along, Alan," he said aloud. He had finished packing his long, handmade leather sea boots, his peacoat and dungarees in his seabag before the mate came to stand at the cuddy door.

"You're bound for the shore, bosun?" Gaskill said.

"I am, sir," Alan Kennard said, and watched the way the mate held the belaying pin behind his back.

"You got permission from the master, then," Gaskill said in his flat Tyneside voice.

"No, sir." He drew shut the throat lanyard of the bag, made it fast.

"You're a British subject," Gaskill said. "You're on the articles of this vessel for another voyage. You oughn't to leave her, bosun. The master might say you'd broken the law."

"To hell with him," Kennard said slowly, "and to hell with you. I'm bound for the shore. When you can get another crew to sail this bastard, you'll find a new bosun, too."

"A foolish way to talk." Gaskill brought his hand around and showed the heavy locust belaying pin. "I could have you written in the log for mutinous talk."

"Maybe," Kennard said. His voice sounded calm. But the rage had begun to gather, to coil inside him like an enormous spring. It was composed of many elements, yet the only ones he recognized were his fear of the shore so recently conquered and the weary, bitter, tortured nights he had spent aboard while the other men had gone ashore. They had come back talking of women, smelling of them, satisfied by them. They were bold in the moment and bigger than themselves because of that, also because of the booze. A few of them had always mocked him, then, as his patience left him, hurriedly offered him a drink from their bottles. It had hurt his pride to drink; he couldn't pay back. Yet he had accepted, knowing that the offers were made out of friendship. Now Gaskill would hold him from the shore when at last he was free.

"Maybe," Kennard said again, his voice still calm. He had stooped as if to lift the seabag. But then he lunged at Gaskill and the crown of his head caught the bigger, more powerful man under the point of the chin. Gaskill staggered and cursed, dropped to one knee on the deck. Kennard didn't hesitate. The seabag held on his shoulder, he swung back his right foot and kicked Gaskill squarely in the face. When Gaskill failed to move, when he lay there only thickly breathing, Kennard stepped around him to the gangway. "You swab," he called back harshly from the dock. "That wasn't all for me. Some of it was for the Danish lad."

South Street was a clatter of iron tires on the cobbles, hooves clacking, irregular patches of shadow and the smooth pools of the gaslights. Head towards the Battery, and away from the sailor joints. You meet an old shipmate, you're a goner. It will mean one drink and then another, for you're wild tonight or you'd never have booted the mate in the dial like that.

He kept on the water side of the street and close above him were the bowsprits, the dolphin-strikers and figureheads of the tall wind ships moored there. Despite himself, he slowed to look up at

them. They were spectrally beautiful in the misty night. Give them
a few more years and they'll be gone from the sea. The steamers are
pushing them off it fast. A good time for you to quit the sea, then.
You're no sort of a steamer sailor.

Still, a sense of sadness pervaded him as he climbed the Elevated steps at the Battery. He was leaving all that he knew, all that
had ever given him the right to be proud. This ahead was entirely
strange.

The guard on the Elevated train was an Irishman and realized
right away what he was, told him where to get off on Third Avenue,
how to reach the railroad station. But that did little to diminish his
nervousness. He sat stiff-bodied on the seat just within the door, his
knees drawn up around the seabag, the lanyard wound closely
around his hands. His belief was that the guard and the few people
in the car stared at him with inimical, mocking glances. He noticed
that all the men wore collars and ties and stockings—socks, they
called them over here. You know that much at least, you damn'
numskull.

He looked away from the people, embarrassed by them. The
train was coming into Grand Street. He could see through the
steam-blurred car window directly into the windows of buildings.
A fat man lopped on the edge of a bed and scratched his naked
belly. A woman sat knitting, her nose down close to her work, her
face gaunt in the gaslight. Four small children stood at the window-
sill gazing out with lack-luster eyes. A young couple made love.

"Jesus Christ!" he said, profoundly shocked.

The guard looked over at him. "All for a nickel," he said. "'Tis
quite a ride."

Alan Kennard made no answer. He knew nothing to say. The
city had begun to stun him, strip his sense of determination. When
he left the Elevated, he kept his eyes averted from the people in
the street. You might as well be wearing a sign a foot high that
names your trade. You're Paddy to these folks. Aye, you're stupid,
green Paddy off the pickle-boat.

The man behind the window in the noisily echoing spaces of the
station said there woudln't be a train for Buffalo before morning. "But buy your ticket now and you'll have it."

Alan Kennard stared hard at him and then laughed. "You're
right," he said. "And where might a man like me pass the night?"

"Down the street at the Orienta," the ticket agent said. He was
wide-eyed as Kennard pulled his jersey up from his trousers and

opened the canvas money belt around his waist. "A room for a dollar and whiskey's fifteen cents."

"Very well," Kennard said. He counted the ticket money slowly twice. All of it, save a dollar or so, was to have gone to his mother. Be careful with it, man. You can't say for sure that you'll be meeting Phelim in Buffalo.

But when he was in the hotel room he realized that he couldn't stay. Black grit was on the strip of carpet before the lumpy, narrow bed. The window was stuck and the commode slop jar hadn't been emptied. Huge red roses were on the wallpaper, and the walls seemed to be coming forward, closing in upon him. He experienced a peculiar sensation of disgust that was almost fear. His intense desire was to go back to South Street, to the ships where at least the decks were clean and the wind was in your face.

He took a dollar from the money-belt and folded it tightly and put it in his right-hand trousers pocket. That was for whiskey if he got around to drinking it. The beer money, the nickels and dimes and the quarter, was in his left. But the rest he wouldn't touch.

The hotel barroom was big, bright with polished mahogany, brass, broad mirrors. The barkeeper had a spitcurl; he wore a gold ring around his tie and pink silk sleeve garters with rosettes. Alan Kennard wondered if the man would serve him. He might give you the heave-out. This here's for the fancy and not for your sort. Try it, though. They say the country's different from at home.

"Whiskey," he said to the barkeeper, although he had meant to order beer. The barkeeper nodded, hardly looking at him. He drank it fast and neat, left the change from the dollar bill on the bar. When the barkeeper filled his glass again, he didn't say anything, but this time he drank more slowly. There were tables at the far end of the bar where men and women sat. Some of the women were pretty enough. He admired their wide feathered hats and puffed sleeves, and the ease with which the men made them laugh. Scrape the barnacles off you, get yourself some shore-going clothes and a bit of sense, man, and there'll be a time when you can do that.

The whiskey was taking effect on him. He was extraordinarily conscious of his bodily power. He stood erect at the bar and stretched himself. The muscles drew taut through his shoulders, his back and arms and legs. If one of those women could see you going aloft, or sliding down a backstay to deck. Och, she wouldn't think so much of her shore-side johnny then. You're the strongest man in the room, if not the best. And you should have yourself a woman.

But he forced his mind away from that thought. Women for him were trouble, great trouble. Sure, he'd had them in the ports from time to time when they'd been cheap or he couldn't stand to go without it any longer. But they hadn't taken care of him, not of the need he had. Better to stay aboard. Then you could dream, and there wasn't dirt, there wasn't meanness, nor the haggling, the yelling.

Have another drink. He picked up the whiskey glass, but it was empty. He tapped it on the bar and the barkeeper came and filled it and he drank. The women were laughing. He turned quickly in his self-consciousness, but the laughter was meant for a waiter. The man was a fat, bald German who carried a tray of beer seidels balanced on his arm. One of the women yanked his apron string and he cleared his throat and sang.

The man was good, Kennard thought, but not good enough. It was nothing like his mother could sing, or him, too, for that matter. Keep out, though. Pipe down. Let the waiter sing and you have another drink.

Only a dime was left from the dollar. He brought out a nickel and nodded to the barkeeper. Then he lightly ran his hands down over his body. The whiskey had become a fire that was consuming him. It burned through the barrier between him and the women. He didn't care any longer, and he told himself that he didn't care.

He sang an ancient Gaelic *cronan*, all the longing of his nature let go into it. The meaning of the words wasn't sure to him, but the wild and lovely tonality was completely his. Men along the bar stared up at him in surprise, yet they were silent, and the men and women at the tables were silent. He walked from the bar still singing, and his legs were stiff, his thick soled shoes scruffed back the sawdust. The last tragic phrase left the room in quiet. He could hear his own rough breathing.

"Ye're Irish?" a man at the nearest table said.

"Ulster," he said proudly. "Out of Daigvera, in the County Antrim."

"Set down ennyhoo," the man said. He waved his hand. "Ulster or no, ye sing like the angels. Give us another."

"With gladness," he said. He sang them a jig then, and a tune taken from the pipers, "Maloney's Pig." The fat waiter brought him whiskey and he drank and drank again until he lost count.

You're drunk, he thought once. You're reeking. Watch out or you may end up in a brawl, or have your money lifted. But there was no way of stopping the whiskey. They filled and refilled his glass, and a blond, small woman leaned against him, her arm about his shoulder. "Sing again, sailor," she said. "But no more of the sad stuff. Something happy-like."

He stood lurching and laughing, his hands on his hips, keeping his gaze on her. "What shall we do with a drunken sailor?" he shouted. Then he gave them the song.

His head dropped forward suddenly when he was back at the table and he thought for a moment that he was going to be very sick. But the woman made him get up on his feet. She led him out of the barroom and into the night that struck his lungs with a long, painful blow. "Come on," she said. "Let's go now."

"No," he told her. He shook his head and stared wildly at her. "Stayin' here."

"All right." She slightly smiled before she turned him around into the hotel.

He remembered the room when they walked along the hall to it. He tried to get free from her. "Dirty," he said. "Stinks. Walls—walls."

Her strength surprised him, and she took the key from him and he was on the bed. She had the commode open while he tried to sit up; he heard her in the hall, then the bathroom. She brought back the slop jar empty, slid off her shoe and banged the heel through three window panes. "Get up," she said to him. "I want to make the bed. You and me are going to have it clean and neat."

She went out of the room to fill the ewer after the bed was made. His hands were quivering and a terrible shyness was over him, but he managed to take off his clothing. "Oh, my God," she said when she saw him. She put down the basin slopping and ran across the room to clasp him in her arms.

Afterward, she lay in a position of exhaustion, her body inert, and he stretched out beside her, let sleep come to him. It was fitful and uneven. He missed the motion of the ship, the fine-woven complex of sounds made by timber, wire, rope, canvas and water. That was what warned him; his sense of hearing told him that the woman had gotten up, left the bed.

He heard her bare feet on the grit of the carpet strip. She dressed rapidly, her corset creaking, her petticoats sibilant. He looked over his shoulder at her and she had the money belt in her hands. "You bitch," he said and sprang at her.

She fought him with a long hat pin, gouged his shoulder. Then he had her by the wrist and slung her up, over and sprawling onto the bed. She wept with her face down against the pillow while he counted the money.

"My mother died so I could have that," he said, troubled by the true sorrow in her weeping. "Ask me and I'd have paid you. But steal, lass, no. Not from this man."

She looked up at him, her hat on sidewise, her face convulsed and yellow-shaded against the dull light from the transom. "I won't be any good for a week," she said. "You went at me like something crazy. What's money to a sailor? You'll throw it away in some beer saloon or give it to another whore."

"No," he said, moved to a tenderness and understanding that were new to him. He wiped the blood from his shoulder, then went to put on his trousers, his shoes. "I'm like you. I only got a few years to go before I won't be worth a damn. So I need the money. But here now."

He sat on the bed and counted out the money from the belt. He made two equal piles of the dollar bills. "Take yours," he said. "We're splicing it between us."

"Thanks for nothing," she said. "You're a hard son of a bitch. You should give me all of it for what you did to me." But she quickly grasped her share and put it in her stocking. She started for the door, then turned and came back to him.

"You're right," she said. "They'd make a whore of you, too, if you wasn't hard. Good luck to you, sailor. Give us a kiss."

He kissed her gently on the mouth, and she excited him so that he tried to embrace her. She shook her head and hoarsely laughed and ducked away from him. "Not me, you ain't," she said. "Shoo fly!"

He stood in the middle of the room listening to the clop of her heels through the twitter of the gas jet. Then he said aloud, "You're a bloody fool. But you didn't beat her. Now get to hell out of here. This ain't for you."

The night clerk was asleep with his feet against the lobby stove and he left the key on the desk, went on out into the street. Dawn was breaking, an opalescent crease above the dun mass of the buildings. The wind was from the East and the sea. He breathed deeply of it as he walked to the railroad station. He was sleepy and very hungry, but he wouldn't sleep or eat, he promised himself, until he was in Buffalo. Back in Ireland, any priest would tell him he was doing penance for his sins. And the man would be right.

He dozed, though, once he was in the train. The night had exhausted him and the conductor had to jerk him awake to get his ticket. Then he stared around the car and out the window, possessed by an enormous curiosity. The other people in the car, as much as he could make them out, were Central Europeans. They had just come off some immigrant ship, and the women wore padded cotton jackets, shawls over their heads, and the men had the withdrawn, brown faces of farmers, long mustaches and wistful eyes. Each man had hung on his coat a piece of cardboard that bore his name and where he was supposed to go. Their language was unlike any he had ever heard in the ships, and he felt lonely among them, and somehow ashamed.

They were being shipped out like cattle, he thought. The language was against them and the folks who'd gone ahead of them and already owned most of this land. Look at it. Och, Alan, it's as beautiful as your own Antrim. Be honest. It's more so, and rich, rich.

The Hudson Valley was in the first soft colors of September. Russet faded into gold and gold into silver along the banks. The river was a wide, dark-glinting shaft of purple where the shadows of the mountains touched, incredible blue beyond. He recognized elms, beeches and oaks. They reared tawny under the enormous spill of sun. Hay was gone from the fields. The wheat and the corn had been shocked. The white wooden farm houses were strange to him, and the shapes of the barns, some of the breeds of cattle. But there was wealth in all of it, and it was big, man.

He leaned back his head and shut his eyes. The fellows who ran this country were maybe the most powerful lot in the world. If you went against them, you must be smart and hard, reckoning out each thing you did. It wasn't like the squires in the old country who really cared only for a bottle, a dog or a horse. Here a man could own all of a county, a good part of what they called a state.

You can have no more jiggery-nackery like last night. That's the end of your foolishness. In the ships, you advanced yourself to bosun for the reason that you took the trouble the other lads wouldn't. The length and size of each piece of rope in the ships you learned, and the breaking strain, the cost, not just the splicing, the working of them. The same for canvas and paint. Even the magnetism of the compass you figured out, and old Hjalmar

Bjornsen explained to you the difference between a latitude and a
longitude. If you'd stayed with the sea, in time you would have
sailed as a mate.

Phelim Carmody is much like you. A young man still, and yet
he sailed as bosun in the *Flying Cloud* when she carried a hundred
and five sailors and four mates. But Phelim's a great one for his
whiskey and his women. So he'll always be working for some other
man, no matter how fine a sailor he is. Watch yourself with him.
Take care you don't keep his habits. You're going far now, Alan,
or you're not going at all. So get to use your brains instead of your
back. Remember your father dead at sea for a handful of herring,
your mother alone, miserable and half starved in the dark.

He dozed again and awoke, and this, the conductor told him,
was the Genesee Valley and they were past the Mohawk. The immigrant people were still, most of them asleep. A sick child cried and
the mother sang a low, repetitive lullaby. He had the abrupt temptation to cry as he heard it, then realized that he was weak from
hunger. Enough of your bloody penance, he told himself. At the
next station you get off and buy yourself what they call here a sandwich and some of that slop they say is coffee. Phelim would laugh
straight out at you if he saw you now. Damn the man, anyhow.
You'll be glad to meet up with him.

Buffalo was half city, half town, with brick business blocks,
muddy, rutted streets jammed with fast driven horses, then a
quarter where there were white clapboard houses and churches set
behind elms such as he had seen in New England. He lost his way
often as he attempted to find Phelim's address, but the people he
talked with seemed to be used to men who talked and dressed like
him. The landlady at the boarding-house did no more than wave
her hand from her broom handle and say, "You'll find him down at
The Shades. He's out of a ship, but he should be sober."

The Shades was down in the middle of the business district and
there was a sort of quiet elegance about it that made Kennard
hesitant to enter. But then Phelim Carmody saw him and bawled
out his name, came rapidly striding forward. Phelim wore a brown
derby hat, a long double-breasted coat, boots with elastic sides and
a gold watch chain. He had a cheroot in his hand, Kennard noticed,
and he smelled strongly of barber's lotion. This was hardly the same
man who had been his shipmate for two years, he thought with a
sharp shock of jealousy. Phelim's hand grip was a strong as ever,

though, and his face deeply tanned, the eyes narrowed in the familiar squint from looking long out over water. "Arragh!" he said. "It's Alan himself. Lad, am I glad to see you!"

It was the Liverpool Irish in Phelim, and probably a good bit of whiskey, too, Kennard told himself. Still, he was happy to be with the big, redheaded rascal. Phelim's loud talk meant nothing once you got to know him. "And me to be here," he said. "You look fine, Phelim."

"So I am," Carmody said. He took the seabag from him, pitched it into a corner. "I've been sailing mate of a lumber schooner and just this week got off her. I wanted to be around when you made town."

Alan Kennard had raised his hand in an unconscious gesture to touch his chin stubble and the neck of his coarse woolen jersey. "It's a fancy place we're in, Phelim," he said low-voiced. The room was done in dark wood paneling. The liquor casks, marked with brass plaques, were entered into the walls, and men went to draw their own drinks, made change from a huge heap of silver on a table.

"True," Carmody said, his keen eyes on him. "But for the Irish there's only the best. Come have a drink and don't mind your clothes. They have every sort in here, from sailors down."

Phelim Carmody was full of talk and a high, nervous elation. "It's a great town and a great country," he said. "I'm for it."

"As you might be," Kennard said. He drank his whiskey slowly, gazing at the men in the room, the way they talked and drank and greeted each other. Here was a work day, but this place had the look of the best pub at home when everybody was wearing his finest for the Fair. And, Jesus, man, how they spend their money. Dollars rolling on that table like sixpenny bits.

"I can't drink long with you," he told Carmody. "I had me a big one in New York and my head's as thick as a maul. How about a walk in the town?"

"Sure, sure," Carmody said and slapped him on the back. "Leave your bag there. It'll be safe 'til we're back."

The sun and the wind of the street were welcome to Kennard. He felt the throb of the whiskey drag out, then stop in his head, and the cheroot Carmody had given him had a good taste. "Four railroads they have running here now," Carmody said. "There's iron works and breweries, all kinds of factories. Down that way is

Canal Street and stay away from it. Their barrelhouse booze will kill you if the harpies don't. But the port's beyond and I'd like for you to see it."

"I would," Alan Kennard said quietly. This was the heart of it, he realized. He must study it and understand it. The valleys on the way from New York had been rich. But the lake ahead meant a great deal more.

Tall and jagged rows of grain elevators were along the waterfront. They were painted flat red or a mustard yellow and flocks of seagulls circled them, cawing, dipping, flashing in the sun. The harbor traffic was like nothing he had ever seen. There were heavy side-wheel steamers, schooners built broad in the beam for wheat-carrying, schooners with fine-set square topsails that were piled high with lumber on deck, barges, towboats, scows, cutters, ketches. "Push your eyes back in, lad," Carmody said. "You should ha' seen it in the big days of the Canal. But that was before my time and I have enough bragging to do anyhow."

"How is it up beyond?" Alan Kennard said. He nodded to the Northwest where the sun flamed over the blue-gray water.

Carmody made an instinctively dramatic gesture. He stood with his arms wide, his broad-featured face lifted to the sun. "It would make ten of any other country," he said. "Thousands on thousands of square miles of white pine, Alan, and all fine wood. Then copper, then iron. Past that the prairies and the wheat land. From Duluth, from Lake Superior, it's hauled here by vessel. Then the railroads pick it up. But you have Chicago and Milwaukee and Detroit and Cleveland in between, each growing faster than a hare can jump a ditch. It's a ring-tailed marvel, believe me. A man can make his fortune soon if he wants."

"You're after one?"

"Ah, to hell!" Carmody brayed his loud laugh. "Not so's I'll break my back for it. I've done well in the three years I've been here and I'll do better yet. But them with the big money have to fight hard for it. They're rough, Alan, and smarter than us."

"Maybe." Alan Kennard was watching a grain schooner being warped in to the dock. "I'd like to sail in a craft like that and see the upper lakes. A man would be a fool if he didn't take what he could find. I've had my share of bad times back home and in the salt-water ships."

Carmody cursed him good-naturedly. "I'll take a schooner out with you," he said. "Tomorrow, though. Money's in my pocket and we can have ourselves a night in the German places. Diebold's and Schwabel's and Goetz's and a grand sight more. We'll drink and we'll eat and dance. There's a *fraulein* with a fine pair of bow fenders I can get for you. She'll make you forget you ever saw a ship."

"Not me," Alan Kennard said in a quiet voice. "I had mine in New York. I'd like to get North straight off, Phelim."

"Goddamn you!" Carmody said. "Who's more stubborn than an Ulsterman? I'll ship with you tomorrow. I'll spend the winter logging in the woods with you and in the spring you'll have a pay-off to hold in both hands. But I won't go North today."

"Very well," Kennard said. "Then I'll be seeing you later up there."

"Ah, you're a donkey," Carmody said. "A proper Ulster donkey. Will you settle for just one more round at 'The Shades' before we pick up your gear?"

Kennard laughed at him and hit him lightly on the bicep. "Sure enough," he said. "Just one more never hurt me yet."

They walked stride for stride along the street. Carmody hummed a waltz tune played on a mechanical organ in a barrel-house they passed. But suddenly he stared sidewise. "What's changed you, lad?" he said.

"I'm not sure," Alan Kennard said. "But I guess it's my mother. I haven't told you yet. She died in Daigvera some months back, alone and cold in the dark. With no one to tend for her because I had to be away in the ships so she'd have a potato, a scrap of fish."

"It's not a good death," Carmody said.

"No, it's not," Kennard said. "Nor do I want one like it."

Carmody started to hum the waltz tune again, then stopped. Kennard was aware that Carmody regarded him carefully, as though he was a man the other didn't know well.

CHAPTER TWO

He experienced an ecstasy that grasped him with increasing power as he made his first trip up the Lakes with Phelim. They were in a two-mast schooner carrying farm machinery marked for Northern ports and he sailed as bosun, Phelim as mate. The work was easy after a full-rigged ship; he had plenty of time to study the country.

Erie didn't mean much to him, because they stood out wide in the lake on a long reach and Cleveland and the rest of the South Shore were no more than a dim tracery under heavy wind cloud. But then they ran Pelée Pass and were off Pointe Mouillée and the mouth of the Detroit River. The towboat came alongside, took their line and hauled them. He stood motionless, caught in the emotion given him by what he saw. The trees on the islands and the river banks raised like vast masts, no, more like the spires of cathedrals at home. They were the pines of which Phelim had told him, and the clear quite white sunlight as it fell among them became a rippling golden sheet over the needle beds. Birds were there, small, and bright, and swift. They flew out over the river in curves of flickering color. A red fox was in the underbrush, a half-eaten squirrel in his narrow, dark mouth. Rabbits skittered, leaped. He saw a tall buck that didn't run and only slightly shivered as the vessels passed.

Kennard drew his hands across his eyes. He wanted to sing. He wanted to shout. He turned around and looked aft, wondering that if what he felt was apparent to the owner and master of the schooner. The man's name was Maumee Mike Jacobs, and Phelim had sailed with him before, told him something of his background.

Jacobs was German and had come as a youngster to this country after the failure of the '48 revolution. He had very strong convictions, Phelim said, and had gone to serve in an Indiana volunteer regiment in the War Between the States. Jacobs had been badly wounded, mustered out and as a result of it some people claimed that he wasn't too straight in his thoughts.

Kennard was both confused and attracted by him. This was his first American ship, his first American skipper, and he had been accustomed to the dour, hard ways of the masters of the British flag ships he had sailed. Jacobs was sometimes voluble and almost painfully talkative. He made no pretense at rank or outright authority, dressed like a farmer, looked like one. Now he had turned over the watch to Phelim, was coming forward with a slouched, yet graceful gait.

"Fine country, hah?" Jacobs asked him softly.

"I ain't seen anything like it," Kennard said. He was uncomfortable, uncertain whether he should call Jacobs "sir" and conscious that other members of the crew carefully listened.

"You ever hear of Jefferson?"

"Aye, that I have, a bit."

"Well, this here was what Jefferson had in mind for the people. And some of it the people have got, and some of it they haven't. But don't you mind such now. I'll tell you more of the matter later. Look up to the North'd. High, high!"

It was like a flurry of snow across the pallid silver sky. Yet the motion, the formations were not those of snow. Birds flew there. They held to the South in an enormous crescent made of thousands of white wings and bodies. Along the Northwest wind, faintly pulsant because of altitude, because of distance, Kennard heard their calling and then what he believed to be the majestic beat of the wings themselves.

"Snow goose from Canada," Jacobs said. "They're early. We usually reckon them for after September. But no man can find their nests or their eggs."

Kennard was lost in ecstasy. He nearly forgot where he was and what his duties were. But the snow geese had gone on to the South, out of vision. Jacobs said, "All right. We'll be off Detroit in a jiffy. Keep an eye on your towline. We'll be meeting plenty of vessels."

"Yes, sir," Kennard said stiffly, surprised at the rapidity with which Jacobs changed his manner.

He thought little of Detroit as they swung past it against the river's veering current. Buffalo had been half a city, half a straggling town. But for a man like him who was used to the granite and brick and the solid compactness of even the small Irish villages, Detroit was some sort of a cheap, shabby joke. It had the look of having been planned by an ambitious idiot. The stores were built with extra half stories in front, and the houses were hung with wooden gewgaws and balconies and pillars that didn't fit.

Kennard spit into the brown water and glared at the towboat deckhand. "Take up your slack, donkey!" he shouted in anger. "Do you want us pilin' down on that?" It wasn't until they were above Detroit and out in what he had learned was Lake St. Clair that he realized he had become angry because he still wanted to look at the snow geese.

Lake St. Clair was magnificent, though, and the night breeze brought him the smell of pines. He inhaled the resinous air as he sent the watch to the halyards and sheets in answer to Phelim's command and brought the vessel back under sail. She rapped sharply out from the shore with her lee rail well down, and he was suddenly very tired and very hungry. He went aft to ask Phelim if he could be relieved to go to supper, but as he came up the poop ladder he heard the long drawn slash of sound from the Northern shore.

"So what is it?" he said, a tension through his back muscles.

"Timber wolves," Phelim said and laughed. "Go below and get your supper, man. Then later on you'll have a look at them. They stand higher than the biggest goat in Antrim and they'll take the arm off you with one bite."

"Ah, no!" he said, still not really believing.

"Ah, yes!" Phelim said. "Now get below to your scoff. You have a bloody great lot yet to find out about these lakes."

But it was the captain, Maumee Mike Jacobs, who helped him get most of his Lakes knowledge. While the sailing season drew to an end, Kennard gradually found that he could be at ease with him. There was no barrier of constraint between them such as existed in the deep-water ships, and Jacobs was eager to speak about the region and the entire country and his conception of their meaning.

Kennard and the lean, big-footed captain often went ashore together when Phelim had the watch in port or was occupied with a woman, a bottle. Kennard was still reserved, unwilling to expose to anybody the degree of his ambition. Yet, when the mood was on him, Jacobs talked for hours straight without any prompting.

Their best conversation was in late November. They had brought the schooner into Hammond Bay on Lake Huron to load lumber for Buffalo at a rickety sawmill dock. Phelim didn't mind the yammering, the screech of the saws, the shouts of the mill crew and teamsters. He consented to take the watch and Jacobs and Kennard left the dock along a partly overgrown woods road that for some distance paralleled the shore. Kennard waited for Jacobs to speak, not only out of awe of the other's knowledge, but because of his growing subconscious desire to remain secret about himself.

"Jefferson, now," Jacobs said. He leaned down towards the shorter, stockier man. "I've told you about him."

"So you have," Kennard said. "President. One of the founders of the country. Louisiana Purchase fella."

"Correct as hell," Jacobs said. His sallow face beamed, as if with the inner glow of his love. He spread his arms to the South. "That treaty took in plenty land, plenty, plenty. You're a sailor. Understand that in the old days the French came all the way down from Montreal, up near the top of Canada, straight through to the Mississippi. Only a few miles of portage in between. The French had the whole shebang to themselves, river, lakes, forests. Jefferson dickered them out of it."

"Why? The French had a right to it."

"Yeah, so, maybe. But they couldn't ha' kept it from the English. And Jefferson wanted it for the States. For the poor fellers, because back East the rich were gobbling up all the land. Jefferson aimed for every man to own a piece of property. Make an equalitarian, agricultural society."

"By God, cap'." Alan Kennard ruefully smiled. "You're a man for the words. You leave me bloody well astern when you talk so."

Jacobs was solemn. He held his lanky body erect. "My folks fought in Europe for what those words mean. I fought here. But the deal's not settled yet. The wealthy fellers got behind Jefferson's back, him and the presidents who came after him."

"You told me before. They fixed it so the government paid to build the railroads, then they moved in."

"And took the timber and the copper and the iron, and they've held on, they're making the little feller pay through the nose."

"How? Maybe not around here, but out West there's a great lot of settlers who own their own land."

"Sure they do. But their crops go East over the railroads. If they don't pay the freight rates, their stuff's not shipped out to market. Then they sit and starve."

"Like in the old country, in Antrim. The squire has the little fella licked all the time."

"No, there's a difference," Jacobs said slowly. "Because in this country if a man's smart enough, he can break loose and get squared off for himself. Now, my father, he did. He has him a farm down on the Maumee River and he's doing fine. I have me the schooner and I'll have me more if this doesn't stop the parade." He tapped his chest, and Alan Kennard stared at him.

"Wound I got from a minié ball in the war," Jacobs said.

"I'd like fine to hear from you about the fighting some time."

"Not from me, you won't. But there's plenty others to tell you that. There's books that you can buy when we're back down to Buffalo, too."

They had stopped at the brush-clotted end of the road. The flat, almost black expanse of Lake Huron was before them, marked by small whitecaps and an occasional, distant sail. Kennard took his glance from the lake. He watched the wild life alongshore, trying to identify the birds Jacobs had pointed out to him. Those were redhead ducks, and on down were mallards. The redheads were bound South, but the mallards would stay, Jacobs had said. They were good hunting, good eating. Over in the woods were juncoes. The bright little bastards were cardinals. That sound you hear is a woodpecker. Listen to him go, man.

Kennard put a hand to his head and grunted. "Damn you, cap', you give me so much to think about that my poor noggin aches."

"All right." Jacobs grinned at him. "One more story, then, and we knock off and go back aboard. Down to Michigan in the early days, a Frenchman name of Nicolet was head of a party that came in from Canada. He was bound for a place that's named Green Bay now. The Indians, a bunch of fish-eaters, were on the shore waiting for him. But he couldn't see them too well from out in the lake, so he reached into his kit in the canoe and he broke out a real Chinese outfit, little round hat, big, long mandarin robe. The son of a bitch, he thought he'd made it. He thought he was coming alongside Cathay and he was going to meet the Grand Khan."

"By God, that's a story," Kennard said. "Still, the fella had found something big. This country has a lot that China ain't."

He was silent afterwards on the way back to the ship. He was thinking of Jefferson, and of the men who had built the railroads, the men who had the wealth and the strength and the skill to come on from the East and rip down these forests. Then he tried to imagine the Mississippi and the Missouri, the Ohio, the Monongahela, the Allegheny and all the other rivers and lakes he had heard about, so that he could put them in order in his mind. It was impossible. The design was too huge. They became for him a fantastic whirligig of images, shapes, colors, vistas. To think of them made him a bit drunk, he realized. But he liked the country fine. Aye, this was the place for him.

Phelim was waiting for Jacobs and him as they returned aboard. Phelim was sober, his face stern. "Weather is making up out of the Nor'east," he said. "It'll blow like a bobcast bastard. You want to sail, cap'?"

"Yes, I want to sail," Jacobs said mildly. "We got the crew aboard?"

Phelim nodded and glanced at Kennard with what Kennard sensed was an odd, new jealousy. "He can find 'em."

"Then get the watch on deck," Jacobs said. "There's no real lee here against a Nor'easter. This dock is no good to us. We'd better stand out clear of Forty Mile Point."

"Yes, sir," Kennard said. He had just begun to understand the reasons for Phelim's jealousy. After all, he was an unlicensed man, and Phelim a mate with first class papers. This ship here might be different from deep-water, and maybe Lakes vessels, too, because of the free and easy way Jacobs acted. But it was damn' rare in any vessel that a master went ashore time after time with his bosun. And there was more. Phelim didn't like it that he ducked drinking and raising hell with him. It was Phelim who'd brought him to the Lakes, Phelim who was his old deep-water shipmate and good friend. But be done with such for now. You have plenty of work ahead and so have all hands aboard.

The wind struck with cruel violence soon after the schooner beat free of the land. Jacobs used nothing but a small jib and the mainsail to do it, but then, outside, the jib had to be taken off and the mainsail reefed. There was no man among the sailors competent to go out on the bowsprit and furl the jib. Kennard took off his shoes and shirt, scrambled forth alone along the bowsprit.

Waves smacked him, plucked, smothered, soaked and chilled, and spray filled his eyes and mouth. He clung on and yelled aft to slack the jib halyard. The cloth came down with a snarl, stiff, iron-hard, and he batted at it, fisted it in so he could make fast the stops. He worked by instinct and memory, unable to see. The foot-ropes cut his insteps; water sheeted over him, and as the schooner bucked reeling, he was submerged to the shoulders, once went completely under.

"So, ye bastard!" he told the wind, and scrambled back to reef the mainsail. The sailors helped him a bit there, yet they were frightened, numb, slow to respond. Due to her extreme list, pieces of timber in the deck cargo had begun to slip the lashings and thrash down-deck to leeward. That would foul against, then carry away the shrouds and running gear, Kennard knew. He had to secure the stuff.

But Phelim moved cat-quick forward to him. "Let's get the sail off her first. Take the throat, lad, and I'll grab the peak."

They cast the halyards from the pin rail in unison and the wind rammed them headlong, swung them dangling out overside, just the halyards in their hands to keep them from death. They swerved back, and hung and braced, took their moment and slacked the sail. The gaff, high above the bulging cloud of canvas, gave an ominous creak to the wind's blows; the mast and the stays trembled; the boom shuddered, whinnied.

There was no light in which to see while the spray spurned them, and they called to each other to make sure of the moment. Then they let the sail go by the run, leapt at it and hauled taut the turns of their stops. "You're still a sailor, you Ulster ape," Phelim said. "Now get the deck stuff secured."

"Aye," Alan Kennard muttered. He stared from under his raised right arm at the men of the watch. Phelim had warned him back in Buffalo. Like many Lakes schooner captains, Jacobs sailed with only one mate. The crew weren't sailors in the deep-water sense. They were homesteaders, farmers who worked the Lakes in the season to make a few dollars cash while their wives and young took care of the land. The lot he had here were for sure frightened, and the watch below would be just as bad. But he needed them all if the ship was to live.

"Get them up from below," he shouted to the man next to him, and in the second that he shouted saw the wave. It was black, crested with white. It poised high above the windward side before it toppled and crashed. Kennard found a handhold. He lay flat as the wave descended, then slung off to leeward. But when it was past and he shook his head to get the water from his ears, he heard the faint, terrible cries.

The watch was gone. Four men, those who had been here beside him, had been wrenched away into the hooting darkness by the wave. He cursed, but his instinctive concern was for the ship. His job was to make her live, and nothing could be done for the four.

He dragged the other watch up from the fo'c'sle man by man. He told them, "Your mates didn't draw the luck. They're goners. But the same will be for you 'less you work with me, lads. Take a look-see there downwind. Get what I mean?"

A paralysis seized them as they gazed at the immense white explosion of the breakers on the rocks along Forty Mile Point. Their faces were gray, their mouths purple with cold and fear. But after they had looked, they turned and followed Kennard to work.

He rigged a Spanish windlass, a web of heavy, interlocking ropes led across the deck cargo from side to side of the ship and then tightened with a balk of timber thrust through the center. He was knocked down times past count by the waves. His trousers were torn, his shirt had blown overboard. Ice formed on his body. Ice was slick over the timber he climbed and the ropes he handled. He had no light, and again he worked by instinct, and gropingly the men tried to help him.

A yell came from one of them once and he squinted up to see a side-wheel steamer not two hundred yards away. She had lost her power, was drifting downwind onto the point. Ice sheathed her fore and aft. Her tall stack buckled as he watched, then snapped and fell, then her pilot-house broke apart. "*Lieber Gott!*" said a German sailor beside Kennard. "T'em liddle black t'ings took off her decks, them's men."

Kennard grasped the German by the front of his mackinaw coat and lifted him and shook him. "Work, you swab!" he said. "You want to lay up alongside them on the point?"

When he went aft to report that the deck cargo was secure, Phelim Carmody was at the wheel. Jacobs stood near him, but Jacobs' head sagged and he was almost unconscious. "The man can't take it," Phelim said. "His lungs are bad from that old wound. But I'll keep her off the beach, bucko. I'll hold her to the South'ard till this breaks."

"So you will," Kennard said. "But why don't I take him below and send one of the lads for tea? The lot of them are about froze stiff."

"Do that." Phelim stood with his knees half bent, his face to the battering of the wind. "Then you can relieve me here. I'm like ice meself."

The storm broke in the hour of dawn, went wildly on to the Southeast. Carmody brought Kennard a sweater, a mackinaw and a great mug of tea while Kennard stood at the wheel. "Get yerself warm," he said, "and then bend on the small jib again. We can run for Port Huron, all but steer the course."

Kennard was so cold that his body seemed afire. Tears ran down his cheeks and his hands as he took the mug were wooden, hardly felt the heat. But down inside of him the tea was good. It spread, he thought oddly, like a big golden bubble in his guts, and it took the cold right out of him. "As she goes," he said and gave Phelim the wheel. But he didn't move away. "How's the captain?"

"He'll be up in a bit." Phelim had eased the wheel, let the ship fall off to Southeast-by-East. "He's slept and he's got some strength back into him. Not the strongest man around, Jacobs. But, how do ye like the Lakes now?"

"A man knows his trade here," Kennard said quietly, "or he's dead. . . ." He was silent, thinking of the men who had been swept over the side from this ship, and the fate of the steamer. It was a lesson to remember. No running room here like on deep-water. And fresh water froze a bloody sight faster than salt. The vessels were shallow draft because of the rivers, but they iced up in less than half an hour. Capsize out in the lake or pile all standing on a lee shore. Aye, Kennard, remember.

"Jacobs will be putting the vessel up for the winter at the end of the trip," Phelim said. "He's had enough for the season. You and me will hit for the woods. We'll see how you make out with an axe in your mitts. But step along like a good lad and give me that jib."

"The jib it is," Kennard said. He took pleasure in standing on the fore deck while a pair of sailors scrambled along the bowsprit and cast off the jib stops. He was dry, he was warm, and he figured to stay so. But, more, he was happy in the fact that Phelim was still his friend. With Phelim as his side-kicker, he'd be all right. Sure and it was a fact that the Lakes were hard. A fact, too, that he was a hard man and could beat them. You're here to stay, Kennard. This is where you get yours.

.   .   .   .

Maumee Mike Jacobs laid up the schooner in Buffalo after she was discharged. He wrote letters and sent money to the families of the men who had been lost in the storm. Then he paid off the rest of the crew, went uptown for a final drink with Carmody and Kennard. "I'm bound for the Maumee and the old man's farm to snug in," he said to them. "Maybe a feller with what I got shouldn't keep sailing. But I'll be better in the spring." He threw a silver dollar on the bar for the drinks and held out his hand. "You know where to find me, Phelim?"

"I do," Phelim said, "and when we're out of the woods we'll look for you, cap'."

"Good," Jacobs said. His deepset eyes came to Kennard. "Buy your books before you throw it all away in whiskey."

"Sure enough," Kennard said. He touched his brow with his finger tips in the old-fashioned form of salute. "I'll no doubt have a few more with this Liverpool snorter today, but I'll get the books first."

Phelim cursed them both with good-natured scorn. "You'd ruin my drinking with such talk," he said.

"No, oh, no." Kennard stood with his compact body straight, his dark brown, intense face tilted slightly to one side. "But it's only from the books that I can learn what I want."

"To hell with you!" Phelim was no longer good-natured. "Go buy them, then, and leave me to the whiskey!"

Phelim was more than half drunk when he got back with the parcel of books. Kennard had to sing "Maloney's Pig" and all the verses of "The Swallowtail Coat" before Phelim would pay any attention to him. But then Phelim grinned and tousled his hair. "You're a donkey," Phelim said. "A proper Antrim donkey. But you can sing and you can sail and you're my good friend. So tomorrow we'll hit for the woods. They're logging heavy up around Saginaw Bay. Take your pick. Where would you like to work? On the Flint, or the Tittabawassee, the Kawkawlin, the Pine, the Rifle, the Au Grès or the Au Sable?"

"Jesus and the Saints!" Alan Kennard said. "I could make a song out of them names."

"Not now." Phelim grasped him hard around the shoulder. "Just have yourself a drink."

.   .   .   .

They went to work up on the Kawkawlin. The outfit that hired them was owned by the Nickerson family and it was big. Eighty-five men and twelve teams of horses and oxen were in the camp where they were assigned. The timber they cut was on part of twenty-two square miles the Nickersons held, and it was only a fraction of the family's property in the region.

"Down Easters," Phelim said as he and Kennard climbed off the sled before the slab bunkhouse. "State of Maine men. Tight with a dollar, but loaded to the guards with the stuff."

"A dollar is what they're paying me for twelve hours' work a day," Alan Kennard said. "Aye, man, they're tight all right."

Phelim squinted at him speculatively, standing ankle-deep in the soft snow. "You're what's known as a swamper," he said. "Next below you is cookee and then chore boy. That's not far from the bottom of the pack. But get handy with an axe and you'll work alongside me. We'll be axemen together. Another fifty cents a day you'll get for that."

"Sure, and a fine thing, too," Kennard said without bitterness. Then he picked up his bag and followed Phelim into the bunkhouse.

It was one huge room heated by potbellied chunk stoves at each end. The bunk was in the middle, and he saw that it was exactly as Phelim had described it to him. The men all slept together side by side and closely for warmth under blankets that had been stitched to form one cover. Now, in this moment of twilight, the men were coming in from the woods and he had the opportunity to look them over, discover the origin of the odor that pervaded the room.

Most of them had been in the woods for only a couple of weeks, but they were unshaven, hadn't taken the trouble to wash. Their bodies gave off the smell of sweat made sour-sweet by their flannel underwear and shirts, the thick trousers and coats and woolen socks. Some smoked shag tobacco in short clay pipes; the rest chewed snuff. *Schnoos* was the name they gave it out here on the Lakes, and cans to catch the brownish spittle were all around the room.

"Not for me," he said low-voiced to Phelim.

"Not what?"

"This goat-stinkin' cuddy. Me, I'll sleep in the snow instead."

"To hell and you will," Phelim said. "You'll get used to it. A sailor like you turning finicky. Think of the fo'c'sle in the *Margharita*, man."

"I am. But there you could stick your head out on deck. You could draw yourself a bucket of water for a wash-down."

Phelim, as he had done more and more lately, chose to ignore that. He had swung around and was greeting men in the room whom he knew. Then there was a high-pitched shout from behind:

"Come set to it or we'll pitch it out!"

Alan Kennard was nearly knocked from his feet by the rush of men. "Scoff time," Phelim said, shouldering beside him. "You'll be like them after a day of it with the axe."

The men ate in absolute silence, ravenously and with a terrible earnestness. It was pork and beans, fried meat in great stacks, thick chunks of vinegar pie and pots of black tea. The men reached out, chewed, gulped, swallowed, reached out once more without lifting their heads or their eyes. When they were through, they pushed back from the benches, wiped their faces on their sleeves, belched and broke wind, stepped quickly through the shuffling cooks who still hurried to refill the platters.

Quite a crew, Alan Kennard thought, not surprised by what he saw and able to comprehend it. They're getting their hides worked off, he thought. These lads put out to beat hell. So they eat the same way. He sat quietly with a mug of tea and scrutinized the men remaining at the long plank table.

They were all recognizable types to him. The French Canadians were the most prominent with their red woolen stocking caps and scarfs, the high, hard cheekbones. Then there were Danes and Swedes and Norwegians, flat-faced and small-nosed in comparison with the Canadians, but broad and deep through the shoulders and with fists like clubs. A few had the thin noses, the short chins and fair complexions of Scots. They were taller men, with the same sort of long, sinewy bodies as the few Indians. There were English and Irish and maybe a Welshman or so, too, from the look of them. But of the lot he was interested by the Indians.

Their clothing was the same as the white men's and a number of the Canadians had almost identical faces and probably more than a drop of Indian blood. But even in this speechless room where everybody ate alike the Indians had a different quality about them. He wasn't sure, and he lacked the language to phrase his thought, but he believed that it was because of their hidden sadness. It showed in their slant, somber eyes, the way they sat in a kind of private isolation even as they jostled the men on each side of them while they ate. Your mother was so. She was a gypsy, a Romany, and came from a people different from them around her. All her life, she was off some far place by herself. And these fellas owned this land. Once, it was all theirs.

The recognition depressed him and he rose from the table, stepped past the flatfooted, sweating cooks and out the door into the night. Stars were up, and his feeling of unhappiness left him as he looked at them. Castor and Pollux were there, and the Pleiades; Orion strode over the fragile black tips of the pines although Sirius was still below the horizon. Cloud was across the Northern sky, blanked Cassiopeia, the Dipper, the North Star. It would be bloody cold tomorrow. With a swing in the wind, there'd be snow.

He heard the soft stirring of horses that had just been fed and the low and grunt of oxen. The stable was in back of him and he walked towards it, eager to know more of this place. There must be some doss better than that bunkhouse, he told himself. Even the stable will be better.

A low-turned kerosene lamp hung inside the stable door. He took it off the peg and turned it up, inspected the stalls. One beyond the oxen was empty. It was stacked with clean horse blankets piled on straw. "For you, laddie buck," he said and grinned and slapped his thigh.

Back in the bunkhouse, the men had already begun their night's sleep. They had taken off nothing except their mackinaws and boots, slept in the manner Phelim had explained to him, body to body in the enormous single bunk. His entrance disturbed some sleeper and that one twitched and muttered "Spoon!" and they all rolled over simultaneously, took up position on the other side. He had difficulty finding his bag in the obscurity, and it was much harder to discover Phelim. But he grasped Phelim by the foot, resolutely shook him.

"I'm going to doss in the stable," he said. "Roust me out in the morning."

"You can't do that," Phelim said, his head up over the edge of the cover. "You're supposed to bunk here. But ask the clerk in the van. The same fella who put us on the payroll. His name is Shaw and you're a donkey."

"You'll soon smell worse than one," he told Phelim, and several men sat up to glare at him and curse. "Get out, greenhorn," the biggest of them called, "or I'll bust you in the head!"

The van, he told himself when he was outside again in the snow, was the name here for the company store. It was where you could buy mackinaws, shoe-packs, socks, snuff and tobacco on credit against your wages. But the place would be closed by now, and he had caused enough trouble as it was. He stood indecisive for a moment, then went on towards the van. He could feel against his shoulder through his clothing and the canvas of the bag the shapes of the books he had bought in Buffalo. There was reading he must do this winter. If he was to go ahead, he had to have the knowledge in the books. And he'd never get it among the bunkhouse lot.

A lamp with a tin reflector burned in the van. He knocked on the door and then rested rigidly, selfconscious and very worried that his request would be refused. Shaw was a young, thin and quiet-seeming man. He wore steel rimmed spectacles that gave him a schoolmaster's look and greatly impressed Kennard.

"I'm sorry to bother you," Kennard said in his soft Antrim voice. "But I have a favour to ask."

"Come in," Shaw said shortly. "You're one of today's lot. I'll still sell to you."

"A pair of the shoe-packs, then," Kennard said, "and a coat. But would anybody mind, mister, if I slept in the stable instead of that bunkhouse?"

Shaw had moved behind the counter towards a shelf. He stopped and slid his glasses up on his forehead, stared sharply at Kennard. "You don't like the bunkhouse, I take it," he said.

"Och, a man could launch a boat in there on the smell alone."

Shaw put back his glasses with a slow gesture. He came to the counter and leaned his elbows on it. A smile was changing the angular lines of his face and then he laughed aloud.

"Don't mind me," Alan Kennard said defensively. "I'm new to the country."

"Stay new, as far as the bunkhouse goes." The laughter was still in Shaw's voice. "Sure, you can sleep in the stable. Just watch out you don't set it afire."

"That I will, and thank you. Now let me have a look at the gear."

Shaw held out the big ledger for him to sign when he had chosen his shoe-packs and coat. But Kennard opened the money belt. He smoothed the dollar bills one by one before he pushed them across the counter.

"You must be a Scot," Shaw said, the laughter wrinkles back in his face.

"A first cousin to them," Alan Kennard said. "I'm out of County Antrim, in Ulster."

Shaw shut the ledger, gave him change from his pocket. "The chore boys get a call at three in the morning," he said. "Then they call the teamsters. I'll have them give you a shout."

"Thanks again," Kennard said. "I'm grateful to you."

He was in the stall in the stable and had begun opening the package of books when Shaw came through the door. "I forgot," Shaw said. He held out a dollar and a half in silver. "I was charging you Nickersons' mark-up prices for credit and not what the stuff costs cash. Goodnight, Antrim." But he didn't go; he stood looking down curiously at the books. "What have you got there?"

"It's what the master of a ship told me to read for the improving of my mind. History is one, geography another, and some other stuff the fella in the store said I should have. In the spring, y' see, I want to sit for my pilot's license. I'm by rights a sailor and no wood-chopper."

"I can see that," Shaw said. He motioned at the books before he started away. "When you're through with those, come around to me. I've got a whole lot more."

. . . .

He had no watch, but as he figured it, he had read until almost midnight. When the tall teamster bawled at him and he staggered up to his feet, the night was achingly cold yet and the teamster told him that the time was about a quarter past four. He stumbled by the man and outside, rubbed his face and neck with snow, banged his hands together for warmth.

Men had just been called in the bunkhouse. They stood in a long, loose line relieving themselves, then clumped in to breakfast. He joined them and found a place next to Phelim. Phelim was sour with sleep, hoarse-voiced. "I'll show you where you get your axe and your flaggin's. Then you're on your own. But watch the axe. They edge them champion sharp in this country."

The stuff called "flaggin's," he learned, was the cold meat put out by the cooks for the midday meal in the woods. Big loaves of bread and pots of tea went with it, and each group or crew carried their own. When he touched the blade of the axe given him by the foreman of the swamper gang, he realized that Phelim had been right. He had never used such a marvelously sharp blade. Some of the hard block of fatigue fell from him as he hefted the helve in his hand, went with the others out along the tote road.

Dawn came slowly through the trees, a thin lilac suffusion first, then vivid, in wide bands of scarlet and orange light. The iced trunks of the trees took the light. They glistened. A refraction from them spangled the air and the snow, gave a peculiar luminosity to the small clouds of moisture made by the men as they breathed.

Alan Kennard lowered his axe. He gazed at the beauty and it made him feel as he had that day aboard Jacobs' schooner in the Detroit River. You're unfaithful, he thought wryly. You're forgetting the beauties of your own Antrim. Then he raised the axe, breathed deeply and swung. His body had become warm, his muscles limber. It was sheer pleasure to work.

The gang he was with cleared an extension of the tote road. Along the road itself the logging teams constantly passed, the alert, big-hooved Percherons with their powerful necks and quarters tightened to the loads. They pulled huge single logs on *travois* in the Indian style, returned from the river with the trace chains slowly jangling on the hames. Their drivers were mostly the French Canadians and those men had a soft grace as they walked, talked in gutturals to the teams. It was the spans of oxen that hauled the heavy loads and the oxen skinners who made the noise. Far down the tote road, Kennard could hear them as they snaked out of the woods. "Gee, now! Gee! You—haw!" The skinners' calls were repeated in a chorus that was very much like music, and above them all day long was the ringing of the axes. Their sound was set off by the whicker of saws, the strident warning cry as a tree was about to fall.

He couldn't help himself. His curiosity was too great and he turned to watch each time that day when he heard the call of "Timber!" The tree described a slight, erratic spiral along the sky. It shuddered, veered faster, faster. Then it fell with a whopping and groaning crash that echoed over the frozen ground. Squirrels scampered. Grouse beat their wings out in the underbrush and slanted off in gray-brown streaks to further safety. The eyes of the Percherons rolled a bit, and nerves twitched the ears down, up. The men who had stood watching and listening muttered, "There she goes" and turned back easily to their work.

Alan Kennard was more thrilled than he had been since he had stood his first trick at the wheel of a full rigged ship. That's for you, he thought. It takes real skill and heft to drop them. Soon now you'll have the full knack of the axe and you'll go join Phelim at it.

He was two weeks with the swamper gang before he was sent to work as Phelim's partner. His life had been established in a quite regular pattern by then, and each night after supper he read for several hours before he fell asleep in the stable. Phelim considered him queer for sleeping there and told him so, but he disregarded the big Liverpool man. There were nights, of course, when the type raced and looped, blurred all over the page and his head slid forward on the book. But there were others when what he read completely absorbed him and he read on and on, and occasionally Joshua Shaw came to visit him.

He and Shaw talked about what he read. He tried within the limits of his vocabulary to give the other the sense of his new knowledge. The thing was expanding, taking growth in his mind. La Salle, Marquette, Nicolet, le Sieur Du Luth, they all had their place, and with them Gentleman Johnny Burgoyne and Pontiac and

Rogers and Perry. It was like a tapestry you saw on the wall of one of the old castles at home. But this was life, and the men were real, not faded figures woven in the cloth.

Joshua Shaw had a great deal to tell him, more than Maumee Mike Jacobs. For Shaw was a college man; he had gone to Yale College in Connecticut. Shaw took the parts one by one and showed him how to put them together. It wasn't any longer just La Salle sick and part starved in a suit of greasy buckskins in a bark canoe, or Burgoyne drunk on a horse fumbling through the woods with his cocked hat on sidewise. The story was of the taking of the whole continent.

"And the big men haven't grabbed it all yet," Shaw said. He sat with his back against the side of the stall, a piece of straw in his hand.

"What d' you mean?" Alan Kennard said. "Can a bunch like the Nickersons miss?"

Shaw grinned at him. "Sure. They're too goddamn' greedy, one way or another. They have two hundred thousand acres of timber land around here—two hundred thousand acres. You could throw Antrim into it and never see the place again. But all they'll do is strip the timber, go on West to another huge chunk until they reach the Pacific coast and have to stop."

"You're saying, then, that they'll leave a lot behind."

"Correct."

"But other fellas can't be as narrow as them. They must know there's a lot more to the land than the timber." Kennard gave him a slow, searching glance. "A fella like you, for one. What are you doing out here, Josh? You didn't go to that college just to be a bloody clerk for Nickerson."

"No," Shaw said. He twisted the piece of straw in his hands. Then he balled it up and pitched it over onto the back of the softly breathing ox in the next stall. "I'm after iron, Antrim. I'm an iron-master from 'way back and so is everybody in my family. We've been running forges and furnaces since Colonial times."

"So you'd be after the iron out here."

"I have been, and I've found it."

They were silent for an instant, staring at each other, measuring each other. Here was a man who had already helped him plenty, Alan Kennard thought, and who might help him a huge lot more in the future. Somehow, too, in his day and way he could do the same for Shaw. "Where did you come upon it, Josh?" he said.

Shaw grinned, but his eyes were hard and thoughtful behind his spectacles. "There's no secret," he said. "Up on the Vermillion range, in back of Superior. My father and brothers worked it with me for several years. Then we went broke. We weren't very smart."

"You?" Kennard was shocked.

"That's right. We had our ore, sure enough, and everything that went for the working of it, fuel, limestone and all. But we were too far from our markets. It cost us too much to ship the stuff out of there."

"But now they're building a canal at the St. Mary's Falls," Kennard said. "The place that on the chart is called the Sault Sainte Marie. Some general, a fella name of Poe, he has the job."

"When he's done," Shaw said, "we'll operate. We still own our ore." He rose to his feet and shook the straw from his clothing. "Catch some sleep, Antrim. That axe is waiting for you in the morning."

"Och, so it is. But before you go, man. Once you were telling me you had some books of your own. Could I borrow them?"

Joshua Shaw gave him his characteristic grin. "I have one at least I'll lend. It's different from what you've been reading, but you'll like it. Goodnight now."

He found a lot of strange words in the book that Shaw lent him. It was also written in what Shaw said was poetry. He had to slow down a good deal to get the meaning, and much more often than before he dropped asleep as he read. But he went back to it every night, and now he was working with Phelim, he had an added sense of confidence in all he did. You'll finish the thing before spring, he promised himself. Just stick with it.

He and Phelim made a fine team in the woods. Phelim was a bit sarcastic with him at first, but then when he saw his skill with the axe they worked in perfect unison. It was a source of constant pride to both of them to fell the trees.

They stood on opposite sides, taking alternate strokes. He let Phelim set the pace, so aware of the man's nature that he could gauge his action to the second. Phelim's axe came up, back over the wide shoulder, dropped in that sure swerve of silvery light. Now it's you. His feet were set wide in the snow. His right hand slid up the smooth wood of the helve almost to the head, and he marked where he was going to place the stroke, brought his gathered body quickly swinging forward, all of his weight behind the axe.

The blade bit deep and true. It made a *cuh-chock!* sound and the force of the swing sent a little shiver of concussion through the helve into his hands and arms. The big, resinous chip was still spinning in the air as he pulled clear, gave Phelim room to swing.

Stroke and stroke, stroke and stroke, without a word said, just their bodies poising, swinging, coming back ready. Then it was time for the big six foot saw, the quick swipe of kerosene across the blade, and afterwards the wedge, the maul, the last few strokes.

She creaked now as they worked. She had started to sway. They looked aloft to see how she would fall, and she was right, was going as they had planned it. They jumped back. The gap had widened where they cut. A groaning shudder was through the tree. Phelim put his hands to his mouth. "Timber!" She seemed to stagger like a human being in serious pain. Then she dropped and it was all at once, the descent making a ripping thunder among the other trees. The little black ants came over the snow by the thousands, climbed the rawness of the stump and massed where the resin pooled. Kennard pointed. "We're ants, too," he said. "No bigger, as a fact."

"Them books has got your wits," Phelim said. He had out and was lighting his stub pipe. "But I still know what you mean. Ten minutes for that one. A dollar and a half a day and found for us, and for the Nickersons the tree is worth a hundred. So we'll stay poor and they'll stay rich."

Alan Kennard shook his head. "Come on," he said, "you Lime Street booger. What's money to you who spends it with both hands? We can be rich, too, in our time."

"To hell you say," Phelim told him. They were moving on to the next tree. "I've snaked a month's pay out of Shaw already. We'll have whiskey in camp tomorrow night and the next day's Christmas. You've forgotten, by Jesus."

"No, I haven't," Kennard said. "And I'll share the cost of the whiskey with you. A drink in this country will go good on Christmas."

There was whiskey all over the bunkhouse Christmas Eve. It seemed that the drivers making the trip into Kawkawlin Center had been bringing in loads steadily, leaving them in the custody of Joshua Shaw. Some men had two, some had three bottles, and right after supper they started to drink. Shaw came into the bunkhouse near nine o'clock and stood staring around the room. "The Nickerson brothers are here," he called in his clear voice. "They want to come in and wish you the season's greetings."

"So w'at do we get?" Big Sven said. Big Sven was a Swede, a top-loader and the toughest fighter in camp. He sat by one of the stoves stripped to his red flannel underwear, a bottle stuck inside the shirt, another within the waistband of the pants. He lurched up, spread his arms. "Last year, they give us dry prunes. Sons of bitches, tell 'em go home."

"You're a goddamn' fool," Shaw said quietly. "They brought a couple of roasting pigs and a five gallon jug of rum."

"It's you, you who bought," Sven bawled. "Yah, not them stingy-fist fellers. I know you, Shaw."

But the door was open behind Shaw and two small, neat men stood there. They must be the Nickersons, Alan Kennard thought. They both wore heel-long black cloth coats with fur collars and seal-skin caps. Steel spectacles such as Joshua Shaw wore were perched on their expressionless faces. Their cheeks and lips had no colour, and only the high, strong bones of the noses gave an indication of their character.

"A Merry Christmas to you, men," they said in unison. One lifted his right hand, the other his left. They smiled, and then like appari-tions they were gone from the smoke-vague room. Shaw tried to go after them, but Big Sven sprang and caught him, tossed him over his shoulder. "You stay, Shaw."

"Let me down, you box-head," Shaw said. "I was just going after my violin."

"Yust you bring it," Big Sven said. "Don't fool around with them fellers. They make me sick my stomach, and I want to drink whiskey. Why, yah, by God, I drink now!"

Alan Kennard was uncertain about the details; the whiskey had put a numbing warmth through his brain, relaxed him to the point where all he wanted to do was sit and drink. But suddenly one of the Scots, an angular, fair-haired man, was out in the middle of the floor and he had a bagpipe and he was playing it.

The Scot stalked as he played, stiff-legged and straight in the back, with an arrogance in his manner that was also in the music. It was the old tunes, one after the other, and Kennard was trans-ported, taken into depths of remembrance that contained a poign-ancy, a beauty which were beyond language. The streamers on the bagpipe were of the Gordon tartan, and obviously the piper had been a soldier in his day. So this mixture of men respected him, and anyhow the music made its own appeal to them.

It was the French Canadians and the Indians who were affected most of all. The Canadians tapped their feet in flawless rhythm; they stalked in imagination stride for stride with the piper. The Ojibways and Winnebagos sat together in a tight knot, as did the majority of the men who were part of a national group. They were immobile and very watchful, drank much less than the others. But the pipe music set their eyes afire. They responded to it gradually, and their hands met, almost silently clapped out the time. Ancient is ancient, Alan Kennard thought, and who ever could prove that a Highlander wasn't half a savage.

The piper ended his playing with "The Flowers of the Forest." He stood absolutely still for the lament, and the room was so quiet that against the quavering lift and fine, thin sob of the notes there was only the crack of stove chunks, the shush of eave snow dropping.

"Yaisus, Yaisus!" Big Sven shouted, overcome by the silence the piper left. He was on his feet and waving to his countrymen to gather with him and sing. But Jean Rotin, a top-loader and a leader of the Canadians, had tears on his face and was still sobbing because of the lament. It was impossible for him to keep silent any longer, and he called to Big Sven, "Us first." Then all the Canadians began singing "Alouette" in chorus.

"Big Sven, he's not too happy about that," Phelim said beside Alan Kennard. "Him and Jean Rotin had a real shindy out on the tote road the other day."

"To hell," Kennard said. "No fighting on Christmas. I'll bust the skull of the fella who starts it."

"You're drunk," Phelim said.

"Sure I am. But batten your big hatch and listen to them sing." The Canadians danced as they sang, and the Indians joined them. They wheeled and sprang and whirled in jigs, throwing back their heads with delight as they roared out, *"Je te plumerai!"* But Big Sven was up, had moved close to Jean Rotin. He grimaced at the strapping Canadian, then screwed his fingers to his nose. "Frawg-eater," he said. "This is Yankee country. You sing Yankee."

Jean Rotin's reply was to kick Big Sven in the stomach. The kick was delivered while he revolved to the singing and it had great momentum. Big Sven dived backward in the air as though yanked by an unseen cable. His arms flapped loosely from his sides and his legs hung wide. He thumped along the floor, then lay slack as an empty sack.

"Hey, Swedes!" a man shouted across the room. He was already running at Jean Rotin. Here we go, Kennard thought with a strange elation. It's a real shindy. His stomach muscles were tensed; his hands were closed into fists and he breathed hard. Phelim had gone into a sort of half-bent crouch and was flexing his arms. "The bastards," he said. "The bastards."

Kennard saw through the room's haze the chore boys huddled protectively by a door, the cooks near them. Their faces were pallid with fright, and some had their hands raised over their heads. The Scottish piper slammed by shouting, "Up, up the Scots!" Other Scots were behind him, then an indiscriminate hurly-burly of men.

But Joshua Shaw was in the center of the room. He held a violin and bow, and he kept them high and out of danger. He blocked the leading Swede, though, sent him sprawling with an outstretched foot. Then he turned on Jean Rotin and kicked him violently just below the right knee cap. Rotin dropped down groaning and Shaw shouted at him and all of them, "*La Paix!* It's Christmas. I want to play a tune."

The men stopped on either side of Shaw. They gazed at him shivering and muttering, heads down, fists still clenched. Shaw gave them no regard. He had lifted the violin; he played it.

Alan Kennard didn't know the name of the tune. It was something he had never heard. But he was aware that Shaw played off key and very badly. The man's better than that, he thought. Shaw's not the lad for poor music. But then he saw the rigour of muscles through Shaw's neck, the whiteness of bone in the knuckles of the tight-drawn hand on the violin. Shaw had taken hell's own chance out there. The Frenchies had knives in their belly scarves and some of the Scandahoovians had picked up axe helves. This would have been a bloody bitch of a massacre.

Shaw lowered the violin and grinned. "Later," he said. "I need a drink. Give me a drink."

Jean Rotin stood lurching, taut with pain. But he held forth a bottle. "Drink my whiskey," he said. "And we sing, *hein?*"

"Sure, we sing," Shaw said. He looked around at Alan Kennard. "You know 'Silent Night,' Antrim."

"Not me," Kennard said, ashamed. "But set up the tune and I'll go along with you."

Shaw and he sang alone for an instant, then Jean Rotin and Phelim came braying in, and the Scots, the Danes, the Swedes and Canadians, even the Indians. At the end of the first verse, Shaw walked to the bunk where Big Sven slumped semi-conscious. He grasped Sven by his undershirt front and pulled him upright. "Now your style," he said. "Sing, too, you box-head. *Stillige Nacht, Hellige Nacht*. Right?"

"Yah, yah," Big Sven said. He stood up and put his arm on Shaw's shoulder and sang with the rest.

Alan Kennard felt drained, weak, and the whiskey no longer buoyed him. You get your nerves raw on such a night as this, he realized. It's almost more than a man can take. Look at them now. They all love each other. Big Sven and Rotin having a drink from the same bottle. Danes with their arms around Indians. Frenchies giving Swedes a loan of *schnoos*. Shaw did it. He made Christmas out of it, and let it be a lesson to you.

The weak feeling passed and was replaced by one of contentment. Phelim had climbed into the bunk, he noticed, and was asleep. A number of the other men were following Phelim. Those who were very drunk sat against the walls or lay upon the floor. They were picked up one by one, pitched into the bunk. The rest stood around Shaw and sang in low voices.

Alan Kennard pushed quietly into the ring. He touched Shaw on the arm and said, "A Merry Christmas to you, Josh. It's you who did it for us."

"Ah, like hell," Shaw said and went on singing. But their eyes had met and the glance passed between them. You're his true friend, Kennard thought. You'll know few men in your life like this one. He turned slowly and walked from the room. Now his emotion was nearly too much to bear. It was necessary for him to be alone in the night.

He had been out in the cold and the dark and the wind for some minutes when from a subconscious channel of thought he wondered about the Nickersons. They had none of Josh Shaw's power with men, and he doubted greatly if they were any smarter. But they were wealthy and Josh was poor, worked for them as a forty dollar a month clerk. But Josh would find his place, and when he did he'd sail right by any lot like the Nickersons. Men wouldn't work for him just because of the dollars. They'd put more into it for the simple, bloody reason Josh was a good lad, respected them and understood them. There was profit to be made from that if you wanted to call it such on the ledger, and it could mean all the difference between winning or losing. Remember, you. Never forget the lads. And now get to sleep. You're good and drunk, you Antrim goat.

CHAPTER THREE

The high, flustering thrust of the March wind was among the trees those days. Sunlight lasted longer, and in among the slash there was the exquisite pastel loveliness of violets. Some of the Frenchies plucked them, wore them in their caps as they came back to the bunkhouse at night. Big Sven told excitedly there of the deer he had seen rutting off in the far woods. He made his body imitate the motions of the buck and the doe, and the men groaned as they watched him, their eyes hot with sex hunger.

"It won't be long now," Phelim muttered to Alan Kennard. "We'll be paid off pretty soon. Then all hands will head for the Center. Every camp does the same. If you think the lads were wound up tight Christmas, wait 'til you're with them in the town. Then they sure as hell cut and go."

"And you, too," Kennard said.

"Aye, me, too." Phelim grinned at him. "But don't think you won't be just as crazy as us. After a winter in the woods, any man is a little bit loose aloft. Josh Shaw has his own girl reserved down at Mamie's place and he stays with her for a couple of days before the drive starts here."

"Let Josh have his girl, and you and me, all the fellas who need one. But ye told me, Phelim, that we'd be coming back here for the drive and that between us we'd save out our money."

"So I did," Phelim said. The cooks had just begun the shout for supper and he and Kennard rushed with the rest. But Phelim kept looking at him, his glance narrow, intense. "Maybe, though, I might break that promise, man. The whiskey might get the better of me, or some little whore. Would ye be leaving me then, to go ahead and sail alone for the season?"

"No." Alan Kennard grimaced. He had been tremendously disturbed and aroused by Big Sven's description of the rutting deer. A dry, queer taste was in his mouth, and an ache of tension had gathered through his loins. He remembered in detail the night he had spent with the whore in New York. "I could go over the side meself for some lass, Phelim. It'd be a pity, though, for we might

41

have a chance to buy a share of Maumee Mike's schooner if we hang onto our money."

"Be Jaisus!" Phelim said. "Forget it, man. Come eat your scoff and you'll feel better."

They went into Kawkawlin Center in a shouting, scrambling column after pay-day. The march was made by the whole camp, and most of them couldn't find room on the sleds or in the sleighs, strode shoulder to shoulder through the slushy snow of the main road. It was already filled with the crews coming from the other camps. Men bawled recognition or curses; there were huge, hugging embraces and a rapid exchange of bottles along the line.

Alan Kennard and Phelim Carmody rode with Joshua Shaw in a company sleigh. They had a pint of red-eye whiskey under the buffalo hide robe and they drank discreetly from it, not willing to draw too much attention to themselves. "A wild lot," Shaw said. "You can never tell what they'll do." He looked curiously into Kennard's dark, strained face. "That means you, too, Antrim."

"And why not?" Kennard said. "I ain't no angel. But I'll be back in camp for the drive."

"They're ambitious, them from Antrim," Phelim said, already flushed by the whiskey. "He don't know that only the pick of the lot make the drive."

"Antrim's among the pick all right," Joshua Shaw said. "Don't you keep on plaguing him. He'll be a better man than you before he's through."

The words had been said in a pleasant, easy voice, but somehow they made Carmody glumly silent. He sat slouched on the sleigh seat, his head lowered, his eyes fixed on the plump rump of the mare that pulled them. Kennard tried several times to form phrases that he thought would take Phelim out of his anger, but squarely and broadly across his mind was the symbol of the town. It withheld all other thought. A shave, he kept thinking, a bath, a few more drinks, clean, new clothes and then the woman. Och, aye, then the woman. . . .

It was Shaw who spoke. He lifted the whip from flicking the mare and pointed. "A goddamn' wasteland," he said. "That's what the Nickersons and their kind have made of this country. It's worse than the Wilderness."

"He means a battle," Phelim said suddenly. "A place where they had a bloody brute fight in the Civil War."

"That I know," Kennard said. But both he and Phelim were staring around them. The land lay stripped, ugly and desolate on either side. Slash was heaped across it among the lesser, cheaper growths of timber the Nickersons had ignored. In the fall, Alan Kennard realized, that might be swiftly swept by fire, and it would be years before the stumps could be pulled and the land put to any other purpose.

Thought of the town had been forced from his mind. He felt a sick disgust that was directed at himself. For a dollar and a half a day, three greasy meals and a flop in a stable, he willingly took his part in such destruction. And all across the country, from New Brunswick and Maine, men like the Nickersons did the same thing. He visualized the country where they had passed, the majestic mountains and the valleys and the splendid, rolling hills before the timber had been taken. He imagined Indians on the forest paths, and the settlers who had patiently, slowly cut out only what was needed in their farming. They had loved the land, respected it. But you, you stupid swab. . . .

He turned and studied the files that jammed the road. They have no understanding. Or if they do, it's very little. Else, why do they go along like this? The country belongs to them and there's many who've fought to make it so. Still, this lot, they set themselves in the hands of the Nickersons. They work like dogs from dawn to night for months and then they head for town and all they've worked for is gone in a couple of days. No future, and no thought of it, no knowing that they've been bought just as their country has, to be stripped, left ruined.

A bitter thing for you to tell yourself, Alan, but a true one. It's a fact you must hang to if you're to go on here and find a life that makes any kind of sense. His glance returned from the road and he found that both Phelim and Joshua Shaw watched him. He stared at Shaw. "Tell me, will ye, Josh," he said. "What the hell do the Nickersons do with the money they pile up?"

"Buy more timber land," Shaw said; "and put more money in the bank."

"They don't spend it on big houses and fancy women and duds for their wives?" Phelim was incredulous.

"Not the Nickersons," Shaw said. "They're too smart for that. Maybe their wives have two sealskin coats apiece and a few new dresses a year from New York. But no more. And you saw the brothers. They haven't changed their coats since I've known them, and it's been a long time."

"But what the gorry do they get out of their money?" Alan Kennard said.

"They're very religious fellas," Shaw said, "and they give a couple of hundred a year to the church. That makes them feel good. But the main thing that they like is their sense of power. They're operating all over the Upper Peninsula as well as here, and they're getting ready to open up along the Canadian border, straight on to the West Coast."

"So they about control the country," Kennard said.

"Yes," Shaw said. "For what they want, they do. That's a fact."

"Ah, stow the gab!" Phelim said. The whiskey bottle was empty and he threw it spinning into the slash. "We're on our way to town. Sing us a song, will ye, sailor?"

Alan Kennard laughed. "There's nothing against it," he said. He set back his head and sang:

> *"While sailin' down Paradise Street one day I did spy*
> *A nice-lookin' damsel who too-ook me eye.*
> *I h'isted my signals, to which she replied,*
> *And a few minutes later I ho-ove alongside."*

It was one of the most famous of the Irish Sea chanteys and Phelim knew it well. He lustily sang the chorus, Joshua Shaw and the men near in the road joining with him. Kennard went on with the second verse, his voice strong and full. He could see the frame buildings of Kawkawlin Center ahead. The stores, the saloons, the Lumbermen's Hotel, the barbershop, Benny's Bon Ton Emporium and the Helsinki Steam Health Bath were all brightly lit. Mamie's place was on beyond the business block at the end of the sidewalk, he knew, and that's where the girls were. But there was no particular excitement for him now in the knowledge. You'll have to watch yourself. No getting so drunk you spend all your pay-off. No falling hard for a girl and letting her take it off you. Do that, man, and you'll finish up like the land the Nickersons have worked over. You won't be worth a good goddamn.

Joshua Shaw had great difficulty with the mare on Main Street. Lumberjacks surged across it in constant motion. They jammed the wooden sidewalks and the planks boomed with the thud of their boots. In front of the saloons, they stood four and five deep, shout-

ing their orders and grasping wildly for the bottles of beer that
were tossed out to them. Men who had hitched to the rails and
posts along the street were backing their animals, taking them
away, and the mare shied, nervously whinnied at the swirl of bodies
around her. "Where you fellas going?" Shaw said. "I'll have to take
her down to the livery stable. She'll kick some shanty boy's skull
in if I don't."

"Look for us in the Tin Horn," Phelim said as he and Kennard
pushed from the sleigh into the street. But then, after Shaw was
gone, he grunted with laughter. "You won't see that lad again," he
told Kennard. "Not if you don't meet him down at Mamie's. He's
a sly card and he knew he couldn't get a hitch on the street. He'll
be quick on his way to his girl."

"So let him go," Alan Kennard said. "I don't blame him. This
ain't no barrel of fun."

"Pipe down!" Phelim said quite savagely. "You're talkin' more
like a ruddy parson every day."

"You're right," Alan Kennard said. His friendship with Phelim
was under new, great strain, he sensed. The winter had done it,
while he had lived alone in the stable, read the books and talked
for hours with Shaw. But Phelim had always been his friend, must
always be. He clasped Phelim's shoulder with an affectionate gesture. "I've been stuck too long in camp. Them books have got me
all fouled up. That makes me the first lad to buy a drink."

Inch by inch, foot by foot, they worked their way forward into
the Tin Horn. It blazed with light, reeked with the bodies of the
men who tried to reach the bar. Six barkeepers, sweat slick on their
faces and their celluloid collars, held forth bottles of beer to the
outstretched hands. They took back silver dollars and rumpled bills.

"A dollar a bottle?" Kennard said.

"A dollar a bottle," Phelim Carmody said. "They sheer ye closer
than a Welshman does a sheep."

Kennard had bought a round and Phelim had begun an attempt
to buy another when the shout came from the door. "Benny's givin'
away a suit!" the man called. "Who wants it, shanty boys?"

The convulsive movement of the crowd was so violent, so rapid
that Alan Kennard had a momentary feeling of fright. Nearly every
man in the saloon turned and headed for the door. They elbowed,
kicked and shoved, yelling at each other or for the sheer delight of
yelling. But once he had his feet solidly under him again and went
along beside Phelim, Kennard was glad.

He had been suffering intensely from claustrophobia. The heat, the smells, the clamor and confusion had given him the desperate desire to get out into the open air. He had been too long at sea, he thought, and in the clean, wide spaces of the woods to like such as this. A young Finn who stood behind him had become sick from the beer and wretchedly vomited. Other men were so drunk they could hardly keep upright. A pair of Frenchies, both very drunk, were making love, one stroking his companion's cheek as he pressed against him.

But it was more than that, Kennard thought. He had seen plenty of the same in the waterfront joints around the world. Deep down, what bothered him was the recklessness that had started to seize him. It was as if you'd slipped from the topmast and you were plunging, plunging, plunging and you didn't care. Christ, it was great, bloody fun to go. But you hadn't slipped. No, you'd been pushed. And what pushed you was the months, the weeks and the hours, aye, even the time of each axe stroke you'd spent in the woods. A dollar a bottle for beer. A dollar and half a day you got in the woods. Keep on, keep on and you'd spend it all. Two, three days of the town and you'd have nothing left. A winter gone, six months out of your life. What's wrong, Kennard? Are ye a weakling, are ye a fool?

He and Phelim were in the street. They reeled stumbling, for the sidewalk planks had broken under the weight of the men. In back of them glass shattered and there were hooting cries. He looked around to see those who had jumped with their boots lifted right through the front window of the saloon. Big Sven was among them and Sven was crazy with what he'd drunk. The immense Swede went on up the street. He slung men out of his path with wide blows of his arms, stopped only when he was beneath the balcony of Benny's Bon Ton Emporium.

Benny stood on the balcony, light from coal oil lanterns with reflectors broad upon him. He was a small man, paunchy and pale, spectacles low on his nose. His hands held a loud houndstooth check vest and he brandished it at the men in the street. "Listen, listen," he cried to them, and miraculously they were still.

"Any fella," Benny said, "he brings me this vest inta the store, he gets the suit that goes with it for free. Now don't fight, boys. Don't make yourselves no trouble. Benny's place is full of good goods you can buy."

"T'row me t'at!" Big Sven shouted. Then he sprang for one of the pillars that supported the balcony and swarmed up it towards Benny.

Jean Rotin came out of the crowd and pulled him down. He and Rotin braced toe to toe slugging when Benny tossed the vest. Big Sven and Rotin were knocked headlong, lost under the waves of men who rushed for the vest. They rose up and struck a few more blows, but there were too many men around them. They began striking at anybody within reach.

"Jesus and the Saints!" Alan Kennard said. "It's a real daisy."

"Sure and it is," Phelim said. Men were fighting all up and down the street, running out from the saloons, the barber-shop and the hotel. Phelim roughly sighed and measured a man who swung past him. "From Number Nine," he said to Kennard, and hit the man with a straight right shoulder punch flush on the ear.

Two men immediately jumped Phelim, using the wicked French *savate* and the flats of their hands. Phelim fell and was kneed in the face. "Och, ye bastards," Alan Kennard said whispering. The rage shook him so that he panted in agony for relief. He hit one man with a blow to the jaw, whirled and blocked the other, fought with him away from the sidewalk and further along the street.

But his man got from him. There were too many of them fighting. He was kicked, pummeled and struck from behind by men he didn't see and certainly he hadn't struck. The rage had flared out in him, left a dark, steadying calm. He looked down and saw a man with his ear torn off, one who had his rib bones kicked through his shirt. Not for you, he thought in the calmness that had followed the rage. You're a lad who's had enough. Find Phelim and knock off to hell out of this.

He turned towards the Tin Horn, hitting back only at the men who hit first at him. Phelim had crawled against the wall of the Tin Horn; he was conscious and he had spewed up the beer. "Are ye all right, lad?" Phelim said.

"As good as could be expected," Alan Kennard said. He massaged his knuckles and a lump at the base of his skull. "But are they mad, the whole lot of them?"

"Tonight they are," Phelim said. "It's the winter they have to get out of them and then they'll be all right."

"But some slob has got the vest. Look. Sven and Rotin would take it from him."

A thick-shouldered lumberjack from one of the other camps was sprinting up the steps of the Bon Ton, the torn and muddied vest gripped tight. Big Sven was a stride behind him, Jean Rotin a stride behind Sven. They grasped the man and took the vest from him, let it drop to the steps, then they swung him, whirled and pitched him. He landed askew in the street with a crack of breaking bones. But they paid him no attention. They were looking at each other and the vest.

"Now they go again," Phelim said.

"No, they don't," Alan Kennard said. He didn't know whether to laugh or curse. The two enormous top-loaders stood silent on the steps of the Bon Ton. Jean Rotin had just taken a silver dollar out of his pants pocket. He spun it up into the air and it shone glittering in the light from the store. His hands clamped it; one hand lifted and he and Big Sven stared, heads bowed. Big Sven nodded and slapped Rotin on the shoulder in a gesture of affection and defeat. Rotin went into the Bon Ton with the vest, Big Sven swung aside towards Cooley's Own Saloon.

"Let's us join Sven in Cooley's," Phelim said. "It will be a proper show when Rotin comes back with the new suit."

Alan Kennard nodded and walked across the street at his side without speech. He was impressed by the scene before him. The men were all through with their fighting. Those who could walk had gone back into the saloons. It was the injured, the very drunk who remained in the street. They lay in the mud-marked, grayish snow or along the sidewalks, in the rutted and stamped space of the street itself. Light and shadow were uneven upon them, touched the contorted bodies in an irregular design. The light was the shade of dull copper, the shadow purple or deep black. Blood showed brown in it, and the rigored bruised faces drab. A few men could crawl. Others hunkered along on their hands and knees. Most lay still, and they were badly hurt.

A tall woman who wore no hat, no coat and the gingham dress of a waitress came out of the Lumbermen's Hotel. She walked steadily through the blotches of light and shadow and examined each badly hurt man in turn. Her face was expressionless; Alan Kennard could tell her feeling only by the lines of her mouth and her slightly narrowed eyes. "Come now, lads," she said to him and Phelim. "Bear me a hand and we'll take them into the hotel. The doc' will be along in a bit. They can't be left here to freeze."

"Yes, ma'am." It was said in chorus, humbly, as though both he and Phelim experienced a sense of shame for what had happened. One·man was dead, they found, and a second dying; two more had arms and legs broken. They lifted them and carried them at the woman's direction into the hotel lobby, put them down on the *schnoos*-splattered sawdust around the huge stove.

"Get out," the woman said then, her voice suddenly sharp. "Will you never grow up? By Christ, will you never get to be men?"

They knew no answer to that, and they were frightened by her anger, simply stared at her before they left. Phelim cursed in a peculiar, high voice when they were in the street and on their way to Cooley's Own. "She'd have me take the pledge," he said. "She'd scare the liver out o' me, God mark the day. But Hightower is her name and her man was a boss logger 'til five years ago some drunk shanty boy busted his skull in for him right here. He lay in a snow drift under that hitch rack all night 'til she found him."

"You're a cheery bastard," Alan Kennard said. "Let it be a lesson to you, though. As for me, she scared me so sober I'll welcome whiskey."

Phelim gave him a curious glance. "That top-piece of yours never stops, does it?" he said. "Ye're thinkin' the whole time, even in town on pay night."

"So I'll drink whiskey," Kennard said. "Tonight, for a short time, anyhow, I'd be through with thinking. It makes a man too god-damn' sad."

Cooley's Own was packed to the door, but Big Sven saw them from the bar, bellowed that room be made for them. They stood with Sven and drank red-eye neat until Jean Rotin came in dressed in the new suit. All of the men there had been waiting for Rotin, and they clapped, howled, stamped their feet.

The French Canadian had an entirely new outfit. He wore a fawn brown derby hat, a celluloid collar with a snap-on red tie, yellow shoes with high, round caps. He lifted the hat and laughed back at them, aware of the sight he made. "*C'est beau, hein?*" he said. He pulled at a lapel of the houndstooth check coat. "By Gar, this fella, this Jean, he so good lookin' them girls at Mamie's they take him for free."

Phelim Carmody was shaking with laughter. "But where the hell's the vest?" he said.

"That?" Jean Rotin gazed blankly down under the long-cut coat. "What feller needs a vest with suit like thees? Vest, anyhow, that was all tore, all over mud. Sven, now, you buy us a good beeg drink."

Big Sven was close to being very drunk. He blinked at Rotin.

"You got money," he said. "You was paid today the same as me."

"Ho-oh, sure!" Rotin said. "But this stuff—" he pointed to the hat, the collar, the tie and shoes— "it costs me what I got left from drinkin' beer."

"I'll buy," Alan Kennard said and put four silver dollars on the bar. But he slipped back from the bar after that round was drunk. The idea was distinct in his mind and he was determined to execute it before he was submerged in the hot-rising wildness of the whiskey. "You hang onto my place," he muttered to Phelim. "I'll be back."

"Wait, ye slippery Antrim rascal," Phelim said. "You ain't going to Mamie's without me."

"It's not a woman I'm after now," he said, "I told ye I'd be back."

Benny was putting up a shutter to close for the night when he came into the Bon Ton. But Benny lowered the shutter to the floor, moved quickly behind the main showcase. "And you, young fella?" he said. The large, dark eyes studied Kennard from head to foot.

"I want," Kennard said, his tongue just a bit thick with the whiskey, "to rent me a suit."

"This in Kawkawlin Center," Benny said. "A shanty boy, he tells me a suit he'd rent. So, why? You don't mind telling old Benny why."

"No," Alan Kennard said. He stared keenly at Benny, wondering just how far he could trust the man, then certain that he could. It took a Jew to understand him, and, aye, to trust him, for there was trust in the deal, too. Benny must have had it hard in his day, sweated to get the dollars. "Listen, Benny." He leaned forward and talked in a clear, slow voice.

Benny solemnly shook hands with him. "A smart boy," he said. "Your pal, he's a real good fella, hah?"

"He is," Alan Kennard said. "But rough with the whiskey once he's started. Make it a suit like that rig you put on the big Frenchy."

Benny rubbed his hands together in pleased amusement. "Come out of them woods," he said, "and I take you in with me. We do good together in the store."

"Like hell," Alan Kennard said. He was taking off his shoe-packs so that he could get out of his corduroy trousers. "I'm a sailor when I'm out of the woods."

"Sailor, shmailer," Benny said sadly. "I seen them in Bremen, I seen them in Amsterdam and New York. Always hungry, but for whiskey or a woman, or just straight hungry. A fella, he's got to be a little bit crazy to follow the sea?"

"Maybe," Kennard said. He had the rented suit on now and he was looking at himself in the mirror. "It's in my blood, though, Benny. It's my calling. But a man can make out all right with the ships if he knows how."

Benny shrugged. "A fella like you, so. You got ideas, a head that thinks. Tomorrow, you bring back the suit?"

"That's right," Kennard told him and quietly smiled. "But if I was the kind of sailor you was talking about I'd buy the goddamn' thing."

Big Sven was fighting with one of the barkeepers when he returned to Cooley's Own. They stopped to look at him and Phelim came red-faced and belligerent from the bar. "Me old shipmate," Phelim said. He fingered the suit. "A lad I've sailed with for years. Out for a piss he goes and back he comes dressed like a ruddy Regent Street dude. Ye think I'll go alongside o' you into Mamie's place and me in this rig?"

"You want a suit," Alan Kennard said, "go buy you one, you stupid spalpeen. Rotin's got his and he looks fine in it. And I'm not one to start after the lasses in a pair of stinkin' corduroys."

Big Sven had reeled around to them. He placed his arms heavily on Kennard's shoulders. "Good fellers," he mumbled. "Shouldn' fight. But suit, sure." His hairy hands pulled money from both pants pockets. "You buy suits for us. We stay drink whiskey. Is right?"

"Right it is," Kennard said. He took the money obliquely watching Phelim. The Liverpool man had a hand deep in a pocket, brought it out full of money. "I'll be payin' for me own duds," he said. "Here, Alan. You know me size and clip. Get me a rig like the one you're wearin'. But hurry it up, lad. I'm about set for a steam bath and then a crack at the lasses."

Benny counted the money and put it in separate envelopes, locked the envelopes in his safe. "For such a business," he told Kennard, "those boys should give you interest."

"No bloody fear," Kennard said, his voice low but hard. "Out of this, I hope to get hold of a schooner."

He stood in the darkness of an alley for an instant after he left Benny's. You're taking a big chance, he thought as he relieved himself. Big Sven and Phelim might whip the hell out of you for having fooled them. But they're drunk and in the morning they'll have their money back and tonight you'll have to put out for them. That was every dollar they had save the couple on the bar.

Phelim and Big Sven sang, heads together over the whiskey. He elbowed in beside them and ordered a drink, waited for them to be done. "Where's suits?" Big Sven said, blear-eyed and wet mouthed.

"Benny was closing for the night," he said. "It's late and the old fella wanted to go home. But he took the money. He says come around in the morning and he'll take care of you fine."

"Son of a bitch!" Phelim said. But then he laughed. "So tomorrow we go see the lasses in our new gear. Stick out for a drink, Alan. The Swede and me are bust. It'll all be on you tonight, dude that ye are."

They drank some more in Cooley's Own, had another in Dugan's and a bottle of beer in Mitchell's, went from there to the Helsinki Steam Health Baths. The small, stifling place was empty and the pock-marked Finn who ran it said that his customers had all gone to Mamie's. "Clean," he said. "More so than them dirty whores Mamie got."

"You shut your mackerel mouth, you!" Big Sven shouted at him. "My Olga, she's clean like the goddamn' snow. You think mebbe fellers like us should chase each other in the woods fer what we want?"

"Go ahead in," the Finn said. He waved his hand at the steam room. "Don't be botherin' me or you don't get no bath."

The strange state of reverie, of entrance back into what was far past and almost forgotten in his life came upon Alan Kennard while he crouched sweating next to Phelim and Big Sven. The steam put a wall between him and them. He had the impression that he was remote, alone, and somehow would be so forever. The memories he restored gave strength to the impression.

Even as a lad, there in Antrim in the glen, you were alone. As your mother was. You may well have learned the habit of loneliness from her. Remember that she barely spoke to you after your father's death, or to anybody for that matter. It was with the "little people" she spoke. Och, remember how she'd put a bowl of milk outside the door at night for the feeding of them. . . .

So you sat for hours by yourself under the rowan tree. The hawthorn hedge at the side of the loaning, that was your proper, secret place. He could see in imagination the white beauty of the hedge, and he smelled the fragrant blossoms. In the village, none

knew you well, liked you much. You took your few ha'pennies and
tanners that your mother gave you, bought what she'd sent you for,
then scoured away for the cottage again.

It was certainly the hedge that kept you safe. But the river,
too. You lay belly-flat while you fished for the bream, and she'd
smile a bit, your mother would, when you brought a fish home for
the supper. Out on the braes you found blueberries. Eat them 'til
you were sick, smear them into your mouth with both hands. Christ,
you were hungry near all the while.

But she'd sing in the dusk for you. You beside her with the sea
the colours of flowers and the last of the sun on the sails of the
Ayrshire sloops standing off from the Mull of Cantyre. Once and
again you'd get a wee bit work cutting peats. The creel you packed
on your back, for you, the widow gypsy woman's lad, were too poor
to own a donkey. Then you would buy her a small drink of the
poteen. She liked her drop; it stole the sadness from her.

It was on those nights that MacKim came down from the village.
Och, aye, the piper, and maybe he slept with your mother later and
maybe he didn't. Not that you know or that it matters. "I trust to
my God so," MacKim said, standing in the doorway with the pipes
under his arm after your mother has asked him to play. Then he
walked the dooryard and while he brought the wind into the pipes
the waves on the Giant's Causeway played for him already. So you
thought in your head, off in the dark in a corner.

"The Birds among the Trees." "The Green Fields of America."
Aye, and "The Swallowtail Coat." Proud old Ulster tunes and
many more like them. They tore the throat right out of you, to keep
from the sobbing. You wanted to get up, you did. Surely, and play
the pipes yourself. But your mother had them from MacKim. She
played them better than him and he sat and stared at her with his
eyes shining hard in his big, red-whiskered face. Goddamn, it hurts
to think back like that.

You left the two of them in the dooryard. Along the loaning
you went, past the rowan tree, past the mulberry and close to the
path that led to the Causeway. But no further. For you were more
than a little frightened in the night. You wanted close to your
mother and MacKim back in the village where he belonged. Still,
if your mother got pleasure from the poteen and the pipes, let
her be.

Cruel for a young lad, such as that. How to change it? How to
go but the way you've gone? And from her you learned a lot. More

than the telling of the Battle of the Yellow Ford, or of Gig-Magog, nine feet high he was and could run faster than the hounds of any hunt in Ulster. She taught you hardness, and to stand for yourself. All the rest, the stories, the songs, the spells of the "little people," they don't count. Or not so you can notice. But to stand alone and be your own man. She taught it to you so as you'll never forget.

Phelim and Big Sven were getting dressed and he got dressed with them, paid the Finn. Then they went down the street to the barber-shop. "Haircut, shave," Big Sven said, his mackinaw flung behind him on the floor. Kennard sat in a chair against the wall to wait his turn, a *Police Gazette* in his hands. But he didn't read the magazine; he looked blankly at the pages and he hardly heard Phelim as Phelim asked him for money. His mind was away, still back in Antrim. He said over to himself silently some of the lovely names and he saw once more the places.

His mother had let him wander when he was part grown. She, a gypsy, wasn't one to stop him. He had been to Ess-na-Larach. It meant in the Gaelic "the Fall of the Battlefield" and the water came down the glenside in a leaping silver smother. Ess-na-Crub was another. It meant "the Fall of the Hoof" and near it in the stream below he had snared the trout that was speckled gold and brown in the bronze stillness of the pools. Beside another, "Tears of the Mountains," and he'd forgotten the Gaelic of the name, he had found the white heather, the sign of good luck, taken a sprig and put it inside his shirt to bring home to his mother.

The awe was in him yet from Carrickfergus Castle, built long before the Norman time. Magheramore he'd seen also, and Ballyna-hinch. There in the moonlight one night among the great, mossed stones of the cromlech he had thought Red Hugh O'Neill marched past him, sword, shield and all. His mother nodded when he told her. It was the Red Hugh all right, she said.

But of the memories that of Ramore Head beyond Portrush remained the strongest. The East wind took you nearly off your feet up on Ramore. You could see for eighty miles, the Irish Sea before you and Ireland at your back. Away across the sea with the sun aglitter on it and the water the blue of bluebells was Scotland. The headlands rose up like the shoulders of giants. They were dark even in the sunlight, the lochs chopped sharp and jagged under shadow. Then to the North, dim in distance, the Hebrides seemed to rest on the sea with the quietness of sleeping birds.

Phelim shook his shoulder. "Come take your turn, man. Are ye asleep?"

"No," he said; "I'm not asleep." The German barber was deft and he gave himself to him in silence. While the scissors worked and the lather smoothed his cheeks he almost slept. But the smell of the talcum powder and the scented water the barber used aroused him. He began to think of the girl he would have at Mamie's. He hurried with Phelim and Big Sven from the barber-shop, and they were quiet, thinking also, he knew, of the girls.

His was a small one with dyed hair, a broken front tooth. But he didn't mind or wait to find another. His need was great and immediate, and even as he was with her in the bed he was away from her, dreaming of Antrim.

The dreams persisted after he came downstairs into the parlor. He sat in a chair in a corner to wait for Phelim and Big Sven. But Mamie wouldn't let him be like that. She walked over to push her corseted fat against him and ask would he like another girl, like a drink? He stared at Mamie with a glance that almost failed to comprehend her presence. "A drink, yes," he said.

"But them boys are going to be all night," Mamie said, coaxing him.

"Like hell," he said sharply. He was resentful to have been drawn from the dreaming. "I got their money and I ain't got that much."

Mamie brought him the drink and one for herself. She sat and studied him. "Must be," she said calmly, "that you got bugs in your head from bein' in them woods too long. But drink up. The booze'll do you good."

"Och, aye," he said. It was cheap whorehouse whiskey and had been watered. But the alcohol there was in it sent a slow channel of fire back to what he had drunk before. He began to feel giddy, happy and very warm, yet perversely wild. That was because of Antrim, he sensed. He should never have gone there into the mem-ories. They were too beautiful and they'd hurt him.

Only a half a dozen of the older, less attractive whores were in the room. He was the one man except for a pimp by the door. Mamie still sat beside him staring at him. "You look to me like a sailor," Mamie said. "Another of them who's dropped a marline-spike for an axe."

"So I am," he said. The alcohol was making a reverberant and swift beat through his veins. "And I know a sailor story I'll tell ye. But first give me another drink."

He drank that and then he drew a long breath, shut his eyes. He had recalled some of the lines of the poem Joshua Shaw had given him to read early in the winter. The beginning, to hell with that. This was some place near the middle, the part he knew best. Say it out, man. Let them listen as you used to listen to your mother. He cleared his throat and opened his eyes to gaze at Mamie and the other women, aware that they were eager to hear him:

> *"The fair breeze blew, the white foam flew,*
> *The furrow followed free;*
> *We were the first that ever burst*
> *Into that silent sea.*

> *"Down dropt the breeze, the sails dropt down,*
> *'Twas sad as sad could be;*
> *And we did speak only to break*
> *The silence of the sea!"*

He paused. He looked around the room at them. But they were listening, even the pimp. He went on:

> *"All in a hot and coppery sky,*
> *The bloody Sun at noon,*
> *Right up above the mast did stand,*
> *No bigger than the Moon.*

> *"Day after day, day after day,*
> *We stuck, nor breath nor motion;*
> *As idle as a painted ship*
> *Upon a painted ocean."*

One of the whores pushed her hair back from her face. Tears were on her cheeks. "Purty," she said. "This boy knows nice stuff."

Kennard took time to breathe. Then, in a deeper voice:

> *"Water, water, everywhere,*
> *And all the boards did shrink;*
> *Water, water, everywhere*
> *Nor any drop to drink.*

"The very deep did rot: O Christ!
That ever this should be!
Yea, slimy things did crawl with legs
Upon the slimy sea.

"About, about, in reel and rout
The death-fires danced at night;
The water, like a witch's oils,
Burnt green, and blue, and white."

"You cut that crap out!" Mamie said. She took a swiping swing at him. "Don't you go scarin' my girls!"

"It ain't crap," he said. "Lad name of Coleridge wrote it and it's poetry." He knocked Mamie's hand aside with his arm, tried to continue, the compulsion of the language forcing him:

"And some in dreams assured were."

The pimp was coming across the room. He had a blackjack in his hand. "You heard Mamie, shanty boy," he said. "Cut it out!"

Kennard moved with ease, was out of the chair and had it lifted in his hands. "I'll bat your brains loose," he told the pimp. Then, as the man stepped back from him, he laughed. He called forth:

"Ah! well-a-day! what evil looks
Had I from old and young!
Instead of the cross, the Albatross
About my neck was hung."

The pimp had bent down, was rapping on the floor with the blackjack. Kennard knew the signal. It would bring other pimps into the room. They'd jump him and there'd be a shindy here. The whores were running up the stairs in fright now and some of the lumberjacks were coming down. He saw Big Sven with his flannel drawers clutched in one hand, his boots and pants in the other. Phelim was at Big Sven's shoulder and he was all dressed, ready to go.

"All right, lads," Kennard said. He felt enormously strong. The chair he held seemed to be without weight. He watched the pimp and he watched the door into the lower hall. The other house-boys would come from there, he knew. They'd have blackjacks, too, and maybe a knife or so.

But the first man out of the door from the lower hall was Joshua Shaw. His hair was tousled across his head and he hadn't put on his coat or shoes. He was very sober, though, and very sure of what he did. "Put down the chair, Antrim," he said. "No shindy, y' understand?"

"Why?" Kennard shouted at him, out of the rage.

"Because you're a smart lad and my girl's waiting for me to come back." Phelim and Big Sven were down the stairs and in the room. Shaw gazed around at them. "Take Antrim out. You keep your noses clean, the lot of you. Here's the key to my room in the Lumbermen's. Go sleep it off."

They took the chair from him while he protested and cursed. Then they marched him towards the door. But he broke away for an instant at the door. He swung to the big pimp standing there and grasped him by the genitals, yanked them violently inside the trouser cloth. "Bow, ye bastard," he said, "when an Antrim man passes ye by!"

Phelim and Big Sven cuffed him around the head when they had him out in the snow. "Now we can't come back, donkey!" Phelim told him. "Mamie won't let us in the joint."

"Ah, to hell!" Kennard said. "Ye're so sore you want to fight me, then?"

"No," Big Sven said. "You yust go to sleep in same bed wit' Phelim and me. Now you shut your mackerel mouth, I tell you."

He was silent as they walked along to the Lumbermen's Hotel in the cold, clear and white night. He was saying over to himself the rest of "The Rime of the Ancient Mariner."

They slept heavily in the uncomfortable iron bed at the hotel, awoke sour, sullen with their hangovers. It was only after they had eaten two platters of ham and eggs and drunk three pots of tea that they were willing to speak to each other in more than monosyllables. Alan Kennard started the conversation; he explained in detail what he had done with their money last night.

Phelim was furious. His ruddy face hardened with the pull of the jaw muscles and his hands closed. When Kennard tried to meet his eyes, Phelim avoided the glance, glared at the floor. But Big Sven raucously laughed.

"Money I've got yet, hah?" Sven said. "Then you go fetch it, Antrim. You bring it here. No fancy rig for me. I'm stayin' in hotel, sleepin' wit' waitress. Mrs. Hightower, she don't put out, no. But younger ones they take care o' shanty boys, yah, oh, yah. Me, I know."

Kennard got up quickly from the table, worried by Phelim's rage. "Wait, Phelim," he said. "You stay with Sven."

"In a pig's ass," Phelim Carmody said. "I'll have me money straight off and no more of your bilge."

They went through the dining room past pale and subdued shanty boys and into the lobby, out of the lobby onto the porch. Then, as he had expected, Phelim grasped him by the mackinaw collar, swung him. "So what would ye do?" Phelim asked tight-mouthed. "What kind of tricks are ye out to play? This thing I don't like at all, at all."

"Maybe you don't," he said shortly, his own rage not far below the surface of his thought. "But it's for the good of both of us."

He had the belief then that Phelim was going to strike him. His nerves flexed in anticipation; he set himself for the blow. Phelim moved away from him, though, went the length of the porch and held the rail with his hands as, Kennard thought queerly, he might steady himself while in a storm at sea.

"How?" Phelim said harshly. "Tell me how before all the friendship I have for you goes out of me. Ye've been pressing me hard, Alan. For months now, I've been thinking that ye have the idea you're a better man nor me."

"Bugger such talk!" Alan Kennard said. "There's no truth in it. Still, here's what I must tell ye, Phelim." He walked to Phelim's side. He took Phelim's arm and looked searchingly into his face. "You were bosun of perhaps the greatest ship of all times, lad, and you can't forget it."

"One of two bosuns," Phelim said stiffly. "We carried two aboard the *Flying Cloud*."

"Aye. But there were fifty-some men to a watch. You're proud of having sailed in her. You'll always be."

"So what, then? I've gone beyond that. I have me pilot's papers for the Lakes. I could sail master of a vessel, should I want."

"There," Alan Kennard said softly. "Now you make my kind of sense. Your way, though, you'd still be workin' for wages, hired out to some other man. I'd have you—and me—sailing for ourselves."

"You mean you'd like to buy out Maumee Mike Jacobs' schooner."

"Exact ye are."

"But with what, rope yarns?"

"No, Phelim, no. With the money we've saved through the winter, and notes he'll take from us. Mike's a sick lad. That which he has is not easy cured, if ever. He won't be sailing long, and I doubt that he'll try to fit himself out this season."

Phelim stared out into the street, weirdly empty now after last night. He filled his pipe with shag and lit it. "Ambition's got ye," he said. He was dimly smiling. "You'd make me a skipper whether or no I like the idea."

"Right again," Kennard said in that same soft voice. "Phelim, what's the sense of goin' on as ye've been? The luck can't last. Take last night here. Ye might have got an eye poked out, or your skull cracked wide. In the woods, too, there's a lot of chances. Get hurt bad and ye can feed your pilot's license to the gulls for all the good you'll get from it."

"So you'd keep me off Skid Row," Phelim said with open mockery. But his eyes were serious, thoughtful. "Who'd sail mate if ye talked Mike into letting us have the schooner?"

"Me."

"Be Jaisus! You're a fine man with the palaver, but you're not yet a citizen and you have no license."

"Josh Shaw will fix the citizen part. He's cosy with a judge in Cleveland, some fella who knew his family in the East. You can help me with the mate's part of it."

Phelim coughed over the pipe stem, then he broke into open laughter. "That's hard to get, that pilot paper. All of one lake ye have to memorize, lights, depths, shoals, every aid to navigation on it. Written questions, too, by the barrel."

"I'll learn 'em."

"Damn me." It was Phelim who now spoke softly. "I think ye will."

"Then let's shove off. We get the money from Benny and start back to camp."

"This mornin'?"

"Sure, man. I've already got the books, the charts and the rest of it in camp. I sent for them right after Christmas."

Phelim Carmody hit him affectionately but hard across the shoulder. "I understand," he said, "what Shaw meant when we were talkin' on the way in here. He's watched you with them books. What'll ye be, Alan, another like the Nickersons?"

"Hell, no," Alan Kennard said flat-voiced. "The style they work,

the timber will soon be gone from this country. But with a ship a
man can always turn a dollar." He looked up, thinking that he
would find a smile on Phelim's face. Phelim was grave, though, and
didn't speak until they were on the steps into Benny's. "A ship, be
Christ!" Phelim said. "With any luck, man, you'll have a fleet!"

There were ten days between that day and the opening of the
spring drive. Alan Kennard and Phelim Carmody passed them back
in camp doing odd jobs, but most of the time working on Kennard's
preparation for his license. Shaw returned to camp on the second
day, and both he and Phelim advised him to read nothing while
he studied and memorized the details of Lake Huron, the body of
water he had chosen as the one he knew best. He lay awake at
night and visualized it in his mind, each bay, each cove, each point
of land, lighthouse and beacon, range and reef. When the drive
started, he had it all solidly in his head.

He was greatly excited by the drive. Here was highly skilled if
very dangerous work. The ice was going in the Kawkawlin. It
cracked, snapped, then buckled under the tremendous weight of
the logs piled from bank to bank at the end of the tote road. The
best of the shanty boys, Big Sven and Jean Rotin among them, were
back from town. They helped run the logs and they went at it with
a proud, fierce eagerness.

Their winter clothes were discarded. Now everybody in camp
but the cooks and the chore boys wore thin denims and boots whose
steel caulks had been carefully sharpened. The denim pants had
been given care, too, and cut off in zigzag patterns above the boot
tops, one leg shorter than the other for a reason nobody knew
except that it was logger tradition. It was like the songs you sang,
Alan Kennard thought, or the way you laid down line clockwise in
a ship. There was a reason for them somewhere, but it had been
long forgot.

He went out on the logs with the others when the drive began.
The reservoir dam beyond the camp had been opened, dynamited
free. Water from there came in a black, ice-crusted rush against
the logs. They groaned, they flung one against the other with a
terrible and grinding fury. Jean Rotin ran them as a deer would
run in the woods; he caught them with his pike pole or a peavey,
sent them fully out into the current. Big Sven and Phelim and some
of the others did the same, although they weren't as fast, as lithe,
maybe as daring as Rotin.

Alan Kennard came back on shore after the first few hours. He had just seen Rotin ride a log down through a timbered sluice where the logs bucked and climbed and whipped higher in the air than Rotin's head. But the Canadian kept on going. He sprang from log to log, seeming to sense infallibly which one would hurl upward next. Men lined the sides of the narrow sluice to watch him. They cheered and waved their hats and caps. Rotin took time to grin at them. His black, thick hair, his white teeth flashed in the sun. He was one hell of a man, Kennard decided, and he was also a god-damn' fool. . . .

They ran the logs from the Kawkawlin down to Saginaw Bay. It took them weeks of terrific labour, heaving the piles from the banks where they had been left in the winter, then following along to clear the jams. The jams made the real danger, Kennard found. Men lost their hands, their legs or lives in them. At a shallow in the river where the scum ice still held, Jean Rotin was momentarily trapped. Two logs crashed together, one rolling, spinning upon that which held the Canadian. Rotin jumped, vaulting aside with his peavey to give him distance. But the upper log grazed his left foot. The boot and red woolen sock were torn from it. He fell headlong and the logs under him were in motion, macerating and ripping like immense teeth.

Phelim Carmody went out and saved Rotin. He dragged him upright, carried him in his arms until Big Sven got there. Then, between them, they brought Rotin to shore. Rotin was cursing over the fact that he had lost a new boot. But when they put him down on the bank, Kennard could see the blood on Rotin's chin; he had bit through his underlip to keep from crying out in pain.

"No more," Kennard told Phelim that night in camp.

"Ye're right," Phelim said. "I had my share today. The liver was scared out of me worse than when you squeezed the pimp. But we stick with it. We finish it out. It's a job for men, this."

"Och, aye," Alan Kennard said; "and you're one of them, ye red-head rooster."

They paid off in Kawkawlin Center after the drive had gone on to Saginaw Bay. Then they visited Benny, bought a couple of plain serge suits, took the stage to the railroad. But not many men were with them; most of the crew had stayed in the Center. "The faster to spend their pay," Phelim said wryly. "They'll be bust sure as hell in a day or so. Ye were right in all ye told me at the Lumbermen's. Enough of loggin', though. Get your mind now on that license."

"No bloody fear," Alan Kennard said. He had shut his eyes and in his mind he saw the chart contours of Lake Huron. "I'll have it for you next week. Then I'll go see Maumee Mike."

Spring was lush green along the Maumee River Valley when he went to talk with Mike Jacobs. He had the new pilot's license in his pocket and a letter from Phelim in Buffalo. There had been no sign of Jacobs in Buffalo, Phelim had written, and the schooner was still tied up at her winter dock.

Alan Kennard realized why after he had sat for a while on the farm house porch with Mike Jacobs and Mike's father. The winter hadn't helped Mike. His skin was yellow, tight to the facial bones, and the large-pupiled eyes far back in the skull. Mike wore a shawl around his shoulders, another around his legs. He coughed a lot, and when he talked his voice came wheezing and broken over the barnyard sounds and the nickering of the young calf out in the pasture.

"I ain't the man to lie, Antrim," he said. "And it's got me. My Pop knows, and my Mom, too. The good old goddamn' galloping consumption. Johnny Reb's minié ball started it. Being out on the water season after season didn't help. Now the doc' says six months, maybe a year. But I'm not leaving this house. I'm not taking any schooner offshore."

He was still, the convulsive coughing a frightful wrack that shook his body backward in the chair. Blood frothed at his lips and he wiped it away. "Damn me," he whispered. "Go and fetch Antrim a slug of whiskey, Pop. He was bosun for me last season, and this one. . . ."

"You shet up," the old man said. He was small and curved with age, made haggard by grief. "I bring whiskey, yes, but you shet up. Doctor says that."

"Been here since the '48," Maumee Mike whispered when his father was in the house. "Ain't got the language straight yet and never will."

"Listen, Mike, you pipe down," Kennard said. He felt a bitter commingling of sorrow and shame. What the hell was he doing here with a bloody bare four hundred dollars to buy a man's schooner? It was a wonder the old man didn't chase him off the place with a pitchfork. Maumee Mike was too sick to talk—more, do business.

But somehow Mike Jacobs divined his thought. Mike reached out and put his sweaty, feverishly hot hand on Kennard's. "You fellas, you and Phelim," he said, "take the schooner. The money don't matter. Leave me what you have and I'll write up some notes for the rest."

The old man was back on the porch. He carried a silver platter and a cut glass decanter, three glasses. He filled two glasses full, put half a finger of whiskey into the third for his son. Then he gazed at Kennard with penetrating eyes. "Good luck, sailor," he said. "Make lots money out of the schooner. Doctors, medicine, they don't come cheap."

"To hell," Maumee Mike whispered. "This fella and Carmody are crackajack sailors. They'll do fine."

But the whiskey, or possibly the thought of his son's death seemed to have fired the old man. He took Mike's hand in his while he kept looking at Kennard. "Me, I fought in the '48," he said. "*Prinz* Klemens Wenzel Nepomuk Lothar Metternich was one great son of a bitch. We was whipped. I come here. Mike, though, he fought in the other war. With Grant he served. In the Army of the West. So, yes, the Eleventh Indiana. Snow, wet, no blankets, and they march, march. Then they're at Fort Donelson."

"On the Cumberland," Maumee Mike whispered, as if prompted by a memory that was too keen to be withheld.

"Fifteen thousand they have," the old man said. "Twenty-one thousand the slavers have. They charge, they charge, and three batteries against them in cross-fire. Abatis, big, high, out of tree tops, in front of them rifle-pits. But they go up. Yes, they go, with the bayonet. The woods is set afire by the artillery. The wounded die, or that night they freeze. But the boys go back. They take them rifle-pits and they chase them slavers runnin'. My Michael, my son was there."

The old man stood up and turned his head aside. Alan Kennard could tell by the motions of his shoulders that he was soundlessly weeping. He went to the old man and embraced him. "We won't forget," he said. "Not us lads who sailed with Mike."

"Come on, Pop," Maumee Mike said. "Get pen and ink and paper for me, will you? Antrim knows I got mine at Donelson. But now I want to give him a contract for the schooner."

They had another drink when the contract was drawn up and signed. But Maumee Mike's energy was about exhausted. He sat back in the chair with his eyes nearly closed, his lips compressed to restrain the coughing. The old man glanced at Kennard. "You stay for dinner," he said, "and I drive you to the two o'clock train."

"No, thank ye," Kennard said. He motioned towards Mike. "You got things to do here and I can walk to the train." He crossed to where Mike sat, bent down and took Mike's hand. "Ye know what I'm thinkin' and what Phelim will think. So long, Mike. I'll write ye soon, or Phelim will. All the luck."

"The same, sailor," Maumee Mike said, and smiled at him.

It was the first time in his life that he had ever kissed a man, but as he brushed his lips over Mike's forehead Alan Kennard felt no hesitation. Here was a man he more than respected. For Mike Jacobs he had deep, lasting love.

CHAPTER FOUR

When he had first arrived in the Great Lakes country it had all appeared strange, confusing, too vast to fall within his understanding. But after the season sailing with Maumee Mike and Phelim and then the winter in the woods, it began to take shape for him. He could distinguish the parts from the whole; he told himself in sailor talk that he had his bearings.

His sense of confidence increased with that fact. He discovered that he was now able to go ashore in Buffalo or Cleveland or Chicago and bid for cargo, make rates with the shippers and merchants who wanted their goods moved by water. Maumee Mike's schooner, the *Procyon,* was well built, a fast enough sailer for her rig, her tonnage. He secured a number of cargoes in straight succession and through most of the season he and Phelim and the crew of farm boys were kept busy. Phelim took his duties as master lightly in port, but seriously once offshore, got drunk no more than a couple of times a month. Alan Kennard was content. They were paying Maumee Mike a steady ten percent on their contract with him, also reducing the notes Mike had negotiated with the bank in his home town.

Kennard was aware of the gradual change in himself. He understood that voyage by voyage he emerged forth from his old habit of loneliness. The time had been too long while he'd stayed aboard the deep-water ships, surly and frightened and in an odd way supercilious. "Och, aye, supercilious you were," he said aloud to himself one night off Mackinac Island as the schooner headed South into Lake Michigan with a load of lumber for Chicago. The word was new in his vocabulary, as were a number of others he had learned during the winter, and he deliberately used it. "Proud to be a sailor and nothing else. But scared to go ashore, you dolt."

He crossed the poop deck with his slow, deft stride, keeping an eye on the draw of the canvas and the stooped Swedish boy at the wheel, but in his mind reviewing what he thought of now as the wasted years. He recalled the ports whose streets he had walked, half grasping the meaning of the signs, getting nothing of the peoples' talk, their purposes or how they led their lives. He had been forever a stranger, a sailor briefly in from the sea, and the sooner gone the better for him. But no more, Alan.

You're an American, a citizen here. You're a mate and you'll be master, in a couple of years owner of this schooner or one like her. The people count for you. Life's not like the old focsle days on the deep water. Half of you's sailor still, but the other half is shore-going merchant. Lose your accent and your salty way of talk. Get to know each of these cities well and who's in them and runs them.

He had already begun to work on that, and during the voyages up and down the Lakes through the splendid gold and silver weeks of high summer he added greatly to his knowledge. A man named Grover Cleveland was big and getting bigger in Buffalo. Chicago, that was Potter Palmer and Marshall Field and the Armours, the Swifts, the rest of them who had survived the fire with their fortunes as big as ever. Jay Cooke had Duluth and forty thousand acres around it; he'd make plenty of boodle out of the place before he was through. Jim Hill, a smart, tough little man they said he was, operated big in St. Paul and the valley of the Red River of the North. Hill was a railroad man, but he was in grain, too, owned elevators, was buying boats to haul his bulk cargoes down the Lakes. Keep your eye on him and don't forget. "Hog's Eye" they call St. Paul, so remember Hill by that. Cleveland, though, Cleveland's the busiest town of them all. You've forgot Milwaukee, but that's wheat and barley, the German brewer folks, the Uhleins, the Pabsts and the Schlitzes. They live in them big fancy brick and stone piles out on the West Side over the lake. You'll be sailing past there tomorrow. Take a look at them houses through the glass. Get back to Cleveland. There's more to Cleveland than all the rest put together.

Colonel Oliver Payne is the richest bucko in the town. He works for the little fella, though, the man Josh Shaw told you about. John Rockefeller is his name. Sure, a farm boy who came up to town and was a book-keeper on the docks before he got ass-deep in the oil business. He's got his part of the Mesabi ore and they say he's hot, too, for the Superior copper. So's the other fella, Mark Hanna. Another farm boy, and as tough and bright as they come. Him and Rockefeller they work together when the spirit's on them, or alone, and Josh says Rockefeller is knocking hell out of Vanderbilt on his New York Central freight rates. Wooden tank cars is what Rocke-feller uses and maybe there'll be a day when you'll see tank vessels on these runs. Watch out for Hanna more than Rockefeller. Hanna's family has been in the Lakes shipping business since before the war. They had a scrap with the Merritt brothers up on the Mesabi over ore land and they dumped them flat. . . . Hanna, he's a king-pin man, and there's others around Cleveland Square that can empty your pockets faster than catch a mouse in a plug hat. Pickands, and Mather, they're shipping men who need a weather eye kept on them. Josh Shaw knows them well; they're from Down East, like his people, and the town is full of their kind.

Andy Carnegie over there in Pennsylvania has got the heave-away on the lot of them. He's steel and he's big and he's rough and he's smart. In the Mesabi range after ore, too, and he has his share, will no doubt have his ships when he wants them. Detroit you know little about for so far you haven't had many cargoes for the place. But if you keep in with the doings of the Cleveland Square gang you'll know what goes on the whole length of the Lakes. Iron and copper and timber and wheat and meat and coal and oil and dollars. Och, aye, it's a real lash-up for you. Damn you, though, man. Don't go talking that way. No more of your "Och, aye" and as for "lash-up" it's good aboard but not ashore. . . . Get straight-ened out, Kennard. Remember—you're an American.

Yet to have it full in your head you should think of the rest of the folks, them like the lot in the woods last winter. They're more than just shanty boys breaking their backs for the Nickersons. East Buffalo is awash with Polish people; they bring them in by the trainload from New York. More of them are in Cleveland, down on the Flats and outside of town, too. Italians also, and Irish, and what they call Hunkies. Bejesus if you know where that last lot comes from, or what kind of lingo it is that they speak. But hard workers, good men. The Irish, they're cops they are, like in New York. But some, too, are in the Pennsylvania mines along with the Welsh and the Scots and the English before them. Some of the black folks they have around, too, come up from the South. "Niggers," they call them, or "darkies" if they don't mean it nasty. Back home it was "Naigers" we called them, but no harm done, and you never seen one 'til you went to Liverpool in a ship. The farm folk are of the old stock, out of the Eastern states and they'll never make a potful of money the way they work the land.

But in Wisconsin you got Danes coming in after the Nickersons and their like and they know a cow and how to care after her. Up to the North you have the Norwegians, Swedes and the Finns.

From a cold country to a cold country and damned if they don't like it. Nebraska they say is full of them and all winter long they sit in under the snow and pick their noses and wait for the harvesting of the wheat. It's a rough time they have, what with the snow and the short summer and the way the railroad lot handles them on the freight rates. It's trouble there'll be, too, before they're through, because they're not men to stand still while they're getting screwed. The same goes for them in Chicago and already they're talking of the Knights of Labor and the organizing of unions. A Christian Socialist Party they've got, that still has a hard hand for the priests.

You're with them, Alan. You have to be, dollars or no. It's them alone who in time can keep you from getting scuttled by the big fellas like Hanna or Rockefeller. The wheel must be round, and the labouring man is one half of it. Be smart, though. Watch out for yourself. Each man in this country has a chance for himself. You'll be a long time forgetting how the bunch from camp threw away their pay in town last spring. If a man has no brains, you can't pour them into his head. Phelim is a sign of that; Phelim has them, but be damned if he'll use them any more than he thinks he should. So there'll be a day when you go sailing right past Phelim and him standing looking at you surprised as all get-out. It's a fight all the way, and you don't, you'll go with the Indians and the Frenchies. You'll end up with an axe in your hands out in the woods. No good. . . . It's going to be Mister Alan Kennard. Then Captain Kennard. Sure. Sure it will.

He met Joshua Shaw in the Weddell House bar in Cleveland in late August. Shaw realized the change in him as soon as he saw the stocky body in a well-pressed suit, the browned face under a five dollar derby hat. They shook hands with both of them conscious of the warmth and strength of their friendship. "Let me buy," Shaw said. "Then you tell me how you're making out with the *Procyon.*" Here was a man, he thought, who was bound certainly for the top, and he wanted very much to hear what he had to say.

Alan Kennard relaxed some of his usual caution as they stood and drank. He talked openly to Shaw of his ambition, how next season he hoped to become half owner at least in the *Procyon.* Business was good, he said. He had enough cargoes lined up for the rest of the season and plenty of promises for next year. "And what goes with Phelim?" Shaw said.

"He's busy riggin' his jib-boom into some doxy down on the

Flats." Kennard turned the whiskey glass slowly around on the dark wood of the bar, his glance gone from Shaw's face. "Phelim would like to be back on deep-water. He's had about his share of the Lakes for a while. But I'll keep him with me 'til I'm ready to go master meself. Phelim and me, we're true pals. But now, Josh—" he looked keenly up—"tell me what goes with you."

Joshua Shaw took time to buy another drink. He was considering just what use he could make of this man's alert intelligence and ability. "My family got together another pile of money back East," he said. "They've all moved out here, the whole damn' clan. We're about to start working an open-hearth furnace at Bellport with our own ore brought down from the Mesabi."

"Bellport," Kennard said; "that's a wee bit town on the lake eighteen, twenty miles West of here. There's a dock and water enough to sail up to it. A good place for you. But how would you get your iron out, Josh?"

Shaw wryly smiled. "My father and my brother and I have been dealing with Hanna. We'll swing it through him and probably use the Erie. But first we have to finish our plant and the Soo Canal isn't open yet."

"A schooner's not much for the hauling of ore," Alan Kennard said without hesitation. "When you're ready, I'll get me a steamer."

They stood in silence then for a moment while around them in the warm, whiskey scented room men talked and laughed and called for drinks. "Don't drive yourself too hard, Antrim," Shaw said. One of his hands went out to Kennard's shoulder.

"Ah, to hell!" Alan Kennard said slowly. "I was brought up in poverty and I've just left it. I want no more. So let's have another drink before I get back to the ship. I'll be dischargin' her whilst Phelim is having his fun."

"Take some time out and get these books and read them," Joshua Shaw said. He had pencil and paper, was writing a list. "They have to do with steel making. It's going to be the big business on the Lakes for years to come."

"Thank ye," Kennard said. His eyes were solemn with gratitude as he took the list. "You'll be in Bellport now, Josh'?"

"That's right. Mother has rebuilt a house we bought there. Send me a letter and I'll come into Cleveland and pick you up. Maybe in the fall after you lay up you can spend a week or so with us."

"Sure," Kennard said in his new manner. "That I'd like fine. So long now, Josh. Take care."

He and Phelim Carmody laid up the *Procyon* at a Black Rock dock in Buffalo the first week of December. It was bitter cold, with a great, yowling Northwester on the lake, and both of them were glad to leave the vessel. But before they left her they sat in the galley close to the range and counted out their money. They had a thousand dollars free apiece with the crew paid off, all bills and their commitments to Maumee Mike met. "I'd like to go over and see the scalawag," Kennard said, "and tell him how we've done for the season, make plans for next year. The doctor says no, though. The Old Man has written such to us. Mike must be near the end of it."

"So he must." Phelim had gone to the range and the tea kettle. He poured himself a mug of tea and added whiskey to it. "The summer's done him no good and this whore of a winter will finish him. Write the Old Man if ye will, Alan. Make your deal with him."

Alan Kennard rested motionless. "If Mike dies," he said, "we'll have to buy the schooner outright or get ourselves another like her. But the deal we have here is rare."

"I know as much," Phelim said. He inhaled deeply as he drank, reached over and opened the draft of the range wide. "Mike's too weak to talk, and if you want her for next year you'd better get it in writing from the Old Man."

"You'll be with me in the spring, Phelim?"

"That I will."

"You're sure?"

"Sure, goddamn ye, man!"

"But you have your gear all packed as if it's away for the deep-water you are."

"And I am. Liverpool's what I want to see again, and the Lime Street lasses. Bejaisus, even me own family. No more of them woods camps for me. Another winter o' that and I'd be talkin' like the squirrels or chasin' them for comfort. I'll catch me a ship as able sailor out of New York, jump her on the other shore and back so again in the spring. I'll have most of me money still left."

"You'll have rope yarns left, that's what you'll have. I'm not countin' on a dime from you in the spring."

Phelim Carmody wheeled on him hard-eyed, his mouth tight. "How about you?" he said. "Are you for another go at it with the Nickersons or their like?"

"No, not me." Kennard gave a barking sound of laughter to break the sudden tension of Phelim's anger. "Enough of that, too,

I've had. It's Josh Shaw I'm going to see at Bellport. Then I'll take a look-see around Patigowoc."

"Your ambition's got ye by the neck," Phelim said, "and you'd throw the tow-line on me, haul me after. But you're still a good man, Antrim, and I'm still your friend. Tell me, though. What in the name is there at Patigowoc? When ye speak of Shaw, I understand. The other, no. It's no more than a spit-kit port there on the Bouche de Mouche."

Alan Kennard was tempted to tell him fully, to explain in detail what he had seen along the shore of the bay beyond Patigowoc when they had made their last voyage there a month ago. But Phelim was in no real mood to listen, he decided, and he wasn't convinced himself. First he had to check over the books on steel making that Shaw had told him to get, then talk with Shaw, afterwards go back to Patigowoc. "Ah," he said, "there's little, Phelim. I had me the idea maybe we could get some lads to cut off the second quality timber there, raft it out so we could pick it up and sell it in the spring. The Nickersons had rights to that land, but only for the pine. They may have left the woods in such shape that no good can be made from the place."

"More likely than not," Phelim said. "Go get your gear and let's hit the dock. I'm for New York and a big, tall, fast one that will haul me home in a hurry."

"Then douse the fire," Kennard said, "and lock up here. I'll lock the cabin, make sure them plough-jockeys left the dock lines led out right."

"Cautious is the name for you," Phelim said, bent to shake down the range. "Damn me if you shouldn't ha' been a cleric, Antrim."

"And you an altar boy." There was snow on deck. Kennard gathered a handful, pelted Phelim hard behind the ear. "Say your prayers!"

"I'll tear the liver out o' you," Phelim shouted. But he was grinning as the snow slipped down his neck.

They parted on Delaware Street in front of the railroad station. Phelim was half drunk and very happy; he hardly looked back as he shouldered his bag and moved off into the crowd. Alan Kennard watched him with a peculiar sensation of loss. After all, he told himself, Phelim was his only link with the past. Phelim was going home, and just a few hours' sail from Liverpool was Antrim. . . .

"To hell," he said aloud. "And what would you do in Antrim?" He turned around and started back along the gray-slushed street.

You have the letter to write to Mike and to Old Man Jacobs. Then get off a telegram to Josh Shaw. Tell him to meet you in Cleveland in the morning. Maybe you took the facts wrong from them books. But the stuff you saw up along the Bouche de Mouche was sure enough limestone. And limestone's what they need in plenty for the making of their steel.

Joshua Shaw drove a handsome pair of chestnuts harnessed to a shining cutter. He wore a coonskin coat and cap and was wrapped in a buffalo robe. "A wee bit different from last winter," Kennard said as he climbed in beside him and the chestnuts trotted smartly off across the Square.

"The Shaw clan was broke then," Joshua said. "Now we're not. My brother, Cottrell, married into one of the wealthiest insurance families in Hartford. But even before that Dad had his stock sold in the new plant."

"Stock?" Alan Kennard said. "But, man, you told me you won't be operating for some time to come."

Joshua Shaw grinned, his light blue eyes low lidded in the wind. "You're an American all right," he said. "I've seen your papers. I realize, though, that I must still explain to you about what is rather vulgarly called stock manipulation."

"That will make me a better American, hey?"

"Perhaps a wiser one." Shaw pointed with his whip. "Hanna and the rest of the boys are great for waving the flag, and a stock flotation for them is an everyday job. Who do you think owns these street railways?"

"Marcus Hanna."

"Go to the head of the class. Now, though, let me tell you how he got to own them."

Alan Kennard was silent when the chestnuts swung the cutter in from the road along the lake bluffs, whirled it on through the white, small village flanked with rows of elms and to the tall house at the end of the village street. Sight of the Shaw home was enough to confirm the thought that had formed in his mind during the drive. Josh was his friend and he'd never hide anything from him. But Josh wasn't alone in this. There was Josh's father and his brother, and they were men who dealt closely with the likes of Mark Hanna. It would be best to meet the father and the brother, get to know the family lash-up before he talked to Josh about limestone.

Joshua gave the chestnuts over to a man who came running

from the barn after they were in the driveway. "Rub them down well, Harry," he said. "They've had a long pull."

"Yes, sir," Harry said and led the team away. Alan Kennard stood gazing at Harry, at the huge red barn with its white trim and lightning rods and rooster wind-vane, then at the house. His gesture was mechanical as his eyes rested on the house; he reset the angle of the brim of his derby and he reached inside his coat and straightened the knot of his tie.

"We live pretty big," Joshua Shaw said with care, "but we're really simple people." His friend was very uncomfortable, he realized, and was vaguely angered by the knowledge. It was quite possible that Antrim had never before visited such a house as this as a guest. He might have warned Antrim, told him something about the house, his mother, his father, Cottrell and Cottrell's wife and Jane. Yes, Jane in particular. But there's no way right now that you can. It's all too complicated. Antrim must figure it out for himself. Don't worry, though. The man has an awful lot of sense in that head of his.

"The house," Kennard said soft-voiced, "is just like them I seen down on the Eastern shore. Maine, I mean, and Massachusetts. Damn me if she's not a beauty." The short December sun was beginning to set out across the lake. It threw a lurid bronze light onto the lawn where the wind had drawn fragile patterns in the snow, piled drifts wave-like around the hedges, the plants and shrubs. The great elms were stark yet magnificent. Their trunks had a dark gray shade and icicles spangled the powerful curves of the branches. Their shadows, also gray and dark, but wavering a bit along the sun-rimmed snow, reached forth to the house.

It was of three stories, the design so bold as to give it an almost box-like appearance. There were long white brick chimneys at each end, though, and even the shape, the fashioning of the clapboards had grace of line. Everything was white except the window shutters and the broad front door, and they were deep green. The fanlight over the doorway was delicate, high; what Alan Kennard recognized dimly to be a Grecian design was along and above the doorway and each window. The window panes were small. They took the sunlight and shimmered with a warm, quiet light. But candles already burned within. He saw their straight and pale flames, and the big brass door knocker, polished brighter than any brass he'd seen at sea, seemed to beckon him forward uncontrollably into the house.

He was profoundly touched, moved closer to tears than he had been in many years. To be a guest in a house like this, bejesus. To have as a friend a man like Josh here. All your life, even home in Antrim, you've been alone, man. And what you called home was a hovel, a byre alongside of what's before you. His hand went to Shaw's arm, gently grasped it. "A beauty," he said soft-voiced again.

"An old-timer for this country," Joshua Shaw said, troubled by Kennard's obvious emotion and somehow not liking it. "One of the original Nutmeg lads who came out with Israel Putnam was the owner. He drew up his specifications after he'd cleared his land, sent them East to an architect in New Haven. That's why the place reminds you so much of those back on the coast. It's identical to them, although over the years it got into bad repair. We've done plenty of work on it. Mother even had pine and chestnut paneling taken out of her family's place in Sharon and sent here to fix this up. But come inside. No sense freezing our ears off here."

"Sure," Kennard said. He rubbed his ears briskly, nervous with the apprehension of how he should greet Josh's family. "A snort of whiskey now, that would do fine."

Joshua Shaw gave him a quick sidewise glance. "Take it easy," he said. "Mother's a little bit on the stuffy order. Her folks were Puritans, y' see, and she hasn't got over the fact. But when Dad and Cottrell get back from the plant we'll have a nip. Dad keeps his supply hid away in the library."

A maid in a black dress, white, frilled apron and cap opened the door for them. She curtsied and said, "Good afternoon. Mrs. Shaw and Miss Jane are in the living room, Mister Joshua." The maid took Joshua's cap and coat, and Alan Kennard could feel the sweat on the palms of his hands as he let her take from him his coat and derby, the small handbag he had brought. You'd have reckoned a girl like this beyond you in your Antrim days, he thought, and here you are big as life and under full sail as a guest. Don't disgrace yourself or Josh. Walk straight and simple and make your bow to the Missus like a gentleman. Then keep your big yawp shut until you're talked to and then have Josh handle the gab.

The two women in the long and shadowy room sat within a flush of firelight. One was young and prim-looking, he saw, and the other gray-haired and prim. Josh's mother, he prompted himself. The Puritan. Set your course for her and come up short abreast of Josh. His sister, the other must be, and mark the eyes she has. They're the color of violets and deep as the sea. A bloody poet you would be getting to be at a time like this, Antrim. Can't ye keep your wits about ye? It's among civilized gentlefolk ye are.

His rage with himself and the beating of blood in his ears held him from hearing clearly the introductions Joshua Shaw made. He bowed to Mrs. Shaw and to Joshua's sister, but all he could say was a mumbled, "Ma'am" and "Miss." Like you were in the loaning on the way from the village at home and you met the curate's wife and daughter. Damn ye, though, you're no longer without shoes to your feet and a lad with herring smeared in your hair. Act as a man, you who would go so high.

Joshua had drawn chairs to the fire for them and they sat next to the mother and daughter. Joshua talked, his voice light and easy as he described how he had met his guest. But he no longer called him "Antrim," Alan Kennard discovered. Now he was "Alan" and Josh was making a point of it to explain to his mother that he was part lessor of a vessel.

Mrs. Shaw sat in a mahogany rocker, her small, thin body erect. She had some knitting work in her hands and her eyes remained on it nearly all the time. But when she looked up her glance was searching, sharp, and she had already studied his hands, Kennard knew, and was aware of what he was. But some of his natural calmness had come to him and he was capable of studying her in turn.

She wore a dress of heavy lavender silk with a lace collar stiffened by whalebone. Her wedding ring was simple but the brooch at her throat contained a big, precious stone that shone with the light of the fire. From her husband, Kennard thought. A gift from him and she wears it to please him. Her face was bland, almost without wrinkles except for around the eyes and high up on the prominent forehead. Her hair was gray, parted in the middle, severely drawn back. Her eyes, when he caught them in their rapidly lifted glances, were of the color of gun metal and flat and cold, a bit bloodshot. She needs spectacles, he told himself without wilful malice. But she's too ruddy proud to stick them on that wee, dainty nose. A very handsome woman she was in her day.

Jane Shaw sat nearest to him. She was a pale blonde with her hair piled high on her head. Although her skirt was plain, she wore a bold candy striped shirtwaist, and there was a look in her narrow face that subtly aroused Kennard. She wasn't beautiful, not nearly as much so as her mother had been. Too much angularity was in the jaw lines. She had her mother's prominent forehead and wide-set eyes, but those were attractive only because of their unusual color, their depth. She seemed to look past him and never directly at him, and he tried in vain to meet their regard.

But Jane Shaw was joining in the conversation with Joshua. She sat forward in her straight-backed chair and let her gaze flick in the oblique across Kennard's face. "So you're a sailor," she said. "Tell us, please. Where have you sailed?"

"Och," he said, and could have bitten his tongue for use of the word, "all over the world. China, India, Spain. Where the winds blow, I've been, Miss Jane."

"Did you hear him!" she said. She had stopped slowly fingering the cambric handkerchief in her lap. She glanced at her mother, then her brother. "Where the winds blow——"

"Yes," Mrs. Shaw said; she didn't lift her head. "Sailors have that way of talk. Mr. Kennard, Joshua. Would you like to have tea with us?"

Alan Kennard took his signal from Joshua for that, shook his head and said, "No, thank you, ma'am."

"I guess we'll wait for dinner," Joshua said. "But where's Dad and Cottrell? Are they still over at the plant, mother?"

"They are. Mr. Shaw has been expecting that shipment of ladles all the day. Just an hour ago, just before you arrived in fact, they arrived. I believe Mr. Shaw is eager to get them off the flatcars as quickly as he can. Dinner will probably be delayed."

"Then we'll go over to the plant." Joshua stood straight, his hands at his sides. "You'll excuse us?"

"Of course." The knitting needles gave an emphatic click. Alan Kennard obeyed it as he would an order given aboard a full-rigged ship in a gale. He swung in unison with Joshua to leave the room. He was extremely conscious of the fire's sighing snap, then the bang of his heels over the waxed, smooth floor planks. You must get yourself new shoes, man. Some with elastic sides and thinner soles, like Josh wears. These you're wearing are too bloody heavy. You could step masts in them and sail them on the lake.

He and Joshua walked part of the way to the plant without speech. They could see it in the darkness, huge and skeletal, and the reflector lights past it where the men worked at unloading the flatcars. "My people have been working iron since before the Revolution," Joshua said. "Our forge was right below Lime Rock on Sharon Mountain. That's on the Housatonic, in Litchfield County, Connecticut. It's still pretty wild country, and during the Revolution it was wild as hell. The British could never find our forge. There were only two in the region that ran all through the war. We supplied musket shot and cannon ball to Washington."

This isn't the true thing Josh wants to tell you, Alan Kennard thought. He's leading up to something. Give him plenty of scope. He'll get around to it in his own style. "What did ye use for fuel?"

"The local timber. We put it in charcoal form, of course, and brought it to the forge in big wains. It made fine iron, better than they're making today with coal. But we burned up too much wood. Five or six thousand cords was gone in a month's run-off."

"That'd mean about two hundred acres of timber land you stripped a month. The stuff can't be grown to keep such a pace."

"You're right." Joshua was staring ahead at the black-silhouetted bodies of the men around the flatcars, the enormous steel ladles on the cars, the blanketed teams and the spans of oxen that stood in a steamy, confused mass. "It's why we gave up in Sharon and came out here to try our luck. My father was a colonel of Zouaves in the war, Antrim. He's still more soldier than iron-master."

"I get you," Alan Kennard murmured. They were close to the flatcars now and passing the teamsters and the ox-skinners. Those men cursed in low voices, and Kennard heard, "The goddamn' colonel. Him and his pig's ass son. They'll keep us here the night, they will."

Nerves pulled at the corners of Joshua's mouth, but he kept on as if he hadn't heard. "I guess from the look of it," he said to Kennard, "that Dad seems to be having trouble getting the ladles off."

A tall, square-shouldered man stood in the center of the bluish glare of the coal-oil lanterns. Alan Kennard recognized him at once as Joshua's father. The facial characteristics were the same, and the carriage of the body. But Mr. Shaw wore a short goatee and a stiff, spiked mustache. A military style cape was about his shoulders, and beneath it Kennard saw a braided Prince Albert coat, a wide silk cravat, striped trousers. The proper dandy, he told himself. Back in England, he'd be senior officer of some Guards regiment. A younger, more slender man rested in the outer circumference of the lantern light. He was dressed very much like Joshua and must be Josh's brother, Cottrell. Even in this moment, though, he could make out that Cottrell wasn't of equal caliber. He seemed a softer, easier Josh, his features a bit blurred and feminine, the mouth pursed up in what with Josh would be an expression of outright rage.

Mr. Shaw was shouting at Cottrell. "Bring your man up here again. Get the pry-bars set and the oxen can hitch on. Move, damn you, Cottrell!"

"Yes, sir," Cottrell said, but he remained still, and in back of him some of the teamsters and workmen laughed.

"Come with me, Antrim," Joshua said. He stepped in among the lanterns propped on boxes in the snow, over the thick plank and beam ramps placed along the sides of the flatcars. "I'll have you meet my father."

Mr. Shaw stared fiercely at his elder son. "That stupid freight manager sent us everything but the crane car."

"I spoke to him this morning, sir," Joshua said, "and then to Mr. Hanna. Mr. Hanna regretted that he asked you to take delivery on the ladles so soon. But there's been a wreck on the line over near Conneaut. They have great need of the crane car to clear the line. Sir, I should like to present to you my good friend, Mr. Alan Kennard. I'm sure you've heard me talk of him."

Mr. Shaw allowed himself a quick nod. Alan Kennard pulled his feet together, put his hands at his sides and said, "Sir." But Mr. Shaw, he knew, had barely seen him. Mr. Shaw had nothing on his mind but the big brute steel ladles and his pride.

"Your brother has been of small help to me," Mr. Shaw said. "And that fella, Grigor, the one you hired as foreman, refuses to understand English."

"Where's Tim Brooks?" Joshua said.

"A four-by-eight snapped," the colonel said, "and Tim had his leg broken. I've sent him to the doctor."

Joshua walked up the ramp onto the car where his father stood. He bent down and examined the vast ladles and the pieces of timber that were under them. "We should wait for the crane car, sir," said. "This way of working is quite dangerous."

"It might be days before we get the crane. But there's our plant." Mr. Shaw made a dramatic gesture off into the darkness. "A number of orders are waiting for us, all under contract, and time is of the essence."

Alan Kennard wasn't quite sure that he understood what "time is of the essence" meant. But he didn't like the look on Joshua's face or the grins of the men behind Cottrell Shaw. He jumped up on the ramp and joined Joshua and his father. "Josh, lad," he said low-voiced, "it's perhaps that I can help ye. Come daylight, we

could rig a sheer-legs here and then a double tackle. Then we'd
sweat them brute bastards down the ramps so that the ox spans
could get at them easy."

"Who's this man?" Mr. Shaw said.

"My friend," Joshua said simply. "Go ahead, Antrim. I'm with
you. But where could we find tackle heavy enough for the job,
and the timber you'd want for sheer-legs?"

Mr. Shaw shouldered his son aside. He gave Alan Kennard a
straight glance. "Explain to me, please," he said, "what sheer-legs
are."

"They're long, strong timbers," Alan Kennard said. "You take
a pair of them and rig them like this." He lifted two fingers and
crossed them almost at the tops. "There you put a good cross lash-
ing and below you brace them at the bottom. Then you hang your
double tackle from the top and get along and h'ist your load."

"You talk like a sailor."

"I am, sir."

Mr. Shaw very slightly smiled. "Some of the Erie Railroad's
fine new telegraph poles are over there at the end of the siding.
They could be used."

"Father," Joshua Shaw said slowly, "you've worked the men
at least sixteen hours today. They're too tired for such a job now."

"Tomorrow is Sunday." Fury was in Mr. Shaw's voice. "And to
get this tackle of which your friend speaks a trip would have to be
made into Cleveland. Too much time has been lost already. I want
the job done tonight."

"Not tonight, sir," Joshua said. "I doubt if the men will even
begin it for you."

Mr. Shaw cursed in a passionate voice.

"Grigor," he yelled; "come here!"

The foreman was swart and squat and recently had been very
angry. His face had a pallor under the high cheekbones, his thick
hands kept twitching. He came forward, but his eyes were baleful
in the lantern light. "Your fat'er," he told Joshua, "he treat me like
I'm army. And enough army I had from v'ere I come. No, men
don't do no more vurk tonight."

"Excuse me, sir." Alan Kennard had half-turned to watch Mr.
Shaw's face. "If you count on me to do your riggin', it won't be 'til
daylight. I couldn't see to handle the gear right."

Veins were distended in Mr. Shaw's temples. His teeth were

against his under lip. But he had control of himself; the fury was
subdued. "Then we will wait for daylight on Monday," he said.
"Grigor, dismiss your men until that hour. Gentlemen, let us go to
the house. It's well time we had some dinner."

They let him walk on ahead while they followed at a few paces,
Joshua on one side of Alan Kennard, Cottrell on the other. "I don't
know," Cottrell muttered. "It's beyond me. But somehow you managed to whip him. Between you, you make quite a team. You don't
even have to have Grigor."

"Listen," Joshua said, "there's one thing I want to tell you,
Cottrell. Maybe you think your father's a martinet. Maybe you go
so far as think he's a dirty, stiff-necked son of a bitch. But so long
you live, you'll never be the iron-master he is."

Cottrell Shaw laughed at that. He put back his head in the
moon-thinned darkness and laughed with obvious delight. "Certainly," he said. "You're iron-master enough, though, for both of
us."

Kennard frowned in speculation at the stiffly striding, proudly
held man before them. Then he glanced aside at the brothers.
There was hell's own amount about this family that he didn't understand, he told himself. But he was in pretty deep with them already,
might be deeper yet.

Mrs. Shaw stood right inside the front door of the house. She
greeted her husband with a quick kiss, took his cape and sealskin
cap herself. Then she kissed each of her sons and gave Alan Kennard a surprisingly warm smile. "When would you like dinner,
Mr. Shaw?" she said.

"In just a few minutes," he said. "First, I wish our guest and
Joshua to accompany me to the library. We have a small matter
to discuss. Cottrell, I expect that your wife is awaiting you."

"Yes, sir," Cottrell said and also smiled. He bowed to his mother
and the three men, went rapidly running up the broad main staircase.

Something happened to you once you were inside this place,
Alan Kennard thought. You've seen ships change a man, but never
before a house. Maybe it's her, though, the old lady. She's sure
different now than when you were here before with Josh and the
daughter. At the same time, she's the same down underneath, calm
and steady, knowing what she's about the whole time. It must be
because the house is so much hers; she runs it top to bottom while

she goes ahead giving His Nibs, here, the idea he's the big potato.

Mr. Shaw had walked across the hallway and to the door of a room where firelight glinted. Kennard and Joshua followed and Kennard looked around with swift, eager glances. He was trying to comprehend the house, grasp the meaning of its beauty and its charm. But there was no chance for that now, he realized. He'd have to do it more slowly; His Nibs had his mind on the drink Joshua had mentioned.

They drank bourbon in water glasses without water, and the whiskey came from a cabinet in the paneled wall that Mr. Shaw unlocked with a key attached to the end of his watch fob. "To Ulysses S. Grant," Mr. Shaw said; "a fine soldier and a fine man."

"Yes, sir," they both said; they lifted their glasses with his. They rested in front of a huge log fire built in a fieldstone fireplace and Alan Kennard wondered how well, after the hours of intense nerve strain, he would take the glassful of whiskey and the heat. But a maid was already softly rapping at the door. She said, "Please, sir, Mrs. Shaw says dinner is to be served."

"We will be there directly," Mr. Shaw said. He put the whiskey bottle and the glasses back in the cabinet, locked the cabinet. Then he drew from his waistcoat pocket a small, thin silver box. It contained charcoal lozenges and they each took one. "For our continued good health," Mr. Shaw explained patiently, but Kennard could see the brief contraction of muscles about Joshua's mouth. This bit about the charcoal was so that Her Nibs in there wouldn't catch on that they'd been drinking, but she must know bloody well. She had timed them so they could have no more than one fast snort.

Mrs. Shaw, Jane, Cottrell and the girl who was Cottrell's wife sat before a fire in a room off the dining room. Cottrell's wife's name was Lucinda and she had been pretty until she got pregnant. Now her skin was sallow, her hair dull. There were purple marks under her eyes and her eyes were red, as though she had been crying a great deal. Lucinda embarrassed Kennard. She held her hands constantly over her lower body, and she blushed when he was presented to her. Cottrell stood at her side, and he must have opened his own supply of liquor, for he smiled broadly and his voice was high and happy.

Alan Kennard looked from one to the other of them again, wanting to understand them and their relationship. But Mrs. Shaw had risen; she and Mr. Shaw were moving in to dinner. Kennard slipped over next to Joshua and whispered, "I've never ett fancy. What do I do?"

"You sit across from me and watch what I do," Joshua said. "But relax. Just start from the outside with the silver and work in. Mother serves a fine table and you're hungry. You won't have any trouble."

They all bowed their heads over the long, candle-lit table while Mr. Shaw said grace. He talks to God as if he knows him very well, Alan Kennard thought. No doubt about this family being real serious about its church-going. He was relieved when grace was finished and the two maids had begun to serve. He was able to tell as a North of Ireland man that the huge table cloth was of pure damask, and he was determined to compliment Mrs. Shaw on that.

But Mrs. Shaw only permitted him to speak to her once while the oyster soup was served, then the roast lamb, the baked potatoes, the stewed celery and tomatoes, the prune whip. She and Mr. Shaw had been carrying on a conversation to which Kennard had carefully listened. It had to do first with the shockingly bad quality of the *Cleveland Leader,* afterwards the nomination of James A. Garfield for president. You had to admit, Mr. Shaw said, that Garfield was a local Ohioan, indeed a resident of Cuyahoga County. Also, Blaine had allowed Robert Ingersoll to make the speech of nomination for him. Any man who gave himself into the power of such an avowed atheist deserved to receive defeat.

Jane Shaw had been sitting in silence. She looked up towards her father and said, "But if it had been a member of the Order of American Union, would it have been all right?"

Mr. Shaw brought his napkin slowly to his lips, and at the end of the room one of the maids gave a harsh, short gasp. So, Alan Kennard told himself, Miss Jane's gone and done it. That Order of American Union, they're Catholic-haters they are, and last summer over to Manitowoc when one of them talked to Phelim, he dumped him ass-past-ears into the lake. A sorry subject the lass has taken up.

"Tell me, Mr. Kennard," Mrs. Shaw said from her end of the table. She sat quite erect, her face without expression. "Do you happen to belong to the Roman faith?"

"No, ma'am." Alan Kennard fingered the slender silver spoon beside his plate. His fingers closed on it and he could feel the metal bend as the gust of anger rose up through him. "My father was a fisherman lost at sea when I was a wee lad. My mother was a Romany, what you might call here a gypsy. I'm a man of no religion. None."

"I see," Mrs. Shaw said, and nodded. Her gaze returned to her husband. "Shall we leave the table?"

The feeling of constraint, of hard-checked anger stayed with Alan Kennard for some time after they had left the table. But Joshua and Cottrell made a great point of talking to him in the tremendous living room before the fire, and then Jane and Lucinda came to them. "We'd like some music," Jane said. "Father and Mother are willing to join us. Why don't you?"

"Of course." Joshua put his arm lightly about his sister's shoulder. "I'd be very unhappy if Alan didn't hear us. And you should hear this Antrim man sing."

They went grouped together into the music room, Mr. and Mrs. Shaw hand-in-hand. How fast they change, Alan Kennard thought. You can't reckon them at all yet, man. But the anger had gone out of him. He was capable now of noticing the gilt-pillared clocks over the mantels, each with its proud eagle and village scene, the bull's-eye mirrors also with their eagles, and the grace of the furniture, the marvellous textures which he knew to be mahogany and cherry and walnut, satinwood and rosewood. The rugs underfoot were old, old, and faded but still lovely. The whole place had a sense of age about it, although it was nothing like the great family homes back in Ireland into which he had peered as a lad. Here every single thing seemed to be treasured, kept safe and perfect from the years.

He slowed with Joshua in the main hall for a moment and took a look at a framed crest that hung on a wall. It had a tartan border, and the sett of the cloth was dark forest green, a clear and lighter green, a flaring red. It was famous in the glens of Antrim as well as Scotland.

"A demi-lion." Joshua was reading to him the meaning of the crest. "Gules, holding in the dexter paw a sword, proper. Our badge is the red whortleberry."

"And if you're from Tordarroch and the Clan Aidh, then," Alan Kennard said, "you were in the Rising in '15. You were among the best of the troops the Earl of Mar had. My mother had a song she sang about you. It was given her by pipers."

"So," Joshua Shaw said, his eyes alight with emotion. "You must tell my father what you know of us."

"Not me." Kennard laughed, the memory suddenly back on him. "I'm a gypsy's son."

Joshua stared strangely at him. "Then look at this," he said. He drew Alan Kennard across the hall. The yellowed parchment within the frame was a commission. It granted the rank of ensign in the Ancient and Honourable Artillery Company of Boston to Lucius Cottrell and bore the date of 1638. "My mother's family. They went on later to Connecticut and Lucius's son served as an aide to General Gates at Saratoga."

"I'd ha' guessed that," Kennard said, "by your brother's name. But what does it mean to you, Josh?"

"Many things," Joshua Shaw said. He squeezed the other man's bicep hard in a sudden access of feeling. "Many things, friend. Let us go and join the family, and you will sing."

The music room was paneled in dark-whorled beechwood. Alan Kennard saw that it contained a piano that held a soft gleam under the firelight, a tall harp and several music stands. Lucinda was at the harp and the rest of the family had ranged themselves along the opposite wall. She was no longer self-conscious, leaned easily to the strings.

It came to Kennard as he listened that he was extraordinarily happy. Only once since he had left Antrim had he been carried into such secret recesses of the heart. That had been last winter in the camp on the Kawkawlin when the Scottish piper had played and then, after Joshua had stopped the fighting, they had all sung. But it had been brief, something torn out of a night of drink between days of hard, dangerous work.

Lucinda played with consummate skill, and she had been trained by a fine master. In her hands, the harp gave beauty that reached far into the dimness of the early world. He didn't know her music, nor did he care. For him it was enough to be here and listen, be carried away with ecstasy.

She stopped at last and Cottrell went to her and kissed her, led her from the harp to a big wingback chair in a corner. It was the turn of Joshua and his father, and in his present mood Kennard wasn't surprised when they played violin duets. Kennard looked around once, took himself from their music to watch Mrs. Shaw.

Her face was rapt with the tremulous calling, the surge, the sweep and then high, fine mesh of notes. She sat forward in the chair and grasped the arms in the identical posture of her daughter.

They looked for the moment very much alike. The difference between them was lost, submerged in the music.

Father and son glanced at each other and smiled and lowered their bows. "Now, Jane," Mr. Shaw said, "you and Cottrell must play for our guest."

"May I suggest, sir," Joshua said, "that Alan sing a solo for us? He sings very well and Jane can accompany him."

Some of the limpid quality that had been in the eyes of both mother and daughter disappeared as they glanced at Kennard. They were doing their best to be polite, he knew, but music meant a great lot to them. He could tell by Lucinda's glance of sympathy what she had suffered when she first became a member of this group. If you flat one note, Antrim man, you'll be as welcome to these folks as a Jesuit with a torch in his hand.

"Come on, Alan," Joshua said stubbornly. "Step over to the piano. Jane will accompany you."

Jane got up and walked with him to the piano. But her mouth was a flat, colorless line and she said brusquely, "I don't know if I have any music to suit you."

"I'm a bog singer and a man for a chantey," he said. "It'd best be simple." There was sweat on his brow as he seated her on the piano bench, opened her music folio. The others were silent behind them; he could hear the roughness of his breathing, the rustle of the pages of the folio and the slight creak of her starched shirtwaist when she lifted her arms, spread her fingers on the keys.

The song was called "Kelvin Green" and he had heard his mother sing it. He couldn't read music, though, so he was forced to tell Jane, "Play and I'll make out as well as I can with you."

He was bad in the first passage, better in the second. Then he really sang. He put his heritage into it, the loneliness and misery of his youth, but, too, his love, his instinctive passion for the glens of Antrim.

He stood still when they were finished. He didn't look down at Jane or around at the others. His pride was rampant in him; he wanted to sing again and he wanted them to ask him. It was Jane who spoke. "Mother, did you hear?" she said.

"Bravo!" Mrs. Shaw said. "Bravo!" She clapped her hands. "Do sing again, Mr. Kennard."

"One more I'll sing alone," he said. "Then ye must all be in it with me."

Jane was reaching for the folio. "Which number?" she said.

"No," he said. He smiled at her. "For this they have no music yet. It's one from the sea."

Jane moved from the piano bench, left him by himself. He stood slowly inhaling and setting himself for "Shenandoah." Memory of Antrim had brought him to memory of the sea. He had failed to realize until now the degree of his longing for the open, rolling water and the feel of a tall-masted ship beneath his feet. He walked as he sang, back and forth just a bit alongside the piano, and his hands stretched out as though he grasped a rope. His eyes were shut towards the end; he was seeing the ship.

They closed around him when he was done. The men slapped him on the back and the women smiled into his eyes. "Superb," Mr. Shaw said. "I should have liked to have you in my regiment in the war, sir. But of course you belong on the sea."

"Ah," he said seriously, "I'm not a patch on you folks. You'd mind if I sang together with you?"

Jane played while they all sang. Mrs. Shaw had a clear contralto, Jane and Lucinda pure-pitched sopranos. Cottrell could go to bass and meet Mr. Shaw's booming voice. Joshua kept to the baritone with Alan Kennard. They gave themselves to "Rock of Ages" and "Abide With Me" and later Stephen Foster's songs, ending with "Flow Gently Sweet Afton."

Mrs. Shaw halted them. She indicated a clock across the room and said, "I regret to say this, but it is a quarter of twelve and tomorrow is the Sabbath." She stroked her hand over Lucinda's hair. "You, too, my dear, must have your rest."

They went forth into the hall elated, laughing, humming bits of the songs they had sung. "If you will excuse us," Mr. Shaw said to his wife, "I have a final word for Mr. Kennard and Joshua. Good music has kept me from it."

"I shall be waiting," Mrs. Shaw said. The gaiety had left her. She was stern, almost grim as she faced her husband. Then she motioned to Jane and Lucinda and Cottrell, sent them up the stairs before her.

Mr. Shaw took the bottle eagerly from the cabinet in the library. He filled the water glasses right to the brims. "To you, sir," he told Alan Kennard. "You have given us one of the happiest evenings we have passed in our home in some months."

"Thank ye very much, sir," Alan Kennard said, aware of Joshua's nervousness and anxious to be out of this room. But Mr. Shaw wasn't content. He lifted a candle off the mantel, led Kennard to a daguerrotype framed in scrolled leather. It showed himself in his Civil War uniform. The pose was proud to the point of arrogance. The cocked, flat-topped cap, the short jacket with its ornately braided frogs and sleeve loops of rank, the sash, the floppy Zouave trousers and the pointed boots added to the effect. Yet the eyes beneath the thrust of the cap visor were deep-set and somber from staring at death. The mouth lines were harsh, long, and the big revolver and the sword were worn by a man who had held them often to kill.

"When I was as you are now," Mr. Shaw said. He drew himself up consciously to his extreme height. "I'm looking forward with the utmost confidence, sir, to what you shall do for us on Monday. To move those ladles should be a completely routine job for you."

"Father," Joshua said, "we've been told that Mother will be waiting. Hadn't we better go to our rooms?"

"At once." A look of scornful hatred crossed Mr. Shaw's face. "It's already the Sabbath. Go ahead, gentlemen. I'll tend to the candles. Goodnight."

Alan Kennard went to bed in a canopied mahogany four-poster. Joshua had opened the window for him, stood in the doorway of the room to say goodnight. "I guess," Joshua said in his slow manner, "that you've found out by now that we're something of an odd family." Joshua paused and stared across the room. This is it, Kennard thought rapidly. He's about to explain it to you. Joshua smiled, though. "We don't have a furnace when we very well could have. Candles, instead of lamps, and for that matter, gas light. Still, the plumbing you used before works all night. Sleep sound, old sock. I'll call you in the morning."

"Thanks, and the same to ye, lad," Alan Kennard said. A candle in an exquisitely shaped and frosted chimney was on the bed table. He blew out the flame, lay back with his hands beneath his head. The house, he had already recognized, made sounds very much like those of a vessel. They kept him awake despite his great need for sleep.

He listened to the tightening and expansion of floor planks in the hall. Beams flexed in the night's cold. Icicles which had gathered on the eaves cracked and fell with a soft, delicate plop into the snow. The branches of the elms had their own cracking sound under the tension of the frost. From the lake, a mile or so away, he figured, came the rumble, then retreat of breakers. The wind was from the Northwest, hauling North. It was hoarse along the shingles here, hooted in the chimney tops. A chipmunk scratched somewhere, busily, without interruption.

Ah, to hell, he told himself. Get to sleep. He began to drowse, but sleep itself was still distant. His mind was occupied with the Shaw family. He once more attempted to understand them. Something's wrong, and yet you can't put your finger on it. The old man, he's strong, and no doubt he was a ruddy fine soldier, is as good an iron-master. The old lady is no weakling, neither. You couldn't find a better than Josh. He's solid all the way. That daughter, Jane, now, she might be a little on the fey side. She's smart, though, and obedient of her father and her mother, and a fine one on the piano. As for Lucinda, she'd been crying before you met her. But that might well be for the fact that's her first kid she's carrying. Her man's not of the strongest and he was well fouled-up when you and Josh come upon him and the old man. Still, Cottrell is all right. Whiskey, no, whiskey's not the answer, neither. And tonight there with the music they was the whole lot of them happy as ticks in a new mattress. It's just that you've never been around with such as them before and aren't acquainted with their ways. A fine family, they are. A handsome one and happy one. Get to sleep.

He slid further towards sleep and then stopped. Pride prodded him from it. He was back in Daigvera. He and some of the other village lads stood before the Bell and Whistle to get a good close look at Lady Innish's brake and dock-tailed gelding. But Paddy Shea, him who was from the village himself and her second coachman, let fly from the box with the whip.

It wasn't the butcher's son Shea hit with the whip, or the tobacconist's or the green grocer's. To hell, no. It was the gypsy's son, the one with his father dead, his feet bare and half the seat of his breeches gone. Sure, sure, and goddamn you if I'll ever forget you, Paddy Shea.

You couldn't get hot at Paddy alone, though. They'd done it themselves, the lads of his own age. Stoned him, bejesus a dozen of them, the length of the village street and out across the bridge. "Romany!" they'd yelled at him. "Whore's son!" And some of the stones as big as cuckoo eggs and him with a cut on the side of his head wide enough to put your hand in. But he found a piece of wood on the bridge, a post of some sort that had been knocked off the load of some waggoner. And he chased them with it, and the bridge was old and narrow. When they'd pelted their last at him, all they could do was run. He'd whacked their backs for them, and Gig Coates, him whose uncle was postmaster, he laid him flat with one on the noggin. They had let him be after that. Aye, they had.

Alan Kennard rolled over in the bed. His fists were clenched. The stream of remembrance ran fast for him, and it was black and violent. He recalled game wardens who had caught him in the bitterness of winter when he and his mother were starving and he had ventured onto some estate to snare a rabbit. Once he had managed to kill a badger and the warden who found him had beaten him until he could barely walk home. But he had gone back to the same estate that night near dawn, stolen a plump chicken, left the feathers scattered on the snow as though a fox had done it. They had to eat, both his mother and him.

There were mates in the big, skysail-yard ships who had given him similar beatings while he was a young sailor and before he learned to keep his mouth shut, obey any order at any time. He named the mates and placed them beside those of the game wardens, the village boys of Daigvera and Paddy Shea. "Ah, ye bastards," he whispered, his face against the soft pillow, "if ye could only see me now! But, wait. I'll go back to Daigvera at least, and master and owner of vessels I'll be, with a gold watch chain across me vest big enough to lead Paddy Shea around by the nose."

The hatred and the ego dropped out of him with that. He was able to laugh at himself. Maumee Mike would be ashamed of you. Mike is the sort to tell you straight off that you're a damn' fool to be thinking so. Ambition, that's all right, and an honest desire to get ahead with yourself. But as for going back to Daigvera to make them know what you've become. . . . Damn you, you miss Mike. He's the one man to keep you to the course, better for it than Josh, and that's an odd thing for you to say. . . . Will you now get to sleep?

He slept with his head down into the pillow, his arms flung out on either side. When Jane Shaw came into the room, when she came and sat on the edge of the bed, he didn't hear her. She pushed her hand under the covers and gripped his shoulder, slowly tightened her fingers on the muscles there.

Alan Kennard started, sprang up towards her. His hands clasped her throat and he almost threw her from the bed before he saw who she was. "Lass, lass!" he said, his voice low with shock. "Never rouse out a sailor like that. A sailor sleeps alone. But what would you be doing here?"

"I came in," she said, "to have you tell me about the sea." Starlight was on the snow of the lawn. It slanted in faint reflection through the window and across her where she stood beside the bed. He saw that she wore a long flannel nightgown with a ruffled collar and that her hair hung loose about her shoulders. She was prettier now, he realized, and far more dangerous.

"But this is past the middle of the night," he said. "And it's brute cold."

"I know," she said. She ran her hands under her hair, swung it back from her shoulders. "I chose the time." Then she jumped up into the bed with him. "Move over! Would you have me get pneumonia?"

"You're daft," he said. "Get out of here, Miss Jane. Go back to your own room. Name of Christ! Your father or your mother might find you here."

"Don't worry too much." She was arranging the covers, the pillow. "You're not the first. Go ahead, sailor. Tell me about the sea."

Alan Kennard rested on his back with his knees pulled together, his hands flat at his sides. The girl wore some sort of scent, or maybe it was just her hair. It was pervasive, started a flow of warmth along his body. He could also feel her bodily warmth, and the way she lay, there was a depression in the bed and he had to strain to keep from her.

"The sea?" he said, only because speech was better than silence. "Who am I to talk about that? I'm an unlettered man, Miss Jane, with no gift for the gab. Be gone now. Please."

"No," she said. "Tell me about the sea. Do it in the same fashion that you sing."

He uttered a savage curse. "Why do you bother me so?"

"Because I want to know of the sea, and you're a man who's been there. Ever since you said it, I've been saying it to myself. 'Where the wind blows'. . . ."

"Ah, the wind!" he said. "The cruel son of a bitch! About that you'd like to know, hey?"

"Yes. But it can't always be cruel."

"No, not always."

"So tell me of it."

She lay on her side facing him. But she lay quietly and there was space between them in the bed. The strange fact of her being here and her insistence had started to arouse his imagination. He returned to the sea in a series of images that were so swift, so poignant and yet so much a part of him that he had no words for them.

"Be patient," he said, although now he was no more than barely conscious of her. "I'll try to get the words for you." Then he was absolutely solitary, taken from her by his confrontation of the sea.

It gleamed for him, and smashed and roared, yammered, whispered, slipped glistening under moonlight, was silent, dull under snow, frothed like magic golden lace across the crescents of atolls where palm trees bent perpetually to the West with the strength of the trade wind that reached seven thousand miles unbroken over the world.

He was on the Antrim coast in summer. The tide was out here beneath the huge gray tangle of rock of the Giant's Causeway. His bare boy's shins were cast in elongated distortion on the surface of the silver pool where crayfish crawled. Beyond, the sea had that color of flowers. But suddenly the wind rose. It beat the sea into black crests and ridges and mountains that fell clashing on the land. He ran, the sunlight and the crayfish forgotten, afraid for his life.

He rowed off that coast in winter. The sea was the shade of dirty canvas. The waves didn't break; there were no crests to them, nothing except the long, terrible tumbling out of the East. Gulls flew above the waves. They cried out, mournful in the tremor of the storm that had blown for a week. Ice scummed the bottom of the boat where the frozen fish lay. John Rourke's seaboots made a hollow thumping, starboard, then port, then starboard again as the boat rolled to the sea anchor's drag. Rourke had died last night of exhaustion in the cold. When he went forward to the bow to haul in the anchor line, he stumbled with his weakness against Rourke. The cap Rourke wore dropped off into the sea. He snatched for it, thinking of the widow, the three young children at home. But the sea was faster, stronger. The cap slewed astern. It sank.

Past Gibraltar, the sea was like a vast and unflawed jewel. There was a brilliance that hurt the eyes. Dusk shattered the brilliance, though, and then made striations that faded from violet to rose to amber and pearl along the coast. The coast was all mountains, rusty in the dusk, the ridges like the blades of knives. Fires burned there in the watch towers where the *carabineros* kept lookout for the smugglers from Africa. But high in the ship, up on the main royal yard as the canvas hung loose in the last of the wind, sun touched. The sail was a blazoned shield and the ship lay purple above the sibilant water.

The Hoogli was brown. The same flatness was in the mud houses on the banks. Wind, when it was down-river, brought the stink of the burning dead, the sounds made by the vultures.

You were aloft and the night was full of moonlight. You fisted the canvas, furled it while the ship leaped with what might be typhoon. But the ship's leap sent white, quivering wings out from under her bow. The bow was black, a slender anvil that struck the sea with a repetition of blows that made the ship shudder through every frame and plank and mast and shroud and spar. Astern, the wake squirmed. It was a shining serpent left by the ship for the sea. You laughed in delight, in great joy and triumph as you watched. This ship could outsail typhoon.

The men stood on deck with their hands shut hard. They had been waiting since the mate had told them. "Mauritius," the mate said. "We'll pass it by broad on the stab'd bow." There it was, a shadow among the shadows of the sea. Breeze was from the land and so gentle, slow that the ship hardly moved. They leaned over the side towards that slight pulsation of air. The smell of roses, more roses than the men had dreamed could exist, was borne to them. One man wept and banged his hands against the bulwark rail. Another laughed, softly caressed his watch-mate's bare shoulder.

Off Cape Horn, in the agony of that passage, you forgot that there was anything but wind. You were beaten, bruised, turned half-mad. Breathing was torture. Standing on your feet as the huge, green-marbled waves combed inboard was a miracle. You hated the wind. It was your lasting enemy.

But in the South American towns as you came back aboard right after dawn the wind was your friend. The Trade blew sweet among the palms, swung the mangoes so that you could catch the ripe fruit in your hand. Your girl walked with you down the cobbles of the street still fresh from the night's coolness. She grinned, told you words that the Trade caught, flung away. You didn't care; you only grinned back. That out in the sparkle of the bay was your ship.

Up in what the old-timers liked to call the Horse Latitudes it was different. The sun was on the ship until paint cracked and tar bubbled in the deck seams. Long masses of seaweed dragged from the sides. Turtles with eyes like stones floated on the brass planes of the sea, swam off only when men chased them in a boat. You got down on your knees and prayed for wind then. You asked for Bristol Roads, or even Hull and a load of coal. . . .

Alan Kennard came back with that same tightening clasp upon his shoulder. He stirred and moaned, cursed. "You're not telling me," she said. "You keep it all to yourself."

"Ah, to hell," he said. "I don't know how."

"No?" she said fiercely. "No?" She was very close beside him and her body pressed against his. "Then let me know this way."

He pushed her from him, but her nightgown was gone, she was naked. He took her in his arms even while he cursed at her. She was laughing. He heard her and didn't care. That was too late, he dimly thought. He had been too long at sea.

They were quiet after a short time. She had been desultory in her love-making, drew from him as soon as he had achieved his climax. Her breathing was regular, his rough and with a nasal undertone. He wished now that he could see her face. Remorse was on him, remorse and also a quick-kindled anger against her.

"Why did ye do it?" he said. "Take such a chance?"

She didn't answer, and he realized that she was putting on her nightgown.

"Answer me!"

"What is there for me to say? You've had me, haven't you?"

She had started to get out of the bed. His fingers found her wrist. He clamped them until she writhed and grunted with pain. "Talk, lass. I'd know. Ye can have almost any man you want. But you pick me, your brother's friend, and right in your family's house."

"You're hurting me."

"My sorrow! I'd know, though."

She amazed him then by the rapidity with which she came close to him and began to talk. A lot of it he didn't get. It was too confused, incoherent. But towards the last he understood her fully. "I want to be a painter," she said. "Express myself. Live my own life. Can someone as stupid as you comprehend that? My music is nothing to me, just a little trick for the family to keep me from going insane. . . . But painting. . . . Cottrell's got the real musical talent and look at what's happening to him. Slowly devoured, as though mother were a python and she was swallowing him whole."

"Make sense. This is wild stuff ye talk. Pythons and the like.

What's wrong with Cottrell? But to hell with him. What's wrong with you?"

"I want to paint," she said in a fierce, wild voice. "I want to be an artist, go live my own life. But mother won't let me. I must stay at home, marry, settle down. Because I'm a Shaw and she was a Cottrell. In Connecticut it was different. There I could steal away and go up the forge brook, or off on the mountain. Even then mother had me followed. She thought I might be meeting a man —some man of whom she couldn't approve. She's terrible. Believe me; she's an awful, awful woman. If only she would let me go. . . ."

Frightful weeping broke over the words. The spasms of it shook her body and the bed. Alan Kennard knew no more than to put out his hand, smooth it across her hair. "Josh can't help?"

"Joshua! He's the one person that keeps the family together. It's enough for him to stand beside father. If he didn't, father would be a drunkard. You don't know, I say. You're a fool. She won't break me, though. She won't do to me what she's done to Cottrell and has almost done to father. I'll get away from her. I'll shame her so that she'll be forced to let me go. Then—" the thin arms swung out as though she passed through an invisible door— "I'll be free. Paris. Paris, yes, and London, and Rome, and Siena and Venice."

"You talk daft. Please, Miss Jane. You'll wake the house."

She laughed, and she had lifted up so that in the final flare of starlight he could see her face. It was at once terrible and beautiful, uncanny with the luminous intensity of her eyes. "Do I care?" she said. "I'd disgrace you and a hundred more men to be free. I shall live like Georges Sand, like Rosa Bonheur. Hear me? D' you understand?"

He got out of the bed and he was shivering before his feet were firmly on the floor. "Come on," he said. He had her by the arm. "You must go to your own room now. Ye don't, I'll call your mother. You're not well."

"I'm well," she said. She had wrenched from him, was staggering head-down towards the door. "It's just that mother isn't. In her pride, mother's just a bit insane. . . . Goodnight. Thanks for nothing. I thought that if you could tell me about the sea I might escape for a bit right here."

The door opened, shut, and she was gone. He listened for her footsteps, but they were less loud than the creaking of the floor planks in the hall. He was bewildered and shocked and afraid. It was impossible for him, though, to divine the reasons for his fear, so he climbed back into the bed. He pulled the covers tight and curled up his body as he had when he was a little boy and his mother had spoken too long of witches, goblins and bog lights. He slept with his teeth locked, to keep himself from crying out with the fear.

He passed the morning in a continuous effort to maintain control of himself, act as he should. After Joshua called him and he had shaved, bathed and dressed he went down to breakfast. All the family was there and their manner was very much the same as it had been at dinner last night. Jane was eating a tremendous plate of ham and eggs and fried potatoes, as were the others, and he did his best to eat the food, keep his eyes from her. Och, stop it, he thought. Act the man you're supposed to be. If later you have to talk to Josh, so you do. But don't disgrace him now.

They rode to church in two sleigh-loads, Mr. Shaw driving one, Joshua the other. Alan Kennard rode on the front seat of the leading sleigh with Mr. Shaw. "I'm not a man to break the Sabbath," Mr. Shaw said in a hurried voice. "But after dinner, do you think you could find your way clear to go into Cleveland with Joshua and get the equipment you need for the ladle operations?"

"Sure," he said. "Them chandlers are willin' to turn a dollar on Sunday as well as any other day. A fella I know down on lower Superior is our man."

Mrs. Shaw and Jane rode on the rear seat, and Mrs. Shaw leaned forward under the robes. "Have you explained to Mr. Kennard about the church?"

"I am doing so, my dear." Mr. Shaw shifted the whip to his left hand, ran the free hand down over the jerk of nerves in his cheek. "It's Congregational," he told Alan Kennard. "We attend regularly although we're not wholly in accord with their forms of worship. We hope very soon to have a new minister here, one of the real sort who has received his theological training in Scotland."

"Yes, sir," Kennard said dully. He was lost in last night, in Jane's wanton action and wild speech. Here she rode beside her mother as prim as could be, a small, fur-trimmed hat aslant over the narrow face, her hands in a huge muff. Maybe tonight, though, it might be Harry, the coachman, who was visited, or some man from the village she'd met at the church. Keep your mind off that. Steer with

the fact that after dinner you're going to Cleveland with Josh and
then you'll have a chance to talk.

The church was of plain white clapboard and poorly heated,
the people solemn. That was all that Alan Kennard noticed except
that Mr. Shaw called forth "Amen!" at certain points in the sermon
and the organ was off-key. His tension had greatly increased during
the service and it was all he could do to sit through the long and
formal dinner. Jane appeared to take particular care in speaking
to him, and once he recognized from Mrs. Shaw's covert, malevo-
lent glance that she was completely aware of what had happened
in the night. He grew sullen under her look; he almost put his
napkin down and left the room. But thought of Joshua restrained
him. Josh is your true friend. You've done enough now without
doing that. Wait, man. Be calm. You've been through worse.

Harry brought around the matched chestnuts and the cutter
for him and Joshua. Mr. Shaw stood on the doorstep fingering his
watch fob as they climbed in and arranged the robes. "We'll expect you back in time for supper," he said. "The team is fresh,
Joshua. Drive right along."

"Yes, sir," Joshua said. Then Harry jumped back from the chestnuts' heads and they sprang snorting along the driveway, snow
clots slung from their hooves a quick tattoo on the splash-board.
Alan Kennard smoked a cheroot Mr. Shaw had given him at the
end of dinner. He rarely smoked, and the heavy tobacco after the
rich dinner made him a little giddy. Sweat was on his forehead and
the bridge of his nose. He wanted to be any place but here, he
thought. Bejesus if in any way he wanted to tell Josh about last
night. But you must.

"Josh," he said in a hoarse voice," last night——"

"I know," Joshua Shaw said. He was reining the chestnuts
down to a steady trot on the shore road. "You don't have to tell
me."

"But, goddamn it, I do." His body trembled under the robes.

"No. All of us know. Mother, Father, Cottrell and Lucinda."

Alan Kennard brought himself to look around at his friend. He
wanted to put his hand on Joshua's shoulder, or Joshua's hand,
and he didn't dare. "I'm sorry. Jesus Christ, if I'm not. But I've been
too long at sea, I guess. Too long without women. So a woman,
anyone, your sister."

Joshua Shaw gazed down the hilly, winding road to Cleveland.

"You're hurting yourself by this," he said, "and of course you're hurting me. But me much less than yourself. Because y' see, Antrim, my sister has done it often before with other men. Back East, the thing reached the point where I couldn't bring my college-mates home from New Haven, and there were men from all over Litchfield County after her. She'd meet them in the woods, or in the forge at night, or in her room. With her, it doesn't matter."

"Why, Josh?" The words came breathily, in a kind of gasp from him. "Is she mad? Last night, I didn't want her. But she got into the bunk with me. She. . . ."

Joshua Shaw's face had gone a blank white; up around the cheekbones there were two small patches of scarlet where the blood congested. "No," he said, "she isn't mad. She's quite magnificently if terribly sane. The whole business is a contest of wills between her and Mother. Jane wants to be her own woman and Mother won't let her. In the end, I believe, Jane will win."

Joshua was silent. There was only the sound of the cutter, the slur of the runners over the snow, the vibratory mutter of the whiffle-tree, the harness wine and the thud of the chestnuts' hooves. "I might have told you," Joshua said. "I wanted to. Then I thought it best that you find out about us for yourself. Because I don't know the answer except that—" he was furiously blushing now, from his coat collar to his cap brim—"I'm for Jane. How great an artist she'll be, I have no idea. But she should be free from Mother. That's her right as I see it. What do you think?"

"Ah," Alan Kennard said, his voice partly strangulated with the impulse to weep, "I just bloody well don't know. It's fierce, that I can understand. How much can pride take, though, Josh?"

"A lot. What Jane did, or Mother did to Jane, drove us out of Litchfield County. And now. . . . But that's another story. Y' see, Mother wants to possess everything that comes within her life. She absolutely owns Cottrell, and just recently she's started taking over Lucinda, lock, stock and front sight."

"You say her folks were Puritans?"

"That's right."

"Back home in Antrim, they still call them Round Heads. I'm no man for the priests, but the Round Heads sure played hell in Ireland. They left the place awash in blood. A hard-case gang."

Joshua Shaw was panting like a man who had just climbed a long hill. "Yes. And day and night, year after year, she's after my father."

"Who's winning?"

"She is. He had his one respite in the war. He could go away then and restore his pride, prove himself to himself in battle. But at the end of it he had to come back to her. That's why last night he showed you his picture in uniform, and, while I'm on it, I guess that's why I showed you the family crest and the Artillery Company commission. We're proud of what's gone, we Shaws."

"We're friends, man. Tell me and tell me now. What can I do to help?"

Joshua Shaw moved to look fully into his face. "It's very difficult to say. Father has got us fixed up in all sorts of propositions in Cleveland. We can't get at our Mesabi ore yet, so he's signed a contract to use low-grade Pennsylvania stuff. Our coal is coming from there, too, and our limestone. We'll be paying freight rates that would make your teeth float if I told them to you. But Dad is the old style operator. Back East, the men he dealt with were all men he knew personally, and his father had known their fathers and so on."

"But not here, though."

"Goddamn it, no. Over in Cleveland this little fella, Rockefeller, is setting up a corporation idea that's going to change everything in business from top to bottom. He's pulling in firms one after the other, either forcing them in with him or driving them to the wall. He's got secret, preferential rates with the railroads. He buys cheaper, ships cheaper, sells cheaper than anybody against him. Maybe, before he's through, he'll take over all the country. Anyhow, he can kick the shins off a man like my father who thinks of being a gentleman first and in business afterwards."

"I don't go with that gentleman talk."

Joshua Shaw grimly smiled. "Neither do I. That's why I'm sticking around with Father. I want to give Rockefeller and the rest of his stripe a real run for their money. Our family knows how to make steel fine, and we should be able to learn how to ship and sell it in any sort of a market."

"Josh, I've been holdin' out on you," Alan Kennard said. Emotion so constricted his throat that he coughed violently. Then, before he went on, he spit elaborately out into the snow. "I think I know where there is a whole great brute lot of limestone that you fellas might use. Mind, I'm not sure, or I would ha' spoke before. But that ain't true. I was holdin' out—until I seen what kind your folks were, and seen you with them. I'm a man who's had more hard knocks than I need, and if your father, say, was to act high-tone to me, I'd never ha' said a word about the stuff."

"Quite right, too," Joshua Shaw said quietly. "Where is it, Antrim?"

"Up along the beach at a wee bit town called Patigowoc."

"That would be on the Bouche de Mouche River, on the Lower Peninsula in Michigan."

"You have it. Phelim and me was in there for a load of lumber a couple of months back. There was no doxies around for Phelim to chase, so I went ashore for a walk around. The Nickersons cut over that land a year or so ago. Jesus, but it's a fire trap now. But the stone, soft and yella-white, sticks right out of the underbrush at you. Limestone it must be, and acres and acres of it. You remember them books you told me to buy?"

Joshua nodded, watching him.

"One o' them says the average blast-furnace charge for one ton of pig iron, you need sixteen hundred pounds of coke and a thousand pounds of limestone. Now that makes limestone pretty damn' important, don't it?"

"It surely does."

"So would ye be interested, Josh? Would it help you and your family, and I mean. . . ." Alan Kennard stared away from his friend. A sudden start of tears had just come to the corners of his eyes. He soundlessly cursed himself for a weak fool. You act so out of shame. Because last night you were a stupid sod and slept with this man's sister. Josh has just got through telling you that this friendship in business is a lot of bilge. Slap the hatches on it. Get yourself straightened out, you who go blattin' around like a colicked calf.

"There's all sorts of limestone, Antrim," Joshua said slowly. "And all sorts of deals to be made on it. Do you know who owns this?"

"I don't, no."

"Do you know if there's been a survey on it?"

"That I don't, neither."

"Then I'd keep quiet about it until you've found out. There's no good in talking to Father; we're under contract already for what we need for the year's run. But go up there to Patigowoc when you leave us and check it again. Find the owner and see if the deed is clear. Then send me a letter and I'll come up and take samples. From then on, let's hope it's what we want."

"Right, bejesus." The chestnuts trotted over the slush of the outskirts of Cleveland now, the runners clacking, rasping on cobbles. Alan Kennard looked ahead, aware that a great deal of the heaviness was gone from his heart. "We can jump through the side door of the Weddell House and have a quick one. Just one, maybe two, before we go roust out that chandler. He's going to soak us double for it's being Sunday, and that's a fact."

Joshua smiled. "You want a drink," he said, "where you can stand in peace and know Mother isn't waiting just outside. Well, so do I. And, Antrim, when we get back home, don't give a thought to Jane. She—she only uses her men once."

Alan Kennard was sustained through that evening and night by the knowledge of the solidity of his friendship with Joshua. It allowed him to be calm at supper, and afterwards when the family gathered in the music room for Sunday service. Hymns were sung; Mr. Shaw read from the Thirty-fifth Psalm:

"Plead my cause, O Lord, with them that strive with me: fight against them that fight against me.

"Take hold of shield and buckler, and stand up for mine help.

"Draw out also the spear, and stop the way against them that persecute me: say unto my soul, I am thy salvation.

"Let them be confounded and put to shame that seek after my soul: let them be turned back and brought to confusion that devise my hurt.

"Let them be as chaff before the wind: and let the angel of the Lord chase them.

"Let their way be dark and slippery: and let the angel of the Lord persecute them.

"For without cause have they hid for me their net in a pit, which without cause they have digged for my soul."

The voice was sonorous, yet impassioned, and echo came back upon echo from the walls. Alan Kennard sat with his head lowered. He looked furtively at Mrs. Shaw, at Jane, then Joshua, Cottrell and Lucinda. Their faces seemed impassive; they seemed to show only the polite boredom of a Sunday night family service. But the servants had been called to be present and stood just within the doorway. Harry, the tall, bony-faced coachman, stood glowering as if the words Mr. Shaw read were directed straight at him. The cook and the maids were Irish, and the cook kept plucking at her lips as though about to break into tears.

It's cruel, Kennard thought. As cruel as they come. Harry

must ha' been in the bunk with her, Jane, and the servants know it. That cook will be packing her duds and on her way soon. She'll give the priest an earful next time at confession. But the one His Nibs is talking to is his own wife. . . .

Mr. Shaw snapped shut the brass buckled Bible. "Let us kneel and pray," he said.

The prayer was long and for Alan Kennard in the main unintelligible. It contained many Biblical illusions, usages of speech that were beyond his comprehension. He was grateful that his knees ached; he could think about them and not about this family or the meaning of the Bible passage or the wandering, secretly desperate prayer.

When Mrs. Shaw said "Amen" in the same instant with her husband, they all rose to their feet. The servants disappeared, Harry with a backward glance at Jane. Mrs. Shaw nodded to Lucinda. "Time for you to go to bed, child. Time for all of us." She turned to Kennard. "Would you mind if the women folk watched in the morning when you lift the ladles?"

"No, ma'am," he said, keeping his eyes steady on hers. "But it won't be much to see."

She gave him her unusual laugh. "You let us be the judge of that, Mr. Kennard."

There was no invitation to the library that night, no hasty nightcap. Mr. Shaw went upstairs with his wife, his footsteps heavy and stiff, his face remote with a look of inner, distant calculation. "How about you?" Joshua said to Alan Kennard. "You want to sit around and read the papers for a while?"

"No, not me," he said. "I'm ready for the bunk. That was quite a ride today, lad."

They climbed the stairs side by side, walked so along the hall to the door of Kennard's room. "You should get a good, sound sleep," Joshua said. "So long, Antrim."

"So long, lad," he said and entered his room. The door latch could be locked, he found, and he locked it, then undressed, got into bed and blew out the candle. He cursed when he remembered that he had forgotten to open the window, clambered out again. But with the window open he remained for some time there, resting against the frame. He didn't want to go back to bed. The bed made him think about Jane. From Jane, he knew, his thought would go on to Mr. Shaw, Mrs. Shaw and Joshua. And he couldn't help solve their problem. The whole thing was too goddamn' big for him. All he could tell himself was that it was bloody strange how that gray-haired old seagull could go ahead and wreck a good family. If he was His Nibs, he'd up and bust her one in the chops. Or he'd pack his gear and leave her, and to hell with her, the children, the house and the business, too. Every man had his own right to lead his life. But who are you to say? You've got little enough idea of how to get along yourself. Back in Antrim, you were just a lad; you had no way of telling what went on among the folks in the village. One thing alone, maybe, that always there was a slew more women around than men, like your own mother for instance, and a man could take his pick. Here, though, the style in America seems to be that a woman passes her husband all the orders, tells him every change of course he makes.

The wind was chill through the window. Kennard shuddered, abruptly conscious that he was very cold. He got into bed and drew the covers up, arranged himself for sleep. Thought of Jane kept him awake for another hour or so, and he began to understand vaguely why Joshua had taken her side. Then his mind slid around to the fashion in which he would rig and use the sheer-legs and the tackle in the morning. He fell asleep working out the formula for the breaking strain of three-and-a-half inch rope, five-eighths wire.

It was supposed to be difficult, he realized about eleven o'clock of the next morning. Still, for him it was simple. The gear was good. He had rigged it right. Joshua and the foreman, Grigor, had the hang of the job now, went right along with him. So all he wanted now was out of here.

He waited, though, standing a bit aside from the apex of the sheer-legs, really taking sharp pleasure from what he had done. The ox-spans had just started to pull on the first load. Their skinners thwacked them with the long goads, loudly wailed the commands.

Slack went out of the fresh, soft yellow Manila line he and Joshua had bought yesterday in Cleveland. The ox-spans were in rhythmic motion and the muscles of the immense fore and hind quarters quivered as they moved. A chittering came from the sheaves of the big wooden blocks at the head of the sheer-legs. The oxen moved more slowly; the ladle, broad wire straps passed around it, teetered, swayed widely, lifted a bit, was in the air.

The ox-skinners stared around, goaded their spans and yelled. They had the load; it was theirs now to slide down the ram, drag over the snow to the furnace. Grigor's men had watched in diffident silence, working only when they had received an order from him or Joshua. When the ladle swung into the air, though, and the ox-spans took it away, they gave a hoarse, cursing shout that was very much like a cheer.

Mr. Shaw came over to Alan Kennard. He held out his hand. "Very well done, sir. My congratulations and deepest thanks."

"Don't talk too fast," Alan Kennard said, liking the man but embarrassed by the language he used. "Let's see how the tackles cast off and if the next one can be h'isted as easy."

"I have no doubt about that."

"Sure, you don't." He left Mr. Kennard and went over to help Joshua and Grigor cast off the tackle lines, make ready for the next load. Then he spoke swiftly to Joshua. "I'll be getting out of here now," he said. "You and Grigor can handle the rest. You don't need me."

"But Mother's expecting you for luncheon."

Alan Kennard glanced over at the sleigh where Mrs. Shaw and Jane and Lucinda sat. They were erect and eager, hands lifted to their eyes in the clear sunlight as though at some game or tournament. "You come with me while I talk to your mother. You tell her I got to go, Josh. Tell her any goddamn' thing you want. But. . . ."

"I understand," Joshua said softly. "Where are you going, Patigowoc and the Bouche de Mouche?"

"That's right. I'm after that limestone land."

"Write me, then."

"I will."

They had been walking slowly towards the sleigh. They stopped beside it, uncovered their heads and bowed. "Mother, my friend is a busy man," Joshua said. "He insists that he must leave right away on reasons of business. And all I can say is that we're grateful to him and have kept him long enough."

"But of course." Mrs. Shaw's smile was suave. "It is a pleasure to have had you with us, Mr. Kennard. Thank you for all you have done for us."

"Thank you, ma'am, for your hospitality. It's been fine meetin' you, and the young ladies, too." He bowed to each of them in turn, put the derby back on his head with a light clopping sound. "I hope to see you again."

"It will be a pleasure," Mrs. Shaw said. Jane said nothing; her glance was away, off over the lake. "A pleasure," Lucinda said. "And next time you come, you must sing more for us."

"Thank you," he said, and took off the derby again, turned in the snow with Joshua. Mr. Shaw caught up to them when they were part way to the cutter and the blanketed chestnuts. "You're going?" Mr. Shaw said.

"I must, sir. I've got a job of me own to do."

"Certainly. But of course." Mr. Shaw slid a mitten over the spikes of the mustache, the goatee. "I had only hoped that you would have one more drink with an old soldier before you left."

"I'll be back, sir, if you'll have me."

Mr. Shaw didn't smile. "You must come." He drew off the mitten. "Goodbye. Good luck, and a great deal of thanks."

"Yes, sir," he mumbled, very eager to be away.

Joshua went with him as far as the cutter. "Harry will drive you to Cleveland," he said. "I'd better stay here with this."

"Sure you should. So long, Josh. I'm sorry—What I mean is, things will be better."

"Write me," Joshua said. His hand grip was prolonged and tense. Then, oddly, Joshua reached up and stroked his face. "Take care of yourself. We need you."

"Ah, to hell!" Alan Kennard said and got up into the cutter.

Harry spoke to him very little on the way into Cleveland. But when he did it was about Jane. "How'd you and her make out?" Harry said. "Was she hot for it, and all of a sudden cold?"

Alan Kennard didn't calculate the blow. He simply swerved on the front seat of the cutter next to Harry and struck the coachman a short and hooked punch to the side of the jaw. Harry lost both reins and whip. He lurched sidewise out of the cutter and into a snowdrift. Kennard had time to look down at his thrashing feet and legs before the chestnuts bolted. They ran for several miles. Kennard hung on and cursed them and cursed Harry. He stretched down finally and seized the reins, backed and turned the cutter, went back for Harry.

Harry stood wide-legged in the road. He spit blood and waved his hands. Alan Kennard stared at him, the hatred a galling force that compressed the words upward, out. "Get in, ye dirty son of a sow," he told Harry. "Don't say a word to me or by the Jesus I'll beat the brains loose from your stupid skull. Y' hear me? I'm a friend of Josh Shaw's, a true friend. Get in, I said!"

Harry got in moaning. "Shall I drive?" he said.

Alan Kennard handed him the reins and whip. He didn't look at Harry or speak to him again until they were in Public Square in

Cleveland. Then, when he was down from the cutter, he pointed to the blue-green lump on Harry's jaw. "Tell them back in Bellport," he said, "that you got that in a barroom here. Ye don't, the next time I see you, you'll have no jaw."

Harry lashed at him savagely with the whip, but Kennard was ready for that. He had already ducked, was leaping to the curb. He heard the whicker of the whip lash, then Harry's cursing, the grate of the cutter's runners as it was turned. After that he paid no attention. His tremendous and consuming desire was to get to Patigowoc and the limestone land. Only then, he knew, would he really be able to do something for Joshua or himself.

Patigowoc was miserable in the lock of midwinter. The frame hotel that had been built when this was prime timber country was shut, as was the saloon next door. The single street looked mean, depressing as Alan Kennard entered it with Jake Reem, the local postman. Reem carried the mail from Napta City, the rail-head and county seat, to Patigowoc, and he had told Kennard that he could stay at his house.

"Old lady ain't much of a provider," Reem said, "but it's better'n you eatin' outa cans at the general store. Town's fell to pieces since the Nickersons left. Never was much anyhow."

Alan Kennard was in a dour mood, not given to speech. He didn't like the look of the town and now he didn't like the idea of having come to it. This for him was a strange kind of business. He was no land-grabber, no fella to go shuffling and snooping around after titles and deeds. But Reem regarded him curiously.

"You want," Reem said, "I'll take your bag over to the house. That's it, the third one on the left. Then I got to put up my horse. I'll be over to the store, though, right away with the mail."

"Sure," Alan Kennard said and reluctantly drew the horse blanket that had served as robe from around his legs. Barn swallows pecked over the few horse droppings in the street as he walked towards the store. All the houses had hay piled against them at ground level to protect them from the snow, and Monday morning's wash hung stiffly frozen, flapping on the lines. A wooden Indian, his features long since defaced by some drunken shanty boy, was on the porch of the store; snuff, tobacco and patent medicine signs were nailed around the door which had a felt weather stripping. He pushed it open and the odours of dried prunes, peppermint candy, snuff spittle, drying wool and a hot-burning wood stove were in his nostrils.

Eight men and a woman were in the store. They all stood still and looked at him. A young man with an anxious squint and black sateen sleeve guards was behind the counter. "Do anything fer you?" he said.

Shore-going folks, Kennard's subconscious told him. Then, as his conscious mind caught hold, make sense. "Yeah," he said. "You run the store?"

"So, I do." He was given a moist hand lightly powdered with flour. "Lars Keiberg is the name. But wasn't you in here last summer?"

Smart. A young Dane and he's smart. Must call himself a go-getter. Bet he plugged the shanty boys hard in their day. "That's right. Name of Alan Kennard. Mate of the schooner *Procyon*. We was in the river in August and November to pick up lumber."

"I was in Detroit in November," Keiberg said, as if in apology. "My wife was running the store."

Alan Kennard faced around at the group by the stove. The woman was making a semblance of inspecting some yard goods, but the men just stood and looked at him. They'd stand there, he realized, until they'd learned his business, and if they didn't Keiberg would tell it to all the village within an hour. "I was thinkin'," he said, "that my partner and me—he's skipper of the schooner—we might make a deal to haul the timber that's down along the river. Who owns the land there?"

"Well, a fella name o' Sigurd Svenson," Keiberg said cautiously. "Swedish fella. But he's gone now."

"Where to?"

"Well, we don't know. Him, his wife and kid, they cleared out right after Svenson he sold his timber rights. That's about four years ago."

"Goin' onto five," a man at the stove said.

"Goin' onto five," Lars Keiberg said. "Anything you'd like here, Mister Mate?"

"A tin of them sardines and a pair of shoe packs. I guess nobody'd mind if I went down and took a look at that land, would they?"

"Shucks, no," two men at the stove said in chorus. Lars Keiberg said, "Ain't nobody lived on it since the Svensons left. Fella'd have a hard time finding the boundary lines, even. You need a notary public, I'm one, and there's a public surveyor over to Napta City."

"Sure," Alan Kennard said. But that was the extent of his

patience. He put on the shoe packs, paid his bill in silence. Outside on the porch he met Jake Reem with the mail sack. "You goin' down there, huh?" Reem said. "Ain't much to see except slash and more slash. Old Svenson place is on the left-hand side of the road. Kids broke inta it and it's in kinda bad shape. Missis Svenson, she was Ojibway. Usta have a lot of them Ojibways around here. Great fish-eaters. Fishin' all the time."

Kennard held his street shoes out to him with rigid hands. "You mind," he said, "stowing those with my bag when you get back to your house? I want to get down to the river while the light lasts."

"You wait just a few minutes," Reem said, "and I'll go with you. I'm acquainted out there."

Alan Kennard didn't answer, moved more rapidly down the street. He had heard around the world that Irish were curious folk, that they talked a lot, drunk or sober. But you take a Midwest town in the winter. You take a town like this and you feel as if a thousand fellas were talking to you at once and all of them with nine pairs of eyes a foot high in their heads. Couldn't they let a man be?

His nerves were quiet by the time he came to the river road. He looked out over the Bouche de Mouche and the slate-dull sweep of Huron and with the lake wind in his face he felt better. Partridge drummed in the underbrush where he passed. Juncoes flew up in veering flight, and he heard the racket-rack, racket-rack of a wood-pecker in a dead pine.

Wind had flung the snow from the limestone outcroppings along the river shore. He stooped and touched it, picked up samples and put them in his pockets. Then he swung inland, wallowing through drifts and climbing small ledges. All of it was limestone under the thin topsoil. He marked ridge after ridge where it showed, and it must go on, he calculated, for an area of several hundred acres at least.

But Svenson, the man who owned the land, was gone and the men at the store didn't know where. They had no reason to lie; there was no reason why they should. As far as they could figure, he was only here after what timber was left after the Nickersons had scalped the pine. Maybe he could learn more from Keiberg when he went back to the store, or from Reem while he had supper at his place. But he still could take a look at Svenson's house.

It was on the river road and at the top of quite a steep hill. Beeches and a few oaks, a horse chestnut and a sugar maple grew around it. Once it had been a simple log cabin with a slab and sod roof, and that had probably been built by the wife's folks, the Ojibways. But Svenson had made it pretty neat, put in windows and an iron-hinged door with a porcelain knob, laid a regular white pine floor and a brick chimney, covered the inside walls with newspapers, then wall paper. ╳

But the stove and all the furniture were gone. A rusted piece of pipe swayed dismally in the stove hole with the pressure of the lake wind. Broken window lights let in the wind to stir the litter on the floor. There were stale, dry piles of defecation in the corners left by bums or village kids, and piles of sodden newspapers stripped from the walls that bums had used to sleep on for the night. The bedrooms showed the pallid marks of pictures on the walls, a chafed spot made by a bedstead.

Alan Kennard felt a vague sense of grief, of defeat. These folks had left for good. They weren't going to come back. Still, in a corner of the smaller bedroom he found a tattered *McGuffey's Reader*. The pages had been gnawed at by wood mice, and rain had leaked upon it from the roof. The child's writing was almost illegible. It said: *Minna Svenson. Her Book.* Then, below, and obviously written at a later date in a firmer hand: *Chicago*.

"Bejesus, then," Kennard muttered against the quavering of the stove pipe, "you're bound for Chicago. It's where this family went. The lass wrote it so."

He found out only a small amount more about the Svensons that night as he had supper with Jake Reem and his wife, talked with Lars Keiberg in the store. Svenson had been the village school teacher; he had taught school for years here after coming out from Sweden. His wife was a pure-blood Ojibway, and there had been Ojibways on the land along the river before there was a village. They used to say the land belonged to them, but they'd all moved away except the one Svenson married. Svenson was smart. He had filed title to the land in his own name over in Napta City at the county courthouse.

"How much?" Alan Kennard said.

"Mebbe two hundred acres, mebbe a bit more," Keiberg said. "But I notarized the deed before Svenson filed it, yaas, so I did. You want a notary any time, I'm one."

"Sure," Kennard said. "You got any idea, though, where the family went?"

"Chicago. That's what they was sayin'. Nobody knows for certain, though." Lars Keiberg took a chew of snuff, worked it against his right upper gum. His eyes in the shaded lamplight were wide in their scrutiny of Kennard. "All the timber land around here ain't in Svenson's name. I got some. I can get more. You like for to make a deal?"

Be careful, Alan Kennard thought. Be ruddy well careful. This bucko is knife-sharp. "Not now," he said. "First, I have to talk to my partner. Carmody's his name and he's down in Buffalo, waitin' to hear from me. Him and me will be back up here later. Then we'll likely make some business with you. Now give me a sack of them peppermint drops. Bill Reem's wife looks to have the sweet tooth good."

"She has," Keiberg said solemnly as he filled the sack. "You mind if I close up the store?"

"You go ahead." His dime was down on the counter. "I'll see you in the morning, mister."

But he was up at dawn with Bill Reem, rode with Reem to Napta City. He wanted to check that Svenson deed in the court-house, he had decided during the night. If it was right, then he was going on to Chicago. Two hundred acres of limestone was a lot. Enough, sure as hell, to put him in operation so he could supply Josh Shaw. . . .

The deed was in the Napta City courthouse. It was in the name of Sigurd Svenson and for two hundred and thirty-four acres running parallel to and inland from the Bouche de Mouche River. For a two dollar bill to the clerk, he also discovered that the taxes had been paid by Svenson from an address on Halsted Street in Chicago. But for the last three years the taxes were in arrears.

"Fella might be dead," the clerk said. "Or he might be broke. Sooner or later, though, the county's goin' to put up the land for public sale. We ain't the kind to wait for our money too long."

"Right," Alan Kennard said softly. "I get you."

It took him long, gritty, uncomfortable hours to reach Chicago by train. He was hungry and dispirited when he arrived. The doubt had again returned to him; he couldn't bring himself to believe fully that this was the right thing for him to do. But you're here, Alan. And what else is there for you to do? If you want to get ahead in America, you must cut and run for yourself, not wait for life to push you along in the fashion of Phelim.

The janitor at the Halsted Street address was reasonably talk-ative. He told Kennard that, yes, he had known the Svenson family, he had known them well. But Svenson had died three years ago.

"Come out here from some place in Michigan with a pocketful of money. Usta be a schoolteacher. Yeah, that's him. Put the whole shebang in Hyde Park real estate. They took him, them sharpers. He dropped apart just like that One Hoss Shay. Then his heart went bad on him. Died right upstairs here. The wife and the young girl moved out after that. The wife was some kinda Indian. Never said a word to you unless you spoke first." The janitor squinted. "You ain't an Indian, are ya, mister?"

"No." Alan Kennard's face was somber. "I'm a Finn."

He went back to Buffalo after that. He sat in the furnished room he had shared with Phelim and read books or he walked the docks, went down to Black Rock to take a look at the *Procyon*. Several times, he started a letter to Josh Shaw. But there was no good writing, he knew, not until he had some definite word about the ownership of that land.

It was in the second week of March that he got the black bordered card telling of Maumee Mike Jacobs' death. Although his savings were much lower than he liked, he bought a new black suit downtown, took the first train he could get.

Maumee Mike's mother and father and relatives were to him oddly self-contained during the funeral ceremony. He was accustomed to the passionate, terrific grief of peasant Antrim, the laments and wailing and tearing of hair, of flesh, the drinking and eating, the constant note of emotional abandon. These German-American people in their stiff and correct clothes appeared to have no outward feeling for the dead. He was the only one who wept over Mike's coffin in the parlor.

But there was an honor guard of the local GAR post that accompanied them to the cemetery. The clayey earth flung back from the grave lay red against the snow where the guard formed to fire the volley. The men were no longer young; their faces were gray in the misted sunlight. When the reverberation of the volley rolled back through the valley, crows cawed on the branches of the willows. The sound was as harsh as the weeping of Maumee Mike's mother. She clung to her husband's arm and spoke to him in a low voice in German. Alan Kennard heard her repeat Mike's name, then the bugler began to blow "Taps."

Kennard had the thought that never before had he listened to such poignant music. It's not only that your friend has died. When he went, a part of you went, too. You've tried hard in this country, Alan. You've done your level best. But it's a great place and a cruel one. You needed a man like Mike to help you, show you the way. Now you're out of soundings and off bearings. You don't know where you're bound or what you'll do. Phelim, the wild one, he's no aid to you unless he's right alongside. Sure, oh, sure, you'd go to Josh, but all the family's there. And what can you do with him, empty-handed as you are? For certain, you're no man for the iron trade. It's all you are is a poor, miserable lout of a sailor without a ship.

He sat alone in the kitchen with Old Man Jacobs after the relatives were gone. Mrs. Jacobs had fed them, given them coffee cake and coffee; a bottle of *schnapps* was on the table. Old Man Jacobs looked at him from red-rimmed eyes. "Let's talk simple, Antrim," he said. "I'm tired. Soon, too, I must go to my wife."

"So what would ye say?" Alan Kennard said. He was heavy-hearted, knew in advance the words the old man would say.

"The doctors and the funeral got it all from us. All but the farm and the schooner. The farm I must keep for my woman, for after I'm gone. But the *Procyon*—she must be sold. You got the money?"

"No."

"Your friend, Carmody?"

"No."

"You can raise the money for her?"

"I greatly doubt it." Alan Kennard rose to his feet. He took the old man's puffed, rheumatic hand. "Sell her, Pop. There's other schooners for such men as Carmody and me. But, if ye like, I'll tend to the sale for you."

The old man shook his head. He uncorked the *schnapps* bottle and poured a drink for Kennard and one for himself. Then he clinked glasses. "It's enough that you should lose her. Good luck, Antrim."

He wasn't sure why he did it, but he went to Chicago instead of Buffalo after he left the Jacobs' farm. No hope remained to him that he might come upon the Svenson family, make a deal for the limestone land. But he vaguely realized that he had spent too much time in Buffalo, and anyhow the *Procyon* was there. Chicago was a town he didn't know too well; he'd better get the hang of it. And in the season he could catch a mate's job aboard some schooner.

That thought made him grimly laugh. His savings were down to three hundred dollars. Even Phelim, carousing around with the Lime Street lasses, might come back with more of his pay-off left. Ah, to hell, to hell with it all. He wrote a letter to his landlady in

Buffalo asking her to send on the rest of his things, and another to Joshua Shaw giving Joshua his address. Then he bought himself a pair of overalls and a second hand mackinaw, started to look for work.

The foreman of a construction job on Diversey Street gave it to him. "Carryin' brick," the foreman said, "and two dollars a day is the pay. Right wid ye?"

"Right with me. So when do I start?"

"Now, me lad. There's yer hod. Get to it."

He had carried his sixth hod up onto the scaffolding where the bricklayers worked before the memory came to him. Then he cursed aloud and the bricklayers looked around at him. But he was on his way back down the ladders, saying over to himself what the old timer had told him outside the Commissioner's in Cleveland when he had got his license.

"There's just one thing you can't do with them," the old timer said. He pushed his splayed hand out towards the new license in its tight roll and ribbon. "You can't eat 'em."

CHAPTER FIVE

The winter was for him dull and miserable. He lived alone in a cheap furnished room, ate badly, slept worse, and when he drank to escape his boredom, he entered into moods of profound depression. He told himself that he was getting nowhere. His luck was out. All the fine dreams had fallen apart, and here he was on the beach, another defeated man whose pride was bitter in his mouth.

Even in the spring when he sailed as mate in a Chicago-owned schooner he still felt no satisfaction with his life. He should have the limestone land, be on the way to put over the deal with Joshua and ready to become of some consequence ashore. Instead, he sailed in a goddamn' work-house ship that took any kind of cargo and had as master an old, soured Prince Edward Islander who left him in charge of the loading and discharging in each port. His time away from her was extremely limited, and in many ports he had no desire to go further than the dock. The ports either bored him or tempted him too much to give up his trade as a sailor.

He developed an interior thought pattern in the image of a dark cave from which there was small chance of escape. While the season passed, the habit grew upon him more and more to keep silent among his shipmates. He spoke hardly ever except in the way of business to the young second mate, and with the captain he was as cold-mannered and formal as any clipper ship mate. The Prince Edward Islander had a blue-veined nose, a raucous voice. It was his pleasure when on deck to shout every command.

Alan Kennard disregarded him. He retreated back in his mind upon the fact that he was an excellent sailor, just as good if not better than the captain. His one delight during the season was to exert his seamanship, apprehend any order the captain might give him. The captain regarded him first with anger, then with respect and understanding. A tacit truce was established between them; they let each other be most of the time and the captain took out his wrath on the second mate.

They were in Buffalo in September with a cargo of wheat and

had just gone alongside the elevators to discharge when Kennard saw Phelim Carmody. The Liverpool man stood jaunty in a double-breasted liver brown suit and a lighter brown derby hat. He smoked a cheroot and his free hand was pushed deeply into his coat pocket. The sunlight through the dusty air magnified his body, and the gulls swerved about him as though he were some heroic statue. Alan Kennard swore softly and jumped down from the schooner's 'midships rail.

"Hey, you," the captain yelled after him from the poop. "You got dischargin' to do."

Kennard answered him forcibly and obscenely. Then he joined Phelim. They thumped each other on the back, held each other by the arms and closely stared.

"Hard times?" Phelim said.

"Not what I like, no. That old bastard works me like a lascar. But what would you be doing, Phelim?"

"Mate in a Pickands and Mather steamer. Carrying ore. I wrote you from the other side, then when I got back out here."

"My landlady in Chicago don't forward any mail, and we haven't been in there in months." Kennard paused. He sensed something new, something different about Phelim. He had the sudden impulse to leave him before he learned what it was. "You know that Maumee Mike is dead," he said slowly.

"So," Phelim said. "I heard it here in the port when I got back. Then I got word that you were sailing mate of some jackass schooner. It was after that I lined up the steamer job."

"You like the steamers?"

Phelim Carmody looked down at his cheroot. He brushed the ash off the tip with a fingernail, started to relight it. Then he pitched it away, over the string-piece of the dock. "Yeah, I do," he said. "They're regular. They get you into port when you're supposed to get in. Y' see, Alan, I married a lass whilst I was back in England. Bejaisus if I didn't."

"You dog!" Kennard said and laughed at him. But it was the reason for Phelim's confident bearing, he realized, for the calmness and steadiness which were now a part of the man. "Who is she?"

"A Birkenhead lass. But as Irish as me. Her folks went out there in the Famine. I met her in Lime Street one night when I was less sober than I should ha' been and I took her for a doxy and she slapped me face. For a bloody fact, she knocked me flat on me ass. So I gets up and I asks her pardon."

"And the next thing you know you're married."

"For a fact."

A jealousy that was a consequence of his loneliness, his feeling of frustration, brought the words to Alan Kennard. "What's her name? Where is she now?"

"Aileen's her name. It was Aileen Meagher before I married her. Right now, she's up at the Genesee Hotel waitin' for me. She come down from Cleveland when I wrote her the ship was putting in here. We got a little flat in Cleveland. But I wanted to line you up, bucko, and I heard you were due in today. Will you come up to the hotel later and have a bit of scoff with me and Aileen?"

Alan Kennard blushed and was aware that he did and tried to stop it. "Good Christ," he said, "things ain't the way they used to be, Phelim. Your wife comes down special from Cleveland, you don't want to spend your time gamming around with some old shipmate. You probably got to get back aboard pretty soon."

"You let me worry about when I got to get back aboard," Phelim said. "And what you're talking about, there's all winter for that. You come alongside the hotel at six o'clock, see? When you meet Aileen, you call her Peggy. That's what I call her and she likes it fine."

"All right, then," Kennard said. "So shove off out of here before one of them gulls ups and fouls your hat."

He was thinking of Phelim and Phelim's wife when he went back over the side. But the captain rested there to meet him. "What kind of language was that you used to me, mister?" the captain said.

"Ah, to hell," Kennard said. He gazed hard at the captain. "You want me to pack my gear?"

The nostrils of the blue-veined nose fluttered, drew inward. "No," the captain said. "But it sets a bad example for the crew. Take over from the second mate now, will you, mister, and when she's empty see that her rose-boxes are clean and the holds swept down?"

"Sure," Alan Kennard said. He laughed. "But at five o'clock I knock off. I'm bound uptown for dinner."

Phelim and his wife were in the bar when he got to the Genesee Hotel. The light was a bit dim and for a moment he couldn't distinguish her features. Then he saw that she was a true Irish blonde, and tall and lovely. Her hair was the color of corn husks just after they had been touched by the first frost. Her skin was the famous Irish milky white, her nose small, narrow, slightly snubbed, and her underlip full. Her eyes, as far as he could determine their shade, were clear blue, set beneath wide brows. A thrill of animal excitement ran through him; muscles and nerves tightened in his groins. She had fine breasts, rounded arms and a magnificent body. Here was a woman to give Phelim all he needed in the bunk and more.

She spoke with the lilting Liverpool Irish accent, and the sound of it, her beauty and her sheer physical magnetism entranced him. He hadn't been near a woman in months; it shocked him to discover how great his need was. Then he forgot that as he began to tell her stories of the days when he and Phelim had been shipmates.

Phelim sat back and drank and quietly listened. His wife drank drink for drink with him, and Alan Kennard hurried his own, wanting to remain gay and hold her attention. When Phelim spoke of dinner, Kennard was already drunk. He fought the alcohol grimly, but his tongue was thick, his lips numb, and he had the impression that his skull steadily contracted, creating a piercing pain in his brain.

He had only vague knowledge of where they had dinner and what they ate. The food was hot, though, and it sobered him some, and at the end of dinner Phelim said, "Come on back to the hotel with us, Antrim. I've got a bottle in the room and I want to have Peggy hear ye sing."

"It's the Antrim folk who sing fine," Aileen Carmody said. "That will be a pleasure. Do come along."

"Sure I will," Kennard said. He was wondering desperately if he could sing at all. Memory of the Shaw family, of Jane and Joshua and all of them had sprung abruptly into his thought. Jane's image stayed with him. He linked Jane somehow with this blonde, beautiful woman. If Jane could be like her, now. If only Jane. . . . You're drunk, you joker. Sober up. Get your feet under you and walk straight. Would you make a fool out of yourself, out of Phelim and his wife?

Phelim and Aileen sat on the side of the bed in the hotel room. He sat on a chair facing them, his collar opened, his tie knot loosened. Phelim passed the bottle and it was the real Irish, stung the throat like a gigantic hornet. "Sing, Antrim," Phelim said. "Give us 'The Swallowtail Coat.'"

"No, I won't," he said strangely. He was being lifted and swung and hurled by the whiskey. He put his hands down on the frame of the chair to keep himself from falling to the floor. "Want to talk to you. Tell you something. . . . You, Phelim, and you. 'Peggy,' he said for me to call you. That I will—'Peggy'. . . . Phelim, ye remember Josh Shaw?"

"That I do," Phelim said. He didn't pass the bottle any more. He had placed it on the floor beside the bed, the coverlet over it. Kennard blinked at it and wet his lips with the end of his tongue. He could use another drink. Maybe that would stop him from talking about the Shaws, about the limestone land and the widow and her daughter. But damn him if he could stop now.

"Well, I went last winter there to Bellport to visit Josh," he said in a blurred, yet deliberate voice. "I met Josh's mother, his father, his brother and sister and sister-in-law. The whole kit and kaboodle o' them. And what a bitch's brew I walked inta. Excuse the word, Peggy. Excuse the word."

His head went forward to his chest and he was wordless for perhaps a minute. But Phelim and his wife were also still. They waited for him, he slowly realized. You're their guest. Phelim's your old shipmate and friend. He started to speak again and went on to tell them the story, all of it, saving nothing, not even about Jane or what Joshua had to say of his sister or how Harry had talked and he had knocked Harry from the cutter.

He had no recollection later of the space of time he took to speak. But he remembered that without interruption and without more than an infrequent grunt from Phelim he told of the Bouche de Mouche limestone land, the Svenson family, the unpaid taxes.

He felt better when he was through, sobered and quiet and at his ease. His eyes raised to them on the bed and he found they looked at him with an almost impersonal kind of curiosity, as though he were no longer Phelim's old friend. "A most peculiar do," Phelim said. He stood up from the bed. "But ye should get along back to the ship, Alan. In a few hours I've got to go aboard me own. Write me, you donkey, care o' the company in Cleveland. And when the season's done, come and see us there. Right, Peggy?"

"Right indeed," she said. She had risen to her feet and she walked to where Alan Kennard still sat. She drew him upward to his feet, her hands strong and firm upon his arms. "Goodnight," she said. "Don't think too hard of the limestone and the rest. You'll make out fine in America."

"Thank ye," he said. He was incapable of saying anything more. Phelim had turned and begun to unbutton his coat and vest. Kennard stumbled forth into the hall, and the key clacked as the door was locked from within. They may not like you for being soused, he thought, but at least you're square with yourself. No holding out this time. You told them the truth, man, and when you did it you proved yourself a true friend to Phelim.

It was hashed up badly, the way you explained. Go back in the fall and see them, though, and give them the thing full straight. And, too, you must go over to Bellport and see Josh. He's still your good friend. Now put your feet down, one and then the other. This is the street that'll take you to the ship. Stop tacking so bad. You're a lad who can walk all right while carrying a load.

That was a bad fall on the Lakes. Gale followed gale down from the Northwestern flatlands. There was ice in all the ports to be thrashed through laboriously as the ship was brought to dock, and outside when the gales blew full, there was ice on deck, and on the halyards, the sheets, every bit of working gear. The old Prince Edward Island captain took to his cabin and emerged from it only as the vessel was entering or leaving port. He drank a great deal and by the middle of November he had pneumonia.

Alan Kennard nursed him as best he could; after all, the old fella was a real sailor. But in each port the young men who formed the crew got off the ship. They had various pretexts that meant the same thing: they wanted to be at home with their families. He cursed them out for what they were, still they didn't rise to anger in answer. Their reason for sailing was the simple one of making money for the farm. They'd pay off on the steam thrashing machine, or buy a new plow, another team, a hundred more Plymouth Rocks, a boar to take care of the sow, the new parlour set like the stuff down in Flint and Kent's. They possessed no sailorman pride. He had listened to them through the season and should have known. They weren't sailors and didn't pretend to be. It was just the miserable, lonely apes like him who were.

He picked up a few replacements in Detroit, two men more in Port Huron. They were the vagrants of the Lakes who in the height of the season jumped from ship to shore after one trip, making just enough money for another good, long drunk. He took them out of the back rooms of beer saloons, the doorways of gospel halls and rooming houses where they hadn't paid the rent. He kept them sober and he made them sail and he brought the schooner into Chicago with the Prince Edward Islander comatose in his cabin.

The owners of the schooner had their offices down on La Salle Street. They were quite surprised when he explained the situation to them, and they went so far as to say they would send an ambulance out for the captain. "You have your master's papers, Kennard?" Froler, the senior partner, said.

"I'll have them by spring."

"Then consider yourself the new master of her," Froler said. "And hold yourself ready to outfit her and sail her for us."

"I'd like that in writing," Alan Kennard said; "if you don't mind." He felt no particular elation over the advancement. Master of a schooner, hell, he'd figured that for himself a long time back. It didn't count for much. The schooners would soon be gone. They were being pushed off the water all the time. Steamers got the trade these days, the kind in which Phelim sailed. And even skipper of one of them wasn't what he was after. He wanted that limestone land.

Froler punched the button of a hand bell on top of his roll-front desk. A skinny clerk in an alpaca coat appeared at the door. "Write out a contract for Mr. Kennard," he said. "He's going master of the *Aroosta* in the spring. Make it the same as the old one."

"But for twenty-five more a month," Kennard said. "I'd like an even two hundred.

"No good," Jaeckel said. Jaeckel was the other partner, a younger man with a florid face and sideburns. "We can't afford it, Kennard. The money ain't in schooners any more. You take one-seventy-five a month from us or you take nothing."

Alan Kennard looked down at his hands, cracked from exposure, calloused with the weeks of hauling lines when there had been no-body else aboard to haul. He should get angry, he thought. He should get to his feet and tell this pair of La Salle Street dudes to stick their contract up with the corners out. But he wasn't going to. No, not him. He was scared. He knew where he could grab another job as mate, but not another as master. And he needed money. The bloody damn money. Without that, he was whipped for good.

"I'll take the one-seventy-five," he said.

"All right," Froler said. He jerked a finger. "Wait in the outer office. Sign your copy when the clerk gives it to you. We'll mail you yours."

They didn't shake hands with him, and they didn't wish him luck or say goodbye. He simply picked up his hat and walked out into the outer office where the clerks sat on their stools in the same postures as seagulls along a harbour breakwall. The clerks were beaten men, subdued and withdrawn. Give him another half dozen years and he wouldn't be any different.

He bought himself a pint of whiskey after he left Froler and
Jaeckel and Company. He was supposed to go back to South Chicago and the ship. But bugger the ship. Let the second mate tend
to her a while longer. They were all through for the season anyhow.

He drank the whiskey walking back and forth along the lake
front. His musing mood led him far down the dunes. He stumbled
among driftwood and through crab grass. His shoes filled with
sand; several times he was chilly struck by spindrift flicked up from
an incoming wave on the beach.

"Master," he kept saying to himself. "Master of a vessel after
all your waitin', workin', and it don't mean a damn' thing to you.
Ah, to hell. Get out of here and back aboard. You're going sour.
Soon you'll be as bad as the old Prince Edward Islander."

He floundered back over the dunes in the copper-ribbed, magenta dusk and found a hansom cab on Wabash Avenue. "Take me
to South Chicago," he told the driver. "Over to the docks on the
river."

"You know what that's going to cost ya?" The driver leaned part
way down from the box.

"Don't give a goddamn," he said. He was immediately belligerent, grabbed the hem of the driver's overcoat. "You drive me, that's
all." Then his mood inexplicably changed. He took the pint from
his pocket. "Here. Have a snort."

The driver squinted at the bottle. "Not enough there fer to wet
a chippy's throat," he said. "You better keep it, mister. Get in,
get in."

"Ah, to hell!" Alan Kennard said and flung the pint into the
gutter. He got in, sprawled across the horsehair-smelling seat, fell
asleep. But before he slept he decided that when he had laid up the
schooner he would go to Cleveland, then to Bellport. It was important, he drowsily realized. He had to see Phelim and Peggy, and
Josh and the whole damn Shaw family. They're your friends. And
you're so lonely it hurts. It hurts bad.

Phelim and Peggy Carmody had a second floor flat in a re-
modeled house on Ontario Street. It was right past the Doan
Tabernacle where Moody and Sankey had held their revivalist
meetings, and Alan Kennard was reminded of the singing, the impassioned shouting as he came to it from the Superior Street via-
duct. Give you something to talk about besides your own troubles,
you dumb-head. Be decent with the folks this time and when
Phelim passes the bottle don't go drinking it like you was mad.

Peggy answered the door. She wore a loose wrapper and a house-cap over her upward-drawn hair, and Kennard saw at once that she was pregnant. It made him glad, brought him in a fashion he didn't clearly understand closer to them. "And so how is Mrs. Phelim?" he said gaily, holding forth to her the pound box of chocolates he had bought down at the Union Depot.

"Fit as a fiddle but getting bigger every day," she said. "I'll have a son for this man not long from now."

Phelim stood behind her in his shirtsleeves. He looked squarely into Kennard's eyes, then took his hand in a strong grip. "How's Antrim?" he said.

"I've been better," Alan Kennard said, "and I've been worse. In the spring, though, I go master of a schooner name of *Aroosta*. What's with Phelim?"

"Me, I'm no more than a Pickands and Mather stiff," Phelim said. "The pay's steady, the job's all right, so I don't complain."

There was a turkey carpet on the parlour floor. The furniture was fumed oak, and the table had a marble top. A hand tinted photograph of Mount Vesuvius was on the wall and a rubber plant was near the window. It looked like the stuff you saw in the window at Flint and Kent's, Kennard thought. Phelim had sure enough done all right. Snug as a bug in a new mattress.

"Sit down, man," Phelim said. "Take a load off your feet." He gave Kennard another square glance. "What about a drink?"

"Sure, I'd like one. But—" he grimaced—"nothing like the last time, Phelim."

They sat and drank whiskey and water while Peggy knitted a baby sweater. She glanced up at Kennard from time to time, and he was aware of the meaning of her scrutiny. *She wants to know if she can trust you, if you're truly Phelim's friend.* "You've seen them folks," she said, "the people who live out at Bellport?"

"Not since I saw you last, no," he said. "But I'm bound there after you've had your share of me."

"It's good to see you, you rascal," Phelim said. "Here we are, both sailin' the Lakes but all season long we don't meet. That's the bloody bad part of our life. A man has no time for his friends, or for his wife, even."

"Back up the cart!" Peggy said. She was smiling, but a small flush of color was along her throat. "You've had no complaints when it comes to me." She rose and put down her knitting, and Alan Kennard was once more impressed by her beauty despite the thickness of pregnancy. "Liver and onions and home-fried for supper. And you, Mister Mate, can go fetch a can of beer. But, Antrim, you can't go with him. You two'd get to drinkin' in the saloon and then me supper would be ruined. You stay with me, see how a meal is cooked ashore."

"It's hen-pecked I am," Phelim said. "Beat blue from the rough talk she gives me. Watch out whilst you're with her in the kitchen. Peelin' the spuds is where you'll end up."

"I'll take my chances with her," Alan Kennard said. "Get along, will you? I've a thirst for beer on me as big as a house, and after supper I'd sing you a song."

"Then I'm gone," Phelim said. "I'm gone in the minute."

Peggy Carmody was serious-faced when she and Kennard stood beside the range in the kitchen. "Antrim," she said; "you're my man's best friend. Tell me straight. Are you in love with the Shaw gell out to Bellport?"

"Bejesus," he muttered, surprised by her forthright honesty. "No, I'm not. So far as I know, anyhow, Peggy. It was just once that I passed a night in the bunk with her. But, why do you ask?"

"Because there's talk here in the city about them, and strange talk it is. They go about with the big people, them such as Phelim's bosses. Hoity-toity. But the girl, she's been seen in hotels around the Square with drummers and worse. The brother, Cottrell, comes in drunk as a flounder although they say that at home he has a small daughter."

Alan Kennard didn't want to meet her eyes. Her gaze was too direct, too searching. He looked around the small kitchen that had obviously been painted by Phelim, at the deal table and chairs, the copper water boiler, a fly that had chosen to crawl up behind the window curtain and die.

"Look, Peggy," he said in a harsh voice. "The last time I was with you, I was drunk."

"Soused to the gills." She gave him a quick smile, and he knew that it was meant to lessen his nervous tension. But his emotion was too great to be restrained. He said, "I don't know what I told you then, and not that it matters. Josh Shaw is my good friend, though, all but as dear to me as Phelim. The old man I like, too, and Cottrell. His wife's a fine girl; she plays the harp like an angel."

"As for Jane? Jane and the old lady?"

"They're hard news. But do I go back out there, which I will, I'll keep clear o' them. It's Josh I want to see most of all, him and the old man. So tell me now, and you won't be hurting my feelings. What would they be saying here in detail about the family?"

Peggy Carmody shook her head. She was slicing bacon, sliding strips of it into a frying pan. "Best that you find out for yourself, Antrim, or have your pal tell you. This much I can say—in all of it, Josh Shaw comes out well. There's Phelim at the door. Go let him in, and no drinking of beer before supper."

"Aye, aye, sir!" he said, and grinned. But he was held in somber thought as he went to the door and let in Phelim with the foam-slopped can.

He forced that thought back into a rear corner of his brain at supper. Peggy had changed into a cleverly cut dress for the meal, arranged her hair with a high amber comb in the back. She carried the conversation, made both men laugh repeatedly, and said nothing as Phelim poured whiskey into their tea. "No bothering with the dishes now," she said. "I'll stack them for later. Sing for us, Alan."

He was touched by the use she made of his first name, and the lingering remnants of thought about the Shaw family went from him. "It's a song from Antrim," he said. "The pipers play it, too. But my mother used to sing it."

It was "The Birds Among The Trees" and singing it he remembered that for months he hadn't sung. Phelim and Peggy were silent when he was finished. True Celts, he thought. They need give you no praise with their hands or lips. It's in their silence that you know.

"Here's one for Phelim. We sang the thing together when we were in the *Margharita,* and a big, brute ship she was, too. Right, Phelim?"

"Sing," Phelim said. "A man shouldn't delay with 'The Swallow-tail Coat.' "

After "The Swallowtail Coat" and for Phelim's pleasure he sang "Paddy Doyle," "Away For Rio," "Dead Horse" and "Haul The Bowline." Phelim joined him in the choruses there and they stamped their feet, clapped their hands.

"I'm tired, lads," Peggy said suddenly. "I'm sorry, but I'm tired. D' you mind if I go to bed?"

"Stupid, that's me," Alan Kennard said. "I should ha' been gone long since."

"Not a bit of it," Peggy said. "If your pay envelope looks like Phelim's, you should save your money. The kettle's on, Phelim. When it's hot, wash the dishes. Then take the spare blankets out of the closet and make up the couch for Alan. You'll spend the night here, Alan, and in no hotel."

"But I'll be a bother to you in the morning and all," he said. "It's best I get along, Peggy."

"No," she said; "it isn't." She came over to him and gently clasped his hands. "We'd like you to have the idea that this place is home for you, too. Goodnight, Alan."

His voice filled with emotion as he thanked her and said goodnight. She kissed you before, he thought, but not tonight. It must be the young one she's carrying that makes the difference. But it might well be that tonight she reckons you don't need such stuff anywhere near as much as last time. Phelim's your friend, and now, too, Peggy is.

He and Phelim didn't speak much as they washed, dried and racked the dishes. But after Phelim had fitted the blankets to the couch he gripped Kennard hard by the shoulder. "Take it easy out in Bellport," he said. "And should you foul up, remember who's your friends."

"Thank you, lad."

"Just do as I say, will you?"

"I'll try, Phelim. I'll do me bloody best."

He lay awake for some time on the unfamiliar couch, missing the action of the vessel and bothered by the street sounds. Then sleep was there for him and he entered gratefully into it. He couldn't think of Joshua or Jane if he was deeply asleep, and in the next room Phelim, Phelim's wife slept at peace. He could hear Phelim snore. That, at least, was familiar. The goddamn' Liverpool man had a snore that was like a whistling buoy you came on outside a harbor. But the harbor was here, inside this flat. . . .

He took the train to Bellport in the morning, not willing to have Joshua go out of his way for him. But he sent a telegram ahead from the Union Depot. "Spend day with you if you do not mind. Antrim." Pretty good, he thought. Just ten words and it got over what you wanted to say exact.

The smoke of the Shaw plant dragged long brown banners over the Lake sky. He saw them as the train jounced to a stop at the little station and he left his seat by the stove. The sight pleased him; it was good to know that Josh had plenty to keep him busy.

Joshua was on the platform in the same coonskin coat and cap, smiling broadly, one hand upraised. "Time you came, Antrim," he said. "We've been looking for you."

"Ah, I've been busy keeping me belly away from me backbone," he said. "A bastard of a work-house schooner I was in all season long. But you seem to be doin' fine."

Joshua nodded, as though abruptly distracted. They were away from the station now and walking over siding rails towards the plant. "How long were you in Cleveland?"

"For the night only. I stayed with Phelim and his new wife."

"Then you didn't hear anything about Jane."

"Yes, Josh, I did a bit."

"From whom?"

"Phelim's wife, Peggy. But——"

"Listen to me, Antrim. I'd better tell you right here." They had stopped and Joshua's face was very grave. "Jane went away last week. Father sent her. He gave her five thousand dollars outright and he settled a thousand dollars a year on her for life. The slaves are freed. . . . But it's had a hell of an effect on Mother, and Father's a different man."

"Your Mom I can understand," Alan Kennard said. "About the colonel, though, I don't." He had no desire to speak. His effort was made only to reduce some of the look of pain in Joshua's face.

"He blames her entirely for it," Joshua said. "His conviction now is that it should have been done a long time ago. And Cottrell— Cottrell's bad; he's drunk the whole damn' day. Lucinda's had a little girl. She wants to take Cottrell and the baby back to Hartford with her. Her family will give him a job in the insurance business. But Mother won't let him go. For her, that would be the final breakup of the family. So Cottrell just stays drunk."

Alan Kennard put his hands on Joshua's shoulders. He looked deeply into Joshua's eyes. "Why d'you tell me this, Josh?"

"Because you're my friend and you'd better hear it from me than from some stranger."

"All right, I've heard it. What can I do?"

"Nothing. There isn't a single thing to do. But come on. We're going to pour at eleven o'clock and Father's on the floor."

They came into the high-roofed plant through a side door. The upper reaches were in smoky dimness, obscure and oppressive, and for an instant Kennard was reminded of his symbol of the cave. But shafts of sunlight were through the tall wall windows, bent upon the benches where the moulders worked. Light also pierced forward from a furnace.

Its source was like a weirdly unblinking eye. Its color was an extreme cherry-red. Mr. Shaw rested before it, peering from behind green goggles. Grigor was beside him, his back black with sweat. "Grigor's about to pull the plug," Joshua said. "The heat is right."

Mr. Shaw had stepped back with a gesture to Grigor. The foreman made movements so swift that Alan Kennard couldn't follow them. He could see, though, the long lines of men who had formed at one side of the furnace. They were in teams of twos, carried small ladles on steel handles between them. Each team crouched, feet spread, bodies tense. Then, as Grigor pulled the furnace plug, they loped ahead.

The molten steel issued forth in a fierce-gleaming freshet. It illuminated all of the enormous place. Billows of radiance swept the shadows. Sparks cascaded, orange, silver, thinly crackling. The men with the ladles had taken on the aspect of giants. Their bodies, limned by the flaming steel, were stupendous in motion.

They trotted across the sand floor with their awful loads. The moulds lay in rows in their thick wooden frames and each received its share of steel. Alan Kennard gasped, his throat constricted. "Hell must be like that."

"Almost every man says the same thing his first time," Joshua said. "But just watch out you don't burn yourself."

Men were knocking apart the moulds. They pulled the castings along the floor to shallow pools of water and the castings were gold-bright, scarlet as the water hissed and steamed, then purple, then black.

"Car wheels and couplings," Joshua said. "We have a contract with the Erie. How'd you like a job?"

Alan Kennard had steam in his throat and eyes. A film of grit was on his skin, his clothing. "You take your job and shove it," he said. "Me, I'm a man for the open."

But Mr. Shaw was advancing across the floor to them and Grigor followed. Kennard smiled widely for Mr. Shaw; here was a man he admired. Grigor stood wiping himself with a bandana while Kennard and Mr. Shaw greeted each other and shook hands. Then he stepped up and held out his hand. "How's sheer-legs?" he said. "You use 'em?"

"Not this season," Kennard said. "Maybe I'm lucky."

"No, not lucky," Grigor said. "You should have job here."

"Enough of that." Mr. Shaw smiled, stroking the mustache and beard. "Each time we pour and there's a visitor here, Grigor or Joshua try the same stale joke."

Things are different, Alan Kennard thought rapidly. Now it's got around to His Nibs bringing Grigor into the talk. Him and Grigor seem to go along fine. A strange lash-up. "They can't give me none of their nonsense," he said to Mr. Shaw. "I'll stick to the ships even if I freeze me neck off. But how about me borrying Grigor for a couple of months next season?" ·

"Seasick," Grigor said. He pressed his spatulate fingers against his stomach. "Seasick, jeeschri'. No boats no more." He turned then, letting his great voice go at the men around the cooling pits.

"A fine foreman," Mr. Shaw said. "The best I ever had. But how have you been, Mr. Kennard?"

"Fair is the way I'd say it, sir. My partner and me lost out on that schooner we had. And another deal—" his glance went over to Joshua—"ain't worked out yet."

Mr. Shaw studied him. "We could use you here, you know."

"Thank you, sir." He was able to sense Joshua's embarrassment. "I wasn't gaffing before. I'll stick with the ships. That's me trade."

"Then let's go and have a wash-up and some dinner." Mr. Shaw drew the heavily fobbed watched out of the waist pocket in his trousers. "It's nearly time for dinner. Mrs. Shaw and Lucinda and Cottrell will be pleased to see you, I'm sure. Joshua, have you told him about Jane?"

They had gone into the sunlight outside the plant door and for several seconds father and son regarded each other. Joshua's face was slightly pale, but Mr. Shaw stood calmly, the big hunter watch still on the palm of his hand. "Yes, sir," Joshua said. "I told him all that I think is necessary."

"Very well." The watch went back into the pocket. "I understand that we're having a roast of pork for dinner. A solid snort of Bourbon wouldn't hurt that a bit, now would it?"

"No, sir." Past Mr. Shaw's erect head, Alan Kennard looked at Joshua and received a solemn, reassuring wink in return.

Mrs. Shaw greeted them in the front hall. Her manner towards Alan Kennard was gracious and relaxed, and watching her closely he found her unchanged. But on the way into the living room he noticed a hot air register placed among the splendid floor planks, saw on the walls spaces where the paneling had been removed for the installation of gas jets. "The slaves are freed," he told himself; that was what Josh had said.

Cottrell and Lucinda were in the living room, Lucinda slim and pretty and smiling. Cottrell was white-sober. Cottrell hung on, Kennard thought, like a man on a high spar in a full gale of wind. He had lost a lot of weight; his clothes didn't fit him right and he kept looking from his mother to Lucinda and back with a nervous twitching of the eyes.

A fire burned in the deep living room fireplace and Mrs. Shaw seated herself before it in her mahogany rocker. "Dinner will be served in just a few minutes," she said. "Do sit down, gentlemen."

"Thank you," Mr. Shaw said. He bowed to her. "But we would prefer a drink." He led the way into the dining room and Alan Kennard took time to glance around behind. Cottrell was on his feet. He had started to go after them into the dining room, then stopped. His mother's eyes were on him, and the open, beseeching appeal in them made muscles quiver in Kennard's stomach. Lucinda stared at her mother-in-law; her eyes held fury and contempt and a pride whose source Kennard could not understand. "Go on, Cott," Lucinda said in a low voice. "Join the men."

"Excuse me," Cottrell said and came stumbling through the door.

The maids were still setting the table. They made an elaborate effort to disregard Cottrell. He shook all over when he reached the others at the sideboard. Whiskey and brandy and wine decanters and an assortment of glasses were there. "What will it be, son?" Mr. Shaw asked Cottrell, his face averted as he poured Bourbon.

"A little sherry," Cottrell said. His lips worked with difficulty to pronounce the words. "Just a smidgeon."

Mr. Shaw poured him half a glassful, put it in his hand. "Here's to prosperity for all of us," he said. "Take your time," he told Alan Kennard. "We have time for several more before dinner's ready, haven't we, Kate?"

"Oh, yes, sir," the elder maid said. "Except Mrs. Shaw——"

"I'll talk to Mrs. Shaw. Have another, Cottrell?"

"No, I thank you, sir," Cottrell said. He didn't shake any longer and his voice was level. "I guess I'll go back and keep Mother and Lucinda company."

Alan Kennard had no pleasure from the whiskey. He was sorry now that he had come here. Joshua was the only one of these people of whom he had any understanding. He admired the old colonel, and he liked Cottrell and Lucinda. Jane had strangely and cruelly fascinated him. But Jane was gone, although the house was dominated yet by her presence. Jane's leaving, her breaking away from them, was reflected in everything the rest of them did. Even the maids responded to it. They moved around this house like people on a tightrope in the dark, and Jane was carrying the light. Deep down, all of them must want to follow Jane, get out.

He was profoundly perturbed, more so than ever before in his life. His sense of values was lost. Since early youth, from the days of his frightful poverty in Antrim, he had always believed that wealth gave power and security. Without it, nobody was safe, and happiness was just a dream.

Sure, he thought, his mind stimulated by the swift, hot lick of the Bourbon, you could be happy for a night with a bottle and a lass. But you couldn't have the real thing. Not the one that lasted. And look at this lot. They have what's needed. But they're tearing each other apart. Jane had to make a whore of herself before she busted out. His Nibs is riding pretty high right now, what with drinking in the dining room and all. The old battle-axe in the next room, though, she hasn't let down yet; she's not through by plenty. They got Jane away from her. They got their hot-air furnace and their gas jets. While she still hangs onto Cottrell and Lucinda hates her guts and she hates Lucinda back. Josh should be married. He should ha' had a wife a couple of years ago. Bring her here? She'd get the same ticket that's stuck on Lucinda. So Her Nibs wins again. She holds top hand and His Nibs better watch out, for sooner or later she'll try to crack him wide.

But don't let it get you down, Alan. You have small acquaintance among the wealthy, and as a fact these here are the only rich folks you know. All of them ain't like the Shaws. Just because they're fouled up don't say you have to do the same. And if you're not after wealth in your life, what the hell else are you going for? It's the big thing straight down the line, in the States, in Ireland, anywhere. You want money. You want to be rich and powerful and strong. The honest way, though. When you have it, too, you won't hurt them around you. This has been a good lesson for you.

Mrs. Shaw had entered the room with Lucinda and Cottrell after her. "Dinner will be spoiled, my dear," she said quietly.

"Yes, my dear," Mr. Shaw said. He put the stopper back clinking in the Bourbon decanter, smoothed his fingers along his mustache. "Shall we be seated?"

They sat down and grace was said and what Alan Kennard guessed was mock turtle soup was served. Mr. Shaw's face was ruddy from the Bourbon. He brandished the knife a bit as he carved the roast, and his voice rumbled through the room.

"A strange age, Mr. Kennard," he said. "One of great changes, in and outside the family. My good wife, for instance, has been long unwilling to have such modern conveniences as a furnace and gaslight brought to her home."

Keep your yawp shut, Alan Kennard sternly told himself. He's talking to hurt her, get his due out of her hide. Remember the Bible stuff he read? "Draw out also the spear." Draw it out, hell. Stick it in 'til she's hoop-legged from carrying it.

But Joshua had come into the conversation. "Don't you think, sir," he asked, facing his father, "that the greatest changes are being made by such men as Rockefeller?"

"Coal Oil Johnny," Mr. Shaw said. He struck hard at the whitish, smooth-grained pork. "Coal Oil Johnny. . . . Yes, no doubt about it, Josh. The corporate idea. Get everybody in or smash 'em flat. But that's been tried before. The Michigan Salt Association—you must have heard of it, Mr. Kennard—they got together secretly in a cabal and they forced prices up double until they were exposed. Harkness was in it, Flagler, Rockefeller, too."

The last plate had been served, but Mr. Shaw still stood. He stared down the table, his eyes narrowed, the carving knife at rest on the roast as though it were a sword and the roast the body of an enemy. "I must say," he said, "that those who make the tremendous fortunes today were men who for the most part could have done their duty with us in the war. But they preferred to pay for substitutes."

He sat down with that and started tearing at a potato and a piece of pork. Cottrell shifted on his chair, the food before him untouched. "Could we have a little wine, sir?"

"Of course." Mr. Shaw waved a hand. "Kate, the wine." He seemed to savor his when it was poured, although the lines of anger remained around his mouth. "Allow me if I quote. It is Thomas Jefferson: 'A wise and frugal government which shall restrain men from injuring one another, which shall leave them otherwise free to regulate their own pursuits of industry and improvement, and shall not take from the mouth of labor the bread it has earned. This is the sum of good government, and this is necessary to close the circle of our felicities.' "

"Excellent indeed." It was Mrs. Shaw who spoke, erect at her end of the table, her shoulders back within the watered gray silk of her dress. "A splendid expression. That would give latitude, though, to such as the Molly Maguires. Anarchy can exist also under such terms."

"I am, madame," Mr. Shaw said hoarsely, "not an anarchist. My sentiments have been with Mr. Carnegie in his troubles with the murderous riffraff. He's a man whom I admire. It is his type that will take care of those who would make the greatest misuse of what Jefferson meant. Carnegie won't fall into the trap of their price cabals and their corporations. Down there at Braddock he's got the finest steel plant in the land, and one man runs it, one man owns it."

"Father means," Joshua said quickly across the table to Kennard, "that Carnegie with his Bessemer process has got them all backed up. They can't touch his prices."

"Touch them?" Mr. Shaw said. "For steel rail, they're not within ten dollars a ton. Carnegie will bring it down to thirty and perhaps more. You mark my word. A Scot, Carnegie. You were aware of that, Mr. Kennard?"

"Yes, sir," Alan Kennard mumbled. The three stiff drinks of Bourbon, the wine, the rich food and the conversation with its odd, nervously strained undercurrent had dazed him. He waited dully for the end of the meal. A few words alone with Josh and then out, he promised himself.

He and Joshua succeeded in escaping the rest after they had left the dining room. Joshua took him by the arm and upstairs. "We'll be quiet in my own digs," Joshua said. "Father passed a standing order long ago that I shouldn't be bothered there."

"But don't ye have to get back to the plant?"

"Not until three o'clock when we pour again. Come on in."

It was a big room with the weak winter sunlight across it from the many-paned windows. Bearskin rugs were on the floor, and on the walls were pronged, blue flannel flags with a white Y, a photograph of a number of young men all crouching on an iron pipe fence and all in high-necked sweaters. Joshua pulled a chair around and said, "Sit down. I'd like to show you something Jane left."

"For Christ's sake, why?"

"A good question." Joshua had been on his way to the closet. He halted and swung back towards Kennard. "But because you're my friend, I guess, and I have no one else to show them to."

"Go ahead, then."

They were three oil paintings in simple wooden frames. Joshua propped them up at the end of his bed where the sunlight reached in clearly upon them. The first was a fall scene, showed trees and a brook, several partly hidden figures. "Our forge stream," Joshua said softly. "Back in the days of the Revolution. 'The Hunters,' she called it."

Alan Kennard got up from his chair. He moved so that he was directly in front of the painting. Jane, he thought. Jane can paint like that. Damn you, man. See the beauty in it.

The trees were white and silver birches, a red oak, a butternut, a clump of beech. Light was broken over them. Their leaves, in the patchwork fantasy of fall, were brilliant or faint, already faded, sere. But the dark water of the stream ran frothing, it flashed against the rocks, gave vaguely back the colors of the leaves in the eddies. Trout were in the pools; leaves floated over them, some whirling, some slow. Moss was on the rocks, among the tree roots. A toadstool tilted, the top heavy with sun. The men wore long red coats and hats the shape of shovels. They had clumsy gaiters and crossed belts, carried muskets.

"Lobster-backs," Alan Kennard said whispering. "That's them, the Sassenach. They're after your forge."

"That's right." Joshua's eyes gleamed. "But they never found it." He took the picture down, lifted up another. " 'April.' She asked me for a name and that was the best I could give."

"You did well. That's enough."

The scene was again the brook, but now the light was coruscant. It leaped at the tender green of the leaves, twisted glinting bands around the sap-streaked tree trunks, was irradiant on the water. Laurel was against the further shadow, a filigree of color so delicate that Alan Kennard moaned aloud. Violets grew on the banks past the moss. A deer, stepping down to drink, had left a sharp hoof print; it was filled with the morning's rain and brightly took the sun. Rinds of snow were still in the shadow of the trees, but they melted, trickled. Where rocks formed a pool, a trout was half out of the water after a coiled brown worm.

"I have no words," Kennard said. "I have nothing to say. But the way she paints, my mother sang."

Joshua was silent. He was taking down the picture, putting up the third. This was a seascape. Wind had the sky, and drove high storm clouds. The cloud was sullen, ripped, yet thick bodied. The sea below surged, broke, resurged with wide crests. Cloud gave the crests a steel-hard, cruel edge, and the troughs were veined in purple, green that was almost black. Far off, beyond the cloud, in the clear gold air of the horizon a single bird, an albatross, flew. He was small against the sea, the cloud, and strong, his wings raised to the wind.

"You know the name," Joshua said.

"Yes, I do." Alan Kennard had been standing with his hands clenched. " 'Where the wind blows.' Tell me, though. How could a man find Jane?"

Joshua gave him a slow, half veiled look. "Father and I don't know. Perhaps we'd rather not. It might be London, it might be Rome or Paris. Father just puts her money in a New York bank for her and that's all."

"Poor lass. Poor goddamn' lass."

"I wouldn't say so. Jane's paid her price and over. She'll be all right. But you don't want to see her, Alan."

"No, I don't. It was just an idea, seeing them. We're fey, the Antrim folk, and they turned me head. But, Josh. . . ." He stepped forward near to his friend. "What's to become of you, the whole family?"

Joshua shook his head and tried to smile. "That's something else I don't know. It's all mixed up, isn't it?"

"Bad. You should have a woman, Josh. Married a couple of years back."

"That can wait."

"For what?"

"I don't know. But Lucinda's on the point of leaving us, Cottrell or no Cottrell. And if she does, her family will take their stock out of the company. They own five thousand shares."

"Then——"

"Don't bother, Alan. There's nothing you can do, that I can do. Mother and Father must have it out between them, and only then will there be an end."

Alan Kennard was forced into motion by his agitation. He strode the room, over to the bookcase, to the windows, the pictures against the wall, the chest of drawers, the door. "I went over the limestone land at Bouche de Mouche," he said. "It's there, more than two hundred acres of it. But the bloody owner is dead. His wife and kid were in Chicago and they're gone. I've been almost off me head trying to find them. That land, Josh, and you with the plant here and me supplying you the limestone, Christ, we'd do fine. I'd have ships of my own, a fleet. The Kennard Line, right?"

"Right." Joshua Shaw stood perplexed, uncertain. He had in the past, he thought, respected if not admired this man's ambition. When they had been together in the camp on the Kawkawlin, it had seemed to him a fine thing. But he was no longer sure. The value of any ambition had been stripped from him. Let it run and it led to what had happened in his own family, his own home. Alan should be content to sail as master of some schooner, work his way later into a well paid job ashore. But a limestone company, a steamship fleet and the chance to make a great deal of money, no. Alan wasn't the man. He was at the same time too honest and too hard. Either his honesty would suffer or the hardness enormously increase.

The latent feeling of depression deepened within Shaw. His life had come close enough to tragedy, and he would do his best to save Alan. Down the hall, Lucinda's baby fretfully cried. It was the signal he needed. "I've got to get back to the plant in a bit," he said. "Let's stop in, though, and take a look at Lucinda's kid. She'd be pleased. As to the limestone deal, Alan, we have plenty to carry us and we're under contract for our supply."

"I thought only to the end of the year."

"We've renewed the contract."

"You wouldn't be interested, then?"

"I'd be a damn' fool if I weren't. You clear that title, and if the land's what you say, we'll talk turkey."

"Good. I can ask no more." They were out the door and in the hall, moving towards the baby's soft, small cries. "I think I'll be on my way when you head for the plant, Josh. Back to Chicago and another crack at finding them folks."

"You have all my luck."

"Thanks, lad."

They halted at the door of Lucinda's room, then tiptoed hurriedly on to the stairs. Lucinda was feeding the baby at the breast and Cottrell lay across the bed, gape-mouthed, drunk and asleep. Out of this house, Alan Kennard told himself. Get out of this house. You don't belong here, ever.

CHAPTER SIX

Again, the winter was for him slow and dull and unhappy. He passed the months in Chicago. Invitations came to him from both Joshua Shaw and Phelim and Peggy to spend Christmas in their homes. He refused them, preferring to be alone in what he once more considered as the dark, miserable cave of his life. When Peggy bore Phelim a nine and a half pound boy and he received a drunkenly illiterate letter from Phelim, he was tempted to go to Cleveland for the christening. But he stayed on in Chicago. He was better off alone.

He lived in a scab-walled furnished room on Clark Street and he had returned to work for John Frawn, the contractor for whom he had carried a hod the winter before. This year, though, Frawn, a County Cavan man with a sharp, quick intelligence, had recognized him as a sailor. "Youse can do more than hustle the bricks," he told Kennard. "I have my wire to be spliced for my rigs, and block and tackle to be overhauled. Start right now."

Alan Kennard was pleased, for the work meant higher pay and he was saving every dollar, had over two thousand dollars in a savings account. Yet the pleasure was momentary. He couldn't release from his mind the fact that somewhere he had missed, that his life seemed to hold no future except work for other men. What's happened to you? he asked himself repeatedly. All your dreams, your plans have gone to hell.

He went several times to visit the janitor at the Halsted Street address where the Svenson family had lived after leaving Patigowoc. But the man knew no more than before; there was no trace at all of the mother and daughter. Kennard gave up in final despair. The county would soon sell the limestone land for back taxes. His chance to get it was gone. He had nothing like enough to bid it in at public auction, and nobody to lend him the additional money. The Shaws were under contract for their limestone, engaged in their own affairs, Phelim was busy being a father and had only his season's pay-off to keep his wife and kid and himself until spring.

Kennard got into the habit of prowling the steam beer saloons when he was through work, drinking far more heavily than he had in the past. He started a fight one night with a stranger who at the other end of the bar said that all Ulstermen were no-good bastards. The man was bigger and tougher than he, and Kennard had his nose broken, an eye blackened, and sprained two fingers of his left hand. He was unable to do his rigging work and John Frawn docked him a week's pay, warned him that the next time he would be fired.

He walked the streets for hours after that. It was a kind of penance, he told himself, and by doing it he might find out what was wrong. He stood in front of the great homes on Prairie and Indiana Avenues, staring at them with a savage hatred, bitterly envying their occupants and in a blind desire for self-escape blaming them for his state. Then he wandered North through the ugly sprawl of the expanding city, over the Rush Street bridge and to the fantastic, enormous pile of Potter Palmer's new house. " 'No titles in America,' " he muttered, quoting a famous old saying of the immigrants about to leave Ireland; " 'no royalty. Every man has a chance.' That fella there's a prince—a prince of dollars. And what chance have you against him?"

But he realized then that the hatred, the envy were futile and he turned back over the bridge, cut away from Michigan Boulevard and out onto the sand dunes. The solitude slowly brought him tranquility. He responded to the plangent roll of the waves on the shore, the sandpipers' leaping and tiny cries, the wind and space and cloud. His thought steadied; he saw himself in what he believed to be true perspective.

Stupid, that's you, for wanting to push too far and too fast. It'll get you only trouble. Forget the limestone land. Keep on with what you know and can do. If you're anything, you're a sailor, and your life's on the water. So study for your master's license. Take out the *Aroosta* in the spring, save your money and there's still a chance at least to own your own vessel.

He kicked a sand-smoothed piece of driftwood from his path, walked rapidly striding towards the city.

His master's license was issued to him in March, and already swallows cheeped over the horse droppings in the streets, boys played with tops and marbles, ducks streaked in arrow-like passage against the wind on the way to the breeding marshes. John Frawn paid him off at his request and he went to La Salle Street and Froler and Jaeckel and Company, was given command of the

Aroosta. A young Hollander named Schooste from Grand Rapids was his mate and they chartered a hansom cab together, took their gear over to the ship.

They were by themselves aboard her for more than a week while the company gathered a crew, but Alan Kennard didn't mind. Schooste had also put in time in deep-water ships, knew and liked his work. They rigged a stage, began to scale and scrape her hull, then paint her. The sun was warmer every day on their backs; Kennard sang long chanteys. Even when his crew was sent down and the farm boys came clumping aboard he kept on at deck work. He tightened up stays, renewed halyards and downhauls, served off wire he spliced. He was back where he belonged, he told himself, and maybe this season his luck might break.

He brought the *Aroosta* into Muskegon for a load of lumber for Chicago the first week of May. His cook had got drunk in Green Bay, the last port, and left the ship, and on the way across the lake one of the sailors had taken over in the galley. But the sailor was nothing like a cook, and as soon as the ship was made fast to the boom inside the harbor, Kennard went up the hill to find a new one.

There was a small, shabby place near the sawmill that was called The Greek's. He entered it and sat down at a table with a red checked cloth, ordered ham and eggs. The Greek might know of a cook, and anyhow he'd get himself a decent meal. But then he began to watch the waitress, his attention drawn to her immediately by the manners of the other men in the room. They were from the mill, rough spoken and careless, still they were polite with her although their glances never left her while she was in the room.

She was small, straight bodied, about eighteen. Her hair was soft brown, worn in a bun at the back of her neck. She had black eyes and broad black eyebrows, long lashes. Her skin was so clear that the brows and eyes had an almost startling effect. The nose was long for the face, narrowly bridged, and the high nostrils flared lightly as she breathed. She wore a thin gingham dress and he saw that her breasts were firm, little. When she came in from the kitchen carrying a full tray, her buttocks went up and down, right, left rhythmically in a motion that ravished Kennard's thought.

He sat fumbling at the ham and eggs, remembering that it was months since he had given himself to a woman. That had been a two-dollar Clark Street whore who had taken him one night in an alley after he had drunk himself close to stupidity on steam beer. Jesus Christ, he didn't even have any memory of what she looked like. But this girl. . . .

He pushed a quarter under the edge of the plate, an enormous tip for him, and went over to the Greek behind the counter. "You know anybody who wants to go cook of a schooner?" he said, his will nervously engaged to keep him from looking at the waitress.

"You ask that one out in the kitchen." The Greek changed his dollar bill, returned to whittling a match stick. "Got to get me another."

"What's the matter, no good? My boys don't want no slop."

"You've et here," the Greek said in a plaintive voice. "You know it's good. But four fights I had here alone last week. Them fellas get worked up lookin' at Minna. Then they're all crazy and they fight. One his head is busted by a chair. Me I have three teeth knocked out. See?" The Greek showed the gap in his lower jaw. "So you talk to her in the kitchen, Minna's mother, Mrs. Svenson her name."

The name meant nothing to Alan Kennard until he was right at the kitchen door. Then he thought, Svenson. Mrs. Svenson. And the girl's her daughter. Nerves jerked in his temples; he started to sweat, the steamy, greasy kitchen air in his face. The girl, Minna, passed him with a tray of dishes and he barely saw her. He was trying to collect his thoughts, decide how he would talk to Mrs. Svenson. But don't be stupid. You need a cook. That's it—you need a cook.

He opened the kitchen door and crossed the sawdust covered floor. A broken shanty boy who clung to his flannel shirt and shoe-packs was at the sink in the corner, slimed above the elbows as he washed dishes. Mrs. Svenson was at the big coal range beyond. Alan Kennard was certain then, and his pride and his ambition and hope formed solidly within him; he was suddenly calm, deliberate, as if he were in a storm at sea. He walked to Mrs. Svenson and took off his cap.

"Alan Kennard," he said. "Captain o' the *Aroosta*, schooner. Carrying lumber mostly, here on Michigan and once in a while over on Huron and down to Erie. I need me a cook. My last one got drunk-up and left me in Green Bay. The Greek was just saying mebbe you'd like to make a change."

Mrs. Svenson wore black yet for her man. Her hair was stringy in the Indian style and her apron had grease splotches on it, but the rest of her was very clean. She regarded him with olive-shaded, piercing eyes. "How many men?"

"Twelve, counting me and the mate."

"What kind of quarters?"

"Good. The cookhouse is 'midships. You'd have a room to yourself."

"My daughter goes with me where I work. What kind of pay for us both?"

"What d' you reckon you're worth?"

"Sixty dollars a month. That's for her and me, both."

"It's a stack of money." Half of that, he thought, will have to come out of your own pocket. The company won't pay it. But don't argue. Not too much, anyhow. This is her all right, the Ojibway from Bouche de Mouche. She owns the limestone land and she don't seem to know the stuff is worth a nickel.

"I'm a good cook," Mrs. Svenson said, "and I've got a good reputation from a lot of camps. Sixty, take it or leave it. But first I want you to understand about my daughter. No man—" a harsh, heavy note was through her voice—gets fresh with Minna."

Alan Kennard put his hands in his trousers pockets. He leaned back against the wall, aware of the enormous weight of her love for her daughter and also that Minna was there. Minna stood by the sink holding a tray. She gazed curiously at him and her mother.

"My ship's run decent," Kennard said. His eyes met the woman's eyes. "No funny business aboard. But I'm loadin' now. I have to clear before dark. The sixty for you and your daughter, that's what I'll pay. You and her get your duds together and come on down. I'll have a sailor on the dock to help you out aboard across the boom. The *Aroosta*, right?"

"Yes, *Aroosta*," Mrs. Svenson said. "You talked to the Greek?"

"I did. He won't mind."

Minna was gone from the kitchen when he left. But as he walked through the front room she looked up at him from a table she cleaned. She smiled a bit and inclined her head, and he could feel the blood rising, tightening around his heart. Watch out, Kennard, he warned himself. You goddamn' fool, watch out. You want that limestone land bad. Don't break your luck. You only found them folks because they're still close around the Lakes.

. . . .

Mrs. Svenson went onto the main deck of the *Aroosta* after supper was cooked and while Minna washed the dishes. The captain,

Kennard, was aft on the poop, she saw. He walked like an Indian, nimble and easy. Sailors came the closest to walking like Indians. But the rest of them here must be farm boys; they moved as if their feet hurt or their shoes were wrong. Svenson had been a smart man and not clumsy, still he had stepped around in the style of a sick duck. It was strange; she hadn't thought about Svenson in several years.

She sat down on a 'midships bitt and wiped the sweat from her face with her apron and began to enjoy the lake and the night and the wind. She was pleased to be away from the shore. The men back there had been after Minna all the while. Sure, there were men here, too, and probably just as eager as the lot in Muskegon. But here she could watch them and Minna better.

She sighed and let the apron drop, ran her hands over her face and her thin hair. Men, big and strong ones, little, dapper, quick talking ones, some who were tough, some gentle, with education and good chances, those who drank and didn't drink, the boasters, the liars, the straight no-goods who as the shanty boys said would hop a hoptoad if they could catch it. All chasing Minna. All wanting her. You're a woman; you know what the thing means. You can't blame them. Or Minna for being attracted. Your daughter's a good girl. Still, she's pretty, and she has a right to like men.

Your trouble is that you're so tired. My goodness, you're like an old fire inside, a lot of ashes and just a little heat, just a little. Some day there won't be any more. Four years now since Svenson died and left you without a red cent. Ever since, you've fought to keep you and Minna alive and Minna straight.

The men of Mrs. Svenson's fatigued imagination grouped into columns. They marched grimacing, leering, gesticulating and calling before her. They opened their clothing and obscenely exhibited themselves. Their eyes were like the eyes of foxes outside a chicken coop; their mouths had wet and shiny lips.

She had the strength left to dismiss the vision. It wasn't as bad as that. Some of the men wanted to marry Minna in the same way Svenson did you. And a lot of them—she smiled wryly at the thought —just want what's under Minna's dress. No marriage. Nothing but that. It's no different, though, from the time when you were a girl. A good thing, and no lie, that you found Svenson.

Mrs. Svenson brought herself to contemplation of the ship's crew. The captain looked to be a sober man, serious and the way Svenson was before Svenson sold the timber rights and got mixed up with the real estate sharpers in Chicago. Svenson, the poor dear, was a schoolteacher and nothing like a quick trader. But keep on with this. Svenson's dead, buried, gone.

The mate aboard here is married and has a wife and family in Grand Rapids. That the captain told you after you and Minna came on. A Hollander, the mate. He won't be any trouble. He'll be dreaming about his folks all the time. Saving his dollars, too, and not drunk in port to raise hell. The crew are farm boys. They still have hay in their hair. Maybe a couple of them will chase after Minna, but not much. They got their own girls back home. That leaves the captain, and you can keep an eye on him all right.

Mrs. Svenson relaxed. The night was soft with a Southeast breeze. The schooner sailed fair before it, the upper canvas rustling, whispering, blocks squeaking a bit as the sails eased and slack ran through the sheets, then was taken again. The water had a sound she had forgotten. She was thrilled and led into early memory.

She sailed Huron with her father in a bark canoe. He paddled aft. She was in the bow. They had been fishing since before dawn. Ciscoes and small-mouth bass were behind her in a sleek heap. They'd eat good tonight. A good, big feed. Her mother wouldn't groan all night from the hunger and the younger children cry in their sleep.

Long ago. You had nearly forgotten. Sure, because they're gone, the whole shebang of them. Svenson told you what it was. Typhoid, and smallpox, and the doctor doing nothing because you were dirty damn' Ojibways. Your father was killed by the bottle. The white men wouldn't let him have a gun, but they sold him whiskey.

Long ago. Long ago. . . . You don't even reckon yourself as Ojibway any more. Still, you are. Remember that *mesabi* means giant. *Erige* means cat, wild cat. Now they call it Erie. Back in the old days the Frenchmen's name for it was *Lac du Chat*. Svenson explained it to you. He knew a lot and he didn't have any use for the whiskey, and because you were Ojibway didn't mean anything to him. But when he went to Chicago those men took him apart the way your father would take a white man's trap apart. Right there, Svenson was like your father. He couldn't put the pieces together to make it work any more. So he died. They might as well have shot him.

Mrs. Svenson looked up, aroused from her meditation by Minna.

Her daughter had just slammed back and hooked the cookhouse door. She walked over the slightly pitching deck in high-buttoned shoes, and she wore a tight skirt and a fresh shirtwaist. Mrs. Svenson smelled orris root and toilet water; she noticed that Minna kept to the beam of light that came from the cookhouse doorway, and that the bow lookout had turned and faced aft, that the wheelsman and the captain also watched.

A bleak wrath settled upon Mrs. Svenson. She realized that despite all her effort Minna would defeat her. It wasn't just that men wanted Minna. The girl was eighteen. She needed a man, and pretty soon she'd have one.

Kennard had come to the forward rail of the poop. "Step along aft," he said, his voice lifted lightly by the breeze. "Here's a good place to sit if you don't bother my helmsman."

"Come on, Ma." Minna plucked the sleeve of her mother's dress. "That's the captain. He'd like us up there."

"All right," Mrs. Svenson said. She rose aching-bodied, slowly moving. Her mind phrased terms of expostulation, but she uttered none of them, not even to herself. She sensed that it was no good. She'd tried, tried hard. But she was whipped. There were too many men. The best that she could hope was that this Kennard was a decent man, would be good to her girl.

Alan Kennard kept abaft the wheel-box while they were there on the poop. His intention was to make the mother understand that he was no crazy skirt-chaser, and his pride restrained him from too eager overtures towards the daughter. Minna, he found, both tremendously excited him and repelled him. He was startled by the paradox, and hurt. He only very dimly realized that Jane Shaw was between him and Minna. They weren't at all alike, he told himself in a moment of extraordinary perception. One was like a little cat, a kitten in skirts, and the other, hell, he had no words for Jane.

He strode from side to side of the poop deck, giving unnecessary orders to the wheelsman and knowing very well what the sailor would tell his watchmates when he went below. But that couldn't be helped; he had to do something, find some release for this that had him by the guts.

Mother and daughter sat in canvas deck chairs near the starboard rail. He and Schooste had built them for their own comfort, and they were low and long. His idea as he strode back and forth was that Minna's skirt was caught, pulled up by the breeze, although he was able to tell himself bitterly that she would never let it happen with her mother sitting there beside her. Minna got up from the chair after a time and came to join him. The wind pressed upon her, brought the skirt and the shirtwaist back closely about her body, and in the light from the binnacle he saw the curves of thighs and breasts. His breath went short in his throat; he could hardly answer her question.

"We're bound for Green Bay," he said. "Them paper mills hog up timber the way the crew eats your ma's cookin'." The sailor at the wheel looked around at that and Kennard was pleased to shout, "Watch your steering, you. Hold her fine."

"Yes, sir," the sailor mumbled, bent down again to blink at the compass card.

"My, you treat 'em rough," Minna said. She stood right beside Kennard, and he had just discovered to his dismay that he was no more than an inch taller. "Not too rough," he said. "But if the mate and I didn't keep after 'em, they'd handle this like it was a wheelbarrow. You care for sailing?"

"First time." The breeze was in her hair, had loosened the bun. Her arms were raised to fix it and he had the impulse to put his hands on her, smooth them down her hips. He stepped back a pace and put his hands in his pockets. She followed, as though the faint pitching of the vessel forced her. "I like it, though. Just hope I don't get seasick."

"You won't. You seem to be a good, husky girl. Stay out on deck plenty 'til you get used to the motion." He could smell her now, and was conscious that she had fixed herself for him since supper. The toilet water he had smelled before; it was the same kind the whores in Kawkawlin Center used, and the country girls in the small ports around the lakes. The other stuff, that was some sort of face powder and he didn't know its name. But it smelled good. It sure got to him. He tried to smile at himself, keep control of his will, and then a tendril of her hair brushed against his cheek.

He recoiled, his head jerking aside. You goddamn' fool. She's looking at you like you're daft. And so you must be. Are you scared, Kennard? Scared by an eighteen-year-old girl with her mother sitting a short fathom's length away? To hell you are. Take care the old lady don't notice or she'll grab the daughter by the hand and they'll start swimming for the beach. Phelim now, he'd laugh himself silly at you. . . .

Minna had gathered the escaped hair, returned it to place.

"Gosh, the wind," she said. "But where we goin', Captain, after Green Bay?"

"Dunno," he said. The physical expression of his passion was so intense that he shivered, and his stomach and his groins were contained by a cramping agony. "I get my orders from the company after we unload. Might be Chicago, might be Buffalo or Cleveland or Milwaukee. We just haul what they give us to haul."

"That's fun," Minna said; "and the water is so pretty. Better than that Muskegon. Oh, my!" The vessel had rolled a bit coming off a pitch and she teetered around against Kennard. Her hands went to his shoulders, his to her hips. They stood so shortly, gazing into each other's eyes, conscious in perfect nervous communication of their mutual desire.

Mrs. Svenson had pushed herself up from the deck chair. "I'm going down now," she said with the slow manner of speech she had learned from her husband. "I need some sleep. You, too, Minna?"

"Yes, Ma." Minna was free from Alan Kennard. She offered him a short, secret smile. "I'll see you in the morning, Captain. My mother's tired. So am I."

"Sure," Alan Kennard said. He touched his fingers to his cap brim as he had seen Royal Navy men do when parting from their women. "Goodnight, Minna. Goodnight, Missis Svenson."

Daughter, then mother went down the ladder to the main deck. The sailor at the wheel was far off the course. His breathing issued in quick gusts. "My ma," he said, "she usta put saltpeter in our food at home. Or give us the black purge so's we was so weak we'd forget the stuff."

"Why, by the Jesus." Kennard could only speak just above a whisper because of his own torment. "You steer the course. Get back on it, you hay-head! What you need's a calf, not a woman."

"Had me a calf," the sailor said stubbornly, speaking much more to himself than to Kennard. "What I want now's a woman. One like that there. Give my whole season pay-off just for to have her in the bunk for an hour."

Alan Kennard approached him. He gazed across the binnacle light into the sailor's eyes. "You won't have no season pay-off," he said. "You won't have anything but a broken leg from where I hove you on the dock, you bother her. Tell the rest of the lads the same. That one's for me."

"Yes, sir," the sailor mumbled. He blushed as he dragged at the wheel spokes, the passion in the captain's voice too great and too terrible for his comprehension. But Kennard had left him. He was over at the taffrail, staring down unseeing into the wake and cursing himself for a champion, daft fool.

Kennard was sleepless during the night. He writhed and twisted or lay with his hands clamped hard to the bunk frame. His senses were sharpened to the degree where he could determine each change of course, Schooste's footsteps along the poop planks, the tread of the other men as the wheel and the lookout were relieved. He tried to lose himself in that intricacy of sound, evade the knowledge that rested stark across his brain. But he could not, and in despair and amazement he realized near dawn that he was falling in love. It must be love. You've never felt this way before about a woman, you thick ape. But make sure before you go any farther. Maybe the thought of the limestone land is mixed up in this, too. Bejesus if you're not all mixed up.

Then the ability to maintain clear thought left him. He imagined Minna without her clothes, Minna beside him here in the bunk, Minna in his arms and responding with great delight to each small motion he made. Her hair was spread across the pillow. He could bury his face in it, and in the hollow of her shoulder. Their breathing had the same beat; the tide of their ecstasy mounted, mounted again, again and broke in the same instant.

Kennard lopped in the bunk with sweat over his body. He was deeply ashamed. You're like one of them farm boys in the fo'c'sle. No better, no smarter. Would you go marrying a lass such as that? You, make yourself into a legal pimp for a chance at some limestone land and a regular piece of tail? Goddamn you, no. You were born poor; you've lived poor, and all the signs are you'll die the same. Still, in your own way, you've been a man of honor. It's a fancy phrase that, hoity-toity, one you've never used before. But should you hornswoggle the lass into marrying you, Phelim and Peggy would disown you, Josh think of you as a no-good sod. Square away with yourself, Kennard. When you get into Green Bay, go up the town and get some doxy for a pair of dollars. Then you'll have your wits back so you can think and act straight.

He rose from the bunk and drew a bucket of cold water, bathed from head to foot, using strong, astringent soap. It made him shudder after the bout of passion, but he felt better for it, recognized that he had regained his self control. His usual habit was to shave and change into fresh clothing early each morning, and now he debated whether he should. Sure, he told himself as he opened his razor case. Going crummy on deck wouldn't prove anything. Act your regular style. Show the girl you ain't a bit different because of her. That's right, Alan. Steer your own course.

The watch had finished sweeping down when he came on deck. The canvas hose was rigged and the pump clanked and clucked, the water gurgling along the planks. That was familiar, correct, and he stood at ease as he took over from Schooste. But then he saw that although the watch sloshed through the water barefoot, their swabs swung steadily, each man was neatly shaved. Their hair was combed with care; they wore clean shirts, and Tordish, who had been on the wheel the night before, wore his shoregoing clothes, a pink silk shirt, a high celluloid collar, a tie and blue serge pants. His yellow, bulldog-toed shoes were made fast by the laces to the mainmast pinrail.

Alan Kennard looked at Schooste. "A bunch of dudes we got."

"Yah." Schooste was ruminantly fingering the stubble on his chin. "Come on deck that way."

"The cook been called?"

"Sure, Cap'. I call her and the daughter prompt at two bells. They're up."

Kennard stared into the binnacle. He was unwilling to have Schooste see his eyes as he passed the order. "That fella, Tordish," he said, "he's on my watch. But I want you to tell him not to come on deck in no shoregoing duds. Tell him next thing he knows he'll be wearing them on the dock. They ain't the rig for a sailor. Savvy?"

"Yes, sir," Schooste said. But he couldn't hold back his smile, and he added hurriedly, "A crazy booger, huh?"

"Crazy as a loon," Alan Kennard said, his jaw muscles stiff with anger.

Both Minna and her mother appeared on deck after the breakfast work was done. It was a superb sunlit day and the schooner stood under all canvas on the cross-lake traverse for Porte des Morts Pass. Minna had discovered the little ladder up the side of the cookhouse and the space next to the work-boat on its chocks. She and Mrs. Svenson sat there with their feet tucked up under them, Mrs. Svenson with some sewing in her blunt and gray-veined hands.

Kennard regarded them from the poop. But he was more fascinated by the actions of the watch. The sailors took every opportunity to pass the cookhouse and when they did they slowed and looked up at Minna. They flexed their muscles and walked with exaggerated, rolling strides, laughed a lot and shouted to each other in broad sailor talk. If their work brought them aft to the scuttle-butt they wet down their hair, combed it, took time to tighten their belts and smooth their shirts inside their trousers. Tordish, in answer to Schooste's order, had changed from his shore clothing. He wore, though, nothing except a pair of hacked-off overall pants held up by a rope yarn. He strode the deck with his hairless, pimply chest thrust out, his bare heels bumping the planks.

It was for Kennard a source of ironical amusement and also revelation. The crew's popular epithet was "Aw, shit!" They had reduced the words this morning to "Aw, shucks!" or "Darn me!" But he could recall how last night he had called unnecessary orders to the wheelsman, and how in his cabin he had debated whether or not he should shave. You're lucky, he thought, greatly pleased with himself. You caught yourself in time.

The schooner raised Porte des Morts Pass over water scarlet with late sun. The low headlands, the beaches were already amber and dull gold, the pass a chasm of loveliness that opened onto the sunset. Kennard gave the order to come about on the other tack, and creaking, her lee rail low, the schooner ran in from the lake. He stood by the wheelsman, busy with his piloting as he checked the landmarks and took bearings. Still he was aware that the men off watch had gathered near the cookhouse door while they waited for supper. They shadow boxed and wrestled, shouted, sang, jumped nervously from one position to another, the bolder among them peering in the cookhouse portholes or door.

Pack of young fools, he sourly told himself. You'll have to put a stopper on that. But you're young, too. Young enough, anyhow, to almost fall in the same trap.

He ate his supper on deck as the schooner went through the pass, wore around Deathdoor Bluff onto the new course. Minna brought him the plate of pork chops and applesauce, fried potatoes, thick slices of buttered bread. She was silent, her manner deferential, and he realized pleasantly that she was awed by his power of command. "Stay here if your work's done," he told her. No sense in giving the lass the rough end of the stick just because you got stupid and randy. "Tell your ma to come up, too. It's kind of pretty from here, puttin' on down the bay."

"Thank you, sir," she said formally. But she went down the ladder in a graceful leap that showed her legs to the knees.

Alan Kennard disregarded her when she returned with her mother and they seated themselves in the deck chairs. Schooste had come on deck to relieve him, and it was a fine, clear night, a good time to check the compass. The Big Dipper was apparent, a slight gilt scroll against the mauve sky; Polaris hung alone and faintly blue in her corner of space.

He bent and took his Polaris observation, wrote down the error on a slip of paper. Ahead, like wings lifting above the depths of the bay, the lights on Chambers Island and Green Island broke, wavered radiant over the surface mist. "Southwest by a half South is your true course," he told Schooste.

"Southwest by a half South, sir," Schooste said, and the wheelsman repeated it, slacked the wheel.

Alan Kennard moved back and sat on the taffrail, one foot raised to balance himself. He felt calm, fully at peace. But Schooste was making a big business out of checking the lights. "Should catch Peshtigo about now," he said.

"Not for a while," Kennard said. "I'll be around on deck, anyhow." This whole do had its funny side. Schooste was in it; the damn' Dutchman had to act like he was Admiral Lord Bilgewater himself. Just because of that kitten over there in the tight skirt. And look now. Tordish is coming aft, still belly-naked.

The young, blond headed sailor held an accordion under his arm. He stopped at the foot of the poop ladder and looked up at Kennard with respectful eyes. "All right, Cap'n, if I play this?"

"You know goddamn' well it is. But don't you make too much noise and wake up them who want to sleep."

"No, sir. Thank you, sir." Tordish retreated forward with the accordion pulled taut. The other men of both watches waited 'midships where the light from the cookhouse doorway was broad on the deck. Tordish braced himself against the cookhouse and inclined his head so that his hair fell over his forehead.

Romantic-like, Alan Kennard thought, and yet he was stirred by the music. Tordish played quite well. His tunes were the favorites on the mechanical pianos in the beer joints ashore, *Freischütz*, *William Tell*, Strauss waltzes, polkas, a fast two-step.

Kennard had seen it happen before. He wasn't surprised when the sailors formed couples, started skidding, whirling and swaying up and down the deck. Some of them, those who followed their partners, made mock feminine cries and protestations in the accepted fashion, but all of them gazed aft at Minna Svenson. Tordish watched her with a glance of open desire as he brandished the accordion against his chest.

Minna pushed upon the chair arms. She was nearly erect before her mother swung her back into the chair. "You stay here," Mrs. Svenson said.

"But, Ma——"

"You stay here," Mrs. Svenson said. Her face was expressionless. "They'll be in port tomorrow."

Alan Kennard moved to Schooste's side. "I'm going below to catch a bit of shut-eye," he said. "You call me when you raise Peshtigo. I want to take her past the reef myself. And you tell that Tordish to knock off the music at two bells prompt. Him and the rest have got plenty of work in the morning."

He had the impression as he entered his cabin that he was still calm. But when he took off his shoes and stretched out in the bunk, his nerves, his body, his brain and entire being were possessed by thought of Minna. He cursed himself. He looked down with loathing at his body. "Bejesus, she's got you," he murmured. "She's got you bad." He rose and filled the bucket with cold water and bathed. It gave him small relief, though; he lay spasmodically, grinding his teeth until Schooste called to him from the top of the companionway scuttle. His motions, he knew vaguely as he climbed up on deck, were like those of a man held by a frightful fever.

The schooner lay at her dock in Green Bay for several days while Kennard waited for his orders from Froler and Jaeckel. He spent most of it uptown and away from the vessel. But Tordish had got drunk and in a fight in a whorehouse, been put in jail. Kennard had to bail him out, bring him back aboard, and when they arrived Mrs. Svenson was just serving dinner for the crew.

It was corned beef, boiled potatoes, cabbage and fresh apple pie. Kennard's innate sense of frugality forced him to stay and eat it, and as he came on deck Minna was by the gangplank. Minna had on some sort of a cotton suit with a ruffled hem on the jacket, a straw hat that projected forward from her head and carried artificial violets. Long white gloves were in one hand and she wore high kid shoes adorned with pearl buttons.

"I have to go ashore," she said. "That smell—my goodness—it's awful."

Alan Kennard looked around with her at the tremendous upthrust of the paper mill smokestack. It was almost a hundred feet high, they boasted in the town, and one of the biggest on the bay or the river. "Ain't the smoke so much," he said. "The stink's from the digesters. They're full of ammonia and sulphur to soften up the wood."

Minna wrinkled her nose. "And the noise has me about out of my mind."

"That's the drum barkers," he said; "the big iron cylinders where they shake the logs till the bark is off." He had started to cross the gangway and had halted. "You go down on the dock," he told her in a lower, softer voice, "and wait for me. I'll be along in a bit."

"I'll wait," she said.

He found Schooste on the poop. Schooste sat torpid with dinner. "I'm bound ashore," Kennard said. "You got the ship."

"Goddamn," Schooste said. "I thought mebbe I could hit uptown mineself." But then he glanced over at Minna on the dock and his expression changed. "You mail a letter to my wife for me, Cap'?"

"Let's have it," Kennard said impatiently. Now that he had made his choice, now that he had committed himself, he was selfish of every moment away from Minna. You're playing the fool, the back of his mind informed him, but that was dominated by the thought of Minna beside him in a buckboard, along the beach out past Sable Point, just the two of them, no crew, no sharp-eyed old woman or ship or mate to watch. To hell, you've been careful and you got nothing for it. It's done you no bloody good at all. . . .

He talked and laughed a lot while he walked uptown with Minna. Yet he couldn't remember later what he said, nor the reasons for his laughter except that he was happy to have stuck Schooste with the ship. Minna's presence claimed him; the simple fact that he grasped her forearm and that they were together. An instinct of caution prompted him, though, when they were at the livery stable and the horse was being backed into the buckboard shafts. "Your ma mind what time we come on board?" he asked Minna.

"She knows I'm gone with you," Minna said, her mouth lines firm. "She hasn't got any need to worry."

"Then I'll jump over here and pick us up a little stuff to eat. Couple of bottles of beer, too."

"Gee, you're a real sport," Minna said. But the livery stable man had been intently listening, took a lap robe from the rack and put it under the buckboard seat. Color darkened Minna's face; her throat muscles trembled. "Go ahead!" she snapped at Kennard. "Go ahead! If we're going to have a picnic we'd best get started."

He drank four fast neat ryes in the saloon where they made up the sandwiches and sold him the beer. Then he felt capable of going back to Minna. He had driven very little, was clumsy in his handling of the horse until they were outside of town. There, in the open country along the narrow dirt road, he tied the reins to the whip socket, let the horse move at a walk.

Minna sat upright on the seat. She hadn't spoken since they had left the stable, and he had the belief that she was angry with him because of what the stable man had done. But then he understood that she had immersed herself in the beauty of the afternoon. "Pretty, isn't it?" she said suddenly.

"Yeah," he said, willing also in this time to be quiet.

Elms and maples arched above the road. Sunlight struck through them to form patterns that were complicated and frail, and while they shifted with the slight breeze upon the tree tops, they never broke, only undulated on the yellow dust. They were black. The leaves were a tender green, and above, in the sunlight blaze, almost silver. Wild roses grew in the ditches. He reached out and took one, gave it wordlessly to Minna and she pushed the stem through the buttonhole in the lapel of her jacket. A buck rabbit poked his head over the lichened stone of a fence, then, his ears up, jumped and skittered across the road, a file of small rabbits behind him. Minna squealed and clasped Kennard's hand. "Pretty," she said again.

Lilacs grew in a magenta froth of bloom in a farmhouse dooryard. A woman in a blue sun bonnet drew a bucket from the well, waved to them and smiled. Chickens ran in the road after them. The farm dog barked sleepily at the horse and went back to his fleas and a pool of shadow. Down in a field, the farmer called his team musically, his voice slowly fading. A woodchuck sat in a clover patch, pert and watchful, his fat belly glossy with sun. Robins had nested in the roadside trees; the chicks cried with surprise when a bull calf bawled from a pasture.

"Where are we going?" Minna said. She seemed to have become drowsy. Her head nodded and her body was lax.

"Out by Sable Point."

"Nice out there?"

"Dunno. I never been before. But it looks nice from what I've seen from the water."

She was asleep, her head over on her shoulder. Her hat had been disturbed and shoved sidewise. He worked slowly to discover the hat pins, draw them out, then take off the hat. Her body drooped towards his on the seat and he put an arm around her, loosely held her. The fine trees were gone; they were out in open country where the road was a rough track and the sun fell full and hard. He turned to shield her from the sun and the warmth and the supple softness of her body affected him. He kissed her on the lips. She didn't respond. She was limp. He sat back from her, feeling sorrow, a strange shame.

But she awakened after he had driven the horse under a solitary hickory tree. It gave a patch of shade that must have been chill upon her in contrast to the sunlight, for she sat up shivering. She blinked at him for an instant in alarm, as if she did not know him, then smiled. "Gosh, I was sleepy," she said. She stretched her arms and beneath her jacket he saw the shape of her breasts. "Let's get out," he said, the tight beat of blood around his heart. "That's the point over there. We'll have to hoof it."

"Looks like," she said, "that they've been berrying out this way. They made a path. So I won't tear my skirt and Ma won't be angry."

"Yeah," he said, taciturn with the burden of his passion. He had taken the horse out of the shafts, tied the animal to the tree and put down a bag of oats. Now he lifted the sandwich sack, the bottles of beer from under the seat. He hesitated and picked up the lap robe, tucked it under his arm. "You want your hat?"

She saw that he had taken the robe and her eyes were wide. "Leave it," she said, looking at the hat. "Nobody's here to steal it, and I might lose it."

He went ahead of her over the path that led to the point. He held back the brambles and bushes, but once or twice he heard her moan as her skirt or her stockings were caught. "You stay here," he said, "till I find the place for us."

"No," she said. "I'm not staying."

He stared at her. "Why not?"

"Snakes. . . . Might be snakes around."

"Like hell! But you want for me to carry you?"

She shook her head, her mouth puckered in a wry smile. "I'll make it myself. You just keep on slow."

They came out upon a small, shelving strip of sand beyond which the water lay like turquoise flame. He spread out the robe, put down the sandwiches in the shade. But the beer was lukewarm to the touch through the dripping sack. "Got to stow it in the water to cool," he said. "I don't, it'll blow up on us."

"Good idea," she said. "But take off your shoes and socks and put it in good and deep so's to be real cool."

He took off his shoes and socks, then, deliberately, his coat, his tie, collar and shirt. She watched him, he was aware. She was studying the breadth of his shoulders, his muscles, the flatness of his stomach, the depth of his chest. By God, you ain't no Tordish. You're a grown man.

He was out knee-deep in the water when she shouted to him, "Here I come!" She had stripped off her jacket, her shoes and stockings, walked into the water with her skirts up around her knees. "Gosh, it's good and warm. You have to go out more yet, Cap'."

"You call me Alan," he said, and then he heard her screech. She had slipped over a stone, floundered in water up to her waist. He dropped the beer bottles and waded back and helped her out. She laughed as she shuddered. "Cold enough off that darn' rock. No harm done, though." She fingered the dribbling folds of the skirt. "It's cotton and it'll dry in a hurry."

"If you lie down on the robe and stretch out you'll be dry fast enough," he said. He moved to the robe and seated himself on the edge of it. But when he looked around for her she had disappeared. He could see only the dim print of her feet in the sand, hear the rasp of wet cotton behind a bush. He sat very still, his hands locked on his knees. You're pushing for it, he thought. You're getting closer to it all the time, Kennard. But, damn you, are you sure you want it?

It might be something like Jane all over again. And if you dip into this one, it's marriage. You'll have to get spliced to her certain as hell. Then you'll be stuck with the old woman, too. She could turn out like Mrs. Shaw. Bang your skull loose at the end of each trip, tell you how to run your house, how to run your wife, bejesus, too, your ship. You should have put down your two dollars the other day and taken a doxy in the same joint where Tordish took his. But you didn't. You're here, out to buy it for a price that's a sight more than you want to pay. So you're fouled up fine.

Minna was coming back from behind the bush. She carried a sodden garment closely in one hand, stooped down with her head bowed to tuck it within a corner of the robe. Then she sat shyly beside him and he recognized with a flare of passion that it was her drawers she had placed there. All furled up neat. She couldn't stand them wet against her. Now she's got on nothing but the skirt and maybe a petticoat.

His imagination let him expose Minna's thighs. It went on and she rested entirely naked. Stop. You're off your head, man. Her and the mother will have you up for rape. But he turned around to Minna. He took her in his arms and slung her flat on the robe, her hands beating at his back, her teeth grating against his. She made a hoarse sound of refusal, part grunt, part sob each time she could pull away her lips. But at last she lay wide-legged and his hands went over her the way he wished. Her eyes were shut; she was biting her underlip.

For him, it was as if he reeled down off a tremendous cliff. He plunged through the darkness of abysses that were incredibly deep, held no end. Yet he was followed. He wasn't alone in his passion. Some other man went after him to her, and that other man was again himself. They moved very near in the deepest abysses and he could hear the other, make out the horror, the dismay of the voice. "Not you," he thought he heard. "Not you, Kennard. Come back. Our mother has sent me."

He rolled roughly aside from Minna. The congestion of blood in his lower body gave him exquisite agony. He was wracked by it, tormented so that he gasped wretching. But he slid his hands across his eyes to keep him from sight of Minna. "I'm daft," he whispered. "Bloody well off my rocker."

She made no sound. She seemed to lie very still. He released his hands and looked at her. Her body twisted heaving and when she looked at him her eyes held hatred. Then, as he reached toward her, the passion resurgent and commanding in him, she pitched over onto her stomach, locked her arms about her head and wept. He got up silently and walked from her down the beach.

She watched him after a time. She did her best to understand him, the fury of the passion gone and now no more than a dull ache in her brain. He had refused to take her, and from her talk with other, more experienced women, she was surprised and also hurt. It was an insult. A nervous reflex rippled through her muscles and she put her hands strongly against herself. She hated him, hated him, hated him.

But the reflex passed. She lay slack, staring at the sky where small wind cloud drifted. They resembled the Indian canoes her mother had told her about when she was little. Still, you don't want to think about canoes. What's the matter with this man? Just remember all the others who were crazy for you.

Kennard sat at the water's edge. His feet were in it and he had his arms on his knees and his head bent to them. Minna got up, compelled by pride, and walked towards him.

Maybe something's wrong with him, she told herself as she approached. But it might be, too, that he's a good man and didn't want to do you harm. Ma must think he's all right or she wouldn't have let you come out with him. Don't be snappy, or fresh. Just find how he'll act next. You're not too sure of much.

Her shadow, sent in protraction by the westering sun, touched Kennard seconds before he heard the slurred tread of her feet. He brought himself to look up into her eyes, although a perverse quality of his nature demanded that he first inspect her body with the sunlight on it.

"You must figure me for a crazy one," he said.

She stood motionless. "You're a good sight different from other fellas I know."

"Yeah." Calmness had come to him, and he gestured for her to sit down at his side. "I got to tell you this. . . ." He broke off as he tried to prepare the words for her and stared forth across the bay. The water was azure, the sun a fiery crescent; the cloud left strips of dark, pine green below and then the azure returned.

"I'm in love with you," he said. "Yeah, I've been in love with you maybe ever since you and your ma first come aboard. But there's more. About the other."

"What other?" She sat with her knees crossed, just her toes dabbling in the water. She did that so he would believe that she wasn't nervous. It was her impulse, though, to jump up and run away from him as straight and fast and far as she could run.

"You listen, Minna," he said, possessive in the present phase of his emotion. "Your ma's wealthy. You will be, too."

"Gosh, you scare me. You sound cracked."

"I'm not." He wheeled on her, swirling the sand, and in his eyes she saw that he was sane. She started to quiver. It wasn't enough to paddle her toes through the water. She scooped up handfuls and loosed them in sun-gay showers on her ankles and her calves. This man was strange. But not crazy. And he loved her.

He was about to ask her to marry him. Wife of a schooner captain. How'd you like that? Let Ma talk to him, though, and let him talk now. You're not scared. It's just that he's kind of odd.

"You remember Patigowoc?"

"Of course. I was brought up there. Then we went to Chicago. Then Pa got cleaned out and died."

"Your old school book's still in the house in Patigowoc. *McGuffey's Reader. Minna Svenson,* it says. *Her book.* And *Chicago.*"

Her eyes were toubled before she laughed. "You're right."

"So I am." A sort of triumph was in his voice. He looked at her fixedly with an intense gaze. "I've been after you and your ma for about two years. The land over there belongs to you yet. It's got limestone on it, and limestone is worth a parcel of money. They have to have the stuff to make high grade steel."

Minna Svenson wet her hands in the slowly lapping water. She traced her fingers down her cheeks and down her throat. The coolness was good. It took away some of the heat that seemed to be breaking right through her skin. This isn't crazy talk. He means every word he says. And before, remember, he told you to call him Alan. He's a good-looker, too. You could love him, might love him right now. It'd be nice being married to him.

"I've had women," Alan Kennard said with an abrupt burst of egotism. "More'n a few. But when it come to you—" His eyes had become defiant—"I bloody well couldn't. Not without you knowin' about the limestone and that I want to marry you."

"You're nice," she said.

"And when we get back aboard," he said harshly and rapidly, "I'll talk to your old lady."

"Ma would like to know," Minna said. "The limestone, that'd be awful' important to her, because she's worked so hard. Then about you and me, she's——"

"But how about you?" he said. He had risen to his knees, and erect. He pulled her up and held her at arm's length. "Minna?"

"I think I love you, Alan," she said. Then nervous tension made her giggle, and she felt contrite and embarrassed. "Race you down the beach. Loser has to bring in the beer."

She ran as fast as she could most of the way and afterwards slowed to let him win. He stood on the shore while she waded in after the beer. It's different, she thought; he's asked me to marry him. Still, she took caution not to bunch her skirts too high, and back on the beach she retreated behind a bush with her drawers. No two times. That before had been bad enough. And you can afford to wait till you're married.

He gathered driftwood for a fire and she opened the beer and the sandwiches. They sat wordless as they ate, too engaged in thought for speech. Sunset spread gentle and soft upon the bay; night dropped black to receive the stars. The fire burned with a marvelous blue and red flame, and the sand flies were driven away. She was lulled, allowed her body to go supine. He was soon beside her.

"Can I kiss you, Minna?"

"Sure, Alan." Her hands closed on the nape of his neck. "But not like before. That made me kind of scared."

"I love you, I love you," he said tenderly.

It was close to dawn when he brought Minna back to the ship. But arc lights burned on the dock; flat-cars were abreast of the holds and Schooste had cargo whips rigged from the fore and main booms. "Orders for Buffalo," Schooste told him on the poop. "Full load o' pulp paper."

"All right," Kennard said. "Lay below and catch your shut-eye. But how's the coffee pot?"

"A-bilin'," Schooste said. "The old lady's still up. You mebbe will see her with the cleaver."

He stretched to strike Schooste, then restrained himself. "Get off the deck, you!" he said.

"Gosh, Cap', you real serious, hah?" Schooste said.

"I am," he said. "I am indeed so." But aboard was no place to talk to Mrs. Svenson, he knew. It would have to hold over until they were in Buffalo. This ship was too full of big-eared men.

He evaded Mrs. Svenson during the next few days, and was even happy in the fact that it was rainy, windy weather that kept Minna from coming on deck. But after they had cleared the Detroit River and were headed out into Erie the fair weather returned. The tug had cast off at dusk, while the moon and Venus were both apparent in the Eastern sky. The moon rose with splendor and illumined the lake and the ship and cast vivid shards upon the tree-thick shore. There was very little wind, only intermittent gusts out of the West. Series of lucent ripples radiated aft from the cutwater. The canvas slatted grayish brown in the moonlight and the booms and gaffs seemed painted with silver. Middle Sister Island was dim shadow far beyond the bow.

All hands were on deck. They were under the spell of the night, and Tordish played his accordion with unusual softness. Minna had climbed onto the cook-house topside. She sat with her back against the work-boat and Kennard realized that she had made no attempt to greet him. Jealousy darted in his brain. She's paying you back for not coming around the last few days. But the old lady's down there on deck. Go down and make like you want to talk to her and Minna will be off that topside fast.

He sprang lithely from the poop to the main desk and Tordish and the rest of the sailors backed away from the cook-house at his approach. He was alone with Mrs. Svenson. She sat on the wave guard of the cook-house doorway. She didn't look up at him, nor did she speak. But Minna scrambled down from the topside and came and took his arm, and he sensed that there had been many conversations between mother and daughter about him since the ship had left Green Bay.

"Let's go over to the rail." Minna tugged at his arm. "Ma's tired. She doesn't want to talk."

He smiled at Minna, conscious that his nervousness was much less than her own. They moved to the leeward rail and stood there with elbows akimbo and looked out at the glistening lake. The sailors had gone forward, but only a few feet away, and Tordish no longer played the accordion. You never knew before, Kennard thought sharply, what damn' small privacy you got aboard a ship.

"Talk to me," Minna said in a low voice. "Tell me something nice. All I've seen of you the last few days is with a fork in your hand or up there calling orders."

"I love you," he murmured, and to his great delight she murmured back, "I love you, Alan."

It was extremely difficult for him to keep from kissing her. He lifted his hands and gripped them on the rail. "We got to take care," he said to her from a corner of his mouth. "They're all looking at us."

"Yes, I know," she said. "But in Buffalo we can be alone, can't we? It would be fine if we went uptown and had a meal together that Ma didn't cook."

"Pipe down, darlin'," he said. "The whole lot of them are listening."

She gazed around in involuntary vexation at the sailors, then back at him. "All right," she said. "But if we can't talk about ourselves, you'll have to tell me about the sea."

"Goddamn!" he said. The chord of memory had been struck hard. He could hear Jane, and see her. The amassed impressions he held of her came up out of a somber fissure of thought that he had not known was still in his brain. Jane. What would she make of this one he'd just said he loved? Jane, who'd fought and fought, and won at her own rough price. Skinny and prim looking, but with the eyes that went right down through you to the heels. She played for you while you sang. She painted the pictures you'll never forget. The brook and the lobster-backs in by the trees. The other of the brook. That light on the water, and the mark the deer left, the flowers, the trout after the worm. All of Antrim itself wasn't half so fine. And the picture of the sea. Yes, she gave it the name that came from you.

Some instinct of Minna's nature was disturbed. She looked into his face with grave and calculating eyes. Then she stroked the fingers of one hand over his, provocatively, and so that the sailors could see. "If you want to stand here like a hitch post," she said, "I'm going to bed. I like a person to talk to me."

"I will," he said. "I got a story about the sea for you."

It was old Hjalmar Boren who had told it to him. They had been shipmates together in that Leith bark, the *Heather,* his second deep-water ship. He had been off watch and sat with Hjalmar under the wide, trembling shadow of the mainsail. Hjalmar wasn't old. Just that the man had picked up clap three times running in the ports and was no good for deck work any more, could only sail as sailmaker. But the Swede was good at that, and in his own country, before he'd taken to the sea, Hjalmar had been a lawyer, something of the sort. Hjalmar was the one who had taught him to read.

The story, Hjalmar said, was a book story. He sat sewing a patch on a jib clew, careful and yet quick, twelve stitches to a needle length. It was about a Greek, a prince. "The fellar's name was Odysseus. He come from out in the Greek islands, a place called Ithaca."

Hjalmar had lost most of his front teeth in a fight in a whorehouse in Valparaiso. He talked with a little lisp and he kept a wad of Copenhagen snuff high in his cheek. The wind in the sails, the sounds of the watch on deck, the sough of the seas alongside and the chatter of the gear made listening to him a bit hard. But Hjalmar talked in the simple sailor language he understood.

"So go on," Minna said. She nudged him. "You're acting kind of funny again. Please tell me the story."

"Very well," Alan Kennard said, taking himself back from Hjalmar and Hjalmar's telling of the story. "This here's about a Greek prince name of Odysseus. He was a goddamn' good sailor, and, yeah, a soldier, too. He went out to fight a war at a place called Troy. That was another Greek port. The fighting was tough and when it was finished, this Odysseus, he had hell's own time gettin' home."

There was something in there about a wooden horse, but the second mate had been yelling at the watch then and he had missed what Hjalmar had to say about it. Still, he was straight about the voyage home.

"Twenty years this Odysseus sailed. One island where he put in, a woman name of Calypso threw a quick round turn on him. She kept him flaked out in a cave and she said by the Jesus she was going to marry him. But she changed her mind. She wasn't such a bloody bitch after all."

Minna had retreated from him a pace or so, Kennard saw, as if she didn't like the story. But she stayed there, and she kept her glance on him. Mrs. Svenson over at the cookhouse was listening, and the sailors stood in an intent semi-circle up the deck. He raised his voice without self-conscious effort. The habit of story telling was deep in his nature. There were all the nights when his mother told stories and sang.

"So Odysseus, he rigged himself a boat. They used leather for rope back there, and they steered with a long sweep oar in a craft like them they got out in the Greek islands these days. Yeah, square-set and bad sailers when they ain't before the wind.

"Odysseus, he hauled and he tacked and he hauled, but he still couldn't fetch up home. Then he got into hell's own storm. A real bad blow it was. The craft foundered under him. Two days and two nights the poor swab hung onto a piece of her. Then he hit the beach in a river. He was bare-tail naked, the gear all ripped off him in the storm. So when he got up on the beach, he crawled into the bushes and he flaked out there for some sleep.

"There was a young princess from over in a town down the coast. Her old lady, the queen, sent her and some of the other lasses out to wash up the palace bunk gear in this river where Odysseus made the beach. They washed the gear and they were about to shove off home when Odysseus—he was asleep over in the bushes—he woke up.

"He was in a bad way. He didn't have nothing but a bush he'd broke off to cover him. The lasses, they all hollered. Not this young princess, though. She knew a man when she saw one crossing her bow. So she up and talked to Odysseus in the Greek talk, then she took him home.

"Well, her folks, they were sailors, too. They took good care of the poor fella and they give him a fine boat and crew so he could make it home. This time he did. But while he was gone—twenty years he'd been gone, mind you—his wife'd had a lot of men in the house. All o' them had been pushin' her and the other women in the house around. After marrying her, they were, or getting into her bunk. Odysseus, he found this out. Him and his son got together and they killed the whole goddamn' crew of them. Every last bastardly one. Then he passed the order for the place to be swabbed down with fresh water. He had a hawser brung up from shore, and the women had been in the bunk with them fellas, they was hung right outside the door. Then him and his woman turned in. Penelope, that was her name. A smart woman. Better than what most sailormen get to know."

Minna was half smiling at him, not quite certain that somewhere in the story there had been a hidden reference to her. She didn't like that last thing he'd said at all, about this Penelope. But now he was over beside her. He took her hands just as if the crew looking didn't mean a bit to him. "It's about the only sea story I know," he told her. "Next time, you ask me to sing. I sing real good."

"I will," she said with blunt honesty. "I didn't think so much of that."

He walked beside her to the cookhouse doorway. Mrs. Svenson gave him an upward, searching glance and said, "When do you talk to me, Cap'?"

"In Buffalo," he said unhesitantly. "All right?"

"Fine," Mrs. Svenson said. "Good night." She pushed Minna before her into the cookhouse and shut the door.

They talked the night after the ship had docked in Buffalo. All of the crew including Schooste had gone ashore. Mrs. Svenson mounted to the poop where Kennard paced, a piece of rope yarn in his hands. "Sit down," he told her. He indicated one of the deck chairs. "I'll go get Minna."

"No, you don't," Mrs. Svenson said. "Minna's working on a new dress she wants to finish. So we let her be. What's on your mind?"

Kennard was always made unquiet by a ship in port. He resented the fact that there a ship began to lose her identity. The traditional cleanliness couldn't be maintained; people who didn't know how to steer a wheelbarrow came aboard with the greatest of confidence and every kind of a question. The galley had to be locked, and the storerooms, and down in the main cabin men who one way or another had something to do with the owners sat around with their hats on and acted cocky as hell.

But tonight he had given strict orders to the watchman at the head of the dock. The ship lay silent, her lines in good shape, the decks reasonably clean from the sweep-down the crew had made just before knocking off. The wind, what there was of it, was from the lake, clean and fresh, with the sound of gulls upon it and the intermittent song of some Swedish sailor left as anchor watch aboard a steamer.

"Well," Alan Kennard said in the language he had often considered since Green Bay; "I want to marry your daughter. Maybe she's told you as much."

"She has." Mrs. Svenson lay almost inert in the deck chair. "Go ahead."

"I'm a serious fella. Saved my money. I got more'n two thousand dollars in a savin's account in Chicago. You want to see the book?"

"Not now. Minna's young, Cap'. She's just eighteen. She might like to frolic around some before she's through."

"Wouldn't bother me. I'd go right along with her. My best pal, he's mate of a Pickands, Mather steamer, and his wife is like that and they're happier than ticks in a new mattress."

Mrs. Svenson smiled. "I'm glad," she said.

"But I got something else to tell you," Kennard said.

"About the limestone land in Patigowoc, you mean."

"That's right. You and Minna can be rich."

"Ah, stop it!" Mrs. Svenson's gray-veined hands opened and flung out into the shaft of light from the companionway. Her face was swarthy with anger, and her voice rough. "All of you men who come from over the seas have got the idea you're going to be rich. Svenson was one. So I end up being a cook for shanty boys and sailors. How do you know that limestone's worth a damn' plugged nickel?"

"I don't," he said, at once irritated and impressed by her anger. "Still, the stuff belongs to you. The title to the land's in your name.

I've got a pal, too, who's in the iron business. He uses limestone in his plant. He'll go look over the land for you and tell you what it's worth."

"All right," Mrs. Svenson said quietly. "But, first things first. When would you figure to marry Minna?"

"As fast as I can."

"Where?"

"In Cleveland, if I can rig it. My friends, Phelim and Peggy Carmody, could stand up for us. But I'll have to write the company for time off."

"Go on and write. There's no kin nor friends left to Minna and me. I'm Ojibway, and my folks are long since dead. And don't count on me for any money; I haven't got it."

Kennard made a dramatic gesture with his arms outspread. "I'll take care of it all, Minna's clothes, the weddin', the whole lash-up. You were saying you were Ojibway. Well, my ma was a Romany. That's what we called them in the old country—a gypsy."

"Yeah," Mrs. Svenson said mildly; "I understood." She was on her feet, and surprisingly like a man, she held out her hand to him. "Good luck to you with Minna. I think you've got a real girl there. Hang on and I'll send her aft so you can make love for a while."

"Thanks," he said, abashed by the simplicity of her expression. "Thanks a lot, Ma."

Froler and Jaeckel gave Alan Kennard their best wishes and a week off without pay, explaining that they would have to hire another master during his absence. "Bugger them," he told Schooste as he tore up their letter. "I'm piling off this one for keeps."

"And you about to be married? Gollies!" Schooste shook his head. "Jobs ain't so easy to come by, Cap'n. You'll cool down after you and her are spliced. But I can handle the ship until the new fella comes aboard. You head ashore with your folks."

My folks, Kennard thought. You have yourself a family now. You take Minna, you take the old lady along with her. But no yowping about that. You and the old lady get along dandy. She'll be a great help to you later, too.

He clapped Schooste on the back and laughed. "Thank you kindly. I need all the time I can get. But pick up a cook on the beach. Mrs. Svenson's through aboard."

Minna was very excited when he went forward to talk with her and her mother. He had received letters also from Phelim and Peggy Carmody and from Joshua Shaw. It pleased him to know that the

marriage could be held in Cleveland with his friends present and
with the chance to discuss the limestone deal with Joshua. But
Minna said, "I don't have the clothes to go visiting. You say this
Peggy is real beautiful, and the Shaw fella sounds high and mighty
as can be. Look, Alan. What I have on is my best dress."

"Wear the cotton suit," Mrs. Svenson said quietly. "If it was
good enough to catch your man, it'll be good enough to wear in the
train to Cleveland. Then we'll see about new clothes. You start to
pack. I'll be in right away." She winked at Kennard after Minna
was gone. "The girl isn't full grown yet. You have some work on
your hands, you know that?"

"I know," he said gravely. "But don't you worry. We'll make
out."

"Doesn't worry me," the Ojibway woman said. "It's you who's
marrying her."

He hired a hansom cab to take them to the station and the crew
gathered at the rail to see them off. Schooste had bought a bottle,
and he and Schooste had a couple of long drinks in farewell.
Tordish insisted upon carrying the bags from the ship to the cab,
and Minna alternated between blushing and giggling. When her
mother silenced her, she whispered, "The only other time I was in
a cab was at Pa's funeral. I'm sorry. . . ."

Minna slept out of nervous exhaustion in the train, her head on
Kennard's shoulder. Mrs. Svenson didn't bother to wake her to eat
the box lunch she had brought. But as she and Kennard ate the
pork and baked bean sandwiches she said suddenly, "We won't disgrace you in Cleveland. Svenson was a good man. He taught us
some manners. We've just got a little raggle-tailed since he died."

"Sure thing," Kennard said. "But my friends ain't fancy people.
They was, they wouldn't be. My friends, I mean. You have any
liking as to churches?"

The gray haired and haggard woman stared for an instant
through the smoke curtained window. "I'm no churchgoer. Nor
Minna. Svenson was an atheist. You fix it the way you want. But
I wouldn't like it fancy."

"I'll talk to Josh Shaw," he said, perturbed. This thing seemed to
be getting bigger all the time. Minna's weight against his shoulder
cramped him. He suffered from a peculiar sensation of claustrophobia. His desire was to be alone. He had grave doubts about his
love and his future. Then Minna stirred slightly and partly opened
her eyes and murmured his name, lifted her lips to be kissed.

Tenderness, keen passion came to him. He kissed her, fully aware that Mrs. Svenson approved of his action.

Phelim and Peggy Carmody were at the Union Depot to meet them. Peggy wore a wide straw hat and carried a parasol, and Alan Kennard could see the jealousy in Minna's eyes. But Phelim had been drinking; he was ready with his usual jokes and small talk, the charm he could exhibit to any pretty woman. He took Minna by the arm, slung the Svensons' battered straw suit case in the other hand and went off in front with her. Peggy followed amiably with Mrs. Svenson and Kennard found that he was alone and didn't like it. He hurried to catch up to Minna and Phelim. "Trying to steal my girl?" he asked Phelim, more than half seriously.

"Me a married man and a Pickands, Mather stiff," Phelim said. "But, sure I was. She's so pretty she should be stole."

"Aw, go on with you!" Minna said. "You sailors certainly have some talk."

But Phelim Carmody was regarding his friend, concerned by Kennard's new, tense manner. Lines had deepened at the corners of the mouth. The eyes squinted rapidly, and the face was gaunt. It wasn't just the girl and getting married, Phelim thought. Antrim surely wasn't that bad off for a woman. By the glory, though, this family's name was Svenson; the old lady was sure as hell an Indian. Then they were the folks from Patigowoc. The limestone was mixed up in it, too. Antrim was taking a shot at the moon. He was after the sweepstakes good. A bad business. You don't like it. And yet you can't let your pal down. Just keep your yap shut.

"Let's go to our place," he said when they stood at the cab rank. "We can pile you in."

"No." Kennard said. He had just made the decision. "We're bound for the Hollenden. Don't want to squeeze you, what with the kid and all."

"Nothing's too fine for an Antrim man, hey?" Phelim said, incapable of keeping the note of mockery out of his voice.

"That's right," Alan Kennard said. He had sensed a good deal of what was behind Phelim's question and he was angry.

"But at least you can come over and get washed up and have a drink," Peggy said. She stared hard at Phelim. "The big lug has been holding out some real Irish whiskey for you."

"Thank you kindly," Mrs. Svenson said. "We'd like that. Then maybe you'd tell me and Minna where we could go to buy some clothes."

"Go with you," Peggy said, twirling the parasol in pleasure. "Red, here, gets paid mainly in pennies and nickels so I have to make me own clothes. But I sure know where to buy 'em."

Mrs. Svenson took over the Carmody's baby immediately after they entered the apartment. She changed his diaper and wiped his nose, then balanced him on her knee while she drank a glass of the Bushmill whiskey Phelim poured. Alan Kennard sat staring glumly at the rubber plant, lost in himself and unwilling to take part in the conversation. Phelim drank also in silence, his drink heavy and undiluted. Peggy and Minna talked about their shopping trip.

"Now over to Levy and Stearn's," Peggy said. "That's where we go first. You want Madame Ruppert's Egyptian Balm, and the Face Bleach. Sure, and the Almond Hand Cream. Mercy, you been out in the sun a lot."

"Sure, I know," Minna said humbly. "We've been aboard the schooner all the time."

"Then there's Miss Keeney's," Peggy said. "She's up on Euclid across from the Lennox. First class millinery is what she got. Some of the prettiest hats you ever did see. Paris originals, too, the girls say, and I don't think they're lyin'."

"You're spending Antrim's pay in one hell of a hurry," Phelim said. "Take it easy, woman."

"That's all right," Alan Kennard said, perversely provoked. "I got plenty stowed away."

"So," Peggy said quickly, aware of the antagonism between the two men, "you can go over to Ball's, Alan. Superior and Seneca. They have about as nice rings as anybody in town. Better than the red-head bought me in Liverpool, anyhow."

"Ah, you give me a pain!" Phelim said. He was on his feet as he finished his drink. "I'm goin' over to the company. You want to come along, Antrim?"

"No, I'll stay here." Kennard kept his eyes lowered. "I got to give Minna and Ma Svenson the money for their shoppin'."

Phelim took his cap off the deer antlers in the hallway, then looked back. "You're right," he said clearly. "Finders, keepers and losers, weepers. That's what they say in this country, and you better hang onto to what you got."

"Say, listen—" Kennard said.

But Phelim was out the door and his steps thudded on the staircase. The women sat still. It was only the baby who made any sound; he pulled his thumb from between his gums with a soft *plop-*

plop. Peggy's face was very red. "Phelim's been drinking, Alan," she said. "He don't like working for the company too much, and I guess he's a little jealous of you. Captain, while he's sailing mate yet."

"Captain of a jackass schooner," Alan Kennard said. "That's me, and that's no big shakes."

Mrs. Svenson put the baby down to crawl upon the floor. She took the whiskey bottle and poured Kennard another drink. "Here's to you," she said. "You'll sail more than schooners. And now, Peggy, you and me are going to measure up on Minna. She won't get to buy any store dress. Not so long as you know a good seamstress."

"I know a daisy," Peggy said. "She'll fit you slick as a minute, Minna. But you get out of here, Alan. The girl has to take her clothes off so we can measure her correct."

"Very well," he mumbled. He had been greatly hurt by what Phelim had said. Phelim had meant for him to know that he was some kind of pimp. That's right. For wanting to marry Minna, Phelim reckoned him as such. Why, by God, I'll beat the Liverpool sod's brains loose. Like hell you will. Phelim's a head taller than you, and stronger, and just as tough. He's your old and true friend, too, and entitled to his own opinion. You'll have to explain the lash-up to him later. Now get out of here. It's time you did.

"Why, Minna, your neck's just twelve and a half," Peggy was saying, a tape measure in her hands. "And your waist will come in to a real twenty with a new corset. Bust, thirty-six. Arm, twelve. You writin' them down, Ma Svenson?"

"I am," Mrs. Svenson said. "Cap', you were told to clear out of here."

"On my way," he said. He went over and kissed Minna's bare shoulder, made her shiver. Then he placed two fifty-dollar bills on the table. "Buy the best. I'll get the rooms for us over to the hotel. See you later."

But he failed to go in the Hollenden when he reached Superior and Bond. He was conscious of his badly pressed blue serge suit, his unshined shoes and the train grit on his collar and his hat. You need a wash-down and a whole new rig yourself. Josh will tell you where to get the suit. He'll tell you more. Josh can put you straight about this marriage stuff. Never was a man to make a friend out of a pimp, and if he thinks you are, he'll say it straight out.

The Weddell House bar had a calming effect upon him. He welcomed the smells of sawdust and tobacco and wet wood and alcohol. The beer he drank was cool, faintly pungent in his nostrils. This was where he had told Josh that he would meet him. But he was early. He'd have a chance to get his thoughts squared away first. Just slide along easy, Alan. You're right. You're not wrong. . . . His thought went to Minna and he drank the beer faster, rapped with the glass on the bar for a fresh one. He was beginning to get drunk when Joshua Shaw walked in and joined him.

They shook hands gazing closely at each other and then Kennard laughed. "Guess I got a little load," he said. "But what'll you drink, Josh?"

"Whiskey and water," Shaw said. He could see their reflections in the bar mirror, and he was oddly oppressed by the difference between them. Kennard looked like just what he was—a slightly drunken sailor ashore in his best suit for some special occasion. Shaw looked quite dandified in contrast in spite of his steel-rimmed spectacles and the gray in his sideburns. His pepper-and-salt suit was obviously tailor-made and his dove gray homburg expensive. The high collar, the fluffed-out cravat, the pearl stick pin were all popular signs of "the gentleman," and in coming in today he had for some obscure reason brought along a malacca stick with an ivory head and with it a new pair of gloves.

But those were surface indications. Down underneath, he realized, he and this man were very much alike. They were both desperate. They had great need of each other. "So tell me, Antrim," he said, "about this girl you're going to marry."

"Ah, she's like a dream from heaven," Alan Kennard said. He was sweating from the beer, but he had already ordered whiskey for Joshua and himself. "She's a saucy little angel."

Joshua Shaw grinned at him. "Your adjective hinders the metaphor. Still, I understand you. Is she the daughter of the man who owned the limestone land at Patigowoc?"

"The same. Her and her mother are over here at Phelim Carmody's now. We plan to get married in this town. I hope you can fix it for us, Josh."

"I see no reason why I shouldn't. Here's all good luck."

"Thank ye, man. But how are the folks out to Bellport?"

Joshua Shaw gulped the whiskey. "Lucinda's gone," he said. "She went about two months ago and took her daughter with her."

"Bejesus. That can't have done Cottrell any good."

"It hasn't. Cottrell's a real out-and-out drunkard."

"But your mother, and the colonel?"

"Mother's just about the same. It's hard to say about her, though. You know how she is."

"That I do."

"Father is busy making steel. He's at it day and night. His way of keeping from thinking of things at home."

"You'd make me think you've had no word from Jane."

"Nothing. She's in Europe, and that's all we know. But when Lucinda pulled out, her family made it hard for us. They forced us to buy in their shares of stock in the plant for cash. So our cash reserves are knocked to hell and gone, and with some of the weird deals Dad has entered into around the Square, our credit isn't too solid any more. You say Mrs. Svenson came along with you and your girl."

"She did. She did indeed." Alan Kennard slopped a bit of his whiskey in his nervousness. "Josh, are you out to say we might make a deal between us for the limestone at Patigowoc?"

"Exactly. If we could get into that and establish clear title and get it working, we'd both make a lot of money." ✕

"All right. By the God, we will, then. But first let me tell you how I met the girl—Minna, that's her name—and fell in love with her and the rest of it. There's a question you have to settle for me, y' see. Because I ain't no pimp."

"Who the hell said you were?"

"Phelim Carmody, me old pal and ship-mate. But not straight-like. He hinted at it kind of. And now you listen to me and I'll tell ya. But, would you wet your whistle again first?"

"Thanks, I'll wait, Antrim." Joshua Shaw stood uncomfortably, one foot pressed hard against the bar rail. There was enough that was devious and distorted and wrong in his own life without coming upon more of it. But you must listen, he thought. There's every reason why you should. Antrim, this girl of his and her mother may prove to be the salvation of your own family. You've been pressed too long and too far. There's not much else that you can take and not go under yourself.

He listened with part of his mind, detached and remote, while Alan Kennard talked of Sable Point, the Ojibway woman, the night in port in Buffalo with her and the angry words Phelim Carmody had said. The rest of his thought was given to his father, stamping straight-backed through the lurid light as the iron was poured; his mother in the mahogany rocker, steadily knitting or sewing, and always refusing to admit that anything had gone wrong; Cottrell sagged with alcohol, stupid, crying Lucinda's name in the night, sometimes making believe that she was still there in the house; Jane, whose memory was greater than her presence, the piano silent, her room silent, the chair beside her mother's empty. Christ, will Antrim ever be done?

"So there's the end of it," Alan Kennard said. He had talked himself sober. "You're a smarter man than me, Josh, and educated. What would ye say?"

"That you should marry Minna. That I'm proud of you for having been so honest with her and with her mother. As for Phelim, to hell. . . . He can't mean what he said. His wife had it right; he cracked at you out of jealousy and whiskey. But come on. I want to meet your saucy angel. And we'll go over to the Hollenden and arrange for your rooms."

Kennard whacked him on the back in joy. "I thought ye'd say what you did. For the license now, though, Josh, and the weddin'."

They had gone forth into the street, walked narrow-eyed with the sun in their faces. "Leave that to me, too, Antrim."

"But the old lady's of no religion, nor Minna nor me."

"I'll take care of the whole thing." The carking despair had drained out of Joshua Shaw. He was almost as elated as Kennard. "Judge Beek, over there in the court house, is a good friend of Dad's. They were in the same regiment in the war. The Judge will handle the license business for you, and marry you in his chambers. Then, as soon as we can, you and I had better head for Patigowoc to give me a look at the limestone. Will your Minna mind too much?"

"Not if she knows we're out to make a pile of money for us. She's a girl who's had it the hard way. Living nice would suit her very fine."

"Then," Joshua said, "stop on the way back to Phelim's and pick out a dandy ring for her. Bring her out and buy it right away. I'll go with you to Phelim's and while you and Minna are out, I'll have a talk with the man."

"Ah, don't be too rough on him, Josh. He's as much a friend to me as you are."

"I won't be rough." Joshua flicked his gloves against his thigh in an exuberant gesture. "I'll just ask him how he'd like to go master of a limestone-carrier in the Kennard Line."

"By the gorry!" Kennard said. "You've got all the problems settled." Joshua Shaw smiled faintly at him. Not all, he thought. There's still a number that belong to me. . . .

Minna was entranced by Joshua Shaw. She sat in the Carmody's parlor and talked animatedly with him and extended her hand as if it already held her wedding ring. "I told Alan no engagement ring," she repeated. "Golly, the wedding ring cost him a hundred and sixty-five dollars. He's a sport, my man."

"He certainly is," Joshua said, and turned his attention to Mrs. Svenson. She sat in a corner with the Carmody baby asleep on her lap. Another who's run long enough, Joshua told himself. She'll be willing to sit in Antrim's house and fondle her grand children. Don't you talk anything like business to her now. She's sharp; she'll listen to you when you're ready. And you did enough here when you straightened out Phelim.

Phelim and Alan Kennard were celebrating the warmth of their friendship in the kitchen. They had insisted upon buying two enormous porterhouse steaks and a number of bottles of whiskey and wine, and suddenly both of them were cooks. Peggy had objected for a while, at last accepted them and sat down beside the boiler to peel the potatoes and prepare the vegetables they had forgotten.

Mrs. Svenson listened to their racket with her head cocked. "As wild as buck rabbits," she said. "Pretty soon I'll have to go in and quiet them before they shake loose the ceiling. Minna, you're not doing a thing. You go and help Peggy."

"But, Ma." Minna looked down at her new dress. She felt dismayed that her mother would speak to her so before such a gentleman as Joshua Shaw. A sense of her recent importance came to her, and she remained still. Married, she thought. You're going to be married, married. Gollies, what a ring. This dress is a love. Flowered taffeta, that's what it is, and a red as bright as flame. The hat you bought at Miss Keeney's is glazed straw, and the cherries are just as cute. A captain's wife. Perhaps more. Alan and Joshua Shaw have got some deal on about the limestone. They haven't talked to Ma yet, but you can guess. Oh, gee, you're really lucky.

"If you won't help Peggy," Mrs. Svenson said, "then you'll set the table. Or hold the baby. Do you want Mr. Shaw to hold the baby while I do it?"

"No!" Minna stood rapidly from the chair. She was afraid of the baby with his snatching hands, his drooling lips and damp bottom. It was a simple shame that getting married meant that you had to have kids. If only she and Alan could wait for a bit for that. . . .

Kennard and Carmody were in their shirtsleeves in the kitchen. They wore paper bags on their heads in imitation of chefs' hats and they passed a whiskey bottle from hand to hand while they stabbed at the steaks. Minna slipped in under Kennard's arms; he glanced around, his eyes wild with the whiskey, and kissed her. "But you get to hell out o' the galley," he told her. "Phelim and me are the cooks and goddamn' good ones, too. Peggy, she's just here for ballast."

Minna smiled sympathetically at Peggy. "I came to set the table," she said. "You tell me where you keep the silver and the cloth. I can find the dishes myself. Don't you get up."

"Over there." Peggy pointed with the potato knife. "In those two drawers. When this pair of hooligans are through ruinin' the meat, we'll eat. God help us all."

"Amen!" Phelim shouted. He gave Peggy the bottle. "Take a drink for the good of yer moulderin' soul."

The big meal and the whiskey had combined with the noise to give Joshua Shaw a headache. He pretended to join in the hilarity that went on, but he had the feeling of being solitary and in no sense integral to this group. Alan Kennard sang; he and Phelim flung Minna and Peggy around in reels and jigs, stamping the floor with all their might.

A strange place for you to be, Shaw told himself, and a stranger thing for you to have done. Your own concerns are certainly sufficient to keep you busy. Still you've chosen to throw the dice for Antrim. It's a peculiar friendship you have with the man. Why did you go into it so far? He has no knowledge of finance or economics, really nothing except a shrewd native intelligence, his peasant stubbornness and ambition.

You know the reason, though. Earlier today you had it very clearly; you're tired now by these shenanigans, the talk you had with Phelim, with the Judge, with the license clerk, the rest of them. The reason is that your own family has gone so terribly sour that you had best help Antrim get started to salvage it. You can use the Bouche de Mouche limestone at the plant if the stuff's any good at all. That will save you at least twenty thousand dollars in cash outlay in the next year, make possible a new loan for the plant. For you can get the bank to go behind Antrim on the limestone purchase, fix a stock flotation for him, take out your share of the profit by a long range contract with him.

Damn you, however, for a hard headed Yankee conniver. You've always held it against the Public Square gang for deals like this and here you are right up to the neck in one yourself. Have another drink and act up a lot better as a guest. Antrim will be over in a moment to tell you that you're as glum as they come.

He noticed Mrs. Svenson as he poured the drink. She beat her bunion-broad feet on the carpet to the tune Alan Kennard sang, but her face was unsmiling, her eyes sad. She's a person like you, Joshua Shaw thought. She remains in a world that's very much her own territory and where nobody enters. Minna, the daughter, has meant a tremendous amount to her. Minna's getting married, though, and she's already relinquished her, as you've let go Jane and Lucinda, and, yes, admit it outright, poor damn' Cottrell.

Joshua Shaw went out into the kitchen. He found Peggy's feather duster in the closet, pulled a handful of feathers from it. Then he walked determinedly to Mrs. Svenson. "Let's go," he told her. "We can dance better than that lot. We'll give 'em an Indian dance."

"Sure thing," Mrs. Svenson said with a wide grin. She stuck the feathers at random into her hair. Joshua Shaw had taken off his cravat. He bound feathers inside it to his forehead. He cupped his hands around his mouth and gave a prolonged whoop.

The dancers turned and stared. "Indian music," he shouted to Alan Kennard. "Ma Svenson and I are going to do our turn."

"So you're an Indian?" Kennard said, drunk enough to be amazed.

"Never you mind." Joshua Shaw had Mrs. Svenson by the elbows and they had begun to hop, swiftly step, retreat. "I'm a Highlander by blood and it's the same damn' thing."

Phelim brought a wooden wash tub from the kitchen, thumped it for a drum. Alan Kennard added high-throated, yipping cries. They all danced. They only stopped when there was reiterated knocking on the front door.

A patrolman stood there, his eyes bewildered under his helmet brim. "It ain't just the neighbors," he said. "But the fly-cop will be around, and after him the roundsman. The shield might be taken offa me was youse to go on. A real great din you've been makin'."

"Take a drink, Ould Sod," Phelim said, "and send the neighbors and the fly-cop and the roundsman to us and we'll take care of the lot of them. My friend, here, an Antrim man, God help him, is about to be married."

But the gaiety had gone out of them; the tight, glittering thread of their mood was snapped. The women had moved over and sat down in chairs. Joshua Shaw was unbinding the cravat from his forehead. The patrolman took a quick drink, sighed, rubbed his hand across his mouth and returned the bottle. "You're through?"

"That's it." Alan Kennard was looking at Joshua. He wished he could understand Josh better right now. The man had been the life of the party in the last half hour. But no longer.

"I have to be on my way," Shaw said, conscious of the glance. "Back to Bellport tonight and we pour early in the morning." It was awkward for him to pick up his hat and gloves and stick; they made him seem like a snob to these people, he knew. "But I'll meet you all at the Hollenden at ten o'clock Wednesday. Everything's all ready. "We'll go right over from the hotel to the judge's chambers. Thanks a lot, Peggy. This has been a marvelous evening."

They each murmured some answer to him, but Minna was the only one who followed him to the door. She threw her arms around him and kissed him on the mouth. "You're a fine man," she said. "Just fine."

He was instantly aroused by her kiss. It started a throbbing through his body as he went down the stairs. He told himself, you didn't realize before quite why Antrim was marrying her. You've learned. She's hotter than fire. Christ, maybe you should stop out on Payne and see that little milliner who gave you her card. But you can't. You have to go on home. That's right, sonny. Duty calls. Duty and the pride of the benighted Shaw family. Oh, the old Highland stock. . . . Better, much so, that you were Mrs. Svenson's kind.

.   .   .   .

Minna had a huge bouquet of white and red roses and the sensation that she was drifting through a shimmer of radiance. She was extremely conscious of her dress and her hat and shoes and the new corset, all of the new magnificence she wore, and of Alan beside her, so handsome, and Ma and Josh Shaw and Peggy and Phelim.

The judge, my goodness. In a black robe. White hair and skin that looked like shiny old leather. He makes it very dignified and serious, almost like a church wedding. Alan doesn't believe in religion so we didn't go to a church. Later, though, we will. All nice folks go to church. It's the thing to do.

The judge had a voice like a summer river. Minna was carried away in the slow, firm sweep. "Dearly beloved, we are gathered together here in the sight of God, and in the face of this company. . . ."

The language was of a kind she didn't know. The sound of music was given, solemn and marvelous, measured. But the white haired man with the shiny skin was saying words. "Alan, wilt thou have this woman to thy wedded wife, to live together after God's ordinance in the holy state of matrimony? Wilt thou love her, honor and keep her in sickness and in health; and, forsaking all others, keep thee only unto her, so long as you both shall live?"

Alan's voice was deep. "I will."

"Minna, wilt thou. . . ." But the rest wasn't clear to her. It was held on a plane of emotion she had never before reached. There was the ring, of course, and Alan's kiss, Ma's dry, bony cheek, Peggy's plump and wet one, Joshua Shaw smelling of toilet water and Phelim of whiskey.

Then they were in the street. There was a hansom cab and that took them to the Hollenden. People smiled at her in the lobby and in the dining room, and she tried to smile back, but she was thinking of upstairs and Alan. The creamed chicken was good. She wished she were hungry. The champagne corks went *whop!* underneath the napkins just the way she'd always heard they did. But Alan, and this damn' corset was killing her.

They lay together at peace in the big double bed in late afternoon when Alan told her. "Josh and me, darlin'," he said. "We're bound for Patigowoc tomorrow. Josh must have a look at that land and I've got me just three more days away from the ship."

"Oh, no," she said. She moved closer to him in the bed until their bodies touched and trembled. "You're not leaving me behind. Not now, not ever."

"All right," he said, wild for her and yet knowing that he was wrong.

CHAPTER SEVEN

"Golly, I wish we'd have stayed in Cleveland," Minna said. Then, to her surprise, she blushed and lowered her eyes. It was the first time she had ever shown irritation with Alan in public. You should be ashamed of yourself, and with Josh here, too.

But neither of the men answered her. She wasn't sure because of the train noises that they had heard her, although they were both awake. Alan sat beside her on the red plush, gray grimed seat, his now familiar thigh against her thigh. The contact excited her, must excite him, yet he hadn't looked at her when she spoke, nor had Joshua. They stared off into space as if in some secret way they could isolate themselves, get away from her. She experienced a sensation of anger that had behind it fear compounded with jealousy.

Well, darn them anyhow for keeping so gosh-darned still. A fine-looking pair. Both had their coats off; handkerchiefs were stuck inside their collars. Alan was red faced and he sweated more than Josh. Big, shiny drops slid down his cheeks. There were dark marks of sweat around his sleeve garters. His shirt stuck to his chest so that she could see the muscle outline, the curly short mat of hair that yesterday and last night had given her such delight to stroke with her breasts. Josh was just about as uncomfortable-looking, though, and his face bore a stiff expression which to her appeared to be one of peculiar pain.

She was suddenly, almost shockingly aware of her femininity. Joshua sat forward of her and Alan on the pushed-back seat. Their knees touched from time to time as the train swayed, and she could sense by the way he drew instantly away from her how much she attracted him. Her breasts stretched. A rigor was in her thighs. If Ma knew, if Ma knew, she'd slap you silly. You were just married yesterday. But probably that's why. You're acting like a little animal.

Minna rose from the seat compelled by a need for flight. She moved lurching through the lurching car. She hated the car, the train, herself, her husband, all men. But she had ridden only rarely in trains; she was distracted, her compulsion lost. The train seemed to bang, howl endlessly within the filthy envelope of its own smoke. Nothing could be seen beyond the crusted windows except the smoke. Her vision was held to the people.

A woman in a thick woolen dress and with a shawl over her head in this heat sat nursing a baby at the breast. Minna could catch the acrid-sweet odor of the milk, see the white slick of the trickle along the baby's chin. The mother's eyes were shut in the same way as the baby's, and her breath was slow and deep. Three men played cards on a suitcase propped on their knees. They slapped their hands on the straw of the suitcase with a motion like grouse beating their wings out in the underbrush. A drunk who had done a lot of yelling at the depot in Detroit sprawled across a seat with a piece of pie in his hand. It was chocolate cream pie and he was asleep. The stuff spattered drop by slow drop onto his shirt front. Flies were on the pie, on his shirt front. A drummer with reddish eyes and a collar higher than Joshua's watched her as she advanced. I'll slap him, she thought in horror. Darned if I won't. But the drummer kept his hand down and she was past him and at the end of the car.

The ice had all melted in the cooler. The water was sickening, tasted of metal. She gulped to make it stay down and stepped over the puddle in front of the cooler to the toilet. When she was inside and had lifted her skirt and petticoats and started to bend over a whirling gust of grit and smoke came up at her from the bottom of the toilet bowl. She sprang erect crying out, tears in her eyes.

Alan was alone as she returned. He sat reading a stiff piece of paper. She recognized it as the power of attorney Ma had given him in Cleveland. That was part of the scheme to make money out of the old place in Patigowoc. Well, all right, fine.

"Where's Josh?" she said after she sat down.

"He went out for a smoke." Alan had folded the paper, put it in his coat pocket.

"This here's a smoker."

"He's out on the platform. He wanted some fresh air."

"All he'll get is cinders."

Alan looked curiously at her. "Let Josh be."

There, she thought. That's a husband talking. An order right straight off. But I love Alan, love, love, love him. When he puts his hands on me and he holds me so. . . . Stop it. Wait 'til tonight. "When do we get into Napta?"

"Late. We're on a jerk train."

"Couldn't we have stayed in Detroit, Alan? That hotel in Napta, it's not—" She let her voice break off.

"Not what, darlin'?"

"We'll be together," she said. She whispered it to him, her lips close to his cheek, her nostrils gathering his strong smell. "Together. And you'll make a lot of money for us."

"I'll try." His voice was hard, hard and rough, and under her hand on his shoulder she felt the muscles abruptly tense. My man. Smart and tough Alan. Gosh, just think.

She was asleep when they reached Napta City. Kennard had to support her as she staggered slack-legged, heavy against him down the station platform. Only the train crew and some section hands were around the station where the engine fouled the soft air with great, hissing spurts of steam, the carmine flash of coals from the fire-box. Joshua carried the bags and their footsteps were loud over the station planks, over the cinders beyond, then the wooden sidewalk and the porch of the Grangers Hotel. "Two rooms," Joshua said to the blinking man in his undershirt in back of the desk. "Make them the best you got."

"Ain't got but one kind," the man said with satisfaction. "Two dollars for each and you pay me now."

Thinks we're city dudes, Alan Kennard told himself. Like to kick the bastard in the shins. But take it easy. Things go right, you'll be living near to here. Poor darling. He meant Minna. She had hardly opened her eyes since leaving the train. But she flinched instinctively under the brutal yellow glare of the overhead lamp in the lobby, lifted her fingers to her hair and her hat as the clerk stared at her.

"We'll take care of ourselves," Kennard told him sharply. "You just give us them keys."

"Sign the register," the clerk said and held forth a clotted pen. He looked squint-eyed at the signatures. "You stayin' long? You want a call in the morning?"

Kennard ignored him and Joshua had already begun to climb the stairs. They parted in the hallway above. "See you in the morning, Josh," Kennard said. "I'll break out early and call you."

"Goodnight," Joshua said, his back partly turned, his face obscure in the hall light. "Sleep well."

Minna revived some in the room. She took off her outer clothing while Kennard filled the wash bowl and opened the suitcase.

He had a pint of whiskey in the suitcase and he gave her a drink.
"Now no fancy stuff," he told her. "You strip all the way down and
let me give you a quick wash."

"Ssh!" She pointed to the thin pine paneling that separated them
from the next room. "Josh is right there."

"To hell with Josh," he said. His thought was inflamed by her.
"That man's sleeping solid."

But when she was completely undressed she stood trembling
before him. "I can't," she said huskily. "The bed will squeak and
he'll hear every sound and so will the folks in the other rooms and
downstairs, too."

He had been staring at her body, lost in voluptuous speculation.
Her corset had left faint ridges along her hips. Her buttocks were a
bright pink from the hours of riding in the train. The way her
breasts were, and the lines of her legs, oh, my God.

"Don't be silly." Rage locked with longing were in his voice.

"I ain't." She had picked up a petticoat, covered herself.

He cursed and moved over and sat down on the bed and it
squeaked. She cried very softly, motionless with the petticoat
around her. He saw a bedbug on the dirty cotton pillow slip, others
along the edge of the sheet. The section hands were in the saloon
down below. They shouted and cursed, the sounds piercing upward
through the hollow layers of the structure. She's heard worse, he
thought, in the logging camps and in the Greek's in Muskegon. But
that's no reason she should hear more as your wife. And you're no
man to make a woman sleep in a crummy bunk.

"All right," he said. He went to the suitcase and took a drink
from the bottle to steady himself. "You just let me wash you down
and then you change into clean gear and we get out of here."

"It's late, Alan," she said, plaintive in her fatigue. "Where do
we go?"

"Never you mind," he said. He gently pulled the petticoat from
her. "Not far. You're married to me now. You trust me."

He wrote a note to Joshua while she dressed after the bath. She
leaned over his shoulder to read it and he didn't mind. He'd won
his point. By Gorry, he'd controlled himself with her the way she
wanted, but he'd showed her who was boss. A hot little biscuit, this
one, his Minna, quick to jump off the stove.

They tiptoed along the hall and he thrust the note in under
Joshua's door, then they went hand in hand down to the lobby.
"Bedbugs is all over town," the clerk offered solemnly. "Nickersons'

loggin' crews brought 'em and we've had 'em ever since. This here's
the only hotel in town, though, and you won't find anyone to let you
in private such a time of night."

Alan Kennard lost his temper enough to lean across the desk
and grasp the clerk's suspenders, let them snap resoundingly. Then
he waited for the man to respond, laughed as the other gaped and
drew back. "Sharp enough to be a drummer," he said. "You
shouldn't be in Napta, buster. But you see my partner gets a call
at seven in the morning. Got that?"

"Yes, sir," the clerk said and teetered forward onto his stool.
"Seven o'clock."

"Would you ha' hit him?" Minna asked with awe as they walked
along the sidewalk.

"Shucks, no," Kennard said. He felt fine after the incident. "Just
hove him out in the goddamn' street."

The night man at the livery stable was asleep. But he brought
out a good horse and a clean rig when Kennard awoke him. "Going
to Patigowoc," Kennard explained. "Put in some oats and a bucket
for water. You'll have the rig back tomorrow."

"Gosh," Minna said. The horse was loping past the cast iron
statue of the Civil War soldier in the square. "You sure know how
to make people hop around for you."

"Should by now," he said complacently; he hugged her close to
him. "Been in the ships long enough."

"But why are we going to Patigowoc now, Alan?"

"Your old place is cleaner than that hotel. And it'll be pretty
down at the river."

She was speechless, her love, her admiration for him too vast
for her to express them. She sat as close as she could to him, allowed
him to place his hands under her clothing, fondle her. She felt a
new pride. She was his woman; just riding along in the buggy
she'd taken care of him and given him the calmness he always
somehow seemed to need. Golly, though, he was hot for it. Until
they got out there at the river, she'd have to hang on hard herself.

The outer town, the Patigowoc road were in silence and a star-
light-flecked darkness. Trees were big, vague in the night mist
along the ground. Dogs barked occasionally at farms they passed,
and a rooster crowed prematurely at sight of the rig lantern. The
rest was a simple repetition: the sway and rattle of the rig, the creak,
creak of the breeching in time with the horse's slow trot, the hooves
over the sand and stones of the road, the ellipse of light cast from

the lantern in briefly shifting bloom upon the dusty bushes at the roadside. He sat relaxed. He didn't speak. She had the opportunity to look out into the night and recall her early youth.

You never thought you'd be coming back over this road, and in such style, married to a man who's going to be rich. Of course Pa said he was going to be, too. He told you and Ma so the last time you rode here on the way to Napta and Chicago. But you and Ma never really believed Pa. He wasn't the man to be rich. But this one is. . . . Remember, Ma wouldn't even let you wear your new dress that day. Ma, she's keen in her way. Tired, though. She's glad I've got my Alan.

She dozed for a bit, claimed by her fatigue and the langorous quality of the night. When she awoke, they were in Patigowoc. My gosh, the feed store, and here's the hotel and the saloon. Those two are still shut. Back in the old days, when you were a little kid, the shanty boys used to fight outside there. Kick each other. Tear each other's ears off and you and the other kids who were watching would run like a skinned cat. Keiberg's store. He and Pa argued about everything and Pa always said Keiberg talked more than he knew. Jake Freem's. His kid, Joe, about pulled the pigtail off you one day at school. Just because you were the teacher's kid. Over there's where you dropped the bag of candy in the snow. The snow was all slushy and the teams had been hauling all day long. So you couldn't pick them up. Mint balls. Ma gave you another nickel when you came home. You ate them right on Keiberg's porch and you didn't give the other kids a darn one. The school looks bigger than when Pa taught, and the church is the same. Mrs. Minnick has got some fine flowers, but she's stingy. She never puts more than a dime in the plate on Sunday. There's home. The house up on the hill. You used to know just how many steps it took to it from Keiberg's. One day when you were barefoot, a day about like this one's going to be, you found a garter snake right in that rut, and up where the fence is you saw the big son-of-a-gun of a turtle crawling up from the river. He scared the dickens out of you. You ran home bawling to Ma and when she understood she laughed her head off at you.

Alan Kennard had taken her hand, gripped it lightly. "The house is in kind of bad shape," he said. "You won't mind, will you?"

"No, I won't mind." She kissed his cheek. "Not with you around to fix it up."

"You're talking to the wrong man," he said. He had taken the whip from the socket and snapped it at the horse for the hill. "Josh and me get what we're after, you'll have a new house."

"Oh, no!"

"Sure as hell, darlin'." He was laughing, but in the starlight she saw that his eyes were narrowed, contained by a fierce and eager glare. She felt fright, then conquered it. He was a strange kind like Ma. Sometimes he went away from you in his thinking and you didn't know why. But she wanted a big house, too, just as big as she'd dreamed about helping Ma in the woods camps and waiting on table for the Greek. "Let's have towers," she said.

"And a cupola," he said.

"A porte-cochere."

"I don't know what that is."

"It's what I read in a book. Ladies get out of their carriages there safe from the rain."

"Then one of them, too." They were in front of the wrecked house and he swung her down in his arms. The roadside grass was cold with dew and she shivered. "You scared?"

"Just excited. Hurry up, Alan, and make a path. I want to go in there with you."

"That was just an idea I had. You stay outside. It's all dirty."

"I don't care. I'll be thinking about the new one the whole time."

"So," he said. He had unhooked the lantern from under the rig, pulled the reins over the horse's head. "Then we go together." He raised her, balanced her against his shoulder, and with a sliding yet firm stride carried her through the grass to the house.

A bat stirred in the slanted shadows of the front room after the door was open. It flew squealing a thin arpeggio, and for her the sound was almost as bad as the flapped passage past the starlight of the windows. When she moved backward, a plank gave under her and ominously cracked. The other rooms held field mice who ran with a dry rustling and pattering. This wasn't home. She put a hand to her mouth, half ashamed of her impulse to weep.

"You stay here," Kennard said, the lantern high in his hand, the other reassuringly on her shoulder. "I'll be right back."

He seemed to her to stride like a giant through the room. She was proud of him. He wasn't scared of the bat. Alan would knock the bat silly. But hurry. Don't be long. The scream's right up in my throat.

He came back with brown but dry newspapers and a book. The book was in the pocket of his coat and she barely saw it. But it was her reader, she knew, the McGuffey's. She felt a sudden confusion of emotions. Alan made her feel like a little girl with the book. She was his wife, though, and out on the road she'd made him calm, given him what only a woman could. "Why did you bring such stuff?" she said, so that she might restore her sense of maturity.

"Papers will make us a bunk," he said, "what with the seat from the rig. Out under the big maple tree, huh? Grass is short there and we won't get wet."

She was grateful that he had said nothing about the McGuffey's. Papers were just papers, and under the maple she'd be herself again, her married self. He spread the papers neatly beside the rig seat while she stood and watched, then he turned around towards the horse. "You know how to unhitch?" he said.

"Sure, I do." She giggled. "Don't you, Alan?"

"No. I'm a sailorman, not a bloody waggoner."

"You talk stuff like a book once in a while. I'm not so sure I know just what you're saying. But I'll show you how to unharness."

It made her very happy as she released the hold-backs and the traces, led the tired horse out of the shafts. "Now take off the collar," she told him. "Not the bridle, though, or he might run away. There's a halter in under the seat. Tie him to the wheel."

"Yes, ma'am." She realized from the tone of his voice that his pride had been hurt, and at the same time his respect for her increased. Minna's a woman, she thought triumphantly. But he had the bucket, the oats sack. He said, "I'm going down to the river for some water for the beast. You won't be scared alone?"

"Not out here," she said. "It was only that darn' old bat." She made her way to the maple tree while he went to the river. Her fingers worked fast to loosen her corset, her underclothing. She must be ready for him when he got back. The bucket plashed and sucked as he filled it in the river. His shoes crunched the grass, the road sand. The horse snuffled the water and whinnied with pleasure. His shoes were away from the horse, on the slope that led to her. He was beside her; he was prone and she reached out her arms.

She slept for a time afterwards, although not deeply. He was awake, she sensed, and opened her eyes to look at him. He was propped up on his elbows, gazing at the river. What the dickens, it's all full of mist. He can't see anything but the willows and the cattails and the bushes. A strange fella. Now he's gone away from you.

"Alan," she whispered, and touched his hand.

"Yes, darlin'."

"What is it?"

He was silent.

"What is it you're looking at?"

"The ships," he said. His voice was vibrant. It had the quality of an organ in church when the organist was playing really well.

"Ours?" She had sought hard to find the question, unable to follow clearly the intricacy of his thought.

"That's right. The Kennard Line ships. Black hulls, white deck houses and green stacks. The stacks'll carry an orange K. Same green for the flag, and the same orange K."

"Gosh," she said. "You've got it all figured out. But come back to me."

"I don't know what you mean, darlin'." Then he was aware of her gesture, the position of her body. He lay down with her in his arms. But she was aware later, just before she fell into profound sleep, that he again looked at the river.

.   .   .   .

Joshua Shaw had sat up on the chair in his room at the Grangers to keep away from the bedbugs, slipped off it several times and finally slept on the floor. He was very stiff and very angry at dawn. The note beneath the door added to his anger. "Why, damn you, Kennard!" he said. "You and your little Indian belle. I've half a mind to go on home and let you work this out yourself."

But expression eased the anger. He was able to understand how preposterous the words were. Not only was he unfair to Alan, he was unfair to himself. The habit of self restraint he had practiced for so long came into play, and his usual mood of ironical introspection made him smile. He whistled an old Yale beer-drinking song while he washed, shaved in cold water, changed to corduroys and boots and felt much better. Down in the kitchen, though, when he had wheedled a mug of coffee from the blear-eyed cook, an undercurrent of sadness entered his thought.

It was a very small part of his conscious mind that directed him to ask the day clerk how he could reach Patigowoc, then wait at the post office for Jake Reem. He was noncommittal, slow in his speech as he rode with Reem out of Napta City. That bout of anger, he thought, just goes to show you the many things that are wrong with your life. Little Minna attracts you. She has in fact cast a most effective spell. Yesterday in the train and last night in that bug-haven hotel, you were more aroused, more given to the need for sexual satisfaction than you have been in years. Joshua, who comes from the breed of Presbyter, Covenanter and Puritan. Hell's fire for such as you. To covet your friend's wife. A sorry, stupid business, and you know it full well.

"So what you say you was goin' to do in Patigowoc?" Jake Reem said. "Ain't no logging left that's worth a holler. Farming's about played out, too, if a man has sense to see it. But you look to me like some sort of surveyor in them pants and boots. That your trade?"

"It is. I've got some riparian rights to check over down by the river."

The word riparian was unknown to Jake Reem. He admitted the fact and asked for explanation. Shaw gave it to him in a lengthy fashion, going back to etymology and also explaining what that was. He hid behind the talk as if it were a screen that kept him from Reem's scrutiny. The center of his thought remained in solitude, and he considered his own problems, regarded bitterly the way his life had taken.

He saw his life as bleak, as null. The sense of realism he possessed made him recognize that he had been attracted also to Phelim's wife, Peggy. Both she and Minna had a physical appeal which if he allowed it could overwhelm him. Yet there was something other than the physical. Their lives were healthy, happy; they gave real satisfaction to their men and received it in return. Up on the Kawkawlin, he thought, Kennard and Carmody were just a slightly brighter than average pair of shanty boys to you. Kennard made his impression with his desire for learning and the great, damn' drive the man has to get ahead. You took a kind of foppish pleasure in making known the meaning of books to him. In a way, you stuffed his mind in the same fashion you have this dolt beside you. It was a trick that helped to pass a dull winter. Anyway, at first it was a trick.

Then things became different. Yes, greatly different. You envy them their women. You'd like to leap into bed with both their wives. But that's not all the answer, and really just a fraction of it. They're solid, with their feet down square. You're not. Along your empty, solitary way you go, and the best you can turn up is an all night whore at Mamie's, some scared little milliner out on Payne Avenue who hustles you in the back door before the neighbors see.

Fear is the answer. You are literally afraid to go out and take yourself a wife. For family reasons, surely. But you should stand as a man, not let those affect you so that you're denied what's decent, honest—use the right word—healthy.

Here you ride beside this blabber-mouth of a postman and you lie. To him and likewise to yourself. Out of fear. Don't lose sight of the fact. It reaches right to the roots of your life and they're rotten, rotten. You must escape, cut away what's bad before it's too late.

"So like you say," Jake Reem said, "a man he could take over all up and down the river. Have himself docks and fishing, tell the other fella to go plumb to. You aim for that?"

"Not quite," Joshua Shaw said, and was back in the depths of his thought.

Trace through your family. Seek into the pattern that's made you what you are. Always, you've been proud. Shaw, of course. Of the clan that served with glory. Remember pointing out to Alan Kennard the coat-of-arms, and don't forget his response. Back at Sheff', when you were in a game of whist, they had a name for what you did. "Played from weakness." And you went on to show Alan the commission, tell him of the ancestor who served in the Continentals. Father with great care showed him the picture in uniform.

Shaws who with Wallace have bled. Earl of Mar's men. The finest, the right of the line. God, what cheap tomfoolery. Shaws to the right of you, Cottrells to the left of you, and in the middle, what? You don't know. Pride before a fall. Or afterward. Certainly you've fallen, to ride with blabber-mouth to meet your ambitious Antrim pal and his little Indian belle. But you've forgotten fear. That's right alongside of you with blabber-mouth, only far more silent and biding his time.

Don't be such a fool, and so supercilious towards Mr. Reem. He's a citizen, a man duly appointed to carry out his duties as rural free delivery postman for the township of Patigowoc. You're class-conscious, more accurately, a snob. Oh, you've sneaked away from it from time to time. You got along well on the Kawkawlin and the same holds true at the plant. But it's been secretly for your own benefit, nobody else's. You belong to a class—the upper class—and just what the hell, precisely, has it done for you?

A dandy new question. One you must pursue. Because class hasn't helped Father, or Mother, or Cottrell, Jane or you. To the extreme contrary. Those fellows in Cleveland, the gang, have no "class" about them that restricts their actions. They scalp you just as fast as Minna's forebears used to lift hair in these woods. However, calm yourself. Rid yourself of your stupid class feelings and be polite to Mr. Reem.

"Tell me," he said. "Up to here, you've made out a pretty bad report on Patigowoc. But you must have some up-and-coming folks."

"Couple o' them, certainly." Jake Reem wore a wide-brimmed woven straw hat against the sun, and with his patched shirt, his faded overalls he looked like a farmer. Except for the soft hands, Shaw thought, and the weak, irresolute eyes. No farmer survived in this country with those. "Would 'a' been outa here myself long ago wasn't for my asthma. Lansing, or more likely Detroit. My wife's cousin's got a wheelwright shop in Detroit. Fella I guess who's smartest in the village is Lars Keiberg. He runs the general store. Usta have another, name of Svenson. Been gone some time and not long back we heard he was dead. Schoolmaster. He married an Injun Ojibway woman and sold off her timber rights to the Nickersons. Went to Chicago. Now such a matter as yours, riparian and all, Lars Keiberg would like to have his hand in that. He's dipped into plenty already."

"Like what?" Joshua Shaw said, as though idly.

"Don't know if I know for sure. But he's took up options all around the old Svenson place. And he's even put down money the same way right along the street. The old hotel, fer instance, and the saloon, the feed store property. Give me twenty-five dollars for a two-year option on mine. Don't make no never-mind to me, because I ain't selling, and I can use twenty-five with the pay I get on this job."

Joshua Shaw watched the ripple of muscles in the rump of the horse. He gazed at a robin that dragged a worm from the roadside bank and crows that sat stark on a dead chestnut limb. It's out, he told himself. Of course it had to be. No sense in blaming Alan. This Keiberg smartened up just as soon as Alan came and looked over the Svenson land. Well, you'll have to count him in, that's all, and probably you'll have to make his share of the counting big.

"Must be good country to hunt," he said to Reem to keep Reem from recognition of his rapid tension.

"Fella who wants it there is," Reem said. "Deer all through here in the fall. Shoot wolf right off your back porch most any night in the wintertime, and fox outside the next man's chicken coop every night in the week." He laughed at what Shaw knew was supposed

to be a joke. "Been a little buckshot spent, too, by some couple o'
farmers to get their daughters to the altar. Can't rightly call that
hunting, though, can you?"

"There's several names for it," Shaw said, laughing back. But a
flutter of nerves was in his hands, and he put them in his trousers
pockets. "I'd like to talk to Keiberg."

"You'll find him down to the store," Reem said. "That's where
I deliver the mail. Wouldn't be surprised if he'd like talkin' to you.
Ri-par-ian, hey? Ri-par-ian." His glance came shrewdly sidewise to
Shaw. "You think Lars Keiberg might try to sell my house out from
under me, my wife and kids?"

"He can," Joshua Shaw said. "Any time he wants to take up his
option."

"A fact." Reem's lips pursed. "I'll remember that. Why, goldarn
the damn' slick Dane!"

Lars Keiberg stood on the top step of the porch of his store
in the morning sunlight. He rested at ease beside a defaced and
weather-cracked cigar Indian, a chew of snuff up in his cheek.
Shaw recognized him at once without Reem's description. Keiberg
wore black sateen sleeve guards and a city straw hat, a celluloid
collar without a tie. Eyes like a cat's, Shaw thought, a cat that sees
the rat and believes he has it cornered. You didn't figure on this,
but back in Connecticut you never had the idea that Jane would
really leave home or Cottrell become a drunkard.

"My name's Shaw," he said as he climbed the steps and held out
his hand.

Keiberg's hand had the feel of the underbelly of a fish. To grasp
it made muscles contract in Shaw's stomach. The real enemy, his
subconscious mind informed him. The man has a great deal keener
money lust than Antrim.

"Lars Keiberg," Keiberg said. "Your partner's down at Jake's
place with his wife, her who was Minna Svenson. They're havin'
breakfast, and I guess Kennard had a borry of Jake's razor. She
come into being a pretty girl, that Minna."

Joshua Shaw stood still, amazed by the hatred that Keiberg had
set afire in him. "You talk just a bit too fast," Shaw said. "What
exactly is the meaning of all your interest in Kennard and me?"

"Come into the store," Keiberg said. "You and me had better
talk some more." He had sensed the hatred and his pale jaws jutted.
"See, I know why you're here. You're from the Shaw Iron and Steel
Works, over to Bellport, Ohio."

Shaw followed him silently into the store. He kept his eyes on Keiberg, disregarded the stares of the people by the counters and the stove, the thin and angular woman who was obviously Keiberg's wife and counted money at the till. There was a little office at the back. It contained a box safe, a table that served as desk, two chairs, a multitude of drummers' samples, a ledger that carried the primly written legend, *Lars Keiberg, Prop.*

Keiberg swept clear a space on the table. He opened the safe and brought forth several large manila envelopes. "Options," Keiberg said, twitching the snuff wad around against his upper right gum. "County map. Kennard, he made a pretty bad mistake. I got you fellas all hemmed in and you can't get out for much of anythin' to the water 'less I let you."

Joshua Shaw sat down at the table. He watched without speech as Keiberg drew the sheaf of options and the large-scale map from the envelopes. Keiberg spread them out, left them there for him to examine and then sat back in the other chair.

"How did you turn up so goddamned smart?" Shaw asked, the loathing undisguised.

"All Danes is smart," Keiberg said. "Don't you forget it, mister. I figgered what Kennard was doing, soon as he showed up here. So I did some business of my own. Had my own survey made, and my own fella come in and make an analysis of the limestone. It's good stuff, what you and Kennard got, and what I got, too. But, check the map. All is marked off there. That piece, the three-acre one, the title wasn't clear to it when Kennard was last in town. I cleared it; I bought the land. You yust go ahead and try to start up a lime quarry at Bouche de Mouche and don't deal me in. You'll go broke in a hurry, yaas, indeed you will."

Shaw checked the map and found that his hands were so taut the stiff paper rattled. Kennard will kill this man, he thought. He'll smack his head off at the shoulders. But maybe not. Perhaps he has more control than you have. It's a long range proposition for him, and not as it is for you. The problem for you is immediate, or, simply, there is no problem. Therein lies the rub. Recall back in Sharon, when Father and Cottrell and you were going to come West and make a fine new start, a splendid fortune in steel? Shakespeare had language for men who dreamed like you. At Sheff', though, Shakespeare wasn't much, and whatever warning you might have learned you missed. So instead you have a most unmelancholy Dane. How I'd like to crack him on the jaw.

But he kept his glance from Keiberg. He methodically checked each option against the map, studied the map itself with great care. Keiberg had done very well. There was no evasion of the fact. Every piece of land around the Svenson property was tied up by him. The most valuable of all, the river front piece, Keiberg had bought outright; the deed for it was among the papers. Those three acres were potential and vital dock space, for sidings, for berthing the vessels and loading the stone. If you didn't have them, you didn't have anything. The whole deal was no good. And Keiberg had also taken options all along the village street, as the postman had said. Keiberg was out to make himself a wealthy man, and for the initial outlay of no more than a couple of hundred dollars. "All Danes," he had said, "is smart." In light of the evidence. . . . Joshua Shaw put down the map and looked deeply into Keiberg's liquid brown and unblinking eyes.

"What do you want from me and Kennard? Just how much?"

"Twenty-five thousand, flat. Or ten cents a ton for the stone you move."

"That's a hell of a sum. We can't finance any such deal, carrying you on our backs."

Keiberg shrugged. "You want to work the stone, not me."

"Well said." Joshua Shaw shut his hands tight. "But why didn't you go to a bank and get into business for yourself?"

"Me, I'm just a poor country storekeeper. I'm no fella for bankers, big deals."

"You lie," Shaw said hard-voiced. "But that's hardly the point."

"Sure ain't. Now listen, mister. I been waitin' for you. Take that map and check the land. Find your samples, make your analysis. Don't go to insult me. I'm honest, and yust because I was smarter than your partner ain't no fault of mine."

Joshua Shaw laughed as he rolled up the map. "Your logic is impeccable," he said. "As good as your sense of values. I'll need a horse, though, to ride over the land."

"I got one for you." Keiberg was returning the envelopes to the safe. "Saddled up ready over in the shed. I'll drive down with you to the property. You think this Kennard, and Minna, they'd like to come?"

"No doubt about it," Shaw said. "Kennard will in particular. He's what might be called extremely interested."

They had left the office, walked now through the redolent store. Keiberg very slightly strutted. He glanced aside at his wife and at the other people, then back at Shaw. "Your samples," he said, "you can take over to Napta City to the high school for analysis. Fella name of Lipfer, he's the principal and a countryman and friend of mine. Five dollars is what he'll charge only."

"Thanks," Joshua Shaw said. He was tempted to draw his geologist's hammer from his pocket, hit Keiberg with it, hurl the man down the steps. But to what purpose? he asked himself wearily. What would be gained? Folly would only be added to folly.

Keiberg had gone ahead of him across the street. He entered the carriage shed and stopped beside a surrey. A skinny gelding was harnessed to it and hitched to the back was a horse bearing a worn cavalry saddle. "You can handle him?" Keiberg said.

"I can," Shaw said. He stood in the cool, dung-and-leather-smelling shed and measured the stirrup leathers, then mounted. "But be sure you're able to do the same for Alan Kennard."

"Fella don't bother me." Keiberg was up on the surrey seat. His eyes took on a shining quality in the dim light, and his voice rose, reverberated from the roof. "You neither. Get your horse outa here. My wife ain't goin' to stay and run the store all day."

Alan Kennard and Minna were in a dooryard down the street, Shaw saw as he put the horse to a slow trot on the off side of the surrey. Kennard was freshly shaven and red-faced, Minna disheveled, wan. "Step down, Josh," Kennard said, "and come over here."

"No good," Keiberg said. "I know that Jake Freem, he's got a big mouth. He more than likely told you plenty because he's sore I took an option on his place. But you two don't do no talkin' private. You ain't pulling no tricks on me."

"Why, you son of a bitch!" Alan Kennard said. He vaulted the dooryard fence and ran around the surrey to Keiberg. Keiberg jerked the whip from the socket, had the butt lifted to strike. "No dumb fool sailor fightin'," he said. "I ain't for such-a-matter. You get in, Kennard, you and your wife. We'll drive down nice and quiet to the river, then we talk."

"Alan, what's wrong?" Minna's face was white, her hands shaking.

"This here swab would outsmart us on your folks' place."

Minna let the gate smack behind her. Color was in her face again, and it was dark, reminded Shaw strongly for the first time of her Indian blood. She moved to Lars Keiberg on the surrey seat. Her eyes as she gazed up at him were terrible in fury. "You deviled my poor Pa when he was schoolmaster here and couldn't pay his bill at the store. You called my Ma 'a damned Injun' and you wouldn't give her credit, even at Christmas. Hit my husband with that whip and I'll scratch the eyes out of your head, you gosh-darn' skunk, you!"

Joshua Shaw swung his horse close and grasped Keiberg by the shoulder. "She will," he said very quietly, "and afterwards I'll stick them down your throat. Put back the whip."

"All right." Keiberg slid the whip into the socket. "But no more cursin', no more yellin'. I'm a decent man."

"You're what I called you," Alan Kennard said, leaning over the wheel for Keiberg. "Come down to me, swab."

"Let him be, Alan." Joshua Shaw pushed Kennard back. "They're watching us all up and down the street, and the man's right. This is no way to act. You and Minna get in back, there. We'll talk later. Please, will you? I've had just about enough."

Minna strained with her unappeased anger as she climbed in over the wheel to the rear seat of the surrey. She couldn't understand it, she thought. It was too much for her. Lars Keiberg, the skunk. Yes, the dirty skunk. Always making money. Always taking it from other people. Pa knew ten times as much as he did and Pa died broke. And Alan's in trouble now, too. Josh is trying to get him out. Look at Alan, how he sits. Gollies, he scares you.

Alan Kennard sat absolutely rigid. His lips worked, but they made no sound. Veins in his temples trembled. He kept staring at the back of Keiberg's neck, scrawny above the too big collar, smooth and unlined. He'd like to put his hands on that, she knew. Catch it and wring it like a chicken's neck. Alan's half crazy. He doesn't really understand what Keiberg's up to, either. Only Josh, and Josh goes riding along like we were on the way to a picnic. Not quite, though. See how stiff he rides. He's as angry as Alan, maybe more.

The horses had gone shambling up the sunny road to the top of the hill. Keiberg stopped the surrey before the wrecked house under the trees. He glanced at each of them in turn. "Go ahead. Look around and check the map. I'll stay here. You'll find them boundary markers is all cut clear from the brush, Shaw. There's old woods roads, too, that you can folla."

"Thanks," Joshua Shaw said as he sent his horse on at a walk past the house.

Alan Kennard hurried after him with Minna. His feet stumbled on the grass-grown road. He was held by a sensation of unreality.

All that had seemed so fine, so certain last night was now dissipated. He thought dully, you and Josh are into big trouble. Keiberg's taken the ploy away from you. Somehow, the bastard's fixed it to do you in.

Shaw had dismounted. He stood at the side of the road with the map in his hands. "Has he got us, Josh?" Kennard asked.

"Why, you numskull, certainly he has." It was Shaw's abrupt belief that his friend was dull witted and clumsy, had become a man who could only hinder him. The web of circumstance was what the poets called it, and it had been drawn much too tightly about him. From Kawkawlin to Cleveland to Bellport to here. He'd helped Kennard get what education he had, helped him get married. He was doing his best in the moment to see that he made a fortune. Kennard expected a great deal of friendship.

"Don't talk to me so, Josh," Alan Kennard said. He stood with his feet spread, his body bent forward. "You're in this as well as me. Your works will make very good use of the stone from here, and at a big saving. Slack up a little now. Tell me what the trick is he played on us."

"I'm sorry," Shaw said. "Excuse me, Alan. It's simply that you figured wrong about the land along the river. We'll need much more than you thought. The Svenson property has got a little bit over two acres giving on the river. We'll need five, six, perhaps eight. And that there, and that there—" he pointed—"Keiberg has got. You must have figured in terms of the schooners you've sailed, and loading from wagons."

"I did."

"But it will be steamers twice as long as a schooner. And sidings for the cars from the branch railroad line to the quarry. There's no money in limestone, even the best, unless we can ship in bulk, sell that way, and cheap. The stuff will have to be moved fast in the season, and for that privilege we'll have to pay Keiberg twenty-five thousand dollars or ten cents on each ton."

"Holy Christ! He's surely out to rip us. But does his price wreck the entire business?"

"Not quite." Joshua Shaw had rolled up the map, remounted the horse. "Let me take a look at the land and the stone now, collect my samples. There's nothing that you and Minna can do. Rest in the shade and I'll come back for you."

"Very well," Kennard said in the manner he used aboard ship. But that was the best he could muster, he told himself; a couple of words. He'd fouled it up good. Big ambition, small brain. You're a bloody poor business man. If you win out, Josh will be to blame. And Minna. . . . You must have taken one hell of a slide with her. Last night, everything fine—house, towers, cupola, that there porte-cochere, ships, a flag. Your top piece could go for a bollard, Kennard, solid wood from ear to ear.

Minna nervously took his hand. "Come on, Alan," she said. "We just can't stand here."

"Sure not," he said thick-voiced. He led her to where a willow dappled the bank and the river. They sat down, embarrassed by each other's presence and conscious of it and knowing no way to relieve it. Minna pulled up grass, chewed the stems. The soft chewing sound she made started nerves jerking in him. He felt the urge to get up, go away from her, either that or let his frustrated misery forth in wildly shouted curses. He sat still, forcing his nerves to accept her sound.

Minna looked ugly in the sunlight through the willow leaves. She hadn't had a chance to fix her hair while they were at Jake Reem's for breakfast, he knew. Keiberg and Josh had come before she could get to it. But that didn't stop the fact she looked ugly. Her hair was all adrift around her face. Her nose was too long when she wasn't powdered up. The dress was rumpled from the love making they'd done last night and a button was missing from her left shoe.

You stupid dog. If she looks bad to you, just reckon a bit of what she thinks of you. Captain Kennard. The fella who was going to make a fortune, come hell, come high tide. Here you are on your hunkers and the best you can do is make a mock of your wife.

Alan Kennard shut his eyes and tried to sleep. But the sun was hot. His body was cramped from the position he held. Blue-bottle flies came determinedly at him and Minna. A hornet flew over a patch of milkweed, lancing gold and black. It lit on Minna's shoulder. He struck heavy handed and missed the hornet. Minna broke into low, convulsive sobbing.

Out on the river, a boy in a flat-bottomed skiff floated opposite them. He threw a rock anchor over the side, then lopped on the gunwale staring at them. He didn't move, he just stared, and the flies and the gnats or the hornet didn't seem to bother him. Alan Kennard found his scrutiny impossible. "Stop cryin'," he muttered to Minna. "Heave up and get to hell out o' there," he shouted at the boy.

The boy moved enough to lift a hand to his nose, waggle the fingers slowly. His stare stayed unchanged. "I can't stand it," Minna said. "He's like a snake, like a lizard." She jumped up and went running down the road.

Kennard gave himself to an attempt to outstare the boy. He couldn't follow Minna, he realized. The boy would laugh at him. His eyes tired and blurred. He dozed; a blue-bottle stung him on the neck. While he floundered cursing, slapping, the boy hauled in the anchor and drifted on down the river.

Minna came back with dust ochre-striped upon her shoes. "He's asleep," she said.

"Who?" Kennard said, confused yet by the boy and the fly.

"Lars Keiberg, that's who." Her voice was sharp. "Hat over his eyes, mouth open. Darn him. I almost chunked a rock at the horse. Some funny thing if the horse'd drag him in the river."

"Good you didn't," he said severely. "We have to deal with that fella."

"Josh has," she said.

He gazed at her, his eyes part open. Bloody odd, he thought. Ever since you saw this girl you've wanted to put your hands on her and make love to her. Now you hate her, and she's your wife. He turned his back to her, looking out upon the river and not seeing it, his thought taken into devious chasms which he recognized only as those that held defeat.

Minna moved noiselessly along the grass. She kissed him on the neck in the exact spot where the fly had stung. "Alan," she said, "I love you so."

He held her in his arms and then across his knees. "My darlin'. My Minna. We'll always love each other. Right?"

"Yes." Her body lifted under his caress. "That's right."

Joshua Shaw discovered them side by side and asleep in middle afternoon. He was tired by his hours of riding the land, occupied by the complications of Keiberg's demands. He took his little geologist's hammer and lighted tapped Kennard on the shoulder. "Let's go, sailor," he said. "I'm ready for our man."

They sat up hastily pulling at their clothing, but he had gone back to the road. They smiled and kissed in reassurance before they went to him. Kennard kept hold of Minna's hand. His love for her was greater than before; he was proud of the anger she'd shown him. His little darlin' had real spunk.

"You get your samples?" he asked Shaw on the road.

Shaw patted the bulging pockets of his coat. "Plenty."

"Look good?"

"Fine. But I can't tell 'til I've tested them in the lab. Then we have to make our settlement with Keiberg. I checked enough of his land to know that what he says is so."

"But if the stone's good," Alan Kennard said, "can't we tell him to go jump in the river?"

Joshua Shaw contemplated him curiously. "Antrim, you'd better recognize for good and all that we're in a big operation. There's no way to ignore Keiberg. He has us; his land blocks us. We have to deal with him."

"I don't like it," Kennard said. "I hate the bastard."

"My sentiment is yours," Shaw said. "Still, we must be patient."

Lars Keiberg was awake and sitting up in the surrey. He had a small branch in his hand to chase the flies from his horse. "You folks must be hungry," he said cheerfully. "I got root beer, cheese, crackers, such-a-matter at the store. Sell 'em to you same price as anybody else."

"No discount for cash?" Joshua Shaw said. But Keiberg was watching the pockets of his coat and Keiberg said, "Cash or check, I'll take both. Yaas, I will, for big and little."

"You must reckon," Alan Kennard said, sour with a return of anger, "to make yourself a real mucky-muck in the Napta City Bank."

"Sure and I do." Keiberg's face was serious. "Vice president, maybe, and for certain manager of the Patigowoc Branch. Patigowoc's going to be some town, you think so, too?"

"Why not?" Kennard said, and was forced to laugh at him. "With you around, it can't miss."

Joshua Shaw slouched in the saddle hardly listening to them. You've won, he thought. The stuff's here in your pockets. But don't tempt yourself too much. Not until you've made your lab tests can you know absolutely. But if you're right, if this is what you believe, and despite Keiberg . . . He wrenched himself aside from continuation of the thought, afraid somehow to finish it. "Tell me, Keiberg," he said. "Can we get in the courthouse at Napta City today to look over the deeds again? And can I use that high school laboratory?"

"Sure, sure. I'll put you into Napta in another hour. Courthouse will still be open. But I tell you right now the deeds is like I said. The back taxes on the Svenson place, they might be some bigger than you figgered, but that's for you, not me. Minna, here, her Pa usta know the high school principal."

"Mr. Lipfer?" Minna said, breaking her brooding silence. "He was a good friend of Pa's."

Keiberg smiled pleasantly. "Five dollars, like I said before, Shaw, and you make all the tests you want. Lipfer he has a nice wife, too. She keeps a clean house. No bedbugs such as the Grangers. She'll put you up for the night nice and decent."

"Take care," Joshua Shaw said, "or you'll turn into our Good Samaritan." He had his hand in his pocket. He fingered the limestone samples, and his thought had reverted to the dream. The image he saw was of his father's face when he told him the deal was a success.

.   .   .   .

The crude little laboratory was dark except for the corner where Joshua Shaw worked under a green globed student lamp. Kennard stood across the room with Lipfer, the principal, and intently followed each motion Shaw made. He was near to nervous exhaustion; when they had arrived in Napta City, he had gone at once with Joshua to the county clerk's office. They had studied the deeds of the property that surrounded the Svenson place, been assured by the clerk that all of the titles were clear. Then they had learned the sum of the back taxes accrued on the Svenson land. It was six thousand, two hundred dollars. Joshua had violently cursed when they were back out in the street. "Quite a tidy sum we have to pay," he said.

"It is," Kennard said hesitantly. He was worried by Shaw's despondent manner. "But we're goin' ahead, right, Josh?"

"Of course." Shaw nodded, then tried to smile. "I'll meet you at the high school. Have our new-found friend, the unmelancholy Dane, take Minna to the Lipfers'. It will keep him out of the way. I don't want him around while I'm making my tests."

Lars Keiberg protested vigorously against that after Minna had been left at the Lipfer house. "So you fellas don't trust me," he said. "When I'm fair and decent with you. My maps, my options, my land, you seen all of it. I lend your partner a horse, I bring you here. I get Lipfer to open up the school, hurry there, and I fix things so you can stay at his house. So now——"

"Ah, pipe down," Kennard said. "You'll start me cryin'. For what you'll get you can wait. Let Shaw be. He's tired."

"So, sure, I will," Keiberg said. But his glance was hard, scornful as he brought the surrey before the high school steps. " 'Til eight o'clock I wait. Then I go home. Of you fellas I've had yust about enough."

Kennard had known better than to answer. He had jumped out of the surrey and strode rapidly under the elms and climbed the school steps. The smell of chemicals had guided him to the laboratory and he had entered on tiptoe, in awe and painful hope. Lipfer was motionless within the door. "What's he doing?" he whispered to Lipfer.

The bald little man lifted a cautioning finger. "He has finished his chemical tests. Those give the correct amounts of calcium oxide, magnesium oxide, clay, etcetera. What he does in the moment is to use the calorimeter. It's the vessel in front of him. He fills it with one hundred times the amount of water to the weight of lime, takes a temperature reading each minute. But my chemistry is not very thorough. Mr. Shaw must tell you himself. He is a real technician. See how he uses the scales, and, by goodness, he is making a thermal chart. That I have not seen done before in this country."

Alan Kennard felt the weariness pass from his feet through his legs to his back and brain. You should be out aboard the *Aroosta*. Not here. You're into something much too big for you. Ambition's hauled you too fast and too far. He dozed, leaning up against the wall.

Joshua Shaw worked with two parts of his mind engaged. One measured, weighed, checked and evaluated, decided the figures he wrote down on the chart. The other had gone back to consideration of his mother. Why does she act so? Her life is absolutely inflexible. She bends to nobody, no force or influence. Yet she is convinced that all her actions are motivated by love for her family.

The reason can only be that times have radically changed and she has refused to change with them. As a consequence, she clings all the more closely to the faith that the Cottrells have followed for generations. But for her, and for us, her family, it's greater than just faith. It's an entire way of life. If you succeed here, and you will, the formulas are all coming out right, you won't do any better than bring together the wreckage she's caused.

You can't blame her fully, though. She isn't the only one at fault. Father has pretty much the same old fashioned style, and it's very much out of place today. He and Mother keep on thinking things should be as they were fifty, a hundred years ago. The difference between them is that Father understands to a degree what's happened in the industrial revolution. He doesn't know how to whip it; he still instinctively relies upon his clan and his class position for support. So he's come to trust you to carry him through. Not Mother. She's alone, living up there on the monolith of her spirit. She's still as Puritan as Cotton Mather.

For her, the world's become a wasteland. Made so by the dollar. The dollar has ravaged it, come to mean everything and nothing. To her, that's no paradox, simply horrid verity. The dollar. Mammon. They must be repelled, evicted from the spirit. All around her, she sees the dollar take possession. She's therefore more determined than ever that we shall accept her set of values—the true and only life values—or perish.

Well, we've very nearly reached the perishing point. Skidded right to the brink. You've saved the family, though. With this, the downward cycle stops. You'll pile up such a stack of dollars that even Mother will be cowed and forced to listen to reason. The job's not done yet. There's still a lot to go, and you'll be making a lot more money for the Kennards and the Keibergs than for the Shaws. No time to argue, however, and at least Antrim is your friend and you're happy to help him. As to the others, the hell with them. Take what you can get. *Valeat quantum valere potest.*

He examined the calorimeter once more and entered his reading on the chart, then looked through the dimness of the room at Alan Kennard and Lipfer. "I'd highly admire the man," he said, "who would take me to a drink and a good substantial dinner."

"I'm not the drinking kind," Lipfer said. "But I know Mrs. Lipfer she's got corn beef, dumplings and sauerkraut on the back of the stove. And Mrs. Kennard, Minna, is there with her. Between them, they should have a bang-up meal ready."

"Then you go and tell them to put it on," Alan Kennard said. He had roused himself at the sound of Shaw's voice. "We're going to stop by the saloon and buy a pint so's we can have a drink."

"But I have to put out the lights and lock up," Lipfer said. "I can't have any trouble with the school board."

"You won't." Joshua Shaw neatly folded the five dollar bill before he put it in Lipfer's hand. "Let the man hear it, too, Antrim. We'll have to tell Keiberg ourselves. The stuff is fine, just what we hoped to find."

"Good! Oh, how fortunate!" little Lipfer said while Kennard

stood unable to speak. "With such news, everybody should be happy. Please understand, gentlemen. Most of the equipment here has been paid for out of my own pocket. Your five dollars will go to buy more. And perhaps with the quarry in operation, the county . . ." But Shaw and then Kennard had walked past him. They walked without word from the room. Kennard had his head down, like a man who was in pain or about to weep. Lipfer shrugged. There went a strange pair. But they were paying guests in his home. They would bring wealth to the county. He hurried to turn out the lights and follow them.

Lars Keiberg was below in the street. He had been resting on a horse block, and rose up and moved quickly forward. "Well," he said; "well, how about it?"

A mood of extreme reaction had overcome Shaw. He was seized by a sensation of despairing anger at sight of the storekeeper. There were men like this who were always waiting, he thought, always battening on your skill, your energy, the frail resources of your hope. He shoved around Keiberg and over his shoulder told Alan Kennard, "I'm going on to the house with Mr. Lipfer, Antrim. Pick up the pint, will you?"

"Aye," Kennard said. Then he turned on Keiberg. "How about what?" he said perversely.

"You know," Keiberg said. "The limestone, fool."

"Call me fool, huh?" All the pent, the long and terrible ache of waiting took torrential form within Kennard. He was shaken from head to feet with rage. He gasped, and his knees bent; he circled Keiberg with the intent to strike the other man down, smash his head against the horse block. But Lipfer had slowed and stared at them as if at a vision of demons. Knock it off, Kennard thought, informed by some secret recess of will. You're through with brawling. To dump this swab would do no good.

"We'll talk over the deal in the morning, Keiberg," he said. "The stone's good. But we got to reckon out how we can meet your terms."

"Tomorrow noon, then," Keiberg said. "I don't give you no more time than that. You fellas——"

Kennard couldn't control himself. He cursed Keiberg. "You'd pick pennies from the eyes of the dead," he said. "It's a tidy trick you pulled on us. But what you got ain't worth much without what we got. All you can do is put the squeeze on us because your land lays around ours. If that wasn't true, you'd ha' gone to the banks a long time back and made some sort of deal for yourself. So the thing is between us."

"A tough fella," Keiberg said in a voice of fury. "He marries little Minna Svenson to make a fortune. But Shaw does the work. Shaw maybe sleeps with your wife, too?"

"Ah, you swab." Kennard was smiling. "You'd like for me to hit you. It'd make you think you were a man. Go back to your penny and nickel store, you, and count the candy balls."

Perspiration rimmed Keiberg's eyes. An agitation was through his body, and cords stretched prominently in his throat. "I tell you," he said hoarsely. "By tomorrow noon, you close the deal with me or I go to the banks. So I lose money perhaps, because my land ain't worth much without yours. But then you don't get nothing for sure. You can't treat me such. I'm smart, a smart fella. And you been stupid, see?"

Alan Kennard stood there silently until in the early evening shadows Keiberg had crossed the square beyond the monument of the soldier and unhitched his horse and driven off along the Patigowoc road. Then he went towards the saloon to get the pint. But only one drink while you buy it, he promised himself. Two and you'll be angry all over again and you'll start out and catch him, bust his skull like a clam shell. He meant every goddamn' word he said about us being ready for him by noon. If the deal got into the hands of a bank, we'd be sunk, for the bank'd lift the price plenty over what even this bastard has stuck on it.

Joshua Shaw was alternately loquacious and silent during supper. He told the Lipfers a long story about a classmate of his at college who had imported blooded cattle from their home region of Schleswig-Holstein. He afterwards sat dull-eyed and stared fixedly at his plate, even refused to join Minna in praise of Mrs. Lipfer's dumplings. Kennard believed he understood what troubled him. Josh was played out. This meant more to him than he wanted to show. And now the poor lad was falling asleep.

"I'm sorry," Kennard said to the Lipfers. He was going around the table to where Joshua sprawled head down, arms loose. "A long day and last night he had no sleep, fighting them bedbugs at the hotel."

"They're fierce," Mrs. Lipfer said. "As big as cockroaches."

"Bigger," Minna said. "They got teeth like wolves."

While the Lipfers laughed, Kennard lifted Joshua out of the chair, propelled him into the hall and up the stairs. Joshua revived a bit in his room. He gazed thoughtfully at Kennard, then said in a whisper, "No good, old boy. It all of a sudden became too much for me. Limestone, Keiberg, red-eye whiskey and Schleswig-Holstein dumplings took care of my depleted powers. But, seriously, Antrim . . . Your limestone's good for steel manufacture, most of it, and the rest for quicklime, cement and brick, a number of purposes. Keiberg, though, Keiberg presents quite a complication. The only way to pay him off is at his offer of a flat twenty-five thousand. Otherwise, on a tonnage basis he'd skin you alive."

"Why d' you keep on sayin' me instead of us?"

Joshua Shaw rolled over on the bed and stood. He smoothed out the coverlet, then took it from the bed. His back was turned; he was at the washstand when he answered. "You own the stuff," he said; "I don't. If you swing the deal, it's going to be Kennard and Company. And, Antrim, I can't help you with the financing. Twenty-five thousand plus six thousand in taxes is more than I can get from any Cleveland bank where I'm known. You recall I've told you how my Dad has entered into some weird contracts. Well, as a result, the Shaw name in Public Square banking circles isn't in the best of repute. Further, you'll need additional funds, to the tune of perhaps another thirty or forty thousand to get into operation. You have quite a business on your hands."

"That I've guessed." Alan Kennard went to the washstand. He looked searchingly into his friend's face. "You're not drunk, Josh, to talk so?"

"No, I'm not," Joshua Shaw said, and looked at himself in the washstand mirror. His face was blotched with fatigue. A brownish suffusion was through the skin under the eyes, and the mouth lines were slack. "I'm just whipped out, Antrim. Too much of it too long. You've sought me out for help while secretly I've been after you for the same. Getting angry with Keiberg won't change the facts. Always, always there's a Keiberg. The deals never come off the way you plan them; some other fellow has his hand out for your money and he gets it. . . . I tried to fool myself today. I had the idea we could swing the thing. But thirty-one thousand with a possible forty thousand extra on top, no. Not for me. So I should get to sleep, and in the morning go back to Bellport and my family. A splendid future."

"Knock it off, Josh. You're young and smart. The colonel's a fine iron-master, you the same. Your plant is a dandy."

Joshua Shaw put his hands on Kennard's shoulders. His voice

had a broken edge. "You think I'm not affected by what has happened to Jane and Lucinda and Cottrell? My guts are like a furnace after the iron is pulled."

"It's a hard question you ask, man. I have no words for it."

Joshua Shaw smiled, and the expression made his face appear very old, infinitely tired. "Nobody does, Antrim. But now I go to bed. Excuse me to Minna and to the Lipfers. I'll see you in the morning." He raised his hands and moved to the bed. "Goodnight."

"Josh, you're sure," Alan Kennard said harshly, "that you can't help with the deal?"

"No more than I have. It's up to you now, friend."

"Yeah, it is," Kennard said, suddenly fierce. "I'm glad. I asked for it—I got it."

Joshua Shaw reared halfway up in the bed to stare at him, but Kennard had already turned, was gone from the room.

Kennard was very brief in excusing Joshua and himself to the Lipfers. Then he simply told Minna to join him in the front parlor. He pulled shut the sliding doors there and confronted her. "We're stuck," he said as Minna stared blankly at him. "Josh just pulled out on us. We need a lot more money than Josh can raise, and the man's all fouled up inside. His family's in a bad way. Well, that I'll tell you later. But I tell you this now because you're my wife and I married you because I love you."

"Sweetheart," she murmured; "sweetheart." She touched his cheek. "Don't let it mean so much to you. The money, I mean."

"It does," he said, "and I'm going to get it. By Gorry, I will. You sit down now and you be quiet. Let me figure this out. Kennard ain't whipped yet."

She nodded and sat motionless in a chair near the rubber plant while he paced the room. He was at the far end as she slipped out and returned with thread and needle she had borrowed from Mrs. Lipfer. She sewed the missing button on her shoe, glancing up at him from time to time. She felt no perturbation, no dismay. Alan was her man. She loved him. What he said he'd do, he'd do.

Kennard had stopped at the end of the room to examine his hands. He was lost in longing for the past. You were all right when you were a sailor. With these, you made your living, not your brains. Brains is a good word for something you ain't got. Stop it. Stow it away, man. You have got brains. Mark one thing very bloody well now—if you slip here, you'll never have another chance like it. So help you, you won't.

He walked the room, back and over, back and over, to the
rubber plant, to Minna on her chair, to the table, to the bright
tightness of the cuckoo clock on the wall by the door. Money.
What you need is some man to back you and put up the amount
Josh had the idea he could get. Froler and Jaeckel now, they might
do it because they got the ships and they could easy haul the stone.
No, those two would trim you the same way Keiberg has. Get them
in and the deal would be rigged so they'd pick up the biggest part.

Minna had stopped sewing. He noticed as he passed that her
hands were still. The darlin', she must have been pretending for
quite a time to secure that damn' button. His coat brushed against
the needle and thread she had put on the marble-topped table and
he knocked them to the floor. He stooped to pick them up, evilly
struck his head against the table edge. "You stupid ape," he said
aloud. "But you're not the first." The gray marble had been cracked,
the crack repaired with cement.

Cement, he thought. John Frawn, your old boss in Chicago, he
used cement by the carload. Lime goes to make the stuff. That
comes from limestone. Josh said so tonight. Frawn's one of the
biggest contractors on the North Side, spreading out faster than a
County Kerry man can drink whiskey. Holy Bejesus. You had to
hit your head to make sense.

Frawn knows banks. He deals with them all the while in his
business. As Josh can use the stuff for his steel, Frawn can use it
for to make his own cement and brick and the like. You've got it.
You've come upon it, and you're almost there. Frawn will remember
you. He'll come here if you let him know just what the deal is you
have. He has lads working for him, too, who know how to use
steam shovels and dynamite, do quarrying and build a lime kiln
if needs be.

You'll pay dear for it. No doubt about that. Frawn's not the
kind to blink at a dollar when it's waved under his nose. But if it
ain't him it's Keiberg and Keiberg's banks and you can reckon
what'll come of you then. John Frawn is your man. The least you
can do is try him.

"I think we're out of it, darlin'," he said abruptly to Minna. "But
I'll not be sure 'til I send a telegram and get an answer back. Is the
station shut now?"

"Yes," Minna said. She showed no surprise at his words. "After
the ten o'clock train is in, the agent goes home to bed. He's not
the nice kind. He won't open up for anybody."

Alan Kennard gazed up at the cuckoo clock. It was one minute of ten. It would be, he thought. That was the way his luck went. He couldn't have figured this half an hour ago. Works wound and ground and whirred within the clock; the varnished door slapped open and the cuckoo leaped leering, raucously called the notes. Kennard shook his hand, identifying the clock with his misfortune.

Minna regarded him in amazement, startled to find that in this moment her husband acted exactly like a little boy. "Selvey is the next town down the line where the station agent keeps open all night," she said. "Mr. Gluck's his name. Pa used to send messages by him once in a while before he went to Chicago. Do you want to go there, Alan?"

"Aye, that I do," he said abstractedly. Then the cuckoo retreated, the door clicked, closed. "I must get a message into Chicago quick."

"About the schooner?"

"Schooner?" He laughed at her. "I'm through with that. Nor will I go back 'til the day when my last dollar's spent. The limestone land's what I'm after."

"Then let me drive you to Selvey, Alan." She was at his side and held his hands. "I know the road, I've been over it with Pa."

Alan Kennard kissed her hands. "Right enough. You're no doubt a better helmsman in a buckboard than me."

He slept in the livery stable rig while the horse clopped along the road in the misty, mosquito-noisy night. Minna drove with his head against her shoulder. She took enormous pride in her ability with the reins, swatted out at any mosquitoes that flew near him. Josh Shaw, hey? she thought. Well, her man was better. He certainly had more spine to him. And, one style or another, they were going to get wealthy out of the land Pa had saved. . . .

Alan Kennard destroyed several telegram blanks before he gave the Selvey station agent the message he wished sent. Minna stood behind him and read it over his shoulder. "Gee whillickers," she murmured; "you ready to give away as much as fifty per cent?"

"Ain't giving it away." Kennard glared at her in anger, his satisfaction with her driving gone. "I have to offer that much, else the man I want won't stir his stumps at all."

Minna shrugged. "You keep your bad temper to yourself," she said, sharp in her fatigue. "Don't think I drove you over here just to get insulted."

"You go sit in the rig," he said. He kissed her and pushed her towards the door. "You're tired, too."

They both slept on the way back to Napta City, jostling each other as the buckboard jounced on a bump, waking momentarily as the horse slowed to pluck at the roadside grass or a low tree limb. Then, on the square in Napta City, the horse broke into a trot as it smelled the stable and they both sat erect.

"I'm so tired I could cry," she said. "I've never been so tired. But when do you think you'll hear from Mr. Frawn, Alan?"

"Asked him to answer before noon, and if he likes the look of the deal, to be in here on the night train. You read it, though. Why d' you have to plague me?"

"Stop that!" Minna said so shrilly that the weary horse flopped its ears. "I won't have such talk. We're newly marrieds, and you haven't got the right."

Kennard tried to kiss her and she slapped him. Then she sprang out of the buckboard, went at a run across the square. "Minna!" he called after her. "Hey, Minna!" But she didn't stop and a couple of drunks in front of the Grangers saloon sat up and curiously listened.

He stumbled with sleep after he left the livery stable and walked to the Lipfer house. Entering the strange place at night made him cautious. He had bent down to take off his shoes at the bottom of the staircase when Minna moved out of the parlor and kissed him on the back of the neck.

"Come to bed, sweetheart," she whispered. "I'm ashamed of myself."

"Sure, sure," he said. He picked her up in his arms, carried her and was careless of what the Lipfers might think as the steps creaked.

The telegram from John Frawn came at ten o'clock in the morning. Joshua received it and signed for it, brought it to the room and faintly drubbed on the door. Kennard read it wide-eyed, then gave the yellow form to Joshua. "He's coming," he said.

"Who?" Shaw said.

"The man who'll save our bacon from Keiberg. My old boss in Chicago. Wait 'til I tell Minna and jump into me trousers. Then I'll explain the whole do to you."

He took tremendous effort to enthuse Joshua as they sat in the fumed oak dining room and drank Mrs. Lipfer's coffee and talked.

"I need you, Josh. You can't back out. Frawn's a square man, too, not the kind to reef us out of all we've got."

"But fifty per cent," Joshua Shaw said. He rubbed a hand along his jaw. "You must have been pretty desperate last night."

"I was, damn' well so. I ain't no business man, Josh. The knack of the thing ain't mine the way it is yours. Hang on, will you, lad?"

Joshua Shaw smiled. "You'd straighten me out despite myself. Yes, I'll hang on with you. And when the unmelancholy pride of Patigowoc appears at noon, let me handle him. I can give him my check for a thousand dollars as tender of good faith that we mean to take him up on his deal."

"Y' see?" Kennard said happily. "I don't even have the use of such. 'Tender of good faith.' Keiberg, by Gorry, will run over to the high school and look it up in the dictionary before he takes your check. . . ."

Keiberg sat on the porch for a while after he had accepted Shaw's check. Then, as if at some sudden thought, he hurried across the square to the railroad station, from there to the one-story red brick Napta City Bank. Shaw and Kennard watched him all the way. "What's he up to?" Kennard said.

"It's easy," Joshua said. "He was struck by the idea that he'd better find out whether I had that much money in my bank in Cleveland. So he sent a telegram, got his reply, and now he's depositing his check before the bank closes. A smart fellow."

"I'd like to hit him on the head."

"For twenty-five thousand, it should be worth it. But it isn't. Tell me more about Frawn, Antrim. Just what sort of building does he do in Chicago?"

"Ah, let him tell you himself when he gets here," Kennard said. "I'm so goddamn' nervous I can't sit still. Minna and me are goin' for a walk."

"Go ahead."

"But, how about you?"

"I'll stay here, Antrim. Mr. Lipfer's got a *Lady of the Lake* I'd like to read, and I can keep an eye on Keiberg."

Keiberg was again on the steps of the Lipfer front porch when the night train came into the station. He got up and looked around at Kennard and Shaw in the doorway. "Your man headed here?" he said.

"Here," Alan Kennard said. "But we have to talk to him first a bit before we talk to you."

"I can understand," Keiberg said slyly. "You got to get his money out of him to give to me."

"You bastard," Kennard said with deep sincerity, "I'd like to kill you."

"Shut up," Joshua Shaw said and grasped Kennard's arm. "There's your man."

John Frawn wore expensive clothes and a silk handkerchief tucked inside his collar. A brakeman from the train carried his pigskin bag, smoked one of his cigars. Frawn was a real sport, Kennard thought in delight, a big man with big ways. He moved to the edge of the porch beside Keiberg and shouted, "Hiya, John?"

But his sense of confident well-being disappeared after he and Frawn and Joshua gathered about the dining room table. Frawn did the talking and he talked fast. He wanted to see a detail map, he said, the chemical analyses, the titles to the land and the land itself before he put up a cent.

"Some of those things you can see tonight," Joshua Shaw said calmly. "The rest must wait until morning. Another interested party is also waiting for you. Would you like to meet him now?"

"Like hell," John Frawn said. "I'm tired. Give me a drink and I'll go to bed."

"But, John," Kennard said anxiously, "if we square away with you, will you go ahead on the deal?"

Frawn grinned at him through the silver spirals of his cigar smoke. "Antrim," he said, "I wouldn't ha' hauled meself here from Chicago if I didn't have that idea. Fair warning to you and to Shaw, though. If it's a deal and I put in my money, we'll form a corporation and I'll hold a full half of the stock issue."

"So you will." Alan Kennard had waited for Joshua to speak, but Joshua had remained silent, his head down on the palm of his hand. "I grant you that. Now, let's have the drink."

Minna was standing at the window of their room that faced the street. She had listened to the heavy rumors of the men's voices from below, and made mocking gestures when Lars Keiberg got up, went from the porch. Now she heard her husband on the stairs. She rested straining; she attempted to tell by the sound of his tread whether the meeting had been successful. He opened the door, he came in and he was smiling. "Alan?" she said.

"Yes," he said. He clasped her in his arms. "It's going to be all right."

She kissed him repeatedly, but she could sense his nervous tension, knew that for the moment he had enough of her. She moved away from him and to the dresser with the vague thought of getting ready for bed. Her old *McGuffey Reader* lay there. She had previously disregarded it as a link to her past which showed that not long ago she had been a little girl. But she lifted it, pressed her lips to the battered cover.

"You brought us luck," she said, as if the book were sentient. "Through you, Alan found me." Then she began to dance around the room, her skirt and her petticoats high. "And we'll be rich, rich, rich! Won't we, Alan?"

He gazed at her with eyes made bleak by the calculation of how much he would have to give Frawn, Keiberg, Joshua, surely a number of other men. "That we will, darlin'," he said. "In our time. . . ."

Book Two

1884

CHAPTER EIGHT

He was surprised by his eagerness to get out of here. At first it had been no more than a half-formed thought, then he had considered it sort of a lark that he take Minna with him and they sail aboard the ship named after her to Bellport and visit the Shaws while the vessel discharged her limestone. But by now the idea had put a fever in his veins. He had decided that he would sail as master, and he had given his reason to nobody, not even Minna, and he had not clearly established that to himself.

All you want is to be away, he thought repeatedly. Clear of the desk and the office, and, sure enough, too, the house and the town and the land. Back on the water. You're still a sailor, Kennard. And who's to say you can't go skipper of your own ship?

He stood with a nervous, jerky movement and pulled down the top of his big roll-top desk. "To hell," he muttered, meaning the papers he had left inside. "Collins has got the important stuff." He glanced around the office at the fumed oak paneling of which he had been so proud when it was installed two years ago, and he wrinkled his nose and laughed. Like a lad let out of school early is what you are. Except you've let yourself out.

His mind rested very briefly on the edge of the recognition that willfully and alone he had chosen to give up his duties, and he wasn't pleased, felt a sense of haste that sent him to pick up his hat, his gloves and walk to the door. He stopped there, though, while he read in reverse the block letters PRESIDENT in gold leaf upon the opposite side of the plate glass.

President is you. Collins is waiting in the next office and Collins is Frawn's man brought in more than a year ago to act as general manager. Steady so when you go past him. He's to think that because you've assigned Phelim to the new one, the *Daigvera,* you have to handle the *Minna* for a trip and look over the mate before the mate takes her. No lark, mind you. Leave the laughing and the joking aside.

Collins wore a high collar that pinched his thin throat and an alpaca coat that he protected with stiff paper cuffs he put on fresh each morning. He pushed his spectacles up on his forehead and his

213

pale blue but very bright eyes lifted to Alan Kennard's face. "She's not quite loaded yet, sir," he said, "and she still has to take aboard her coal. I just had a man in from the dock."

"Good for you," Kennard said. He lifted from his vest pocket with an unconscious gesture of pride the fine gold hunter's watch that Minna had given him for his last birthday. "But I have to pick up the Missis at the house and I ain't yet packed my gear. I told Boker to be here at three o'clock."

"He is, sir," Collins said. "Have a good trip. My best to Mrs. Kennard. If anything unusual comes up, I'll reach you at Bellport."

"Thank you," Kennard said in the formal way he had learned from the mates in the deep-water ships. He nodded to his secretary, Mr. Tichby, who shared a corner of Collins' office, and to the clerks in the general office beyond. Then he had the front door open and he stood forth in the sunlight.

Boker waited with the bays and the English landau at the hitching block. Boker was the only coachman in Patigowoc and Napta County who wore a stiff hat, a stock and boots and livery. Him and them make a brave sight, Kennard thought. It was his impulse to run, to jump into the landau and tell Boker to give the bays the whip. Instead, with deliberate intention, he hooked his thumbs into the lower pockets of his vest and swung and gazed at the Kennard and Company building.

It was of simple one-story construction, made of brick and trimmed with local stone. Yet Kennard was intensely proud of it. Kennard and Company was cut in bold letters over the door. The white pine flagstaff on the lawn carried the green flag with the orange K and in the land breeze the flag was rigid. You've done well, damn' well. Now get along. You've played the boss long enough.

Boker let the bays go at the canter into Main Street. He took delight in his skill with the reins and the stares he got from the farmers in their wagons before the stores. But Kennard was forced to tell him to slow down. Today in particular you don't want to let the folks think you're a snob. All right, you're president of the company. What you've done and what you're doing has for sure built up the town, made it already almost as big as Napta City. Look at the stores, the Bon Ton, the Emporium, Keiberg's own place. A whole goddamn' new business block. And Keiberg, the tight-pants bastard, really loosened up and spent some money to fix the hotel. But the old timers are jealous. They ain't got much use for you and Minna. Nor the house you built, nor the folks you brought in for the quarries.

Along the wooden sidewalk in front of the business block he could pick out easily the people the old timers liked to call Hunkies. They were the women who had come into the town with the quarry workers. Some were Czechs, and some were Poles and Slovaks and the rest Hungarians. Still they all wore shawls over their heads; they carried their babies on their hips and they talked in a gabble that nobody but themselves understood. They gave him quick, shy glances and the few men among them lifted their caps. Like in the old country, he thought, and you the bloody mah-ster.

"Let's go, Boker," he said, his sense of haste once more keen. "I'm for getting aboard."

Boker put the bays at a fast canter up the hill to the house. Alan Kennard sat back admiring the smooth pull of the quivering muscles and then the house. "The Towers" Minna had named it, and as good a name as any as far as you're concerned. But the space of it is what you like, and the fact that it's built right on the spot where Minna's folks had their old house. The same trees and view, the river and Bouche de Mouche light out there and the lake. Christ, man, you'll never want another after this. Today, though, you don't care much for it. Out on the water for you. No land for a while. Just the ship under your feet.

He jumped from the landau to the bottom step of the porch under the porte-cochere. "Keep them warm," he called back to Boker. "The Missis will no doubt be longer with her duds than I'd like."

But Minna was ready in the lower hall, her suitcase on one side of her, his seabag on the other. He laughed as he kissed her. "You're a sailor's wife for fair. Don't be fashed, though, if I ask you if you have all of my gear."

"All that you had put out to pack," she said. She was looking over his shoulder into a wall mirror and fixing the veil at the brim of her upswept straw hat. "I hope that the Shaws will take to me. They're an odd lot from what you've said, Alan."

"So they may be," he said. "And you'll mix with them fine, fine indeed." Two of the maids were standing in the hall behind, but he picked up the suitcase and the seabag, nudged Minna towards the porch. "I'd like to be out the channel before dark. This for me will be the first time handling a steamer."

Minna had turned to say goodbye to the maids. Then, on the

porch, she gave him a sidewise glance. "You know," she told him, "you're something of an odd cod yourself. A good middle name for you would've been Hurry Up."

"Ah, woman, please!" he said with a trace of anger. "Come along. I want to get to the ship."

The ship was still loading when he and Minna came to the dock. A grayish haze of limestone hung in the air and the line of flatcars was nearly full. He stood on the dock with his hands on his hips and cursed in a strident voice. The mate was a man named Frank Oate whose home town was New Bedford; he had sailed in whalers in his youth, and was, he told Kennard from the afterdeck, unaccustomed to being cursed for something which was not his responsibility.

"To hell with that," Kennard bawled at him. "Why ain't she loaded?"

"There was an accident in one of the quarries," Mr. Oate said, suddenly soft voiced. "A dynamite charge went wrong and a couple of men were killed. I'd reckon, as president of the outfit, you'd ha' heard."

"Well, goddamn you for your lip!" Kennard said. "I got a mind to pull you right off this packet."

"You go right ahead," Mr. Oate said, still softly, "and see if you can find another man like me to sail her."

"Alan, Alan," Minna said. "What's got into you?" The sailors aboard the ship, the workers in the flatcars and at the conveyors were turned to watch and listen, their faces tight with suppressed laughter.

"All right," Kennard grunted, suddenly aware of how badly he had acted. "Send down a man for our gear, mate. We'll come aboard."

"But how about the accident?" Minna said. "And the men who were killed?"

"That's for Collins," Kennard said. "He knows where I am. Let him come and tell me. I sure ain't going out to the quarry. Too late now to do any good there."

"I've half a mind to go back home," Minna said. "You're too rough. You've got no right to talk that way."

"I'm sorry," he muttered. Then, after she had moved reluctantly from him and started to climb the ladder, "Named the ship for you. Now you tell me what I should do and say. By God, maybe you should ha' stayed home."

But if she heard him, she gave no sign, and Mr. Oate met them aboard. Stiff faced and hot eyed, Mr. Oate took the suitcase and the bag and led them forward over the limestone rubble covering the main deck, up a ladder inside the forward house to the door of the captain's quarters. He unlocked the door and with obvious effort brought his fingers to the visor of his cap in a form of salute. "Think you'll find everything squared for you, Cap'n. The steward's name is Merton. All you got to do is ring that bell and he'll be along."

"I know about Merton and I know about the bell," Kennard said testily. "But, goddamn it, we should be ready to sail."

Mr. Oate released a long and audible breath. He was of stocky build, with a barrel chest and hands that were almost as thick at the fingertips as at the butts of the palms. His eyelids flicked, and a nerve at the left corner of his mouth. "The chief has got steam," he said. "It's the cargo; it ain't us."

"Very well, then," Kennard said. He pushed Minna ahead of him and shut the door.

Minna walked straight across the room to the black leather settee. "Why are you so?" she said, sitting erect, her knees and her hands together. "What's got into you?"

Kennard abruptly understood, and he possessed the words to express himself; he very nearly said them: "I've had enough of the bastardly paper work. Of sitting there at the bloody desk and pretending to be the boss man when I'm not. The job's too big for me, the town's too big, and the house, too. This is what I can handle and what I can do. I never should ha' left the ships." Yet the tremendous barrier of his pride kept him silent and made him stand with his feet widely set on the red rep carpet and smile. "I need me a change of scenery," he said. "And, after all, what's against a man sailing one of his own ships?"

"Pshaw!" Minna said, and he saw that her hands trembled as she pulled out her hat pins and undid her veil and lifted off her hat. He pretended not to notice that as he went into the next and smaller sleeping room with the seabag. Minna is most likely onto you, he thought. She knows. A smart one. Maybe, though, she's keeping still because of the other thing, her not being able to have kids. You're a knot-head, Kennard. You love your woman. So watch out, the way you act with her.

It did him good to open the seabag and toss out onto the broad brass double bed the clothes he had worn so much in the past. Just the feel, the woolly, slightly brackish smell of the sweater relaxed him. Mr. Oate had the same sort of a sweater, high neck, close cuffs and all, but Oate was for sure no better sailor. He'd show Oate. The cap was like Mr. Oate's also, and he pulled it down, low over his right eye, and wore it even while he was still dressed in his shore suit and stiff collar. By the time he had completely changed and buttoned up the blue, double-breasted, short coat and taken a look in the cheval glass, he was humming the first bars of "Roll and Go." Minna watched him without expression as he walked out to her.

"I'm going down on the dock," he said. "I want to get the packet loaded. But you change your gear."

"Yes," she said in a flat voice. "I will. I have a scarf and a duster I'll wear. You go ahead. Don't you think about me—now."

He strode the length of the dock impatiently and importantly while one by one the cars were discharged into the ship. The light was slowly changing, fading into dusk, and he was able to see the ship in distinct perspective against the shining river surface and the tender yellow and green of the willows on the far bank.

She was, he thought, despite the instinctive demand of his pride, an ugly ship. An iron box with a bow on one end, a propeller and a rudder on the other was the best way to describe her. Sure, she had the black hull of his dream, the white deck houses, the green stack with the orange K. The steering pole at the bow was bright in gold leaf and carried the spread winged eagle. Her name, *Minna S. Kennard,* was boldly on the counter and the bow plates and the pilot-house sideboards. This trip she'd make him—not him alone but his partners and the stockholders—close to three thousand dollars profit. Still she wasn't what he liked. He'd as soon sail in the *Aroosta* or the *Procyon,* any old schooner. The hell with all steamers.

Collins was on the dock; he came riding a bicycle, his face set and intent, and maybe a dozen of the town kids chased him. "Good evening, sir," he said to Alan Kennard.

"Evening," Kennard said, and told himself, the man's too slick. First chance you got, fire him. He ain't the kind for you.

Collins had dismounted and stood slapping the dust from his worsted suit. Black tin clips held his trousers in at the ankles and he stooped and took them off, and he brushed his hair back beneath his derby and arranged his collar and tie. After that he leaned against the handlebars of the bicycle while in back of him and

Kennard the town boys ranged curiously, heads forward and eyes
luminous in the first of the dusk light.

"You from the quarry?" Kennard said.

"Yes, sir. They sent for me."

"What happened?"

"A dynamite charge went off prematurely. The loader and his
helper were killed. I've got witnesses and I had the proper papers
arranged at the office. Perhaps you should see the papers and sign
them before the ship leaves. That is, if you plan to leave with the
ship."

"I do," Kennard said. He stepped a pace away from Collins
and looked at the ship. The loading was finished. The jerk engine
was pulling the line of cars from the dock. A hose spurted, snorted
aboard as Mr. Oate started the wash-down. Coal was heaped high
in the bunkers aft. The bosun and his gang were securing the
hatches. The draft marks read right. "You mail the papers to the
lawyers in Cleveland. Lothrop and Medor—you know."

"Yes, sir. But as to the families of the men, and in your absence . . ."

"Take care of 'em. See to the funerals, and like that. You're
paid for being general manager, mister. And I've got a ship to take
out."

Collins' lips drew palely together in his dust-streaked face. His
glance went from Kennard over the heads of the town boys to the
crowd of people who had been moving onto the dock. "As you
say, sir," he said. But instead of mounting the bicycle, he pushed it
through the crowd, and Kennard could hear the muttering and the
part-audible cries of "Bastard!"

And so they do, Kennard told himself as he climbed aboard.
That don't mean much to you. Men work. They get hurt, they get
killed. You been damn' near lost at sea a hundred, two hundred
times. It ain't right for them fellas' folks to stick you with the blame.
You hire fair and square. The lawyers will make a settlement that
meets with the law. And, goddamn them all, there won't be
no jobs and no pay and no settlements unless a ship sails loaded
on time.

He went forward up the main deck with a tight, sharp and cat-
like step. The doubt had just come to him if he was competent to
take the ship out of the river himself and at night. He had gone
with Phelim occasionally when Phelim had done it, and ridden as

far as the open lake off Bouche de Mouche light. Back in the old days he had handled the *Aroosta* all right, but she had been sail-rigged, much smaller. You should call Oate up to the pilot-house. Let him handle her for you. There's no sense you putting your ship on a mud bar because of dumb pride. You won't call Oate, though. No, sir, you won't. You can maneuver a ship, this or any other, stem-winder or sail.

But some deep-seated and very great inner need made him enter the captain's quarters before he went to the pilot-house. Minna had a scarf tied over her hair and under her chin. Her duster was of a delicate fawn color and becoming to her. "Helmsman won't watch his work," he told her in an attempt at gaiety. "I can't take you topside."

"Pshaw!" she said. "The way Collins was so serious, I wasn't certain you were going to sail. You were pretty quick with him."

"Now you listen," he said, and he took her by the biceps, his fingers pressing hard. "I got a ship to sail and no time for monkey-shines. Collins and me are all straight."

"Was it about the men killed at the quarry, Alan?"

"Nothing else. But we pay lawyers to tend to that. My job——"

"Don't tell me," she said. "I understand."

"Then come along with me." He purposely let her go ahead of him up the inside ladder flight to the pilot-house. Sudden, perverse desire made him slide his hand beneath her duster, her dress and petticoats and pinch her buttock right at the bottom of her corset. "That's a good big bunk below. Should take us all right tonight."

She glared back and down at him. "Not after the way you've been acting lately, Alan Kennard."

"Well," he said, "I aim to change my ways. Just let us get out in the lake. Then we'll have a bang-up supper and both feel better."

She had reached the pilot-house door and stepped through it, and she didn't answer. But he nearly forgot her presence as he followed. The pilot-house was in shadow except for the glim of the binnacle and the low turned light over the chart table in the corner. The two men by the forward window had been talking in whispers and stopped at once. "Burrell, sir," one said. "Second mate. Steering gear's been tested, and telegraph and lights. Compass is as true as she'll ever be, and there's the heading card. You'd like I test the whistle?"

"Let go with a short toot," Kennard said. "But I want to talk to Mr. Oate."

"He's down on the fore deck, sir, clearing his anchor. If you'd tell me what you'd like to tell him."

Kennard nodded at the gangling man in a straw hat and denim overalls beside the second mate. "That fella to do the wheeling?"

"He's a wheelsman, sir," Burrell said. "About the best we got aboard. Name of Proctor."

"By God," Kennard said. "By God and by Jesus. He looks like a plough jockey to me. But you say so, he can take her. Go tell the mate I'm ready to pull out, mister."

The old and passionate, secret exultation in command was fully restored to Kennard. He saw obliquely that Burrell had seated Minna on a stool at the chart table and out of the way, and that Proctor stood behind the huge oak wheel. Then he tried the telegraph and went to the inboard window and looked below at the ship and the dock.

Acetylene lamps that gave a blue and dazzling glare had been lit on the dock. They made him blink, and he was aware that his eyes were tired and he was tired. You're for it now, he thought. They're all waiting for you to do the wrong thing, Minna and the rest. Your goddamn' temper fouled you up. But get under way. Show 'em, and quick.

Burrell was back in the pilot-house. "Anchor free at the hawse, sir," he said.

"Give the engine-room stand-by."

"Stand-by, sir," Burrell said and rang it on the shiny brass telegraph. The ring-back sounded musically through the pilot-house as Kennard walked to the forward window. Rigor was in his leg muscles and in his hands and his back. There was sweat inside the collar of his sweater. He breathed with irregular exhalations as he picked up the megaphone from the window sill.

The bosun stood below on the fore deck gazing up at him for the order. "Cast off, bosun. But hold your bowline 'til I tell you."

"Aye, sir." The bosun went at a shuffling run to the side of the deck to shout the order to the after gang. Kennard leaned out the window and watched the stern hawsers sag and slip from the dock bollards and smack through the water and aboard. She has a right hand screw, he told himself. Kick her over easy and your propeller wash will push her out from the dock. Then cast off your bowline and give her rudder and you'll be away.

"Slow ahead, mister," he told Burrell. The telegraph rang, rang back and his hands stretched out on the window sill. She was moving. The slow throb of the propeller came up to him through the ship. Down on the dock, the men in the crowd pulled the children back and for him their faces were dim, almost meaningless; he strained to estimate the gap of water between the dock and the shipside. His fingers slipped on the megaphone and he knew that the sweat had spread to his hands. But his voice sounded calm as he called to the bosun to let go the bowline, then ordered Proctor to come easy to port.

"Easy to port," Proctor repeated, and Kennard glanced around to check him. Proctor slouched at the wheel, his chin no more than an inch or so from the spoke tips. He had given her the exact amount of rudder, though, and the ship was away from the dock, heading fairly out into the river.

"Half ahead," Kennard told Burrell, and then, "full ahead. You go below now and make the bosun know I want them deck lights off before we're out of the river."

"Yes, sir." Burrell stopped at the door, one foot lifted for the wave guard. "Current will set us in a bit at the bend."

Kennard smiled. "Thanks, sonny. I sailed this river before you put on your first pair of boots." He went to Minna's side after Burrell had gone below and Proctor was on the course for the lake. "A bit different from the old *Aroosta*, huh?" he said to her.

"Some," Minna said. She raised a closed hand and pressed it against one of his. A folded handkerchief was within it. "Dry yourself off," she whispered, "while the second's down on deck."

He felt exasperation and anger and shame. Minna knows, he thought once more, a new, strange desperation holding him. You haven't fooled her a bit. You could sail a thousand ships from here to hell and home again and Minna'd still understand that you don't run Kennard and Company and that what you've got has come to you through the work and brains of other men.

The ship was at the bend and rounding it. The house was on the point beyond. The heavy late spring foliage of the trees masked a part from his view, but he could make out the towers above the massive main gray slate roof, the cupola, the port-cochere, the sweep of the porches brilliantly lit as was the custom when a ship sailed past at night.

"Can you see Ma?" Minna said.

"Sure, she's there." Mrs. Svenson's stooped, narrow figure was in dark silhouette against the porch light at the front door. She waved, and in unconscious answer, although he was aware she couldn't see him, he waved back.

"What's the matter?" Minna said. She was down from the stool and peering for a glimpse of her mother. "Aren't you going to blow?"

"Goddamn it, yes!" he said and yanked hard on the whistle lanyard. Then he went to the far side of the pilot-house from Minna, stood with his back to her. He welcomed Burrell's return and told the man he was in charge of the ship. "I'm going below. When you're off the light, Mr. Oate can secure his anchor. I reckon you know your courses after that."

"I reckon I do, sir," Burrell said pleasantly. "And Mr. Oate will be up to check me."

"Very well." Alan Kennard faced his wife. "Come on down, you, and we'll have ourselves some supper."

The steward, Merton, was a Negro, from one of the very few Negro families in Napta County. He and his wife had come over the Underground Railway as escaped slaves before the Civil War, were still called "contrabands" by a number of the Napta City people. Merton had served with the Third Michigan Regiment and had been wounded, since been capable of no more than house work. But he had been eager to sail aboard the *Minna* and applied for a steward's job the first trip the ship had made. He wore a freshly starched white coat and an air of easy dignity as he laid the table for supper in the captain's quarters.

His deft attention at the meal lessened Kennard's tension. Kennard had taken a long drink alone in the inner cabin after coming down from the pilot-house. Yet he was silent as he ate the fried chicken, the mashed potatoes, fresh peas and pie. Then, at some quietly told incident of Merton's of when Phelim Carmody had commanded the ship, he laughed.

"Cap' Carmody's a good fella," he said. "Got a fine wife, too. If I don't keep him out on the water more, they'll have the biggest batch of youngsters in town."

"It's not just—" Minna began and sharply stopped.

Merton was busy gathering the dishes, the solid silver platters and salvers Kennard had insisted on buying for the ship. He didn't raise his head or make any sign that he had heard. He spoke only at the door and then said simply, "Goodnight, Cap'n and madame."

Kennard rose to his feet from the table. He cursed his wife. But

Minna held her face in her hands; she was weeping. Kennard went into the inner cabin and took the whiskey bottle from where he had left it in the top drawer of the ornately carved chest of drawers. The whiskey gagged him, though, and he was aware that it would do him no good, that he must talk with Minna, put straight what was wrong.

She sat blinking red eyed when he returned to her. He took her hand and drew her erect, placed the fingers of his other hand around the soft point of her chin. "Look at me," he said in a low and rapid voice. "I've figured out what's wrong with me. Maybe I tell you, then you can do the same. But this ain't right, Minna, not right at all."

She stood submissive, silent, yet meeting his eyes. "My hands ha' gone soft," he said. "I got a belly on me like a barkeep'. I'm not the man I used to be. I'm going all to hell inside."

"That's your trouble," she said in a whisper he barely heard. "You want to be two men at the same time. Gosh, maybe I shouldn't say this, because I don't know how to say any more. But you are two men and they're all mixed up so bad I can't for certain know one from the other."

He cursed, but at himself. "Yeah," he said; "you're right. I'd be like Josh Shaw and John Frawn and Phelim, with a little of Lars Keiberg flung in, too. What I mean is, I just ain't made up my mind. Sailor or business man, and I still like sailoring so fine. . . ." A sob of absolute frustration broke up from his diaphragm. "Did we do wrong, Minna, to take on the house and the quarries and the town and all?"

"No," she said slowly; "of course we didn't." Her fingers touched his constricted cheek and in the gesture was open tenderness. "Folks can't look ahead sometimes, not as far as we're supposed to look. It's sure changed fast since you started the company."

"Me? Hell, no, Frawn and Josh and Keiberg were the ones. I just sit up in front. I'm like that steerin' pole on the bow; you see me first, but I don't handle the ship. You think I know anything big about limestone rates, or demurrage, or compound interest, common or preferred stock? I'm still a roughneck. Still an Antrim sailor who should have his feet on a deck 'stead of up on a desk in an office that ain't rightly my own."

"Now you're talking foolish," Minna said gently. She had disengaged her hand from his, gone to the inner cabin for her duster and scarf. "If it wasn't for you, for your smartness and your grit,

there wouldn't be any Kennard and Company at all. Those other
men, they're getting their money and a plenty of it for what they
put in. Shucks, Lars Keiberg's a wealthier man than you right now.
So don't you worry. You take me out for a walk on deck. What do
you call this deck right here?"

He clasped her to him in affection. "The Texas," he said. "It
comes from the old river boats they used to sail on the Mississippi.
They got a lot different terms than from deep-water."

"I've figured that," she said. She was gradually moving towards
the door out onto the Texas deck. "But you know, Alan Kennard,
since we've been married you've told me mighty little about your
years on the deep-water. Now's a good time."

"It could be," he said guardedly. He had followed her to the
deck and immediately he was soothed by the beauty of the night.
You can't tell her about the sea, he thought. Not the way you told
Jane Shaw that time. You won't ever do such again. But, Minna,
she loves you, she wants to help you, help us both, and she should
know. Bring yourself to tell her.

He took Minna's arm and wordlessly they walked forward, then
aft over the short space of deck. The wind was Northwest and they
could get the balsam scent of the forest, the smell of flowering
shrubs and wild flowers, of vines and moist earth, rotted logs. A
loon cried on some inland pond. Night birds were muted on the
shore. Bouche de Mouche light licked and flashed and dropped like
a great golden sickle astern. Overhead, above them in the port
bridge wing, the sidelight gave a reddish reflection rimmed with a
faint band of mist. Mr. Oate's stride over the bridge planks was
measured, regular, matched the slight roll and pitch of the ship.

"I was once in Spain," Alan Kennard said. The agony of spirit
was gone. He felt calm, at peace. "A full-rig ship she was, a Scot,
the *Heather*, out of Leith. Well, there was this river. Guadalquivir
is the name of it. Worse than the Snakey down to Cleveland, but
longer. Brown, flat land on each hand. Grazing land. Bulls there,
big, rough, black bastards, the kind they use for fighting in the
ring."

"You've seen a bull fight, Alan?"

"Hush now and let me tell you." He squeezed her arm. "Sure I
did and this is the story of it." The memory had emerged for him,
splendid and stark. He saw the ship in the river, and he saw the
bulls, the bright horns, the bunching, quivering withers and the
ripple of the quarters. The hooves thudded the dusty pasture again

and sharp through the dust came the bellowed chorus the bulls
repeatedly made. "There's bulls in Ireland, but none like them. By
God, them on the Spanish river weighed close to a ton and ran
faster than a champion horse. Then we come up to the city. Sevilla,
that's the name. A strange place."

"How, Alan?"

"Dirty, and with a stink to it that would choke a goat. But beautiful, and with great, fine churches and buildings and squares.
Women so pretty they'd tear the heart out of you by a look of the
eyes."

"You must have had yourself a woman there."

"So I did," he said. "A little blackhead and saucy as a new six-
pence. I met her in a joint, what they would call a *posada*." He was
proud to have recalled the Spanish word and in the sweep of memory it aroused he was back in the dark and low and dirty room, the
onion strings looping from the rafters, the wine sour to the taste
but hot once inside your throat. Wine was slopped on the wooden
table, on the stone floor. Over under the chimney hood, an old
woman cooked at a smoky fire. But she was the only one of her
kind in the room. The rest were young, narrow hipped, wore high
combs and shawls that shimmered like a sunset at sea.

"My girl made me dance. Lolita."

"She must ha' got you drunk first." There was no rancor in
Minna's voice, just a deep curiosity. "You're no dancing man."

"So I'm not. But with the wine they got me singing, and then,
by God, I danced." His heels rapped the deck planks lightly; his
fingers snapped in imitation of castanets. "Pretty soon, though,
Lolita and me were in the bunk. When a man's been at sea——"

"That you've told me before," Minna said. "What I want to hear
is about the bull fight."

"Well, the next day is Sunday, and church bells ringing to beat
your brains loose. All hands are in the streets, and after church it's
the bull fight. A cruel thing, Minna. A brute bastard of a cruel
thing."

"Go ahead and tell me."

"The crowd's greater than you ever saw, and wild for it, men
and women alike. Sand for a deck, you understand, and the folks
seated 'way high up all around in this place. A band and it's playing
marches and all kinds of fast Spanish music. Then they come in,
the bull fighters. Like this."

He stepped from her and lifted his arm across his body as though he held a cape. His feet took a deliberate sliding motion, and his head was back, his body stiff. "Flat hats, tight pants, little jackets and them capes all fancy. Then they stand in front of the boss man and they bow. Like so, and they give the man a lot of Spanish talk."

"And the bulls?"

"You can hear them inside, busting to get out the gate into the ring. Your guts get all tightened up. Then they let the first one in. A man is here, a man is there, and the *matador*, the main one, he's there. They've got capes and the bull runs straight after them like a bastard."

Minna had gone to the inboard side of the deck and stood very still. She watched her husband with fascination, trying in imagination to catch the meaning of the excitement behind his words. "Give me that," he said and took the linen duster from her shoulders. "This is the cape, y' understand? I'm the main fella, the *matador*. Here comes the bull. Now!"

Alan Kennard was up on his toes, his feet together, his body arched as he swirled the duster. He kept on talking, but he was hardly aware of the fact. He was on the sand of the arena at Sevilla and before him was the black, frothed bull. "Passes him. Passes him again. The bull is damn' well crazy. He goes around, he goes around, and he falls down on his knees and the *matador* stands and takes off his hat to the folks. Yell, by God, you should ha' heard them yell."

"Did you?"

"Sure. I was yellin' like a drunken bosun. Then they brung in a fella on a horse. He wore big leather pants and the horse had a leather shield on him, too."

"Why?"

"They ran the bull at him. They let the bull gore the horse."

"No, Alan."

"Yeah. But I couldn't watch that. It wasn't much of a horse and the fella had a lance for the bull. Still. . . ."

"Tell me the rest."

"Then they hauled the horse out of there. The *matador's* alone with the bull. He's got a sword now and a new cape. Small, red, and a stick in one end. Like so, see?"

"Yes. Go on."

"And he calls him, the *matador* does. '*Toro!*' he says. '*Toro!*' The bull has blood on him from the horse and when they wounded him before. He charges straight, straight, fast."

Alan Kennard set his feet again. He was completely carried into the past. Minna's duster was the tight red cape and in his right hand he held the sword with the curved point. The bull was close, so close the froth from the flared nostrils splattered him as he made the pass. The bull was turning. This was the time. He drew the sword, he raised to his toes and his right arm, the right side of his body went up and over the slick gray slash of the right horn. The sword was in; the bull was past, stumbling and wavering with the anguish of death.

"Alan," Minna said very faintly; "come back to me."

He gazed wide eyed at her, remembering that, strangely, Jane Shaw had spoken in the same way to him.

"I am," he said. He laughed. "And to hell with bull fights and Lolita. Now I want you."

"Fine," she said. She pressed against him immediately they were in the inner cabin. "I want you real bad. Oh, Alan, I love you so."

He made love to her as he had on that night long ago with Lolita. It was fierce, filled with lust and yet a peculiar gentleness. Minna was entirely responsive to him, moaned out in delight when they gained their climax. But then, instead of drawing the covers up in the manner she used at home, she lay still locked with him. "Listen to me, Alan," she said in a subdued voice. "It's my turn to talk a bit to you."

"Talk away, sweet," he said, and yawned. But she was very serious, he realized, more so than he liked by a good deal.

"I'm doing my best, Alan," she said. "My very best. When you were over in Chicago last to see Frawn, Ma and me went to the best doctors we could find in Detroit. They all said the same thing. I'm all right. That is, I should be all right. They told me to wait. I know you want kids, though, and you want them bad. So I got me one of those electric vibrators they advertise in the papers, and another sort of a machine, what they call an electric flesh machine."

"Hell's bells, that stuff's no good."

"Sure. I know now. So I asked Peggy Carmody to take me to church. Her church. We prayed, and I bought candles, and the priest prayed for me."

"Lot of mumbo jumbo." His face was turned on the pillow. "If Phelim wasn't my oldest pal and one of the best damn' skippers on

the Lakes I'd never 'a' hired him away from Cleveland Cliffs. It's
him and Peggy who brung the Roman church to town. I got no use
for the Papist bastards."

"Alan, please. You can't go against their church. They got their
right to worship."

"And I got mine to say it ain't worth a hoot."

She had reared up on an elbow to look into his eyes. "This isn't
what I started to say," she said harshly. "I was trying to tell you
that every time we're together it's the one that might do it.
Then. . . ."

"Then what?"

"We'll have sons, maybe a daughter. And we'll be close together
forever and nothing will get between us to make trouble."

"Ah, darling." He smoothed his hand along her upper arm, then
her breast. "Don't you worry. We'll make out all right."

"But two years, Alan. Two years we've been waiting." She lay
back upon the bed as if in sleep. He drew a sheet and a blanket
over them, lay quietly at her side. The land breeze had dropped.
It was so still he could hear the slow, thrashing revolution of the
propeller, the murmured talk of Mr. Oate and Burrell up on the
bridge. The tucked-back curtain at the port deadlight hung motionless and he could see the moisture gathered in the folds of the ma-
terial. Fog was coming, he thought. It wasn't far off. And in a short
while now they'd be abreast of Whitestone Point, come about on
the new course.

He slid out from the bed and to the chair that held his clothes.
While he dressed he studied the tell-tale compass set in the overhead. The new course would be East a quarter North for twenty-
five and three-quarter miles. Then you should pick up Port Austin
Reef light and after that you were out in the heavy traffic. North-
and-South-bounders all along the course there, because you were
standing down for Port Huron on a Southeast by East heading with
a couple of degrees change off Sanilac light. In fog, it could be a
heller. He went quickly to the door and up the ladder; on the
bridge, the first fog signal was being blown.

Minna watched him go, her head raised a bit from the pillow.
He's back in it, she thought. The ship has him and he can forget.
Now he'll go ahead living from minute to minute while they blow
the whistle and talk to each other and figure and listen. In the back
of his head, though, it will still be there. He'll keep on wanting to
blame me for not giving him a kid. That's why he gets so angry

all of a sudden. He's ashamed of himself; he figures he's not a real man unless his wife has children. But he won't go to the doctor to get examined. And you can't ask him. That would smash the whole damn' thing. Oh, what shall I do, what shall I do? Dear God, help me. I just don't know what to do.

The whistle whooped again and she cowered in the bed as if she had been struck a blow. Fog was in the cabin. It drifted in opaque eddies, closed tenebrous against the port. She shivered; her body worked with little spasms. I'm afraid, she told herself. As scared as I can be. Alan, come on down back. But he would stay, she knew. He had to stay and handle his ship.

She rose and pulled on her nightgown and robe, the fancy ones she had brought expressly for this trip. The whistle blasts made her open her mouth and give choking gasps each time they sounded. She sat on the chair that had held her husband's clothes and waited, for what she didn't clearly know, except that it must be surcease and the end of the blowing of the whistle.

Her knees met hard together. She put her hands flat-gripping to the chair arms. Her head was bowed, her shoulders hunched, and her hair hung down over her face. She felt utterly alone, in a void of grief too vast for understanding.

You'll lose your mind if this keeps up, she realized. You'll start to scream and just keep on screaming. Think of something besides yourself. The house. The town. Peggy and Phelim's kids. Ma, Josh Shaw. The folks in Bellport you're going to meet.

Her thought went to the house. She walked across the lawns past the hydrangeas and lilacs and snapdragons, up the smoothly curving white limestone drive and the iron deer that Alan had ordered built in Chicago. Then she was on the wide front steps under the port-cochere. The downstairs maid, Katrine, had seen her, came to the door and held it open for her.

She walked along the porch where they'd hung the hammock and put most of the wicker furniture. Ma had liked to sit here the first summer and take the sun. But Ma was ailing. She kept to her own room a lot and only came down on especially fine days. She'd go and see Ma now. "Good afternoon, Ma'am," Katrine said. Katrine was Irish-Polish from Chicago, and she'd worked for big people on the North Side. So had Cook and the upstairs maid, Olga. They liked it here in Patigowoc; they said they could save their money, and there were plenty of single men at the quarries to give them company on their nights off.

The main hall was cool, the floor so highly waxed her shoes made a little rustling creak until she was on the Persian rug. Flowers were in all the vases; they had a sweet, heavy smell that made the wax smell sharper. The front parlor held the odor of Alan's tobacco; it wouldn't come out of the big red plush drapes at the door and the windows and the fireplace. Gosh, she was tired of plush, but that was what you were supposed to have. It said so in all the ladies' magazines.

She liked the space of the room, though; it was big enough to take the overstuffed chairs and the sofas and the onyx topped tables and the pictures with their thick gold frames. Of course, they didn't live here much. This was just for fancy. The best room was the back parlor and the place the architect had told Alan should be called his study. The furniture in there was leather and the fireplace was real, not one of those false-back things. Alan had bought some old prize fight pictures and some pictures of horses, a landscape that had been hand-painted in Ireland. But he liked to sit with her and Ma in the back parlor and take off his shoes when he came in from the office. Then she'd bring him his slippers and he'd go in and have a drink by himself in the study before Katrine announced supper. Real style, like they did in Chicago and Detroit. Next fall, when it was Alan's birthday, she was going to get him one of those velvet smoking jackets over at Marshall Field's. He could wear it fine and it would help him in his mind, too, build up his pride.

Her thought left the house. It concentrated once more upon her husband. He was a queer man. A man who didn't know what was going on inside him a lot of the time, or maybe it was one side that had taken hold, then the other. Like she had said to him tonight. He was two men, and one did one thing and the other did another. Gosh, if you can only get him straight. Kids will do it. Just be patient, patient, patient. Don't start crying. That doesn't do any good.

But the whistle blasts had beaten in through the walls of her control. Her nerves were pierced, shocked. She clamped her hands to her mouth to hold back the screaming. Then she began to weep, the tears rolling down her cheeks to her throat. "Alan," she said soundlessly. "Alan, come down to me. I'm scared real bad."

He had the thought while he and Mr. Oate stood shoulder to shoulder at the forward window of the pilot house. Something was wrong with Minna. She needed him. He felt sharp irritation; it was no time for a man to have his mind taken from his ship. Still, tonight he couldn't let her be too much alone.

"You're a married man," he said without warning to Mr. Oate. "So I am," Mr. Oate said, as if not surprised. "You want to go down and see how your missus is doing?"

"That's right. Keep an eye on things."

Mr. Oate had had five hours sleep in twenty-four. He was giddy with fatigue and by nature sardonic. "An eye, hell. I can't see over the bridge rail. But you go ahead, Cap'n. I've been in some a mite worse on the Banks."

Kennard was at the foot of the ladder on the Texas deck when he thought he heard the other ship. Mr. Oate was blowing the regular signal, though, and he was given to believe that maybe what he had heard was simply the reverberation of that blast in the fog. He opened the door of the cabin and went in. Minna leaped to her feet at sight of him. Her tear-dabbled face, her hanging hair made her look like a little girl caught in the horrors of a nightmare.

"Oh, Alan," she said; "I'm glad you came for me."

"Sure, sweet," he said. "I recollected you had no use for fog." Then clearly but for a split second only he heard the other ship. His hands grasped Minna by the wrists. He swung her up into his arms and with her so ran for the ladder and the pilot house.

"What is it?" she said in alarm.

He didn't answer. He was listening to the approaching ship. All his senses were exerted to the utmost; sight, sound and smell, the training of all his years on the water, instinct itself, his profound desire for self-preservation fused to tell him where that ship was.

She was very close and coming right aboard. A minute more, maybe two, three, and it would be too late to save his ship. He lowered Minna down at the ladder head and leaned out over the bridge wing to make a last attempt to locate the other vessel. A very faint pressure of air came against his face and he could hear the rustle of water. There she was. He had her now. "Mr. Oate," he called low-voiced and calmly, "Hard a-port with all you got."

He stood immobile then, waiting, aware that he could do no more. The other ship, a big steamer, was on the port hand and so near it was easily possible for him to jump aboard her. A dim green blur was her starboard light, the long gray line her hull. He smelled her, the stack smoke and steam, the hot ashes her fireman had just slung into the deck-hoist, the coffee and greasy pork in her galley pantry. "Good Jesus Christ!" some unseen man who must be at her pilot house window said.

"Aye," he shouted. "But what ship might you be?"

"*Onoko,* out of Duluth for Buffalo. Who're you?"

The two ships were running side by side, an air suction soughing between them, the rush of their mingled wash like a miniature waterfall. "*Minna Kennard,* out of the Bouche for Bellport. Don't have your fireman dump them ashes or he'll put 'em aboard me. And haul your ass out of my life. You got running room."

"Yes, sir, Cap'. Sorry, but we didn't see you nor hear you in this stuff."

"Next time do better," he snapped and went on into the pilot house. The young sailor who had been at the wheel was sick with shock; he vomited out the window while Mr. Oate held the wheel. Minna helped the sailor, her solicitous voice calm, but he saw that her face had an extraordinary pallor and that Mr. Oate sagged at the wheel in a posture of almost total collapse. "A fine thing, Cap'n." Mr. Oate said. "Mighty tidy piece of work."

"You need some sleep," Alan Kennard said; "or a drink."

"I'd take both," Mr. Oate said. "What with bringin' her in and loading and all, I ain't had a fair sleep in more'n a day. But you excuse me for a minute. Sailor, get below and fetch a bucket of water and a swab. Sick's one thing; cleaning up's another."

Alan Kennard laughed, greatly excited by the knowledge of the danger he had averted. A man like Mr. Oate wasn't the kind to hand you out idle guff. And Minna was coming over to him. Minna was putting her arms around him and kissing him.

"You saved us, Alan," she said; "ship and all."

"Shucks," he said, using the expression he had learned from her, "it wasn't much. Don't be fooled by the sailor's getting scared sick."

"I'm not," she said, her eyes wide and warm. "Alan, I know where you left the whiskey in the cabin. Could I bring it up for you and Mr. Oate?"

"Sure," he said lightly. Then caution reclaimed him. He moved to start the whistle blasts again and took a look into the binnacle to check the course. The sailor had returned up the ladder with a bucket and swab and behind him came Stuffy Smith, the chief engineer. Smith was a former Cleveland Cliffs man, hired away at Phelim Carmody's advice. He was small and prematurely white-haired with a voice frayed by years of yelling orders through the clatter of the engine-room. *"Onoko?"* he asked. "That was her, wa'n't it?"

"Big as life," Mr. Oate said. "About ran us down abeam. If the Cap'n, here——"

"Aw, knock it off," Alan Kennard said, suddenly self-conscious.

"No, sir," Stuffy Smith said. He wore oil stained white overalls much too big for his thin body. Now he stood drolly stooped, his hand out in illustration. "I'd just come topside fer a pee. Then I hear you holler to the mate, Cap', and I see that big man-eating bastid. Damn' near left the tap running, I was so scared. What was she aiming to do?"

"She must ha' worked in too close to shore off Pointe aux Barques, bound South from Detour. Then they hauled her around and she bore down us." Alan Kennard turned. Minna was standing in the doorway. She had taken time to change into a shirtwaist and skirt, had her duster about her shoulders. "Golly," she said, "if I'd known Mr. Smith was going to be up I'd have brought another glass."

"Ma'am," Stuffy Smith said seriously, "I'm a bottle drinker from 'way back. "You just let me have my turn."

They all laughed at that, but Mr. Oate was buckling at the knees. "Go down and call Mr. Burrell, sailor," Alan Kennard said. "Tell him he's to relieve the mate." Then, the bottle in his hand, he poured the whiskey. "One for you," he told Minna and made her keep a glass. "I'll go along with the chief on the bottle."

"You needn't bully me." Minna grinned at him. "After what you did, I'd toast you with anything handy."

Alan Kennard had gone to stand at the forward window. He made an effort to appear nonchalant as they drank his health. But he felt immense happiness. You proved yourself all right a bit ago, he thought. You're surely a sailor and about as fine as they come. And you and Minna, how you love each other. That's what counts. Time being, forget the rest. . . .

.   .   .   .

Lake Erie was resplendent under the early morning sun as Minna awoke. "Fog went with the dawn while we were in the river," Kennard told her. "You get yourself dressed. Time you do that and have breakfast we'll be into Bellport."

He had made love to her again during the night, and her sensation was one of languid delight. "Chase along," she said. "I don't want you peeking at me. I've got a brand new dress for the occasion."

"I know," he said, looking back at her from the cabin door. "You're sweet on Josh."

"No, sir, I am not!" Yet she flushed a bit after he had gone. Maybe Alan was right, she thought. Poor Josh had nobody, and from all the tales she'd heard, that mother of his was something. Alan couldn't really mind if she paid Josh a little special attention.

The new dress was white piqué with puffed sleeves and a tight bodice, flounces at the waist and a considerable bustle. It showed all the best features of her figure, and her dressmaker, a sour old woman from Napta City, had been shocked when she had chosen the design. She wore with it a cap she had ordered from Field's in Chicago. That was also white piqué, was peaked and stiff-crowned, very much resembled in general style the one which Alan wore. Her shoes were shiny white kid with pearl buttons, and her stockings white silk. She left off two of her usual petticoats, took enormous care with her hair so that the bangs were spread evenly beneath the cap peak.

After all, she told herself happily as she stood before the cheval glass in the cabin, you're a sailor's wife. And you can wear this when Alan gets enough money to buy his yacht. You're a vixen, too, Minna. You truly are. Not wearing all your petticoats and a white dress on a bright sunny day. What does it matter, though, if your legs can be seen a bit? Josh is just an old family friend. You don't mean any harm.

The whistle was being sounded up on the bridge and she shivered with a tremor of last night's fear. It was meant as a signal for the men on the dock at Bellport, though, she realized, and took a moment more to bite her lips to make them red. Then she tightened her veil, pulled on her gloves and went up the ladder to the bridge.

Alan was in the starboard bridge wing, she saw, and not to be bothered. The wind was from inshore; it wouldn't be easy for him to dock. Mr. Oate, down on the foredeck, was watching anxiously, and young Mr. Burrell by the telegraph looked nervous and excited. Not Alan. He's as calm as a clam. Golly, he's certain an A-One sailor. You ought rightly to go down and put on those petticoats.

"Half ahead now, mister," Kennard said to Burrell. " 'Midships the wheel."

The blunt bowed ship seemed to swing straight for the dock, then suddenly veered as the engine and wheel orders were changed.

"Full astern. Stop her! Hard a-stab'd, the wheel. Give them your bowline, Mr. Oate. Stick out aft, bosun. Very well. Heave in both."

Minna sighed in a confusion of feeling. Josh Shaw was down on the dock wearing the kind of starched cotton suit and polka dot cravat she wished she could get Alan to wear. She took out her handkerchief and gayly waved at him. He waved back, but not with his customary smile, and he asked, "Is Antrim there?"

Kennard pushed past her quickly into the bridge wing and she stepped aside. Business, she thought. That's all that pair have in their minds. The devil with them, then. I'm sorry I didn't stay home.

Merton was cleaning up the captain's quarters when she came below. "You'd like for me to be ready to take your bags ashore, madame?" he said.

"I'm not just sure that I'm going ashore," she said. "You keep right on with your regular work, Merton."

She sat stiffly on the settee, her skirt spread out so that it wouldn't wrinkle, her handkerchief drawn taut in her hands. The ship had been docked for fifteen minutes. She had counted each minute by the clock on the bulkhead. Alan should have brought Josh here long since. That was ship style, the same as in the schooners. A captain brought his guests to his cabin for a drink. She felt Merton's eyes on her as he passed in and out with clean towels and linen. "Excuse me, madame," he said finally.

"Sure, Merton."

"I didn't hear much, but the men down on the dock are talking panic. Looks like a big bank in the East has just gone bust. General Grant's mixed up in it someways."

"Oh, my glory!" The handkerchief balled in her hands. "I wonder, has it anything to do with Mr. Shaw and his family. Is Mr. Shaw aboard?"

"He is, madame. Him and the Cap'n are in the pilot house."

"I thank you, Merton." She rose, tempted to go to the pilot house. But Josh and Alan were on the ladder to the Texas. She smiled at Josh, knowing that she must. "Minna, good morning," he called. "My, you look handsome."

She dropped him a partly mocking curtsey and said, "You're not so ugly yourself, sir." Then she noticed her husband's face, and recognized that he couldn't dissemble nearly as well as Joshua. "Tell me the news, Alan," she said to him.

"Read it," Alan Kennard said. He threw a rumpled copy of the *Cleveland Plain Dealer* down on the cabin table. "It's all there."

"Ah, no, Antrim," Joshua Shaw said. "Don't put the girl through that." He sat on the settee and faced Minna. "Get us a drink and I'll explain. You ever play 'London Bridge' when you were a youngster, Minna?"

"Yes, I did." Her lips were stiff, the words slow.

"Well, it's tumbled down. To mix metaphors, the wolves have at last got their teeth too near to General Grant's jugular. He had a banking house, Grant and Ward was the name. Perhaps Antrim's told you of it."

"Never." Alan Kennard was taking out the whiskey bottle. "She has no head for business. And why the hell d' you have to go into it with her?"

Shaw gazed across the cabin at his friend. "For the very good reason that in a little while I propose to take her up and have her meet my mother. You see, Minna, our former president, the illustrious general, has been gulled, trapped, fleeced and ruined. He had the idea 'til yesterday, according to today's papers, that he was worth two and a half million dollars. Then, after the word had been broken to him of how he had been used, he found that he had personal assets of one hundred and eighty dollars and that his firm owes more than eighteen million. Quite a discrepancy. It's brought about the collapse of the Marine National Bank. Also, in all probability, it will create a national financial panic. My mother's family have been very warm admirers of the general. A great part of their funds were either in the Marine National or invested with the Grant and Ward outfit. As large stockholders in Shaw Iron and Steel they'll be tempted to pull out from under, protect themselves with what they've got left."

"So it comes around to hurting us, too." Minna reached and clasped one of Joshua's hands. This was bad, she understood, very bad, else Josh and Alan wouldn't be so worried. You'd like nothing better than to cry. Still, with them like this, no. Look at Alan. He can hardly drink his whiskey.

"That's right," Alan Kennard said. "It hurts us bad, through Josh and what might happen to the plant and to our business. Panic like Josh talks about can close us up in short order. We ain't got enough money to go ahead if we don't work the quarries and the ships steady."

"I don't understand business," she said in a burst of unashamed emotion. "All I know is that I care for you both a great, great deal, and no matter what, I always will. So there!"

"Aye." Alan Kennard's voice was rough. His eyes as he regarded her and then Shaw were intent, very keen. "You spoke a lot of truth, Minna."

Joshua Shaw was on his feet. "Don't take anything wrong, Antrim," he said. "You have no reason. . . . Will you go ashore with me? You and Minna?"

"We will. Minna's been ready for half an hour and more. All I have to do is tell the mate where I'll be."

They went in silence from the ship and up the long flights of wooden steps to the bluff above the dock. Mr. Shaw stood there, erect, expressionless until they were right before him. Then he swept off his Panama hat and bowed to Minna. "A pleasure," he said. "Bellport has been visited by no one lovelier."

"Oh, sir," she said; "such talk!" But he had stepped aside at once with Josh and Alan had followed. She was able to hear their voices. "Any word?" Josh said.

"Yes, and bad. Marine National is certainly a goner. The panic has closed everything up tight in New York. But my wife's people, may God help them, seem to consider that in some fashion we're beholden to them. They telegraphed me for an immediate cash loan of fifty thousand."

"We haven't got it," Josh said.

"I told them as much," Mr. Shaw said slowly. "The answer within the hour was to warn us that by tomorrow noon they would put up for sale the block of stock they own in our plant."

"That'd just about wreck us right now, father."

"I'm aware of it."

"What I got ain't too much," Alan said. "But you can have full use of it."

"Thank you kindly, Antrim." There was a note almost like that of laughter in Joshua's voice. "But our predicament is so bad that we need to settle it ourselves."

"Gentlemen," Mr. Shaw said, "we have forgotten the lady. And Mrs. Shaw is awaiting us, is eager to serve an early dinner."

"You've told mother?" Josh said.

"I considered it my duty," Mr. Shaw said. "My belief has always been that the plant was a family concern."

"On paper," Josh said.

"But drawn up, witnessed and made legal by lawyers," Mr. Shaw said. "The Cottrells are now taking advantage of the fact. No more of it, though, gentlemen. Not until after dinner."

Mr. Shaw sat beside Minna in the carriage that took them to the vast white house. He pointed out the plant to her, made her promise that after dinner she would go with him to see the three o'clock pouring. She was amazed at his perfect control, and her only clear thought was that he was like some stage actor going through his lines in a play. But, golly, inside he must be feeling a whole sight worse than you.

Mrs. Shaw met them half way across the lawn to the house. She wore a canvas apron and gardening gloves, carried shears, a basket. So here she is, Minna thought. I wonder, when she touches the flowers, do they shrivel all up? But the basket was full of roses and they were beautiful. Mrs. Shaw talked of them. "You must take some home with you, my dear. They can be put in the ship's icebox for you and they should keep very well."

"Thank you, ma'am," Minna said, stumbling on the smooth path. The brother, the one she knew to be Cottrell, had just come to the front door. He was very drunk. He stooped far over as if under an enormous weight. His face was yellow welted with red; his hands had red, wet welts across the backs.

"That's Cottrell, my brother," Joshua said. "Whiskey's a disease with him, Minna. Don't mind. He doesn't eat with us. Somehow today he got away from his nurse."

"I sent the nurse off this morning," Mrs. Shaw said clear voiced. "I couldn't stand the man's surliness any longer. Tell me, Mrs. Kennard, was the trip from Patigowoc pleasant?"

"Oh, yes, sure." Minna had been holding her teeth against her under lip. Cottrell swayed from side to side in front of the doorway. He had a smell about him. It was like that of a sick animal, she thought, one that had been hurt in a trap in the forest and had got out only to slowly die.

"Sure wasn't so pleasant last night," Alan said, and she was deeply grateful to him, admired his ability to speak with calmness. "Nearly cracked up with the *Onoko* a bit South of Pointe aux Barques."

"Which boat is she, Antrim?" Joshua said. They moved forward into the house and Mrs. Shaw had her arm around Cottrell's shoulder. She led Cottrell upstairs, talked to him in short, soft words.

"First bulk ore carrier built," Alan said, his eyes on Cottrell. "Laid down over here in Cleveland. A good vessel. They should treat her better."

Minna was dazed, on the point of being sick. Alan had described this house and these people to her many times, and yet, in the moment she lacked the power to look upon them as real. Even Josh seemed to have changed. They all talked and acted like in a play, made Alan do the same. She couldn't do it. No, she couldn't forget what had been said aboard and at the top of the bluff. Any more than she could forget the one, Cottrell, who was upstairs now.

Dinner was served. She sat and made herself eat, gave monosyllabic answers to Mrs. Cottrell. Alan looked strangely at her more than once, but she couldn't help it. She just couldn't help it. Let them play that things were all right. What she wanted to do was go hide off by herself and cry and cry.

But at the end of dinner Mr. Shaw took her out into the open air. He didn't talk at all. He smoked a cheroot while they went from one flower bed to another. Then he said, "Would you like to see the plant, Minna? We'll be pouring the iron at three o'clock."

"I'd like to fine," she said; "and, gosh, I'm sorry for you."

"Don't be, Minna." His hands briefly touched hers. "It won't do you any good. But please wait here. I'll go fetch your husband and Josh. I can understand why you don't wish to return inside."

"Thank you, sir," she said. While he was gone, in the few minutes he gave her, she stood at the side of the lawn and let her emotions go in rapid sobs.

Josh and Alan seemed quite gay once they were with her and Mr. Shaw in the carriage. You had yourself a cry, she thought, and they had themselves a whiskey. Well, all right, let them. They need it. Golly, golly, what's going to happen?

They were at the plant gate, had started to go in as the gateman shouted. It was Joshua who swung around. Then, seeing the stiffness of his body and hearing the gateman, they all turned.

Flame flared and leaped and twisted at the windows of the white house. A maid was on the lawn and she frantically rang a hand bell. She stood in the shadow of the trees, wore a gray uniform. The uniform was on fire. She gave the appearance, before she fell and rolled across the lawn, of being a huge flower.

"Jesus Christ," Mr. Shaw said. "Christ, have mercy. I should have known better." He grasped the whip and beat the horses, shouted to the gateman. "Get them from the plant, Dominic. Every man. Send somebody to the village."

Minna clung to Alan on the way back. She kept her eyes shut. It was her belief that the whole world had gone mad. Then, on the lawn where Mr. Shaw stopped the carriage and ran, she was afflicted by the heat of the flames, looked at the house.

Yellow flames were over the walls. Red flames streaked with black smoke held the windows. The roof creaked, caved, and flame was through it like an upthrust pillar. Glass jangled in explosion; the paint made a low, hissing, bubbling sound. Alan had run after Josh and Mr. Shaw. She was alone in the carriage. Do something. The horses are about ready to break.

She took the reins and drove the horses back to the fence at the edge of the lawn, tied them there. Then she got out and started to return to the house. But the maid who had rung the bell was on the lawn. Minna knelt down beside her. The woman was conscious although very near death. Minna cradled her head, lifted the terribly charred hands from the grass. "What was it?" she whispered, compelled by horror.

"Cottrell," the woman said. "He pulled the tip from the gas jet in the hall. I seen him as I was clearing table. I went to turn it off, stop him. So did the missus. But he grabbed holt of her after he lit it. He wouldn't let her go. That's when I got afire. Aiee, I hurt!"

"Be still," Minna said. "The doctor will be here soon."

"No, it's too late. Just say me a prayer, dearie."

"Our Father," Minna began, but the woman was dead.

Joshua found her. He staggered to her side and dropped down on one knee. "Did you learn anything?" he whispered.

She nodded.

"Was it Cottrell?"

"Yes."

Joshua's glasses had been broken, but the frame was still in place. His hands knocked it off as he pressed them to his eyes. "The house was very old, and dry. Yet he must have opened the gas jets all over. When Dad and I got there, we couldn't do anything. We couldn't even go in. They were still standing in the front hall, though. They were—" his voice lowered, lifted resolutely as though this he must tell—"they were holding each other in their arms."

"Josh, darling," Minna said. "Poor, dear man. What can I do to help?"

He gazed at her, his eyes vacant with defeat. "Nothing," he said. "Mother started our downfall, Cottrell finished it. Thank you for your comfort. But simply wait for your husband to come back and take you to where the world is sane."

It was, she remembered later, Alan who took care of the entire situation. Maybe because he had become used to trouble and death on the sea and because both Mr. Shaw and Joshua were in such bad shape. Late that afternoon, in the family carriages, he sent them in to the Hollenden House in Cleveland with Piotr, the heavy-shouldered foreman from the plant. Piotr wouldn't let them talk with any of the reporters in the lobby of the Hollenden, and he carried out Alan's orders and ushered them upstairs to a suite. But Minna could hear the newsboys in the Square yelling the headlines of the story before Alan came in from Bellport.

"You all right?" he asked her hoarsely.

"I will be," she said. "I need a bath and a change of clothes. But how about you?"

"Don't mind about me. Where's the others?"

"In there." She indicated one of the bedrooms. "Piotr's with them. He and I thought— Well, Mr. Shaw was acting a bit wild, and with the windows right close and Josh kind of sick and all."

"Yeah." Alan Kennard smoothed his fingers slowly along the heat-inflamed skin of his jaw. "I know what you mean. But you order supper up for them. Make them eat it. I'll send word to the ship to bring your clothes over. But I got to get ahold of their lawyer and I got to reach Jane. You go right ahead and do like I say."

"Yes, Alan," she said, pervaded by some of his determination. "You should eat, too, though."

"Eat?" He glared at her. "I'm trying to keep the whole kit and kaboodle from going to hell. Pipe down. You got your orders."

He sat at a table in a corner of the parlor of the suite, his head in his hands, while the bellboy took her directions for supper. Then he went out and the clamor in the hall was renewed; the reporters were trying again to question him. "I'm from the Associated Press," she heard before the door slammed. "Is it true, Captain, that there was suicide involved?"

The door panels blurred Alan's answer, but the tenor of his voice alone was enough to let her know that he cursed the man who asked the question. There was another sound, a dull, bumping one. Golly, she thought, he up and hit that reporter man. But it was just the waiter with the trays. "Did you see Captain Kennard in the hall?" she murmured to the waiter after she shut the door.

"I did, ma'am. The news-writers were on him like flies. But he got into the elevator and he's gone downstairs."

He'll send wires to Jane, wherever Jane is, she told herself, and to Jack Frawn in Chicago. That's what he'll do. He's fighting like you never saw him do before. So calm in the middle of this. And you went and gabbled at him, you little ninny. You should have more sense.

"Supper's ready to be served, ma'am," the waiter said. "Should I call the gentlemen?"

She stared hard at the waiter. "No," she said. "Those reporters paid you to get the Shaws out here. There must be some question they want you to ask. Go on now. Leave!" She motioned for him to give her the bill, picked up a pencil to sign it.

"Cash, ma'am," the waiter said. He was grinning. "That's what the manager said when I brung this up. 'Cash for any food served.'"

She flushed to the roots of her hair. Alan had forgotten one thing. She had no cash, and this wasn't the time to call for the manager. It all seemed like a trick against them, a dirty, rotten trick. She went to the door of the bedroom where the Shaws and Piotr were and lightly knocked. "Piotr," she said; "I need some cash."

The waiter was right at her shoulder, tried to look into the room when Piotr opened the door. The big Hungarian grunted at sight of him and hit him a hammer-like blow on the skull with the heel of his fist. "Back!" he said. "I heard you talkin' to the missus. Ten's enough, Mrs. Cap'n?"

"Plenty and more," she said. She plucked the benumbed waiter by the sleeve. "Bring up a bottle of whiskey and keep the change. But next time don't try any tricks."

"Yes, ma'am," the waiter said. "It's just them fellas in the hall put me up to it."

Joshua came out to eat when she called him and after Piotr had given him a drink of whiskey. But Mr. Shaw wouldn't move from the bed in the darkened room. He lay mumbling and muttering, seeming to watch the pattern of the arc light from the Square upon the ceiling. The words he said, though, were those of the newsboys below: "Panic! Big national panic! Bellport blaze! Three dead!"

She shuddered. This was worse in its way than the burned woman on the lawn. Piotr sat between the bed and the windows; he gestured covertly at her. "No, I'll take my turn," she said in a firm voice. "You go out with Joshua and eat your supper. The whiskey's on the table."

"Jane?" Mr. Shaw said vaguely once she was within the room.

"Jane's coming," Minna Kennard said. "Alan has sent for her. Please be quiet, sir, and sleep."

"Jane, you were right in going." The man on the bed lay very still as he spoke. "We should all have gone. But where? You didn't tell us, Janey. . . ." The voice went from a whisper into silence. Then, abruptly, in response to the newsboys' cries, it rose in staccato: "Pap-uh! Oh, get ya pap-uh! Panic an' fire!" She put her hands against her ears and braced her body. Alan, come back. Hurry.

. . . .

The doorman down in front of the Hollenden knew him, and he asked, "Anything I can do for you, Captain?"

"Yeah," Kennard said. "I want a hack to take me to Mr. Aeneas Lothrop's house."

"It's out on Euclid, sir." The doorman waved a hansom cab forward and didn't blink at the five-dollar bill Kennard handed him. "Don't tell them newspaper fellas."

"No, sir," the doorman said as he saluted. "Not me."

Kennard sat back in the cab with his hat low over his face. He was violently perturbed. His feeling was that the cab hardly moved, and yet he could hear the rapid clop of the horse's hooves and he knew that they were already out of the Square. Take it easy, man. Now if ever you have to think straight. Just hope to Christ that Lothrop's home. He's a smart fella and him and his partner have handled Josh's family's affairs for years. And he's your own lawyer, too, and that won't hurt. You can talk to him on the level. No jiggery-nackery or beating around the bloody bush.

"Wait for me," he told the cab driver when they had stopped at the carriage block before the immense house. "I'll be out in a while."

He had thought during the last part of the ride that he had himself under control. Yet as he mounted the porch and rang the door bell he felt diffident and distraught. You're not sure of what you want to tell Lothrop, he realized. Damn you, too, you simpleton, you ain't got a calling card the way Minna said you ought. The bloody maid might not even let you in the house.

The maid stared at him for an instant and then opened the door and asked him to come in. "Mr. Lothrop is at dinner, sir," she said. "They're entertaining. Do you mind waiting for a bit?"

"I would indeed," he said. "You tell Mr. Lothrop for me that it's very important."

The maid ushered him into a small side drawing room where

the smell of the potted plants became at once oppressive. He was sweating profusely and each chair he tried seemed to be uncomfortable. Down the wide parquet hall he could hear from the dining room the high, light clatter of voices, the sound of laughter. You can laugh, he thought, obscurely angry. But not me. What the hell can be funny tonight?

Aeneas Lothrop came erect, smiling along the hall. His thick brown hair was parted perfectly in the middle. He was in a dinner jacket and his shellacked, pointed shoes gleamed. A fop, Kennard told himself with disgust, yet according to Josh this fella was one of the greatest football players Yale ever had. Pioneer Connecticut stock. Smarter than a whip. Watch out with him. He might take you over the jumps, just because you don't know what the hell can be done.

Yet he found as Lothrop led him into a quieter, cooler and bigger room that he was at ease with the man. "I didn't think," Lothrop said, "that you came out simply over the case of those fellows at the quarry. I just got the papers about them from Collins this morning. Your interest is the Shaws, isn't it?"

"It is," Kennard said. "Nothing else."

"A terrible thing," Lothrop said. He stood at the doorway with a bell-pull in his hand. "Let me offer you coffee, brandy, port or whiskey."

"Whiskey," Kennard said. The lad has as steady nerves as a big time gambler, he thought. You did right to come here. He looked squarely into Lothrop's eyes. "We ain't got much time. I come from the hotel and the old fella's gone all to hell and Josh ain't much better. You're lawyer for the Shaws, and mine, too. What can we do to save the shebang?"

"Well, there are several things," Lothrop said. A maid had brought a tray and he poured whiskey for Kennard, coffee for himself. "Tell me, though, what you suggest. Inasmuch as you're such a close friend of the family."

Kennard thought, inasmuch my ass. You want me to play my cards first, bucko. But I'm fixed so I have to. "You know," he said before he drank the whiskey, "that the old lady's folks closed in on them today."

"No." Lothrop sat with one leg crossed over the other, slowly stirring his coffee. "But I'm aware they were caught in the Marine Bank crash. That I heard downtown today."

"They sent the old man a wire and they said they wanted fifty thousand cash or by tomorrow noon they'd put their company stock up for sale."

"A very silly move," Lothrop said. "Putting that much stock on the open market at a time like this might wreck the whole Shaw enterprise."

"But Josh and the old man ain't got anything like the amount of cash that was asked. I know. They told me." Kennard rose impulsively to his feet. He walked over and stood in front of Lothrop. "Look, how long before the old lady's will would be probated? I mean, how much time does a fella have?"

"Well said," Lothrop said, his eyes on his cup. "I think that what you're after is something like this, Captain. With the correct interpretation put upon it by you, say, Josh could be brought under the circumstances to enter into a petition of bankruptcy. He's the treasurer of the company, his father temporarily incapacitated, his mother and brother newly dead, the company affairs already in bad shape. For him to give over the company in bankruptcy to some reputable receiver recognized by the court would only be a very logical step."

"The petition could be put through fast?"

Lothrop looked up and smiled. "Faster than Mrs. Shaw's will can be probated. And with enough speed to keep the Cottrell clan from throwing away their shares. Of course, the thing to do is to find the right receiver, a man acceptable to Josh even at this time of emotional stress."

"Who d' you think?" Kennard said hoarsely.

"My choice is yours," Lothrop said. "I'm convinced that you are an excellent man for the job."

Don't laugh, Kennard told himself, and don't curse. Try to act just as slick as this operator. "Well," he said, "I ain't too qualified for work like that. The court might object."

"My recommendation and that of my partner," Lothrop said, "would be presented to the court. Without bragging, we are both very well known to the local judiciary."

"And the Cottrells?"

"They'd be automatically blocked from selling their stock until you as the receiver saw fit."

Kennard shook his head from side to side in open admiration. "You're way out in front of me, mister," he said. "Give me another whiskey, will you? I've had one hell of a day."

"Nor are you finished yet," Lothrop said gravely, bent over the whiskey decanter. "There must also be some sort of agreement drawn up between you and Josh whereby later, at a stipulated date, he is recompensed."

"What d' you mean by that?"

"It's wholly possible that during your term as receiver a bid might be made to you for the Shaw Iron and Steel Works. The net sum of the sale should revert of course to Josh."

"Now I get you. But I'm willing to give Josh share for share interest in my own company, and make him vice president to boot."

Lothrop smiled again. "I'd say, rather, that instead of stock you be given a flat sum of money for your services. Fifty thousand dollars would be a good figure. And in addition you would take Josh into your firm as vice president. Agreed?"

"Just about," Kennard said. His head throbbed and his eyes smarted. The whiskey he had drunk was sour in him, and abruptly he had an intense dislike for Aeneas Lothrop. "Who you figuring to sell the Shaw Works to? Yeah, and what's your price for the deal?"

"I have no man or men immediately in mind," Lothrop said quietly. "Yet I wouldn't be surpised if some local combine were formed to offer a reasonable bid. As for my price, it will be ten thousand and you'll find it on my bill at the end of the month."

Kennard was forced to laughter. "By Christ, you sure know your cards."

"Then we're agreed." Lothrop was on his feet. "Josh and his family are protected and you have proven yourself his very good friend."

"Yeah," Kennard muttered, unable to withstand the cold, precise drive of the man's logic any longer. "Yeah, let it be so. I ain't got the head to go any further against you."

Lothrop bowed to him. "Excuse me for a moment while I say goodnight to my wife and guests. Then you and I had better go to my office. This will demand a considerable number of documents. Help yourself to the whiskey should you like."

Kennard waited for him numbly and was numb and almost speechless as they rode to Lothrop's office in the hansom. His mind was confused; he suffered a severe headache, and the day's events, the details of the plan Lothrop had evolved were a vague chiaroscuro in which he could no further define right from wrong. You're helping Josh, he told himself. That's the main thing. You make a few thousand for yourself, it don't matter. Just couldn't stand and see the whole shebang go to hell. . . .

He roused himself a good deal, though, when he returned to the Hollenden with Lothrop. He was thinking of Joshua Shaw and what Joshua would say and do. Minna would be there, too, he realized. She'd be curious; she'd ask him what the deal was about and damned if he could tell her right off. Better Lothrop did. Lothrop could put that along with the rest on the bill.

The reporters were gone from the lobby and there were no curious people to press about them in the elevator. Joshua and Minna sat sagged half asleep in the front room, and that meant that Piotr was in with the old man. Kennard sat down on the couch beside Minna, took her hand in his and whispered, "How are you, darlin'?"

"About worn out," she said. "Why have you been away so long?"

"Mr. Lothrop and me had things to figure. You go in and go to bed. We have to talk to Josh for awhile."

"No, I'll stay," she said. She was gazing curiously across the room at Joshua and Lothrop. They sat at the table in the corner and the lawyer had his briefcase open and some documents neatly piled. He spoke slowly to Joshua, calling him "old boy," his arm up and around Joshua's shoulder.

"In simple terms," Joshua said, his voice toneless and halting, "until Mother's will is probated, Dad and I still have the major voting interest in our stock. And as treasurer I could enter the company into bankruptcy."

"Provided that you have your father's signature on these also," Lothrop said.

Joshua's face was without color. Piotr had washed it in Bellport after the fire, but it had been hurriedly done. His eyebrows, his ears and temples and underjaw still carried smudges of soot. They gave him a peculiar comi-tragic appearance, as if he were a clown who wasn't quite certain of his role. Now nerves throbbed in his temples; scarlet mottled his cheekbones. "I dislike doing this," he said stiffly. "Dad should be seen by a doctor. He's not himself at all."

"Listen, old boy," Lothrop said. "I must be blunt with you. What the Cottrells demanded today is simply the beginning of what's ahead. We're on the verge of a tremendous national panic. All your creditors will be after you in a matter of days, or hours. Your company with its present lack of assets would be swept down the drain. Bankruptcy proceedings are your only way out. So accept what's offered here."

"How about it, Antrim?" Joshua said. His nearsighted eyes had contracted into a fixed stare. "It will help you and yours, won't it?"

"That's a fact," Kennard said. "But the deal's been made to save you."

Joshua laughed with a sound that was barely audible. "I'm among friends," he said. He took the long legal sheets and signed them slowly where Lothrop indicated. Then he pushed himself up from the table and took them in to his father.

Lothrop broke the silence that had come upon the room. "Your husband has done very well tonight, Mrs. Kennard. You should be extremely proud of him."

"Just why?" Minna said in a tense voice.

Lothrop offered her his smile. "There aren't many opportunities when a man can help a friend and help himself in the bargain. The Captain has succeeded."

"I don't know as I understand you," Minna said. She was looking sidewise at her husband. "But it doesn't seem right, not for him, and not for you." Her movements as she stood were clumsy with fatigue. "I'm going to bed, Alan. In the morning I'll have you tell me—if you can."

.   .   .   .

Mrs. Svenson once again got into the habit of sitting on the porch nearly all day long that summer. The downstairs maid, Katrine, or Minna fixed her chair so that it faced the lovely bend of the Bouche de Mouche where the ships turned coming and going. She could see the glint of the river, the open lake, the sandy, curving shore, and on the lawn close in front of her squirrels played and robins pecked and a mole who knew the gardener's habits dug stubbornly under a croquet wicket.

The doctor from Napta City had begun to give her drugs for what ailed her, the tumor that was, he said, way deep inside, and so she suffered very little. Minna had made a soft cushion for the chair; her son-in-law had brought her a fancy Japanese bamboo fan from Chicago, and Katrine, who had become more her friend than a maid, supplied her regularly with cold lemonade. She was wholly content to pass the hours here, retreat further and further into the past, led to it by the familiar view of the river and the lake, even these trees which were all part of her first memories. Yet there were also the people, and they formed increasingly their lives about her.

Alan Kennard was seldom at home. He was busy in Chicago and Cleveland and Toledo and Buffalo, finding cargoes for the ship, orders for limestone that would keep the quarries running. He was tense, remote when he came back. New lines were along his jaws and in his forehead. He smoked big, black cigars and quietly drank a lot of whiskey. It was one dusk when the whiskey had him that he talked to her. He took a chair beside her in the delicate violet light, sat nervously swinging his leg back and forth.

"You hear folks call me a sharp dealer?" he asked abruptly.

"Not so's I could notice," she said. "I'd ha' whacked you with this—" she lifted the fan—"if I did. But what brings you to such a question as that?"

"Things folks have been saying behind my back. Lars Keiberg for one. Minna for another. By gorry, yes, Minna in particular. I don't like it, Ma."

"No reason why you should. If it's true, it's true, and not a thing you can do. If it's a lie, you're man enough to take care of it."

He hoarsely laughed. "You don't get around, Ma. You just set here."

"But you spoke of Minna."

"I know I did. She thinks I treated the Shaws rough when the lawyer and me got them to go into bankruptcy. The way she reckons, I took advantage of their trouble, made them move the way I wanted. But they'd ha' gone under in the crash if I hadn't. And now with their plant being sold, they're getting thirty cents back on each dollar. Josh comes in as vice president here at good pay and without havin' to buy too much stock. He's safe, the old man's safe, even his sister and his mother's no-good folks Down East."

He stopped to light a cigar and in the bluish bloom of the sulphur match she studied his face. An unhappy man, she thought. It's this country. The dreams keep tearing him up inside the same way they did Svenson. But he's tougher than your man; he fights a good sight harder.

"I can keep running," he said swiftly, as if he had read her thought, "where plenty of fellas have failed. We have contracts to deliver steady to the combine that took over at Bellport, and to half a dozen more big steel companies down on Erie. I've been working on the other end of the business, too, with the building trades. That was in the deal I made with Jack Frawn last month when I bought up his interest and got rid of his wise monkey, that Collins. We're going to make all the slake lime and brick and cement we can handle. Josh Shaw will be in charge of it and take on Collins' old job, too. Ours is a real company. Sure, I've had to give plenty of credit, but we'll get our money back with a nice profit to boot when these goddamn' hard times are over. Y' see, Ma, only the small men have gone under. The hard-headed fellas are still around and in business."

She was glad that in the rise of darkness he couldn't see her face. Here was Svenson's kind of talk. In his time, too, Svenson had tried to make her believe in the majestic dreams. "You tell this to Minna?" she said.

"Some." The cigar ember glowed as he inhaled. It showed his face gaunt, the cheeks hollowed, muscles knotted at the jaw angles and the mouth rigid.

"Why not all? Maybe she'd change her tune if she knew."

"No. She just don't care."

"You two are in trouble, Alan. Now you tell me why."

"Ah, hell! Over two years and she can't have kids. She's sweet on Josh Shaw, too."

Mrs. Svenson sat upright in the big wicker chair. "That's fiddle-sticks," she said. "Alan Kennard, you're talking loose and foolish."

"I am in a pig's eye." He flung the cigar out into the driveway. It made a quiver of sparks among the fireflies there. He stood and gazed down past it at the lawn slope, the trees and the river and the ambient leap of Bouche de Mouche light. "All this I give her. But even before the Shaws' house burned down, even before that tough old seagull and that skidrow Cottrell went and killed themselves, she was sweet on Josh. What's a man to expect? Ain't I worked hard enough for her?"

"A woman expects children, too," Mrs. Svenson said in a flat voice. "You might be to blame as well as Minna. Take yourself to a doctor and get examined. It wouldn't hurt, either, if you stayed home a bit more and gave her a little more consideration. Minna's the kind who likes affection. But I've never seen anything wrong between her and young Shaw, and I doubt me if I will ever."

"Fine talk." He had come to stand spraddle-legged before her and inside the house lights were turned on, showed her his eyes wild and furious. "You should ha' seen your daughter over to Cleveland after the fire. 'Poor Josh.' 'Dear Josh.' A lot of goddamn' bilge.

Like he was her lover, or some scared little kid. Me, I don't want any more of the Shaws. I've had my share and as soon as I can——"

"You be still," she said fiercely. "That's what you'll do, Kennard. They'll be here tomorrow and we're going to entertain 'em."

"Who fixed it?" He bent over her in anger.

"I did. The sister, Jane, is coming in from Europe and bringing a friend with her. She wants to see her peoples' graves, get her affairs put straight."

"Minna must ha' let you know."

"She did. And Minna had the word from Mr. Shaw, not Josh."

Alan Kennard slapped his hand against the porch railing. He cursed with the fervor of his youth, using words that Mrs. Svenson had failed to hear in the woods camps where she had worked. She gazed at him neither shocked nor surprised, just with her own rage growing, solidifying.

"I run this place," he said. "You don't, Minna don't."

"Be damned if you do," she said. It was an old phrase of her husband's and he had always pronounced it with a slight Swedish accent which she unconsciously copied. "This place belonged to me long before any dollar-hungry sailor came up from the sea. You want trouble, I'll get it for you. Mr. Shaw gave Minna to know that one reason Jane is coming is because the Cottrell folks have started suit against you for the way you sold out the Shaw plant."

Kennard laughed, but it was a hoarse, dissonant sound. "You'd scare me?" he said. "Or you'd try to buy another husband for your girl, one that'd give her kids?"

"No," Mrs. Svenson said. "I'd only fit you to your boots. You've become a bit too big for them. You're into some few things you don't like much and they've turned you sour. So you bully Minna, take it out on her. But not me you don't. I know what makes you tick and just how to stop your clock. Ambition's your trouble. You want to be the biggest man on the Lakes. Forget that for a while. Go in and have a drink. Whiskey will help what ails you."

"Why, goddamn you!" he said. But he turned and went in through the door.

She sat there for quite a time after he had gone. She felt spent, drained by the fury of her emotion of the moment. You may have been wrong, she told herself dully. But he needed all of that. He asked for it, the cocky rascal. Not quite a rascal, though, your son-in-law. He's a better man than most who might have married Minna. The dreams have got him, like you figured before. He'd be as big as the country, and there's very few that can. . . .

Pain had worked in under the edge of her last dose of drugs. Her excited nerves responded violently to it. She sat and twisted hunched sidewise in the chair. She called Minna's name, then Katrine's, but her voice was without sound. When she attempted to stand up, thinking of her own room and her bed, she collapsed and dropped asprawl on the porch.

It was Alan Kennard who heard her. He was in his study, a glass in his hand. His acute hearing told him what had happened. He finished the whiskey before he went out to her. This was going to be bad, he knew. Minna was at the top of the first flight of stairs, and Katrine and Cook and the other maid, Olga, were at the kitchen door. They'd been listening to all that he and the old woman had said at the end. It had been said real strong and loud. All right. Come on. You're ashamed of yourself and showing the fact to them will make little difference. Tomorrow, the servants will spread the story all over town.

Minna was breathless with terror and anger. "You'll kill her," she gasped, "the way you act."

"Out of my way," he said and went on into Mrs. Svenson's room, the thin, bony body in his arms. "I admit I'm wrong. Would ye have me tattoo it on my chest?"

"No, Alan." Minna had begun to loosen her mother's clothing. "Just show her and me some human kindness. Since we've been back from Cleveland you're a man I hardly know. And now this Jane and her friend are coming. We have to entertain them."

"Fancy language you use," he said harshly. "My woman's gettin' to be a bloody lady." But he patted her on the shoulder as he said it, and when she stared up at him his expression had become that of remorse. "I'll have Boker fetch Doc' Chapin. The doc' will tend to her."

"It's no use. The doctor told me. Only these." Minna touched the bottle of pills on the side table. "They hold back the pain for a while. Then she needs more, and more. Oh, Alan, she's going to die."

"Darlin'," he said, "don't take on so. She'll live a long time yet."

"Like this? With the pain at her, as if she was an animal in a trap?"

"Then may she die soon." His arms were around Minna; he held her tenderly. "It's a rough road she's on. But you forgive me, Minna?"

She gazed into his eyes. "I do," she said strangely. "You have your own kind of pain, too. Let me be with her now, Alan. I have to get her to bed."

Mrs. Svenson had full memory of the evening when she awoke. It was dawn. A hush was on the land and water. The birds were not yet awake in the trees, and very softly the breeze that came with the sun riffled the leaves, gave a susurrus that soothed her. She lay motionless in contemplation looking out into the gold-banded silver light that carried upward gleaming the moisture of the dew. Then, from the dock, the bass bray of the whistle sounded.

The *Minna* was sailing, she knew. Captain Oate must have done loading and blew the whistle to get his crew aboard. The theme of her contemplation continued. If she'd been hard on her son-in-law last night, there had been reason. But there had been reason on Kennard's side, too. You'd be a fool if you didn't admit to that. He has lots to irk him, and a great deal to feed his pride. The ships run this river because of him. The quarries are here and operating because he's stuck everlastingly to it, and the town's built up, folks have money in their pockets. The whole shebang's a going concern when half the country is bust and broke. No wonder, then, that Alan Kennard is a cocky man.

Another whistle blast rent the river quiet. The *Minna* had pulled away from the dock. She was bound out. Mrs. Svenson lay waiting for the blast that would be sounded when the ship was abreast of the house.

The blast came, echoing, shattering the final fragments of the dawn. Robins awoke in the trees. Magpies and jays called. Down on the town road, a dog barked at the baker's wagon and in all the chicken yards the roosters crowed. Mrs. Svenson turned slightly on her side. She had heard the slur of bare feet in the next room; Alan Kennard had got from bed to watch his ship sail.

He went back towards the bed and she could hear his voice and Minna's in muted talk. They must have made peace, she sensed, for there was the sudden light lilt of laughter from Minna, the kind of laughter a woman gave only when she was joining in the act of love.

Mrs. Svenson listened with care and no feeling of shame. The brief, dim cries, the creaks, the rustling and panting were for her an avenue of escape to her own past, to the times when in robust joyousness she had welcomed the passion of her man. This body had once offered Svenson all that he desired. It was, she recognized in a sharp, rapid descent into self-loathing, no longer the same. Now it rotted and within that rottenness she was forced to live. No man would ever again. . . . Your own daughter when she undresses you has to. . . .

She jerked around on the bed, stretched out her hand for the bottle of morphine pills. Take them all. Gulp them straight down. They'll send you where you should go, woman. No use your living any more.

But her hand slowly released from the bottle. No. You can't. Last night you helped. You might very well help again. Listen to them in there. They're happy. By your standing up to Kennard you brought them together again. Each hour you live has got some worth. If Svenson was around he'd tell you that sure as sure. Take just one and it'll kick the pain back out of you for a time.

She took the pill and drowsed, and roused from the drowsy state into further contemplation. Her thought went forward to the day and the people who would come to the house. This Jane Shaw, she must be quite a girl and with more spunk in her than the rest of the family wrapped up in one parcel. Jane's friend was English, from what Josh had to say, a sculptress. A funny word, the kind that used to make Svenson laugh. You don't call Jane, who paints, a paintress.

But keep the thing straight in your head. You have half an idea that back in the old days Kennard had doings with Jane. It might be part of why he was so jumpy last night. His old sweetheart come visiting and he's married to a half-breed and you're as much an Indian as was ever born into your tribe. Alan Kennard's worried by that and for a fact you can't blame him. It might be a little rough this afternoon. Mr. Shaw, though, he's your good friend; he'll be handy to stop any bushwah that might get started. The local folks you and Minna and Kennard know how to treat. There's Keiberg, of course, and that rack of bones he calls a wife, and Phelim and Peg Carmody, then Doc' Chapin and his wife from Napta, and the little fella, Lipfer, who was such a friend of Svenson's, and his wife. They're mixed up kind of, but they'll do, and Minna has got plenty of drink and food and games for them. You just sit on the porch and watch and get to know Mr. Shaw better. He's a nice old man.

There was the slapping sound of slippers in the hall, the rattle of the door knob and Minna was in the room. Her hair was tousled from love-making, her eyes and face flushed and bright. "Ma, you look better," she said at once.

"You, too," Mrs. Svenson said. "It seems like you've put things straight with your man."

"I have. He's sorry for last night."

"Then help me up out of here. I'll bathe myself, but you'll have to fix me into that dress. What time do you expect your folks?"

"After dinner." Minna had her hands on her mother's sinewy, dark-skinned arms. "It's to be an afternoon lawn party. That's how the editor of the *News* over to Napta City told me he was going to print it."

Mrs. Svenson kept back the involuntary grimace of her pain. "My, just imagine. The old folks when I was a youngster used to gut their fish where you got that croquet."

"I know." Minna stared at her mother. "But there's no need to mention it. Times have changed."

"They surely have," Mrs. Svenson slowly said, "and you can count on me to remember the fact. You stay out of the bathroom, I thank you. I can still go and make my water alone."

Alan Kennard had asked her before the party started, then put a big slug of whiskey in Mrs. Svenson's glass of lemonade. She welcomed it later when the tension became quite extreme. Peggy Carmody was an unexpected source of trouble; she resented with open scorn Jane Shaw's friend, Enid Gormley. The English girl was thin and pale, her blond hair plainly worn under a small white duck cap, her costume identical to Jane's, a simple shirtwaist and skirt and short jacket. But her accent was unmistakably English and upper class, and with the exception of Jane, the other women all wore large hats and ruffled organdy dresses. "We'd heard we were to play croquet," Jane said in tacit apology.

"Too bad," Peggy Carmody said, her Liverpool Irish accent intentionally broad, "that it can't be cricket or that other shenanigan, polo."

Jane gave her a steady look. "You're big enough and strong enough," she said, "to play them both. Come along, Enid. We'll take sides against the men in any style they want."

Doctor Chapin came from the East and he was quick to follow them out onto the lawn. Then Joshua Shaw hurried down the steps from the porch with Alan Kennard and Mr. Lipfer. Mrs. Lipfer, a slight woman with a big hat and a parasol, regarded both

Mrs. Svenson and those already on the lawn, then took the steps, opened the parasol and moved as near her husband as possible. A sensible person, Mrs. Svenson thought, one who can look at both ends of the question. But the Carmodys were still on the porch with the Keibergs and Mr. Shaw. Minna stood irresolute on the top step beside Peggy Carmody.

"Don't play no games," Lars Keiberg said in answer to a glance from Mrs. Svenson. "Stuff's not for me."

"Well, I'm going to play," Minna said. She took off her ostrich plume hat and handed it to her mother. "I'm not any old stick-in-the-mud to be left out. What do you say, Peggy?"

"Nothing," Peggy said, "but that the English should stay in England."

Mrs. Svenson lifted her fan and swiped Peggy across a broad buttock. "Go beat the stuffing out of her, then, that's how you feel. Get along, too, Phelim. You're as Irish as your wife."

"That I am," Phelim Carmody said, and grinned. "Let's us take a hop out there, Peggy."

"In these?" Peggy said. She pointed down at her high-heeled shoes. "With them wearing the like of sandals?"

"Go stocking-foot, then," Phelim said; he swung her rapidly around. "It's not you nor me who'll spoil the game."

Peggy broke into laughter at that and flipped off her shoes beside Mrs. Svenson's chair. She paddled happily with Phelim across the lawn and chose a mallet and was instructed in the play by Joshua. Mrs. Svenson sighed, then took another long pull at her drink. "Lars Keiberg," she said, "they need a score-keeper and you're a man who can count quicker than most."

"So I do," Keiberg fingered the satin lapels of his coat. "You'll excuse me?"

"You go right on," his wife said nasally. "You wouldn't make no company here anyhow."

"Give the lady a glass of lemonade," Mrs. Svenson told Mr. Shaw. "Then you sit down and we'll have a nice talk."

"Gladly," Mr. Shaw said. The wrinkles of anxiety had disappeared from his high, ravaged face. "My daughter has some things of interest she has told us about Europe."

It was for Mrs. Svenson inconsequential talk, and she was aware that Mr. Shaw meant it to be. In a low-toned, easy voice, lounging back in his chair, he described the Crystal Palace, the escapades of Prince Edward, the discoveries recently made at Pompeii. She bent her head and smiled and nodded, but her attention was held by the group on the lawn.

Little Enid Gormley and Peggy Carmody battled furiously against each other. Peggy had just been given the chance of a shot at the English girl's ball; she had knocked it with a tremendous sweep far off the lawn into a hydrangea bush. "Oh, well hit!" Enid Gormley said. "I must say well hit."

"Sure and you might," Peggy told her. "Next time, I'll whack it in the river." That was said smilingly, though, and Enid Gormley smiled back. Mrs. Svenson glanced from them to Jane Shaw.

Jane stood watching her friend with thoughtful eyes. Joshua, aided by Boker, had found the ball, brought it back. "Here, Enid," he said. "You must play it from the boundary."

There's perhaps a good bit more than friendship between Jane and the English one, Mrs. Svenson thought. Years ago, you saw the same thing with women of your tribe whose men were gone. They lived together like man and wife, and in this pair Jane's the one who rules the roost. But it wasn't without purpose that she had her friend come along. She'd give her to Josh if she could arrange that. Her purpose now is to get them together. A smart and clever girl, Jane.

The game was finished and Lars Keiberg loudly named the winners. "All right," Minna said, her hand on her husband's arm, "there's claret punch for those who want it, and who's hungry?"

"To hell," Alan Kennard said. "Phelim and me at least will be drinking a little whiskey. Josh, you and the Doc' come have a snort with us. Keiberg, here, and Mr. Lipfer, they're teetotallers. Lemonade's their ration."

"Thanks, no, Antrim." Joshua walked beside Enid Gormley; they were headed towards the summer house at the edge of the lawn above the river. "It's too hot for whiskey. But when you choose to serve your food, Minna, do give us a shout."

"Yes, of course," Minna said carefully, and her glance was on Jane. "What would you like, Miss Shaw?"

"To be most honest with you," Jane Shaw said, "I'd like a drive through the town and a look at the quarries. But that can wait. I'm ravenous, really. A glass of your punch and then some food would be splendid."

"I'll take you around," Alan Kennard said. "You're right about the provender. You never saw in all of Europe such a ham as Minna is ready to put out."

"Alan," Minna murmured to him, "don't talk so."

"And why not?" he said.

"It's nouveau riche."

"Noovoo reech," he repeated, mocking her. "Well, what we got's new, but by the Jesus we ain't 'reech.' Stop the chatter and lay out your food."

Jane and their other guests had gone past and for an instant they were alone on the lawn. "You like Jane, don't you?" she said tensely. "You always have."

"After a fashion, yeah," Alan Kennard said. "But that don't mean I don't love you, Minna."

"You'll take her for the ride, though."

"Sure, I will."

"Just you two."

"No. I'll have Boker to drive us. Listen, girl. Don't be going after me. I meant no harm before. But I'm not the man to put on side with folks like Jane."

"Oh, be still!" she said and ran before him up the steps and into the house.

Jane had found a chair next to Mrs. Svenson's. She sat calmly, waiting for the older woman to begin the conversation. Here in this gray haired and gaunt woman, she thought, was gathered a great deal of the power behind Alan Kennard's throne. Joshua responded to it, and her father, Minna certainly, and that strangely misplaced Dickensian character, Keiberg. An Indian and a woman who has seen very many things, learned the answers to the problems which have for so long perplexed you. She may not care for you, she may not trust you, and it'll be a pity if she doesn't. For Enid and Joshua are hitting it off very well. What plan you have has begun to succeed, if only very vaguely.

"You and your friend," Mrs. Svenson said, "you'll be on your way back to Europe soon?"

"No, madame, I don't think so," Jane said. "From what I understand from Joshua, it'd be best for me to stay until the Cottrells have brought their suit into court."

"Kennard's got good lawyers. They'll see to it that the thing is settled in your favor." Mrs. Svenson turned around and looked deliberately into Jane's face. "He's a changed man since you knew him last."

"That I can appreciate," Jane said. "He has come quite a way, and I admire him for it."

Mrs. Svenson lifted the fan as if to strike at a passing fly. But behind it she gazed out at the summer house where Joshua sat deep in conversation with Enid Gormley. "We've tried to get your father and your brother to stay here with us. They won't, though. Their damn' man's pride keeps them in that cheesebox hotel of Keiberg's. You can't find it comfortable."

"We don't," Jane said. "It's perhaps the worst hotel in which I've ever been. And I'd forgotten that anybody in America could cook so badly."

Mrs. Svenson smiled with her. "You could come stay with us," she said. Mrs. Svenson looked through one of the tall French windows behind her. Minna with the rest of the guests stood at the dining room table as Cook and Katrine started to serve the consommé, the potato salad, the ham, the roast beef and turkey. Buffet, Minna called it, Mrs. Svenson remembered. What was buffet, though, about that? She'd sit on right where she was and eat.

"I'd rather we didn't stop with you, madame," Jane said. "Allow me to explain, please."

"What's your reason?"

"Your daughter wouldn't like it."

"That's about right," Mrs. Svenson said. "Minna's a troubled woman. She'd like to have children and she can't. Things could be better between her and Kennard. But, if you don't stay at the hotel?"

"Heavens," Jane said, "women like Mrs. Keiberg might be shocked, but Enid and I had the idea this morning that we'd like to pitch a tent down on the beach by the point, live there. Enid could do her sculpture right in the open and I'm very eager to make a number of landscapes. We walked as far as we could towards the place, then we got stuck in the brush."

"My people in the old days," Mrs. Svenson said, "used to have a trail through there. But the lumber people left it full of slash. You go in and fetch Phelim Carmody out to me, Miss Jane. He can get the company launch and take you to the point. Bring me a plate of food and one for yourself. Ham's what I'm pleased to have, with some of the potato salad, a bit of the breast of turkey."

"Yes, madame," Jane said. "I'd be gratified, too, if you asked Captain Carmody to call to my brother and Enid. Josh in this moment wouldn't welcome a sisterly shout."

Mrs. Svenson tapped Jane's knuckles lightly with her fan. "You have more gumption," she said, "than either your father or your brother. Enid should make Josh a fine wife."

"You think so?" Jane gazed back as if in surprise.

"So do you, my dear," Mrs. Svenson said. "Hurry it up now. I'm hungry, and you'll want to have Phelim take you out to the point before dark."

Alan Kennard had quickly given his permission for the use of the launch to the point. But he had insisted that first Jane go with him and see the town and the quarries. Boker had the shiny English station wagon ready, drove them straight-backed and proud through town. Jane sat listening idly to Kennard, her thought still with Mrs. Svenson, with Joshua and Enid.

"This here now," Alan Kennard said, "is the business block. Keiberg built it. His name's on it. See?"

Jane looked forth reluctantly and then without conscious knowledge her artist's instinct was engaged. The town was an ugly but also fascinating hodge-podge. Keiberg's creation, of red brick and brownstone, had preposterous cornices, an attempt at grandeur in the form of gray marble columns at the front. L. Keiberg, 1883 was cut into the stone there. The lower floor was occupied by the Patigowoc Branch of the Napta City Bank and the windows heavily barred with iron. The windows in the two upper stories told in variously sized gilt lettering of Lawyer; Mrs. Johannsen, Modiste; Painless Dentist; Surveyor, Real Estate; Mortgages and Insurance. The Bon Ton beyond was in an old clapboard building given a coat of bright red paint and with some of the worst of the Bowery sweatshop finery on display. A. Pakatos, Meat and Vegetables was next, a broad awning up against the sun, and the barber shop with its gay-striped pole, L. Keiberg's General Store where a wooden Indian stood beside chipped snuff and spavin cure signs, the Patigowoc Post of the Grand Army of the Republic that shared quarters with the Woodsmen of America and bore a lithograph portrait of James G. Blaine in the dusty window, Gilligan's Saloon, decorated at the bat-wing doors by double posters declaring for Stephen Grover Cleveland. Across the way, of course, was the Patigowoc Hotel, uncompromisingly hideous in the afternoon sun, a drunken and solitary drummer asleep in a rocker on the narrow slice of porch. The feed store, riotous with swallows, flanked it, after that the livery stable, the blacksmith shop, a short stretch of clipped lawn marked by whitewashed stones and the one story, solid brick building that carried the graven sign over the main door of Kennard and Company. A tall flagpole was at the edge of the lawn; from it flew the national ensign and below a flag with a green field and an orange K.

She felt a peculiar sensation that was at once pride and jealousy and fear. Antrim, here, the dark visaged, tautly held man at her side, had achieved this while her people, with all their wealth, their tradition, had broken themselves in the swiftly flowing and cruel tide of American life. "You've done a fine job," she said to him.

He made no answer, just smiled at her, and she was allowed to return to her own thought. That frightful hotel housed her father and brother. She was a rootless wanderer. Her mother and Cottrell —don't think of them. Antrim, though, lived in what was close to luxury. His house was vulgarly appointed, yes, and his wife a rapidly souring half-breed. But there was a great deal that was vulgar also in the homes of the wealthy in the East, the entire bourgeois class as you've seen it in England, France, Germany and Italy. Disregard the obvious and the petty. Seek back as well as you can, Jane, to the sources. While you're with them, you must give all possible support to Father and to Joshua.

"You'd care to ride down to the docks and have a look?" Alan Kennard asked her abruptly. "The *Daigvera* is loading and about to sail in a few hours."

"No, I wouldn't." Her voice contained a note of weariness. "The impressions are too much for me to catch all at one time, Antrim. And Enid and I were down there early today. We saw your other vessel sail."

"But you wouldn't mind a ride around the quarries?"

"That'd be interesting, yes."

He gave the order to the coachman and she sat back in the solitude of her thought. The Shaw blood, she pondered, mixed with that of the Cottrells, may well have run too thin. This man is a peasant, his mother a gypsy, his father an illiterate fisherman. He has a toughness of fiber, a compulsion to get ahead that no doubt your people lost generations ago. Compare him to those you saw on Main Street, the shawled women, the wives and daughters and mothers of his workers, Middle European nearly every one of them, still half believing that somehow, somewhere the streets of America are paved with gold. He possesses the same belief; it sends him through torments of ambition into which Father and Joshua refuse to go. He's representative of the new America, and that means he's as ruthless with himself as anybody else.

"Where's it going to end, Antrim?" she said.

"What?" he said, staring narrowly at her.

"All this."

"Ah, hell," he said, and she knew that he would deliberately give her a literal answer. He was past exposing his inner self to her. "Once the country's got the election under its belt and Blaine's in, things will be better. Keiberg has a scheme to run in a trolley line from Napta City. There's talk, too, of building a bowling alley and a roller skating rink out back of the business block. We'll have our own high school next year; the kids won't have to pack over no more to Napta."

She slowly nodded. The coachman had whipped the team into a canter; they were at the outskirts of the town. A few farm buggies clattered by, the men raising their hats to Kennard, and along the road on the porches of the unpretentious houses the women who sat and rocked looked up and waved. "You're the big man," she said.

"I'm one," he said. His mouth lines were wry. "Keiberg's the other."

The carriage swung. They were off the town road, following one that paralleled a pair of white powdered steel rails. She saw small, lopsided shacks with tar paper roofs, miserable rows of privies, the tattered clotheslines of the poor. Children ran half naked among the shacks, their legs coated with the limestone dust. Goats yammered where they rested tethered to shrunken bushes. The sun shone on the walls of the single clean building; it was surmounted by a cross.

"Your workers' homes," she said without emphasis.

"That's right. Goat Town, the old timers call it. Don't tell me. I know it stinks. But Keiberg owns the land, asks all the rent the tariff will bear."

"Joshua wrote me," she said, "how Keiberg maneuvered you when you came here to start operations. Why don't you take him aboard ship and tie a rope to his leg and tow him for at least fifty miles? He is an exceedingly nasty man."

Alan Kennard shrugged. "Business is business, Jane, and like I said, Keiberg owns the land. Then there's a side angle, too. Him and me are plugging for Blaine heavy in the county. We're both of us for high tariffs."

She was wordless, and it forced him to go on. "Your folks' law-yers over in Cleveland, Lothrop and Medor, they're busy as get-out in the Hanna gang. Hanna's for Blaine for president. Hanna's a man who can talk to judges. We don't want to lose the Cottrell case. That would put a big dent in you the same as me."

"Yes, that would," she said absently. She had just recognized the huge figure in the cart that came towards them. It was Piotr Stykowsky, who had been floor boss in the Bellport plant in those days that seemed so distant. "Piotr, how are you?" she called, and waved her hand to him.

Piotr reined in the horse that drew the cart. He gazed at her unsmiling. "I been worse, Miss Jane."

"But what are you doing here?"

"I come wit' your brudder. First at the kilns, then dynamite boss."

The cart bore on its side the inscription of Kennard and Com-pany. He lowered his head, then splattered spit over the letters, slapped the horse forward at a trot. "Why you Hunky bastard!" Alan Kennard shouted.

"Don't," Jane said; she seized Kennard's arm. "If you make trouble for him, you make it for Joshua also. They're good friends."

"Too good," Alan Kennard said. "Josh should know better."

She was still, knowing nothing more that she could say. The coachman had put the team in motion and they had gone by the neat little chapel, were at the top of a ridge. "Hold up here, Boker," Kennard said.

Below them were the quarries. Dust drifted, eddied in chrome yellow banks through the air. Drills rattled in what was to her a demonic chorus. Steam shovels swung with the ponderous motions of mastodons. A train was loaded from the conveyors. The locomo-tive rasped a signal, started. Out of sight in a further quarry, a dynamite blast shuddered thundering. A column of dust rose that blotted away the sunlight. The horses jerked and Boker had dif-ficulty in holding them, looked sidewise at Kennard.

"You don't want to see the brickyard and the kilns, Jane?"

"No." She had hardly heard him. She was creating in her mind the details of a composition that would encompass this scene. It would be called "Ghosts." The half-naked children in the fore-ground, then what was ahead here. The train crew, the workers at the drills, at the conveyors, on the steam shovels, crawling up out of the pits were alike ghostly pale with limestone dust. The

stuff had penetrated their skins, their hair, their clothing and
coarse, clumsy shoes. "Let's get back. I'm eager for that ride on
the water, out into a place that is clean."

"Very well." He was scowling. "Put the whip to 'em, Boker,
and take the short cut home."

Mrs. Svenson had refused to go upstairs with Minna at the
arrival of darkness. She was content to remain on the porch and
finally Minna left her and Mr. Shaw alone, went in to give orders
to the maids about a meal for those who had made the sail to the
point in the launch. Mr. Shaw had been tempted to go along, Mrs.
Svenson realized, and had only stayed because of her. But right
now she had no talk for the man; her thought was occupied by the
way Jane had acted after her ride with Alan Kennard.

Jane had gone straight to her brother, taken Joshua's arm, led
him to the summer-house. They had stayed talking there until
Phelim Carmody had blown a whole series of toots on the launch
whistle. The others were already aboard in a gay group under the
canopy. They had brought pitchers of the claret punch, a bottle
of whiskey, and Peggy Carmody, hatless and still shoeless, reared
her head from under the canopy and bawled loudly, "Come on,
yez! All aboard who's goin' aboard!"

Enid Gormley climbed back on the dock and ran up the slope
to the summer-house, marched sister and brother out holding them
by the hands. Phelim cast off fast and opened the engine wide.
The sharp-bowed launch with its red and white canopy, mahogany
hull and cluster of people around the glistening brass engine and
stack made a brave sight on the river. But Alan Kennard stood
aloof at the bow, as far away from his guests as he could get.

She's rowelled him, Jane has, Mrs. Svenson thought. She's
rowelled him hard. And I doubt now if there's ever been anything between her and the English girl but friendship. She's so
angry with Josh that if there was she'd never let Josh get next to
the little one. Watch out, Kennard. You've got much more of a
fighter in Jane than you have in Minna.

Mr. Shaw stirred in his chair and politely coughed. "A happy
time," he said, "in an unhappy world. It's been a glorious day. I'm
grateful to you for it."

"Why me?"

"You made it so," he said softly.

"That's fiddlesticks."

"No, madame. Permit a contradiction. I'm a defeated man, one who has suffered perhaps a bit more than his share. But I have also witnessed many things, and own some of the powers of observation that are peculiarly yours." His voice dropped; he sat with his hands, his body loose.

"What you need," she said, "and me, too, is a drink of Alan Kennard's whiskey. You can find it. And while you're about it, bring me out that afghan robe in the hall. My feet get cold once the dew is down."

The whiskey warmed him. He stood and walked before her as he spoke again. "In my youth," he said, "in the Litchfield County of Connecticut, I saw the last of the old order. Farmers, madame, who met you on the road were reading Tacitus or Livy in the original. Even the meanest of men knew their Ben Franklin, their Tom Paine, and every chapter of Scripture."

"You miss such?"

"Greatly, madame. They were a simpler, better, certainly a more thoughtful lot. The war in which I fought engulfed them. The world hasn't been the same since. . . . 'Mine eyes have seen the glory.' Yes, we sang that going into battle. But only at first. In Washington, in New York we saw the wives of the profiteers who sprinkled gold and silver dust on their hair, openly jeered at the shabbiness of our uniforms. Their sons stayed at home. For a pitiful five hundred dollars apiece, they bought all we gave. But at the angle of the wall at Gettysburg——"

"I've heard that you were there. Tell me of it."

"No, I thank you." He very slightly smiled. "There are too many others these days for me to exhibit my share of vainglory."

"You might mean Mr. Cleveland and his aspirations."

"I might, but I don't. Rather, I think of them who wrap themselves in the flag as they steal our country wholesale from us. What's happened to us, madame? Have we gone daft, that they can take it from us as they do?"

Mrs. Svenson spread her hands down over the afghan. Minna had knitted it for her and it was very soft and fine. The warmth of it was welcome, and on the point, she saw, they had built a driftwood fire, sat about singing. She would have to wait hours, probably until tomorrow, before she got a chance to talk to Jane.

"Come to me," she said to Mr. Shaw, "I just don't know, sir. When I was a girl here, things were right enough for us Indians. We fished, we hunted, we scratched ourselves and we were happy. Much like, I guess, your Litchfield County. It was the timber folks who did us in. They rode the war, too, made their piles from that. And now—" she lifted her hands palms upwards in an instinctive gesture of her youth—"I'm an old, sick woman in a rich man's house."

"My wife's people," Mr. Shaw said harshly, "were passionately of the Puritan faith. Not even at Yale College did I ever find any more devout. They would tell us, I'm sure, that what were courage, steadfastness and a great desire for liberty have become simple avarice. Perhaps in all honesty they were right."

Mrs. Svenson nodded. She had heard Minna in the hall, coming to take her to bed, and she was glad. Fatigue had crept upon her and with it the pain. But the thing had been worthwhile; she had made a true friend of this man, a friend she needed. They, both of them in their secret hearts, were simply hanging onto life. The dark gate was ahead and from it they couldn't turn back. Svenson would be pleased to know that she had such decent company on her journey.

"I have enjoyed it, sir," she said as she rose to grasp Minna's shoulders. "Do call more often. We like having you here."

"Madame, I'd be delighted," he said. He bowed to her and to Minna, and for an instant, just as she went in the door with the pain jagged up through her, she could see him in his uniform and how his eyes had shone while he still had hope and strength.

CHAPTER NINE

Doctor Chapin had told her, and also the specialist, Doctor Fitzgerald from Detroit, yet Minna could not quite believe it. She was pregnant. After ten years of marriage, at the age of twenty-eight, she was to have a baby. The doctors were gone now; Katrine had shown them down to the porte-cochere and Doctor Chapin's gig. You're alone. If you want, cry.

Minna cried softly, stretched out full length in the big double bed where she and Alan Kennard had so often lain in love. What will Alan think? It will make more of a change to him than to you. But, Golly, a baby, your baby. Her crying stopped. She was still, her hands up behind her head. The calm of the late June afternoon was through the room. Upon the ceiling, the leaf designs of the tree branches close against the windows began to fade, to merge. The long glass curtains appeared to be made of fine copper mesh, catching the light so that it entered in a subdued, dim flood that was almost colorless after the radiance of high sunlight. Every sound on the river, on the lawns, in the house was known to her. She felt completely at peace. She no longer in any way doubted the doctors.

They weren't sure of the cause, they had admitted. But how did that matter? You're going to have a baby, Minna. Yes, you. A baby, a baby. Right here in this bed you'll have him. It must be a him for Alan. So, a son. That will be along in the winter. You won't mind, though. Your house is warm, your husband rich; Doctor Fitzgerald will come back from Detroit to be with Doc' Chapin.

She got out of bed and went to the full length mirror across the room. The nightgown she wore was a fancy one, put on for the doctors. She took it off and in the lustrous yet almost colorless light examined her body. Doc' Chapin said your womb may have tilted. You've ridden horses with Alan, and bicycles. But Doctor Fitzgerald said it might be a chemical change. Something that's happened to your blood or Alan's. Don't go on standing here like a ninny. Katrine could come upstairs and find you and you'd scare the wits

268

out of her. Put on some clothing, my dear, and make it really nice.
Alan will be home tonight and then you'll tell him.

The dress she chose was one he had brought her last month
after a trip to Chicago. It had been made in Paris, and was, she
knew, very expensive. The lace of the bodice was exquisite, the
silk of such quality that she felt keen pleasure as she fingered it.
Perfume for your hair. A bit behind your ears, on your throat and
between your breasts. The sheer silk stockings he bought you,
too. And the slippers that hurt your feet a bit but are so pretty.

Olga came to turn on the upstairs lights while she was arranging her hair. "Oh, ma'am," Olga said; "I should ha' been here to
put your lights on ten minutes ago. My, how nice you look!"

Minna smiled at her, greatly tempted to tell her the news that
pervaded her entire thought. But, no, she decided. It was six years
ago that Boker got Olga in trouble. Alan had to fire Boker, you
had to take care of the poor girl and get her out of town with Doc'
Chapin's help. She lost her kid. Now, if you told her, she might
hate you like the very dickens.

"Mr. Kennard's coming home tonight," she said, and moved
past Olga into the hall. "I'll be glad to see him."

Olga stood with her sallow face slanted in the glare of the hall
fixture. "Ma'am," she said just above a whisper, "the doctors was
here this afternoon. Did you have any luck?"

"Yes," Minna said; "yes, I did. I'm going to have a baby, Olga."

"By God, how good!" Olga said. Her hands were clasped together. "How happy I am for you!"

A sudden compulsion to weep was upon Minna. "You don't
mind?"

"Me? Not me nor the whole darn' town. Ma'am, they'll all be
happy for you. Everybody's been waitin', hopin'.'"

"Thank you, dear," Minna said, and before she would weep,
went on down the stairs.

She walked slowly through the ground floor rooms, seeing them
in a new fashion, as a mother. Her son would crawl, toddle, walk,
run here. The tidies would be pulled out of place, maybe some of
the drapes ripped, pieces of bric-a-brac, vases knocked down. You
won't care. Later on—she was in the high-ceilinged dining room—
when he's big enough you'll give birthday and Easter and Hal-
loween parties for him. A dozen kids at this table and your son
at the head, shouting the loudest, eating the most, and by all means,
you immodest woman, the handsomest.

The speed and intensity of the visions had begun to tire her. She felt a need to recapture the mood of peaceful contemplation that had been hers in the bedroom. She went onto the front porch and took the chair that her mother had habitually occupied.

It gave her direct recall to the past, where there was no longer any excitation of the emotions. She was surprised, looking back into that time, that the years which had seemed so slow in passing had in reality gone very fast. Among all of it, there were only a very few sharp distinct memories. There was the death of her mother in the winter of '85, and the next spring the death of Mr. Shaw. They had been strangely close towards the end, those two. It had made some little talk in the town, not that they had cared, and codicils to both their wills asked that they be buried side by side. A good thing. Darn the silly talk anyhow. Now it's every bit forgotten except by you.

Time's like the river out there; a lot of stuff gets carried away out of folks' lives without their knowing. Just think, Minna, how many nights, how many days you've sat like this and waited. Waiting for Alan. Waiting for ships. Waiting, too, deep down in you, and hoping, hoping, hoping for a child.

She started slightly in the chair, wrenched from the smooth, narrow avenue of memory by the footsteps behind her. Katrine stood there, a gray and stooped figure in the hallway light. "I brought ye a shawl, ma'am. Just to slip about your shoulders. Always, when the dew's down——"

"—You brought a shawl to my mother."

"I did, ma'am."

"I was thinking of her, Katrine."

"And so was I when I went to fetch the shawl. A good woman, Mrs. Svenson. May the Saints bless her."

Minna looked around, scenting the odor. "You've had a drink, Katrine. Have you and Cook been at the bottle again?"

"No more than a small nip," Katrine said without hesitation. "Y' see, ma'am, Olga told us what you told her. But I'll put the bottle away from Cook. I won't let her get drunk, not tonight, what with your news and the Captain comin' home and all. I'm happy as a lark for you, ma'am, and so's Cook."

"Thank you kindly, Katrine." Minna held out her hand to the servant's rheumatically puffed hand. "It means a great deal to me. You know."

"I do, I do." There was a glitter of tears up under Katrine's eyelids. "Two I had and lost them both, then my man. But if you'll excuse me, I'll get to Cook before she gets to the bottle. A tough woman she is, once she's started."

Minna listened to the creaking footsteps in the hall, the thudding thwack as the pantry door swung, then Katrine's aroused treble, Cook's deeper, rougher tones. "Leave be of me!" Cook said and then was in the hall. She was a pace ahead of Katrine when she reached the porch.

"This old owl," she said, and brandished her arm at Katrine, "would keep me over that stove 'til I sizzle. But I'll ask you personal, ma'am. Would the Captain like mint sauce with the roast tonight? And maybe a nice prune whip after wid his coffee?"

"He would, I'm sure, Cook."

"Then he'll get them. For you, now you're goin' to be a mother, I'll keep you fine as fine can be. But tonight's the Captain's. He'll be a happy man."

"Shoo!" Katrine shouted at her. "Would you stand and gabble while your roast falls apart in the oven?"

"I would not," Cook said; she wheeled and went shuffling back through the hall, Katrine again a pace behind her.

Bouche de Mouche light was breaking, lambent along the water. The great gold blade in its sweep touched the windows of the house that Joshua and Enid Shaw had built far out upon the point. They gleamed, and Minna thought, curious, but they haven't turned on their own lights yet. That's just what they are, a curious lot. And they're bringing up their children the same way. A boy and a girl, two years apart. How lucky. I wonder, will you have any luck like that?

Her mind slid away from the conjecture, returned to Joshua and Enid. Their love affair, then marriage had been another of the high places during the last years. Enid had carried out the plan with Jane after that lawn party here, and camped for the summer on the point. Mr. Shaw had got them a fine, wide-flied tent through some G.A.R. official he knew. Joshua had built a fireplace for them, called each evening after work in the company launch with their groceries.

My goodness, the talk in the town then. Down around the saloon, they were saying that those two swam bare-tail off the beach. A couple of men full of beer on a Saturday night had rowed out there in a skiff and gone ashore, right up to the tent. They'd hooted and hollered, carried on as though Jane and Enid were really bad women. But Jane had come from the tent with a hatchet, Enid with a frying pan, and the men ran for it like scared boys and only later on, when the men got drunk again, was anybody able to learn the story at all.

Jane never said anything. She went back to Europe that fall. Then without notice, even to Alan or you, Enid and Josh went over to Lansing and got married. Josh worked through the fall and often after dark and when it was cold to build a log cabin on the point for him and Enid. Nothing much more than a shack, exposed to the Northeasters, too, with timber wolves around all the time and no way of getting into town except by the launch and later over the ice. Josh was at work every day, though; he got in somehow, on skates when the ice was clear, or on snowshoes, sometimes walking the whole way.

In the spring they started their house. They didn't ask anybody out until it was done. Then they asked you and Alan alone. Remember how funny you felt, because you hadn't seen Enid in nearly a year, and the house, gosh, how strange. Fieldstone and timber. Low, built right in among the boulders above the shore. And a big white pine smack through one corner of the living room. Josh had the windows specially made in Chicago and brought in the men from there to finish the job. When you looked out onto the lake, it was like it was pressing up against you and you could dive in.

All the furniture Enid made herself. Wolf pelts for rugs. The fireplace in the living room so big Alan stood straight up inside. No furnace, though. Just fireplaces in each room. And all around in the living room Enid's sculpture. You're not a cultured woman, no matter how much you'd like to say so. Her stuff sort of scares you. Women with heads shaped like pine cones. Men with great big, thick bodies and little-bitty legs. That one called "The Waves," you understood that, and you should be proud, because it won the prize in Chicago. Jane's picture was something like it, the one she painted out there before she went back to Europe. The mist is on the water just like any early spring day when the sun's about coming up, and the blue heron over among the grass in the cove, you've seen him a lot of times. I guess, too, that she and Enid did go bare-tail swimming after all. Because that's Enid standing naked in the water about knee-deep.

It's kind of odd, but Mr. Shaw wouldn't visit out there. He

spent most of his time here with mother. Talking, or just sitting, and when he wasn't doing that he'd work at the little hand forge Alan had made for him. Every fitting for Josh's house he worked out himself, just the way Josh told him. Beautiful stuff, too. Alan said he could sell it for him for plenty any time he wanted to put it on the market. Not Mr. Shaw, though. He got queerer as time went on and Josh is a lot the same. Think back to the fire in Bellport, of course, Minna, and you have an idea why.

Alan doesn't like Josh acting so queer and living off like that alone with Enid. He says it doesn't give the company a good name, and after all Josh is vice president, handles all the limestone part of the business. Golly, it took everything Mr. Lipfer could do last year to get Enid to send in their kids to school.

Jane, you don't hear from Jane any more. She's off there painting in Italy and France and those other places. Josh has told Alan how Enid has found articles in the European papers and the art journals about her. She's won prizes, too, more than Enid, but Enid doesn't try so hard.

"Mrs. Kennard, ma'am." It was Elmar, the coachman, and he stood in the drive before the porch steps.

"Yes, Elmar." She was pleased to hear the man's voice, be taken from her retrospection.

"Shall I harness up? It's about time for the boat to come 'round the bend."

She smiled at Elmar. He was Boker's successor, a young, bigfooted Dane who had run his own harness shop in Napta City until he had been wiped out in the '84 panic. He lacked Boker's touch with the horses, and he was a temperance man, but he got along well with Cook and the maids, was saving all his pay to start up in business again.

"You know as well as me," she said, "that nobody can tell just when the boat will get in. Fog's setting up outside and the Captain cares little for it. He'll have her on the slow bell by now."

"Sure, so." Elmar shifted his feet uncomfortably in the tight English boots that Alan Kennard insisted he wear. "I forgot that. But Cook, she vas telling me, ma'am, that mebbe soon we'll be having a young Cap'n around the house."

"Cook's right," Minna said.

"A fine thing, by gollies. I'll wait, then, ma'am, 'til I hear the whistle, hah?"

"Yes, Elmar." He went back along the driveway, the boot heels harsh upon the gravel, and once more she was alone and drawn immediately into memory.

Elmar's nasal accent had made her think of the Keibergs. Lars Keiberg had changed only slightly over the years. He was still cautious, secretive, careful with each dollar he spent. But he had expanded his affairs throughout Napta County, was a senior vice president of the Napta City Bank, principal stockholder, according to Alan, in a dozen concerns. His wife, who looked like a mouse and sounded like one, was with Enid Shaw, the town's strangest woman. She appeared at all the church socials, the Ladies' Aid meetings, the Grange suppers, the Woodsmen's picnics. That was because of the fact, though, that Keiberg made her go. She preferred to remain at home in their shabby clapboard house at the end of Main Street.

Four years ago, she'd born Keiberg a son, and you, Minna, were as jealous of her as you've ever been of anybody in your life. Then the poor little fella—Lars, his name was, too—died with the diphtheria. She never came out of that house at all for six months after that, and the ladies who went to call on her were turned away right at the door. Now they say that Doc' Chapin's visiting there again. She must be carrying another. But this time she's not ahead of you. You have your own, and it'll be a better kid than hers any day in the week. Minna Kennard, you most certainly should be ashamed of yourself.

She rose, pushing back the chair. Through the fog over the river, she had heard the sound. It was the *Daigvera*, bound in from the point. The past was erased, and her sense of shame over her feeling for Mrs. Keiberg. She stood braced against the porch railing, straining to see the ship. "Oh, Alan," she whispered, "just wait 'til I can tell you!"

He came up the steps with the light, rapid sailor's tread so characteristic of him. But he's been changed by the years, her inner mind told her, even in the instant that she took him to her and kissed him. The passionate love you've had for each other has almost been worn away by the waiting. "Guess," she murmured to him, suddenly shy, "what Doc' Chapin and that other doctor from Detroit had to say today."

"You got lucky?" The pressure of his fingers against her forearms was involuntarily cruel.

"Right the first time, mister. I'm going to have a baby. Yes, sir, by golly, a son for you, and you can count me in, too."

He laughed and swung her high off the porch and the lace of her dress tore at the shoulder. "Minna, Minna! Holy smokes! Come inside. For this, we got to have champagne."

His access of hilarity was so swift, so intense that without awareness she recoiled from him. When they were in the rear parlor and seated on the couch, she looked at him in deliberate scrutiny. Her slim sailorman had become thick through the body. His hair was gray at the sides, and his cheeks were laced with tight little whiskey veins. The clothes he wore were very fine, what anybody even in Chicago or Detroit would call those of a gentleman. But while she wasn't much for such things, his diamond stickpin and his ring were a little too big. She'd made her grammar better, and her manners. Not him. He liked to talk tough, with lots of profanity. Only thirty-five, that's all he is. Still for a couple of years now around the town they've nicknamed him the "Old Man." Of course you know enough about sailors to know that has a special meaning for them. Not for the townfolks, though, and they use it to him.

She was afraid that he had sensed her mood by the searching, sidewise glance he gave her. But then he laughed. "I'll never find another like you. Jesus Christ, Minna, how I love you! But I ain't the one to deny that it's been tough waiting."

"For me, too," she said.

But he disregarded that. He was shouting to Katrine for the champagne, and Katrine was at the door with it and to say that dinner was ready. At dinner, he made her drink along with him. She took on his hilarity degree by degree, for he was at his most charming. He had seen a Nat Goodwin show in Cleveland, remembering several of the songs and the dance routines.

Olga, Katrine, then Cook and finally Elmar crowded into the pantry doorway at his invitation. He poured champagne for them and burned one of the corks in the wall jet and blacked his face. "Just Pappy now!" he shouted. "C'm on, y'all, Mammy, and dance with me!" They pranced around the table hand in hand, and Cook laughed so hard she cried.

"Off to bed wid ye," Katrine said to Cook with mock sternness. "You'll split a gut, you keep to laughin'."

It was meant as a hint for her and Alan, Minna told herself.

She waved her free hand to them in the doorway, pulled Alan towards the parlor. He whirled her around and around there for a time, singing old Antrim songs of his youth, and then abruptly he was motionless. "I should, goddamn me, take better care of you. Got to think of the boy."

"Alan, there's nothing like that. Not for months yet. I'm perfectly fine."

"Then we could go to bed and it'd be all right."

"Sure, silly." She had grasped his pocket handkerchief, was cleaning the smirch of cork from his face. "But I'm darned if I will with a runaway from a Nat Goodwin show."

"Kiss me," he said, "and I'll even take the pledge."

"No, sir, for that I won't. Whiskey's good for a man like you."

"You mean it sweetens my sour belly."

"Not elegant, but exact." She was smiling.

"I ain't the elegant kind. Let's see, though." He stood off from her, put an arm to his midriff and bowed. "Madame, could I accompany you to your bood-wa?"

"*Mais oui*," she said. It was a phrase Madame Johannsen, the dressmaker, used, and she just barely remembered it. Her thought was surcharged with Alan, Alan in bed at her side, Alan holding her in his strong and demanding arms. She turned without further word and went up the stairs. He was right in back of her, reached up under her petticoats and pinched her.

"Alan, don't!" she said in mechanical protest.

"All I want," he said hoarsely, "is a little bit as a sample."

"You're a rascal. You didn't hear that in a Goodwin show."

"Can't say I did," he said laughing. "It comes from a long way back and from before I met you."

"Where?"

"Ah, to hell." They were upstairs and in the bedroom. He had already taken off his collar, his tie. "No more talk. Let's us make love."

She slept heavily, exhausted by the fury of their passion, and yet sleep was far from him. He lay fully awake and nervous, his mind unready to accept the fact that he was to be a father. Get out of here, he told himself. Go downstairs and buy yourself a drink. You'll never sleep the way you are, man.

He put on his nightgown, a robe and slippers, quickly descended the stairs. Katrine had left the lower hall light burning and he turned it up high. He stood for an instant within the doorway of the front parlor, looking around him. He was oppressed by the abrupt knowledge that this was not really his. It belonged to Minna. Everything in the room showed signs of her. She'd made it different, made it hers through the years.

You've been away too much. Sure, you've ridden the ships up and down for no real reason but that you wanted to be out of here. Business, you said. You got it, too. And a good deal of whoring thrown in. There was a couple of years when you thought you were no more good to a woman.

He walked on, his sailor's night sense guiding him through the darkness of the rear parlor. It's the same. Minna has her hands on it, too. The only part of the whole bloody house that belongs to you at all is the study. Reach to your right and you'll find matches on the table.

The match glared blue, then orange and he was gratified by the accuracy with which he discovered and turned on the table lamp. The room, by God, is yours. He rested in the middle of it, gazing at the lamp-bright paneling, the big, overstuffed leather chairs, the Persian rugs, the tall and broad brass spittoons. Models of each of his ships were on the walls. The wall facing the massive table that served him as desk bore a glass case holding the shipwright's model of the *Heather*, sent out on his order from Leith where she had been built.

Phelim comes here to gam about old times with you, he thought. Many's the bottle you've knocked off together. And Oate and Stuffy Smith, the other senior men from your ships, they'll step along to have a snort on occasion. You've done more steamboat work in this place than down at the office.

He pressed the panel he had designed himself and opened the liquor cabinet, lifted out a bottle of rye. The cigars in the humidor on the table were fresh. He clipped and lit one, sat deeply in his chair, put his feet on the table with his slippers hanging loose. Now you're squared away. No more of that jumpy feeling, man.

"To you, Kennard," he said aloud, and drank from the bottle. "With a son behind you, you'll lick them Cleveland bastards flat." He cursed, banging the bottle against the polished oak of the table. You hate that lot. All along, you've had to buck them. For them, you're still an outsider.

You lack the connections. A good, goddamn word. Yes, sir, the connections. And if you ain't got them, and you know it, sooner or later you're in trouble. Josh or Old Man Shaw might've got them for you if they wanted. But it was pretty late for the old man, and Josh has never chose to lift a hand in that direction. Josh, after marrying his odd cod, don't seem to care anything about putting the company ahead. He'll do his work, just so much, no more. Man's dropped whatever gumption he had.

Lothrop and Medor, now, they could've got you into the inner circle down there to Cleveland. Christ knows you paid them plenty for winning the Cottrell case. The trouble with that, though, was the Cottrells were in so solid in the East. They had their own connections through the Down Easters in the Cleveland gang. The word was passed; Kennard's to be kept out. And nowhere along the line, not yet, anyhow, have you laid onto enough money to buy your way in. Them bastards, they play the game with real big piles of chips.

Have another drink. The hell with you, you Cleveland swabs and snobs. They're that, too, with their sons going Down East to school, their fancy English clothes and all them big homes and churches on Euclid Avenue. Don't you forget you were born on the Antrim shore and when your time comes, ram it to 'em hard.

The game ain't all played yet. The way the country goes, you still have your chance. Look how you've come along in the last ten years all on your lonesome, saving the help you got from Josh at the start. Have another drink. No, to hell. You'd be getting yourself drunk and with the woman up there eager for you the second you want her.

A good woman, Minna. She's going to give you a son. You got to have a name for him, though. Your old man was named Mark. A good name. Minna won't mind, and if she does you'll talk her out of it. So Mark it is. Just a very small drink for Mark. To you, lad. My son, by God.

. . . .

Mark Kennard's first clear memory was of the bed jacket his mother wore. The color was soft pink, the wool very fine, and lying with his head against it he could see as though they were a miniature, magic jungle, the luminous tendrils rising before his eyes. His first sensation was not distinct. It had to do with her smell, a mingling of the odors of her body and her skin, and her breath when the skin of her cheek was against his. That was all confused with the women he came to identify later as Katrine and Cook and Olga. They had different smells; before he knew their names, he knew their smells. Cook's was the strongest, and when she was around you couldn't smell anybody else, not even Mother.

The radiator in his room gave him his initial fright, started his dreaming. He had no words for the sounds it made. He just lay in his crib and listened transfixed as it burbled, chuckled, broke into a slow rasping, another chuckle, a bang. Those sounds he associated somehow with formless, nameless beings who each night grew in the dark. They approached near to the crib, and when they were too near he cried out, and then Mother was there to take him in her arms, walk with him to the other room and to the other bed.

Father was there in that bed sometimes. He had a strong smell, too, but not like Cook's. His voice was deep, as hard, as rapping as the radiator's. One night Father came into the room where the radiator was making the sounds. He talked just like the radiator, and he banged at it and after that the radiator only chuckled a little bit.

He liked Father for that. He began to trust him and watch for him the way he did for Mother. Still, if Father had stopped the radiator, sent away the formless and nameless people, he was to be feared. You can't trust Father as much as Mother; he's not the same.

The Belgian hare was white, with long, shell-pink ears, and called Jules. Later, Mark was to remember that he got Jules on his third birthday. Elmar kept Jules in a hutch with wire on it out beside the stable. Those and other facts about Jules were extraordinarily clear to Mark.

It was on his third birthday that he was bitten by the hare. He was able to run rapidly over the lawns by then, and had already pulled down most of the drapes within reach in the house. His vocabulary was also quite extensive and he entirely understood Katrine when she told him not to go out and see Jules until the photographer came. He mustn't soil his suit, and take care you keep your hands clean, see.

The suit was white. A sailor suit, his mother had called it when she and Katrine had dressed him upstairs in his room. His shoes were white and he wore a round hat with a ribbon his mother said was a sailor hat. "Father's a sailor," she said. "He'll be proud of you in this."

Father came with Elmar and the horses. Another man was along. He carried a box with legs and he had a green cloth. They all went out on the back lawn then, Father, Mother, the man who had the box. Elmar took Jules out of the hutch. He scratched at Elmar, but Elmar knew how to handle hares. He smoothed Jules' ears back and brought him over to Mark. Then Katrine came from the back porch where she had been standing with Cook and Olga. She had a comb; she combed Mark's hair, fluffed it over his shoulders. "Don't you blink," she muttered to him, "when the fella takes the pitcher."

"I don't want any pitcher," Mark said. "I want to hold Jules."

"Here you be," Elmar said, and put Jules in his arms. "Hold him so, Mark."

Mark and Elmar were friends. Mark trusted him because Elmar let him go in the stable and pat the horses, sit up in the carriages. He didn't have any fear when he took Jules from Elmar. He was laughing and stroking Jules between the ears as the man with the box bent down under the green cloth. "My, how cute they are!" Mother said. Then Jules bit him through the hand.

It was through the right hand and in the fleshy part. He dropped Jules, he screamed and clutched his hands together, seized by the pain. Blood spurted onto his suit. Mother, Katrine, Olga, Cook were all jostling him. They all wanted to see his hand at once.

Father and Elmar were chasing Jules. Father had a rake and he whacked and whacked at Jules, hiding in under the back porch steps. "I'll kill the bastard," Father said. "Bite my boy like that."

Father's face was very red. He glared at Mother as she went up onto the back porch with Mark in her arms. "No goddamn' pictures today," Father said to Mother. "I'm goin' to have Elmar destroy this fancy Frenchy rat. And after you've fixed the boy's hand, you take him downtown and get his hair cut right. He ain't to be all sissified up like a girl."

"Alan, I'm ashamed of the way you carry on," Mother said in a low voice.

"You should be," Father said. He was poking after Jules with the rake again. "Never ought to ha' bought the hare in the first place."

The pain of the wound he received from Jules remained dominant in Mark's mind for a considerable period after his third birthday. It held back many other impressions of his third and fourth years, riding with Elmar to pick up Father at the company or at the dock, the smell of bay rum, hair, spittle and dust in the barbershop, the feel of the scissors around his ears, the feel of the blankets high up when in the winter the wind blew so strong the house rocked and on the window pane as he lifted his head he saw the snow patterns shaping, heard the snow, *shush, hush, uh-shush* in the great and wild cry of the wind.

It was the Carmody children who were responsible for keeping the pain dominant. There were four of them who came to the house to play, and they were all bigger, stronger than he. The boys knocked him down, or the girls. Then they kicked him. If he kicked back, they flung him flat, and the biggest boy, Pete, sat on his head for a while. But he liked Pete; Pete carried dead snakes in his pockets, and he knew how to pluck the wings off flies. Some day, Mark knew as Pete squatted on him, he'd be a big kid himself, then he'd do this to littler kids.

The thought was with him the day Father came home from the company and said they were going to go out and visit Uncle Josh and Aunt Enid. Mark was very excited while Katrine helped him get dressed. Uncle Josh and Aunt Enid occupied peculiar importance for him. He had only met them four or five times and then on Christmas Day or Thanksgiving, when there were a lot of other grown folks around. But what Father meant was that today they were going to go out to the point. That meant in the launch, the one with the shiny whistle. He'd have a chance to pull the whistle lanyard. And there were kids out there, Uncle Josh and Aunt Enid had kids. They were small. If he wanted to, he could pick on them.

But he was disappointed in that experience. Father only let him blow the whistle once, and the kids, while they were small, were strong, and the little girl, when he tried to trip her, threw him on his back. Her name was Ariadne. Her brother's name was Owen. They both wore only little short brown pants and no shoes. He felt funny running after them in his velvet suit, and if he took off his shoes, he knew, Mother would tell him he was bad.

So he stayed pretty close to Mother where she sat with the other grown folks in front of the fireplace. They were drinking tea and eating what Aunt Enid called crumpets. He had a couple of the crumpets, and when they started back in the launch it was dark, the wind was blowing and water slapped him in the face harder ever than he had been slapped by Pete Carmody. He got sick all over the cushions in the cockpit.

"Looks like," Father said, "that I've got bloody small chance of makin' a sailor out of this one. I'm glad you're due to have the other."

"Doc' Chapin's not quite sure, Alan," Mother said. She cradled Mark's head in her lap, smoothed his hair. "But I do hope so, for your sake, and mine."

When they were at home and he was in bed, Mark asked her about that. "Why was Father angry for me being sick?"

"Because he's a sailor." Mother's voice was harsh in the darkness. "His way is to have you just like him."

"But you like me still, Mom?"

"I adore you, Mark. Never forget. Your Mom adores you."

"Dad said, though, about Doc' Chapin. What did he mean?"

"That you'll probably have a little brother."

"Who'll sleep in here with me? Who'll be here when the wind blows?"

"Yes. Get to sleep now."

"Sing to me first."

"Mom's tired. Dad's waiting for his dinner."

"Sing to me, please. Please!"

She sang a song that he had never before heard. The words were unrecognizable to him and the sound of it was like the wind at the window. "That's a sad song."

"It's an Indian song. My Mom, when I was a little girl, taught it to me. But now you get to sleep. Dad will be calling up in a hurry."

"I don't like Dad."

"You shouldn't say that. Your Dad's a very fine man."

"I don't care." His hands were at the base of her neck. "But you kiss me and I'll go to sleep."

CHAPTER TEN

It was Alan Kennard's belief that with the birth of his first son he began to feel age. He resented that, and dismissed the thought from his mind, did everything in his power to resist. For a time, he cut down on his cigar and whiskey consumption, when at home took secret exercises in the bathroom every morning. When out aboard the ships he made a habit of working on deck as much as possible, although he often surprised his officers and crews, knew that some of the men laughed at him behind his back.

But with the birth, the rapid flourishing of his second son, Stacey, he could no longer escape. Before, there had been some pleasure for him in the fact that he was called the "Old Man." Now it rankled him, and depressed him. His affection for Mark had always been qualified by the doubt that Mark would become a sailor. He privately considered the brown haired, shy boy something of a sissy; he looked back with displeasure upon Mark's being seasick aboard the launch, irrationally blamed him for the unfortunate incident with the Belgian hare.

Then one lovely May afternoon just after he had come home from the office he discovered how wrong he had been. Mark, gangling and skinny at the age of ten, and Stacey, tubby, red faced and six, were on the side driveway playing catch. The lawn was soggy from a recent rain, and Kennard could see their deep footprints where they had played there, moved from it to the graveled driveway.

Mark had an infielder's glove and a nickel rocket ball. He wound up and threw with surprising skill to Stacey. That's school, Kennard thought rapidly; that's where the lad learned. But Stacey caught bare-handed, and was really too small to receive such speed. The ball bounced on past him and almost to his father's feet in front of the porte-cochere.

"Hey, Pop," Stacey called, happy in the knowledge that he was the favorite. "Throw us the ball, will ya?"

283

Alan Kennard wore a tightly buttoned suit, a high collar and a derby. Elmar hadn't taken the brake on around to the stable yet, sat curiously watching. Olga was out sweeping the porch and she also watched. Kennard, as he stooped and picked up the ball, was quite self-conscious. Throw straight, you flounder-head, he told himself, you're not very good at this.

His throw was badly erratic, slung the ball against the house and nearly through a window. Olga let out a screech and ducked. The two boys stood stiff, staring, and Elmar's face quivered with restrained laughter as he started the team towards the stable. "Gee," Stacey muttered, the horror leaving him enough so that he could speak. "Patsy Carmody throws better than that!"

"Shut up," Mark said. "Go get the ball."

Alan Kennard went on up the porch steps and wordlessly into the house. He had been alone in his study for about ten minutes when Stacey entered. Stacey had been crying, and there was a lump on his forehead. He crawled up onto his father's lap and put his arms around his father's neck. "When you were a boy," he whispered strangely, "you were poor, weren't you? You had to work. You didn't have time to play. And in Ireland the boys don't play ball anyhow. Hey, Pop?"

"Jesus Christ!" Alan Kennard said, caught between amazement and sorrow. He hugged his son to him. "How did you figure that out?"

"I didn't. Mark told me to say it. He cracked me, too. He's bigger'n me. But you wait. I'll get him."

Kennard sat very still. Here, he reflected wryly, was the answer. This boy would be the sailor of the family and canny Mark with his sly ways the one to run the money end of the shebang. A good combination, a real aggregation. He'd tell Minna tonight, and she'd be sure to see it his way.

"Stace," he said, "how would you like to have a boat?"

"One for the bath tub, Pop?"

"Hell, no. One for the river."

"Ain't I kind of little yet for that?"

"Don't say 'ain't.' And you'll grow, laddy. You'll be a sailor before you know it."

Stacey's place in his father's affection was very firm after that. Alan Kennard built the sailing dinghy himself in a corner of the stable, rigged her, sewed her sails by hand, and Stacey was both flattered and fascinated. His judgment of his father changed; the man for him became omnipotent, almost god-like. He went for voyages during the summer months aboard the company ships, and he was allowed to steer, had the compass, the stars, the winds explained to him, visited in the engine-room of the *Diagvera* with Stuffy Smith, saw the vast legs of the main engine lick, flash and fall, blinked fascinated into the ruddy flame of a furnace as a fireman slung in coal. He was going to be a sailor all right. Gee, it was sure some life.

Yet he and Mark remained unbrokenly close. The brotherly bond was strong for them despite the fact that they were four years apart. They skated and sledded and fished through the ice together in the winter, played marbles and tops and ball and cowboys and Indians and follow-the-leader the same way in fair weather. At school, they were the Kennard boys, and fought side by side against any common enemy. The Polish and Hungarian and Italian and Swedish boys respected them, and even the Carmody brothers, the toughest in the town, learned to let them be.

At home, they shared the same big room on the top floor of the house. A lot of their books were there, but their mother insisted that most of them, along with their magazines, be kept downstairs in the library. It looked better, she said, and she wanted them to do their homework and reading where she and their father could watch.

Stacey got to know all those books by title if not by content. The family habit when Alan Kennard was with them during the winter months was to gather each night after supper in the library. Olga had already lit the lamps and the gas log in the black marble fireplace. Stacey and Mark lay on the floor before the wheezing, sputtering log. Their father read the Chicago, Detroit and Milwaukee papers, dozed a bit when his cigar was finished. Their mother knitted or did brocade work, occasionally asked a question about their homework. Stacey had plenty of time to read the books he liked.

Through the cones of lamplight, he stared up at them before he made his choice. *Twenty Thousand Leagues Under The Sea* was next to *Heman's Poetical Works,* and then *The Winning of Barbara Worth,* the red and gold volumes of *Young Folks Library,* bound copies of *Leslie's Weekly* and *Cosmopolitan,* past them *Johnson's Natural History, The Crisis, Hawthorne's Works, Life on the Mississippi, Masterpieces of World Literature, To Have And To Hold, Gullivers' Travels, Paddle Your Own Canoe, Robin Hood, Les*

Miserables, Ivanhoe, bound copies of *St. Nicholas,* and in a corner by themselves because their mother liked them when she read at all, *A Romance of Two Worlds* and *Sorrows of Satan.*

Stacey had tried the Corelli books a couple of times, but while they were frightening, they were too heavily plotted for him, and Mark had told him to wait until he was more grown up. But neither he nor Mark cared for Henty although they got a new one every Christmas, and they had long ago traded their *Ragged Dick* and *Luck and Pluck* and *Tattered Tom* series for some paper-backed cowboy stories. Cowboy stories, he and Mark had decided, were the best, those and *Ivanhoe.*

They were greatly influenced by the cowboy stories the spring they got in trouble with the woodchuck. Mark was thirteen then, and Stacey nine, and for his birthday Mark had been given a single-shot bolt action .22 rifle. That had put quite a strain on the relationship between them, as it clearly showed the difference in their ages. But Stacey in a deal at school with Pete Carmody had got hold of a woodchuck trap, and he had let Mark help him put it out in a field behind the house.

After some argument, they had staked the trap down beside a hole in a patch of clover in the field. Then they had gone home and played ball for a while, tired of it and loaded the rifle. They'd shoot the damn' woodchuck, Mark said. They'd blow his head off. Trapping was no good if you had a real rifle.

But crossing back through the field they came very suddenly on the woodchuck. They were amazed, frightened, and Mark had never before fired the rifle. "Back up," Stacey told Mark. "Else, we'll get chawed. Look at that ole son of a gun!"

The woodchuck had come to his hind legs. He snarled at them. He was big, all of forty pounds. The little eyes were yellow around the rims, but the centers were blood color. His teeth showed, long and sharp and dirty brown when he snarled. When he wasn't snarling he made panting and groaning noises that were just as bad. Where the trap had caught him on the left back leg the hide and flesh were chewed raw. Still he had flattened down the clover around the hole for twenty feet or so, pulling the stake with him. It was the stake and the chain which kept him from getting down the hole. The stake stuck, from the looks of the sides of the hole, and the woodchuck didn't know enough to pull it around so it would slide in after him.

Mark held the rifle across his body. He fingered the trigger, but

, he retreated step by step. "Only one bullet," he muttered. "Should ha' brought more. 'At's a big bastard of a woodchuck. Come on, let's clear out, Stace."

"No, sir," Stacey said. "I want my trap back. Gave Pete a span new top and my bike pump for it. What's a-matter? You scared?"

"Maybe some. But we could get Elmar out here. Old Elmar, he'd shoot—Look out!"

The woodchuck charged low along the ground, his claws making a sharp scrabbling. Mark tried to shoot, and then he tried to run. But the woodchuck was snapping at his legs and he couldn't run far. He dropped the rifle.

Stacey screamed before he kicked out at the woodchuck. He was barefoot and the kicking hurt his toes. That and the sight of Mark with blood along his legs and the woodchuck snarling, snapping started him towards the rifle.

He picked it up and the woodchuck saw him and turned on him. But he held it down in front of the red eyes and pulled the trigger with the fingers of his right hand.

The woodchuck went on past him. It fell down flat, rolled over until the big fat belly was up. The legs twitched and took short, slow motions through the air. Stacey knew it was dead. "Damn, rotten, stupid!" he said to the woodchuck in incoherent rage.

Mark was sitting on the ground. He had his pants back to look at his legs. "I'll get infected and die," he said. "I'm all chawed." He began crying and wiping his hands through the blood on his legs.

"What'll I do?" Stacey said. "You don't want to die."

"Pee on it," Mark said. He had stopped crying and he wasn't shaking any more. That's what the Old Man says to do when you're hurt. Go ahead and pee."

"I can't," Stacey said. "I'm so scared it won't come."

"Then I'll do it," Mark said. "You help me up."

They were wiping off the blood and the pee and making bandages torn from Mark's pants when Elmar ran out into the field. "You little sons of bitches take that gun?" he said.

"Don't you go calling names," Mark said calmly. "Look at the bugger of a woodchuck Stacey just shot."

They went up to their room when they returned to the house. Mark stretched out on his bed and put his arms over his eyes. "I'm hungry," he said, "but I don't want to go down and eat. Olga or Katrine will see my legs and tell Ma."

"Ah, shucks, come on," Stacey said. "I'm so hungry I could croak. Ma's over to the Keibergs. She won't be back 'til nearly supper-time and the Old Man's at the company."

"Nope," Mark said; "I'm staying right here. But you go over and look in my drawer, Stace, and you'll find a quarter. I got it left out of my allowance. You take it and hop downtown and buy us some candy. Get the kind of things you like. You did pretty darn' good with 'at big ole 'chuck."

Stacey stood at the window, pleased and yet undecided. "Raining," he said. "Won't take my bike out in that."

"Then run," Mark said. "You're always saying what a swift runner you are."

"Sure," Stacey said. "Run right smack between the rain drops." But he went to Mark's drawer in the bureau and took out the quarter. "Be seein' you, podner."

Mark lay quite pale and quiet. "Don't eat it all coming home," he said.

Stacey yanked his mackinaw from the closet in the lower hall, but when Katrine called after him to put on shoes he only sprinted out across the porch. He ran all the way down into town and made his choice quickly in the store: licorice sticks, a dime's worth of them, nickel's worth of the candy corn, nickel's worth of lollipops and the same of peppermints. Then he darted into the rain again, and instead of keeping to Main Street cut out across-lots.

Before he had reached the store, he had been able to think of himself as a real Plains scout coming in to tell the cavalry that the Comanches were on the prod. But buying the candy had destroyed the illusion. Now he wanted to regain it. The splosh of mud beneath his bare feet, the soft pressure of the wet grass of the paths against his legs gave him a fine feeling of excitement. He was back on the Plains again in imagination and the Comanches were very close when Fat Mary called to him.

Fat Mary stood in under the porch of the old, tumble-down Hicknam house. She was a big girl, about fourteen and pretty thick. Her father worked on the section gang out of Napta City and folks said he was a drunk and beat her mother all the time. Around school, down in the basement at recess, he had heard other fellows talking about her, but he didn't know just what they meant.

"Hey, come here!" she called to him. "Where you runnin' to so fast?"

"Home," he said, not slowing his stride.

"Well, you can't be in no hurry," she said. "This here's Saturday afternoon. Stop along with me a while."

"Why?" he said.

"I'll show ya," she said. She twitched up her skirt. "C'me here!"

He followed her, oddly troubled and yet compelled by her gesture and the sight of her white, fat thighs. She led him into the cellar, jerking at his arm. "Take it easy, Mary," he said.

The cellar was dark. Cobwebs were all over and it had a sour, nasty smell. A pile of papers and empty bottles was in a corner. Fat Mary took him over to the pile of papers. She lifted her dress high and said, "You know how to do it?"

"What?"

"Jeez," she said. "Another dumb-head."

He backed from her, and his hands trembling, dragged the candy sack out of his mackinaw pocket. "You take this," he said, "and you let me outa here, hey, Mary?"

"Like hell," she said. But she grasped the candy with both hands, stuffed a licorice stick into her mouth with a lime lollipop. "You and me are goin' to have fun. Your brother knows. I showed him. Like this, see. Don't get scared. You run, or if you tell on me, I'll get Gyp' and them others to whop you good."

"Golly," he said in final, shamed protest as he obeyed; "you're eatin' all the candy."

"You shut up and get busy!" she said.

He ran desperately fast the rest of the way home when he got out of the cellar. Mark was in the tack room of the stable with Elmar; they were talking about the Maxwell the Old Man had said he was going to buy. "All right, where's the candy?" Mark asked, a little bit tougher than usual because of Elmar's presence.

"Fat Mary ate it," Stacey said, and then regretted the answer. Mark stepped close to him and pushed him hard in the chest. "That damn' ole Mary's been after you. You're too young for such a matter, hear me! You stop it!"

The push had hurt Stacey, and he was aware of Elmar's staring glance. "How about you, then?" he asked angrily.

Mark hit him at once and they fought from the tack room across the gravel outside the stable, locked bodies, tripped each other, wrestled savagely, Stacey underneath and very much the loser until Elmar separated them.

"Get to hell in the house," Elmar said. "I knock your heads togedder, both."

"Ah, go on!" they said, confronting him. But he turned and got a whip and flourished it and they went subdued, heads bowed, into the house.

Elmar felt amused, and also compelled to tell the Old Man. It gave him a sense of importance when at six o'clock after he had picked up the Old Man at the company office and they were riding back back behind the bays he said, "Them boys o' yours is purty good, Cap'."

"How d' you mean?" Alan Kennard said.

"Well, that Fat Mary, she's young pig around the town. Makes plenty o' ridin' practice for the boys."

"Bare-back?"

"Yes, sir."

"You sure?"

"Yes, sir."

Kennard bit the end from a fresh cigar. He squinted thoughtfully at Elmar. "I hope," he said, "that you ain't lying, and that she's clean."

"I ain't lying, sir. And no fellas I heard of got anything from her yet."

"Very well," Kennard said. He lit the cigar and consciously relaxed. His pride was pleased. He liked the idea that his sons had proven themselves to be so masculine. "I'm glad you told me, though, instead of my wife. Now you keep your yowp shut."

"Yes, sir," Elmar said. He had been debating whether he should tell the Old Man about the woodchuck, and from the Old Man's manner decided against it. Enough was enough. This Kennard, he was a touchy, peculiar fella. Then, abruptly, Kennard chuckled. "Stace," he said, "is kind of young for such as that. Might stunt his growth. Better talk to him."

"Guess you better, Cap'," Elmar said, and touched up the bays for the driveway ascent to the house.

But Kennard kept silent about the matter over the weekend. The boys were likely to get surly with him, he realized, and then he might lose his temper. Minna would find out what had happened and she'd be flustered, all worked up. Shucks, what if the boys had? Good for them, and healthy, as long as the pig was clean, and they had to learn some time. He'd wait on talking to them. If it got to be a habit, that was different.

Mark and Stacey had become reconciled after their fight on Saturday. Mark was placated when Stacey stole a pound box of raisins from the kitchen closet and brought it to their room Saturday night. They sat on Mark's bed and ate the raisins and discussed Fat Mary and the details, as they knew them, of copulation. But, the last raisin gone, Mark said, "You stay away from her, hear? Them fellas she goes with are big and tough."

"Sure," Stacey said with sincere meekness. He was very tired, his body sore and his mind exhausted. He moved over into his own bed and started to fall asleep. But then he caught himself. "Mark?"

"Yeah."

"You still awake?"

"What d' you think, dumb-head?"

"Well, I want for you to make a promise."

"Go to sleep!"

"No, I won't. Not unless you promise."

"So?"

"You don't fight with any of those fellas down at school because of Mary and me."

Stacey, he was a smart little son of a gun, Mark thought. Because he had been thinking just that. He was ready at Monday morning recess to tell Wen Bozsick and Gyp' Lostiano to keep Fat Mary off Stace. They were the two biggest fellas who were with her the most. If they told her, she'd listen, you bet. It could mean a fight, though. Those fellas didn't like to be talked to.

"Promise, podner?" Stacey said.

"Sure," Mark said. "'Cept, one of them bothers me, I'm not going to stand around."

"Listen!" Stacey said, rearing up in the bed. "You're my brother. There's a fight, I'm in it with you."

"You let me do my own fightin'," Mark said harshly. "And you get to sleep. This here's been a day."

Stacey, who was in the fifth grade, didn't get out into the playground at recess on Monday morning until after the fight had started. It was going on over in a corner with a lot of the big eighth grade boys packed close around so that Peg Leg Leary, the school janitor, couldn't see and break it up. But Stacey understood immediately and pushed on through, shouting, "Hey, you let my brother be, see!"

Mark was fighting Wendel Bozsick and getting the worst of it. His nose was already bloody, his jaw bruised. Stacey didn't hesitate; he dived at Bozsick. "All right, podner," he called to Mark. But Pete Carmody tripped him, and as he rose Gyp' Lostiano shoved him down again. "Darn' eighth graders," Stacey said. "Leave go o' me."

Still, he realized, Mark was in the eighth grade, too, and must have asked for this. He'd been hurt some when Pete Carmody tripped him, and he'd best stay out of it. He stood panting and shivering and whispering Mark's name during the rest of the fight. He was terribly ashamed; Mark was about to be whipped good.

Mark wasn't tall enough or strong enough for the Polish boy. Wen Bozsick could get inside Mark's guard and hit almost at will. He kept his right hand constantly in Mark's face, hit with the left for the body. Mark was knocked down three times before Pete Carmody, the best fighter in the school, chose to end it. He stepped forward and stood over Mark. "Friend o' mine," he said. "An' he's had enough."

"You get to hell out," Bozsick said wildly, shaking the blond hair back from his eyes. "He got to say he's a liar."

"Why?" Pete Carmody said. "About that Mary?"

"Don't you go namin' no names," Bozsick said. He looked aside at Gyp' Lostiano.

"'At's right." Lostiano stepped from the crowd. "Shaddap, Irish."

Stacey couldn't contain himself any longer. He had just noticed how Mark staggered weakly to his feet. He gathered himself and lunged at Wen Bozsick. His head struck the much bigger, heavier boy in the pit of the stomach and they went floundering to the ground. Above them Pete Carmody and Gyp' Lostiano fought, and then, amazingly, the crowd was gone and Peg Leg was there.

Peg Leg wasted no time; he cuffed at all of them. "Get in da school," he said. "Get in a da school, the hull kit, kaboodle o' youse!"

The bell was ringing for the end of recess and they broke and ducked from Peg Leg, glad for the bell's sound. The janitor insisted on the story that he had lost his leg at the second battle of Bull Run, while it was well-known that he had been run over by a horse car during a spree in Chicago. But he still possessed the ability to whip any boy in grammar school and most of them in high school, was respected even in Gilligan's, the town saloon.

Stacey stared back at Mark as he ducked into the doorway that led to his own classroom. Mark was pretty banged-up and bloody, all right. Darn' old teacher was sure to send him home with a note to the Old Man. And you're to blame, Stace. You're the one who got in trouble with Fat Mary. . . .

It was raining heavily when school was let out for the day. But Stacey found that there were several beside himself who waited for Mark. Pete Carmody was one, because Pete and Mark were friends, and Patsy Carmody was along because she was Pete's sister. Ingë Keiberg was there, too, not because she was nosey, but she was a friend of Patsy's and kind of stuck on Mark. None of them said anything as Mark came down the stairs from the principal's office, so Stacey knew he had to ask the question. "You get a note?"

"Sure did." Mark tapped his geography book. "Supposed to give it to the Old Man."

"Let's see it," Pete Carmody said.

"Don't you let him, Mark," his sister said. "It'll get all wet in the rain."

"Oh, for gracious' sakes!" Stacey said scornfully. But he was greatly surprised at the attitude Ingë Keiberg took. She was a skinny, usually quiet girl, and one of the brightest in the seventh grade. "You give it to me, Mark," she said, "and I'll tear it up. You don't have to see me do it. You can shut your eyes."

They had been moving slowly in a loose group along the side street from the school to Main Street. Now they stopped and gazed at Mark. He blushed a bit as he looked at Ingë. "Get yourself in trouble if you did."

"As if I care!" Ingë said. "Give it to me."

Mark unstrapped his books and from between the pages of the big geography drew the note. *Captain Alan Kennard* was written boldly across the front. They studied that while the rain drops fell and blurred the ink. "Let's read the note, too," Pete Carmody said. "Why you waitin', Ingë?"

"Don't be goopy," Ingë said. "Why read it? Just shut your eyes."

She ripped the note into many little pieces and let them flutter out into the muddy, rain-pooled street. Pete and Mark and Stacey laughed happily, but Patsy was scared and said to Ingë, "Gee, what's going to happen to you!"

"Listen," Pete told her; "you snitch, I'll whack you good. I sure as sugar will."

"Ah, come on," Mark said. "Let's not start to yappin'. Up to our house we can have some fun playing cops and robbers."

They played cops and robbers until the girls said they were sick of being caught. Then they ate some cookies Stacey got from Cook in the kitchen and went into the main drawing room. The excitement of the day had a disturbing effect upon them; they were unwilling to start another game, and outside the rain dropped in dismal gray sheets.

Old Mr. Duvern, the upholsterer from Napta City, was repairing a chair, and for a time he took their interest. But Mark was nervous, restless, and he had a pack of Black Jack gum. "C'me here," he said to the boys and led them across the room to the huge statue of David and the lamb. The girls wanted to follow, stood back only when they were given a strip of the gum apiece.

The other three strips were masticated and then rolled together at Mark's order. "Ole Dave," he whispered to Pete and Stacey, "he hasn't got one, see. I looked last week."

The statue was massive, of white marble and on a black marble base. David, one hand on the lamb's brow, wore a short robe and stared out into space. Mark climbed up onto the base and began to put the wadded gum in place beneath the edge of the robe.

Patsy Carmody screamed from the opposite side of the room. "That's bad," she said. "It's a holy statue, Mark, and your folks had it brought all the way from New York."

"Ah, shaddap!" Mark said, but Mr. Duvern looked up from his work. Mr. Duvern had a glass eye and he was troubled by it. He blinked at Mark, then at the statue. "Take it off," he told Mark. "You should be ashamed of yourself."

"Go soak your head!" Mark said. He stood defiantly before the statue, his hands on his hips.

"By gosh," Mr. Duvern said; "I should talk to your Ma instanter." He put down his work and moved across the room to the statue. But when he bent to pull at the gum his glass eye slipped from the socket.

It went rolling brightly over the carpet in the chandelier light and right beside Ingë's foot. She stood poised for flight with Patsy in the doorway, but as the shiny piece of glass stopped against the red velvet door drape, she stooped and picked it up, put it in her dress pocket.

"I want my eye back," Mr. Duvern said. "Give me my eye." He looked comical and also horrible with the red, gaping socket, and the boys laughed at him and yelled, "Yah, yah! Find yer own ole eye!"

Minna Kennard heard the shouting in her bedroom. She came swiftly down the stairs and into the drawing room. An intense rage filled her after she had seen Mr. Duvern. "Who has it?" she said sternly, then wrenched it from Ingë's hand. "Ingë, you and Patsy go home at once. You, too, Pete. I'll talk to your mothers later."

Mark and Stacey were sidling through the doorway behind her and she snapped at them, "Stand still. I'm not through with you."

Mr. Duvern was very eager to explain how he had happened to drop his eye. Minna Kennard deeply blushed and went straight to the statue. "You did this, Mark?"

"Nope, Ma," Stacey said. "It was me."

She looked searchingly down into his eyes. "Mr. Duvern said it was Mark."

"Mr. Duvern's wrong, 's all I can say. Mark told him, go soak his head. But I stuck the gum."

Minna Kennard gazed at her elder son. "Were you in a fight at school today?"

"Yes, Ma."

"And what have I told you, and your father, too?"

"Not to fight, Ma."

She was trembling with anger, and instinctively the two boys withdrew pace by pace from her. "Go to your room!" she shouted at them. "Stay there 'til your father comes to talk to you."

"Hey, boy, I guess we're goin' to get walloped good," Mark said when they were up in the room with the door shut.

"Looks like it," Mark said. "But what'd you do, go lying about me?"

"Well, I figured you got enough this morning."

Mark was silent for a moment while the rain rustled and pattered on the windows. "You're a real podner," he said. "Don't you bawl, though, when Pa whacks you."

"I won't," Stacey said. "I ain't that kind."

Alan Kennard had listened patiently to his wife. Nothing of what she said surprised him. It was stuff that any pair of lads might pull. But Minna was right, he knew. He had to talk to them. He left Minna in the library after supper and went to stand for a time before the statue. It was his vague idea that by regarding the statue he could somehow discover the language to use to Mark and Stacey.

But all he gained was the memory of when, with Minna, he had bought the thing. That had been before the house was finished. They had gone down to New York at the architect's suggestion and Minna had bought towels and sheets and pillow cases and drapes and rugs and a whole lot more gear. There had been the stained glass for the hall window, and pictures, real oil paintings, by

Frenchmen and Englishmen. Some had sheep in them, and some doves. One was of a man and woman wearing kind of skimpy stuff and running full speed ahead through a dark wood.

He and Minna put up at the Waldorf Astoria on Thirty-third Street and he recognized some of the Steel Corporation crowd, once it was Charley Schwab, right in the middle of the lobby. He took off his hat and bowed and Schwab bowed back, but Minna wasn't pleased. "He doesn't know you," Minna said. "And he's not going to. Why'd you do it, Alan?"

No answer came to him immediately and he brooded about it. That night he took Minna to the roof garden in Madison Square, got good and drunk while she just sat staring at him. "Buyin' a statue tomorrow," he told her suddenly.

"For goodness' sake, what for?"

"The house. We got room. Maybe I ain't Charley Schwab and maybe I won't ever be. But I got the spondoolix to buy a statue such as him and his kind has."

"You're foolish," Minna said. Still, she leaned across the table and pressed his hand. "Foolish, and smart, too. Go buy it, then."

Now Minna was calling to him from the study. "You'd better get up there. Those two won't think anything of you unless you do."

"Very well," he said. But as he climbed the stairs he didn't think of his sons. The transference had been made in his mind between Schwab and the Steel Corporation crowd and the Cleveland Square gang. That lot over in Cleveland were pressing him. They were putting it to him hard, and today at the company he and Josh had had a long talk about what was almost certain to happen. The Lakes seamen were fixing to go out on strike; the boys wanted more money, and they rated it. The Vessel Owners Association, though, was all against a strike. They were ready to bring in as strike-breakers a whole bunch of deep-water sailors who were on the beach in the East Coast ports. If he backed the strike, the Cleveland Square gang would dump him sure as shooting. They'd go after his ship charters, close him up tight overland, too, because out of Napta City they controlled the freight rates, could make him pay through the nose for his deliveries.

You should be figuring out that situation, Alan Kennard told himself when he reached the top of the stairs at the second floor. Still, here you are fouled up with your sons pulling a bit of a joke with some chewing gum. For the love of Jesus, why can't Minna let be? Ah, knock it off, man. She's a good mother to them, and a fine wife to you. Is it you're so scared of the Cleveland gang that you can't lead your own life? You are not. . . .

He went into the bathroom on the second floor and took from its hook beside the basin his razor strop. Then he went on to the third floor and the boys' room. The light had been burning there as he came to the head of the stairs; he had seen it under the door. But as he moved along the hall it was turned out. He slightly smiled. A smart pair, his lads.

They were in their own beds and noisily snoring. "Mark," he said after he had opened the door and stood inside the room; "get up and turn on the light. Stacey, you ain't asleep, either. Set up, you!"

He walked back and forth before them swinging the razor strop when Mark had lit the gas jet. "Your Ma says you been real bad," he said. "Both of you. Stickin' gum on the statue. And I've been hearin' about you and some pig of a young girl in the town."

"Elmar's a snitch!" Stacey said impulsively. "Don't you believe a word he told you."

"Pipe down," Alan Kennard said. He swung to his elder son. "What the hell's happened to you? You're all tore up."

"Got in a fight at school," Mark said. "Hey, Pop, if you're going to lick us, can we have some supper afterwards?"

Alan Kennard cursed to keep from laughter. "Who'd you fight?"

"You wouldn't know him, Pop."

"Who'd you fight?"

"A fella name of Wen Bozsick."

"Well, I know his old man. He works for me out to the quarry. But you tell me what it was about."

"Migs," Stacey broke in. Wen Bozsick stole a whole slew o' Mark's migs."

"You pipe down!" Alan Kennard roared at Stacey. He smacked the foot of Stacey's bed with the razor strop. "Your Ma says you were lyin' this afternoon about the statue. Now, by God, Mark, I want an answer out of you."

"I'm not going to lie," Mark said tensely. "This fella and me, we just had a fight, that's all."

"But about this Fat Mary."

"No, sir!"

"I know better. Take off your shirt and turn over."

Mark complied wordlessly and hunched himself up on the edge of the bed, his buttocks presented to his father. But as Alan

Kennard struck the first blow Stacey leaped at him. Stacey pummeled his father with his fists. He was wild with grief. "You let 'm be!" he cried. "It was me he was fighting about. Me and Fat Mary. See?"

Alan Kennard dropped the razor strop and held his younger son kicking, squirming and sobbing in his arms. "Steady so, lad," he murmured. "I ain't got the heart to beat either of you now. But how big is this Bozsick?"

"Bigger 'n Mark and heavier," Stacey said. "Mark fought him like a bobcat. He took a real drubbin'."

"I get you," Alan Kennard said. He carried Stacey over to his bed, put him in it and pulled the covers high around the tear-stained face. Tears were under his own eyelids. He was strangely and deeply moved. He had never before sensed just how much he loved both his sons.

"Well, I'll tell ya," he said thickly, embarrassed and made very self-conscious by his emotion. "No fella that big is going to whip any son of mine."

"Ah, gee, Pop," Mark said in perturbation. "Leave him to us. Stace' and me can make a hash of him."

"By God, no!" Alan Kennard said furiously. "Enough back-chat out of you. I'll handle this the way I want. Now get to sleep, both of you." He was at the door before he recognized he had forgotten the razor strop. He turned to pick it up, but Stacey was already there. Stacey slid it into his hand and said, "Goodnight, Pop."

"You little rascal," Alan Kennard said. "Hop back in your bunk. And if I catch you ridin' bareback with any more girls I'll baste you 'til you're bow-legged."

"Pop, you're leaving the light on," Mark said.

"So one takes care of the other, hey?" Alan Kennard said. "I'm onto your game. Don't try it on me again, though. Next time will be real rough."

He was relieved to be out in the hall with the door shut in back of him. He was weak with restrained laughter, bemused by the spectacle of Stacey leaping at him when he had started to whip Mark. But Minna waited at the head of the stairs past the maids' room. She stared at him grave-faced and as he advanced to her said, "I must say, Captain, that wasn't very much of a punishment."

"Ah, to hell with you!" he said, abruptly angry. "I have other things on me mind."

"Such as?" she said with the same bitter note through her voice.

"Going down to Gilligan's and finding the old man of the lad who knocked Mark around."

"You'll do no such thing, Alan. You can't! It's not right."

"Right, wrong, it's what I'm about to do. Sick of bullies is what I am. The Cleveland lot, they'd bamboozle me and fleece me as they see fit. And now me own son has his spots knocked off by some young ape. Well, I'll find his father, and by the God I'll teach him a lesson for his son."

Minna stopped half way down the stairs to the ground floor. "Alan Kennard," she said, "don't go out of this house for any such purpose or I'll be forever ashamed of you."

"So you will be, then," Kennard said. He hung the razor strop on the bannister, stepped to the front door and swung it wide. "Don't wait up for me. If I find the man I'm after and whip him, I may come home soused to the goddamn' gills."

The rain had become a fine mist through which moonlight broke opalescent. Bull frogs were noisy in the river, and one of the first katydids let go the monotonous sound so regularly that Kennard began to repeat it beneath his breath. He slowed on the uneven slate sidewalk that he had demanded the town build to the edge of his property and looked out into the night.

A confusion of thoughts occupied his mind. This was his town. If it hadn't been for him, there'd be nothing like it. Sure, Lars Keiberg owned a big whack and was wealthy, and Josh's money had helped, and Frawn's, too. But he was the man who had seen what could be done.

Right over there was where he'd sat with Minna under that willow the day Josh had surveyed the limestone. Those were his ships made fast up to the dock beyond. The railroad belonged to Kennard and Company, and all the line into Napta City. Past there, though, it was different, goddamn' different.

Because of the bunch in Cleveland. They had no use for him, never had. Neither did the real wealthy fellas in Detroit and Chicago and Milwaukee and St. Paul. He wasn't big enough or small enough to suit their taste. They wanted to own him lock, stock, barrel and fore sight, and if they couldn't, they were out to bust him.

Like now with this strike that was coming. Dog eat dog, and no mercy. Only you ain't any dog, Kennard. And you're not going to lose out to them. You've weathered some tough times before. You can do it again.

He flexed his back muscles, then his arms, pushed the brim of his hat down over his eyes at a belligerent angle. You feel like a scrap tonight, a good, old fashioned shindy. Push my lads around, hey? Send my Mark home bloody nosed. No, by God!

Gilligan's was fairly full when he strutted in wide-legged from Main Street. There were several other places in town that sold whiskey and beer, but Gilligan's was the oldest and the best, and here, he expected, he'd meet the man he sought. Some of the crew members from the company ships in port were along the bar and they looked up at him respectfully and said "Good evenin', Cap'," and Gilligan came over from the end of the bar.

"Irish, Cap'?" Gilligan said.

"Irish it is," he said, "with a drop of water, Mike." He felt a bit uncomfortable, standing so alone. Bozsick wasn't here. The boys down the bar had been talking about the strike, too, when he came in, and they stood still, looking out of the corners of their eyes at him.

He drank his drink neat and coughed at the impact of the whiskey. "Mike," he called to Gilligan, "buy all hands a drink." He seldom came into the saloon any more and it made him feel better to buy a round. It was good to have the lads remember that he'd been a sailor once himself.

But the conversation down the bar was only fitful, about baseball, politics, crops, everything but the strike. He motioned to Gilligan and bought himself another drink. "You seen Istvan Bozsick tonight, Mike?"

"No, I ain't," Gilligan said. He swiped the bar thoughtfully. "Ain't been in. Say, any o' you boys seen Bozsick?"

A slender young coal-passer from the *Daigvera*, a local boy, answered. "He's over to the bowlin' alley. You want him, Cap'?"

This was wrong, Kennard knew. The coal-passer was playing kiss-ass, hoped that by doing a favor he'd get ahead in the ship. But to hell with standing here. You'll be on your way to soused before you fetch up. "Yeah, I do. Get him for me, will ya?"

"Yes, sir," the coal-passer said and hurried from the bar.

Istvan Bozsick was a burly man with a brown, seamed face and huge hands. He came in slouching and stood beside Alan Kennard at the bar. "You look for me?" he said.

"Correct," Kennard said. He braced himself with his back to the bar, not quite certain how he should proceed. But then Bozsick said suddenly, "I got game goin' over to the alley."

"To hell with your game!" Kennard said. "And don't you start out cocky with me. Your boy might reckon he's tough, but you ain't man enough for me."

"What you say?" Bozsick said squinting. "What you mean?"

"That your son dumped mine at school this morning. My boy, Mark. And I'm down here to square away with you."

"Oh, ho!" Bozsick said softly. "Oh, ho! The Ole Man, he can't let his son take own drubbin'. But my boy ain't done no wrong."

"Shut your yowp, you Pole lunk," Alan Kennard said. "Shut up, or put up."

Mike Gilligan came bustling down the bar, his fat belly bulged out upon the mahogany. "Say now, look here, Cap'," he said anxiously. "Let's not have no trouble."

But the quarryman had slid into a crouch. "Irish bastard!" he said. "You don't own me nor my boy. Shut up your talk."

Alan Kennard went for him with both hands, shrilly cursing. They fought the length of the bar, back through the room and from it into the street. Bozsick was a clumsy fighter, but he was possessed of great strength and to hit his body was like hitting a barrel of cement.

Kennard's breath cut short. He gasped as he wheeled and guarded and struck. The face, he thought. Go for the face. You'll bust your hands on the body. Yet to get in at the face meant that he take punishment from Bozsick, and he was hit in the mouth, alongside the ear, in the throat and abdomen. He was reeling, spit blood when Bozsick lurched on the slippery sidewalk. Kennard sensed his moment and hit with a long and terrible overhand right.

Bozsick did a half somersault backwards and lay on his back in the mud of the street, arms, legs, body slack. "Get up," Alan Kennard said. "Call me an Irish bastard, hah?"

But men restrained him, held him when Bozsick rose stumbling and floundered off down the street. "Enough, Cap'," Mike Gilligan said. "You give it to him good."

"All right," Kennard said. He hawked up blood from his throat, allowed himself to be lead into the saloon. "Set up a round for all hands."

He noticed, though, as he wiped his face on a towel given him by Gilligan that no more than half the men drank the proffered round. Those that didn't looked at him with open dislike. They're waiting for you to get out of here, he realized. They think you acted like the cock o' the walk.

"Say, Cap'," one of them, an old Swede, said; "you gonna fire Istvan now?"

"Hell, no!" He straightened, his aching hands tight on the bar. "That ain't my way."

"Sure, sure," the Swede said, expressionless. His name was Nordstrom and he'd sailed for years as wheelsman in the *Minna*. "But you stick with us if we go out in the strike?"

Alan Kennard took a long, rough breath. "I grew up hungry," he said. "I sailed the deep-water ships when the crimps got all your pay and any mate had the right to beat a man's brains loose. You think I'd sell out you boys?"

"I dunno," Nordstrom said slowly. "I yust can't say." He turned then, leaving the full drink on the bar, and walked out, eight men, all of the seamen there, at his back.

Alan Kennard felt a cramping sensation that started at his knees and spread upward through his body. Those lads didn't trust him. They had no use for him. He took a five dollar bill and put it on the bar. "Goodnight, Mike," he said. "Goodnight, all."

They answered him, and there was no warmth in it; they spoke as if he were a stranger. When he was out in the street and on his way home he was ill and vomited. A clammy sweat ran down him. He shivered and his teeth rattled. "Bastards!" he said hoarsely, although he was uncertain whether he meant the men he called the Cleveland Square gang or the men who had left the bar with Nordstrom.

CHAPTER ELEVEN

They sat motionless now around the long, dark table, all of them staring hard-eyed, yet calm, sure of themselves. The one who was chairman rapped his cigar end against the tall brass spittoon beside him and said, "We're about through with you, Kennard. You've heard us out. Go with us, and you get sufficient crews to man your vessels. Go against us if you wish, and we'll break you. In two months' time, you won't have a charter or a contract left. By next season, you'll be busted, completely out of business. Make up your mind; you've had plenty of warning. Are you with us, or against us?"

Kennard rose slowly from his chair. It seemed that for this moment life was very nearly suspended. He could see beyond the window, out in Public Square, a seagull up from the lake that flew pearl-winged through the broad summer sunshine. Down on the Flats, a ship blew as she threw off her lines and started along the winding turns of the river. Hansom cabs, drays, carts, streetcars rattled, clanged; hooves clopped; newsies called their papers. But the group here waited for him, and it wouldn't wait long.

"No, sir," he told the chairman in a heavy, harsh voice, "I don't go along with the Association. I'm for the boys, got a feelin' for them and their rights."

A very slight flush entered the chairman's face. At the corners of his mouth, nerves pulled. He gestured to the stenographer, and her pencil rustled on the notebook page. "All right, Kennard. But when we're finished with you, you'll be lucky to get a bosun's job. Good day to you."

"Why, you—" Kennard began, then checked himself. He picked up his hat and went stiffly from the room while they remained without speech, their eyes on each other, their interest in him lost.

The rage made his jaws ache, and a scarlet haze obscured his vision. He stood for some minutes in the lobby of the building before he could find sufficient control to call Aeneas Lothrop on the telephone. A smooth voiced male secretary answered at Lothrop's office; he said that Mr. Lothrop was at the Union Club and ex-

pected Captain Kennard at any time. "Thank ye," Kennard muttered, and stumbled a bit as he emerged forth into the sunshine of
the Square.

He was numbed by shock; that had taken the place of the rage.
You were warned, he thought dully. Josh explained it to you, if
you didn't already know it for yourself. Phelim didn't lie, neither.
He gave you to understand the chance you took should you stand
up to them. But the way they did it. Holy Christ, was that neat.
Not a word in open anger, not a voice raised. All nice and smooth
and a-taunto. At the same time ripping you up the back, taking all
you've ever made away from you. Are you licked, though? Really
through, Antrim?

He stopped suddenly on the sidewalk and people behind
bumped into him. His hands closed to fists. Not you. Not Alan
Kennard. Fight them right down the bloody line. Pack of swabs.
They're not the lot to order you around, tell you how and when
and why to sail your ships. Lothrop's the lad for you. Smart as a
whip. If anybody can bear you a hand in this town, it's him. You'll
pay for it because he don't come cheap, but you won't mind, so
long as you win. . . .

There were a number of carriages and three automobiles in
front of the Union Club. Kennard slowed and regarded them curiously, aware that it was here he was going to see Lothrop instead
of in the lawyer's office. A very tony fella, Lothrop. That red, long-
snout Renault with the chauffeur in the white coat and cap and
black gauntlets was his. Made a lot of money and married a lot
more. Solidly in with the gang. Still, you have to come to him, and
he wants the men who count to know it. Son of a bitch is playing
both sides of the fence.

The main lounge of the club was somber and quite cool after
the street. Kennard gave his name self-consciously, then waited,
the old inquietude upon him. He wasn't a member; he was still a
stranger in such a place. And the eyes, the faces of the men in the
lounge were much the same as the ones in the board room of the
Vessel Owners. Take it easy, you. Keep a-hold of yourself. You're
all jumped-up and you can't afford to be.

Aeneas Lothrop lifted gracefully from the deep leather chair to
greet him. He wore a pongee silk suit and a figured cravat which
Kennard recognized on himself would look ridiculous. You'd like
to call him a goddamn' fop, Kennard thought, but he rides jumpers
like a fiend and he's one of the best yacht sailors on the Lakes.

"How are you, Captain?" Lothrop asked smiling, and held out his powerful hand.

"Been better," Kennard said, with the belief that his voice sounded very loud.

"Then a brandy cocktail is in order," Lothrop said. "Or would you prefer a whiskey sour?"

"The cocktail," Kennard said. He didn't like the stuff, but by God if Lothrop drank it, he would, too. He sat remembering vividly the time he and Lothrop had arranged the deal to take over the Shaw family holdings. Lothrop had shown no mercy on that; he'd gone in fast, come out faster, although he and Josh had been close friends, their parents and grandparents before them. Shark eat shark. He'll scoff you, too, sailor, if you don't handle this just right.

Lothrop stretched back in his chair. He picked up and relit a thin yellow cheroot he had been smoking. "How did you make out?" he said.

"I told them I was with the boys."

Lothrop didn't move. He watched the spirals of his smoke drift off into a shaft of sunlight from a window. "I thought you would. But, to what advantage?"

"I ain't the kind to sell out my own."

"Well spoken." Lothrop inhaled, exhaled smoke. "I say it as a friend, though, and not as your lawyer."

"Let's square away," Kennard said roughly. "What do you mean?"

Lothrop glanced aside at him and smiled. "Morgan once made a famous statement to Judge Gary. He said, 'I don't know as I want a lawyer to tell me what I cannot do. I hire him to tell me how to do what I want to do.'"

"What I'm after," Alan Kennard said, "is to keep my fleet and my company. Can you help me there?"

"It all depends."

"You talkin' money?"

Lothrop let his vexation show in the tightening of his face. "Not yet. Not my own price, that is."

"You're a slick article," Kennard said. "You'd have me tell you what I reckon to do. But I got no assurance you won't turn and give the whole story to that bunch."

Lothrop shrugged, once more fully relaxed. "It's up to you, Captain. I can't make your decision for you."

"But you can advise me."

"Naturally." The waiter had arrived with the drinks and Alan Kennard slopped some of his as he took it from the tray. Lothrop didn't seem to notice. His glance was on his glass. "Good luck to you, however you may decide."

Kennard drank the entire cocktail before he answered. Rage thudded, pounded, made a dim roaring in his brain. A painful knot was in his stomach muscles. He felt a great resentment against this man. Lothrop was one of them, the enemy. Advise you, like hell. He'd dump you out that window on your head if he was paid enough money for it. You're better off at home with Josh and Phelim, yeah, even talking it over with Lars Keiberg. Try once here, though. Give it a spin. He's going to stick you with a whopper of a bill anyhow.

"What chance have I got?"

"Against the Vessel Owners Association? None. Absolutely none."

Kennard's throat constricted. He coughed with nervous tension. "Explain to me why I ain't."

"Then you must be patient. Would you care for another drink first?"

"No. You just go ahead and talk."

"Just for a starter," Lothrop said, "you're lined up with the wrong people. Labor can't win. They lost the Homestead Strike, the Pullman Strike, all the stockyard strikes and God knows what else. And, by the same sign, the forces opposed to them won't let them win this one."

"Even if all the ships are tied up?"

"Believe me, they won't be. There's too much at stake. Carnegie won't have it, and Rockefeller and Morgan won't have it, nor will Mark Hanna and any of the rest of them who have a big investment in the Lakes. Can you stand up to them?"

"Not alone, no. But I reckoned that if I took a stand, maybe some of the smaller fleet owners would go along with me."

"And cut their own throats. Just consider if you would, Cap', the power Hanna has. I name him because he's a local man and you know what his connections are here with the street railways, his bank, the shipbuilding outfit and the rolling mills."

"Dollar Mark," Kennard said bitterly.

"That's what they call him. And I needn't point out that he's treasurer of the Republican Party and Senator, exceedingly influential in Washington. I admire your spunk, Cap'. But I'd be a pretty poor kind of attorney if I counselled you to buck men of Hanna's stripe."

"You mean," Alan Kennard said very low voiced and slowly, "they're the bunch that run the country."

"Just about." Lothrop stroked a hand up along the planes of his face in a gesture of reflection. "I've had dealings with most of them one way or another, and I've come to appreciate their power."

"So we're just little fellas on the outside lookin' in. Without a goddamn' thing we can do."

"Except to go with them," Lothrop said. "You recollect what happened to the Shaws."

"Some folks say that you and me plucked 'em."

"An unworthy accusation," Lothrop said, and laughed. "But they were bound to lose what they had. They couldn't escape it. If Josh has advised you—"

"Let's have another drink," Kennard broke in with deliberate rudeness. "You can put it on my bill." This man was too slick, too quick with his facts and arguments. By Jesus, take care, or he'll talk you out of everything you own. He works for the other side and so why listen to him? But Lothrop had called the waiter, sat slouched in his chair, an amused expression about his mouth and eyes.

"You talk hard, Cap'," he said, "and in your day you've fought hard. Still, aren't you about through?"

"Say it straight out. You'd have me stand and get fleeced."

"Not a bit of that." For the first time, there was a quality of emotion in Lothrop's voice. "I'm simply trying to make clear to you that you can't win the way you're going. Look at what happened to Debs and Altgeld and Bryan. If Grover Cleveland could break the Pullman Strike, don't you think the same sort of action will be taken with the seamen? Why have militia armories been built in every big city? For what purpose have the blacklist and the iron-clad oath been designed? What's the job of the Pinkertons, and the Coal and Iron Police? Labor hasn't got a chance, I repeat."

"Even under the law, you'd have me think."

"Yes, even under the law. I had a broader conception when I left school and started practice. It didn't seem—" Lothrop's mouth was pulled in a sour twist—"quite as one sided as I've exposed it to you. But I learned. A chap who was at school with me got a letter from Mark Hanna one time. He showed it to me, and I shall quote it to you, Cap', because I have your interests at heart. This friend of mine was prosecuting attorney here in Ohio and brought a suit to annul the Standard Oil charter. Hanna's letter to him said, 'You have been in politics long enough to know that no man in public office owes the public anything.' "

"Ah, hell!" Kennard said. "I've heard that story before and I don't take any stock in it."

"As you like, then." Lothrop had risen to his feet. "Good luck to you. At the end of the month, you'll receive a bill from my firm. But, after today, we won't be able to represent you."

"Scared?"

"You mistake me, Captain. I'm a sensible man, not a revolutionary. Change may come, and it should, but it will be gradual. Please bear my best to Mrs. Kennard and to Josh and his wife."

Alan Kennard reached out and grasped him by the arm. His breathing came fast in his throat and he trembled. "You show no mercy, man. You'd leave me to be wiped out."

"You've asked for it."

"No," Kennard said, the word rasped, almost inarticulate. "I ain't. Or, if I have, I change it. . . . Aeneas, can you get to them in the Association? Tell 'em—you know what to tell 'em."

"I guess I can," Lothrop said. "But let's sit down. There's no rush, and we shouldn't forget we have a drink coming."

The taste of bile ruined the drink for Kennard. He had been extremely frightened, he knew, and to a degree he still was. His lot and this lot here had put him in the middle and banged the hell out of him. But what was the point of losing all you had? They mightn't understand right off, Josh and Phelim and the rest of them, but the way he'd done it, when he went back to Patigowoc the ships would sail, the quarries and the kilns operate. No starvation, no rough stuff, nobody killed or with their brains beat loose. If it was the system, well, it was the system, and you went along if you were smart. No sense wrecking yourself for a pack of wild ideas.

But when Lothrop went to telephone and he sat alone, part of his conviction about the choice he had made left him. He shut his eyes, as if by doing that he could withhold from his imagination the faces of the people in Patigowoc as he explained to them that he was against the strike. Phelim would be the angriest, of course, because Josh really didn't give a goddamn' about much any more. There was a great lot of people in it back home beside Phelim, though, and so far he hadn't reckoned in Minna. She'd have a word to say. She was a firm woman, Minna, firmer with the years. Ah, Christ, sailor, why did this have to be?

.　　　.　　　.　　　.　　　.　　　.　　　.　　　.

Two years ago, at Alan Kennard's insistence, he had installed the telephone. When he heard it in the middle of the night Joshua Shaw thought, that's Antrim calling. He had an instantaneous sensation of alarm: things must have gone wrong in Cleveland.

He got out of bed and walked to the phone in the moonlight, took the receiver from the hook and said quietly, "Shaw speaking."

Phelim Carmody boomed back at him, "'Tis me. The rotten sod has done us in down there, Josh. I just heard from the boys at union headquarters. Kennard and Company is on the list to get scab crews."

"No, oh, no, Phelim. That can't be."

"By the Jesus it is! He signed with the Association at five o'clock yesterday. The boys have been tipped off. They know it for a fact."

"Where is Kennard?"

"Still in Cleveland, from what we hear. But the bastard'll be comin' home. He'll have to, if he'd be puttin' them scab crews aboard his ships."

Joshua Shaw fingered the top of the telephone box in nervous consternation. He looked behind him and saw his wife standing in the doorway of their bedroom, his son and daughter peering in from the sleeping porch. The phone jangle had awakened them. They had heard what he had said. There was no secret left. The time has come, the walrus said. . . .

"Where are you now, Phelim?"

"At the hotel with Frank Oate and Stuffy, the rest of us, the strike committee."

"What do the others think of it?"

"They'd bust Kennard's head, shellack the scabs good. But, are you still with us, Josh?"

"I am, and I will be to the end. The idea of violence doesn't appeal to me, though, Phelim. Give me an hour or so and I'll be over to talk with you. Don't get drunk and keep the bunch sober. Perhaps we'll be able to swing Kennard around to our way of thinking."

"A fine chance, after what he promised us when he went down there. Why ain't we heard from him? Why ain't he played it square?"

"Those are questions I can't answer offhand, Phelim." A vast weariness had abruptly gripped Shaw. "Let me talk to you later. I'll have to think about this."

"Josh."

"Yes, Phelim."

"You won't turn against us, go with him?"

"Not I."

"Good man. We'll be expectin' you. Tell the missus I'm sorry if I roused her outa sleep."

Joshua Shaw hung up the phone and stepped from it reluctantly to face his wife. "Bad news," he said. "But I daresay you've already gathered that, Enid."

"I have," she said. She stood small, slight before him in her thin summer nightgown. "You must know that I've never quite trusted your friend."

"My friend and partner," Shaw said. A swift gust of rage seared him; he struck his left hand into the palm of the right. "Ignorant, vain when I met him, and, despite the years, still the same. He's sold himself for something he'll never achieve."

"Harsh words, Joshua. I wouldn't use them so immediately." Enid Shaw turned; the children were still at the door to the sleeping porch. "Back to bed," she told them. "Your father and I will explain this to you in the morning."

"Is Captain Kennard a bad man?" It was her daughter who spoke, poised as though in extreme terror.

"No, of course not, darling. Now to bed, please. Hurry!"

Her husband had gone to stand at the fireplace. His hands rested on the rough stone mantel, and she could see the way they twitched, spasmodically jerked. She joined him and pressed her body against his. "It's cold, Joshua," she said; "and you're cold. Build up a fire, if you would, while I make us a pot of tea."

"Thank you," he said in a whisper. His arms clasped her, he kissed her. "I need you very much."

"Silly," she said, but she let him kiss her again before she broke away to the kitchen.

It was good for him to gather the birch bark, place the logs, strike the match and then watch the flames flutter. Maybe he wouldn't have his home much longer, he thought, but tonight this still belonged to him. He swung and looked out upon the lake, the view he had grown to love so much.

The pines were stark in the moonlight. The beach at the end

of the point shone silver where the waves rolled over the pebbles and the sand. Bouche de Mouche flashed, a tremendous riband that with the moon's radiance took the color of copper. That flicked across the dock he had built, the boat he had built, the lawn he had cleared, the house he had built. All for what? To give them in resignation to Alan Kennard? He put his head down upon his hands and groaned out of frustrated rage.

His wife stirred the fire when she came with the tea. She pushed forward his favorite chair and wordlessly made him sit in it. Then she pulled up her own, gave him a cup of tea. He drank, unashamed of the tragic expression he knew he wore. Enid was his woman; between them was nothing that resembled shame.

The tea gone, he filled and lit the pipe she brought him. His nerves had become steady, he realized. He would be able to talk with her. "What shall we do?" he said. "I can't stand for this. My life wouldn't have any more meaning if I did."

"Go speak with him," Enid Shaw said. "Try to convert him to your way of thinking if he's really in error."

"And if I can't?"

"Sell out, and get out."

"Let Kennard reap what he has sowed."

"Yes."

"But you love the house. You've been very happy here."

"There are some things that are worth more than houses."

Joshua Shaw's face quivered. He thrust back the chair and strode the space before the fireplace. Watching him, she was keenly aware that he was no longer a young man. He was bald, what hair he had left almost white. His stomach had a paunch beneath the pajama jacket, and there was a sag of hopelessness in the facial lines despite the rigor of his anger. A displaced man, she thought. One who has lost himself and can't find the path out from the maze. You love him, love him dearly, and yet after this night, if he stands by his convictions, he will be to you a third child. Strange, for when you met him it was you who were the weaker person, or so you believed.

Joshua Shaw bent over her. He took her hands. The light of the fire was behind him, gave his body the semblance of extraordinary size. "I know what you're thinking," he said in a voice that was dimly audible, "and you're right. In a little while, I have to go, join the men on whose side I consider I should stand. They're not my kind, not Phelim, not Smith, nor Oate, nor the lesser of them, the sailors and firemen and coal-passers and cooks. But if my life has meaning—"

"—It has meaning, Joshua."

"Then I must cast loose from all that has gone before. Those men deserve more money. They deserve better working conditions, and as I understand them, practically the entire set of their demands are correct. I'm a stockholder, though. From their work, I make a profit, much more than I can make from any skill of my own."

"I might say that there you are wrong."

He tried to grin. "You would flatter me in order to ease my pride but not my conscience. . . . For years, I've been puzzled about why mother acted as she did. At last I think I have the answer."

"You would like to tell it to me?"

"There's nobody else who'll hear it. Nobody else who should. You see, Mother was absolutely inflexible. She bent to nobody, no force or influence. Yet she was convinced throughout that her actions were performed because of her love for her family.

"She was an intelligent woman. The reason for her terrible mistake must have been that the times changed much too fast for her. So she clung all the more closely to the faith, the old, narrow traditions that the Cottrells had followed for generations. But it was really much greater than any faith. It was an entire way of life.

"Father was much like her. He kept on thinking that things should be as they were fifty, a hundred years ago. The only difference between him and Mother was that to a degree he recognized what had happened in the industrial revolution. He still didn't know how to whip the conditions around him. All the while, he instinctively relied upon his clan and his class position for support."

"I have seen that in England."

"I know you have. Mother, though, remained as Puritan as Cotton Mather. She lived alone in the secret prison of her spirit. For her, the world had become a wasteland. The dollar had ravaged it, become to mean everything and nothing. There was in her terms no paradox in that. The dollar was Mammon. It had to be repelled, evicted from the spirit. She saw the dollar taking possession of value after value. Her intention was that her family accept what she saw as true and good, and if we didn't, then we should perish."

"Jane escaped. So have you."

"But at what a price. . . . I'm tired, darling. Enough so that I don't want to fight any more."

"You haven't changed your mind about Alan Kennard?"

"No! Because he to me represents what I've come to call my enemies. But after that . . ." His voice lowered into silence. His gaze was on the lake where the first crest of dawn touched the water roseate.

"We can go to England," she said. "There is that small place my people have. Living there would be very simple, very nice."

"And I'd be a man without a job while you kept on with your art and the children grew up to look upon me as an ineffectual, talkative old fool."

"Not," she said sharply, "if you give Kennard what he has coming today. It's time you dressed and went over there."

"Yes, ma'am," he said. But none of the rage in his eyes was for her, she knew. It was all for his former great friend, Alan Kennard.

.   .   .   .

"So you," Phelim Carmody said thickly, "sold us out. Why? Tell me! Are ye man, pimp or mouse?"

"Pipe down," Alan Kennard said in a fierce voice. He sat at his desk in the company office, and before him the top desk drawer was part open. If he wished, he could slide his hand onto the .32 bull-dog revolver there. By the gorry, Phelim wasn't going to get away with any rough stuff with him. "Make sense, man. I've listened to too much of your bilge. I didn't have you let in to take such as this."

"Bilge, is it? And let in, hey?" Carmody advanced until, leaning across the desk, his sweaty face was within inches of Alan Kennard's. "You have completely forgot. That is what you must ha' done. For a fella brought up in black poverty, a fisherman and gypsy as your people, no, it can't be. You it was who sailed with me in the *Margharita* and I can still see ye goin' down under the fist o' the mate and nary a word could ye say and less could ye do without you got your head banged in. Ah, you know. . . . You know as well as me. 'Tis not only the *Margharita,* but all the other ships and what we seen together here through the years on the Lakes. Look me square in the eyes, Antrim. Tell me straight. Why did ye do us in over to Cleveland?"

Alan Kennard was stiff bodied with fatigue, unshaven and grimy from the train ride from Cleveland. He had drunk a considerable amount of whiskey aboard the train, and it had left him with a seemingly flannel-lined mouth, a headache that he believed any moment might split his skull. There was no patience he could muster for Phelim. The man's words made little sense to him, and most of them he'd heard before. So get rid of him. Josh you can talk to maybe, but not to Phelim.

"Get on with you, Phelim," he said mildly. "Old times don't count. This here is too big a question for you and me alone. Sure, I went with the Association in Cleveland. I changed me mind after I'd talked with the board and with my lawyer. Is it wrong I should ha' done so? The fleet must be kept runnin', and the quarries, the kilns, the town itself. Your way, I'd blow it all to hell for a few more dollars a month for seamen. I gave the boys three watches when the rest of the companies are still standin' six-and-six. The company grub, the wages and the quarters are as good as any on the Lakes. So for such you give me a hard ear? That lot coming up from the coast are deep-water men. You shouldn't be ashamed, but proud, to sail alongside them."

"Ah, the liar, the false-carder that ye are! How about the boys hurt in accidents? Where's there been any extra pay or insurance for them? Which one of us in your ships can be sure of his job from season to season? And where do the firemen and coal-passers aboard the *Daigvera* and the *Minna* sleep? Down in a goddamn' pair o' doghouses built on the after engine-room plates. Stacked like fish in a bin, no fresh air, no quiet, nothin' except the chance o' catchin' the consumption along with half a dozen other diseases. Out in England and Germany and Sweden the boys have unions now. And we'll have ours here. Ye wait and see, two-face."

"Phelim," Alan Kennard muttered, "think of Peg and the kids. Five of them you got and the whole lot growing fast. If you go along with the strike, they'll starve. I won't be able to help you, man. Keep your wits. Be sensible."

Carmody moved with deliberation. He picked up the ornate spittoon beside Kennard's desk and hurled it through the plate glass of the front office window. Then, as Kennard rested rigid, he took the desk weight and threw that through the glass panel of the door to the outer offices.

"Get up, swab," he said. "Outa yer chair and fight. What's the matter? You must have pride enough left to come at me with your mitts. Or is it you're scared to pull that gun from the drawer. . . ."

"You're a fool." Alan Kennard had put his hand on the revolver, gradually withdrew his fingers. You can't, he realized. Not against Phelim, not now nor ever. He's been too long your friend.

"Me." Phelim Carmody's white lipped mouth contorted. "Maybe I am. But an honest one. And you—here's a bit of a gift Peggy sent

you. 'Spit in the *audmadhaun's* face,' she said." Carmody leaned
forward and vigorously spit. "Fight, Antrim. On yer feet."

Alan Kennard sat very still, the trickle of spittle slow down his
shirt front. He no longer attempted to keep his regard upon
Carmody. There was much more to engage his thought. A crowd
of several hundred men and women were along Main Street before
the company building. Some of them had come up onto the lawn.
Those were seamen from the ships tied up in the river. The tougher
among them had taken Carmody's throwing of the spittoon as a
signal. The halyards on the flagstaff had been cast off the cleat,
the company flag lowered to the ground. They stamped on the flag,
tore it apart. But it wasn't enough for them. They were tearing
down the staff, too.

"Tell them," he said to Phelim Carmody, "that Pinkertons will
be in town tonight. If they don't stop, each one of them out there
will get a piece in prison."

Carmody didn't answer. He simply worked his lips in a silent
curse and walked towards the shattered door. The clerks, the sten-
ographers had run out of the building after Carmody had broken
the glass. The big main office was deserted except for Joshua Shaw
and the men of the local strike committee. "You heard him?"
Carmody asked Shaw.

"I did," Shaw said, "and I can't say I admire you too much for
it, Phelim. Violence isn't good."

"He'd bring in Pinkertons," Frank Oate said. "What would you
have us do, kiss his ass?"

"Not quite," Shaw said. "But let's not have any more rough stuff
for a while. Phelim failed with him, I know, and still he might listen
to me."

"Good time vasted," Nordstrom said. "Yust you hit him one on
his head."

Kennard gave Joshua Shaw a long, bleak glance as he halted
by the desk. "You're with them, hey?"

"You've known that right along. But you were supposed to be
along also."

"It got too rough for me in Cleveland."

"Who convinced you, Lothrop?"

Kennard's eyes held surprise. "Not him alone. The Association
promised to ruin me if I bucked them."

"You're ruined anyhow, Antrim. And you could have fought.
Look out there."

"At what? Me torn flag and smashed staff? They'll pay, the bastards!"

Joshua Shaw spread out his hands in the same sort of a motion he would make to a distracted child. "Take notice, Alan, that most of them aren't seamen. They're your quarry-men and kiln workers, and folks who don't even work for you. The town's against you solid, and for the strike. Go out and ask them."

"I'll stay here. I ain't no fool."

Shaw chose the words with care. He kept his eyes on Kennard's, made the other man meet his glance. "You'll wreck yourself and wreck the town, too. All I can do is warn you. But when you took over here, you came into possession of much more responsibility than you knew. It won't be easy to give it away. Nobody wants it but you, and you just can't get up and leave."

"You mean," Alan Kennard said blinking, "that you want to leave."

"I do. As of now, I'm through with the company and through with you. I have eight thousand shares of preferred, two thousand of common that you'll buy from me at par to settle my share of the business. Call in Keiberg from the bank and get me a certified check."

"Look, I ain't got any kind of money like that. You're talkin' about sixty-two thousand dollars."

"Sixty-four thousand, two hundred, to be exact. But get it up. If you don't, I'll put the stock on the open market. Some smart operator who got a hold of that with a couple of hundred other shares might take your voting control away from you."

"Good Jesus Christ," Kennard said, his voice agonized; "I thought you were a friend of mine."

"I was," Joshua Shaw said. "But I can remember what you did to my father and sister and me back some years ago. This is only what is known as unpoetical justice. But go ahead and get up the money. I'll get out the stock for you, and clean out my desk. I hope you can find a low-paid man to replace me, you cheap bastard."

Alan Kennard nearly flung up from the chair to strike at him. "What's the matter with you?" he asked in a frenzy of confused rage. "Why're you mixin' with that pack of rats? I thought all the fight had gone out of you years ago."

"So you bet wrong twice, once on the boys and again on me. I'll be at my desk when you have the check ready."

"All right," Kennard said. His face had a gray shade, and his hand shook as he turned the handle of the telephone.

There was time before Keiberg arrived for him to have a long drink from the bottle he kept in the desk. It brought him back an appearance of calm, but he was thick tongued as he explained the matter to Keiberg, carried the check to Joshua Shaw in the next office. "No hard feelin's," he mumbled when he had counted the stock certificates and Shaw had the check. "Might as well us end as friends."

"Surely," Shaw said. He put the check in his wallet. "But this is going into the general strike fund. I hope the boys beat you ragged. Tell Minna for me she married a jackass."

"You son of a bitch!" Kennard shouted. Shaw had already gone, though, and as he crossed the lawn the people there clapped and cheered for him.

Alan Kennard went back and had another drink from the bottle. You'll be stewed soon, he thought. Knock off. He was staggering when he opened the company safe and put in the stock certificates that had been Shaw's. Get home. You shouldn't hang around here like this. No work today, anyhow. Need some sleep. And tonight, when Pinkertons are in town . . .

He left by the side door, but the crowd saw him and Elmar wasn't there to meet him. The crowd cried curses, and three or four bricks, a couple of beer bottles and rotten apples were thrown. But older men among the seamen kept them back, and he was able to go along Main Street all right and up the hill to his house.

The only peculiar thing was that very few people spoke to him, and even those who did seemed nervous and ashamed. God-damn' fools, he thought. Don't they know I'm doing it for their best interest? Should thank me, not look at me cock-eyed.

Mark and Stacey were playing ball on their usual spot on the lawn. They stopped when they saw him coming along the drive. Neither one called in greeting, or moved. "Hey, you fellas!" he said. Then they whirled and ran around to the back of the house.

Minna met him in the front hall, unhesitatingly kissed him. He gripped her by the elbows. "Something's pretty fishy," he told her. "Seen the boys out on the lawn and they ducked me. You know why?"

"Yes," she said. "I sent Elmar down to pick you up about an hour ago. The strikers caught up to him on Main Street. They ran the Maxwell in the river and stripped the uniform off him, chased him home in his drawers."

"Jes-us Christ!" Kennard leaned back against the cool wood of the staircase banister. "So they did, huh? Well, Phelim's gone, and Josh Shaw is gone. My boys don't care to talk to me and my car's in the river. How about you?"

Minna brushed her lips across his forehead. "I'm your wife," she said. "I'll always love you."

CHAPTER TWELVE

"This is the town team," Mark said in the dark. "They want me to play with them."

"Gee whiz," Stacey said. "That's dandy. But the same position?"

"Sure." Mark pulled his pillow higher and turned so that he faced his brother in the opposite bed. "Gyp talked to me down-street today. Marv Mehaffey has gone to take a job at Studebaker. So they need a first baseman bad, and Gyp says I'm the guy."

"Whillickers!" Stacey said, deeply impressed and also jealous. "Will you wear a suit and everything?"

"Why not? Luke Pares might be the coach, but he's an old drunk and Gyp really runs the team."

"Well, he's captain of high school. He should."

"Like hell. How d' you figure that? A bunch of older fellas play for town. Guys like Sam Greer and Hollis Berger and—"

"I know, I know," Stacey said impatiently. "I've gone to every darn game, haven't I?"

"'Cept when you're out sailing."

"Look. I only sail the dink after school in the week. And I can't help it if the Old Man makes me take trips in the summer."

"You're a lot of gas. You love that. What the Old Man makes you do is no excuse, either."

"Aw, come on!"

"No, sir, I mean it. Down-street, Gyp told me that if it wasn't for the Old Man and the strike they'd ha' asked me to play for town last year."

"He was giving you the bull. They don't hate the Old Man that much."

"You'll find out. Don't you get the idea that folks around here have forgot why the Shaws and the Carmodys and the Oates and all of them left town. And Cap' Oate's wife killed herself, she threw herself out of a window over to Port Huron."

"The Old Man sent her a check." Stacey sat upright, and his

voice was tense. "I asked him out aboard the *Minna* and he told me so."

"But she sent it back. She wouldn't take it. Cap' Oate had to go working as deckhand on a car ferry. What's the matter with you, though? You sore that you weren't asked to play for town?"

"Could be," Stacey said in a burst of complete honesty. "If you can get on the team, I guess I can."

"What a kid!" Mark said. "Listen, stupid, I'm four years older than you."

"So you're pretty smart, hey, Mister Sixteen? Maybe you'd care to get out of bed and try a little hand wrassling. I'll flip you right on your butt!"

"I didn't say anything like that. You're a real good ballplayer, and big and husky for your age."

"Got a better peg than you any day."

"Ah, shut up. You make me tired. You're tryin' to get around to asking me to ask Gyp can you come out for the team. Hell, Stace, you're still in grammar school."

"Anyhow, I could shag flies. Gyp and them could see the way I can peg in to the plate."

Mark was lowering his pillow, preparing for sleep. "All right, for gosh sakes. I'll talk to Gyp, maybe Luke Pares, too. Let's us get some sleep."

"You mind if I ask one more question, Mark?"

"Go ahead."

"You still sore at the Old Man about the strike?"

"He sure caused a bunch of people trouble."

"Me, I feel the same. You oughta see the fellas out aboard the boats when he's not lookin'. They hate him."

Mark stretched out his hand and took Stacey's hand. "Yeah. Lars Keiberg is the only man in town who's got any use for him, and that's just because they make money together."

"Mark, what d' you think Ma thinks?"

"Be quiet! Get to sleep!" There was a rough edge about the words. "Ma doesn't tell anybody anything any more."

.   .   .   .

Alan Kennard had read the *Napta City News* while at the office Saturday morning. When he came home for lunch he was decided. "Mark's playing first base for the town. They're up against Hamatack today. We should go see them play."

"I meant for you to know," Minna said slowly, looking at him down the length of the dining room table. "Both the boys ate early and hopped off."

"Stace going to play, too?"

"Mark didn't seem to think so. Stace is pretty young yet for such-a-matter."

"He's center field at grammar school. He could do it if they gave him a chance. But I didn't reckon Mark was that good."

"The game's at two o'clock," Minna said. She rang for the maid to begin to clear the table, then stood from her chair. "We can take the street car over with all the gang that's going."

"Street car be damned," Kennard said. He glared at his wife. "We got the new Packard, ain't we? George will drive us."

Minna nodded from the doorway. There was no good, she warned herself, in contesting her husband's decisions these days. The gulf between them was already too wide. . . .

George had been chauffeur for wealthy families in New York and Chicago, and Alan Kennard considered that he was lucky to have got him after Elmar. The Packard gleamed as George brought it around under the porte-cochere. He leaped out and saluted, helped Minna in and asked stiffly, "Where to, sir?"

"The ball park at Hamatack," Kennard said. "Follow the car tracks to the right after you get out of Napta City."

Minna sat quite still, the soft rush of spring air pressing her veil against her face. Beside her Kennard rested with his arms crossed, his Panama hat clamped down, a panatella between his teeth. She thought, he looks very important, terribly certain of himself. But he isn't. He's alone. He's all by himself and he can blame nobody for it except himself. You've tried to help and hang onto him, make him see that he was wrong. He's not the kind to listen, though, and if he ever finds out, it will be his own way. Like right now, instead of taking the Packard we should have gone on the street car with the other folks. That way, we'd be doing what the boys have done, show that we still belong to the town, aren't stuck up because the strike was lost and so many people were pushed out of their jobs.

"Why you so quiet?" Kennard suddenly asked her.

"I was thinking."

"You're always thinking. You must ha' got another letter from Enid Shaw."

She lifted her veil so that he might stare fully into her eyes. "Yes, I did," she said. "They're very happy there in England. The children are away at school, and so she has plenty of time for her sculpture. Josh has become quite a water colorist, she says."

"About all he's good for," Alan Kennard said. "That fella was whipped the day the house at Bellport burned down."

Minna locked her hands, although they sweated inside her gloves. She had the keen desire to tell the red faced, glowering man at her side that he was wrong. But that would do no good, now or later. She sat quietly, gazing through the folds of the veil at the countryside. Once, she remembered, this had all seemed beautiful to her, and she had believed that she was very happy.

Past Napta City, they swerved around a street car packed with ball fans. Men and boys stood on the steps and constantly rang the bell, hooted, yelled, waved their hands and hats. "Hamatack rooters," Alan Kennard said. "They don't give Patigowoc a chance. They'll find out."

"Excuse me, sir," George said. He was slowing down. "That man up ahead is in trouble. Shall I help him?"

"Sure," Kennard said. "It's Luke Pares in his old rattletrap. If you can't get it to run, give him a tow. My Christ, he's got the whole Patigowoc team aboard."

Luke Pares' Stanley steamer had been severely treated by a number of owners. It was canted over in the ditch, a cloud of vapor eddying over it, the Patigowoc team around it in anxious consultation. George sounded the Packard's horn and stopped beyond. He appeared very efficient in his dove gray uniform, black puttees and gauntlets as he went back and spoke to Luke Pares. But Pares and the others laughed at him. "Couldn't fix it," Pares said, "if you was the finest mechanic in the state, which you ain't. Go climb in your bandbox and take to hell outa here."

"So he'll carry my boys and still talk like that," Alan Kennard said. He slung his cigar into the ditch and jumped from the Packard.

"Alan," Minna said, "please don't make trouble."

He grinned. "Fooled you," he said. "Nothing like it. . . ." He had opened the tool box, took out the coiled tow rope. "Haul the bastard in, that's what I'm going to do. Wouldn't have that bunch ride with me, but so long as Mark and Stace are with 'em, can't let 'em stay here."

He secured the tow rope to the rear axle, led it to the steamer. "Make fast, Stace," he said. He gave the end of the rope to his son. "Less talk out of you, Pares, and more driving. We'll pull you in.

Start the Packard when I give you the signal, George, then let me get aboard."

"Goddamn me if I know I want your tow rope," Luke Pares said. He was lanky, with a long face and thin, red nose. He stood straight, his hands at his sides, his jaw outthrust. "I ain't one to be owing to you."

"Cut out the bull," Gyp Lostiano said. He was the team captain, dressed in a neat blue and white baseball suit, his glove buttoned to his belt. "We can't hang around all day. Take the tow, Luke. The Captain's doing us a favor."

"No favor ta me," Pares said. But he clambered behind the steering wheel of the steamer and the group swung up onto the seats, the fenders, the running boards and the caved in top. George had gone to the Packard and at Kennard's signal began to tow.

"All right, Cap'," Stacey called excitedly from the steamer. "You get in now. We're doin' fine."

Mark hit him a quick blow across the shin and made him gulp with pain. "Keep quiet," Mark said. "You have to talk foolish, too?"

The Hamatack team was strong, composed mainly of grown men. By the end of the sixth inning, they were ahead ten to one. But their pitcher had become a father the night before, and while his side was at bat he passed out cigars and went behind the bleachers for a drink.

He started to lose his control in the seventh inning, walked two men and then allowed another pair to make hits and bring in a run. The Hamatack manager went on the field and spoke with him, and the pitcher nodded vigorously, rubbed slippery elm across the ball. Mark was the next batter and each time before he had struck Mark out. "Ain't nothing to it," he told the manager. "Strike out the kid and then I'll get the side."

Mark stood nervously at the wooden board that served as the plate. This guy had more speed than he was used to and a drop that just about fell from your shoulders to your knees. Still, he had to make a hit. The fellas before him had, and he could. With two on yet and none down, this might be a big rally.

The first ball was very low and very fast, yet he swung at it. Luke Pares and the others on the Patigowoc bench groaned; the Hamatack pitcher grinned at him. "Gonna bean ya now, boy," he called to Mark. "Watch out, duck!"

That ball was head high. Mark struck at it with all his strength. The shock passed violently through his hands and he knew that he had hit low on the handle of the bat. But the ball was going to be fair, a high, looping fly out into short center field. Run, you dummy.

He ran wildly for first while the Hamatack second baseman and shortstop both maneuvered to field the ball. They cried out in unison, "Mine, mine! All mine!" Then they collided head-to-head, tripped and sprawled, the ball between them on the grass.

Mark saw a Patigowoc runner cross the plate, and another. He touched up on first base, kept on to second when the Hamatack shortstop picked up the ball and overthrew the plate by a yard. Mark took time to look at the crowd. His mother had her veil back and she was smiling. His father yelled as loud as any of the Patigowoc fans and he pounded George so hard on the back that George lost his cap. Ingë Keiberg was in the bleachers with some of the girls in her class at high school, and she yelled, too, held up her hands to him, the palms and fingers together. Stacey had been on the end of the Patigowoc bench, had rolled off and was twitching with laughter on the ground.

Stace was all right, Mark thought, a darn good kid. You'll never have another brother like him. Don't forget the Old Man or Ma, either. They came out to see you play. Come on now. We got to win this game. . . .

The Hamatack pitcher went out at the end of the eighth inning. But Patigowoc had tied the score by then, and the man who replaced him, the regular left fielder, immediately got into trouble. Gyp Lostiano put a line drive triple into the trees at the boundary of the field, stole home on a wild pitch. The next two men struck out, and on the Patigowoc bench Luke Pares said, "All you fellas have t' do is hold 'em. We got the game."

Mark was emboldened by the run he had scored. "How about my brother, Luke?" he said. "Give him a chance."

"Him?" Pares said. "With us only one run ahead? I ain't crazy."

"Go on, Luke," Gyp Lostiano said. "I've seen the kid field and he's good. He got a better peg than Mark. And he don't need to come to bat. Put him out in right."

Luke Pares frowned at Stacey, taut with eagerness behind Mark. "Drop a fly on me and I'll kill ya," he said. "I'm only doin' this because your brother ast me. Get out there in right. Play deep."

"Yes, sir. Thanks, Luke," Stacey said, and wheeled on the full run for right field.

The first two outs in the last half of the ninth inning were made by the infield. Mark strained to make sure of his catches at first base. He was worried about Stacey. The kid was pretty small to be out there. Shucks, all the Hamatacks needed now was one dropped ball. Then they'd get into a rally and take away the game.

He stepped back of the bag and onto the grass when the third Hamatack batter came to the plate. Cover deep. It's their captain and he hits lefty, always hooks to right field. Nail it before it gets to Stace. Gosh, you were wrong to ask Luke to let Stace play.

The Hamatack captain hit the second pitch a bit below the waist. He drove it veering right down the first base line. Mark went for it and it took a violent hop off his glove hand, was past him far out into the field. While the Hamatack captain thudded on around first, Marked turned and bawled, "Hey, Stace!"

Stacey played in a pair of khaki trousers unbuckled at the knees. They flapped and his bare feet flashed as he chased the ball. It bounced erratically, and he juggled it, clung to it, then poised and threw to Mark.

Mark was more than twenty feet into the outfield. He took the throw at his shoulder and revolved towards third base. The Hamatack captain was going down to third, stretching it all he could. Mark panted. That was a long peg. But Gyp was covering third. Sure as hell, if he made the throw, Gyp would tag the guy.

He brought the ball back in a snapping motion, set his feet, stiffened his knees and threw. The ball licked in a yellow-white streak. Gyp Lostiano got it. He held it firmly in his glove as he tagged the runner and the umpire cried, "Yer out!"

Alan Kennard felt limp, unable to move or speak. But when he glanced aside he noticed the glint of tears under his wife's veil. He gripped her around the shoulder, strength, confidence abruptly restored to him. "Some pair of lads," he said. "Look, Minna."

"I am," she said, and now she was smiling.

The Patigowoc team carried Mark and Stacey on their shoulders. They hurled Stacey up into the air, let him almost touch the ground, then tossed him again. Luke Pares danced out in front, and took the team over to the Packard. "Shake hands, Cap'," he said. "I'm sorry I was a dumb-head before."

"To hell," Alan Kennard said hoarsely. "Us folks in Patigowoc are all friends."

Those words returned to him during the evening when he sat alone in the study and had a drink from his private bottle. He was lucky, he knew. Mark and Stacey had done it for him, pulled him

back into the town. But wasn't that Mark smart, though? Getting
Stace to play, making the gamble that Stace could play just right.
Time you pushed off Mark on his way out of here. Send him East
to school, to the fanciest one you can find. Yeah, and send him to
college, the same kind of place, Yale, Williams, Princeton, Harvard.
He'll be the kind of fella like Lothrop, take over the business end
of the lashup for you. Stace, though, you hang onto Stace. He's
your sailor in the family. Stace will go ahead with the ships where
you let off.

Alan Kennard put the bottle in the wall closet and climbed
the stairs to his boys' room. The door was shut and through it he
could hear them and they were talking about the game. He waited
for an instant, oddly unwilling to break their conversation. But
then he opened the door and said, "Hey, you fellas" and entered
the room.

"We're all right," Mark answered. "We were just shooting the
bull a little before we went to sleep."

"What I heard outside ain't bull," Kennard said. "Mark, how'd
you like to go Down East to school, some big place where they got
a jim dandy ball team?"

"Well, I'm not sure," Mark said. He turned over on his side to
glance at Stacey, but Stacey's face was averted from him. You'd
like to go, he thought. Down East is where they play the real ball
and have the good coaches. Today was all right, still what the
fellows felt isn't going to last. They've got no use for the Old Man.
Which means when you come right down to it, you and Stace, too.
"If I went, then—"

"Hell's bells," Kennard said flushing. "One of you has got to
stay home. Think of your Ma. Don't you up and ask me, Mark, to
have Stacey go along with you."

Stacey had swung around to gaze at Mark. "I don't want to go,"
he said. "But you should. You're the real ball player."

"Hear your brother?" Kennard said. "He'll stay home. He's
bound to be a sailor."

"That's right," Stacey said, his eyes still on Mark. His voice
was calm, contained no bitterness or jealousy. "I like steamboatin'
good. A lot better than ball."

"O.K., then, Pop." Beneath the level of the beds, Mark reached
out and quickly touched Stacey's hand. "Thanks a lot. It'll be just
great."

Alan Kennard kissed them both, briefly but with open affection.

He recognized only when he was out in the hall and on the way downstairs that he had said nothing to Minna yet about his decision. Ah, she won't mind, he told himself. She's your woman, and what you say, she'll take.

He hummed a few bars of "The Swallowtail Coat" as he came to the doorway of the bedroom he and Minna shared and saw her at her dressing table. She held a comb in her hand, was busy with her hair, but had caught his reflection in the mirror. "I'm glad about today," she said.

"Me, too," he said. He stooped and put his lips gently against her cheek.

Book Three

1915

CHAPTER THIRTEEN

You felt the loneliness worst, Minna thought, when you came here into their room. It hadn't been changed much, and when they were home together they still used it, slept in the same narrow, iron-frame beds, though they were both really grown men, Stacey as well as Mark.

Minna sat down on the edge of Stacey's bed. How long, long ago, Stace down with the whooping cough and Mark just over the mumps. Then Stace got the mumps, too, and was a very sick boy. You can't quite remember the year, not that it matters any more. But Stace is close; you can reach him handily. This new boat he's aboard is the *James K. Oliver*. Second mate of her, too, and you're proud. Any man who can ship second mate with Phelim at Stace's age is a real good sailor. Maybe the Old Man's not happy that Stace has gone to work in the Harkness Line, but you don't care. It all goes back to the '04 strike and what happened then. If Stace wants to work outside the Kennard Company, let him, I say. The Old Man has had his way plenty and enough. More than once back in the strike he nearly broke your heart. The boys haven't forgotten. You can't.

Minna, what kind of talk is this? You're a lucky woman. There's a great deal to make you happy. You have your two fine boys. The Old Man. This house.

This house. . . . Don't lie. You and the Old Man rattle around in it like a couple of peas in a dried pod. You should have given it up years ago, when Mark started going Down East to school. Because you weren't happy afterwards, and Stacey wasn't, nor the Old Man. And Katrine's gone. Olga, too, along with Cook, Harry, Elmar, George, my golly, how many of them. These girls you've got aren't like the old ones, all Polish, using their own language between them in the kitchen and just waiting for a job in a war factory before they up and leave.

She spread her hands out beside her on the worn coverlet. It was a warm and exceptionally quiet June day. A wasp rasped at the window screen which Stacey had punctured years ago with a shoe he had thrown at Mark and which she had repaired herself rather than tell her husband. The mower clacked over the lawn past the porte-cochere and on the rear porch one of the maids gutturally laughed.

No sound inside, she thought. Sixteen rooms full of silence. She got up from the bed and went to the window, but the wasp had flown away. The silence seemed to close in upon her like an unseen and immense wall. She needed conscious effort of the will to stand and read the titles of the books her sons had left, then regard in the corner an old hockey stick of Mark's, the handle tape loose and peeling, behind it Stacey's favorite fishing rod. The reel on the rod was flecked with rust. You should have it cleaned. Better, clean it yourself. What else have you got to do? But maybe Stacey would be angry. It's his rod and he left it there.

She walked across the room to what had always been known as "Mark's side." Photographs he had brought home from Andover when he had graduated were hung over his chest of drawers. One was of the sixth form, white pants, double-breasted blue coats, Mark with his hair parted in the middle and scowling. Mark, Mark. You'll be home soon, dear. The picture next to it was of the baseball team, and Mark, a big A on his sweater, was in the middle because he was captain.

Captain of Andover and varsity at Princeton this year. Your son. But, why did you do it? She meant her husband. Sending Mark to school Down East chopped our life all to pieces. Mark's friends aren't ours any more, nor Stacey's either, come to that. They're nearly the whole lot Easterners, talk different, act different, dress different and don't give a good, simple damn for our kind. Alan Kennard, you're the strangest ever, and sometimes, I declare, I'm not sure if I still love you.

The memories were bitter; she had no desire to arouse them. Yet they occupied her mind. She recalled poignantly her husband's efforts to take her and himself into life beyond Patigowoc. They had rented for a summer a cottage at Lake Geneva, and they had been snubbed over and over. She had pointed out to him in a fury of revulsion one evening that the people with whom he wished to associate disliked his speech and practically everything else about him. But he had persisted the next summer in taking a place at Lac La Belle. There, through business connections he had in Milwaukee, he arranged it so that they were invited to a number of parties. But at the fourth one he happened to hear his hostess referring to him as "the Squaw Man."

After that, he was content to go on trips to Detroit and Cleveland and Chicago and New York. His life became very solitary, and
his single relaxation was to relieve the captains of his vessels, sail
in their stead while they were on vacation. But when Mark came
into prominence at Andover, he had told her, "We got to go down,
Minna. We got to see the lad play in the Exeter game."

They had gone, and for both of them it had been a painful,
nervously exhausting experience. He had bought a suit at a Fifth
Avenue tailor's in New York for the occasion, did his best to im-
prove his grammar. But she sensed at once that Mark was embarrassed by their presence, and when the game was finished,
without waiting for supper with Mark, they took the train for
Boston and home.

Princeton now, she thought. Mark's sure to ask us down for
the Yale game. He must, if only because he loves us. But you don't
want to go; the Old Man doesn't want to. We're smalltowners.
Patigowoc is just about our speed. And, come to you, you're content to stay here. You've been head of Ladies' Aid and Mission
Society, run the church bazaar more times than not. Since Peg Carmody left, you haven't had a real close woman friend. Sure, you see
a good deal of Brigitte Keiberg, but that's on account of Mark is
sweet on Ingë. Just imagine, that measly little stick of a woman
with spunk enough to get Keiberg to put up money for his daughter to go Down East to school. Pride. Lars Keiberg must have the
same kind of pride as the Old Man—what the Kennards can do,
well, by golly, the Keibergs can, too. Foolish. Because what's Ingë
going to do when she comes back here all full of that fancy education?

Down along the shore road, through the hush of the heat-heavy
day, Minna Kennard heard the sudden sputter and rattle. The mail-
man, she told herself. Rick Skodoska on his Harley-Davidson. What
a lot of noise. They should make him get a better machine. But
that lets you know he's coming, and the town's so big, they're talking about next year having three-four fellas do the work. Hurry
down, though. There might just be a letter from Mark.

Rick Skodoska stopped only long enough to wink at the maid
and hand her the mail, then sent the motorcycle down the driveway in a slash of gravel. "Here, Ma'am," the maid said; "the Chicago
papers and a letter from Mister Mark."

"Thank you," Minna Kennard said, keeping her temper. She
put the papers down on an arm of a porch chair, sat and read the

letter in Mark's graceful, neat script. It began, "Dear Mother." How many years, she wondered, had he called her "Ma"? But her attention had been caught by the lines below; her breath rose short in her throat and her knees trembled, her hands shaking so that the words blurred.

"Dear Mother,

"When you receive this, I will be on my way to France. A bunch of my chums and classmates have decided, as I have, that we can't stand by any longer and see Europe taken by the Huns. We have signed up for ambulance service with the French Army, and some of the boys are even asking their parents to help contribute for ambulances. Don't worry. I'm not asking that of Dad and you, although if Dad could see his way clear to send a couple hundred simoleons to the International Red Cross, it would be bully. Please —please, Mother—don't worry about me. I've been thinking about this for a long time, and I know it's the right choice. The damn Prussians have to be stopped or else civilization will end.

"Last weekend, I saw Ingë in New York. We had dinner and went to the theater together, then talked over the whole situation. She agrees with me perfectly. She says she'd go, too, in a minute if she wasn't a girl. Of course, a man on his way to war can't demand too much, but Ingë and I came to an understanding over the weekend and we're engaged. I got her a ring, and if the bill comes in from Tiffany's, don't be surprised.

"Tell Dad for me that it isn't costing me anything to be sent out. People in New York—no names, please—arranged everything. My stuff from school will be home soon, freight and parcel post. I'm sorry I couldn't finish out the year and that you and Dad missed seeing me play the Yale game. But I'm in a much bigger game, and am I proud to have been asked to play!

"I haven't much more time now, as the folks who are sending us out are giving us a small farewell party. But I want you to know that I love you very much, and Dad, too, and, of course, old Stace. Remember that Ingë is to be your daughter-in-law. I'll write you and give you my address as soon as we arrive in Paris. President Wilson and the 'peace at any price' fellows keep me from doing it now.

"*Vive la France!*

"Your son,

"Mark"

She was still slumped in the porch chair when Alan Kennard came home for what in recent years they had accustomed themselves to speak of as luncheon. "Here," she said tight-voiced, and gave him the letter.

While she had waited for him, two thoughts had held her. The first was the cause of immense relief: Stacey was safe, couldn't follow Mark. Back in '13, the year he was a senior in high, Stacey had torn a knee ligament in a football game. That would keep him out of any war, safe, safe, safe. . . . The second was for her husband. The Old Man might be very angry and hurt that Mark's letter had been sent to her, not him. But if he feels hurt, you won't care a lot. He's done the same to a lot of people in his time.

She had attempted then to think of Mark, Mark in uniform, wearing a helmet, driving an ambulance through the dark, shells bursting around him, rockets across the sky and bullets everywhere. But her mind had refused the thought. It was too terrible for her comprehension, and she withdrew from it.

Alan Kennard read the letter standing before her on the porch. Red mottled his face. His neck distended and he breathed fast. "By God!" he said, crumpling the letter into a pocket. "My son, yours, Minna! Ain't he done fine!"

"No," she said; a rigor of hatred was in her body. "He hasn't. Mark has no part in that war."

"What the hell d' you mean?"

She abruptly wept, her head down, the tears splashing her dress. "Let me be," she said. "I just want my boy."

"A woman for you." Kennard beat his hands hard against his sides, strode the porch and wheeled back to her. "I'd go to Canada tomorrow and enlist if I reckoned they'd take an old fella like me. The bloody Huns got to be stopped. Don't forget I come from over there. Don't forget they've raised a regiment right around the place I was born. They'll whip them sauerkraut bastards, drive 'em back across the Rhine quick as not. Come on. Get a'holt of yourself. Mark's done a damn' good thing. You wait and see. He'll end up a captain or a major, with medals. I know Mark."

"You fool," she said over the hiccuping gasp of her sobs. "Won't you ever understand?"

He glared at her and stooped forward. "What?"

"If you hadn't sent Mark Down East to school he wouldn't ha' gone to war. That's for Easterners, not for us. Who else around here has enlisted in a foreign army to get all shot to bits?"

"Ah, you talk like them sauerkrauts in Milwaukee. Sure, it's our war. You should be proud. Mark's a hero. But come to the table, woman. I'm hungry and I want to get back down to the company. I'll send the Red Cross a check right today. I have an idea, too, of who the fellas are in New York who shipped Mark out. They'll let me have the lad's address over there to France. He'll lack for nothin', not Alan Kennard's boy."

"Go eat," she said. The maid was at the door and staring. "I'm not hungry."

"Very well," he said. He stamped on into the house. She heard him in the study: the jangle of keys as he opened the liquor cabinet, the clink of the whiskey decanter stopper. Then he started to sing "Tipperary." But he knew only part of the words, went from it to "Gerry Owen."

She smiled as the tears still rolled her cheeks. Stacey was hers anyway. She could keep him from that cocky, muddle-headed man in there. When Kennard went into the dining room and sat noisily eating and talking with the maid, she rose from the chair and climbed the stairs to the bedroom.

The impulse was strong upon her. She lowered herself to her knees beside the big double bed and prayed. "Dear God," she ended, "please bring my son home to me." She got deep comfort from the prayer, and as she wrote the telegram to Stacey she was calm. She waited, though, until Alan Kennard had left the house before she called Western Union. There was a bond between Stacey and his father, she knew, that she hadn't succeeded in breaking yet. Let him hear from Stacey about the telegram. . . .

.   .   .   .

Sandusky Sam, the deckhand on the twelve-to-six, the young Italian coal-passer and the oiler on the same watch and Fancy Pants Stevens, the steward, were waiting by the ladder down into the hold. They had the bat and ball and a couple of mitts. "How about it, Stace?" Sandusky said as Stacey came down off the bridge. "Play a little ball before we put into Deposit?"

"Guess I might," Stacey said. He looked down into the huge hold of the ore-carrier. She was upward-bound and light, and yesterday the deckhands and deck-watches had swept and washed it down. It was a good place to play ball when the light was high like this.

Sandusky had a pretty fair arm, so did the coal-passer. Fancy

Pants wasn't much, or the oiler, but the ball was old and battered, so soft a man could dig his fingers into the cover and anybody could throw a curve. They threw the ball around a while and then chose sides and started a game of one o' cat.

The light was clear except over in the wings where shadow stretched. The strong-backs put bars of shadow out in the middle of the hold, too, and occasionally a gull flew across the sun. But when Stacey came to bat he took the first pitch. He hit it hard, and Fancy Pants, who was pitching, ducked down to save himself.

Stacey lost sight of the ball. It was high, he realized as he ran. Then he saw the flash of flight. The ball had gone the full four hundred-foot length of the hold. It struck right up against the forward coaming and bounced, showed clear in the upper sunlight and was gone.

Sandusky scrambled fast up the ladder to deck. They could hear his thick soled shoes banging over the deck plates towards the starboard side. "She's a goner," he shouted down; "an' she's our last one. You sure knocked her, Stace."

"Yeah," Stacey said. "I sure did."

He went to the bridge after he left the hold. A rind of fog was upon the water; the Northern shore of Huron was hidden behind it and the sun had dissolved into a lemon-green blur. Phelim Carmody came out of the pilot-house, one hand inside his shirt to scratch his belly, his carpet slippers flatly slapping. "Better stand by aft, Stace," he said. "I'm goin' on in."

"All right, Cap'." Stacey squinted. "But I can't even see that goddamn' dock."

Phelim grunted and spit snuff juice into the windless air. "Come into Deposit with a sack over my head. So can the Old Man. You'll learn. Get on aft."

They had the wires down and were taking the coal aboard when the dock boss shouted up out of the fog. "You got a Kennard aboard?"

"Second mate," Sandusky shouted back importantly. "He's right here."

"Telegram for ya," the dock boss said above the rumbling crash of the coal. "Bring it aboard?"

"Be obliged," Stacey said.

Max Karig, the deck-watchman, and Sandusky peered curiously at him as he opened the telegram. "Anythin' wrong, Stace?" Karig said.

"Nope," Stacey said. But he turned aside from them and stood alone. His emotion was vast, and yet not defined. Mark in the French Army, he thought. The son of a gun off to the war. Ma isn't happy, though. She doesn't like it and she said as much. Mark must have just up and joined without letting her and the Old Man know first. Ingë, she was in on it. I'll bet on that. Else, he wouldn't go. They're in love bad. Poor Ma. She must be real worried, and the Old Man wouldn't be any help to her. Bet he's prouder than proud.

"Hey, Stace!" Phelim Carmody boomed from the bridge. "Cast off yer wires, then stand by the hook. I'm bound on up."

The ship was wrapped in fog. Stacey could barely make out the pilot-house as he walked forward. No reason, he told himself, for Phelim's going on up. We could stay at the dock until this clears. But Phelim is like the Old Man; they sail in weather that would scare the liver out of any other man.

Along the reaches above Deposit, the fog moved and shifted, swirled with the very slight currents of land breeze. It clung close against the skin, though, and only down against the shipside was the water visible, a thin, brassy strip that led to the little white ruck the bow wash made. The rest was the fog: ahead and astern, port and starboard and overhead, a gray that was like the inside of a clam shell that had just been opened.

Max Karig stood on lookout about eight feet past Stacey at the anchor windlass. He wore a blue and green checked shirt and the bow apron was painted white. Still to Stacey he was a wraith that smelled of Beechnut chewing tobacco, red lead and Albany grease. Stacey coiled again with care the sounding lead line he held. Seven, eight, no, nine boats were astern of them, also bound for the Soo. They tagged after Phelim, knew him for what he was and let him pilot them. In a shake now, Phelim would be calling down for a cast.

"Let 'er go, Stace!"

"Let 'er go, sir!" Stacey took the wooden toggle between the second and third fingers of his right hand. He swept the sounding lead in a half circle, out, back, out back, then cast. The splash was dim, the line thrummed a bit as he gathered in slack over the wire side rail. The line was opposite him and there was strain on it. He had bottom.

He heaved in hand over hand, the spattering line loose-coiling at his feet. The two strips of leather were inboard, the toggle, the three strips of leather. Go slow. He was almost to his depth. He ran his right hand along the closely woven line. That was it. He turned aft to face Phelim unseen on the bridge. "By the deep, four!"

"Y' got mud fer bottom?"

He bent down to finger the tallow charge in the heel of the lead. "All mud! Must be in near to the bank."

"Very well. Now bend yer ear."

Phelim's trying for distance by echo, Stacey thought. Maybe he's got some idea where we are. I haven't. I got buggered up down off the last range. Mark in the French Army. Son of a gun. Get my glass knee fixed and I could join. Hang on, though. No time for such-a-matter. Give Phelim a hand with the distance.

The first and second and third blasts rent into the softness of the fog. The sounds went out wide. Then they narrowed, bent into vaguely crossing clashes of resonance. Astern, the other vessels were blowing. Phelim cursed; his slippered feet thumped the bridge.

He's at the speaking tube, Stacey thought. He has to talk to Stuffy Smith. Years ago, when they had sailed for his father, Phelim and Stuffy had worked out a bearing system for use in fog. The chief engineer stood directly below an engine-room ventilator. Sound came much clearer there than topside. Stuffy swung the ventilator around to meet the echo, read off the bearing on the cross pieces at the bottom of the shaft.

But Phelim shouted into the speaking tube, "You plough jockey bastard! That ain't nowheres near it. Yer wrong as hell." The speaking tube cover shut with a snap. "Walk out the port bower a bit, Stace. I'm about to drop her. Ain't a thing coming down. Must all be tied up at the Soo. But Lennert and them others are chasin' me hot and Stuffy's gafoozelemed. When I give you a holler, put three shots in the water."

There was a white dapple of moisture on the anchor windlass. When the steam came pounding, rattling through the pipes and he opened the petcocks the vapor was licked away at once by the fog. He locked in the windlass and released the brake a bit and took the devil's claw off the port chain. This is good work. Taken years to learn it. But Mark's out at the war. Damned if I shouldn't join him. Shoot a gun as good as Mark any day.

The rust-red chain links came steadily clanking up over the wild cat as he gave steam to the windlass. A couple more. All right, shut down. He shut down the steam and over his shoulder shouted, "Ready to lower."

Phelim Carmody was bellowing to the ship astern through the megaphone. "You got it, Lennert. Pull out an' pass, you want." The fog bounced and brandished his words and the words of Lennert's answer. "Dumb bugger!" Phelim told him, then, "Let go, Stace!"

Stacey gave the chain another short forward kick with the windlass and slacked off the brake.

The weight of the anchor seized the chain. It went running out over the wild cat in a showering leap of blue sparks. Rust from the links pecked Stacey's face. The first fifteen fathom marker whipped up, over the wild cat, down through the hawse pipe. Close the brake some. Slow the strain.

Max was back from lookout to watch him and give a hand. I don't need Max. I can do it myself. But if I send the fella back up to the bow he'll be sore. He'll tell the gang in the focsle that I've been pushing around like the Old Man's son. None of that crap. Let him stay.

Phelim Carmody had rung the engine room telegraph to *Stop*. The bell jingled and jingled back. Over it was the splatter, the splash, the running clangor of the chain. There's the second marker. The whole fore part of the vessel had begun to vibrate. Even when she's loaded she does this. Slow down some more. Pay out easy.

The third marker was coming up onto the wild cat. It went into the dark cavity of the hawse. Shut the brake. "Give me a hand, Max." They braced their feet on the slippery plates and swung straining at the locking wheel.

"We near Six Mile?" Max said.

"I don't know," Stacey said. "I don't think the skipper does. You keep on lookout. I'll chase Jericho down from the wheel so's you can go get your coffee."

The vessel had taken all her forward scope. The current and the anchor caught her, brought her back astern. Stacey stood on the bow apron with Max holding his knees and stared down into the water. The chain led well off. She rode fine. He told that to Phelim.

"Come up for yer coffee," Phelim said. "Them pig-jumpers has all gone to anchor, too."

Phelim sat in his specially built chair in the pilot-house with his feet on the window sill and his undershirt open so that he could scratch his belly. "You be sure to bring up the sugar bowl, sonny," he said to the deckhand. "Harkness ain't broke yet, nowheres near it. And tell the steward we want some pie. None of them dinky samples o' his, but pie. Bring some cheese along when you come."

"You'll have the kid thinking he's a waiter instead of a sailor," Stacey said as the deckhand went down the ladder.

"He ain't a sailor," Phelim said. "There ain't many around. You and me are among the few." Phelim eased himself in the chair and glanced at Stacey where Stacey leaned on the window sill staring out into the fog. "What's the news?"

"Mark's joined the French Army."

"No, fer Christ's lovely sake."

"Yeah." Stacey had bent down, was massaging his right knee. "Get an operation on this and I think I'll go join him."

"And break your Ma's heart wide. Stace, ain't the Old Man done enough to her?"

"I don't know what you mean."

"In a pig's furry. Sure and you do. Look. I'm your friend, even if I ain't no more the Old Man's. Your mother now, too, she's about as fine a woman as comes. But be damned to such talk. I'm from out there, too, and don't ye forget. So's Peg. Many's the night last winter Peg and me talked about me goin' back to bear a hand, whatever. No, though. No's the answer fer you and me alike. What are we doin' here but haulin' iron ore? Where's the great part of the ore goin'?"

"You sound like Bryan."

"Bryan be buggered! The ore goes into guns and the guns to the Allies. Let Mark go fight. Bejesus, now you can't stop him. Mark's no sailor, though. You are. So stick to sailin'. It's your job. Here, right here, you can serve best. And with the knee—"

"All right!" Stacey snapped, intense with emotion. "You've got me convinced. Slack off, Cap'."

"Very well," Phelim said softly. "Shake hands on it, then. And give a toot on the whistle for that deckhand. He must be eatin' out the galley on his own."

CHAPTER FOURTEEN

They found little to say to each other here in the stillness of the early evening. It was a hot, oppressive night with a waning moon and the tree toads busy. The Old Man, when they had come out on the porch from dinner, had taken off his coat, collar, tie and shirt. But Stacey kept on his shirt and tie; Ingë had telephoned during dinner to say she would be by in a bit. You're only home for a couple of days, he thought, and she may not see you again soon and she's got the idea you're a roughneck sailor.

His thought went from Ingë to his mother. She had gone up to bed half an hour ago, her face wan in the hall light. The war years had worn her down, Stacey realized, and now Mark's being wounded has added to that. The Old Man's not the kind to be of much help to her, not any more. When Ingë comes by, ask her. She'll know, because she and Ma have got to be real close.

"How long," Alan Kennard said abruptly, "is the *Oliver* goin' to be in drydock?"

"Two-three days. It's a main shaft bearing job and a propeller overhaul."

"You got to get back down to Detroit?"

"Not before she's ready to sail, no."

Kennard turned slightly in his chair. He studied his son unblinkingly. "When you going to give up sailing for Harkness and ship out with your own outfit?"

"After the war, I guess." Stacey's voice was flat, slow.

"Phelim Carmody must ha' put the high sign on you for fair."

"I still got plenty to learn and he's a man to teach me."

Kennard snorted. "Come to me, I'd send you out skipper of the *Minna* tomorrow. You're ready for master."

"Thanks, Pa. I'll wait for a while."

The stillness dropped between them then, and they spoke only to curse at a mosquito. When Ingë came up the driveway in her father's Buick they got up eagerly to greet her. She wore a light pongee dress and white slippers; her hair had been blown loose; she was smiling, seemed very gay. She kissed them both on the cheek. "Home is the sailor. Good to see you, Stace."

"Good to see you, Ingë. How you been?"

"Worried, frankly. But I got a letter from Mark today. The wound isn't too bad. He'll be all right. And he sent some photos, and his chief of section put through a whole big box of souvenirs. They're in the car. Would you get them?"

"Sure," Stacey said. But he went reluctantly to the Buick. Your brother is a hero, and no fooling. A medal, a wound, souvenirs, a girl like Ingë. You, you're chief mate of a rust-pot ore boat. Same old run every week. Christ, you've got so you know it in your sleep. No medals, sport, and no wounds. Girls—you know the whores in Buffalo and Duluth and Two Harbors and that's about all.

He carried the big box up onto the porch and his father said, "Bring it in the house, Stace. Better light and we'll get away from them goddamn' mosquitoes."

"How about Mother Kennard?" Ingë said. "Wouldn't she like to see all this?"

"Gone to bed," Alan Kennard said. "You show it to her tomorrow. Now you go ahead. Let's us hear the letter."

Ingë sat beside one of the fringed lamps in the drawing room to read the letter. The light shone on her brown hair and her flushed cheeks. Stacey watched her entranced. Skinny Ingë, that's what we used to call her. Some difference.

He lost the meaning of the letter after the passage where Mark explained that he suffered from shell fragmentation in the left shoulder and arm. Almost three years since Mark had been away. Ingë faithful to him the whole time, or so it looked, anyhow. Some fella, Mark. Always out in front of you.

The letter was finished and Ingë was passing around the photographs. Mark in a helmet and long overcoat, mud up to his knees. Mark in a peaked cap, his uniform all clean and wearing the medal. Mark and some other men and their ambulances. Mark in Paris with the Arch of Triumph in the background. Mark. . . . Aw, to hell with him. Stacey put the photographs in order and handed them to Ingë.

"Open up the box, Stace," she said. "The things in there he sent to you."

Stacey took out a Death's Head Hussar cap with the skull and bones insignia, a spiked leather helmet bearing the *Gott Mitt Uns* design, a *Gott Mitt Uns* belt, an officer's sword in a gold-scrolled scabbard, a rusted sawtooth bayonet, a handful of Iron Crosses.

"That's Mark all over," Alan Kennard said, his voice rough with pride. "Never misses a trick. Bet, on top of this, he could come home and give a better lecture than Guy Empey any day."

"The hell," Stacey muttered, but Ingë had heard him, and she laughed. "All I want," she said, "is to get him home. But he won't come. With us in the war now, I think he'll transfer to the American Army."

"Right over there," Alan Kennard said passionately. "Infantry. Mark's a fighter."

Ingë was returning the souvenirs to the box, her glance obliquely on Stacey. "Father Kennard," she said in the manner she had acquired at her Eastern school, "might I be so bold as to suggest we have a drink?"

"Well, by God!" Alan Kennard's eyes flashed. "Do your folks know you touch the evil stuff?"

"What they don't know," Ingë said, "will never hurt them. Right, Stace?"

"Sure," Stacey said. His father was walking past him into the study and to the liquor cabinet. He waited until he and Ingë were alone. "You must have some hot times down there at school."

"Not school," Ingë said. "But weekends in New York and New Haven. . . . Hard for a girl whose sweetheart is overseas."

"Must be." Stacey felt awkward with her glance steadily lifted to his, and in an odd, inexplicable way, angry. Ingë appeared to sense that. She stepped forward to him around the box and put her hands on his shoulders. "Stace," she said rapidly, "let me say that I understand. You're doing a bang-up job yourself and the men like Mark are getting all the glory."

"I don't care."

"Yes, you do, and you should."

"Army turned me down again last week. Navy won't even look at me."

"Stace, don't be a boob. You're really helping to win the war. I'm proud of you. Mark is."

"Cut it out!"

She shrugged, although the smile was still about her lips. "Go out in the Buick," she said, "and you'll see my music box on the rear seat. If you bring it in, we might have a dance."

"What is it," he asked, troubled, instinctively suspicious, "one of those gramophones?"

"Of course, silly. With some dandy records. We all have them down at school."

Alan Kennard had poured bourbon and water and they stood in the drawing room and solemnly drank to Mark. Then, his glass empty, he started towards the porch. "You two have your dance," he said. "Too goddamn' hot in here for me."

"Look," Stacey said when he and Ingë had danced twice around the room, "the Old Man's right. It's too damn' hot. And I'm no good at that kind of Eastern step."

"I think you're silly," Ingë said. "But never yet have I beaten a man over the head to get him to dance with me. Steal us another drink, and then maybe we could go out aboard your boat and have a swim?"

"My boat's in drydock in Detroit."

"Sap! I mean your sloop. The boat Father Kennard bought for you."

Stacey brushed sweat from his forehead. "You must miss Mark plenty," he said.

"Get us the drink," she said quietly. "Any more talk like that and I go home."

They said goodnight to Alan Kennard on the porch steps, then carried the gramophone, the records and a bathing suit that belonged to Ingë down to the dock at the edge of the lawn. The bathing suit had been tucked in a front pocket of the Buick, and Stacey hadn't been surprised when she produced it. This had all been planned, he told himself. He didn't know how it was going to end, but he knew what had begun it. Ingë missed the hell out of Mark. He was Mark's brother, talked and acted a little like him, was a better substitute than anybody else around. Watch out, sailor. You can get into a whole parcel of trouble tonight.

The red hulled Old Town canoe that the Old Man had bought for Mark and him while Mark was still in high school rested on a pair of sawhorses on the dock. Stacey ran his hand over the hull. It had been carefully sandpapered, repaired this season. He recognized the Old Man's work in the smoothness of the eye splice in the painter and out at her buoy in deep water the sloop gleamed under the moonlight.

"I haven't been down since I've been home," Stacey said. "The Old Man fix them up for you to use?"

"For you, Stace. Perhaps I'm a buttinski, but he misses you terribly. His greatest ambition, I guess, is to have you sailing for him in the company."

"You know why I'm not."

"Yes. Because you're foolishly proud. You haven't let yourself forget the strike."

"And, by God, I never will." He had hefted the canoe up from the sawhorses, careened it and dropped it into the water. "Take your slippers off before you get aboard. Don't want any holes poked through the bottom."

"Stace Kennard, I'm so peeved I could slap you! How many times have I been out in this thing?"

"Mostly you and Mark, not me. Mark's no sailor, neither are you."

He had gone down into the canoe after putting aboard the gramophone, the records and her bathing suit. She stood white faced on the dock, her slippers in her hand. "Don't try to take your unhappiness out on me," she said with violence. "It's not my fault that you can't get along with your own family."

"You'd better go back where you belong," he said. "I'm not the boob you think."

"Oh, oh, you!" she said and threw a slipper at him.

. He caught it laughing at her. "Miss New York," he said. "Don't they pitch any harder than that Down East?"

Her answer was to spring down into the canoe, squat on the bow thwart. He glared at her. "Out. On the dock. No more of your guff."

"Really?" She had seized the gunwales. "How would you like to be capsized? Push off or I'll do it."

"Guess you would, by God." He was forced to grin. "So let go the painter. That's the best way to start a capsizin'."

"You're a fool!"

"I heard you before."

"Stace, please, let's go out to the sloop. I didn't expect anything like this from you."

"Figured I was too dumb, you mean."

"It might be worth your while to know that Father Kennard can hear nearly every word we say."

"No skin off my neck. Let him figure what he likes. I'm my own man."

"I never," she said, "never!" Tears of frustrated rage were on her high cheekbones. "Stacey, I can't bear any more. Believe me. . . ."

"Hell," he said, made ashamed by her tears. He cast off the painter and thrust the canoe out from the dock. His paddle strokes gave undulant silver streaks to the black water astern. There was no sound from the house, none on the water except the paddle gurgle. He could clearly hear the treetoads and the thin whisper of a rising breeze through the willows. She sat without motion, her head down, her hands on the gunwales. This is wrong, he sensed again. He straightened and drove the canoe with a long stroke. "We'll have wind. You want to sail out past the light?"

"It doesn't matter," she said. "I just don't care."

But when he had the canoe alongside the sloop her mood changed. She leaped quickly onto the sloop's fore deck, helped him secure the canoe to the mooring and cast off the sloop. "Let's put up the sails fast," she said. "I'd adore going out into the lake."

"Wind's against us for that," he said. He was in the cockpit and had placed her possessions on the settee, was shaking out the mainsail. "But we'll get down to the point. Can you h'ist the jib?"

"Yes, sir." She gayly laughed as she spraddled the bowsprit. She worked out along it and loosened the stops, came back inboard and led the sheets through the fairleads. "Heave away." She had kicked her slippers up against the cabin housing before she had gone onto the bowsprit, padded aft with her stockinged feet firmly spread.

He hauled upon the jib and mainsail halyards and took them to the cleats and sheeted home the jib. The sloop heeled nicely as he put the tiller down; he sheeted the main and crouched on the after cockpit gunwale. She stood at his side watching the moonlight on the canvas, the irradiant bow wash and wake. "Fun," she said. "More fun than a barrel of monkeys. Stace, we shouldn't ever fight."

"Sure," he said. "But watch your records before they slide off onto the deck."

"You know," she said, "I think you're afraid of me. Each time I try to be nice to you, you pull away, say something mean."

"You're Mark's girl."

"Mark's in France, four thousand miles from us. He has plenty of French and British girls to keep him company. You should hear the stories I've heard. Any American ambulance driver on leave in Paris owns the place. Champagne parties day and night. Asked out to the best homes, and to the best beds."

"You talk rough."

"With reason. . . . French officers I've met in New York have told me they were just as jealous as could be of the Americans."

"Why didn't you give some of the Frenchies a whirl?"

"I have." She was blushing. She swung around to meet his gaze. "Not what you might think, though." The breeze had shaken her hair and hair pins rattled from it onto the cockpit floor. She pulled, let them all fall. "What I mean is, they kiss very nicely, and one, a captain, a Blue Devil officer——"

"Keep going. Tell me. I won't snitch to Mark."

"I could slap you! But that's all."

"Then these Frenchies, they didn't get into your pants."

"Are you for the rest of your life going to talk and act like a toughie sailor?"

"I'll never go East to college, and that's a cinch. Stand by the jib. I want to put her on the other tack."

"Why?" she said. "Why not sail back? All you do is fight with me."

"Aw—"

"Don't say 'Aw hell!' If I have to listen to it once more, I'll scream."

"Really?" he said in imitation of her manner. He headed the sloop into the wind, then let the sheets and halyards run, went forward and dropped the anchor. She was fisting and stowing the mainsail when he came aft. "You're doing your best to be difficult," she told him, "and I simply won't have it. Let's play a tune or two and then take a swim."

"You have the whole proposition figured," he said. "Right down to the suit."

"Stop being a boob. Wind the machine."

He grinned as he turned the gramophone crank. "Say I'm a nice boy."

"Not until you play 'Honolulu Lu.' "

"Is that your pet?"

"One of them. Gollies, you haven't got a suit, have you?"

"No."

She had stopped the record. "Then let's go skinny-dipping. I'm game if you are."

"You'll freeze your tail off when you come out."

"Is that the best excuse you have?"

He said nothing. She had already begun to pull her dress up over her head.

Her breasts were soft white and her nipples very dark. He was surprised by the curves, the fullness of her body. "There." She stood with her head lifted; her hands were at her sides. "How do you like me?"

"Oh, goddamn it, Ingël!" he said.

"Wait a minute," she said. "This is a swimming party." She jumped to the gunwale, braced herself and took a flat racing dive out into the water. He yanked wildly at his clothes and dived in and swam after her. But she hadn't swum far. She was floating, lying on her back with her hands moving just a bit about fifty yards from the boat.

He could make out the shape of her breasts and her legs through the water. He swam close to her and tried to touch her, his passion and his eagerness keeping him from speech. She pushed him off and swam away, all around the boat. He followed, angry with her, with himself, indistinctly thinking of Mark but aroused by the knowledge that she would finally have to go back to the boat.

He stayed in the water after she went aboard. She was Mark's girl, he told himself. She was a nice girl, not like Fat Mary or the rest he'd had, and her trouble was that Mark had been gone too long. But she smiled down at him from the deck. "You're still shocked," she said. "I don't believe you've ever had a girl."

"You're a liar," he said. "And put your clothes on."

"How many have you slept with?" she said.

"More than a couple." He was up over the side, standing on the deck close to her.

"Where, fibber?" One arm was crossed over her breasts, but she made no attempt to shield the rest of herself.

"In Duluth, in Cleveland, a slew of places. But how many fellas have you had?"

"Are we going to ask questions all night?" she said.

He threw her down on the cushions of the settee and held her there. He wept in to her wet hair when it was over, but then she sat up and played the gramophone. "I don't see what's wrong," she said. "We're young and healthy. You don't have to give me any

of that silly talk about being untrue to Mark. Neither do you have
to tell me you love me. It's very simple—we both needed this. I was
about to lose my mind."

He caught her in his arms again, passion back in him. Then she
said, "Come on down in the cabin, silly. Some darn fisherman
might see us here. Bring the cushions."

The breeze increased near dawn and they shivered, lying together in the low, lightless cabin. He brought in their clothing and
he told her to dress. "Not yet," she said. "I want another swim. If
I'm going to have a child, Mark will be the father. Don't you
know that a good, brisk swim is what you should suggest for me?"

"I don't know half the bilge you talk," he said. "Some of your
friends Down East ha' sure given you queer ideas."

"But the swimming works," she said. "Let's be practical."

He set the sails and hove up the anchor while she swam alongside. "All right." He took her under the arms and hauled her on
deck. "We're bound home. The Old Man could be waiting up
for us."

"Not to mention my mother," Ingë said. She was shucking her
dress over her head, pulling up her pants beneath it. "But, I can
handle her, and it was a very nice experience. I feel ever so much
better."

"By Christ," he said, "you sound as if you'd just eaten a box of
candy! Do you love Mark? D' you still want to marry him?"

"Of course, simp. Mark's my darling. But I just couldn't hold
off any more. I've heard so much about it, and read so much.
After all, that's what women are supposed to be good for in the
world."

"You stump me," he said. "How will you explain to Mark?"

"Mark won't ever know. It's our secret, Stace, unless by absolutely foul luck I have to visit a doctor."

"Get up for'd, you." Stacey was hoarse with anger. "Take the
boat hook and don't miss the buoy. I have half a mind to dump
you overboard with your music box around your neck."

She held the boat hook and she swerved it back and forth ten-
tatively, as if prepared to strike him. Then, though, she grinned.
"My, what horrid manners. But you won't blab, not to Mark or anybody else. I know you, Stace Kennard. . . ."

They moored as quietly as possible, and hauled the canoe onto
the dock without sound. But after they had climbed the lawn
they saw Alan Kennard was still on the porch. He sat asleep, snor-

ing. "One of life's awkward moments," Ingë whispered. "Push the
Buick for me like a good boy and I'll start the engine down the
road. Not so much noise and maybe he won't hear."

Stacey shoved with all his strength and the Buick creaked,
rolled and gathered momentum down the slope. Ingë's hand as she
waved back at him was a vague white flutter. He was in the house,
up the stairs when the motor clattered.

Alan Kennard reared erect from the chair wide awake. "Son of
a bitch," he said. "Makin' such a noise this time of night." Then he
identified the motor sound and heard the door being shut on the
top floor. Stace and her. They must ha' been at it for sure out there.
Good mind to go bust Stacey one right in the snoot. But, for what?

He climbed stiffly through the cold, mist filled house to his and
his wife's bedroom. She had left a side lamp burning and he turned
it off, finished undressing in the dark. Before he got into his bed,
though, he walked to where Minna lay. He reached out and caressed her buttock. Your woman. Always will be, and a good thing
she don't know about this. She'd be all hurt and flabbergasted.
Don't you ever open your big hatch to her. The kids tonight didn't
do any real harm.

CHAPTER FIFTEEN

She was very tired. The music hurt her head. Several of the guests, Phelim and Stuffy Smith among them, were already drunk, and the Old Man wasn't very far behind. Minna Kennard stood at the foot of the staircase in the flower littered hallway and tried to draw her breath more slowly, then smiled as Ingë danced past her with Jerrod Bishop, the best man.

Ingë was a lovely bride. That little white cap set on the back of her head above her smoothly waving hair was handsome. The grandmother in Denmark had sent her the wedding dress, and for a time Minna and Brigitte Keiberg had thought it rather old fashioned. But Ingë gave it elegance. The lace was very fine, the bodice low cut; Ingë had laughed when they had protested that it was too low cut. "If Grandmother approved," Ingë said, "why should Patigowoc object? Don't be a pair of fuddy duddies, my dears."

There was something hard and hidden about Ingë, Minna Kennard thought, just as there was about Mark. Perhaps that was because they'd delayed their marriage so long. Three years after the war, almost seven years all told, they'd been engaged. For one reason or another, Mark had kept putting it off. He'd wanted to stay in France as an officer attached to the American delegation at the peace conference. Then he'd gone to the Sorbonne for a year, and at last come home, only to go on West and work as a fire warden up in those mountains in Colorado.

Ingë hadn't seemed to mind, though. She had stayed Down East a lot, visiting old school friends and going to the Art Students League, coming back to Patigowoc only when Mark did. It was the war, the Old Man had told her. Mark had been all beaten to hell out there in France. And if Ingë could stand for it, why couldn't she? Let them two settle the business in their own way.

Well, they had, Minna told herself once more and brought the stiff self-conscious smile back to her lips and walked from the hallway on into the drawing room. Mark danced with Ingë; he whispered to her. She nodded and broke from him and ran towards the stairs.

"Hey, hey, Ingë!" the bridesmaids shouted. They were Easterners and Ingë had dressed them beautifully in pale blue taffeta. They made the local women look dowdy, Minna Kennard knew, herself included, and they had dominated the party from the start. Most of them had been dancing or at the champagne table with the ushers. But they ran for the door after Ingë, jostled happily to get into position to catch her bouquet.

Minna looked from them back into the drawing room and the rooms beyond. Here's where the difference showed. The ushers followed the bridesmaids, and Jerrod Bishop, of course, and Mark and Stacey and the Old Man and Lars Keiberg when his wife led him by the hand. The rest, though, even the young ones, and they were from Patigowoc and Napta City and Hamatack and Detroit, they didn't. They felt out of it. For them, Ingë and Mark had become Easterners, folks apart.

The Reverend Neubel who'd done well enough down at the church sat in a corner with a silly kind of a grin on his face. He wasn't used to drinking and the Old Man had fed him a couple of stiff jolts of Canadian Club and hooked it up with champagne. Phelim and Peggy and Stuffy Smith were here because Stacey was their friend, had personally asked them. A lot of the others had been invited by the Keibergs and had accepted because it was the biggest wedding in this part of the state and they could get all they wanted to eat and drink.

"All right, chickens!" Jerrod Bishop shouted.

Ingë had just tossed her bouquet. The little blonde and saucy girl whose name was Jo Ann Ashley caught it. She turned and smacked Jerrod Bishop on the cheek with it. "Refuse me now, you dog," she said.

"Would you take advantage of a drunken man?" Bishop said. The champagne and the dancing and last night's bachelor party in Detroit had put a high shine on his thin, long face. But the scar was an ugly red along his jaw; nerves jumped and flickered around his eyes. "No more *reformés* for sale. Mark's the last. United we fall."

"United," Jo Ann said harsh voiced, "you drink and go flat on your faces. The war's over. Remember?"

Jerrod is Mark's old room mate at Andover, Minna Kennard thought. He got Mark to go to Princeton. They were in the war together. Jerrod was wounded twice, much worse than Mark. Oh, how lucky you really are. And Ingë. That little girl is just crazy for Jerrod, but he won't have her, not at all.

Mark was in the hall, a champagne bottle in each hand, his cravat dishevelled, sweat on his brows, and yet in command of himself. "Drink, children," he said. "Come one, come all."

The haggard lines left Bishop's face. He put his arm around Mark's shoulder. "Sing for us. Let's sing *'Les Fraises et les Framboises.'* "

"You have the wrong man," Mark said. "Ingë and I have to catch the four o'clock. And I have to change."

"*Très bien.*" Bishop took one of the bottles from him. "Then we'll sing without you. "Go on, Mark—" he was almost shouting, his eyes narrowed—"change!"

He went half way up the stairs after Mark. Then he swung around and gestured down at the ushers. "You know it. Let's go!" His voice, strident, filled with an awful anger, rang out through the hallway into the drawing room, slashed through the tune the band played, flattened the babble of conversation in the drawing room.

> *"Eux! Dans leur bureaux d'affaires,*
> *Dans leurs bordels et dans leurs bars,*
> *Font la politique et les guerres.*
> *'Guerre jusqu'au bout et à outrance,'*
> *Qu'ils disent, 'Allez-y, les gars,*
> *Pour le salut de la France'—*
> *La France à Eux—*
> *Les Merdeux!"*

Jo Ann had slipped out of the hallway and stood beside Minna Kennard. The girl stumbled as she walked, and Minna had the thought that she was about to be ill. She grasped Jo Ann by the arm. "You don't feel well, dear?"

"Well?" Jo Ann dully repeated the word. "Thank you, I'm fine. Just dandy. But that brute up there singing, that stupid, wilful fool. . . ."

"But what does the song mean?"

"It's terrible. He and Mark and the others brought it home from France. A lot of filth, blaming the profiteers for the war. In France, they'd be jailed for singing it. But Jerrod persists. He says he can't get it out of his mind."

"You love him, don't you?"

"I do, I really do, Mrs. Kennard."

"Then——"

But Jo Ann had gone on, and she was ripping Ingë's bouquet to shreds and mumbling, "I'm going to get drunk. Soused as a goddamn' flounder. Let him sing his song!"

Mark had come out to the top floor landing with the first verse chorus. Ingë was at the door of her room below, staring up at him. "Is Jerrod mad?" she said. "He shouldn't sing that here. Somebody might understand French and be frightfully shocked."

"He's no more mad," Mark said slowly, "than I've been. Finish your dressing. It'll be over in a moment. Jerrod will drive us to the station."

"Yes, Captain," Ingë said. "Is that all the captain has to say?"

"Please, ninny. I love you, still I can't control that pack of wild men completely. Show them champagne and they think they're back in the war again."

Ingë touched her fingers to her lips. "I understand. Forgive me. I was just wondering about the local people."

"There's the rest of our lives to consider them," Mark said. "Get dressed, darling. We haven't much time."

Stacey had been with the group around the Old Man. Phelim was there, and Stuffy Smith, Lars Keiberg. Friction still existed between Phelim and the Old Man, although they had shared a quart of Canadian Club and worked persistently at the champagne. Keiberg was no help; he had asked Stuffy Smith if he got as good wages with Harkness as he had with the Kennard Company. "Go scratch yer ass, ya money-countin' bastard," Stuffy said in answer. "Ya think I'd tell ya that?"

But when Jo Ann Ashley went wavering towards the champagne table Stacey left the group. The Old Man would have to handle it, he decided, or Phelim. He'd done his best. And the little seagull over there was making heavy weather. He pulled down self-consciously the lapels of the cutaway the Old Man had rented for him in Detroit, moved to Jo Ann's side. No sense not trying. You didn't find a job like this around Patigowoc every day.

"How's Jo Ann?" he said and took a full glass from the table.

"Miserable," she said. She thickly belched. "More champagne than I know what to do with and no man. Are you a real, honest-and-no-faking man?" Then, before he could speak, she put a hand on his arm. "Certainly, you are. You're Mark's brother. The sailor one. Can sailors dance?"

"Try me."

"No. I'd rather not dance. I'm too squiffed. But let's go for a walk. Bring a bottle. Better, bring two bottles. I'm going to float right straight back to New York on champagne."

They had gone out through a side door and onto the lawn when the burst of yelling and clapping rose under the porte-cochere. "Ingë," Jo Ann said. "They're leaving. Jerrod's taking them to the station. You'll have to ravish me later, sailor."

"I won't forget," Stacey said. "Let me carry that bottle for you. It's dragging you down by the bow."

Jerrod Bishop drove a green Packard roadster with the top down. Ribbons and old shoes and the Just Married sign had been tied to it, Ingë's and Mark's luggage put in the back. Ingë darted across the porch ahead of Mark, leapt into the Packard while the rice began to spatter. Mark followed and then Bishop, so drunk he staggered. But Bishop started the motor and threw the car into gear. It slewed down the driveway in a ragged parabola, one pair of wheels canted up on the lawn. Stacey dropped the bottles of champagne and told Jo Ann, "Don't get excited. It'll be all right." Then he began to run.

The Packard hit the left hand gate pillar with a grinding shriek. Water jetted from the radiator; the windshield shattered musically and a tire blew out. Stacey pulled Ingë clear first, Mark and Bishop after her. None of them was badly hurt. Bishop had a gashed forehead and that was all.

"Stupid, aren't I?" Bishop said. "Thought the goddamn' thing could at least low-hurdle."

"Haul out your gear, Mark," Stacey said. "Sit down and take it easy, Ingë. I'll get another car."

"Thanks, old boy," Mark said. He had his arms around Ingë, was holding her close. "Sorry to bother you."

Several cars were parked past the porte-cochere. Stacey picked a Hupmobile because the ignition key was in the lock. But as he got behind the wheel Jo Ann joined him. "Can't ditch me," she said. "How's Bishop, banged up enough to deserve mercy?"

"Not much," Stacey said. "But don't be too rough on him. He's only drunk."

Mark took the wheel of the Packard while Stacey shoved with the Hupmobile. They had the Packard out of the gateway, in the ditch of the main road before the crowd could get down from the house. "But do drive slowly, Stace," Ingë said, "I'm so scared my knees still knock."

"A hell of a way to go on a honeymoon," Bishop said. He sat in the rear seat, his head on Jo Ann's shoulder. "Bride arrives in Bermuda with water on the knee. No good. *Epouvantable.*"

"You be still," Jo Ann said. "All we need for comedy is to look at you."

Ingë kissed Stacey on the lips at the station. It stirred him very deeply and his fingers dug into the shoulders of her travelling suit. "Good old Stace," she said. "Always around at the right time."

"Sure," he said. He stood back from her, confused by her kiss and her self control. She hadn't kissed him since the night they had been together aboard the sloop, and had told him the next time they had met that they could never have a "repeat performance." He had a sensation of profound shame as he turned to take Mark's hand and say goodbye.

But people who had followed from the wedding reception jammed onto the platform. They had brought champagne and shouted, danced and sang until the train arrived. Stuffy Smith's shirt was outside his trousers, flapping around his knees. He wore an usher's top hat and he insisted upon putting the luggage on the train. Then he climbed on behind Ingë and Mark and it took Stacey and Phelim Carmody and Alan Kennard to pull him off. His father was smiling, Stacey saw, yet as soon as the train was out of sight his mouth dragged into harsh, taut lines. He's drunk, Stacey thought, and he'll be drunker yet. You'll have to keep an eye on him. Ma's had it rough enough as it is.

Alan Kennard was aware that his mood had changed several times during the day. With the departure of Ingë and Mark, though, it became openly wild. He invited everybody at the station back to the house, was furious when they didn't accept. Those who remained were only a few: Phelim and Peggy Carmody, the Keibergs, Stuffy Smith, Jerrod Bishop and the ushers and bridesmaids and Stacey. It was queer maybe, but he rated Stacey in his mind behind the growing haze of alcohol as being one of them who didn't rightly belong here. To hell. Why bother thinking? Have another snort.

The band had been paid and was gone. The caterer's crew had cleaned up and stolen about a case of champagne and was leaving. The bridesmaids had changed out of their wedding clothing, and the ushers. Stacey and Jo Ann Ashley had carried Bishop upstairs, made him change from his cutaway. Car after car left the driveway while he stood with Minna and Stacey and the Keibergs and shook hands, nodded, smiled, repeated the same stale, empty phrases.

Over. All over, Kennard. Finished with engines. You hope to Christ that Carmody and his woman and Smith and the Keibergs get out of here. They're no friends of yours. You got no real friends any more. You found that out today. Go and have another snort. Try to act human just for Minna's sake. Give her a fair shake, no matter what the bloody else you do.

Minna and Peggy Carmody and Brigitte Keiberg were in a corner of the drawing room talking. Minna looked very tired, but she didn't seem to mind the fact that he was drunk and couldn't walk straight or that Stuffy Smith was trying to wrestle with David, then mounted the lamb.

Smith sprawled from the lamb onto the floor. Phelim Carmody, red eyed drunk, picked him up. "What ya need is 'nother drink. You, too, Kennard."

"Yeah," Kennard said. He took them into his study and opened a fresh bottle of Canadian Club. Stacey joined them as he poured, and he was glad. Good to have Stace around. Kind of stewed, too, from the look of him, but he might be handy.

"Wealthy fella," Stuffy Smith was muttering. "Big ship-ownin' man, this Kennard. Yessir. Ships. Limestone. Lime. Bricks. All kindsa goddamn' stuff. Champagne. Plenty an' more to float a ship. Prohibition. Volstead Act. But Kennard's got champagne, got C'n'd'n Club 'n all kindsa booze. Where's champagne, Kennard? You think, now them Easterners 're gone we gotta drink whiskey?"

Stacey stepped between his father and Stuffy Smith. "Whiskey is the life of man," he said, quoting the old chantey. "I'll drink whiskey when I can. Whiskey for a sailor. Don't you go back on your own kind, yuh goat."

"Called me a goat," Smith told Phelim Carmody plaintively. "Some first mate you got. Don't like him no more than 's ole man."

"Ah, pipe down!" Phelim Carmody said. He had drawn aside one of the drapes at a rear window of the study. He pointed out towards the back porch. "Bastard if I can't count about two hundred empty bottles. What d' you say we have a turkey shoot? Bottle shoot—same thing. Get us a gun, Stace. Go out on the lawn an' we shoot. Bet I can shoot better'n Stuffy, any of you."

"Go ahead," Alan Kennard said to Stacey. "You know where I keep the twelve gauge and the shells. Goddamn' bottles will just be in the way anyhow. We'll throw 'em in the river from the dock. Take turns shootin'." He moved around to face Carmody. "Make a little bet. Five dollars a bottle."

Phelim Carmody cursed him laughing. "I ain't got your kind of money. Fifty cents, that's my speed."

"All right, fifty cents. Get the gun and the shells, Stace. Let's go." The women protested when they tracked through the drawing room. But Alan Kennard wouldn't be shaken. "No harm done," he told his wife. "Promise ya we won't shoot each other. Where's Keiberg?"

"He don't shoot at all good," Brigitte Keiberg said nervously. "And he's out on the porch taking a nap."

"Let him sleep, then," Kennard said. "Just wanted t' know if he'd give me a free shot at his hat. The square-head slob. . . ."

"Come on, Pa," Stacey said quickly, his hand tight on his father's arm.

Stacey brought the bottles down to the dock in a wheel barrow, kept the shells in his pockets and loaded the gun himself. But the heavy recoil of the twelve-gauge had a sobering effect; they were all quiet and calm before they had finished the bottles and dusk was over the river.

Peggy met them on the porch. She stared keenly into Phelim's eyes and asked him, "You ready to go?"

"Get one for the road and I will be," Phelim said.

"Make it quick," she said. "The Keibergs ha' left. We're the last. You comin' with us, Stace?"

"No, I don't reckon so," Stacey said. He watched his father with a sidewise glance. "Phelim says I can jump aboard in Detroit."

"Like hell!" Alan Kennard said. "You work for Harkness, you work for Harkness. Don't want no man saying I kept my son from his ship. You go along with them. Stay here, all hands. I'll fetch the bottle."

They drank in almost complete silence, Peggy taking the bottle firmly by the neck. Then she hugged and kissed Minna Kennard and said, "Goodbye, darlin'. It was grand. I wish them kids the best luck in the world."

"Thanks, dear." Minna Kennard leaned against a jamb of the front door for support. Exhaustion had slowly absorbed her body. She ached from her head to her feet. You're old, she thought, and it isn't just the wedding. Look at Peg, fat, gray-haired. Only yesterday, you told herself how pretty she still must be. You're gray-haired, too, and skinny, and sick inside. What's happened to us? Alan and you. Stace is going with Peg and Phelim and Stuffy. You'll be alone here with Alan. The idea makes you afraid. . . .

Alan Kennard and Phelim Carmody were awkwardly shaking hands. "No sense," Kennard said, "to hammer the hell and gone to Marine City tonight. That ain't much of a car you got, either. You could stay with us, push off in the morning."

"The car runs all right," Phelim Carmody said. "And Stace is the lad to navigate it for us. Take care. Thank ye."

Alan Kennard attempted to keep Minna on the porch with him after the battered Chevrolet had rattled away from the porte-cochere. But she said, "I'm simply worn out. I have to go to bed. If you want supper, one of the maids will fix it for you."

"A fine thing!" he said in a bitter voice. "Our son married and off to Bermuda on his honeymoon. My other son off with a man who works against me and hates my guts. Now my wife, she'll go to bed. And I'm left, bejesus, to drink alone."

"Alan, dear-heart." Minna came back to him from the hallway. She ran her hands over his cheeks and kissed him. "I feel so tired I'm sick. I just can't stay with you. Come up soon, though. Promise me."

"For sure," he said, and forced himself to smile. "It's been a day, a week for you. Get along with you. No harm done for a man of me age to have a drink by himself. I'll be up soon, don't you fear."

He sat on the porch in the gathering darkness, a bottle of Canadian Club between his feet. Near nine o'clock, the *Daigvera* sailed past fully loaded and Clarence McCune, the captain, sounded the whistle. That cheered him for a bit, and then his feeling of enormous despondency returned. He fumbled for the bottle and found it empty, staggered as he got to his feet and went into the study. "Son of a bitch," he said, "you're about as drunk as a man can be. But, what difference, what difference to anybody?"

Minna heard his sobbing when she awoke in the night and went to the bathroom. She put on her robe and slippers, descended the stairs. He sat in his chair behind the desk in the study and his head was down on the blotter; the blotter was marked with his tears. "What's the matter, Alan?" she said, stroking his hair.

"All of it," he muttered. "Everything. Somewhere, the whole lash-up's gone wrong."

"Oh, Alan," she said, "you're tired and drunk. Come to bed. What you say isn't true."

He lifted his head and glared at her. "No? I've made a Down East snob outa Mark. He'll go into the business when he comes back, but that don't mean much. He's a cold and hard fella, harder than me, and he lives by himself in his head. If he really loves Ingë, that's God's own miracle. He's been unfaithful to her plenty, and her to him. Stace—he ain't got any use for me. You saw tonight what happened. A Harkness stiff, same as Phelim."

"I can't take this, Alan," she said whispering. "Months ago, Doctor Durand told me to watch my heart. Get up. Please, please. Here. Take my hands."

He sat limply resistant, sobbing again and brokenly cursing. She pulled him to his feet, moved him part prone out to the hallway. He fell down there and she got him up and made him mount the stairs. He slid from side to side, once nearly over the banister rail. Her breath burned her lungs, her throat; through her mind like a vast and discordant drum beat went his words about Mark and Ingë and Stacey.

She staggered more than he as they entered their bedroom. "Take off your clothes," she gasped. "Get into bed."

"You don't love me neither," he cried at her, then flopped face down onto the bed. "I ain't no good. You hate me, too, like them others do."

"Oh, you poor man," she said. But it was too faint for him to hear. She hardly heard herself. Pain jolted her heart with frightful force. Her lungs constricted. The room swayed, revolved, and the lamp was a blur, her husband's figure a phantom. "Alan!" she called as for an instant the pain released.

He snored. "Alan!" She groped towards him along the side of the bed. The pain closed riving and she collapsed and went to her knees on the floor. Her head met her knees; she gasped out as if by that she could reduce the pain. It became steadily greater. She knelt unconscious, head still to knees.

Alan Kennard found her so in the forenoon. He cradled her in his arms and placed her on the bed, aware in the depths of his remaining drunkenness that she was very ill. Fright sent him out into the hall, to the head of the stairs. The maids came running after he called and then he went to the telephone.

Doctor Durand was quite blunt with him. He had made his examination, written out his orders silently. "How much chance she got?" Alan Kennard asked dry-mouthed.

"Not much," Durand said. "You'd better get Mark home, and Stacey, just as soon as you can."

"You mean she's goin' to die."

"I don't mean to alarm you, but she hasn't a chance. A few days at the most. Good day, sir."

"Good day," Alan Kennard said mechanically. It was one of the maids who had been standing outside the bedroom door who reminded him that he should send the messages to Mark and Ingë and to Stacey.

A chill sweat was on him as he went to the telephone. Minna dead. Always, somehow, he'd figured that he'd go long before her. But he'd fouled that up, too. Life without her. Without Minna, his darlin', his love.

CHAPTER SIXTEEN

Ingë had been dozing in the sun on the terrace when the Negro boy from the hotel came with the cablegram and shuffled his feet and coughed until she noticed him. She thanked him and gave him a shilling tip, but the warm weight of the sun was still upon her when she stretched out again on the rattan chair. She yawned and told herself that it was some foolish message from Jerrod or one of the others. It could wait 'til Mark came back. He could enjoy the laugh with her. Then, though, she thought, something might be wrong in Patigowoc, your family or Mark's.

Her long fingernails ripped the envelope. She sat up to read, narrowing her eyes against the sunlight. Patigowoc was up at the top. So it wasn't funny. The words were cut out in strips, pasted to the paper. *Mother died yesterday.* The period was on a little separate strip. *Funeral tomorrow unless we hear differently from you. Father all right and same your folks. Please dont hurry home. Love. Stacey.*

The first shock of understanding stunned her. She slowly began to cry. Tears ran from her cheeks onto her neck and between her breasts. She shivered. "How terrible," she said. "How ghastly!"

She tried to reread the message and the tears made rainbows before her eyes through which she could not see. The grief was now sharp within her. She stood, strode the terrace, the cablegram crumpled in her hand, her hand beating against her thigh below the hem of her bathing suit.

After a while the tears stopped but she made no further attempt to read the message. She gazed out across the terrace past the whitewashed wall, the whitewashed, neat cottages and over the emerald planes of the sea beyond the harbor islands into the West.

She was taking herself back to Patigowoc, to "The Towers." Mother Kennard helped her dress one of her dolls. They were cutting flowers in one of the beds beside the grape arbor. She was being bawled out and sent home after the boys had fixed up David and poor, funny Mister What's-his-name, the upholsterer from Napta City, had lost his glass eye. Then the acute anguish of her loss blocked out memory. She was just walking the stubbly grass of the terrace, not even feeling its rough thrust against her bare feet.

How long she walked she didn't know. But she grew fatigued, and a sense of her surroundings returned to her. She could cry no more. The grief was too great. She went into the cottage, and the shadow and the cool tile underfoot made her shiver. She was shivering yet as she stepped onto the rattan matting in the bedroom.

Her bathing suit stuck about her knees and she fiercely kicked it free, threw it into a corner. Then, as she put on her *peignoir* and her mules, a degree of calmness came to her. The *peignoir* was lovely and long, Patou had designed it. The mules were warm and made her feet seem small. Mark had said they were cute.

She sat at her dressing table. In the mirror her eyes were puffed and ugly from the crying. She forced herself to comb her hair, a long stroke and another one, another. That's it, Ingë. She powdered herself and put on lipstick. Her lips pouted, she smoothed the lower one with the tip of her right little finger to get the lipstick even.

Mother Kennard dead. Don't be a sap and cry. The warning came last week from the Old Man. But she cried, her head down on the table, her hand groped out for the ball of the cablegram.

The Negro maid came to the door. "Missis, you all right?" Then the maid came into the room. She stood right beside Ingë. Ingë could smell her, the fresh starchy dress, the cheap cologne water the girl used to hide the body odor that was from some glandular trouble. The maid touched her shoulder. "You're 'avin' real bad trouble."

The "a" sound was very soft in the verb; the girl's voice was soft, tender. Ingë brought her head up. Ten shillings a week, Ingë thought, and the poor girl must stand here and see me cry. Last week she had given Henrietta an old dinner dress that her mother had packed by mistake. Henrietta had worn it to a rum-and-shrub party over in Somerset and been a frightful hit. She was Henrietta's friend for life. But there was no reason for Henrietta to cry.

She tried to tell Henrietta so and the crying stopped her. She put her hand on top of Henrietta's hand on her shoulder. They both cried, the girl's narrow body shaking harder than her own. Then Ingë was able to say, "You go away, Henrietta. You let me be. I'll be better that way. It's bad news from home. Mr. Mark's mother has just died."

"Oh, dear goodness!" Henrietta said. Her worn and slop-heeled shoes went creaking out of the room, into the living room and the kitchen. The back screen door opened, shut. Henrietta was sitting on the rear step in the sun. She was shucking peas, imported Canadian peas, into a pan. The empty pods made a little thump, the peas themselves a rattle. Henrietta continued to cry. She blew her nose with the back of her hand.

My mother would fire a maid for that, Ingë told herself. It was expressed in a deliberate effort to become calm. But it made her like Henrietta all the more. Henrietta and she were friends; Henrietta felt for her and Mark, so she cried and had to blow her nose.

Ingë put on fresh lipstick and powder. She hid the cablegram behind her lotion and perfume bottles and picked up one bottle that was named *Extase*. She had bought it in New York last year, but she had always believed it too exotic and heavy-scented to use to attract Mark. Her reason for doing it was unclear, yet she put drops of the perfume behind her ears, on her throat and on her breasts. She lay on her bed with the pillow pulled up behind her head and waited for Mark.

The crying had given her a drowsy, weak sensation. She drifted away from herself into involuntary recollection. When she heard the rattling of Mark's bicycle on the road she was surprised. She had been very far away.

Her thought had gone to Alan Kennard and in recollection she had called him the Old Man. He would be very lonely with his wife dead. Stacey would come home as a result, go to work for the company. And Stacey, when he was off the ships, had no other place to live except with his father.

There was a complication for her and Mark. She and Mark had planned, for a time at least, to live with Mother Kennard and the Old Man. Not now you can't. With Stacey in the house, things would become rather difficult. Perhaps Stacey wasn't in love with her, still he refused to get married. He liked to play the field, he said, and a sailor was a fool to get hitched. He means, Ingë thought with a trace of fear, that he doesn't trust any woman after what you did to Mark during the war.

Don't consider Stacey or the Old Man any more. You'll simply have to handle them when the time comes. You must realize, though, that you can't stay with your own people. You detest your father. Your mother is a miserable, frightened frump. In a week, you'd be fighting with both of them. Mark and you simply must have a home of your own.

She looked up smiling, for Mark had come into the room. "How are you, boy?" she said. She patted the bed at her side. "Sit down."

Mark blinked from the effect of shadow after sunlight. Coral dust was on his suede golf shoes and gray flannel trousers. Splotches of sweat showed through the front of his polo shirt under the houndstooth jacket he wore, and where the shirt lay flat against his skin she could see the curve of his chest, the dark tan shade of the skin. Mark was her man all right. He was her lover.

"I'm half-boiled, darling." He was walking towards her. "They've invented a drink out at the club that they call the 'Seventy-five.' You know—boom! I've had seven. I'm feeling no pain."

She wondered, shall I tell him? If she told him now, there would be an intense emotional scene. No doubt she'd cry again, and Mark's grief was something she couldn't calculate. She'd never seen Mark badly hurt, but underneath his reserve, his contained, quiet manner, he was very sensitive and he'd adored his mother.

"I had the idea," she said, "that you might make us a drink. But after those Seventy-fives you'd probably blow up." He was sitting beside her on the bed. She smoothed her hand along the back of his neck, down over the fine, short hairs at the nape. It excited her every time she was close to him. Maybe it was the way his hair grew, the certain way he always moved, or his long, dark lashes he had inherited from his mother, or all those things put together, or none of them. His hands were hard and tight on her shoulders. "How was your game?" she said.

"If I can use a two iron the way the pro' showed me, I'll crack ninety. Come on out tomorrow with me."

"I shall, but I'm such an awful dub I won't go around with you. As a consequence, I'll probably end up in the bar and get tight."

"Silly," he said. "No, you won't." His hands were going from her shoulders to her arms and breasts. She thought once more about the cablegram. Later, she told herself. If I stopped him now, it would just be too cruel. "Close the door, darling," she said.

Afterwards, lying in the lilac gold-stippled darkness, she told him. He was relaxed, almost asleep, but she knew that if she did not tell him instantly she would lack the courage for some time to come. "Mark," she whispered, "we got a cable from Stacey this afternoon. Your mother is dead."

Mark lay motionless. He stared at the ceiling. His thigh was against her thigh and he drew away a little bit in a reflexive, unthinking movement. The pain was a knot. It formed and squeezed in the center of his chest. Then it was up in his head and he knew, fully knew.

He sat up on the edge of the bed and struck one hand against the other with short and flat blows, palm to palm. He didn't look at her, nor did he cry. Now, she realized, he was alone in the grief as she had been when Henrietta had tried to comfort her. But Mark was frightening her. He should say something. It wasn't right for him to keep absolutely silent.

He turned around and looked at her and found she had drawn the *peignoir* over her body. "Why didn't you tell me before?" he said.

"I just couldn't, Mark. I cried and cried before you came home. Henrietta tried to stop me and I kept right on. It's terrible to miss anybody like that."

Mark had seen the cablegram. He went over to the dressing table and read it. "Stacey is a good man," he said. He had a vision of Stacey in the big, dim house, sitting with the Old Man in the study, calming him, keeping him sober, and talking to the reporters from the county and Detroit papers and talking to the undertaker about all the barbaric details that went to make a funeral. "The Old Man didn't want us to come out. Last week, he told us that Mother's condition wasn't too bad. He should have let us know the truth."

"No, I don't agree." Ingë was behind him and had her arms around him. "We couldn't have got a ship to take us home in time. It's quite likely, too, that she was unconscious up to the end. If we——"

"You're troubled about going home, aren't you?"

"We'd promised ourselves a month here, Mark. Don't think I'm selfish. I'm not. And I loved your mother very much."

"We'll take a ship home," Mark said, "just as fast as we can get one. The Old Man will need me, and Stace. After all, I've never hit a real lick for the company. Think of the years I've lost. . . . Or do you want to think about them?"

"What good would it do if I did?" She kissed him lightly on the forehead. "Go take a shower and change. We'll go over to the hotel and see about ships."

"You're marvelously calm."

"I told you before that I wept and wept."

He looked down into her eyes after he had stood from the dressing table stool. His right hand gripped her chin painfully, and she could sense the rigidity throughout his body. "The war knocked you around, too. . . . We'll never be young again, will we?"

"Never, Mark. But if you keep this up, I shall become hysterical. Do go take your shower."

"*Très bien,*" he said. He stood hesitant for an instant and she had the belief that he was about go on, tell her his innermost thought. But instead he crossed the room, took off his clothing, went in and started the shower. She stared after him, greatly perturbed, then told herself, wait, there's time yet, you must learn to let his nerves uncoil like a series of springs. If you don't, you lose his love for good.

He stood in the shower for many minutes. It cooled him and quieted him and yet his control was broken through and he wept. The sobs came from deep down in his abdomen. They hurt him in their intensity, made him bend forward. He was ashamed of himself. You're crying, he thought, because of the effect of those drinks and of making love. Get yourself together and out of here.

But Mother. . . . He saw his mother at the station when he had returned from Europe in 1920. He had worn a civilian suit and she hadn't known the meaning of the ribbons in his buttonhole. She had nearly wept in disappointment. "Oh, Mark," she said, "perhaps I'm stupid, but I thought you'd still be in uniform." The Old Man had been behind her and said hoarsely, "What the hell, the war's over two years. I'll bet the boy ain't even got his glory suit any more." That night, from the bottom of his foot locker, he had taken out his American uniform, put it on, medals, Sam Browne belt, fourragère and all. He'd worn it to dinner and his mother had sprung up to embrace him and the Old Man's eyes had shone. All during dinner, mother kept her glance on him, asking him again what each decoration meant and once leaning over to finger the cords of the fourragère.

A gesture of love. The greatest he could give her. And you hated doing it because you hate that filthy bitch of a bloodsucker war. Good thing she didn't understand that song Jerrod sang at the wedding. She died thinking you were a hero who had performed some tremendous service for humanity. Mother dear, I assure you that you're lucky to be dead. Because there will be more wars, and worse ones. . . . I know. I saw what happened at Versailles, Clemenceau and Lloyd George tearing Wilson apart. The Germans in the Ruhr with the Senegalese standing guard over them. The men who served with me and even then didn't have enough and went to join the Koskiusko Squadron and fight the Bolsheviks in Poland. Or joined the Legion to fight Moors, or went to Central America in a banana revolution. To kill, to keep peace dead. . . . So I'm happy that you're gone. For your sake, dear. Goodbye.

Ingë stood outside the shower curtain and called his name. He stuck his head forth, the water dripping, his eyes almost vacant in their regard of her. "Whiskey and soda," she said and held out the glass. "It'll do you good, boy." There was a note of eagerness, of keen desire to help in her voice. It brought him back out of the shades of thought about his mother. "Thank you, sweet. Have you one for yourself?"

"In the bedroom. I'll get it." She raised it to his glass. "Here's to your mother, Mark. I know what you have been wishing—that she shall find peace."

"You're right," he said, and came from the shower and kissed her quietly on the lips. "I'm all over it. She's gone to join the others, if you understand what I mean."

"I do." She smiled. "And I'm very glad. Mark, let me in here now. Then I believe we should dress and go to dinner. If we were to spend the evening alone, we might slip back again. Into talking of her, and thinking of her."

"You know," he said; he was smiling, "you often surprise me. Neither of your parents has your looks, nor anything like your brains."

"If we weren't man and wife, Captain, I'd be forced to think that you were out to make an attempt on my pearly pink body."

"That's in the back of my mind," he said. "But it can wait. I'll make it wait, at least through dinner. Let's go to the hotel. I have to get off a cable to the Old Man and Stace and check on ship schedules. We might even have a dance."

"Then you want me all dressed up."

"Of course. Aren't you the prettiest bit on the island?"

The night became green with moonlight as he fixed his studs and put on his dinner jacket in the bedroom. He could smell the night: the sharp dryness of cooling coral, the grass, the flowers and shrubs and cedars in a richer, heavier layer of odor, then seaweed and the sea. You won't have much more of it, he thought. You'll be back with the limestone dust in your nose, behind a desk in the office next to the Old Man's. *Grand commercant.* Certainly, a real beeznees man. Trained for it by Phillips Andover and a year and a half of Princeton and leave out the goddamn' war. *Ça ira.* It has to be. The Old Man can't run the company forever.

Henrietta knocked gently upon the door. "Missis Kenna'd," she said. "Missis Kenna'd."

Mark opened the door. "Oh, sar," Henrietta said. She held out her hand. "I sorrow for you."

"Thank you, Henrietta," Mark said. He took her hand. "Mrs. Kennard's in the bathroom."

Ingë had heard them. She came out wearing her brassiere and a pair of close-fitting, short silk pants. The brassiere accentuated her breasts. A little trim of lace was around the pants and they just covered her buttocks. Against her tanned skin the garments seemed preposterously useless. Henrietta gave her a glance of absolute adoration. "Missis Kenna'd," she said, "Missis Petherton's boy, Phillip, he at back door. He come for to say some person phone for to know if you and Mister come to party tonight."

"That's Grace Sigenay Morris," Ingë said. "You tell Phillip I'll call Mrs. Morris from the hotel in an hour. Give Phillip a shilling for me."

"Yes, Missis," Henrietta said. She looked back once more from the doorway at the pants and the brassiere.

Ingë met Mark's eyes. She made a quick gesture with both hands upraised. "I forgot about it," she said. "Grace asked us to a party tonight over at Coral Beach. I'll get dressed right away and phone her and tell her no."

"But why don't we go?" Mark said. "Mother would like it for us. You know that."

His control is nearly perfect, Ingë thought. He has more sheer will than the Old Man himself. You can't match it. Your thinking's guided by your senses. Let's say your emotions. Stuff over there on the bed is where you're at your best.

But Mark still watched her; he waited for her answer. "Fine," she said. "Make us another drink while I finish dressing. There's no sense arriving at one of Grace's parties sober. Nobody else will be."

She was glad when Mark left the room. She had just begun to realize the full extent of his personal power. Who would win, she asked herself, if Mark and the Old Man were contemporaries? What would happen when the time came that Mark believed the company policy should be changed? Mark was the Old Man, but he was more, too. He had his mother's Ojibway blood to help him be calm and quiet, hidden in his intentions. Should there ever be a real fight between Mark and the Old Man, she'd bet on Mark. Perhaps, though, that was due to the fact that she was so much in love with him. Goodness, the other men you've had, Stace included, are nothing in comparison. She patted the bed as she passed it on her way to the closet to get out her dress.

The hotel bar was packed. The golfers hadn't left yet and people were arriving for dinner all the time. Mark and she stood down at the end where the barkeeper made space for them. The barkeeper had served at Mons and the Somme and he knew Mark's war record. He bought a drink on the house, then some Canadians with whom Mark had played golf came over. They weren't sober, and paid Ingë lavish compliments, started to talk about the war.

"Come on," Mark murmured to her. He was pale under his tan. "This was a mistake. Let's get out of here."

"Right now, darling. You go ahead and I'll follow."

He regained his composure when they were in the lobby. "The cable and the ship info'," he said. "Sit down. I shan't be long."

She watched him as he stood at the desk and talked with the round faced Bermudian clerk. He had put his miniature medal ribbons in the buttonhole of his dinner jacket lapel, and the clerk looked at them with open curiosity, asked some question. She was unable to hear the answer, but the clerk flushed and moved to the far end of the desk from Mark. Then Mark walked back to her.

"I sent the Old Man and Stace all our love," he said. "The best thing we can do for a ship is the *Narissa* next week. I told them that, and to go ahead with the funeral, of course."

"All right, Mark," she said.

Outside in the dark and riding alone down the Shore Road on their bicycles, they talked very little. She was disturbed by his silence, and she had drunk enough whiskey to bring forth the question. "If you hate the war so, why do you wear those ribbons?"

"I'm not quite sure." He veered his bicycle over so that their handlebars almost touched. Ahead of them on the white road toads leaped in the beams of the acetylene lanterns. She reluctantly took her glance from the toads and stared at Mark. A film of sweat was on his face. The war was very close to him now, she sensed. "It started off as a great big, goddamn' adventure. You remember when I used to meet you at Mouquin's. All the waiters leaving. Everybody talking about '*La Belle France*' and '*les sales Boches.*' The same thing down at Princeton. You wouldn't be a real man unless you went. So we did. . . . Then it was fear, fear of being called a coward that made you stay. After I was wounded and my leave was up, I was an *evadé* for more than two weeks. I simply couldn't bring myself to go back. Jerrod had to drive back from the section and fetch me."

"Where were you?"

"Billy-goat drunk in some whore's apartment on the Butte. Jerrod knew her. That was the only way he found me. Mother— mother had the idea right to the end that I was a hero, didn't she?"

"Yes. But let's not talk any more. It's such a nice night."

She was thinking of the funeral, had already imagined the details. The body slack and brown skinned, the thin hair carefully combed back, the ornate coffin, the massed, unlovely flowers, the Reverend Neubel in his too long coat, her father and mother moving through the crowd with just a slight suggestion of sorrow, Stace quiet and tight nerved and solemn wearing a black tie and a stiff collar and explaining again and again to the out-of-town people that his brother and sister-in-law were in Bermuda, couldn't get back. The Old Man would sit by himself. People around him, of course, but still by himself. Oh, if only Phelim and Stuffy and some of the boat people could be there. They'd see that the Old Man got a quick drink. They were his kind and they were the ones to handle him if anybody could. Stace would have to do the rest, but he was capable, not as capable as Mark, still able to do the job.

"Here's where we turn off," Mark said. "This is the path to the Middle Road."

"Take it easy," she said. "I'm out of breath."

They stood at the side of the road against a wall while she got her breath. The darkness was purple with an undercast of mauve. Out in the sound the water was black marble very dimly touched by the light of stars. Along the shore the houses rested pale and for the most part quiet. The breeze was enough to rattle and chafe softly the palm fronds overhead. From time to time carriages passed them on the way in to Hamilton.

The Negro drivers sat erect, crying to the horses, making their whips snap. The people in the back seats were usually couples, a man and a girl or two men and two girls. They laughed and sang, talked in the loud excitement of alcohol or sat held close as they kissed. The ruddy cast of the carriage lights caught the faces and Ingë said suddenly, "I don't like people."

"You're people, too," Mark said. "But if you feel that way, we'd better not go to the party."

She swerved her bicycle around towards the path to the Middle Road. "No. I think the party will be fun."

They stopped again on the Middle Road. It was before a big and old house set within wide lawn behind a high wall. Ingë had remarked the house before, the wine-purple of the poinsettia and the hibiscus reaching like strange flame up over the grayish coral walls, the sheer, startling beauty of the flamboyant tree at the corner of the garden that faced the sea. "I remember this place," she said. "Henrietta told me once she used to work here. Up beyond is where they grow the Easter lilies. Just thousands and thousands of lilies."

"You sound like a local real estate agent."

"I might," she said. But she knew that she had taken him from thinking about his mother and the Old Man. "Listen, Mark." Inside the house on a piano just slightly out of tune someone was playing Grieg. "When I'm old, I'd like to live in that house."

"You're going back to Patigowoc and live in your own house."

"Not now," she said. "We'll live at 'The Towers.' "

"Don't be so generous." He stared at her, leaning across his handlebars. " 'The Towers' is an enormous place for you to maintain."

"You wouldn't like it, though, if it were shut up. And where would the Old Man and Stacey live?"

He laughed and she was pleased to hear the sound. "I've often thought that you were much more of a Kennard than a Keiberg. Still, I want my own home. And let that pair of sailors get a woman to keep house for them. They'll get accustomed to it."

"How selfish you are!" she said, then laughed so that he would understand that her words weren't entirely serious. "You'd like me all to yourself. *Pasha* Kennard and his one-woman harem. Shall I get myself some filmy trousers and curled-up slippers?"

"You'd look well in them." Mark dropped his cigarette and ground it into the coral dust. He got on his bicycle and motioned to her. "I'm hungry," he said. "Let's get to the party."

She said as they rode side by side, "It's supposed to be a very good party. Grace Morris is filthy rich. You'll meet her new husband here tonight. He used to be a room clerk in some hotel at Saratoga. She met him there at the races last summer."

"I'm going back," Mark said. He stopped his bicycle and cursed. "I have no desire to be with folks like that tonight."

"Darling," she said; "darling. You needn't talk with them except to say 'How do you do?', 'Thank you' and 'Goodnight.' There's to be a big bonfire, and chicken and caviar and champagne right on the beach. We can sit by ourselves in the dark. But if we want, we can find somebody nice with whom we can talk."

"Will some *type* get up and imitate Al Jolson?"

"I doubt it very much. Grace isn't the kind for that."

"I'm difficult," Mark said. "I'm acting like a damn' fool."

"You don't seem so to me."

He caressed her cheek. "I adore you," he said.

They rode in single file, Mark ahead, down a rutted sandy path between small, wind-bent cedars. From over the shoulder of a dune they could suddenly see the russet reflection of a bonfire on the beach. They halted, jumped down from their bicycles. A gramophone was playing and they heard the voices of people who had already had a lot to drink. "What's Grace's new name?" Mark said.

"Morris."

"I've got it." But instead of going on he stood staring out past the dunes at the sea. He realized that there was no further sense in holding memory back. He had to speak or he couldn't go to the party and be with those people. It had been bad enough at the hotel, worse on the road, and Ingë would understand.

In a voice which was low and unconsciously took the rhythm of the sea, he told her, "I wear the ribbons, I suppose, because I must insist to myself that I was proud to be in the war. But when I look back, what I see is death. I taste death. I smell it. Men burning in tanks. Men rotting in trenches while the rats gnaw them. Bodies like a log jam in a river at home in the spring. And blinded men, crippled men, brutes, maniacs. Stabbing the prisoners, blowing them up with hand grenades, turning machine guns on them when they were in columns of hundreds. At Verdun, when they tried to stop the looting, sixty-two military police—Frenchmen—were hung up by Frenchmen on the meat hooks in the butcher shops. I saw them; I helped take some down. And in the Forêt de Retz. . . ."

"Mark, must you?"

He glared at her and then gradually the glaze went from his

eyes. "No. But remember later that I'm a little bit crazy. Anybody
who went to that war long enough is a little bit crazy. Because
I was, I stayed out there as long as I did, and then spent the year
in Colorado. I couldn't face you, or my family."

"I guessed as much, Mark. There are others like you."

"Thank you," he said. "I won't speak of it again."

"I didn't mean that."

"You should." He was stumbling on through the sand towards
the bonfire. She had to run to catch up to him. "Mark, kiss me." He
turned and kissed her, his lips stiff and cold. "You love me?" "Yes,
of course I love you," he said. "Then we'll be all right," she said.
"I promise you, darling."

He laughed at her, his arm around her waist. "I believe it when
you say it. Strangely, I do. . . ."

Their hostess held a five gallon goldplated cocktail shaker
beside her. She poured them very chill and strong Martinis. Her
husband gave them plates of chicken and potato salad and caviar
and they moved away along the beach. The other guests were tour-
ist Americans, Bermudians and Canadians and a few officers from
the British regiment in garrison.

Ingë knew people, nodded, smiled, waved to them, but kept
on steadily at Mark's side out beyond the center of the firelight.
The bonfire was of high piled driftwood. It was built at the base
of a small cove. Old and jagged coral rose on three sides back from
the little strip of beach where the guests sat on steamer rugs. Out
in the cove was a pinnacle of coral. Around it entered the breakers
from the open Atlantic. They swept the cove mouth in somber,
phosphorous-veined masses, then toppled, rushed the coral in a
spume of recoil.

The fire was beginning to burn down. A British officer in uniform came to Mark and Ingë with a bottle of whiskey. He glanced
quickly at Mark's ribbons. "Cheers," he said. "Must have a nip
while the piper plays. The fellow's former Canadian Black Watch,
works as a barman at a hotel here. But they say he won the Princess
of Connaught's medal, and I doubt if she gave it to him for just
fiddle-dee-dee."

"Good of you," Mark said and took the bottle. The officer had
wandered off down the beach and he and Ingë were by themselves
again. The bagpiper was striding the beach in front of the fire.
He was bringing the air into his pipes and they gave odd squeaking
and squawking and bleating sounds.

Mark held Ingë's hand. "The Old Man would like a thing like this," he said. But then he realized that the Old Man if he were here would try to dominate it with his stories, the outright force of his personality. Failing that, he'd sit in glum silence, or curse the people for being stupid, go away.

The Old Man was rough, Mark told himself. Back home, he'd have trouble with him in the company. No sense evading the fact. It had to be. Mark pulled the cork from the bottle and handed the bottle to her. "Good luck to us, darling."

"The same, old dear."

He took the bottle from her and drank and watched the piper. The man strutted at the water's edge. He wore a pair of blue serge trousers and a white shirt. He didn't look like a piper, and he had rolled up his trousers above the knees. The tartan cloth of the pipes swelled. The drones lifted. The music was suddenly magnificent.

The piper played tune after tune, strathspeys and reels and laments and marches. The music rose and rose again in the shadowed cove. It was fierce and yet tender, wildly harsh and as soft as the sibilance of the breaker wash up over the sand.

At first as they listened they applauded and some of the British officers called out to suggest a tune. But now the piper had been given a bottle of whiskey and he had drunk his share of it. He was out on the pinnacle of coral in the cove and climbing it step by step as he played. He stood at its top with the great, dark-shining reach of the Atlantic at his back.

The fire was down to embers. The faint scarlet glimmer of light went only part way up the pinnacle. The piper stood in darkness until the half moon broke and ascended.

It seemed to incite him and his playing. He held the traditional, ancient posture, head back, elbows out, feet spread with his knees slightly bent. The rush and the hiss and the sighing retreat of the sea made counter-point for what he played. Mark thought, this is barbaric and wonderful. The Old Man has Scottish blood on his father's side. The Scots are a great people. In his way, the Old Man is great.

Mark drank from the bottle. He was giddy, drunker than he had ever been in his life. He leaned his shoulder against Ingë. His wife. She understood him. The horror. That didn't matter to her. Between them, they'd lose it. He needed her very much now that Mother was gone.

But then his thought was lost in the music. He was led to crests of ecstasy where he believed that he stood alone against all the winds of the world. The winds subsided and in the depths of a lament he wanted to hold his head in his hands, weep as he had only heard women weep.

It was finished with a lament. The piper came stalking down off the pinnacle, the fire making a bright, small shield of his face. Mark lurched up and went to him. He wasn't sure of what he would say to the man, still he must speak. The Old Man would like it if he did. "Magnificent," he told the piper. "Really fine."

"Thank ye, sir," the piper said.

But Mark wouldn't let him go. He knew in the mazes of the whiskey what he wanted to say. "Sorry my brother Stacey wasn't here to hear you. Real sailor. Man you'd be glad to meet."

The piper gave him a blankly pleasant smile and went on up the beach. *Merde, alors,* Mark thought. I didn't put it over at all. The man didn't understand what I meant to say. But Ingë was beside him and clasped his arm. "Come on, old boy. We're going home."

"To the Old Man and Stace?"

"Yes." Her grip increased. "But that's not until next week, remember? Now we're going back to the cottage."

"Damn the cottage," he said. "I want to go home."

CHAPTER SEVENTEEN

Alan Kennard stayed up late the first night at sea. He had sat in the smoke-room talking animatedly with anybody there until the steward had closed it. Then he had gone below to his cabin for his topcoat and climbed to the boat deck. He took enormous pleasure from the windy, salty night; he was back on salt water, he told himself, if only as a bloody passenger.

He was aware that the decision to make this trip hadn't been entirely his own and the fact also pleased him. Mark and Ingë and Stacey, too, had worked to get him to go away. They said he needed a rest, that he hadn't had a real vacation in years. And the company was running fine. Mark, he was a real corker when it came to selling, and Stace, damn him for not finding himself a wife, was sure the man to handle the ships. Between them they didn't leave him much to do any more.

Let out to pasture, Kennard thought. That was one way to say it. But it wasn't exactly so. He was still the president of the company. He had the stock control in his own hands and could go back any time he wanted. If he didn't like the way he found things in Europe, he could always hit for home, back to Bachelors' Hall with Stace.

A bell was rung on the bridge: one-two, one-two, one, the notes drawn long upon the wind. A bigger bell answered from the focslehead, followed by the lookout's shout: "Lights 're burning bri-ight, sir!"

"Aye, aye!" That was the senior officer of the watch on the bridge. Alan Kennard was tempted to go forward to the bridge, introduce himself and pass the rest of the watch there. But the skipper might not like it. You wouldn't too much if you were skipper of her. Don't be acting like some goddamn' Johnny Come Lately. You're sixty and some, man. You've been at sea before, stood your share of watches. Chop along and hit the bunk. There's plenty of good-lookers for you to check among the women, and no doubt tomorrow before the day's out the skipper will ask you up onto the bridge. Mark fixed it so the chief steward knows who you are and will pass the word. That Mark, he's smart. Next president of Kennard and Company. The fella for the job, too. Stace is a sailors' sailor, but the lad lacks something, and it ain't just a wife. . . .

Alan Kennard dreamed as he slept. There were several parts to the dream, and they merged. In one part he was a young lad again in Daigvera. Another part had him at his present age and at Mark's house on the point opposite the Bouche de Mouche light, his three grandchildren around him, the smallest one, the girl who was named Minna after his wife, on his knee. From the laughter of the children he reverted to the sound of keening. He sat under the rowan tree and it was his mother who keened.

Agitated by the dream, he flung out an arm and it struck against the bulkhead, awoke him. "Steady you go," he said aloud. The dream fragments were still distinct. "Here you are on your way to Ireland so there's no reason your gettin' in a sweat about the old days. Sure, you were lonely, and many a night hungry, nothing in your belly save ache and wind. But you're wealthy now, a rich man. You'll find your mother's grave and get her a great, fine headstone. Then off to Belfast and Dublin and London and Paris to see the sights, live like a sport. Take it easy, man. Sleep sound."

Daigvera, coming to it in a rented car from Ballycastle, was a shock to him. It wasn't that it was so drab, so small against his memories. It was that he no longer belonged here at all. The cottage was gone, a rough stone-walled cow byre in its place. He couldn't find his mother's grave, and the Town Hall was closed for the day, nobody in the public house recalled his name.

He stood there in the musty, beery semi-obscurity of the public house bar and realized that he was a stranger, more, a foreigner. He had lost the knack of the talk although always he had prided himself that he still possessed it. In Belfast he had taken care to buy a grey felt hat, a cane and gloves. But he was a Yank to those who stood around him; they could tell by his suit and shoes, his accent, his manner and the way he spent his money. Ah, to hell with it all, he thought. You're a fool to have come back. Mark and Stace, by God, they put over a swindle on you.

The driver of his car was dozing behind the wheel. He woke the man abruptly and said, "Take me to Belfast."

"And now," the driver said, because before on the way from Ballycastle they had talked congenially, "you surprise me. I thought you was one, sir, to go see the Glens and the Gray Man's Path, Carrick-a-Rede and the like."

"The hell with 'em!" Alan Kennard said. "Ireland's not for me."

The driver was still, his face red with anger. But as he turned the car out of the High Street Kennard heard him mutter, "Ye Yankee bastard!"

Belfast had nothing to keep him and he took the first ship for England. The passage was foggy, with a choppy sea, and he spent his time in the bar with a group of English commercial travelers who were attracted by his clothes, wanted to know about America and shared his views about Ireland.

It was clear, high, beautiful summer in England. On the train to London, during a time of marvelous crepuscular light that lasted nearly until ten o'clock, he became entranced with the countryside. Ireland was as fine, he told himself, and nowhere was there anything like the Glens. But you couldn't bring yourself back to a place that was gone. His Daigvera was of the heart, not the head, and between him and that was fifty years. A long time, man. A long time indeed. . . .

He spent a month and a considerable amount of money in London. He stayed at Brown's Hotel, using a letter Mark had written for him, he went to a Saville Row tailor for six suits and a dinner jacket, picked up a sedate looking but fiery little whore in Piccadilly who had a furnished flat in Kensington, took her to the night clubs, the music halls and race meetings. But she was the paid mistress of a Royal Navy commander and when the commander returned from duty at Malta it was sensible, Kennard knew, to go on to Paris.

He wrote two letters home his last night in London. One that he sent to Mark and Ingë was filled with information about the sights of London that he had got from the hall porter. The other, to Stacey, was about the whore and the race meeting. When he had mailed them, he wryly laughed. It wasn't that he was scared to tell Mark and Ingë the truth. But they might think him an old goat, and deep down underneath he still reckoned Mark as a stuffy Easterner.

The Channel crossing from Dover was clear and he stayed on deck watching the cliffs fade, the lights of vessels, then the headlands of France. You're adrift on the land, he realized. Only out on the water do you have your feet under you. Ah, Minna, I miss you darlin'. A whore's no real satisfaction after you and maybe I did wrong to climb into the commander's bunk while he was out of it.

Paris, the honking, hurtling taxis and the exclamatory, asperate language confused him. He felt extremely lonely even in the Ambassadeurs Hotel, the Folies Bergères, Harry's New York Bar. The whores were too flat breasted for his taste, and the Americans he met either supercilious, very young or loud. Wholly on impulse he went on his second morning to the American Express and asked for the address of Jane Shaw. The clerk who gave it to him explained that it was in a small village back from the Mediterranean in the foothills of the Maritime Alps. He tipped the clerk and made reservations on the overnight train from Paris to Nice. They could keep Paris. He liked the Arch of Triumph with the little blue flame bending in the wind in the dark, but the people, Jesus Christ, the way they waved their hands and hollered, they drove him crazy. In Nice, he could rest up and get to understand a bit of this talky-talky. Then he'd go see Jane. Might be she'd be glad to see him. What the hell, he was only drifting anyhow.

Jane lived in a pinkish red villa on a red hillside. She had sent a telegram to him at Nice telling him to come, but he was met at the gate by a sallow woman in a sleazy black bombazine dress and rope soled sandals. The woman gave him a hard stare and said, "*Attendez.*"

He stood for perhaps five minutes in the beating sunlight outside the gate, shifting from foot to foot and becoming more and more angry before he heard Jane's voice. "Come in, Antrim," she said. "There was one particular nuance of light I must have."

She sat under a eucalyptus tree before an easel. She wore a loose cotton dress and was barefoot. Her hair was completely gray, hung to her shoulders, and her face was brown with years of this sun. She put down her brush to take his hand, then the maid brought a chair and he sat. "D' you mind," Jane said, "if I go on painting? It's my favorite time of day."

"No," he said, knowing nothing else to say. For a time he looked over her shoulder at her canvas, but the composition didn't make sense to him and he slowly fell into sleep, his hat over his eyes. When he awoke, the easel, the palate and brushes and paint box were gone. Jane had turned in her chair. She faced him.

"Minna must be dead," she said.

"Some years back," he said. "Spring of 1920." He felt no constraint with Jane. She had become an old woman, and still she wasn't a stranger. She had met him in the way he had pretty much expected. To Jane, Jane always came first.

"I'm sorry to hear it," Jane said. "D' you miss her?"

"Yeah. A hell of a lot."

Jane lit a cigarette, one of the kind that came in the blue package and had the smell for him of wood shavings burning. She stretched her thin, sinewy legs, ran a hand back through her hair. Her eyes squinted in contemplation. "You have the look of a rich man, Antrim."

"I am. Company's worth a couple of million. I got eight vessels and the biggest limestone business in Michigan. Mark, he's done damn' well, too, with the cement and brick side of it."

"Mark's your elder son. The other's name is Stacey."

"You got a good memory."

"Joshua wrote me about them."

"What's happened to Josh?"

"He was killed in the war. Both he and his son. They joined the British Army." Her hand brushed briefly across her eyes as if suddenly the sun were too strong. "I suppose you'd like a drink, and some food."

"Sure," he said. "But I don't want to put you to trouble, Jane. I got the car out there, with a driver. What say you and me go some place and have a nice lunch? Pick any place you like."

Jane smiled, standing from her chair, and he saw that her body was scrawny, angular, that she moved with a decided limp. "I seldom leave here, Antrim. I find no reason to do so. Would brandy to drink suit you, and a ham omelette?"

"Sure, dandy. But I figured——"

She was going on to the house and he let his voice drop. A feeling of resignation claimed him. There was no sadness in it, simply acceptance of the fact that Jane was old, fixed in her ways, and that for her what he wanted didn't count. She's almost like an old maid, he thought, though Christ knows she ain't that. One thing you didn't figure was that she'd be living alone. You reckoned she'd have some woman pal around, maybe even a man, one of these Frenchies with the slick hair and talk. But she's sailed past that. Finished with engines.

"Do come inside, Antrim," Jane called from a side doorway. "It's considerably cooler and what little ice I have won't last long."

The room into which she led him was long and pleasant with shadow, the floor set in red, uneven tiles, an immense hooded chimney place in one corner. The furniture was dark and heavy, comfortable, and he sat fully relaxed in a chair with a broad leather back. Jane poured brandy and soda for him, but none for herself. "I gave up in the war," she said. "Before that, I used to drink too much."

"Were you in the war, Jane?"

"I was a nurse with the French."

"My boy, Mark," he said proudly and quickly, "was with the French. Then the A.E.F. Got a couple of medals."

"Splendid," she said, but there was no enthusiasm in her voice, and she added at once, "I've told the maid to feed your driver. The poor man shouldn't sit out there unfed in the heat."

Alan Kennard revolved the brandy glass in his hands. He savored the bouquet and then drank gulping. Might be that he'd been wrong to come visit Jane. He felt now as if he was slipping down over a cliff into an unknown darkness. Jane, she was still goddamn' odd. You couldn't tell what she was going to say or do next. But you just can't get up and shove off. You ain't that rude, and you're hungry. Stick around a while more.

Jane had lit another cigarette, the smoke drifting pallid through the shadow. "What was your reason for leaving America?"

"Dunno." He set the empty glass on the table near him. "Mark and Stace ha' got the company running so good there wasn't much left for me to do. They gave me the idea to come on out and visit the old country."

"And how did you find it?"

He shrugged. He held out his powerful, stubby hands in an unconsciously dramatic gesture. "Not for me, Jane. What I knew when I was a lad, that's all gone. Couldn't even find my mother's grave. Couldn't even. . . . Ah, to hell with it!" He stared at her, sitting tensely forward in the chair. "You happy?"

"Yes," Jane said softly, "I'm happy. Let me fill your glass."

He drank eagerly. "But back in the old days you weren't."

"Antrim, I've given up thinking about them. It's—the French call it *recherche du temps perdu*. Seeking for what's past, and lost. Why? Why should one? I've emerged from that, then survived a ghastly war. There's another war or wars ahead. Meantime, I paint and live, and am happy."

"I don't follow you," he said. "Not about the war stuff anyhow. And here you are alone. You got no family, nobody. When your time comes to die——"

"—I shall still be happy." She motioned around towards the table. "Luncheon's ready. Let us eat. But bring your glass and the bottle."

He became quite befuddled by the brandy after luncheon. Jane had to direct him twice to the primitive bathroom and in the mirror there he saw that his eyes were red-cast, his lips shiny, wet and loose. He straightened his tie and scowled, told himself savagely to cut it out. But he was being buffeted by heightening waves of memory. They formed in a whirligig fashion, spun through his mind.

When he went back to Jane in the living room, they were moving very fast. The pair of chestnuts in the snow outside the Weddell House bar, Josh, more snow. Josh again, the huge white house, candles, Josh, snow, a lavender silk dress, that was the old lady, Josh, a candy striped shirtwaist, that was Jane, the old lady, Josh, Jane, candy stripes, snow, the old lady, the colonel, Cottrell, snow, candles, Jane, old lady, Cottrell, Lucinda, old lady, drink, dinner, drink, dinner, Jane, piano, sing, sing, laugh, old lady, colonel, Josh, stairs, bed, bed, snow, dark, Jane.

"I sang 'Kelvin Green,'" he said to the gray-haired Jane. Pronouncing the words broke the spell of the whirligig. Keep on talking, he thought, and you'll make yourself sober.

"Yes, you did," Jane said. "Would you like some coffee?"

He blinked at her. "That's right, sober me up. But you, you can get away from yourself without booze. Me, I can't even with the stuff."

"Alan, to be honest, I never suspected you wish to do so."

"Ah, g' on!" he said. But it was true, he knew. Never before this. No. You never wanted to get away from yourself until now. Why? Ask her. Maybe she can tell you. Another question was in the way, and he blurted the words:

"Shouldn't you kick me to hell outa here? I ain't any fun to you."

She smiled and shook her head. The maid had entered with a tray and she took off the coffee pot and cups, filled a cup for him. "You give me perspective," she said. "If you do nothing else, Antrim, you show me I wasn't mistaken to get away from my mother."

"What part's your mother got in this deal?"

"The forces that wrecked her are having their effect on you."

"G' on! My life's a lot different than hers. She was all mixed up by the old time stuff. She wanted your old man sober, Cottrell sober, all hands singing hymns and church-going. Christer, that's what she was."

"But lost in the same fashion you are. She hated the world, was afraid of it. You're driven by fear, Antrim. That's at the base of your life." Jane had gone from her chair to light candles in the room. Their flames wavered, lifted and steadied as she stepped over to him with the coffee cup in her hands. She looked down into his eyes. "What are you after? How far are you going to go before you stop being afraid?"

"Goddamn you!" he said. His thought was arrested by remembrance. He was in bed in the white house at Bellport. He listened to the tightening and expansion of floor planks. Beams flexed in the night cold. Icicles which had gathered on the eaves cracked and fell with a soft, slight pop into the snow. The branches of the elms had their own cracking sound under the tension of the frost. From the lake, a mile or so away, he figured, came the rumble, then retreat of breakers. The wind was from the Northwest, hauling North. It was hoarse along the shingles here, muttered down the chimneys. A chipmunk scratched somewhere busily, without interruption. When Jane came into the room, when she came and sat down on the edge of the bed, he didn't hear her. He had been asleep and his dreams had been of Daigvera, his mother, poverty, loneliness, the village lads who had picked on him because he wore tattered pants and was a gypsy's son.

"Tell me," Jane said, her eyes knife keen, knife hard in the candle light.

"Sure I will," he said hoarsely. "I ain't afraid of anything or anybody. I've built up a fine, thriving business. Minna, I took first class care of her. And the boys, I've made real men of them. Both at the top."

"But at what price?"

"Ah, you mean the strike, that old business."

"No. I hardly know of that. I mean what's inside you right now, what you tell yourself when you're alone in the night."

His desire was to curse her again, but strangely he recognized the futility of it. "I miss Minna," he said. "That's about all. Maybe worry a bit about the business. You, though, Jane. You run away, and me, I stayed and fought."

"So through the looking glass we go," she said. "Antrim, there's little else that I can tell you. Except that you've sold your life to other men. You don't own yourself; they do."

"I'm a free man from the freest country in the world. You'd tear me down outa jealousy. You have no husband, no children, nothing savin' them paintings. It's me who's sorry for you, Jane. Still, I didn't come here to tell you this. I thought maybe——"

"—We could be happy," she said. "*Jamais de la vie. Jamais.*" She was limping across the room and when she returned she had his hat and gloves. "Go on down to Nice. They have plenty of casinos for your kind. You might make a great pot of money, so much that while you're playing you can forget what's happened to you."

He stood, his pride hurt, rage burning at the back of his mind. He took the hat and gloves, then gave her a short nod. "Thanks for the drinks, and, yeah, the food. When I write home, I'll tell the boys I saw you."

"Don't bother," she said. She had opened the door for him. "Goodbye, Antrim."

Back in the hotel at Nice he ordered a bottle of brandy sent to his suite, then he stood on the balcony overlooking the Promenade des Anglais and the sea. He drank the brandy gulp by gulp from the bottle and after an hour or so, staggering drunk, he sang "Kelvin Green." People below on the promenade gazed up at him in the night and some few waved their hands and he waved back.

But there was a knocking on the door to the hall. Bellboy to pipe me down, he thought. Dump the son-of-a-bitch. He started in and tripped against a chair leg, sprawled, went down grunting. The door slowly opened; he tried numbly to get to his feet. "Oh, you poor man." It was a woman and the voice was American. "Can I help you?"

"Just a little drunk," he said. "But you can help me."

She pulled him up onto the small, stiff divan. The effort made her pant, and he was aware that she wasn't young, wore a corset under the expensive evening dress. "I'm Mrs. Venner," she said when she had her breath. "Judith Venner. I have the suite next door. As I came in from dinner, I heard you singing. It sounded so nice. Then I heard you fall and I took the liberty of opening the door."

"Glad you did," Alan Kennard said. "Don't know why I'm so drunk, but I reckon I need a little company. Where's my bottle?

Had a bottle. Get the bottle and we'll have a drink and sing a little song."

Her scrutiny of him was swift. "You're Alan Kennard, aren't you, from Michigan?"

"That I am."

"They were talking of you at luncheon today, people I know here."

"Ain't as famous as you'd make out."

"But yes you are," she said laughing. "Your arrival's been mentioned in the *Daily Mail* and the *Herald*. Ships, isn't it, and limestone?"

"Spoke to some fella in the lobby, but didn't know he was a reporter. Let's have a drink. And a song. Used to be a big singer in my day."

Mrs. Venner touched his cheek with her fingertips. "I'll be right back," she said.

She returned wearing a soft silk dressing gown and she smelled of freshly applied perfume. On the make, Alan Kennard thought out of his old habit of caution, and beef to the heel like a Mullinger heifer. But she'll do all right in the bunk and you got the chips to afford her.

They sat side by side on the divan while they sang "There's a Long, Long Trail Awinding," "Take Me Out to the Ball Game," "Mother Macree" and scraps of "Shenandoah." He drank from the bottle between songs and when they reached "Shenandoah" he was only mumbling. She helped him up from the divan into the bedroom, then the bed. He tore her dressing gown yanking at it, but she made no protest, slid it off and moved confidently in next to him. He had a moment of desperate fear about his physical ability and began to sweat. She was very competent, though, and he went to sleep at last in her arms.

The hangover swung like a gigantic hammer inside his skull. Each time he raised his head he cried out dolorously and lowered it back onto the pillow and hoped for further sleep. The pain stayed, kept him awake. He was aware of the woman beside him in the bed. He by degrees recalled last night and her name. "Hey, Judith," he croaked, "get me an aspirin. This here thing is killin' me."

"Right away," she said. He drank and gulped and she stroked

the back of his head and he felt better. "Goddamn," he said, "why'd I go and tie into that one?"

"You were lonely, dear," she said.

He stared at her, sober, calculating. She looked pretty if too plump in daylight, and he remembered how well she had done in bed. "Come back," he said.

"My goodness!" she said. But she came back and she was as good as she had been before.

"Should keep you around," he told her. "You're the kind who knows her work."

"I suppose I should be insulted," she said, "but I'm not. You excite me. I like being with you."

"Bilge. Who's keepin' you?"

"Now you are too rough, Alan. I'm a divorced woman. I've been divorced for years. My husband's remarried and my daughters are grown and married." She lightly laughed. "I'm a grandmother."

"Where you from?"

"Tacoma, Washington."

"What you doing here?"

"I have enough money to travel, and I like men. Before you, I...."

"Before me, what?"

"Well, it was young men, professional *gigolos* usually, and I had to pay."

He was propped up on an elbow to look at her. "Goddamn me if I don't think you're on the square."

"Do you think I would have answered your questions if I weren't? You're awfully direct, you really are."

"But you don't mind."

"No."

He got out of bed and went to the bathroom. He returned to find her at his dressing table fixing her hair. "Alan, I saw the nicest little villa at Villefranche yesterday," she said. "I almost took it. These hotels are so expensive, and if you have a villa you can do just about what you like."

"You and me in the villa, huh?"

He stood behind her and she raised her head and kissed him. "That's right. It would be dandy. You see, I have a number of friends and we could entertain a lot. You wouldn't be lonely any more."

"Go get dressed," he said. "We'll have ourselves some food and take a ride and see the villa."

His months with Judith Venner were reasonably happy ones. She was a good hostess and unfailingly complaisant and often insistent in bed. Her friends were a mixed, rather peculiar group, and they represented, he discovered, a cross-section of Riviera society. Some few were English, others White Russians, Swedes, Belgians, Brazilians, Americans. One Englishman, a cotton mill owner from Manchester, was wealthy, owned a huge villa in back of the Beau Site Hotel at Cannes. The rest lived in varying circumstances, but they all had presentable clothes, enough money for the casinos or an occasional dinner party.

He became at his ease among them. The men soon called him by his first name, didn't resent the fact that he refused to lend money, and the women ignored his rough speech. But when he was with them, even when he was alone with Venner in the Villefranche villa he was able to withdraw from them, regard his life in retrospect.

He saw it now as unguided, without purpose beyond the limits of his personal ambition. What Jane Shaw had said to him hadn't shaken his belief in himself in any fundamental way, but he recognized that she had been right in telling him that through the years he had taken the orders, obeyed the will of powerful men who thought of him only in terms of an inferior. They were the Morgans, the Rockefellers and Hannas and Goulds and Carnegies. Back years ago, at the time of the seamen's strike in '04, Aeneas Lothrop had explained it to him. By Christ, he was lucky to have come along as far as this.

You think about it, the news from the States wasn't good. The Von Sweringens were about to take the count, Mark wrote, and so was Sam Insull with his goddamn' opera house and hot-air schemes. It had been one beaut of a year, '29, but nobody seemed to be pulling out of the stock market crash the way Hoover had promised. Fellas were jumping out of windows in New York. Stockbrokers, sure, but men who'd made a lot of money for themselves. Maybe he'd have to cut down on Venner, tell her to let one of the maids go, or get a smaller car than the Alfa Romeo. That ate up gas like a bastard, and Raoul was sure enough a dandy chauffeur, but just as sure he was making rake-off deals behind his back with the local garage.

Mark hadn't written him yet to lay off spending money; there was always at least ten thousand in his personal account with the Bankers' Trust. The financial statement for last year, too, was a corker. Mark had sent it over with a lot of pride. You know the figures; you got them in your head. Investment in real property and equipment, and that doesn't mean the ships: $463,328. Other investments, which means the ships: $6,400,550. Cash: $82,137. Materials and supplies, that's the limestone, the brick, the rest of it: $244,868. Total working assets: $245,703. Capital stock, and you've kept it down on purpose so's you can control it: $65,000. Unmatured funded debt: None.

None, by God. You sit in dandy shape. Offhand, you can't remember how many tons your ships hauled. But for '28 you do remember, and '29 was a good sight bigger. Short tons only, just hauling ore for other companies from Superior, 153,679 tons. And you got a good rate, 1.06 mills per ton per mile. That ain't saying a word about your stuff, the limestone, the brick, the cement. Man, you're rich and you're going to hang on to what you got.

But some of them here on the coast are taking in sail. They're headed for home and the simple life. No more dough. They got cleaned in the stock market. Should ha' known better. Mark would've told them. "Keep out of the market," Mark said, way back in early '28. He was talking about a piece some fella from the Cleveland Trust Company had printed. Six hours for stock tickers to handle the business done in five hours. Six days for the brokerage house clerks to handle the paper business done in five days. Stock market shut Saturdays. Brokers' loans getting bigger by a hundred million a week. Leading stocks on the market bringing in from dividends about half of what it costs to carry them on margin.

Mark knew. With a smart son like him, you can't go wrong. Maybe you'd better talk to Venner tonight, though. She won't take to it nice. She likes you for one thing, sailor, your pile of chips. She spends with both hands, and you stop her, you stop the parade. All right. You can make yourself another parade.

Alan Kennard had been standing on the terrace of the high-perched villa. Dusk had shut on the sea and town below. Nightingales were singing in the mimosa. Cicadas were among the olive trees on the lower slopes. A workman on the way home down the steeply curving road on his bicycle sang "Ramona" in a high, sweet tenor. Kennard poured himself a whiskey and soda and went back onto the terrace. There was the subdued roar of a powerful motor.

The Alfa Romeo climbed fast up the mountain, slung in through the gateway with a blaze of headlights. Raoul jumped out, nimble and handsome in his white cap, white, black trimmed coat, black britches, and long black gauntlets and puttees. He opened the rear door and Judith Venner stepped out onto the gravel tipsily smiling.

Not tonight, Kennard thought. You won't talk business to her. She's drunk and she must have lost her shirt at the casino. All you can do is give her a job in the bunk. But tomorrow you get squared away with her. You tell her no more Alfa Romeo, just one maid and no losing five thousand francs a crack on the wheel.

Judith Venner didn't argue with him when he told her in the morning. "Then it's finished," she said and sat and wept. That depressed him. He picked up his hat and stick, walked down through the shining walls of sunlight to the port.

An American destroyer was at anchor in the harbor, the first liberty parties ashore. He entered a bar frequented by seamen and at once the flat sounds of the American voices were pleasant in his ears. For a while he drank by himself, then got into a conversation with a bosun's mate, a chief electrician's mate and two gunners. The chief electrician's mate was an old timer and had sailed the Mediterranean in the war. He had stories of the Café Verdi in Genoa, the Galleria in Naples. Kennard raked out his early memories and told of Seville and the bullfight, held their awe with a description of a full rigged ship under all sail.

He was comfortably drunk when he left the café and started climbing the mountain to the villa. Good thing to come in sober, he decided. There was stuff he had to finish with Venner and the walk would sweat the whiskey out of him.

The Alfa Romeo was in front of the villa, but Raoul wasn't in sight. He went up the steps, across the terrace, into the room Venner had taught him to call the salon and to the door of her bedroom. The door was shut. He opened it.

Judith Venner and Raoul lay naked on the bed. They were locked in a spasm of fornication, Venner writhing and panting, her face rapt. Kennard shut the door and went to his own room. His feeling was that of vague embarrassment. He felt as if he had come upon Venner seated in the bathroom. He had never loved her or particularly trusted her, known from the beginning of their relationship that she liked to give herself to young men.

He had enough cash to pay the maids and two of them packed

his bags for him. He wrote out a check for Raoul's wages, a check to the sum of ten thousand francs for Venner, then had a maid call him a taxicab by telephone. Venner made no attempt to appear before he left, although from behind the door he heard her speak unevenly to Raoul. Tonight they'll have one hell of a last ride in the Alfa, he thought. He said goodbye to the maids, shook hands, got in the taxi and told the man to drive him to the American Express in Nice.

You're bound home, Kennard. This winds it up. You're too old for such tricks. Mark and Ingë and Stace will have to get along with you. A good thing to be back in Patigowoc. The goddamn' depression will probably cut business a lot. You'll take over the marine super's job again yourself, send Stace out as skipper of the *Minna*. He'll like it better; he likes being on the water instead of behind a desk. You were the same in your day. Bet Mark will be glad to have you home. And, hell, man, you're a Michigander. It's where you belong.

CHAPTER EIGHTEEN

The Old Man was asleep in his chair now, Stacey noticed, and the *Saturday Evening Post* had slipped off his knees onto the floor. A flicker of the flame from the gas log in the fireplace cast across his face, marking the pouches beneath the eyes, the lace-fine network of red veins on the cheeks, the sag of the mouth and jaw muscles.

Stacey thought, he's really old. He's going for seventy soon. A hard worker in his day and a hard liver, topside, bottomside. He's just about the last of his bunch, too. When Phelim went, well, that only left the Old Man. But there's fight in the rooster yet. Back two years ago in France, he was keeping some woman. Remember the night he got drunk and told you. No bones about it. He met her in a hotel so they went and played house together. Mark was scared when Keiberg's bank folded. Not the Old Man. Cost him about three hundred thousand with what the company had in there, but he didn't yipe. Keiberg was the family because of Ingë, so what the hell.

Reflection about his father gradually changed Stacey's mood. Since dinner, he had been content to sit beside the fire and talk and read. He had become restive. Up through his subconscious rose the knowledge that this was his father's house, not his, and this his father's study. Each night after dinner, if his father wanted his company, he was invited here. But if he chose to go into town or visit Mark and Ingë, the Old Man resented it. He was thirty-two years old and a papa's boy. No wife, no kids, nothing but this old geezer, the slab-sided Dutch housekeeper and the house. It was still a good house. He didn't want to leave, and he liked the Old Man. But nights when Mark and Ingë didn't have him over and the Old Man fell asleep early, he wondered why he hadn't married.

Stacey walked to his father's liquor cabinet and poured himself a drink. There was no sense fooling. He knew why he hadn't married. Just hadn't found a girl yet who he liked enough to let her put the towline on him. Sailing was his life. When he wasn't doing that he wasn't worth much, and damned if he was going to give it up. And a Lakes sailor was only home for about four months out of the year, might have a night ashore with his wife half a dozen times in a season. That put a lot of temptation in front of a woman the way he saw it.

Mark was a real handsome guy, a hero. Still Ingë had gone for him while Mark was off to the war. He wasn't as good-looking as Mark, not by a lot, and for certain he was no hero. So what would any wife of his do, with him out pushing some vessel around most of the year?

Ingë was wise to him; she understood. She'd stopped some time back telling him he should get a wife. Could be that Mark had the idea, too. They had him over at their house plenty, and their kids, well, he wasn't going to kid himself, but he was a good deal more than just Uncle Stace to them. Outside that, not being hitched was kind of no good. A man had to watch he didn't get shot in the fanny by some angry husband, or pick up slobs along the water-front and put on his best suit and go to the fancy joints in Chicago or Duluth or Detroit. So all right. That's how it is.

Stacey put the bottle and glass back in the liquor cabinet. He took another look at his father slumped in his chair, mouth part open, then went to the kitchen. Mrs. Van der Haas sat under the overhead light beside the coal range knitting a pair of socks for her grand niece in Saginaw. "Going down-street," Stacey said to her. "You hear the Old Man floundering around, tell him for me he should go to bed. Some night he'll slip out of that chair and catch his pants afire on the gas log."

"Folks I know," Mrs. Van der Haas said testily, "have done away with them things a long while ago. Steam heat should be enough for a body."

"You talk to the Old Man," Stacey said. "I'm just the star boarder around the joint." He let the pantry door wheeze shut on its spring and went to the hall closet and took out an oilskin coat, an old hat. He could hear the drumming of the rain standing there.

He rested for several minutes out on the porch. This was March rain, but there was still ice in the river, in the St. Mary's below the Soo locks and off Whitefish. The boats wouldn't be moving for weeks, and the Old Man had decided to outfit only four of them. Business was real bad. A lot of the charter contracts made last fall had been cancelled out. No cargoes to haul; steel production down fifty percent. Limestone, brick, coal, wheat nearly the same. Hoover, the Great Engineer. Some way to run a country. Every-thing's bound to hell and it won't be long before the Old Man will have to take in slack and start laying off hands at the quarries and the kilns and crews for the boats, too.

Stacey pulled the hat brim low and latched the collar of the oilskin and walked slowly into the murky and chill night. It was a little after nine o'clock, but most of the lights in the houses were already out. Saving electricity. Sitting in the dark, probably, or already in the bunk. Pop and Mom counting up what bucks they got left and where Pop will find a job when Old Man Kennard lowers the boom. Rough. The Great Engineer, he certainly fouled it up.

Gilligan's front door was locked and barred, as it had been ever since Prohibition began, but a light showed in the rear room. Stacey hesitated. He could go in and have a drink. Most likely, though, Pat Gilligan would be snoozing at one end of the bar and the only customers would be hanging onto a glass of that pissy beer. No good. If he bought whiskey, he'd make the guys sore, and if he bought beer they'd think he was a smart guy who wanted to make out he was the same as they were.

He passed Gilligan's and kept on to the Ace Lunch. Nobody was in front of it or the pool hall next door. A lousey night, Stacey thought. Condensed vapor obscured the window of the Ace Lunch. He stared in, water dripping from his hat brim, and saw Wen Bozsick sagged in a booth, the big blonde waitress, the new one from Grand Rapids, on a stool at the counter reading the *Chicago Examiner*.

Stacey's finger had cleared a space on the glass. The blonde turned on the stool and saw him through it, let go of the paper and put a hand to her hair. Stacey opened the door and stepped in.

The blonde stood up from the stool. Her hands on her hips, her body blocking the aisle between the counter and the booths, she said, "Wen ain't here."

Wen Bozsick had served in the Forty-second Division in the war. He had lost his right leg and the local American Legion post had helped him start the lunchroom. Veterans from all over Michigan came to visit him, and he had gone faithfully to every Legion convention, but during the last year many of the veterans had been broke, sought him out for a loan or a free meal.

"Hey, take it easy!" Bozsick called from the booth. "This guy's a friend of mine. Stace, meet Agnes."

"Another high pockets," Agnes said. "I know 'em."

"Agnes ain't too happy tonight," Bozsick said rapidly. "Set down,

Stace." He gestured at Agnes. "You put on your coat, baby, and go over to Gilligan's and get us a pint."

"I ain't going out in that rain," Agnes said. "And I ain't got any money."

"You know you got the money," Bozsick said with anger. "It's in your bag. You stop by Febhauser's, too, on the way back, and buy a nice sirloin steak. Don't you worry, Febhauser'll open up. Just ring the upstairs bell. How about a good hunk o' meat, Stace?"

"Looks like you got one there," Stacey said after Agnes had slammed the door and gone. "But where you been, sport? You been closed for two weeks."

Wen Bozsick was very thin. He played constantly with the gold plated nail cutter at the end of his watch chain, although, Stacey saw, the watch wasn't on the other end. Wen didn't wear his pair of diamond rings, or the ruby cuff links. When he looked up, his bloodshot eyes contracted in a nervous blink.

"Stace, I've fed enough fellas free around here this winter to make a whole damn' company of the National Guard. I never seen it so tough in my whole life."

"Then you'd better dump Agnes. She's the kind that costs money."

"Agnes don't really work here. She does, but her and me are married, Stace. I had to do it to keep the bank from getting the place. Agnes has dough."

"By God, I'm sure surprised."

"You don't know Agnes. She was head waitress over in the Pantlind, and her former husband, he usta have a fine undertakin' business in Jackson. She's been around. I ain't saying, of course, that it's a shame a guy like me has to get married."

"You leave me holding the sack around here all by myself."

"That's no kidding. But how many boats will the Old Man run this season, Stace?"

"Four. That's what he said."

"And how about ashore?"

"I don't know. He and Mark have been talking. It's not my end of the business. I just sit around the company and scratch until the boats are ready to sail."

"But if the Old Man lays off heavy, the town goes straight to hell. Bad enough as it is."

"Needn't tell me. Look, Wen, I'd like to buy the pint and the steak."

"Ain't I said Agnes has dough?"

"So you haven't got your rings. And your cuff links. Here's five bucks. You take it or you're no friend of mine."

Wen Bozsick squirmed around to give his artificial leg more freedom. "You're the best fella in your family, Stace. Never could get to like the Old Man, and Mark, I dunno about Mark and Ingë, they ain't snotty, but they ain't been friendly, either, since we was all kids together."

"Knock it off," Stacey said. "Forget it!"

Agnes was back. She had the pint in her coat pocket and the steak wrapped up in paper. "Now," she said, "I suppose you'll tell me to cook the thing without me even having a snort."

"That's complete one hundred goddamn it percent correct," Wen Bozsick said. He snatched the pint from her. "Get out in the kitchen. Stop insulting me and my friend."

"You louse," Agnes said. "You bum. For this I get married, and maybe four times a week you're any good in bed. If I was to go to the bank tomorrow——"

Bozsick was on his feet, swinging at her, and she ducked, ran behind the counter. He trapped her there and hit her on the jaw. "Don't hit me again," she said; "I take it back."

"Hit ya!" Bozsick sat down in the booth with Stacey. "I'll kill ya! Bring us a pair of them shot glasses from the kitchen. Me and my friend, we drink it neat."

Agnes walked slowly to the booth. "He don't hit hard," she told Stacey. "If he did, I'd leave him, the ape. But all day long I'm here just watching him with that watch chain. Hocked the watch, the rings, the links in Detroit so's he could take care of his old buddies. And the bunch that comes in here. 'Order o' Grape Nuts.' 'Order o' Wheaties.' As a fact. When it's bacon and eggs, they make a hop for the door without payin'. But he sits and he looks at me and he tells me to go get him a pint and a steak."

"Stace, here," Wen Bozsick said distinctly, "is Cap'n Stacey Kennard. Father's Old Man Kennard who runs Kennard and Company. Brother's Mark who got that big, snappy place out on the point. So you keep your mouth outa this."

"Ah, let Agnes sit down and have a drink," Stacey said.

"You're a gentleman, Captain," Agnes said, "like my former husband."

"Listen—" Wen Bozsick said, but Stacey was pouring a drink. He seized his glass and over the brim of it stared at Stacey. "As a fact, Agnes has got it pretty good, Stace. Hunnek's ain't got enough merchandise in on them counters to fill the front door. The Arcade's about to go bust any day. Folks are scared silly. When old Keiberg's bank went, a lot of people took it real hard. What's the answer, Stace? Don't the bright guys like your brother know no answers for the deal?"

Stacey had started to lift his glass, but then, because they watched him curiously, he said, "Mark tried to explain the proposition to me once. It's all about supply and demand and commodities and capital goods. The thing goes back to the war, and the stuff that was destroyed there. But don't blame Mark. He's doing all he can, the Old Man, too."

"Everybody says so," Agnes said. She filled the glasses again. "Mr. Mark Kennard is known to be very handsome and generous. His wife is some looker, too, and having those three kids didn't hurt her figure none. But what are we all going to do to keep alive?"

"You go cook the steak, baby," Wen Bozsick said. "With that around, you don't need to ask no such question."

Agnes rose and smoothed back the gilt-yellow wings of her hair, slid her dress more evenly over her hips and plucked at her girdle. "French fries, Stacey?"

"Yeah, please," Stacey said. He didn't want them, and he didn't want the steak. But Wen was his friend and hungry. Before he left here, he was going to lend Wen more money. At least enough so Wen could get back the stuff he'd hocked in Detroit.

He stood for a time in the rain on Main Street after he left the lunchroom. It was his intention to go into Gyp Lostiano's pool hall and see the bunch, but thought of Mark held him back. You know when you're down-street here how different you are from Mark. You and Mark aren't the same any more at all. Some place along the line, you split apart, Mark and you. He's a good fella, he's all right in his way, but it's not yours. And Ingë, shucks, she just rides in Mark's wake these days. She's his wife and she went Down East to school the same time he did, they have their own friends, folks from Detroit, Grosse Pointe, like of that, and as far as the town goes, it doesn't mean much to them. But it means a lot to you. This is your town for keeps.

There were twenty-five or thirty men in Gyp Lostiano's place. Most of them sat in chairs along the walls, and only one table was being used. The rest are too poor to play, Stacey thought. Goddamn it anyhow. He nodded to Gyp behind the cigar counter, to Hank

Ling and Saavo Minc and Ralph Jenkins and young Mike Stykysky and Giusepp' Pastlieri whose old man was the town bootlegger.

Ralph Jenkins had been out of town for almost a year and Stacey went over and shook hands with him. Ralph was a Negro, but he wore the best suit in the room, seemed handsome, well fed in contrast with the other loungers. Ralph had been playing pro ball, Stacey remembered, and last year there'd been talk of his getting a tryout with some Tristate League club. "Come on, Ralph," he said. "Let's us shoot a game."

"Like to, Stace," Ralph said. But as he moved to the cue rack Stacey saw that his trouser cuffs were frayed, his shoes cracked. Stacey followed him to the rack. "Let's call it off," he said. "You can shoot rings around me. I'm no match for you."

Ralph smiled. "I've got enough for one game. Go ahead. You crack 'em."

Stacey slowly chalked his cue, a smarting sensation behind his eyelids. This was tough and no kidding. He'd played ball with Ralph in high school. He and Ralph were old time friends, and he'd like to lend him money. But he'd already slipped Wen Bozsick thirty, and if he started here with Ralph he'd end up giving out dough to nearly every guy in the room.

He ran the cue back and forth through his fingers to get the feel of it, then lined up the cue ball and cracked hard. While he stood back and watched Ralph make his shot, Saavo Minc asked him, "How many company boats sailin' this year, Stace?"

"Four," Stacey said. "Should be a wheelin' job aboard the *Minna* for you. Giusepp' can go firin' on the *Daigvera*. Rest of you better see the Old Man. He's hiring. Not me."

"Your shot," Ralph Jenkins said. He spoke without emphasis, but Stacey told himself, he's a Negro. No job aboard for him, not even as waiter this year. Like in the old days. He could play for the high school because nobody could rightly stop him. Wouldn't let him on the town team, though. Main reason, I guess, he went back with his family in Detroit.

Stacey lost the game. "Here," he said to Ralph Jenkins and threw a dollar bill on the table. "Double or nothing for the next one."

"All right," Ralph said quietly; "it's a bet."

Ralph won the game and picked up the dollar bill. "Thanks, Stace."

"Welcome," Stacey said. "What d' you say you, me, Saavo,

Giusepp' and Mike and Hank go have a beer over to Gilligan's?"

They nodded, but stiffly, and none of them moved. Little, wry-faced Saavo Minc said, "We got no dough, Stace. You know that."

"Christ," Stacey said, "I got dough. Some left out of last season's pay. What good's it going to do a single fella like me? Might as well put it in beer."

They laughed then, and followed him, and at the door Saavo took his arm. "Stace, lemme bring along a friend of mine."

"Sure thing," Stacey said.

Saavo's friend was short, broad through the shoulders and chest, with a tanned, scarred face and small blue eyes. He wore a leather windbreaker and dungarees, had the look of a working man. But his manner was assured, his voice low, and Stacey had an immediate feeling of curiosity about him. Saavo had introduced him as Walter Brod; walking through the rain towards Gilligan's, Stacey said, "Where you from, Walter?"

"Here and there," Brod said. "Just came through from the coast last week."

"'Frisco to Detroit in four days," Saavo Minc said. "Some guy. Jumped the Rocky Mountain Limited in Salt Lake and rode her straight through to Chicago. Yard bulls would ha' killed ya if they caught you, Walter."

"They failed," Walter Brod said, his voice dim in the rain. "For which, of course, I'm glad."

"You should be," Stacey said. "The bulls are playing tough these days. Had a deckhand last summer in the *Minna,* he jumped ship and tried to ride a freight to go see his folks in Omaha. Kansas City police beat the hell out of him."

"A no good bunch," Saavo said. "Killers who've got no use for the working class."

Pat Gilligan started up from his doze at the end of the bar when Stacey knocked on the door. He let them in, staring with open disbelief at the men behind Stacey. "What the hell you got, Stace," he said; "a convention?"

"Sure," Stacey said. "The Apple Knockers League of Napta County. Set us up some beer."

They took their beer to a table in a corner and sat down and talked desultorily about how the Cubs were shaping up in winter training. Then Saavo Minc said, "You think us fellas would be any better off, Stace, if we had a union on the Lakes?"

"I don't know," Stacey said. "We've got along pretty good without one since the old days. A man who really wants to work, he can get a job."

"I'm not Lakes born," Walter Brod said. "But I've shipped out here, and I've shipped deep-water, too."

"So you're union, huh?" Mike Stykyzky said.

"I sure am," Brod said. "Even before the depression, a man who wanted a job on the Lakes had to know the right skipper, the right chief engineer. I don't mean the cheap jobs, deckhand, wiper. But oiler, deckwatch, wheelsman, you've got to be a Marine City boy, or a Rogers City boy, or a Patigowoc boy, something like that, to hold a good job steady. A man doesn't have connections, he's out of luck."

"You don't like the Lake Carriers," Stacey said. "You don't figure they hire right."

"That's a scab book they make a man carry," Brod said. He looked around at the other men at the table and all of them nodded in confirmation. "The Lake Carriers is anti-union as hell. And ship out of one of their halls and you're stuck for a five or a ten for the guy who hires you."

"Aw, hell, no!" Stacey said.

There was a moment of constrained silence. Saavo broke it. "Lake Carriers can be pretty rough, Stace. You got to admit that."

"Look," Brod said to Saavo Minc, "the man's a skipper. His father owns Kennard and Company. Don't think he's going to take our side."

"Walter's a real advanced thinker, Stace," Saavo said. "Worked with the Wobblies out on the coast. Used to be a Spartacist back in Germany."

"What's a Spartacist?" Stacey said. All the beer was gone, but he delayed ordering another round, interested and to a degree angered by Brod's attitude.

Brod was rolling a cigarette. He looked up from it squarely into Stacey's eyes. His voice was deliberate, harsh. "The Spartacists were a group of revolutionaries. They took a licking because they were ahead of their time. In the dialectical sense, Germany wasn't ready for them."

Stacey thought, look up dialectical in the dictionary home. You don't like what the guy's saying, but you don't know enough to stop him. He sat uncomfortably still, waiting for Brod to go on.

"See, what happened in Europe and Germany is going to happen here, too," Brod said.

"You're talking revolution," Stacey said. He glanced at Saavo Minc, worried that possibly Saavo had the same ideas as Brod. But Saavo and the others didn't seem to see him; they intently watched Brod.

The stocky, scarred man was smiling. "Right as hell," he said. "And no man alive can stop it, Captain. Look at what's happening in Washington. All through the country. The people have had just about enough."

"Let me buy a round," Ralph Jenkins said. "Talk like this makes a fella thirsty."

They laughed at that, but Stacey held Jenkins back by the arm. "I'm buying," he said. "I told you guys I would." He went to the bar with the glasses and Pat Gilligan muttered to him, "Your new pal, Brod, is a red-hot Red. Folks are sayin' he's got a regular Bolshevik cell organized out in Hunky Town. Father Ryan put it in his sermon last week, told all good Catholics to stay away from the guy."

"Yeah?" Stacey said as he picked up the filled glasses. "Well, I guess he's not going to contaminate me."

Brod raised his glass to him back at the table. "Willing to listen?" he said.

"Let's have it," Stacey said. "Maybe my old man runs Kennard and Company, but I wear my own pants."

"So, good," Brod said, his intonation slightly German. "It is enough to mention the commercial crises that by their periodical return put on its trial, each time more threateningly, the existence of the entire bourgeois society. In these crises a great part not only of the existing products, but also of the previously created productive forces are periodically destroyed. In these crises there breaks out an epidemic that, in all earlier epochs, would have seemed an absurdity—the epidemic of over-production."

"That's straight Bolshevik talk," Stacey said. He was on his feet, prodded by anger whose source was obscure to him.

"It's the Communist Manifesto," Brod said.

"You know it by heart, Walter?" Saavo Minc said.

"Sure," Brod said. "I learned it that way when I was in jail once back in Europe." His glance caught upon Stacey. "But it's made the skipper sore."

"Listen, you," Stacey said, leaning over the table towards Brod. "I'm a local fella. I was brought up here. These guys have known me since I was a little squirt. We're all the same, all friends."

"Except," Ralph Jenkins said flat voiced, "that you're skipper of the *Minna* and your folks run the town."

"So if you don't like it, Ralph," Stacey said, "why are you sticking around?"

"Couldn't find work anywhere else," Jenkins said. "Not that I got me a job now."

"See what you mean," Stacey said. The rage had dropped away and he felt a little foolish. After all, he'd asked these guys in for beers, and no matter how you tried, you couldn't get around the fact that the Old Man was the big cheese in town. Mike Stykysky, Hank Ling and Giusepp' Pastlieri were getting up, leaving. "Thanks for the beer, Stace," they said. "So long, fellas."

But Saavo and Brod and Ralph Jenkins stayed at the table. "I won a buck from Stace," Jenkins said. "I'm goin' to buy a round."

"Save your money," Stacey said.

"Let him buy, Stace," Saavo Minc said. "He wants to. What the hell, what's a man to do with a buck?"

Stacey shrugged, the embarrassment he had felt in the lunchroom again upon him. He looked across the table at Brod, but Brod was rolling a cigarette, his blunt fingers very deft and sure. Saavo sat with his hands under his chin, a tense expression about his mouth. "Walter and Ralph and me are going over to Detroit tomorrow," Saavo said.

"What's in Detroit?" Stacey stared at him. This wasn't the same quiet, almost sissy kind of guy he'd known in school. Saavo had changed. He wasn't too certain of Saavo any more.

"The Ford workers are pulling a march tomorrow," Saavo said. "Out at River Rouge. It'll be a big demonstration."

Ralph Jenkins was back with the beers. Stacey looked at him. "You in this, too?"

"Yeah, I am," Jenkins said. "Least, I plan to have me a look at it. Shucks, Walter is one of the leaders."

"But what the hell's the march for?" Stacey said.

"A demonstration of solidarity," Walter Brod said. "Ford has thrown them out of their jobs; you know that. Now they're ready to insist that they have the right to be fed."

Stacey sipped his beer. "I don't want to get mixed up in any demonstration. I never worked for Ford."

"Nobody said you did," Saavo Minc said. "But you ain't like the Old Man or your brother. You're a good guy who knows how to get along with working stiffs. Wasn't for you, Stace, there might ha' been trouble around here before this. Why don't you pile-ass along with us tomorrow? Maybe see something you could tell to the Old Man, or Mark. You don't need do anything. Just go for the ride and take in the march."

A constriction of sudden emotion held Stacey's throat. There was trust in Saavo's words. Saavo trusted him and so did the others. They wanted him along because of that. Maybe Brod was some sort of Bolshevik operator, but not Saavo, not Ralph. And what the hell harm could it do if he went? All he was doing was hanging around waiting to outfit the *Minna*. And years ago there'd been that old strike when the Old Man had sold out. Phelim had never forgotten it. Because of that, Phelim had broken for keeps from the Old Man. If Phelim was around, he'd tell him to go.

"I'll go," Stacey said, "just for the ride."

"We figure to stay out of trouble, Stace," Saavo said. "We'll set in my jalopy and watch, that's all."

"O.K.," Stacey said. "Because it's like I said, I never worked for Ford. I got nothing against Hennery."

They shook hands with him when they said goodnight, first Walter Brod, then Ralph, then Saavo. "See you in the morning," Saavo said. "Down-street in front of the Ace. Eight o'clock. Take care."

The top of Saavo's jalopy leaked and in the morning they all bunched in the front seat to keep out of the rain. Stacey had slept badly, fitfully dreaming, and a strange nervousness still gripped him. He spoke little and let the other men talk, but for the most part they also were content to ride in silence.

When they stopped at a traffic light on East Jefferson Avenue coming into Detroit the white policeman yelled, "What the hell you doing, all jammed up with a nigger?"

Stacey could feel the tension lock Ralph Jenkins' body. His own hands closed and he started to yell at the policeman, but Saavo put the jalopy in gear, went past the light. "A Ku Kluxer," Saavo said then, "the knuckle-head son-of-a-bitch."

"Save your breath," Walter Brod said. His face was hard-lined in the grayish light. "We all know them for what they are."

A policeman wearing a rubber cap-top and rain cape halted the jalopy out near River Rouge. He made Saavo bring it in to the curb. "Where you fellas going?" he asked Saavo. But Walter was getting out, and he had taken a bundle of leaflets from under a newspaper on the rear seat. The policeman swung around with his club raised. "Come back, you Commie bastard!"

Walter Brod ran on along the dark, rain-sheeted street. "All right," the cop said. "Get out, all o' yuhs. No sittin' around here. This ain't a ball game."

They moved around the policeman without speech. Behind them, through the fog and the rain, they could hear the people. They stood back on the curb, shoulder to shoulder, strained with nervousness.

The people marched in a loose and sprawling column. Some carried placards and others had leaflets, and it was Stacey's impression that one tall, white haired man had an American flag. But he wasn't sure about that; he was too nervous now to think clearly, for the marching, singing, shouting column was meeting with the police.

The police bunched before a big building that belonged to Ford. Some policeman was shouting orders and whistles were being blown. The people stopped, started forward, stopped, moved again, and abruptly there were the shots, the screams, and the people were running back.

Policemen and men in civilian clothing with clubs and guns ran after them. They hit the people from behind. They knocked them down and kicked and jumped on them. Ralph Jenkins was panting like an animal in pain. "They oughten to," he said. "They oughten to do that."

"There's Walter," Saavo said in a rough voice. "They got him and they been beatin' him. Look how he is."

Saavo was off the curb; he started to run up the street. Ralph Jenkins caught him and brought him back. "Here," Ralph said, still panting and working his lips and the muscles of his face. He took off his hat and coat, gave them to Saavo. "I'll get him outa there. I'm the boy who knows how."

Ralph ran with ease and power. Some of the policemen and the heavily set men in civilian clothes saw him coming, but he ducked them, was past them, close to the pair of men who were kicking Walter Brod where he lay sprawled on his back. Ralph hit one man with the side of his hand at the base of the neck. Then he wheeled and kicked the other and that one went back as though doing a jackknife off a board in a pool. Then Ralph had Brod in his arms and was running with him.

But he couldn't run as fast as before. The men with the clubs closed around him. They grasped his clothing, slowed and tripped him, pitched him down. "Hey, cut it out!" Stacey yelled, as though the men in the street would listen to him if they heard him. "Let the guy be!"

Saavo Minc was crying. But he gripped Stacey's wrist. "Come on with me, Stace."

"Don't fight 'em," Stacey said. "I'll talk to them."

"I'm Stacey Kennard," he said as the policemen gathered in around him and Saavo up the street. "That man works for me over in Patigowoc."

"Which fella?" the nearest policeman said. "The nigger?"

"Yes."

The policeman lowered his club a bit. "How about the other one?"

"He does, too."

"Well, they ain't neither of them going to do you much good," the policeman said. "We just kicked the ribs outa the nigger and the other fella's nose is where his mouth usta be. You got any proof of who you are?"

Stacey's hands shook so much that Saavo Minc had to hold the wallet for him while he pulled out his driver's license. "All right," the policeman said, beads of sweat and rain falling from his eyebrows as he stared down at the card. "You can take 'em away, Kennard. But don't let 'em come back here no more. Next time, they'll get killed."

"Thank you, officer," Stacey said, but with his hands down in his coat pockets. If he took his hands out, he knew, he'd clip the man, try to tear off his face.

Over at the jalopy, while he and Saavo were helping Ralph and then Walter Brod up into the rear seat, Ralph suddenly turned sidewise and began to vomit blood. Walter Brod's eyes were smashed shut, but he was still partly conscious, and he said, "Turn him over, Stacey. Hold his head up. He's having a hemorrhage."

"Ain't no use," Saavo said, beside Ralph in the jalopy. "He's dying. Oh, Gawd, the whole car's gettin' full of blood."

Stacey got in the jalopy and lifted Ralph's head, did the things Walter Brod had told him to do. But Saavo had been right; Ralph was dying. He died with his head held against Stacey's shoulder, the pungent, sweet torrents of blood pouring down Stacey's suit and shirt. Stacey drew gradually away, let the body slide back.

Saavo Minc was seized by hysteria; he was weeping and moaning, asking Stacey, "What'll we do? My Gawd, how we goin' to get rid of the blood?"

"Don't worry about the blood," Stacey said. "Get in there and drive. We have to take Walter to the hospital."

"But how about Ralph," Saavo said, "all horrible like that?"

"We'll take Ralph back home," Stacey said, the first real impact of the horror beginning to reach in to him, so that his own words were hysteria-blurred and dim. "To Patigowoc and his folks. It's the best we can do. Drive, Saavo. Start 'er up!"

.   .   .   .

"You must," Ingë said. "The Old Man called and asked expressly that you go in and talk with him and Stacey."

Mark stood across the living room from her, fingering one of the gold-and-white faience dogs on the fireplace mantel. He kept his glance from Ingë. He felt uncomfortable, somehow uncertain when his eyes met hers. "What could I do if I went?" he said, still standing there and fingering the smooth, cold surface of the china.

"Straighten this out," Ingë said, "as you've always straightened things out in the past." She walked towards him, and from upstairs where the nurse put the children to bed there came a quick burst of light laughter. Ingë slowed as she listened to it. "The children are tucked in. I could go with you. If you'd like to have me, Mark."

Mark gazed at her against the background of the deep and shadow-soft room. It represented her personality, her taste; he had let her plan practically the entire house with the architect and the interior decorator. What else, he had reasoned at the time, had she to do? Being cooped up in Patigowoc was cruel enough for a woman of Ingë's ability. But she'd been happy here. She'd thrived, in fact, and perhaps despite all her surface sophistication she was by nature a small town woman. She was certainly acting without much subtlety now.

"You couldn't go," he said, "dressed like that."

She was in front of him, put her hands upon his shoulders. "Silly. All I have to do is throw on a coat." She glanced down briefly at her new low-cut dress. It was of jade velvet, showed her figure to superb advantage. "D' you like this?"

"Stacey and I aren't close any more," he said. "And goddamned if I approve of his actions today."

"Oh, Mark! He wasn't actually in that fight. He isn't to blame in any sense."

"Then what's he doing mixed up with an agitator, an outright Communist like this man Brod? Why did he get into a brawl that's a disgrace to the whole state?"

"If you hurry up," she said, "we could be back in time for dinner."

"Not with Stacey all charged up and the Old Man yelling his head off."

"Then Mrs. Van der Haas will find us something to eat over there." Ingë moved from him. She took two cigarettes from a leather box on a side table, lit them simultaneously, placed one between his lips. "Relax, sweet. It's not as bad as you think. But do let's go."

His scrutiny of her was slow and open. "You want to have Stacey see you in your new dress, don't you?"

"Yes, I do."

"Then wear your mink over it. He'll be sure to think that you're a rotten capitalist bitch and I'm no better."

Ingë didn't reply. She had gone to the closet off the paneled hall. She took out from it his hat and topcoat and her mink coat. She stood waiting for him holding the coats and the hat, her plump, handsome face quite calm.

There were cars with stickers on the windshields in the driveway at "The Towers." Mark noticed them and spoke of them to Ingë. "Reporters," he said. "Let me do the talking."

Mrs. Van der Haas opened the front door, but the reporters were right inside. One had a camera and a flash bulb gun. "Mr. and Mrs. Mark Kennard," he said. "Vice president of Kennard and Company, aren't you? Say, Mr. Kennard, did you have any knowledge of your brother's friendship with the dead man?"

"What man?" Mark said.

"Ralph Jenkins, the ink spot that got rubbed out this afternoon."

"No, none." Mark pushed Ingë in front of him. "Go ahead on in, dear. I won't be long."

"Well," the other reporter said, "did you have any knowledge of your brother's friendship with the Communist agitator using the name of Walter Brod?"

"None at all."

"You seem to come from the conservative side of the family. Mr. Kennard, what are your views about the Communist menace?"

Mark swung open the door. "I have nothing more to say," he said. "Get out. Get out!"

"You want us to quote that, Mr. Kennard?"

Mark jumped at the reporter who had asked the last question and thrust him stumbling out the door. The other one followed immediately, but calling back, "I guess we'll get a statement from you about Communism before we get a company dividend declaration, hey?"

"You're in fine shape," Ingë told Mark as he joined her in the drawing room. "Pull yourself together. I'm surprised. You know you can't push those fellows around."

"This is our house," Mark said in a voice of fury. "They have no right here. It's a violation of basic privacy."

Ingë had dropped her coat onto a chair. She touched her hair, her dress, looked at herself in a mirror. "Stacey and the Old Man are in the study. For goodness' sake, don't make trouble."

"One goddamn' fool in the family is enough, you mean. I agree. Go ahead." His voice was still furious. "Show Stacey your dress."

Stacey sat at one side of his father's desk, his father opposite him. The whiskey decanter, glasses and a pitcher of water were on the desk. Alan Kennard had been drinking heavily and his eyes were cast with red. But Stacey was very sober, very pale and quiet.

"How about it, Stace?" Mark said. "Let's have the story."

"It was straight murder." Stacey looked from him to Ingë and his eyes blinked almost shut. "I told Pa. There's no sense telling it again to you."

"Let 'm be," Alan Kennard said. "The lad's had a rough time, Mark."

"But what in the name of hell," Mark said, "were you doing over there in such a shindy?"

"Mark, don't talk like that," Ingë said.

"Those guys were friends of mine," Stacey said. "They asked me and I went with them and I'm glad that I did. I learned something. Any objections?"

"Yes," Mark said. "I think you were a stupid bastard to go. We're responsible people, with a reputation to maintain. You're a Kennard, master of a Kennard vessel. So, you have to get mixed up in some sort of a senseless hunger march. By God, Stacey——"

"Have a drink, Mark," Alan Kennard said thickly. "You pour a snort for all of us." He pointed to Ingë. "Time we took it easy. Easy, I say, goddamn the both of you!"

Stacey had risen from his chair. He and Mark stood chest to chest. Stacey was trembling, sweat on his face, his lips set and his hands stretched with the fingers wide. "Because a man's hungry," he said, "he can't protest, huh? That's how you figure. You snob bastard. Get out of here before I knock you on your head."

"Your trouble is," Mark said, "that you're just a big, overgrown kid. So you saw a few people shot and killed. What d' you think I saw in the war? Stop being so excited. Sit down. Don't try to get tough with me."

"Yeah?" Stacey said, his face congested, his voice raucous. "So maybe you'd like to tell me, too, that you're against the folks who marched today."

"I'm for law and order," Mark said. "Not hoodlumism like that. You just got played for a sucker, that's all. Take your heart off your sleeve. You're supposed to be a man. Remember?"

"Why, you smug son-of-a-bitch!" Stacey said. He stepped back to gain balance, then struck at Mark's head.

Ingë had been pouring the whiskey from the decanter into the glasses. She stepped swiftly between Stacey and Mark and took the blow on her bare upper right arm. The force of it spun her around and she landed asprawl in a corner, her hair shaken loose about her face.

Mark took time to look at her, and Stacey let his hands fall to his sides. Alan Kennard, moving very fast, locked Stacey's arms. "Not in this house," he said. "Not my boys. Mark, ye act like a loon. Get your wife on her feet. And out of here. You, too. I'll see you in the morning at the company. Ingë, darlin', are you all right?"

"Of course." Ingë was stiffly smiling. "It didn't hurt much. I'm sorry, Stacey, those people got killed. The whole affair is shameful. Goodnight. Goodnight, Father Kennard."

The men were wordless gazing at her. She brushed her hair up onto her head with her fingers, secured it with a pin taken from the number scattered on the floor, straightened her dress and walked easily striding from the room. "Ingë!" Mark called at her, but she refused to look back and he went after her out into the hall and from the house.

Alan Kennard had released his arm lock on Stacey. He grasped a glass and pushed it in Stacey's hand. "Woman for you," he said.

Mrs. Van der Haas peered at them from the drawing room. "You men fit to eat?" she said.

"Throw it on," Alan Kennard said. "We'll be in."

They ate little and in silence and returned to the study. Alan Kennard turned up the gas log against the dampness and afterwards slumped in his chair. Stacey would talk when he was ready, he thought. No sense in pressing the lad. But Stace had seen more than folks get killed today. It was now that you couldn't reckon Stacey any longer as a lad. He was a man grown. See it in his face. Mark did him no good, nor you either, up to here. Ah, to hell, you wish you knew more. Your son sits and looks at you and you got no words for him. The best you can do is keep your big yap shut. Should he like, he could trounce the hell out of you, too. Strong as a bull. Lucky for all of us Ingë stepped between.

Stacey's despair was absolute. It kindled an anger, though, that slowly became consuming and centered upon his father. He kept his gaze on his father's face. The old goat is sober, he told himself. The scuffle with Mark and the food took the edge off the booze. So don't wait any longer. Ask him. Get it over. You have to know. "Pa," he said, "which side you on?"

"Look, Stace, all my life I've been with the workin' man. What the hell am I but one meself? I've never changed. Mark, though, I can't get through to him——"

"Leave Mark out of this." Stacey sat erect and his voice rang in the room. "It's you and me now. Where the hell did you go wrong along the line?"

"Stace, if you'd have at me, you're having at yourself. I've made you what you are. From the time you were a snot-nosed lad, I've worked to make you as best I could."

"Yeah. But the '04 strike. And all that came after it."

"The '04 strike, that's back a donkey's years. What's that got to do with us?"

"Phelim was your best friend. He left the company because of it. His wife wouldn't even ask you to his funeral. Josh Shaw left you, too, a bunch of other fellas."

"Ah, Carmody made you bitter in the years you sailed with him."

"Maybe. But how about you? How about all the chances you had to square away?"

"What the blazes d' you mean?"

"Here you are a rich man. With Keiberg busted, the richest in the county. All along, you could have done plenty. When McKinley was running, when Teddy Roosevelt was, and Wilson, the whole bunch of them."

"Ah, lad, lad! You lower the boom on me too fast. I was for McKinley, no matter that Mark Hanna run him into office."

"That's what I mean. You could've bucked McKinley."

"What, and him bringing prosperity with him? Don't be a loon. Roosevelt, I was for him and the Bull Moose. Keiberg said I was wrong, and Keiberg was right, but it goes to show you where my heart was. Wilson wasn't my kind of man. He took us into war and right tonight we're still paying for it."

"Coolidge and Hoover, they're your kind?"

"Yes and no, Stace. But why all the questions? I've been a lone wolf in me life. The Cleveland gang have kept me busy seeing to it that the company was kept afloat. If you have it in there, get it out of your head that I've had the chance to swing elections, buy senators and congressmen and the like. What they do in Washington has got me beat."

Stacey's eyes hooded over. He passed a hand across his brow. Then he fingered his shirt, and his father sensed that Stacey was thinking of the blood that had been on his shirt this afternoon. "You're a rich man," Stacey said. "The company runs and just about owns this town. Ford's rich. When things got tough, he fired his help and let them starve. I'm wondering, will you do the same?"

"And now!" Alan Kennard said. He banged his hand resoundingly against the desk top. "So we have it! My own son, master of my flag vessel, he asks me such a question. . . . Stacey, I have no answer for you. I'm too old to stand up to you man-to-man or I'd take after you in the minute. You have no trust in me?"

"I don't know," Stacey said, his voice muted to a whisper. He stood and came close and bent down and looked into his father's eyes. "You're a strange fella. So am I. Today over there— To hell with it. I'm beat out. I'm going to turn in."

"You won't join me in a snort before you go?"

"Sure, I will."

Alan Kennard poured the glasses full. "To us, Stace. Good sailin'."

"Good sailin', sir," Stacey said out of deep habit. But as he put his glass down empty he again looked keenly at his father. "Don't screw me up. You know where I stand now. Goodnight."

CHAPTER NINETEEN

Saavo Minc was the chairman of what came to have the name of the Action Committee. He explained it to Stacey early in July when Stacey brought the *Minna* in to load limestone for Indiana Harbor. "The Old Man and your brother are gangin' up on us," Saavo said. "They got a joker up their sleeve. A straight thirty percent cut across the board for all Kennard employees. Mark's goin' to announce it Wednesday."

"You sure?" Stacey said. He and Saavo were at the counter in the Ace Lunch and he lowered his voice to the tone Saavo had used.

"Positive," Saavo said. "My cousin, the good-lookin' one, Arabelle, she's been transferred from accounting and works in Mark's office. Mark's sec'etary let her see the statement the ad agency wrote for Mark to give to the papers."

"Crews get cut, too?" Stacey said.

"Crews, too," Saavo said. "Everybody who works for Kennard Co. I got a copy of the statement. But I don't carry it with me. It's hid home."

Stacey looked out the window into Main Street. A paper banner across Hunnek's store front said Foreclosure Sale. The Arcade, closed in June, was boarded up. As many as fifty able-bodied men stood under the canopy of the Bijou Theater. Guys the Old Man has already laid off, Stacey thought, or fellas who worked out of town and lost their jobs and are hanging around hoping to grab something here. Like hell. The Old Man hands them this.

"I'm going over to the company," Stacey told Saavo, "then back aboard."

"Will ya pull the crew off the *Minna*, Stace? Wednesday mornin', as soon as Mark makes his announcement, we figure to throw a picket line out at the quarries. In front of the main gate. We got signs, the whole thing set up."

Stacey laughed and slapped Saavo's shoulder. "I'll let the boys decide their own minds. But I'll be pushing off. Where can I find you?"

413

"In here, mostly. Wen's on the committee. Him and Agnes ha' staked us all they could."

A new guard whose face was unknown to Stacey stood at the top of the steps at the company building. He carried a club; there was a Smith and Wesson .38 with a pearl grip in an ornamental holster on his right hip. "Hey, wait a minute," he said to Stacey. "Not so fast."

"I'm Captain Kennard," Stacey said; "you dumb bugger. Stand aside or I'll whack you."

"Yes, sir," the guard said. "I'm sorry, sir." He drew open the glass-panelled door.

Stacey stopped in the outer office. A number of the typewriters and adding and stencil machines had covers on them, he saw. No more than a dozen typists and clerks were working. The office boy sat reading a copy of *Cowboy Stories*. Fred Stiles, the sales manager, had his feet up on the desk in his office and his secretary's desk was empty. This in the last two weeks, Stacey thought. The Old Man has sure been laying them off plenty.

Mark was dictating a letter to his secretary. He was in his shirt sleeves and seemed relaxed. "Good to see you, Stace," he called. "Go visit with the Old Man for a minute and I'll be in."

"I want to talk to you," Stacey said. He stood in the doorway until Mark had finished. Mark's secretary was a pretty girl and she smiled at him and said "Hello, Captain" as she passed. But he was walking forward to Mark. "Let me have it," he said.

"What?" Mark said.

"The statement for the papers. The one you're going to give out Wednesday about the wage cuts."

"I don't follow you," Mark said. "There is no such thing. If you've been talking to Saavo Minc, he's a liar and a fomenting little bastard. We're about ready to have him run out of town."

Stacey stretched a hand across the deck. "Come on, Mark. I don't want to have to take it from you."

"You're not very bright," Mark said, a flush of rage up in his throat and cheeks. "There's a lot I could tell you, but that will have to do." He pressed a buzzer on the side of the desk and told his secretary, "Ask Captain Kennard, Senior, to come in my office, please. And the guard."

Alan Kennard walked from his office with his usual nimble stride. "Hey, Stace," he said heartily. "A quick trip. Meant to get down to the dock and meet you. But you load in the morning."

"Not me, I don't," Stacey said. "How about this wage cut, Pa?"

"Straight thirty percent," Alan Kennard said without hesitation. "Has to be, Stace. Last week Mark and me done nothing but check the figures. Company will go bust if it ain't put into effect. You're not with Minc and that lot, are you?"

"I told you back in the spring," Stacey said. "So I say it again. You're throwing the town square on its back and you don't need to. We have dough in the bank. Carry the folks. Thirty percent cut means they'll starve."

"Stacey," Mark said in a controlled voice, "do you want to check the figures with me? Fred Stiles will show you the sales reports for the last quarter. You've been around the ports. You know what conditions are. Why must you argue with us? It's an absolutely necessary step."

Stacey moved sidewise quickly and bumped into the guard. "So you call in this guy. If you can't convince me, he will. O.K. I'm convinced—that you're full of bilge to the ears. You pair of cheap connivers."

"Now, Stace," Alan Kennard said. "Don't go flyin' off the handle. Sit down. We talk it over. The *Minna's* sailin', ain't she? You got a full crew and cargo."

But Stacey had turned and shouldered the guard backward. Then, as the guard stood silent and confused, he walked past him out the side door.

"A fine departure," Mark's lips were white and he spoke violently. "Easier, though, than I thought it would be. And he also let us know that his bunch has got hold of the statement somehow. It won't be bad on Wednesday."

"I ain't so sure," Alan Kennard said.

"No?" Mark said. He had taken a card from a drawer of his desk, lifted his telephone. "Wait 'til I get in touch with Detroit. This can solve a lot of problems in a hurry."

"Ah, you talk big," Alan Kennard said. "Don't go buyin' trouble, Mark."

"You'd like to lose your company?"

"Hell, of course I wouldn't."

"Then let me handle the thing. I've taken enough from Stacey and his kind. No more backing down, not from me. I haven't forgotten the time he hit Ingë."

"He meant to hit you, ya donkey, and you had him hot."

Mark was busy speaking into the telephone. Alan Kennard

waited for a moment, but Mark did not raise his eyes or indicate that he had heard him. Kennard moved slowly from the office, pulling the door shut after him. He was vaguely ashamed of Mark and of himself, yet he realized that there was nothing in his power to change this. Little by little, Mark had taken over the running of the company from him. You're an old man, a real old man. If a shindy comes up Wednesday, you wouldn't be much good in it, one side or the other. . . .

. . . .

Stacey marched in the middle of the front rank. Saavo Minc was on his left and Perry Jenkins, Ralph's cousin, was on his right. Over beyond Perry was Hank Ling who wore his uniform coat with the ribbons and carried the flag. In the column behind were the crews off the *Minna* and the *Daigvera,* about a hundred of the quarry and the kiln workers, with them the men who had come from Detroit and Flint and Dearborn and Grand Rapids and Napta City. All told, they were more than two hundred, and they kept in step along the road while some of them sang "Arise, Ye Prisoners of Starvation!" and the rest shouted the chorus where they didn't know the words.

The out-of-towners were the ones who knew the words, Stacey found. Saavo had got them in this morning before daylight. He had told Saavo and Wen that he didn't like having outsiders, but their answer was that you couldn't swing a strike with just a few local fellows. "Mark's called in goons," Saavo said. "The State cops are goin' to be around. It ain't no clambake, Stace."

Stacey lost his feeling of doubt about the out-of-towners when at the top of the hill and in front of the main gate to the quarries he saw the State police. They had parked their cars and motor-cycles along the road. Fat old Moritz Becker, the mayor, was there in his car, a patch of sweat black on the back of his dusty coat.

"Becker is scared," Saavo said. "Mark's got him on the string, but he knows we're voters, got our rights."

"We're not breaking any law," one of the Detroit men said from behind. "All we're out to do is organize the place, see you fellas have union conditions. Tell 'em that, Kennard. No trouble unless they start it."

"Yeah, sure," Stacey said. But his stomach muscles had begun to quiver. His eyes smarted and his breath expelled hissing between his teeth, he kept clearing his throat, thinly coughing. He could smell blood. It was Ralph Jenkins' blood. He saw in imagination Walter Brod's beaten, blue-pulped face.

A sergeant of State police stood before the watchman's shack at the gate. He had his gauntlets stuck in his belt and rested with his feet broadly apart. The rest of the State police watched him. They were still, their eyes hard, but quiet.

"Head on home, Kennard," the sergeant said clearly. "Stay here and you'll get yourself all jammed up. This riff-raff is out for no good."

"Shut up, you two-bit Cossack!" Hank Ling said. "Keep moving, fellas. He got no right to stop us."

The sergeant stood back against the wall of the shack, his thumbs hooked in his belt, and they went on and formed a single, loose line outside the wire fence and the gate. They walked back and forth there, the placard signs on their shoulders or held straight in front of them, and Stacey told himself, a lot of them must feel just as big a fool as you. There's nobody around who wants to go through the gate to work. They're scared, or they won't take the lousy new pay.

But then up the hill from town he saw the buses coming. Clouds of dust were over them in the gleaming summer air. There were three of them, and they were all full. "The scabs!" Saavo Minc was shouting. "Don't forget we tell each one, 'So you don't believe in a union, you must believe in starvation.'"

"That's too long," Stacey said harshly. "I told you it was too long. All we do is give out the leaflets, tell 'em to stick together with us."

The mayor was out of his car. He came across the rutted road with a State policeman on each side of him. Before he started to speak, he looked over his shoulder and down the hill at the buses. "Fellow citizens," he said, "as your mayor, and as a man who believes in democracy and the real ideals of the American people, I ask you——"

"Horse shit!" several of the out-of-towners shouted in chorus. They kept it up every time after that when the mayor tried to speak. But the mayor did not stay long. He went back to his car. The buses were at the top of the hill. They were stopping; men were getting out.

Those men wore work clothes and had dinner pails and thermos bottles and packages of sandwiches. They looked nervous, unhappy. Not much fight in them, Stacey thought. But Bill Geoghall and three of the other town policemen led them, and in the last bus, just getting out, were maybe twenty of the heavy-bodied men in civilian clothes who had fought against the hunger marchers at River Rouge.

Mark was with the goons, wearing a Panama hat and a spotted silk tie, and a white suit, his shoes freshly shined. A pushover, Stacey thought. That's how Mark figures.

But after that he had no time to think about Mark. The State police sergeant began to lead the first of the scabs towards the gate. The pickets shouted the slogan and held out the leaflets. "Stand back, you!" the sergeant shouted. "Let these men through. They have their right to work."

"Well, don't you go pushin' me," Hank Ling said. "This here that I'm carrying is the national flag."

"Back up," the sergeant said, "or I'll run you in." He brought his boot heel down across Ling's instep and jabbed him in the stomach with his elbow. "You trying to create a riot?"

There was yelling, shouting, motion all along the picket line now, and Stacey saw that some of the scabs were trying to slip through the line and get over the fence instead of trying to come through the gate. The line was being broken. Men gathered in groups of fours and fives and sixes, some pickets, some scabs. But nobody was fighting yet, Stacey told himself; it was still peaceful, and not a guy had gone through the gate. If they stood around and talked it out, everything would be all right.

His rage had ebbed and he had his head turned to look for Mark when Bill Geoghall hit a picket. The sound of the club made him moan. Then several men were shouting, "Get the dirty slob!"

Bill Geoghall's cap pitched up into the air, his coat with the brass buttons and the badge, and his pants. He came staggering out from under the men who kicked and punched him, one hand across his stomach, the other over the back of his neck. But the other town police were striking with their clubs, then the State police. The goons walked in steadily at the wavering line.

"Let's go! Let's go!" Saavo Minc shouted. "Don't let 'em break us, fellas!"

The State police sergeant whirled and hit Saavo slantingly across the ear with his club. Saavo went down sagged at the knees, his mouth open. A group of the out-of-towners jumped the sergeant and struck at him with blows that sounded like an axe against a tree. Stacey ran around the group. He was thinking of Ralph Jenkins again and he wanted to meet the goons.

He moved fast when he reached them, punching for the head, eager to see blood. He was pretty lucky, he dimly sensed. They didn't know yet how well he could fight. Three of them were on him, at work at his face, chest, stomach and kidneys when some of the out-of-towners reached him. They drove the goons back across the road and stood and laughed and called foul names.

But Mark was out in the road. He had put on a pair of pigskin gloves. His shiny shoes were set, the Panama hat jammed low on his head. "Come on," he told the out-of-towners. "Take me!" They sprang at him and the first one knocked him stumbling. He caught himself, hit with both hands before he went down beneath their feet.

"Hey, goddamn you!" Stacey cried. He meant the out-of-towners. "Let my brother be!"

A goon slammed him in the mouth then and he reeled, his arms up to save his face. The goon came at him rushing and too wide open, and Stacey thought, now, and gave a short, jabbing punch to the groin. He sprang as the goon screamed and fell, ran towards Mark.

His impulse was unclear. There was nothing definite that sent him to help Mark. But he was thinking of Mark and the woodchuck, Mark in the fights outside school, Mark beside him by the gas log while they read *Ivanhoe* together, Mark in the game against Hamatack, Mark home from the war and not even in uniform.

He straightarmed a man who was getting set to hit Mark. The man swung startled, his hands down, and Stacey struck him on the chin. "Haul ass out of here, Mark," he said.

"I will like hell," Mark said, and he was grinning. "We're brothers, aren't we?"

"Yeah, sure," Stacey said. Then he received the blow at the base of the neck. He moved to save himself, to look around at least so that he could see the man who had struck him. But the pain was too sharp, the darkness too rapid in his brain. He stumbled from side to side when the other blow came that hurled him headlong and unconscious in the road.

CHAPTER TWENTY

Stacey was sitting on the porch when Mark drove up under the porte-cochere. He had recognized Mark's car while it was still on the river road, and ever since he and his father had returned from the quarry this morning he had been expecting Mark. "Hya?" he said in his usual manner.

"I'm pretty good." Mark walked along the porch to peer at him in the darkness. "How are you?"

"All right. I've been better, but I've been worse." Stacey sat still, not yet ready to look closely at Mark. He was uncertain of his feeling about Mark, and although he had expected him he didn't know how Mark felt or what he planned to say or do.

Mark took a chair beside him and Stacey could hear him grunt with pain as he sat in it. "How is the Old Man?" Mark said.

"Upstairs and asleep since supper. He was pretty excited before and had a couple drinks too many. I got him to go and flake out."

"Fair enough," Mark said. Then they were both quiet. A radio played somewhere down in town and out on the river fish leaped with a quick, delicate plopping. Stacey thought, I wonder why the guy came here if he doesn't want to talk. But maybe Ingë sent him, maybe the mayor and the cops, to see what you're going to do next. I doubt that, though. He most probably just came on his own.

"Do you know," Mark said, "it's a damn' strange thing, but I haven't been there at the quarry since I was a kid."

"Me either," Stacey said.

"It's curious," Mark said, "that we should have stayed away so long. Can you figure out why?"

"Sure." Stacey stroked his hand along his puffed jaw in reflection. "It was a dandy place to play as a kid, but after the strike I always thought the guys didn't want me around there."

"You and I were pretty close then, and still you didn't tell me."

"Not straight out, no. But we talked about the rest of the stuff. The way Luke Pares used to act, and that."

"You mean the ball game at Hamatack when the Old Man came over in the Packard."

"Sure."

"But how about the quarries?"

"Shucks, I just got in the habit of staying clear of 'em," Stacey said. "Might ha' been I was scared that some guy who was sore at the Old Man might dump me in, or chunk a rock at me. The same for the brick yard and anywhere there was a bunch of fellows working for the Old Man. Except out aboard. I always reckoned that I belonged on the ships and nobody'd bother me. Why you asking, though?"

"Because," Mark said, "we've both suffered from a kind of guilt complex. I know you don't like fancy language, but that's the name for it."

Stacey stared at him. "A hell of a time to find out," he said. "You'd make me think that what happened to us as kids, the old strike, I mean, ties in with this morning."

"It does," Mark said gravely. "It most certainly does. But there wasn't much solved this morning, Stace, as far as you and I are concerned."

Stacey was suddenly nervous. He hunched forward in his chair. "Did Ingë send you over to talk to me? Or the mayor, or the cops?"

"No, not at all."

"Well, I ain't talked to the Old Man about anything serious since I came home and got myself back together again. And the boys, Saavo Minc and the bunch, haven't called. But you've got stuff on your mind. What is it?"

"That in many ways you were right today, sport, and I was wrong. We have to stand behind the town. If we can possibly do it, our job's to keep the place running."

"Not pull a Ford and just let 'em starve." Stacey intently regarded his brother. "Take back the thirty percent cut. Right?"

"For as long as we can," Mark said. "But it's our town. The Old Man and you and I have made a damn' good living out of it. If we went ahead and put through the cut——"

"Listen, fella!" Stacey gripped Mark hard by the wrist. "You tell me right now how much the cut idea was yours and how much the Old Man's. Because I went in for you today and I got my head banged. Down-street, if I walked into the Ace Lunch, I'd get it again."

Mark nodded at him, making no attempt to free his arm. "I saw the need for the cut first and then the Old Man backed me up."

"But he's still president of the company. And anti-union as hell. He wouldn't listen to us. What he'd say would be that we'd wreck his company."

"I don't quite agree," Mark said. "I think that between us we can make him see the light."

"You'll have to talk the business stuff."

"I'm prepared to," Mark said. "I've been thinking it over all afternoon. Just before I came here, I was down at the office and went through the books once more with this in mind."

Stacey was getting stiffly to his feet. "I'll go break out the Old Man," he said, "but before I do, Mark, answer me a question. You tell Ingë you were coming here?"

"Yes." Mark smiled. "I didn't tell her why, though. It will be good for her to find out later."

"You're a sport," Stacey said admiringly from the doorway. Then he climbed the stairs to awake his father.

Alan Kennard was by turns sullen, abashed and furious. He cursed both Stacey and Mark. "It'll never work," he said. "Not in Christ's green world. You boys out of your minds?"

"Not a bit of it," Mark said. "We've just come to the conclusion that we're obligated to keep the company running at full force and without any wage cuts."

"You!" Alan Kennard said with scorn. "But it's my goddamn' company. And out there this morning I saw how you two chumps acted. A sorrier sight I never want to clap my eyes on."

"Then clap your eyes on me," Stacey said. He had been fired by his father's rage. The steadiness he had been able to maintain with Mark was gone and in its place a tumult of anger. "You don't take the deal, I'm pulling out right tonight. You should be sick of going down-street and meeting folks who hate your guts. What you living for? Why're you so selfish with your money?"

"Stace, take it easy," Mark said. "We can't decide anything sensible this way."

"Hear that!" Alan Kennard yelled at Stacey. "So you'd pull out, hey? Go back to Harkness, I suppose. Well, these days you'd be lucky getting a job wheeling. But I ain't to be taken over by no Coxey's Army, no bunch of Reds and agitators. Next thing I know, you pecker-heads will sneak in a union contract on me."

Stacey was so furious that he had taken a stride forward towards his father. Mark restrained him. He held Stacey back while he said in a subdued but clear voice, "If Stacey goes, I go with him. We're solid in this. We've had enough, more than enough of your kind of tactics."

"Well, I'll be buggered," Alan Kennard said dimly. He had come downstairs in his pajamas and bathrobe and slippers. He felt oddly and suddenly defenseless against these two strong, determined young men. This morning at the quarry he had seen them fight, and then he had been very profoundly touched by their love for each other. From where he had stood behind the state police, he had advanced and picked up Stacey, brought Stacey home. Yet nothing that he had witnessed or that he had believed possible had given him the thought that they would be so united against him.

Dismay almost overcame him. His sensation was one of a frightful loneliness. Your sons, he thought. You can't lose your sons. But they're serious. Look at 'em. They mean it; they'll walk out on you. And then where the hell will you be? Up the bloody pole all alone. . . .

"Boys," he said plaintively, "sit down and let's talk this over like intelligent fellas. You know the finance end of the company good, Mark, and if you ain't all the way out of your head, you must have some sensible plan."

"I have," Mark said. "You want to hear it?"

Alan Kennard spread his hands. "Go ahead. I'll listen."

"The whole thing's a gamble," Mark said. "We simply bet along with the rest of the folks that the country will come out of the depression before it's too late for all of us."

"Roosevelt talks that way," Alan Kennard said in renewed rage. "You've got your ears flattened back by him on the radio."

"Pipe down!" Stacey said roughly. "Let Mark have the deck!"

"What we'd have to do," Mark said, "would be to mortgage everything we have. But the Cleveland banks would give us loans and carry us. Then in turn we'd give credit to any customer who rated it, keep right on producing and delivering and picking up the charters we can get. Then we ride it out to the end, win or lose."

Alan Kennard rapped himself dramatically on the skull. "My son has rocks in his head for brains. You know what them Cleveland swabs would do to us, Mark, if we missed a mortgage payment by a day? They'd pick up Kennard and Company lock, stock and sight. You and your wife and kids would starve. Stacey, here——"

"Never you mind about Stacey," Stacey said. "He'll take care of himself. So, what d' you say? You for it, or against it?"

"You're crowdin' me awful' fast and hard, boys." Alan Kennard scratched his back and his chest. He shuffled up and down the porch, glancing from Mark to Stacey, then at the river and the somnolent, softly lit town. His sons watched him steady-eyed, and at last he turned and looked into the house. This place with him here alone. No good. And they'd go. Sure as hell they'd pull out and leave him. "Give you my answer in the morning."

Mark laughed at him. "We want the answer now. If you agree with us, I should be in Cleveland tomorrow. But just think of what it will mean to the town. You'll be a hero. I mean it. All the bad old memories will be forgotten. . . . Alan Kennard, the man who made Patigowoc and didn't forget it in its hour of need."

"That's crap."

"Not too much," Mark said. "Now let's have your answer."

"Yes, goddamn ya," Alan Kennard grunted. "Yes! And if one o' you bothers me again tonight, I'll smack ya down."

"All right, Pop," Stacey said, the joy warm and potent in him. "We won't."

Mark was already at the porch steps. "Goodnight, you two. Take care."

"Yeah, we will." Stacey waved to him. "Me and the new town hero. . . ."

* * * * * * * *

Alan Kennard lived in a state of suspended emotion throughout the rest of the summer and into the fall. He stayed home more and more from the office and let Mark handle the company's affairs. He had been greatly shaken the night he had been forced to his decision by his sons, and he still looked upon what they did with despair.

Hoover's defeat only added to his sense of hopelessness. The next thing to happen, he told himself, was for Mark to miss a mortgage payment in Cleveland. Then the whole bloody shebang came clattering down. But if it went, he had to blame them both, Stacey as much as Mark, and Stace was the one he secretly loved the best.

Admit it, man. There's no sense hiding the fact. With Stace out aboard all summer, all fall, you know just how much you miss him. Look here tonight. You alone by the goddamn' fire. Yeah, alone. That old hay-bag in the kitchen, that old Mrs. Van der Haas, she don't count. And Stace is up in Duluth with the *Minna*. Mark got him a grain charter for Buffalo that will bring us a good five thousand bucks clear. Tomorrow, though, they close down the season. Official end of it and no more insurance on any vessels. . . .

He was unable to remain seated any longer and got up and went to the liquor cabinet. But the doctor had warned him not to drink. He banged the cabinet door. His thought returned to Stacey. The lad's pushing it hard. No insurance and a big cargo. If he loses the ship, we lose the works. Just as simple as that. By God, I warned him and Mark and now we're in it good. Should have a chart here, and your radio don't tell you what you want to know.

His large scale charts of the Lakes were on the walls of his office. The company radio operator was on duty there, too, and the operator would know when the *Minna* had cleared Duluth for the Soo. Kennard buttoned his collar and pulled up his tie as he went to the door of the kitchen. Mrs. Van der Haas sat underneath the light by the range knitting.

"Goin' down to the company," Kennard told her. "Mark calls, you say I'm there."

"Button yourself warm," Mrs. Van der Haas said. "It's cold out and when I come in, it looked like snow."

"By God, if you ain't a fine one for news!" Kennard snapped at her. But when he stood on the porch he realized that she was right. He went back for a heavy overcoat, a muffler. The wind was from the Northwest with a rising velocity. The willows shivered and shuddered down along the shore, white-caps were beginning to form in the open reaches of the river. He stepped cursing from the porch. Up off Whitefish tonight, this would bring snow, then ice.

Snow flurries were in the air along Main Street, and only a few people were out, but they recognized him, nodded and smiled, said, "How ya, Cap'? Good evenin', Cap'." He was intensely gratified by their greetings. They were his friends now, meant him to know it, and just a few weeks ago they'd been his bitter enemies. Strange, but he'd never realized that this had been Minna's town, and Mark's and Stacey's, but not his own until after the strike.

He recalled as he walked the scene at the end of the fight at the gate to the quarries. He saw Stacey go to Mark, Mark get hit, then Stacey, and in his nerve centers still was the shock of hurt and pride and futility.

His sons. More, the parts of himself. He'd made them what they were. This happened only because he'd forced them to it, without understanding half the time what he was after. What the hell was it you thought you'd find, Kennard?

All the long years you been chasing something. "Get ahead," you told yourself. Be better than the next fella. Rich. Man like Carnegie, or Hanna, maybe, Jim Hill, Morgan, one of them. You almost made it and somehow you missed. Got no idea why you did, but you did. Right now, you're not willing to say that you might have been smarter, tougher, taken better hold of your chances. Ah, slack off. Don't need to lie to say you're happy and you've got your sons, your daughter-in-law and young ones, this town and some friends again. Think of the way it was after Phelim and Peggy pulled out, and Josh. You were about as alone then as a man can be. No more. . . .

He crossed the snow-crusted company walk, went up the steps. Only the night lights burned in the offices, but out in the extension Turner Phillips, the radio operator, sat at his set, a green eyeshade over his upper face, a carton of coffee from the Ace Lunch at his elbow. Turner had served a hitch in the Navy in the war, later been operator in several of the Kennard ships. He was a good man and knew his work, but his wife was sickly; he'd been happy to stay ashore and handle the key here.

"Evenin', sir," he said to Alan Kennard.

"You talked to the *Minna* lately?" Kennard said.

"Just came off, sir."

"How's she making out?" Kennard tried to keep the tension from his voice.

"She made the Soo. They locked her through and she's bound on South."

"Bet the weather ain't good."

"No, sir, it's not. Wind West-nor'west. Gale proportions before morning. Storm warnings out all over. Nothing moving much."

"Except the *Minna*."

"Yes, sir, the *Minna* and a couple of car ferries."

"Mind if I sit down?"

Phillips looked at him startled. "Sure. But I won't raise her again for an hour or so unless you tell me."

"Don't bother. I'll be in my quarters." But Kennard hesitated. "How's that coffee, hot?"

"Fair."

"Then I'll go fetch us some more. I figure to be here till the

storm blows out. Goddamn it, Turner, if she stays up Nor'west, that
can mean ice."

"Yeah," Turner Phillips said; "it can." He put down the head-
piece in front of the set and swung in his chair. "My boy, Dan, is
at the house. The old lady was figuring to send me over some meat
pot pie. Had it for supper. Damn' good. Dan could bring some over
for you, and stop at the Ace and get us some fresh coffee. No sense
you're going out in the snow, Cap'."

"Can't fool an old timer." Alan Kennard shrilly laughed. "Don't
like the snow any better than you do. O.K., I'll be in my quarters.
When you call your old lady about the pot pie, thank her for me.
You get any word from the *Minna*, just ring my phone. I'll be in."

"Yes, sir," Phillips said. "Meantime, why don't you try to get
some shut-eye?"

"I will," Alan Kennard said. "I sure as hell will."

But he couldn't sleep although he lay with his eyes shut on the
leather divan in his office. He kept looking up at the charts on the
walls. He visualized Stacey aboard the *Minna* in the bends of the
St. Mary's, the dark-winding water under the snow, the dark and
vague shore where tonight the ranges wouldn't show worth a hoot
and in among the pine trees the wolves would be howling. Colder
than the hammers. For a fact, chilly right in here. Knot-head of a
janitor might burn a little more coal; the joint was about freezing.

Kennard turned up his overcoat collar around his chin. He purposely closed his eyes and sought sleep. No need, he thought, for
Turner Phillips to tell him. He should catch his shut-eye. Studying
the charts didn't do any good. That wouldn't bring Stace and the
Minna safe into Buffalo. Let Stace do his own worrying, and you
get your rest.

He had dozed off when the phone on his desk rang and he
sprang to grasp it. "It's me," Turner Phillips said. "The boy just
brought the pot pie, and he got fresh java, too. I've been talking to
the *Minna* again."

"What she say?"

"Not too good, sir. She's out of the river and past Detour.
There's ice. The Coast Guard is talking about more of it all down
Huron, in St. Clair and the Detroit River and Erie. Every kind of
craft is supposed to stay in port."

Alan Kennard cursed. "You call the *Minna* for me. I'll be in.
This ain't no night for Stacey to run for Buffalo."

Phillips rapped out the *Minna's* call letters three times before her operator came in. Kennard had written his message and Phillips sent it fast. Then he sat bent forward as he waited for the *Minna* to reply. He ran off the words on the typewriter beside him; Kennard read them one by one.

"Buffalo out right now. Bad sheet ice. Rudder trouble and vessel adrift. Coast Guard informed and will keep touch you. Tell Captain Kennard no reason worry. More later."

"Son-of-a-bitch!" Alan Kennard said. "That's a man's luck for you. Night like tonight, with the weather where it is, she'll drift down ashore. Coast Guard better get out there in a hurry."

"They will, sir," Phillips said. "Those fellas don't slouch around. Like Captain Stace said, don't you worry. That there under the napkin is the pot pie. Coffee's in the container."

"Don't want no food, no coffee." Alan Kennard was erect, and he turned and reached for the telephone. "I'm bound up the lake."

"Huh?" Phillips said. "Tonight, Cap'?"

"Yes, goddamn it. And I'm takin' the *Daigvera* and the best crew I can raise in town. Coast Guard, all the Coast Guard will do is haul the *Minna* back into Detour. But she's bound for Buffalo. Charter says so, and we don't get paid if she don't make it. How about you, Turner? Do you want to do a little steamboatin'?"

Turner Phillips lifted the napkin from the dish that held the pot pie. He opened the coffee container and pushed the dish and the container towards Kennard. "Known you some few years," he said. "Fellas have called you a bastard, and fellas called you crazy, too. But I'll go, sure. Now let's eat."

Alan Kennard picked his teeth ruminantly while he used the phone. He was calculating just how long it would take to gather a crew for the *Daigvera*, put coal in the bunkers, fire the boilers and get her ready to sail. She had been laid up out of commission two weeks ago. Part of her regular crew didn't live in town and had gone on home. Still there were men enough around to make a crew, and like Turner Phillips, once he'd talked to them, they should want to go. What the hell, this was their town, too, the way things were, and they had a piece in the company the same as he did, and Stacey and Mark.

Mark, now. There was a man he hadn't thought about. Might kick up plenty of stink about the whole idea. No articles for the crew. No insurance on the *Daigvera*. Why risk the *Daigvera* out in a blow when the Coast Guard could take care of the *Minna?* Lot of bilge like that. Sure, both vessels didn't have their insurance, but that load of wheat in the *Minna* was worth the gamble. Explain it right to Mark and you'll get him on your side.

Mark came down to the *Daigvera* at the dock in the hour before dawn as the last of the coal was rattling into the bunkers. Ingë was with him and drove their car. Mark was pale faced and grim, and Ingë, as well as Alan Kennard could make out her face in the snow gusts, shared Mark's feelings. He met them on the Texas deck and took them into his quarters.

"What's the idea?" Mark said at once.

"Simple," Alan Kennard said. "I'm goin' to tow the *Minna* into Buffalo."

Mark was shaking the snow off his coat over the mat at the door. He laid the coat, his hat, his gloves and muffler on the settee before he spoke again. Then he went across the room and grasped his father by the biceps, gazed sharply at him. "Are you all right?" he said.

"I'm fine."

"But this is crazy as hell. The Coast Guard is taking care of the *Minna*. Stace and his crew are in no serious trouble."

"Does that put the wheat alongside the dock in Buffalo? Get us our charter dough? I'm after the money, Mark. We need it. You go ahead and tell me we don't."

Mark was still, glancing at Ingë on the settee. "Listen to me, Father Kennard," she said. "Mark and I love you a very great deal. We respect you. But for you to take this boat out in a gale——"

Alan Kennard laughed. "Take her out. Bring her back. Her and the *Minna*, too. So head for the dock. I got work to do."

"All right," Ingë said softly. "I told you, Mark, that it would be this way."

"You mean I'm a stubborn old bastard," Alan Kennard said.

"Not quite," Mark said. "But you sometimes don't like to listen to reason. Have you a full crew?"

"Enough to sail her," Kennard said. "A couple of 'em are scared. But they'd feel worse if they was to be left on the dock and called cowards. You keep a man on the set at the company, Mark. I'll have Turner callin' in to you. About six hours now, I should put me a line on the *Minna*."

"Yes, sir," Mark said, his voice subdued and melancholy. He stood motionless while Ingë kissed, embraced his father. The grim expression had returned, but when he advanced his eyes were gentle. "Take care of yourself, skipper. A lot of people around this place love you."

"And now by God!" Alan Kennard said. He was deeply moved. He brought his son to him and kissed him on the cheek. "You run things while I'm away. But it's all squared and a-taunto. No reason to worry."

"Give our best to Stace," Ingë said; tears were on her rounded, bright cheeks. "Tell him we love him, too."

"Out o' here!" Kennard said with anger. "No goddamn' cryin'. What kind of a sailor you think I am?"

Mark and Ingë stood on the dock while the lines were singled down, the deckhand brought aboard, the headline cast off. Kennard waved to them from the bridge and gave a short blast on the whistle. But then he forgot about them as he shaped his course for Bouche de Mouche light. He only remembered abreast of "The Towers," for the headlights of Mark's car cut along the driveway there, and he told Joe Caspar, the mate, "Sound three blasts."

The sounds issued mournful, attenuated in the wind-hurled snow, and Kennard stamped quickly across the bridge to the lee-ward side. He didn't want to look at his house. He didn't want to think about it. What he was after was to bring the wheat into Buffalo and both his ships safe to port. But he was tired, an old man that should get more shut-eye than he'd had last night. Huron wasn't going to be too bad once he had the towline on the *Minna*. Down the Detroit River in the snow would be the corker. He'd have to be on the bridge all the time then, pilot her himself.

"Joe, I'm bound for the bunk," he told the mate. "Set her for Detour 'til you get word from Stace. Then call me."

Joe Caspar was young and ambitious and had welcomed the chance to sail as second in command of the *Daigvera*. He nodded vigorously at Alan Kennard. "I'll take her right on up, sir," he said. "You sleep as long as you want. Dave Hogan is all ready to relieve me."

Alan Kennard thought as he left the bridge, I'll trust you now, not later, though. Get into them Detroit bends, there's one fella who'll handle her. That's me.

The *Minna* was heavy with ice, the towline between her and the Coast Guard cutter coated with it, glistening in the brief shafts of midday sun. Spectacle Reef was still in sight down astern of her, and nerves gathered in Alan Kennard's hands when he took over the bridge from Caspar. It had been goddamn' close, and he'd have hell's own time towing her. She was down by the bow with the ice, and the way she answered to the cutter's haul, her steering gear wasn't worth a hoot.

"So you, mister," he said sharply to Caspar, "break out the buntin' and tell the Coast Guard she's ours. I'll fall downwind on her. You have our line ready. When the cutter casts off, we give the *Minna* the line on the same bow. Can you make the signal?"

"Yes, sir."

"Have you got the boys to handle the towline?"

Joe Caspar blinked and snow particles dropped from his eye lashes. "Yes, sir. I know my work."

"Then make the signal and send Hogan up here and get aft. Move along. Handsomely."

It gave Alan Kennard a peculiar sensation of triumph when he backed the *Daigvera* downwind and recognized Stacey in the bridge wing of the *Minna*. He waved, shouted onto the wind, "How ya, Stace?"

Stacey did no more than wave back. He stood in a posture of fatigue, clinging to the wind-dodger of the bridge. Snow was frozen to his cap, his coat and mittens. His face had been stung a raw red; tears of eye irritation clotted on his cheeks. A rough one for Stacey, this, Alan Kennard told himself. The men of the *Minna's* crew moved clumsy-footed along the foredeck. Fatigue had them, too, and the bosun, usually alert, staggered stooped from side to side.

The captain of the cutter had lifted his megaphone. "You bound for Buffalo, Captain?" he called.

"I am, goddamn it!" Alan Kennard called back.

"You're crazy, sir. Take your vessels into Patigowoc. You'll be lucky to make that."

Alan Kennard laughed and the wind struck bitter in his throat. "Happen to be a sailor. You cast off and we'll make Buffalo fine. Report us, if you want."

The cutter captain shrugged and swung and gave a hand signal to his men aft. The windlass began to growl as aboard the *Minna* her towline was cast off. Alan Kennard stared aft aboard his own vessel. Caspar waited tensely in the alley by the engine-house for his signal. "Let 'em have it!" Kennard shouted. "Stick out!"

Aboard the *Minna,* the bosun shuffled with sudden alacrity. He put a heaving line smacking onto the *Daigvera's* fantail. The towline was bent on to it, slipped aft through the sullen gray water. Stacey had shouted down from his bridge; his mate and the bosun and the sailors were hauling in the towline.

"Easy, now," Alan Kennard said in through the open pilot-house door to the wheelsman. "Ease her another spoke, man." The two ships were within a hundred feet of each other, but if he started the *Daigvera* ahead fast, he might snap the towline and Christ knew when he would get another one aboard her. "Slow ahead, mister."

Hogan sent the engine-room telegraph handle over in a small, dim arc. "Slow ahead she is, sir."

"Make it half."

"Half ahead, sir."

" 'Midships, the wheel." Alan Kennard stepped out of the snow and wind into the pilot-house. He didn't need to look aft any more; he could feel the strain in the vessel. The line was secured and he had his tow. Through the forward window, he waved to the cutter. "See you in Buffalo!" he yelled.

But the cutter captain had gone from the bridge. The cutter had come about, was bound across the wind with a big flutter of spume at the bow. Had enough of us, Kennard thought. Well, the same goes for him. Don't need no government haul in my business. Wait for Roosevelt to tend to that.

He went into the chartroom and lay on the settee and dozed after the two vessels were fully on their course down the lake. His legs ached, and his back; his eyeballs had been burned by the wind and they smarted, disturbed his sleep. "Snort'd do you good," he muttered aloud. But he was aware that he would not take a drink. Today, tonight was the time for him to keep a clear, sober head. Damn' shame Phelim was dead. The Liverpool prancer was just the man to have a piece of this. Fight, shucks, now he and Phelim were fighting on the same side.

The two mates kept the watches down the lake and to the light-ship and Port Huron. Then Alan Kennard took the bridge again. He had eaten a substantial supper, drunk three mugs of coffee, and he felt keen, full of energy. But the snow still persisted although the wind had lowered, and he had difficulty with his bearings in the St. Clair River. "Bad here," the wheelsman, an old-timer, said to him, "it's gonna be a bitch down below Detroit."

"Ain't you right," Kennard said. He sat on a stool at the part-opened forward window, peering forth into the snow that dropped

slow, heavy, thick. In this moment he wished that he were home
in bed, and he was oppressed by the knowledge of his age, the
warning of the cutter captain. When he reached for and pulled
down the whistle handle, his wrist was stiff and pained him. But
Stace will hear it, he thought, even if nobody else does. Keep the
law, too, and keep Stace awake. But it's still a long, dirty drag from
here to Buffalo.

Joe Caspar came on the bridge to relieve him at eight o'clock.
But Kennard refused to leave. He'd sit around, he said, for a look
at the range lights. This Detroit was a no-good place on a dirty
night.

The rumble, the scuff, the clunk of ice were gone. The ship's
head yawed with the current; they were in the river. Joe Caspar
stood cursing in the bridge wing and Kennard understood why. The
light tower at Grosse Point was a hundred and eighty-seven feet
high. It had a visibility of fifteen miles. But they were down abreast
of the yacht club and almost under the light and they hadn't seen
it yet.

Kennard took his muffler from the radiator, knotted it about his
throat inside his oilskin coat. He kicked his feet against the radiator
to find if that wouldn't help reduce the pain, buttoned his sou'-
wester strap, smoothed his mittens up and went out onto the bridge.

The city was a citrus green shadow. The docks, where the current rippled, laid a thin, dull, black border upon the shadow. Wind-
sor was unseen. The weather held from there, and it was a white
pelt of snow that clogged the eyes, spattered obscurity. "A good
night for bootleggers," Caspar said. "They'll be running over like
wild."

"You go inside and keep warm and tend the whistle," Alan
Kennard said. It was his intention to be alone. He had to trust to
instinct, to memory to run the river, and he could do it best by
himself. He hooked his elbows over the canvas of the dodger and
stood on one foot and then the other to alleviate their ache.

His mind rushed down the paths of the past and informed him
of the course changes to be made, and he called them in to Hogan
and the wheelsman. But to go back into the past stirred memories.
He remembered the Detroit Yacht Club in sunlight when he and
Minna had boarded Bob Oakman's *Mamie O.* Sure, Minna in pink
organdy and as cute as a bug's ear. That was the day of the Harns-
worth Trophy Races. They had a special speed course up North
of Belle Isle. It was quite a day for Minna, real social, everybody

nodding and smiling aboard the big yacht and the racers out there whipping the water.

Not many days like that for Minna, though. Most of the time she was stuck in Patigowoc. She used to go back in her head, too, and talk to you about the old times when you were home. Because what she had didn't make her too happy. Maude Adams in "All the Comforts of Home" and Adams just eighteen, slim, slick as a whistle. "Floradora." Minna could sing "Tell Me" and she'd get you to sing along.

Poor Mrs. McKinley, Minna would talk about her, then she'd cry, then she'd feel better. But Mrs. McKinley had lost her two kids and her mother. She was an epileptic by the time her husband came to run for president. Everybody knew it. Woman had fits.

Minna was real happy at the Fair over in Chicago, though. You can see her now walking around the lagoon, riding in the launches as if she wasn't a sailor's wife and had never been aboard one before, looking at the statues, the fountains, dragging you from the Hall of Manufactures into that dump they called Liberal Arts.

Better down on the Midway. There was the Irish Village, all right enough in its way, and the Hindu jugglers, the goddamn' Ferris wheel with the women squeaking and grabbing at their skirts and then their hats and then their skirts, the South Sea Islanders, Old Vienna, the Wild West show, the Algerians and Cairo Street and Sandow and Little Egypt.

Alan Kennard crossed the bridge limping. He could barely discern the sailor on lookout at the bow. The *Minna* was no more than a pallid, insubstantial shape astern. Snow walled, roofed the river. Wind flung the snow, sent it flat over the water, upward and aslant, often in the shapes of animals, weird creatures, people of Kennard's imagination. But he knew where he was; he had calculated.

Through a rift in the snow he had established Ecorse light. There was Grassy Island. Next was North Channel and Mamajuda. You should get Grosse Isle and the South Channel ranges pretty soon. Hold her as she goes for a bit. You're doing fine, man. You're a sailor and no bloody mistake. . . .

His mind retreated to the memories. Bryan, big brow, big voice, the mane of hair as pretty as on any horse. "We have petitioned and they have mocked. We petition no more." "You shall not press down. . . ." But the fella ended up a wind-bag. They took him apart at the seams. Did that with a lot of fellas. Not you, though. Back astern there in the *Minna* is almost half a million

bushels of wheat. Means the crops from twenty-two thousand acres
of farm land. Take thirty trains of sixty-five cars each to haul it
overland. Make four and a half million loaves of bread. That'll
feed the hungry Down-East, and, yeah, put a couple thousand of
dollars in your pocket where they belong. You've worked for 'em.

Remember the immigrant folks who were with you on the way
to Buffalo after you'd got Phelim's letter? Well, it's them, their kind
and kids who grew the wheat. Wheat, you carried it with Maumee
Mike Jacobs and in the *Procyon*. You've hauled every goddamn'
thing that will go into a hull on these waters. Worked in the woods.
Helped make the country. Grew along with it.

Memory strayed. He was in Seville at the bull fight. Minna
stroked his hair, whispered in the night. He heard his mother
keening. The lads threw stones at him and he ran. The names of
his ships were *Minna* and *Daigvera*. They were the first, the oldest.
Then *Glenarm, Ramore, Glenariff, Ardglass, Coleraine, Carrickfergus.* "Antrim has nine glens, but Glenariff is the most beautiful
of them all."

Steady up now. There's Boblo light just breaking and the Elliott
Point ranges. You'll have to make your turn. "Mister," he said in
the window to Caspar, "I'd like a snort of java, and a sandwich
maybe. I'm half froze."

"Hogan's here with me, Captain," Caspar said. "He came up to
relieve. Why don't you come in and sit down a bit, or take a little
flop on the settee?"

"Sat down," Alan Kennard said, "I'd never get up again. Sonny,
come left with the wheel 'til I tell you to check her. Then steady
up fast."

The coffee when he drank it seemed to burn a hole through his
exhaustion. But the exhaustion closed again, ran and throbbed and
pounded in his body, and the only way he could escape was by
entering into memory.

He was in the stable with the oxen and the horses and more
snow than this was outside. The book he read belonged to Josh
Shaw. It was written by a man named Oliver Holmes. The words
were kind of hard for him, and he'd had Josh explain them. So some
of them had stuck:

"Through our great good fortune in our youth our hearts were
touched with fire. It was given us to learn at the outset that life
is a profound and passionate thing. While we are permitted to scorn
nothing but indifference, and do not pretend to undervalue the

worldly rewards of ambition, we have seen with our own eyes, beyond and above the gold fields, the snowy heights of honour, and it is for us to bear the report to those who come after us."

Maumee Mike talked that way when you got him talking. What the man meant was the war. Yeah, his war, Maumee's. You can still hear the bugle blowing taps and the goddamn' crows cawing. Old Colonel Shaw, he was in the same war. Big days. But Josh died in a different one, and no friend of yours. Jane. She'd get a laugh out of you and that Venner bitch. Not tonight she wouldn't laugh at you, though.

Now you really mean something. No man can do it better. Maybe you never got over to Mark and Stace what your life's about. Hard thing. You ain't the kind to write, speak like that fella named Holmes. Didn't want to hurt anybody. If you did— You know sure as hell you did. So you take this way of paying off. You figure Stace has done his share, Mark, too. A good pair of boys. Real men. Remember the ball game at Hamatack? And Mark home from the war, no uniform, no medals, no big load of bull?

Caspar and Hogan had come out onto the bridge. They stood on each side of him, Alan Kennard was aware. He stared at them. "What'll it be, gents?" he said, but his voice was a croaking whisper.

"Just raised Bar Point Lightship, sir," Caspar said. "You been out here a good long time now. Come in and get off your feet. We're clearing for the lake. Hogan and me can handle her."

"No! Like hell," Kennard said in a louder voice. They had him by the elbows, though, and they half carried, half dragged him into the chartroom. He collapsed once he was on the settee. A roaring of congested blood was in his head. Fluctuations of intense heat passed through his body. He gasped, and the racked rasp he heard was the sound of his breath.

Blankets were piled over him. The steward was there, and Turner Phillips, Nate Moise, the chief engineer. "Ah, to hell," he murmured at them, yet they stayed, and he listened to them talking, puzzled by what Moise said. "Better get a message to Stacey," Moise said. "The old fella's kickin' over awful' slow."

Then Kennard understood. "I ain't," he said. "Don't you go worrying Stace about me. I'm goin' to make it."

The energy to pronounce those words drained him. He seemed to sway on the settee, and to rise, veer around up against the chartroom deckhead, out into the snow and the night. He shivered, his teeth rattled. It was colder than the hammers in the night. But when he pulled back down under the blankets the heat was consuming. He was in fever and asked for water.

"You're a sick man, Cap'," Turner Phillips said as he gave him the water.

"What ha' I got?"

"Looks like pneumonia," Phillips said. "But you just rest easy and keep your hatch shut. The boys will bring her into port."

"Good bunch."

"Don't talk, Cap'."

Turner Phillips's face wavered out of focus. Kennard saw other faces. They were those of the dead. Maybe you're dying, he thought, and was unafraid, only curious. The faces faded, merged, separated, hung alone and distinct. One with a beard, thin gold earrings, a skin the color of teak. The bosun off the *Margharita*. Minna, smiling, young, as he had first known her. Then Minna's mother. Josh Shaw while he squinted in lamplight. The old lady, Mrs. Shaw, and his own mother, Minna's mother. His mother wore a shawl. Look into her eyes and you saw death for fair. Not that you give a goddamn. You ain't afraid. . . .

He slept and in sleep he dreamed. Mark and Stacey sat beside him on the steps of the porch at "The Towers." They were both in knee pants and had been playing ball on the lawn. "Don't ever get fouled up," he said to them. "Money's all right. But me, I've never cared for it too much."

An inner, far off voice said, "Speak the truth, Kennard. You've been chased by hunger all your days. That's your trouble. Scared of hunger, scared of being poor."

He wrenched himself from the dream and up out of it shouted, "Hey, Josh! Hey, Phelim! C'me here!"

Turner Phillips bent over him and pulled the blankets up, bathed the sweat from his face. "Take it easy, Cap'. We're almost in. Things are going fine."

"How far we got?"

"We can see the breakwall."

"Buffalo, you mean."

"That's right, Cap'."

He struggled from the settee, trailing the blankets behind him. Agony struck his chest like the blades of knives. He stepped into the pilot-house, grazed by the wheelsman, reached the forward window and gripped the sill and clung. The breakwall was there, and the city. He turned and saw the ship steady astern. Stacey was on the bridge with his face lifted to the city.

Alan Kennard made a small gesture with one hand. He was waving to his son. "Take her in," he mumbled. His knees gave, and he fell backward and Phillips and Caspar caught him. "You hear me?" he asked.

"Sure, Cap'," Caspar said.

Alan Kennard was still. His head swung loose as they took him into the chartroom, put him on the settee. They left him alone after a time and in a moment of consciousness while the heat and the agony subsided he realized that death was very close for him. He felt no desire to fight it. This was right. He'd sailed his courses, come full circle. "Minna," he whispered eagerly. "Me true darling."

•